I0772352

DRAGON GUARD
THE SKYSTONE CHRONICLES BOOK 2
BLAKE & RAVEN PENN

GOOD LUX CREATIVE

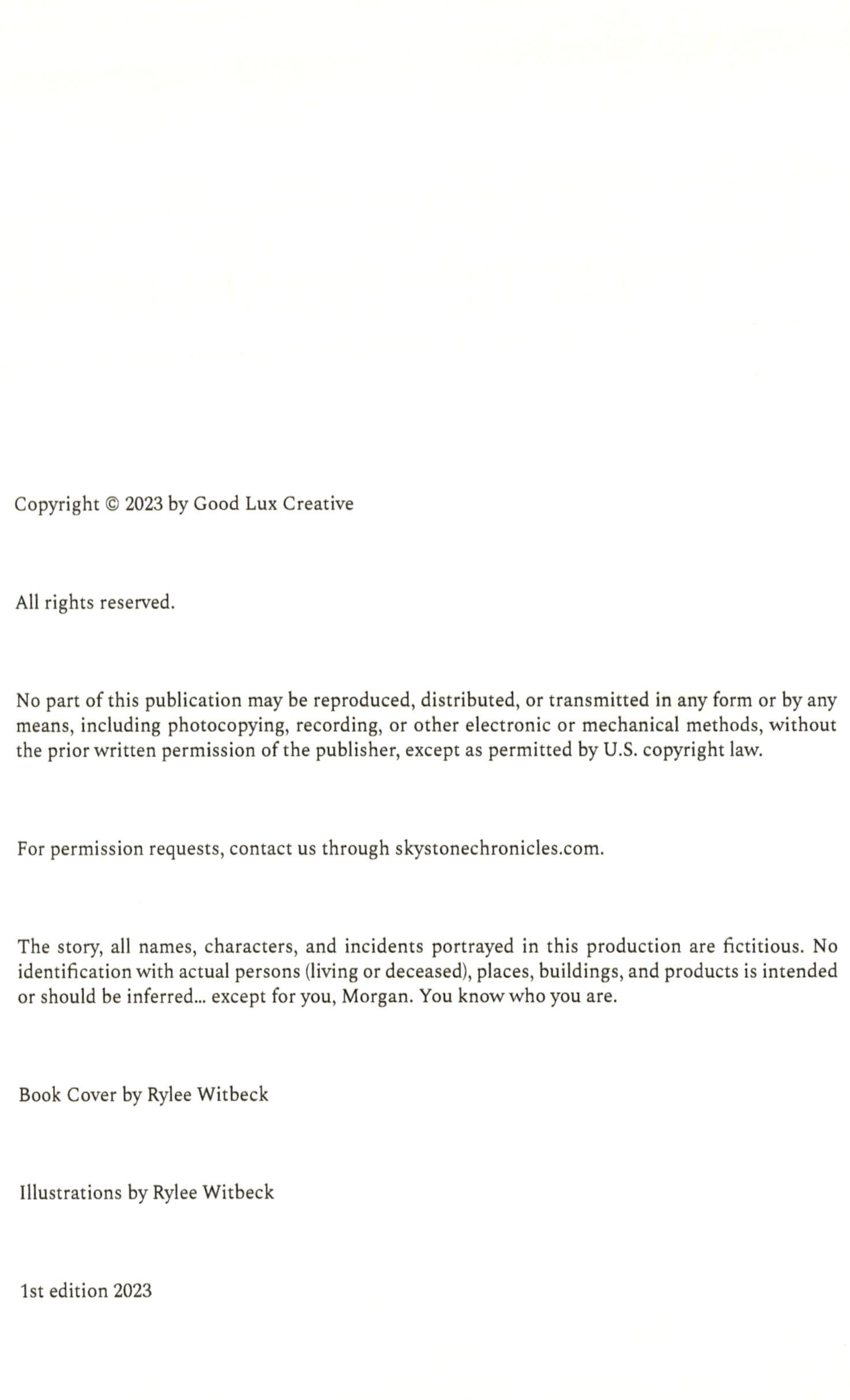

Dedication

For Our Kids

We hope these books are among your favorites someday...
when you can read

CONTENTS

Dear reader,

In our travels across worlds,
we've gathered many stories of
heroes. Those heroes always face
an unseen enemy.
May this book help you face yours.

Sincerely,

Blake Penn

Raven Penn

the skystone chronicles

The Land of
EVGARD

THE SKYSTONE CHRONICLES

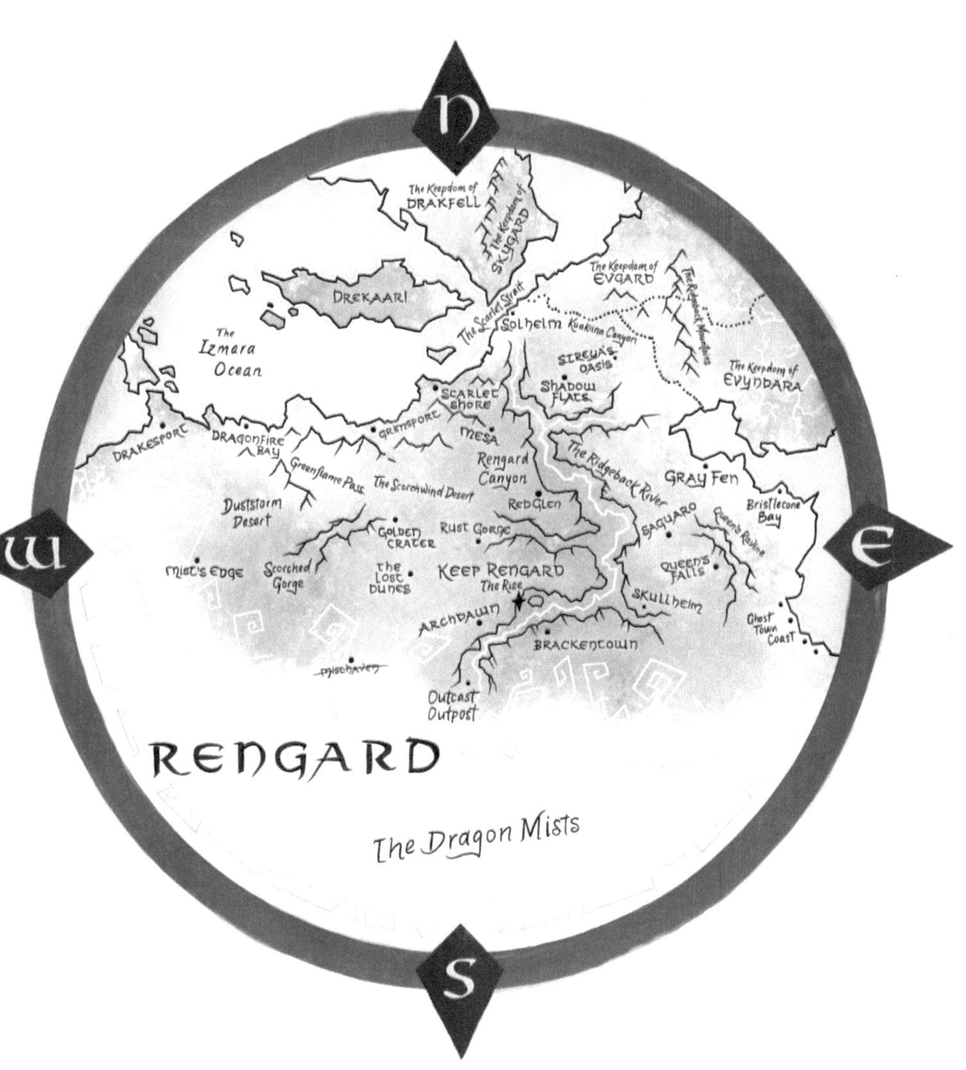

The Land of
RENGARD

N
W
E
S

The Keepdom of
DRAKFELL
The Keepdom of
SKYGARD
The Keepdom of
EVGARD
The Redneck Mountains
DREKAARI
The Scarlet Strait
Solhelm
Kuakina Canyon
The Keepdom of
EVYNDARA
The
Izmara
Ocean
SIREYA'S
OASIS
Shadow
FLATS
Scarlet
Shore
Grimsport
MESA
The Ridgeback River
GRAY Fen
DRAKESPORT
Dragonfire
Bay
Greenflame Pass
The Scorchwind Desert
Rengard
Canyon
RedGlen
Bristlecone
Bay
Duststorm
Desert
Golden
Crater
Rust Gorge
SAGUARO
Queen's Ravine
Mist's Edge
Scorched
Gorge
The
Lost
Dunes
Keep Rengard
The Rise
Queen's
FALLS
Archdawn
Skullheim
Ghost
Town
Coast
Misthaven
BRACKENTOWN
Outcast
Outpost

RENGARD

The Dragon Mists

The Ethereal Triad

The chart below shows the nine types of etherarchy common among worlds. Your world tends to call these effects "magic" or "supernatural." We use the term etherarchy because it is the command of ether that accomplishes these mythic effects.

Any person who can command etherarchy is a magi. They fall into one of three groups.

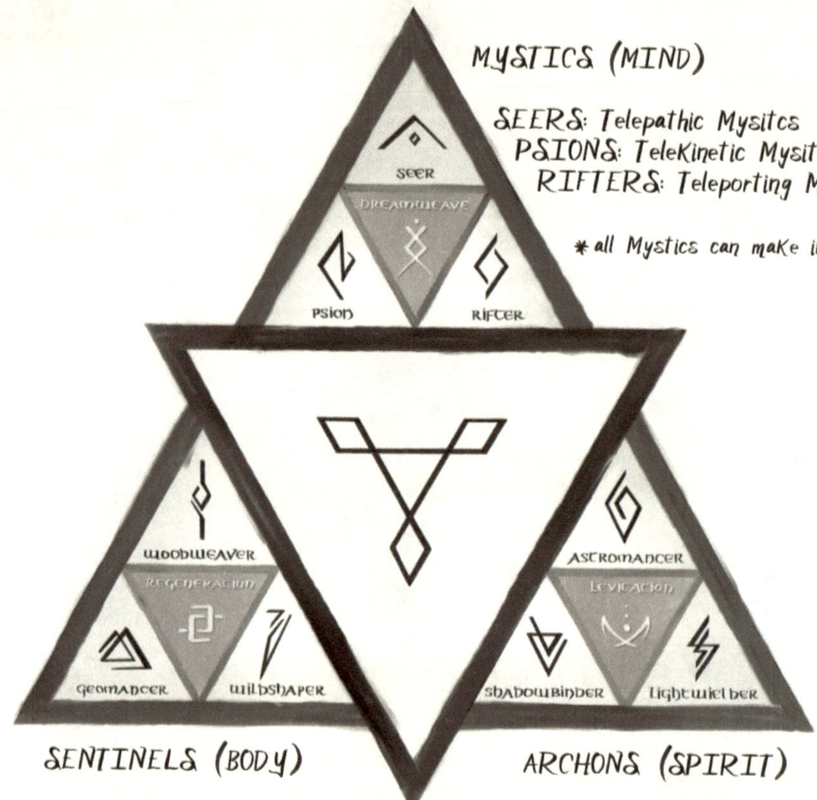

MYSTICS (MIND)

SEERS: Telepathic Mysitcs
PSIONS: Telekinetic Mysitcs
RIFTERS: Teleporting Mysitcs

*all Mystics can make illusions

SENTINELS (BODY)

GEOMANCERS: Earth-based Sentinels
WILDSHAPERS: Fauna-based Sentinels
WOODWEAVERS: Flora-based Sentinels

*all Sentinels can regenerate

ARCHONS (SPIRIT)

LIGHTWIELDERS: Light Archons
SHADOWBINDERS: Dark Archons
ASTROMANCERS: Ether Archons

*all Archons can levitate

*A note on silver: It is common knowledge that all etherarchy is nullified on contact with silver. This is why Mage Hunters wield silver weapons, and why Evgardian Keeps have silver lined cells designed to hold magi.

the skystone chronicles

PREFACE

A Brief Guide to Evgard is included in the back of the book, or you can check out skystonechronicles.com for more information on the world.

Also, signing up for our mailing list will even get you a free short-story set in the world of Evgard!

Now, without further ado, we hope you enjoy *Dragon Guard*!

After defeating the Black Valkyrie in Keep Drakfell, Asher and his friends left their outlander home to become Knights of the Torch. Each member of their old heist crew met with the legendary Farseer and the other leaders of the Knights to receive their next assignments. Asher, his best friend Kai, as well as Eliana, the Princess of Drakfell, headed off to the land of Rengard, first to retrieve a case of valuable intel for the Knights. From there, they planned to make their way to the Ridgeback Mountains so that Elle could start training as a true dragon rider.

But Asher and his friends aren't the only ones the Farseer has been seeing in his omenfires.

Reflection I

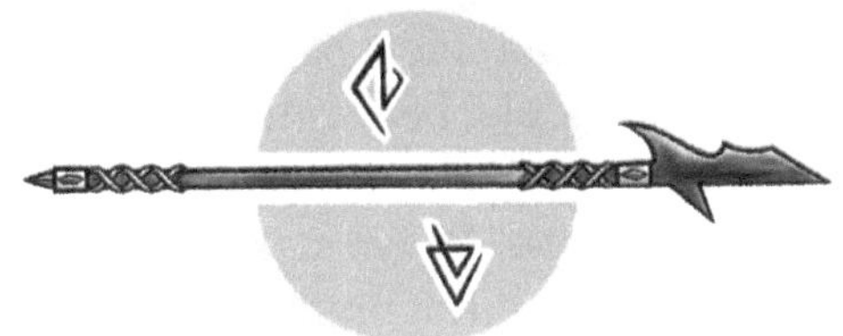

I cy stillness.

The frigid water rushed around Vidya's ears. It filled her nose and stung her eyes as it surrounded her.

She squeezed her mouth shut, swallowing the last bit of air she'd taken in before leaping through the portal. If only she'd taken a bigger breath.

Withering into nothingness in the salty water were the red robes of the Farseer. No, not the Farseer. An illusion.

A drakking illusion. Vidya couldn't believe she'd let herself fall for the Knights of the Torch's trick. She'd been so focused on obtaining her prize that she'd acted impulsively. Foolishly.

Now, she and her entourage would pay the price.

Her four Mage Hunters floated weightlessly to her left and right, their dusky blue cloaks flowing with the current while their heavy armor pulled them down toward the sea floor. The last embers of golden light from the portal winked out, leaving them in complete darkness to await their deaths.

No.

Vidya was not about to die at the bottom of the sea because of some trick from the Knights of the Torch. She wouldn't let Solrac win that easily.

Put me back in control, a soft, feminine voice echoed in her head. *I can save us.*

Vidya hated not being in command of her own actions. But she was running out of air.

She closed her eyes, letting go. She felt the other being slip into her soul, her presence filling her chest, arms, legs, and mind.

When Vidya opened her eyes again, her glowing, lightning blue irises lit the water. Power rushed through her, from her core to her fingertips.

She traced a psionic rune, more blue light trailing from her finger as the rune appeared over her forehead like a sapphire in a crown. Raising her dragonhook spear high above her head, she reached out with her other hand to telekinetically grab hold of her Mage Hunters' heavy armor.

Drawing her entourage close, Vidya's shadowbinding power surged first through her own body before flowing into those of her Hunters. They appeared as shadows of themselves, their bodies not quite solid. It was a form of etherarchy that Vidya herself didn't understand. But the being controlling her radiated confidence.

With a burst of otherworldly might, Vidya pushed her spear upward, clinging to it until her knuckles turned white. She accessed her archonic levitation ability as well, aiding the telekinetic push against the spear.

Vidya and her Mage Hunters shot upward, and it was as if their semi-incorporeal bodies weighed next to nothing. They flew through the water like a meteor cuts through the sky.

Finally, they broke the water's surface. Vidya gasped for breath as they launched into the air. She scanned her surroundings for somewhere to land, recognizing the salty scent and the outline of mountains along the distant horizon. They were in the dead center of the Dragonstorm Sea.

Drak, Vidya mentally swore.

The Soul Reaper's anchor, her companion reminded her.

Vidya strained to continue their ascension as she fumbled in her pocket for the white, runemarked stone. She felt more precious ether drain from her as she activated the stone, dropping it below them toward the water.

Just before falling back into the sea, the portal spun to life. Rather than the telltale gold rim of etherarchy, eerie blue light edged the rift.

Vidya felt her Mystic ether well run out as a headache split across her forehead, the rune there vanishing. Likewise, her chest felt so tight she thought it would burst. She was almost completely drained of power.

Vidya went limp, barely conscious as she felt the other being's presence leave her body. Both she and her four Mage Hunters fell through the air, disappearing into the portal below.

A hollow feeling filled Vidya as she and her Hunters came tumbling out the other end of the portal. Through blurred vision, she saw familiar black stone walls and a silver swan insignia adorning the large black door. They'd come through right where Vidya had left the exit anchor.

Swan Spire.

Vidya had turned the tower into her own personal sanctuary. It stood overlooking the Mage Hunter Academy, on a high cliffside in the heart of the Ridgeback Mountains.

Beside Vidya, her Mage Hunters breathed heavily as their waterlogged cloaks drenched the black, painted slats of the wooden floor.

Vidya gasped for air. Her lungs felt like lead.

But she was alive.

You're welcome, the voice purred inside her mind.

"Come in."

Vidya's voice was ragged as she spoke. The door creaked open to reveal the shadowy silhouette of a tall man with angular horns sprouting off the back of his scalp amidst his dark hair. A gleaming silver pauldron graced his shoulder, and the long, dusky blue cloak of a Mage Hunter swept off his back as he entered Swan Spire.

"The Ursadon," Vidya said as he stalked toward where she sat.

"The Black Valkyrie," he replied in an accented voice, using her title. Few knew her true name, which was the way Vidya liked it. At least, it was the way things had to be.

"Take a seat," she gestured toward a finely-carved, black wooden chair opposite her. A shudder ran through her body—a lingering effect from both her fight with the Farseer and subsequent escape from the Dragonstorm Sea earlier that day.

The Ursadon sat down, the dim sunlight from the window streaming onto his face through black curtains. It shone off of the deep violet scales along his hairline and cheekbones. A spiraling, white ether scar crept along one side of his jawline. The Drekai Mage Hunter stared at Vidya expectantly through his bright, dragonfire green eyes.

"Things did not go as planned in Keep Drakfell." Vidya coughed, a wet, hollow feeling aching inside her chest.

"Perhaps you need some time to recover," the Ursadon replied.

"No," Vidya snapped. "There's no time to waste. If I am to capture the Farseer and obtain his ether well, I need more power."

"What would you have me do?" the Ursadon asked, loyalty coloring his otherwise flat tone.

"I'm sending a group of enforcers to arrest the Captain of the Guard in the Canyon Keepdom. I've uncovered evidence that Captain Cenrik is in league with the Knights of the Torch."

The Ursadon's brow furrowed. "Well done. But what do you need from me?"

Vidya's lip curled into a smile. "You're my best Hunter. I need you to take Cenrik's place as Captain over Keep Rengard's army."

No sooner had the words left Vidya's mouth than the Ursadon was on his feet, his dragonfire green eyes flashing.

"No. I'll go anywhere across the realm other than there."

"Why ever not?" Vidya pouted, feigning ignorance.

"You know *she's* in Keep Rengard."

Vidya gave a light chuckle. "Exactly why I thought you'd want to go. To be close to her."

"Her daughter is about to join the guard there. I can't go."

Vidya's voice hardened suddenly. "You *will* go."

The Ursadon pressed his lips into a tight line.

"You will," Vidya repeated. "You said yourself that I need time to recover. Until then, I need you to do some digging—Have you heard of one called the Liberator who leads the Coven of the Gray Ones?"

"I've heard of them, yes." The Ursadon's jaw tensed.

"I need you to go to the Canyon Keepdom, where the Coven is based, and find out the identity of the Liberator."

"I told you, I can't go to Rengard."

"Then I have no choice," Vidya spoke with sweet sharpness. "Either you do as I say, or I send you to the Soul Reaper's laboratory and you become a skymage tonight."

The Ursadon growled in his throat. "You're no skymage. I'll never become what you are."

He's too weak-minded to wield our power anyway, the voice whispered in Vidya's mind.

Vidya smiled. "I thought not. In that case, congratulations on your appointment as leader of the Keep Rengard army, Captain Zoren."

CHAPTER I: THE DRAGON CHASM

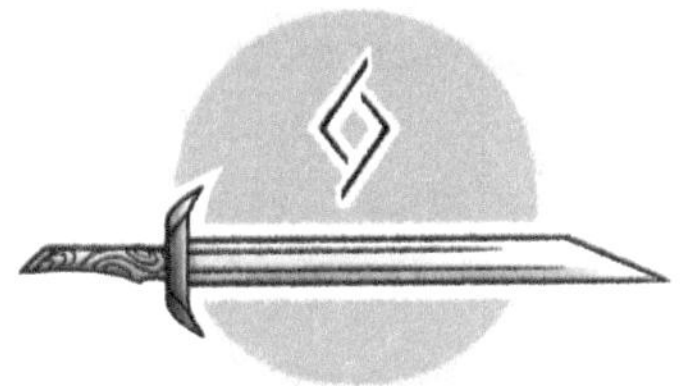

I squared my shoulders as I stared into the gaping redrock chasm, pretending that facing down a few dozen wild dragons was no big deal. But inside, my stomach was in knots.

Clanking sounds from long, seaxe-style swords mingled with creaks from recruits loading their scaleslayer crossbows. The blazing desert sun warmed the sandy red stone beneath our feet, the heat only adding to our anxious energy.

"Here you go, Solvai," I said, passing my best friend a long, newly-sharpened dragonhook spear. "The one you were sparring with yesterday had a splintering haft, so I brought a replacement."

"Oh," Solvai took the spear, weighing it in her hand. "Thanks, Meleya."

"And Brigan," I said, turning to my other best friend. "Your cloak isn't latched properly—There you go."

"Thanks, Meleya." Brigan's warm brown eyes sparkled at me as I smoothed his gray recruit's cloak.

I tucked a few flyaway locks of hair back into my long, white scaletail braid, racking my brain for anything else we might have missed.

"Did you both hydrate enough this morning?"

"Yes, Meleya," both Solvai and Brigan said in unison.

"Do you have your backup weapons?"

"Meleya." Brigan gave a dimpled grin. "I get the sense you're a little on edge."

"I'm just checking," I raised my hands defensively. Though he was absolutely right. We were about to head into a gigantic chasm to face our deaths—Of course I was on edge.

"Yes, we have our backup weapons," Solvai patted the tomahawk hanging from her belt.

"Are they sharpened?" I raised a dark eyebrow.

"You left whetstones on our pillows last night," Brigan reminded me. "So, that's a definite yes."

A commander's voice boomed across the mesa. "Recruits to the platform."

My friends and I exchanged glances. This was it.

Nine.

My heart dropped into my feet as the large, heavy platform jerked downward.

Eight.

The metal creaked as the commander spun the crank. We hugged the platform's center as it descended into the chasm. The harsh sunlight overhead dimmed, the striped, weather-worn orange walls rising up on our left and right.

Seven. Six.

Thud. The platform hit the sandy earth at the bottom of the chasm. We scrambled to get off, clouds of red dust puffing up around our boots.

Five, four, three...

The chains tightened as the commander pulled the platform back up to the top, removing any chance of escape. I'd heard lectures on the Dragon Chasm, how it was the best way to separate the strong soldiers from the weak. Keep Rengard's ultimate test that ensured it had the most powerful army in the realm.

Two.

But watching them unbolt the heavy gate at the other end of the chasm, it became very clear that this was no classroom.

One.

With feral roars, wild dragons spilled from the cave within the rock. Serpentine wyverns launched into the air, jets of lime green dragonfire spraying from their jaws. Four-winged evren shrieked like something from the void as they shot out of the cave. The ground shook as mighty wingless drakes bolted across the chasm toward us.

I lowered my eyebrows, gripping the handle of my seaxe. The long, single-edged sword felt familiar in my hands. The blade was sturdy, the angular tip sharp enough to cut through dragon hide.

For many of my fellow recruits, this would be their first time facing a wild dragon. But I'd spent my childhood roaming the canyons with the nomads. This wasn't my first dragon rodeo. Plus, these dragons were young, probably even less experienced than we were. But they were still wild dragons.

With a warrior's cry, I was the first to charge across the chasm. Then Brigan joined in, followed closely by Solvai and the rest of the recruits.

We screamed until we ran out of breath, but the dragons were still several yards away. It turned out the chasm was a little longer than we'd thought.

We inhaled deeply, then gave another battle cry.

This time we timed it right, clashing against the dragons with a discord of roars, shrieks, and clangs. I came up against a fierce, towering drake that reared up on its hind legs and raked its claws toward me.

I ducked, then rolled out of the way, red dust from the ground streaking across my pale gray recruit's cloak. I launched out of the maneuver and landed on my feet. Then I whacked the flat of my sword down on the base of the dragon's tail. It whirled on me, its fiery green eyes fixed on my dark brown ones.

It took a lot of willpower to not strike at its heart then and there. I could practically hear Dad's voice screaming at me in my head.

A wild dragon never hesitates, and neither should you.

That's what he told me the day he gave me my first dagger. The dagger was one of my fanciest possessions—Dad had stolen it from a nobleman before I was born. With a northern-style sloped blade and a handle carved from a dragonmoose antler, the dagger now served as my ever-present backup weapon, hidden inside my boot.

But today wasn't about killing as many wild dragons as we could in order to survive. Today, the commanders hoped for as many new soldiers as possible to bond a dragon of their own. Not all of us would, of course. Most squads had at least three or four non-riders. But bonding a dragon made a soldier a lot more effective when it came to defending the keep.

A bonded dragon was different from a wild one. Dad always said that the bonding process changed something in the dragon's soul, advancing it beyond a savage animal.

Never kill a bonded dragon, Meleya, he used to say. *They have souls as refined as yours and mine.*

I stared up at the narrowed eyes of the drake, my heart thumping wildly. Every drill instructor who'd ever tried to explain the bonding process had used words like 'connection,' 'sharing,' or the ever-helpful phrase, 'you just kind of feel it.' That didn't seem to be doing a lot for me now.

The dragon let out a low, throaty growl, looking confused as to why the tasty human wasn't fighting back. The veins in my forehead would've burst had I focused any harder on trying to forge a connection.

I didn't feel anything, but then again, I wasn't sure what I was supposed to feel. Hesitantly, I raised one eyebrow.

Big mistake.

That seemed to snap the dragon out of whatever befuddled trance it'd been in. It flared its nostrils, vertical pupils shrinking as it breathed in my scent.

Drak. One look told me that not only had I failed to bond the dragon, but it had just caught a whiff of my ether well. As much as wild dragons enjoyed the taste of regular people, it was the ether inside us magi that drew them to the keeps.

The drake sucked in, jaws wide. In the back of its throat, I saw the sparks of green dragonfire ready to roast me on the spot.

Experience kept me from running away—that would only get me scorched from behind. Instead, I dove toward the space between the drake's forelegs.

When the dragonfire blast came, I was already scrambling underneath the drake's scaly underbelly. It was the perfect spot to take a stab at it, but just because the drake hadn't wanted to bond me didn't mean it wouldn't want to bond another recruit.

I got to my feet and rushed back toward the thick of the action, where the other recruits were busy trying to bond dragons of their own. It looked like a few had already succeeded. One gray-cloaked recruit sat astride a pale blue wyvern, already flying out of the chasm toward safety. Another held on for dear life as his wingless drake crawled straight up the canyon walls like an enormous lizard.

Circling the air above the chasm was a group of soldiers on wyvernback. They allowed the newly bonded pairs to pass over the high edge, but each time one of the wild dragons tried to escape alone, the soldiers used their dragonhook spears to redirect them. For the dragons, there was no getting out without a rider.

I scanned my surroundings, looking for another potential bond. I had to get out of here too, before any of the commanders watching from the ledges above noticed that the dragons wanted to get to me more than the others.

A scream from Solvai made my heart drop. I spun around, gaze honing in on my friend as she looked upward with wide eyes.

I was at her side in a second, seaxe ready to take a swing at whatever dragon was daring to threaten her.

"What is it?" I frowned, seeing no dragon asking for me to hack it to pieces.

"Did you see that?" Solvai shrilled.

"Where?" I demanded, knuckles whitening around the hilt of my sword.

"It was just there," Solvai said, pointing at absolutely nothing. "A violet-scaled hummingbird. I've never seen one this far west before."

My adrenaline rush vanished in an instant. "Drak, you bird nerd."

"Sorry," she blushed. "Their beaks are so interesting, though. I hope I can remember so I can carve it later."

"There will be no carving later unless we make it out of here alive," I warned.

Behind her, I caught sight of a four-winged evren rocketing toward us in a blur of sapphire-colored wings. At the same moment, a white wyvern jumped at us from the side, teeth exposed. I gulped. Both clearly wanted a taste of ether.

Violet-scaled hummingbirds forgotten, Solvai and I maneuvered as one. Time seemed to slow as Solvai bent low to jab at the wyvern. At the same moment, I went high, rolling over Solvai's back with my seaxe arcing to slash at the evren.

I hit the evren right across the belly, and bronze dragon blood sprayed across my face and hair, standing out against the snow white strands. By the sound of the wyvern's pained screech, Solvai's dragonhook spear had struck true as well. Both creatures retreated to nurse their wounds, neither of them interested in forming a bond.

"The commanders *have* to put us on the same squad after that," Solvai said with a grin.

"They'd better," I smiled back. "Now go get yourself a bond."

Solvai nodded, then hurried back into the fray. I felt my muscles relax as she left. I didn't want any of my friends near me and my dragon-attracting ether well.

Come on, Meleya, I thought to myself. *Bond a dragon and get out of here before the commanders realize what you are.*

I could picture the distress on Mom's face if anyone were to find out I was a magi. Already, more dragons were looking my way, eyeing me with barbaric hunger.

I had to find a bond, and fast. My gaze flashed back and forth as I looked for a nice, calm-looking dragon.

I almost missed her, with her rusty orange scales that blended into the chasm walls. A regal, majestic drake oversaw the action with intelligent, green eyes.

She stretched her neck upward and opened her jaws wide. Instead of dragonfire, she breathed out crackling, gold lightning. My breath caught—she was a mythic dragon with etherarchy. A Lightwielding stormscale drake.

I darted toward her, praying to any of the three goddesses willing to listen that the other hungry dragons wouldn't follow me.

The drake watched my approach with curiosity. I tried to calm my soul, preparing to attempt another bond.

But before I got the chance, another recruit eclipsed the dragon from my view. Edrea sneered, stabbing toward me with her dragonhook spear.

I leaped backward to avoid getting skewered.

"What in the void?" I protested. "We're only supposed to be fighting dragons today, not each other."

Apparently, Edrea didn't care. She came at me again, and this time I blocked with my seaxe.

"Stay away from that stormscale drake." Edrea's black eyebrows lowered into her usual scowl. "She's mine."

"If you want her that bad, then try to bond her yourself," I said, blocking another blow from Edrea.

"You don't think I already tried that?"

"Then let me—"

"If I can't have her, neither can you," Edrea snapped.

I ground my teeth in frustration. Edrea was honestly wasting time guarding the drake when she could be out trying to bond another dragon? I wished I could say that surprised me, but throughout boot camp Edrea had always been one to scratch my scales. If the commanders assigned us to squads on opposite sides of the keepdom, it would be too close for me.

"That's ridiculous." I glared, losing my cool. I pushed back her spear with my seaxe, then with a grunt, I swung back.

"Find your own dragon, snowhead," Edrea said, spinning to block my blow. "Or better yet, go back to the dirty nomads."

I leaped toward Edrea, sword raised. She held the haft of her spear between her hands to block me, and my blade hacked into the wood, leaving a notch. My cheeks flushed with frustration.

"At least the nomads taught me manners," I barked.

Suddenly, a flash of lemon yellow came careening toward us from the heavens like a shooting star.

The brightly colored dragon plummeted, knocking straight into both Edrea and me. We screamed as we went rolling across the sandy floor. I managed to hold onto my seaxe, but Edrea's spear went clattering in the opposite direction.

Soot. I'd let myself get distracted. No doubt the evren was here for me and my ether well. The yellow dragon shrieked, pulling upward as it violently flapped its four wings. It was already circling back to take another snap at us.

"Drak, snowhead," Edrea swore as she caught sight of her spear. It had snapped in half right where I'd been whacking at it. "Look what you did."

"Maybe if you hadn't been gatekeeping dragons, we wouldn't be in this situation," I responded.

The evren must've noticed that Edrea was defenseless, because it raced toward her, jaws open wide.

Edrea cried out again, scrambling to get away. But she was going about it all wrong, running straight ahead, in line with the dragon's flight path. Any second, it would either roast her alive with a jet of dragonfire, or simply catch up and sink its teeth into her flesh.

I ground my teeth in frustration and let out an annoyed growl before jumping between her and the evren.

I maniacally swung my sword in warning toward its legless underside. Rather than get stuck with a blade, the evren pulled back at the last second, opening its four wings to catch air and halt its momentum. I leaped toward it, still slashing.

The evren backed up, flapping its wings rapidly. I kept coming at it, and out of the corner of my eye I saw Edrea scuttle toward the bladed end of her broken dragonhook spear. She grabbed it, then turned toward me.

We locked eyes for a split second before she grimaced. Then she dashed away, probably to try and bond another dragon and let me take care of the yellow evren myself.

Thanks a lot, Edrea.

The evren lashed its long, scaly tail toward me. It snapped against the back of my hand, knocking my seaxe to the ground. I inhaled sharply, cradling my hand.

But the evren wasn't finished. It reared back its head, preparing to blast me. I crouched, ready to duck under its belly and run.

At the last moment, the evren went cross-eyed. Instead of spraying me with dragonfire, it let out a massive sneeze.

That caught me off guard, especially when along with the sneeze came a white blast of energy. Pure ether—this dragon was an Astromancer, a starshot evren. The ether shot toward me like a dart, and I leaped backward, falling back into the dirt. The white ether blast hit the earth between my legs, a jagged, white mark spiraling across the red chasm floor.

The evren sneezed again and again, each outburst sending another blast of ether shooting at me from its mouth. I scrambled backward on my hands to avoid getting hit.

Sneeze after sneeze, the ridiculous evren got closer and closer. Before long, my back hit against the chasm wall. The evren had me trapped in a somewhat concealed alcove in the rock. I realized with a degree of horror that the commanders watching us wouldn't be able to see me here, which meant I was on my own, even if things got bad.

I cringed, covering my face with my hands as the creature reared back for one final blast.

Chapter 2: The Captain

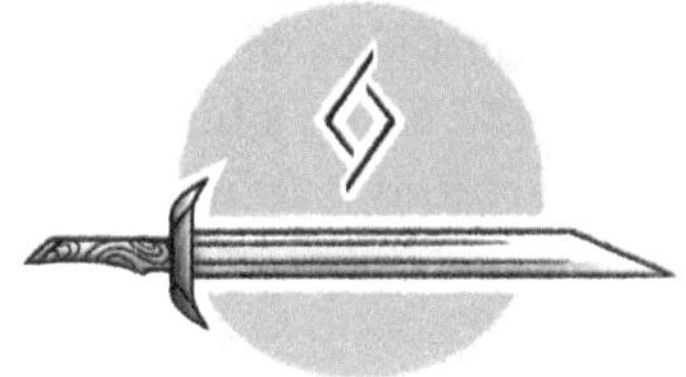

The dragon's astromancy-powered sneeze never came.

I dared to open one eye, peeking at the dragon. Its dragonfire green eyes were no longer narrowed to slits. Rather, they were round and shining as they caught the rays of sunlight streaming into the chasm.

Then it hit me like a strong gust of wind.

Not the evren, but the feeling.

Calm filled my heart, despite the tension and chaos surrounding me. My anxiety about the Dragon Chasm and the worry about Solvai and Brigan getting through it melted away. Even the darkness that always plagued the back of my mind—the fear that I'd fail my parents—vanished for that one beautiful instant.

As I stared at the bright yellow evren, it was like I was hearing music, too—A spirited melody, like a flute rising and falling. It captivated me.

Before I knew it, I was runetracing.

Tiny threads of golden light trailed from my finger, and the mystic rune for the Sight appeared, hovering over the center of my forehead.

Then I blinked.

All at once, a set of brilliant new colors bloomed to life before my eyes. Glowing, rust-colored clouds danced along the horizontal lines in the canyon rock. I could see the uniquely colored auras of every creature and person in the chasm—the action of the battle like a clashing of rainbows.

But the aura that drew my attention was the one right in front of me. As I watched, the evren's soul went from a muted yellow to a vibrant, lemony gold. It exploded with beams of light like the sun.

One of the beams seemed to reach toward me. I reached back, holding out a hand toward the dragon's aura. I watched with wonder as the light encompassed my hand, forming a golden cuff around my wrist—an ethereal symbol of our newly-formed bond.

In turn, I saw a coil of fiery indigo light slip from off the tip of my finger and float toward the evren. The piece of my aura formed into a shiny, blue-violet triangle right over the evren's heart.

The dragon landed on the ground, folding up his wings and standing on the claws at his wing-joints. Using the claw at the hinge of his right forewing, the evren scratched vigorously at the scales over his chest. A bright yellow scale fell to the ground in front of me.

The evren's heartscale.

I watched as the indigo piece of my soul filled the void left by the dragon's heartscale, then picked up the yellow scale the evren had dropped before me. The moment it touched my skin, I felt the bond solidify as a flash of white-gold light bloomed from my hand.

The smooth, triangular scale fit perfectly in my palm. I felt a series of musical notes play in my heart, and I smiled as I realized that it was the evren communicating to me through our bond.

The evren seemed to smile back, his tongue hanging out of his mouth as he panted gleefully. As I studied the evren's face, I realized that the panting wasn't the only thing that reminded me of a puppy. His short snout and erect ears brought to mind the wolf-like snow dogs that lived in the northern keeps. Sharp horns curved backward off the top of the dragon's head, and ridges ran down his neck and tail.

Gold light played at the edge of my vision, and I realized I was still using the Sight.

Instantly, I stopped focusing on the etherarchy. The rune hanging over my forehead went out and dissolved into gold etherdust. The brilliant colors and lights of the spirit plane vanished, giving way to the relative dullness of the physical world.

My head was buzzing, my pulse out of control. What was I thinking? Using etherarchy out in the open? Not just in the open, but while the commanders observed us?

My eyes flew to the chasm ledge high above where I sat. The yellow evren had backed me into a tight corner of the redrock. It would've been pretty hard for anyone to catch sight of the golden rune over my forehead from so far away.

Nobody was screaming the word 'magi' or mounting their dragons to swoop in and arrest me. I'd gotten away with it—for now.

Still, I was furious with myself. I needed to be more careful.

A growl pulled my focus. While the commanders and my fellow recruits hadn't noticed, another handful of dragons must've picked up on my ether well. A whole group of them stalked toward me.

I felt a tug from whatever ethereal string tied my heart to that of the sneeze-happy evren. He nudged me excitedly, enormous eyes bouncing between me and his back.

In theory, I knew exactly how to ride a dragon. I'd studied for three years at Keep Rengard, the finest boot camp in the Canyon Keepdom, and probably all of Evgard.

I cautiously grabbed hold of the spine at the base of the evren's neck and swung one leg over his scaled back.

"Are you sure about this?" I asked the evren, aware that the ether-hungry wild dragons were getting closer.

Ping! My new evren's reply played in my heart like music as he crouched.

One of the wild drakes leaped toward us, and at the same moment, my dragon launched us into the air. I yelped as the drake's claw just missed my leg.

My evren gave an enthusiastic shriek as we soared upward and out of the chasm.

The rich orange fabric of my brand new cloak, made to match the redrock of our land, fell over my shoulders and down to my calves. I was an official soldier of Rengard now.

We stood in the front row of a huge stone amphitheater not far from the Dragon Chasm. A few juniper trees shot up at odd angles from gaps between the stones and small, bristled spineweeds filled in most of the cracks in the rocky seats.

In the seats behind us sat the army of Rengard. Not all of it, of course. Many squads were on duty at the main keep or posted in neighboring towns or outposts. But a couple hundred orange-cloaked soldiers had come to welcome us into their ranks. I even spotted a few members of the nobility's high guards back there, their cloaks of black with orange trim setting them apart.

A flat, stone surface at the base of the amphitheater's seats served as a stage. Beyond the stage, assistants to the dragon keeper helped round up our new bonds. While we went through our induction ceremony, they'd take our dragons back to Keep Rengard's stables.

Beside me, Brigan and Solvai held their heads high. Solvai hadn't bonded a dragon in the chasm, but Brigan stood with shoulders back, his new rusty orange heartscale hanging from a cord around his neck. It perfectly matched his new cloak. It was somehow fitting that despite Edrea's best efforts, Brigan had bonded that regal stormscale drake from the chasm.

He looked like the perfect soldier, his thick, black hair cropped short on the sides with the top pulled into a smooth ridgeknot style. Despite all we'd gone through in the Dragon Chasm less than an hour ago, not a hair was out of place, except for that little corkscrew curl he always pretended just happened to fall perfectly over his forehead.

Brigan turned my way, a dimpled smile playing at his lips.

"I'd ask which dragon was yours, but with a heartscale that bright, he's hard to miss."

Brigan nodded toward where a couple of assistant dragon keepers were struggling to get a certain yellow evren to stay still. My dragon hovered a few feet in the air, his four spastic wings beating fast. He flew in tiny circles, chasing his own tail.

I gave Brigan a shrug. He chuckled.

"I put in a good word with a couple of commanders," he said. "I'm almost positive they're gonna put you, me, and Solvai on a squad together."

"Glad to see you putting your title to good use," I replied.

"No point in being the Heir Duke of Keep Solhelm if you can't swing a few favors for your best friends."

"So you'd consider being your squadmate a favor? Sure it's not a curse?"

"Whoa," Brigan folded his arms across his broad chest. "Curse? Don't go accusing me of being a magi now."

He gave another winning smile, but my jaw tensed at the joke. I turned away.

Brigan frowned. "Meleya—"

The sound of marching cut him off. We both stood at attention as Keep Rengard's nine commanders took the stage. They all wore their full uniforms, from the oversized pauldrons on their right shoulders to the gleaming ravenhelms on their heads. Six of them had ascension armor incorporated into their uniforms—pieces forged using the shed scales from their own bonded dragons.

After the commanders came the Captain of the Guard. Captain Cenrik's ascension armor chestplate and gauntlets were a vibrant shade of sage green to match the heartscale he no doubt wore around his neck under the uniform. He took a step forward, and golden lightning crackled across his scaled ascension armor in a display of power—lightwielding etherarchy granted to him through his dragon's shed scales. The crowd watched on with respect as Captain Cenrik raised his right fist to the left side of his chest.

"For Evgard, unite," he shouted in a deep, resounding voice.

Every member of the guard, including our row of new soldiers, raised our fists to our chests in the same gesture.

In booming chorus, we answered with the Guard's Salute.

"For Evgard, we serve. For her flag, we fight. For her people, we protect. For Evgard, unite."

The last word echoed across the stony amphitheater and out into the rugged desert terrain beyond. A few dragonbirds—Solvai would probably know exactly what species—fled their perches among the junipers at the sound.

"Be seated," Captain Cenrik ordered, and we obliged, settling in for what would no doubt be a long welcome speech. "Before we announce squads, I'd like to thank you all for your service. What an honor to serve alongside you all these years. And to you new soldiers..." Cenrik gestured toward those of us sitting in the front row. "I only wish I'd have had the chance to work with you."

Murmurs ripped throughout the crowd. Brigan, Solvai and I looked at each other. What was Captain Cenrik saying?

Captain Cenrik went on, confirming our suspicions. "But the time has come for me to step down. I wish you the best of luck. May the goddesses favor you and our great keepdom."

There was a small uproar as Captain Cenrik, his face a neutral mask, began to walk off the stage the same way he'd come. A pair of armored men met him at the edge of the amphitheater, one subtly taking hold of the back of his arm as if they were worried he'd try to run or something. It took me a second to realize what uniforms the armored men were wearing.

Silver pauldrons with the symbol of a sword through a triangle on them. Silver swords sheathed at their belts beside hanging silver chain whips. Long, dusk blue cloaks.

My heart sank. Years on the run, hiding among the nomad caravans made it so I knew that uniform all too well.

Those were Mage Hunters.

I was so focused on the action surrounding Captain Cenrik that I almost missed the new arrival taking center stage. But when he spoke, I felt my blood run cold.

"Soldiers of Rengard," his accented voice was commanding, yet somehow flat and emotionless.

He too wore the dusky blue cloak and silver armor of a Mage Hunter, though his was adorned with pieces of black and amethyst ascension armor. His helmet had been modified to accommodate a pair of black horns curving off the top of his head, and a long, dark purple tail coiled around his legs. Patches of black scales grew along his knuckles. The symbol of the Captain of the Guard had been set above the Mage Hunter mark on his oversized pauldron.

I heard a single word uttered over and over in the whispered conversations of the guards behind me:

Drekai.

Please, I prayed to the goddesses. *Let it not be him.* But I knew of only one Drekai Mage Hunter throughout all of Evgard.

He removed his helmet, revealing an ether-scarred face. The white scar crept along his jawline, across the patch of scales growing along his right cheekbone and into his hair. The jagged, spiraling scar sent a shock of white through his dark hair as well.

I remembered the day he got that scar.

"That's the Ursadon," Brigan muttered beside me, using the name the realm had given the famous Mage Hunter. They called him the Ursadon after the dragon bear, because he always tracked down his magi targets, never missing even one.

None, except for me.

My hands balled into fists as the man just stood there, perfectly still. He stared out over the crowd for a full minute as he waited for us to go silent.

Then, just to prove who had the authority here, he waited another minute while the last embers of conversation went dead, had funerals, then completely decayed.

Finally, he resumed speaking, his cold, monotonous voice filling the amphitheater.

"My name is Zoren," he said. "I am your new Captain of the Guard."

CHAPTER 3: THE BUNKER

Other than the fact that the Ursadon's appointment to Captain of the Guard had me panicking inside, it was a perfectly normal evening.

The deep orange sunlight streamed through the window, shining onto the bunker's tan adobe walls. The bunker wasn't much, with only enough space for a stone oven and iron stovetop, a couple of shelves, one countertop, and a long, rickety table.

Solvai sat at one end of the table, her whittling knife moving carefully up and down a block of wood. Behind her on a shelf stood a few of her finished pieces—a delicate ridgebacked wren with intricately-formed wooden feathers and a complicated model of a pair of ashfalcons in flight. On the top shelf was the first piece she'd ever made here in the bunker—a crudely carved falcondrake patterned after the small charm she always wore around her neck. The last gift from her soldier father she'd never gotten to meet. He'd died in combat while Solvai's mother had been expecting her.

Solvai stuck out the tip of her tongue in concentration as she worked. I had the feeling that the block of wood in her hand would soon take the form of a violet-scaled hummingbird.

Meanwhile, I'd taken over the countertop as I restlessly measured flour and dumped it into a wooden mixing bowl. I flipped open the small, waterproof pouch clipped to my belt and pulled out a saltshaker. Almost more than the backup dagger in my boot, I never wanted to be caught without it. I sprinkled some into my cupped hand before tossing it in with the flour.

Brigan sat at the other end of the table, leaning back in his chair against the wall. As usual, he hadn't stopped talking since we got back to the bunker after the new guards' ceremony. Brigan threw out topic after topic, hoping to spark a heated debate.

"Gauntlet down," Brigan said, hoping to get one of us on the defensive. "I bonded the best dragon of any of the new soldiers today."

Solvai didn't look up from her carving. "Does it get better than a lightwielding drake who perfectly matches your new uniform?"

Brigan smiled. "She does, doesn't she?"

"That may be so," I said, playing right into Brigan's hopes. "But—and I'm just gonna throw this out there—my dragon can fly."

His eyes lit up. "Whoa, Meleya throwing down a gauntlet of her own. Are you saying evren are better than drakes?"

"Definitely. When you're fighting a wild dragon, being able to fly will always give you an advantage. Sorry Brigan, but drakes are objectively lamer."

"Says the girl who bonded the most brightly-colored dragon I've ever seen. Tell me, what advantage do you get from being a living signal flare, broadcasting your location to every enemy for miles around?"

"I think Meleya's dragon's cute," Solvai said, rushing to my defense.

"Exactly what every warrior wants to hear," I mumbled, roughly pouring a cup of milk in with the flour. The white liquid splashed up onto the sides of my mixing bowl.

Out of nowhere, I felt a little rush in my heart, followed by a curious, plinking melody.

Brring-a-ling?

I froze midway through grabbing a mixing spoon. Was that my dragon?

Feeling kind of silly, I channeled my thoughts into a response.

Buddy, is that you?

Ping! my dragon affirmed musically through the bond.

Huh, I thought. *Can you like... read my mind whenever you want?*

Tring? I got the impression that the evren wasn't sure what I meant. Maybe he'd understand emotions better. Through the bond, I tried to convey how vulnerable the idea of sharing my every thought made me feel.

Bing-bong, he replied, and somehow I knew he was letting me know that while he could sense strong emotions from me through the bond, my thoughts and mind were still my own. I could let him in or out whenever I wanted.

I relaxed at that. Dragon or not, I didn't like the idea of having anyone inside my head.

Tring-a-ling, my evren thought, sending a somewhat melancholy string of notes through the bond.

I miss you too, I thought back, the corner of my mouth quirking into a half-smile.

"I wish they'd let us see our dragons before placement trials tomorrow," I said out loud.

"Same," Brigan agreed.

"Don't worry," Solvai said, wood curling off of her block as she moved her knife along its edge. "My mom's the best dragon keeper in the realm. She'll take good care of them."

I began incorporating the milk into the flour mixture as Brigan leaned back even further in his chair. Suddenly, he snapped his fingers.

"Gauntlet down," he said, moving on to a new topic. "Spears are inferior to seaxes."

That got Solvai to look up from her work, a glare on her freckled face.

"Sorry, Solvai." I shrugged. "I have to agree with him on this one."

"Not a fair debate when two of you are swordfighters. Next topic," she ordered.

"Fine," Brigan said with a conspiratorial smile. "Gauntlet down: Captain Cenrik stepping down isn't retirement—he's secretly under arrest."

"What are you talking about?" Solvai frowned.

"Did either of you see those Mage Hunters escorting him away after the ceremony?" Brigan asked.

"No," Solvai replied. "The only Mage Hunter I saw was the new Captain of the Guard. I didn't know they even allowed Drekai to be soldiers, let alone lead the army."

I tensed at the mention of Zoren. I felt a nervous pit forming in my stomach as I seized my mixing bowl and turned it upside down, shaking it a few times to drop the sticky dough onto my flour-coated countertop.

"He's not just any Drekai," Brigan said. "The Ursadon is a realm-renowned Mage Hunter. He takes all kinds of high-profile magi hunting cases across Evgard. A few of my parents' friends have hired him to clean up their keeps."

The pit in my stomach grew at Brigan's choice of words.

"So what's a Drekai doing living on the mainland?" Solvai asked.

"Nobody knows," Brigan said ominously.

I know, I thought, biting my tongue as I forcefully began to knead the dough. Mom told me Zoren came over from the Dragon Isles with a group of Drekai in order to spy on the Mage Hunter Academy, deep in the Ridgeback Mountains. It didn't take long for him to turn his back on his own and join the Hunters himself.

"How about this," Brigan said eagerly. "Gauntlet down: Drakfell betraying Evgard was a good political move."

"How can you even pretend to argue for that?" Solvai asked. "Everyone knows Drakfell's king brought ruin to his keepdom by turning traitor. As we speak, Keep Evgard is sending in enforcers and platoons to quell the uprising."

"So you don't think the Knights of the Torch can match Keep Evgard's forces?"

"I don't think the Knights of the Torch are anything more than a myth. Sure, maybe they were a thing hundreds of years ago, but not anymore." Solvai set down her carving tools to emphasize her statement.

Brigan leaned forward in his chair, excited by the controversy. "Counterpoint: I heard that the leader of the Mage Hunters, the great Black Valkyrie herself, lost in a fight with the Knights of the Torch's patron, the Farseer. If that's true, I doubt Evgard's few platoons can stand up to Drakfell when it's supported by the Knights."

Solvai rolled her eyes. "The Farseer? Really? It's all Drakfellian propaganda."

Brigan stood up, fire in his eyes. "Gauntlet down: The Farseer is a real person, not just a legendary figurehead."

"You really think there's some mystical, red-robed man running around the woods, popping up to save magi in need like in the old stories?"

"If there is, he's doing an awful job," I gave my dough a frustrated slap, then continued kneading it with a vengeance.

My friends stared at me for only a second before Brigan nodded. "That's true. We're executing more and more magi each day in hopes that it'll somehow stop the more frequent skyfalls. My parents write that we've had two skyfalls in Keep Solhelm within the past month alone."

"Just think," Solvai said. "Now that we're officially in the guard, we'll get to fight when the next skyfall comes." She sighed, a faraway look in her eyes. Brigan and I exchanged knowing glances.

"You'd have made your dad really proud," I said as I finished kneading.

"You think?" She smiled. "At first I was sad that I didn't bond a dragon in the chasm this morning. But my father wasn't a dragon rider either, and that never stopped him from leading the charge against a pack of wild ridgerunners, or single-handedly slaying a wild third ascension drake."

Solvai absently rubbed the carved falcondrake charm that hung from the chain around her neck. The corner of my mouth turned up on one side. Brigan and I had heard Solvai's favorite stories about her courageous father many times.

I grabbed another handful of flour as I prepared to separate the dough. As I reached into the sack, a puff of white flour shot out and rose into the air.

I jumped as a tiny cough sounded from above, followed by a series of angry chitters. The three of us looked up to see an irritated draccoon chastising us from his place in the rafters.

"Sorry, Dusty," I chuckled as the creature waved his tiny black fists and thumped his spiked, ringed tail in rage.

Dusty must not have been satisfied with my apology, because he spread his stubby arms wide, revealing skin flaps that ran along his arms and connected them to his sides.

Oh no.

Using his arms like makeshift wings, Dusty launched himself from the rafters and glided down, straight onto my flour-strewn countertop.

"Hey," I cried out, throwing my arm between the draccoon and my dough as he hungrily tried to grab at it. "You can have one when they're done, if you're a good little draccoon."

Dusty chittered some more, narrowing his beady eyes at me. Then he leaped off the counter, scurrying across the floor and up Brigan's leg.

"I got him," Brigan said as Dusty slunk up his torso and around his arm to perch on his shoulder pauldron. Brigan carefully walked over to a wooden support beam in the corner of the bunker, letting Dusty off so he could climb back to his home in the rafters.

Dusty squeaked gleefully as he darted toward one of the beams directly above me. With a little smirk, he held up an armful of tiny objects.

Then, one by one, Dusty dropped the objects down toward me.

"*Dusty*," I scolded as I caught an extra hair loop, a pin bearing the insignia of Keep Solhelm, and a leather cord necklace with an orange dragon heartscale tied to it.

"You scaly little thief," Brigan protested, reaching for his bare collarbone. "I don't know why we keep you."

Dusty gave a little victory squeak as Brigan glared.

I chuckled. Brigan had threatened to kick Dusty out of our bunker many times before. But I knew that even if he tried, Dusty would come right back. My friends may've thought Dusty was just some sneaky little draccoon who wanted a free meal and people to harass every once in a while, but I'd known Dusty long before Solvai, Brigan, and I found this old, abandoned bunker. Dusty had been one of my only friends growing up on the run in the canyons.

And he wasn't even real.

Well, that wasn't technically true. Magi's ethereal familiars were real, in a manner of speaking. My dad had formed Dusty using dreamweaving runes before I was even born. Together, they'd terrorized the nobility of Evgard, stealing trinkets and coin whenever they got the chance.

Nowadays, Dad used Dusty to keep an eye on me while he and mom couldn't.

I passed Brigan back his things, then carried my balls of dough over to a pot of boiling oil. I dropped the first one in, and it made a satisfying, sputtering sizzle as it fried.

"Mmm," Brigan said as the scent of rich, fried dough filled the bunker. "Gauntlet down: Meleya's honey fry bread is the tastiest thing in the realm."

"Can't argue with that," Solvai said.

"It's my mom's favorite," I said, looking out the window toward the late afternoon sun. I needed to hurry up and finish before I lost my chance to see them tonight.

"We could come with you, you know," Solvai said cautiously.

Brigan nodded. "I'd love to finally meet your parents."

"No," I responded a little too quickly. "Trust me, guys. Spydra Prison isn't a pleasant place to visit."

"We can handle it," Solvai said as she and Brigan watched me. I didn't look up as I used a slotted spoon to pull the fry bread out of the boiling oil.

I knew my friends were willing to go with me to that place to visit Mom and Dad. But that was because they didn't know the truth about *why* my parents were locked up. If they'd known my mother and father were illegal magi, I doubt they'd have been so eager to join me on the trek to Spydra.

"No," I said firmly. "I have to go alone."

Chapter 4: Nine Minutes

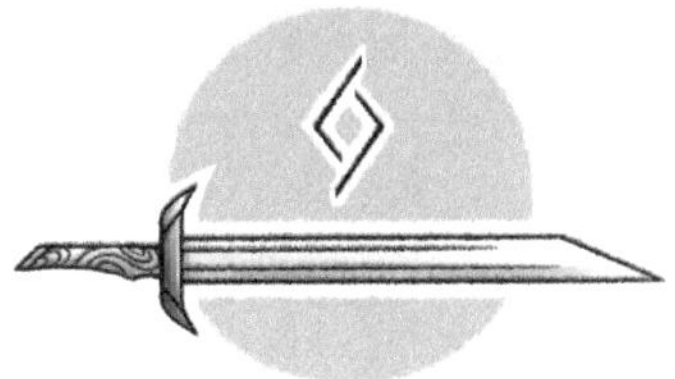

With a large basket of fry bread tucked firmly under my arm, I stood overlooking the edge of the Rise.

Nestled between the high, majestic red walls of Rengard Canyon, the Rise stood tall and proud. For the nobility whose estates and gardens flourished on top of the butte, it was easy to forget the commonfolk of Keep Rengard who lived along the river in the lower town.

During my first several weeks as a recruit three years ago, I'd commuted from the lower town up to the Rise each day. Basic training took place just outside the grand, white adobe Keep Rengard citadel, but with my parents locked up, I'd been living in the hollow of a rock near the base of the Rise. I'd stayed there until Solvai found out and she and her mom took me in. As head dragon keeper to the king and queen, Lorelai lived in an apartment attached to the stables, only a scale's throw away from the training grounds. The accommodations were quite nice by commoner standards, and Solvai's room had plenty of space for an extra tenant.

The nobility saw little reason to leave the grandeur atop the Rise, so getting up and down without a flying dragon was an ordeal. Once again, I thought about how nice it would be if I had access to my dragon tonight.

Ping! A single, happy note penetrated my heart.

I chuckled, then thought back through the bond. *Hi there yourself.*

Yeah, flying down the Rise would make things a lot quicker. But still not as quick as if I was allowed to use etherarchy. As a Rifter, I could've been at the prison entrance in seconds. But if I did that, it would just make it that much easier for them to lock me inside once they found out I was an unregistered magi.

I stepped back from the edge and made my way to the narrow stone bridge that spanned the distance between the Rise and the canyon's edge. The king of Rengard always kept a high mage who specialized in geomancy. The registered Geomancer kept up the arch, ensuring it never eroded away, and in times of peril they'd use their etherarchy to break down the arch so that Rengard's enemies couldn't get onto the Rise.

I found it a little contradictory—for a realm that banned and executed so many magi, it sure didn't mind relying on them to protect itself.

I got to the gatekeeper on duty at the bridge. I was already reaching for my coin purse to pay the fee when she stepped aside, waving me through.

"Thank you for your service," she said, nodding to my orange cloak. I nodded back with a smile, stepping onto the top of the arch.

The king's current high mage had done her job well. While the bridge looked dangerously narrow and delicate from afar, the surface felt wide and strong as I crossed.

On the other side of the bridge were two pathways. One veered north along Rengard Canyon's upper rim, toward the majority of the keepdom's major cities, while the other led straight off the canyon's edge onto a geomantically-formed staircase. The stairs made long, questionably safe zigzags all the way down the cliff face.

I hurried down the steps, the air getting cooler once the canyon wall cut me off from the sun's rays. I didn't want to waste time—the prison closed just after sunset.

As I approached the bottom, the bustling sounds of Keep Rengard's thriving port greeted me. The dock was lined with merchants selling everything from drakefish to dust scarves or cactus juice. They called out, trying to draw business to their stands and shops. A longship had just pulled into port, and a few men and a couple of bonded drakes carried heavy sacks of goods down a ramp off the boat.

As I headed down the dock, people nodded to me with respect. A few even hurried out of my way, thanking me for what I did to protect the keepdom. I felt a little strange, especially since I'd only been made a guard earlier that day and had yet to actually fight off any wild dragons. And, of course, there was the voice lurking in the back of my mind reminding me that if these people knew I was secretly a magi, they'd have a very different reaction.

There was much less hustle and bustle at the south end of the port. One smallish river longboat floated there, a ferryman leaning against the post that tied the boat to the dock. He nodded when he saw me coming, then began untying his vessel.

I stepped into the boat and held out a copper mark, the usual fare for a trip downriver. But just like the gatekeeper on the arch, the ferry driver refused my money. He did, however, accept a piece of fry bread.

Soon, the noise of the trading port gave way to the quiet stillness of the canyon. While they'd built walls and placed sandbags all along the edges of the water to guide the river near the port, out here, the Ridgeback River wound freely through the deep canyon. Drakalope hid in the grasses near the sandy banks while falcondrakes soared above. I spotted a bighorned craghopper using its clawed hooves to scale the cliff. A large shadow passed beneath the boat—an aquadon with its long neck and tail, and four flippers paddling at its sides.

Occasionally, we floated past a home built to hug the canyon walls or a family ranch. I saw a few vegetable gardens growing in the canyon bed as well.

I sighed, wondering if I'd ever have the kind of life where I could grow a garden of my own. I loved the idea of cooking with fresh vegetables that I'd grown and harvested myself. But such a thing was out of the question while I was a soldier. I'd be living in the barracks now, on and off duty too often. They may even send my squad to one of the outer cities like Rust Gorge or Brackentown.

And once I was finished working off my parents' six-year sentence by serving in the guard, they'd be banished to some wasteland far away from the realm proper. Either the wilds of the Island of Drekaari, or perhaps the northernmost mountains of Behrfell. It was so cold there that not even the wild dragons came to terrorize the towns. Certainly too cold to hope I could grow tomatoes and squash.

We rounded a bend in the river to reveal a heavily painted canyon wall. The reddish surface had been defaced with words written in coppery dragon's blood. 'Death to all magi,' was one phrase that always made my skin crawl.

Sticking straight up from the loose redrock at the base of the wall were nine spears. Atop each spear was the dry, horned skull of a different wild dragon. Painted in more dragon's blood on the left cheekbone of each skull was the symbol of each of the nine magi types. I saw the lightning-like symbol of the Lightwielder on one and the angular lines of the Geomancer on another.

Finally, my eyes came to rest on the symbol scratched onto a sun-scorched wyvern skull at the end of the lineup. An elongated, open diamond with extended lines slanting off the top and bottom. The symbol of the Rifters.

I shuddered, clutching my basket of bread closer. As if the writing on the wall hadn't been bad enough.

At least the anti-magi monument served as a landmark between the Rise and Spydra Prison. I was getting close.

Before long, the entrance to the prison came into view. It was nothing more than a weather-worn wooden sign and a hole in the rock. I thanked the ferryman and stepped off the boat onto a crude dock, then followed the dirt path lined with a charming little dragon bone fence and a few more hollow, desiccated skulls.

I'd only made it halfway along the path when a voice called out to greet me.

"Well, if it isn't Meleya of Misthaven," said a cheerful guard, getting up from his chair beside the hole in the rock that served as Spydra Prison's front entrance.

"It's that time of week, isn't it?" I called back, smiling as I approached.

Ulf wore the same guard's uniform as I did, though his was a lot more snug around the middle than it once had been. Although, his fitness wasn't the reason they'd relegated him to such a lonely post so far from the Rise. Rather, it was his dragonfire green eyes and the ruddy scales on the tips of his pointed ears. Ulf was a half-born, part human and part Drekai.

"Look at you," Ulf said. "Orange cloak and everything. Congratulations."

"Thanks. Speaking of congratulations, how's your wife? Are you a proud father yet?"

"Any day now." Ulf gave an uneasy almost-smile. "I'm so nervous."

"Don't be," I said. "You'll make a drakking amazing dad."

"Thanks. Although what worries me most is that the little thing will come out looking... well, looking like me."

Ulf shook his head, almost subconsciously trying to get his curly mop of hair to cover his scaly, pointed ears and bright green eyes. I knew exactly what he meant.

I reached into my basket, pulling out a cloth-wrapped parcel. "This is for you and your family."

Ulf's face lit up. "This isn't honey fry bread."

"With honeybutter."

Ulf whistled, unwrapping the parcel. "I'd better sample one now—gotta make sure it isn't poisoned or anything."

I snorted. "Of course."

Ulf took a massive bite, and I could hear the light crunch of the bread. He closed his eyes contentedly, and I felt warmth flood my heart.

"So," Ulf said, chewing. "How was the Dragon Chasm? I remember how terrified I was when I went though—and I was in my twenties when I joined the guard. Can't imagine doing it when I was—how old are you again?"

"Almost seventeen."

"Can't imagine," Ulf repeated as he shook his head. Then he glanced upward at the fading daylight. "Soot," he swore, smacking his lips. "Sun's almost down. Better get you in there before the prison closes."

With that, Ulf reached into his pocket and whipped out a thin, metallic rod about the size and length of a mixing spoon.

My pulse raced at the mere sight of it. The rod was made from pure silver—the perfect tool for checking to see if someone was a magi.

I held out a hand, forcing a blank expression onto my face. Ulf hurriedly pressed the silver rod into my open palm.

A feeling like icy-cold lightning shot through my skin and up my forearm. Freezing pain made me want to cry out and reel backward.

But on the outside, I didn't flinch. I didn't move a muscle, looking down so that Ulf couldn't read the pain in my eyes.

"Still not a magi," Ulf said routinely, pulling back the silver and sending a wave of relief through my hand. "Head on in. And thanks again for the bread."

I nodded to him once more before heading into the open mouth of Spydra Prison.

During the Dragon Wars, the nobility of Keep Rengard had decided that they didn't want magi prisoners held so close to them in the dungeons at the Rise's citadel. So they repurposed the abandoned spydra tunnels, turning them into a lovely, totally bleak prisoner getaway.

I walked for several minutes down the familiar, torchlit caverns. Each one was twisting and narrow, with strangely smooth walls bearing gritty, spiraling patterns on them, the result of being carved from the rock using the shadowbinding venom of giant spydra long ago. All of the giant spydra had supposedly moved on from the cave network, and now only a few of the tinier multi-headed dragon spiders still lurked. I occasionally caught sight of one of their black shadowsilk webs spun between the crevices of rocks.

But the deeper I went into the tunnels, the more worried I became that the giant ones may not have actually abandoned their old caverns.

I passed a few caverns that led to the non-magi cells closer to the entrance. They kept the dangerous prisoners at the back.

Suddenly, an aura of coldness fell over me, and I knew I was nearly there. In the flickering firelight, silvery streaks of paint flashed along the walls. Already I could feel the silver acting like a dampener on my ether well, and I knew that it would be hard for me to channel etherarchy here. Not that I dared to try.

The silver-infused paint got thicker the closer I got to the magi prison cells. I took one final turn, heading into a completely silver paint-lined cave.

"Meleya!" two voices shouted in unison.

"Mom, Dad," I said, running the last length of the tunnel to get to them.

For the past three years, the separate cells at the end of the tunnel had been their home. Each cell was built into an individual cavity along the back of the cavern, both with a gated wall of silver bars blocking them in as well as keeping them apart. But I knew that when they reached through the bars at the edge nearest each other, they could just touch the tips of their fingers together. The only price was the sharp pain from letting the silver touch their arms as they did.

"I made fry bread," I said, holding up my basket.

"Aw, soot," Dad said, his slight northern accent coming through. He had a teasing glint in his eyes. "I was hopin' for dragon fritters."

"Ivar," Mom scolded him through the bars of her cell.

"Kiddin'." He threw up his hands.

"Next week, I promise," I assured him as I sat facing the corner formed by their cells. Both Mom and Dad sat as well, as close to me and each other as they could be without touching the silver. I buttered each of them a piece of fry bread and passed it through the bars, then finally made one for myself as well.

I bit down into the bread, the taste of sweetness and salt dancing on my tongue. It was perfectly crisp on the outside, with a tender, moist interior.

The bubbles in the bread made the perfect pockets for catching pooling honey butter.

"I've said it once, and I'll say it again," Dad said between bites. "Mels, your cookin' is the only reason I have to go on in here. These'll get me through another week."

"Thank you, Meli," Mom agreed.

I beamed at them, gazing into their faces in the low torchlight. Dad looked a lot like me, with his shock of white snowhead hair and suntanned skin. He had a short, dark stubbly beard and laughing eyes. The Psion's silvermark cut into his left cheek matched the silver in the bars and painted onto the walls of his cell.

"How's Dusty?" Dad asked, licking the fingers on one hand as he held out the other for another piece of bread. I set down my own piece to butter his next one.

"As much a troublesome pickpocket as ever."

"Glad to see he's keepin' up our old skill," Dad chuckled.

Mom rolled her eyes. They were dark brown, almost the exact same shade as mine. Her face was beautiful, though most people couldn't see past the burns that dominated the left side. Through all the angry red scarring, I could still see the silvery lines that formed her Rifter's silvermark.

I cringed and looked away. Even now, her burn was hard for me to see. Every time I did, I remembered the day I walked into our family's tent and saw Mom pressing the hot coal into her cheek, a scream escaping her lips as she tried to burn away her mark. I'd only been seven years old, and not knowing what else to do, I'd run up to her and tried to get the coal away.

Looking down at my palm, I could still see the scar the coal had left on me. It was small, but Mom had been more upset about my burn than hers.

I closed my fist.

"I brought last week's scorecard for the game," I said, reaching into a corner of my basket. "Ready to see if we can take Dad down?"

Mom gave a small, smug smile, reaching for a stack of well worn cards from a corner of her cell. "He doesn't stand a chance."

"Hey, no gangin' up," Dad protested as Mom dealt us each a short stack of cards. Reddish brown dust from the roads we'd traveled together filled the cracks and lined the edges of each one. Dad and I carefully reached through the silver bars to take our cards.

We chatted as we played, too aware that our time together was running short.

"Tell us about your week," Dad said, laying down a six of stars to start the round as he gestured to my cloak. "Love the new look. It's almost like you're a real guard or somethin'."

"Hey," I said, laying down the twelve of stars beside Dad's card. "I *am* a real guard."

"That's right," Mom said, playing the starry-robed Mystic card to take the hand. "You're out of basic training this week." She frowned deeply, and Dad and I exchanged worried glances.

"It's not a big deal," I said hurriedly. "Nothing's changed at all so far. I'm basically a glorified doorkeeper." I looked to Dad, who subtly gave me a grateful nod.

Mom played another card. "But don't new guards have to fight wild dragons as a sort of initiation?"

Dad rushed to answer. "The Dragon Chasm's an old tradition, though, right?"

I played into Dad's response. "Yeah, that's an old tradition for sure."

An old tradition that they still do every year, I thought.

Mom looked between the two of us, deep skepticism behind her eyes. I swallowed. I was never a very good liar.

"Meleya?" she prompted as she started the next hand.

Dad gave me another warning look, but I was cornered. I replied, "Okay, so maybe they had us in close proximity to a few wild dragons. But I was completely safe. And..." I grinned excitedly, quickly taking my turn in the game, and then reaching for the bright yellow scale tied to a cord around my neck. "I even bonded a dragon."

"You didn't," Dad said. "You should've said right away! Congratulations, Mels."

"What's the dragon like?" Mom asked, concern still etched onto her scarred face.

"He's this highly-energetic evren. Mythic too—an Astromancer."

"No way," Dad grinned, then turned to Mom. "That's a good thing, right, Freya? A dragon with etherarchy'll help keep her safe for sure."

Mom didn't answer. Dad played his next card and plowed on.

"What makes you say astromancy? Starglass claws? Ether shielding along the scales?"

"Ether blasts," I said. "He blows little ether comets when he uh... when he sneezes."

Dad cracked up at that, slapping his knee.

I continued. "In fact, I think I'm going to name him Sniff."

Prrring, my dragon sent an approving note through our bond.

"And you were right, Dad," I said eagerly. "About dragon's souls. Remember what you said about the bonding process making them different somehow? It's true. It was like I saw the dragon's soul change and come to life as I bonded it."

"Really? I knew it!" Dad leaned forward. "What about Solvai and Brigan? Did either of them—"

"Did you say you *saw* the dragon's soul come to life?" Mom said, her hand coming to a hard stop as she gathered the cards to take another round.

I faltered, realizing my mistake too late.

"Uh... no," I stammered. "What I meant was, I mean, I could tell in the dragon's behavior and stuff."

"Freya," Dad started.

"No," Mom said, involuntarily raising her voice. "You saw it through the Sight. You used etherarchy."

"You know I know better than that—"

Mom's eyes welled up with tears. "Meli, how could you?"

"Freya," Dad said again, getting to his knees. "She's fine. There's no need to—"

But Mom wasn't finished. "You can't risk your life like that, not here. Not when they're watching you."

"Mom, please. I was careful—I'm always so careful."

"It's not enough. You think this is bad?" Mom gestured at the silver cell all around her. "You have no idea the things they do to magi. Death comes in a thousand different flavors with them."

"Breathe, Freya," Dad pleaded.

"No," Mom went on, getting to her feet with shaky knees. "This isn't safe. Meleya, you have to get out of here. You have to leave the keep."

"No, Mom," I said, getting to my feet myself. "If I leave the guard, they'll execute you and Dad."

"We can't know that," Mom said, doing a terrible job of reassuring me. Her eyes went round and unfocused as she grew increasingly hysterical. "At least you'd be safe."

"What does that matter if I lose you two?" I stuck out my chin.

"Mels," Dad said through his teeth, shooting his gaze toward Mom. I bit my tongue.

"You have to get out of the Canyon Keepdom," Mom said, and I couldn't tell if she was talking more to me or to herself. "If she can just get to Skygard, there's a chance. She'd have to go far to the northwest, cross the Scarlet Straight where there are fewer Mage Hunters." She squeezed her eyes shut, a couple of tears falling across the rough, burned skin on her left cheek.

"But there are Mage Hunters all along the border," she continued, inhaling and exhaling rapidly. "Lining it from Drakesfjord through Solhelm..."

"Freya, breathe," Dad urged, pressing up against the icy silver bars and reaching as far toward her as he could. "Slowly, in... out..."

Mom covered her face with her hands as she fell to her knees.

Guilt hit me like a crashing wave. A thousand memories from living with the nomads bubbled up inside me, and I felt tears prick the backs of my eyes.

Suddenly I was seven again, walking though one of the smaller canyons in eastern Rengard. We'd been traveling with the Dunefox caravan, and I remembered being glad—this was the longest we'd been with the same caravan that I could recall. Mom wore a dust scarf all the time to cover her silvermark. She liked for Dad and me to wear ours too, to make hers seem less out of place, but I always pulled mine off. It got too hot out there under the sun all day.

The caravan had stopped to make camp for the night. Mom and Dad worked to set up our dragonhide laavu-style tent, while Dusty the draccoon and I played together in the dirt nearby.

Before long, a couple of other kids came over with a ball and asked if we wanted to play. I remembered being thrilled by the chance to play with friends my age. It was hard being a nomad amongst nomads.

We laughed and kicked the ball around the sandy canyon floor. The other kids loved Dusty, who would chitter and dart away every time the ball came near him.

Before long, a bigger kid joined us. He kicked the ball so high that I couldn't reach it even when I jumped. It sailed over my head, bouncing into a deep ravine. The other kids and I stared at the ball as it rolled down the crevice and out of reach.

The other kids shrugged and began to disperse. But I felt my heart sink. I wasn't ready for my new friends to leave.

I looked around to make sure nobody was watching, aware even then that my etherarchy was bad. Dangerous. Then I lifted a tiny finger and traced the rifting rune—I'd seen Mom use it many times before, though she tried to hide it from me.

A small portal opened up in front of me, a gold light-rimmed tear with white inside it. Looking into that whiteness, I could make out the other end of the portal where the ball sat wedged between two rocks. I reached through the portal, hastily retrieving the toy before letting both rifts and the rune over my forehead dissolve into etherdust.

I turned to call out to the other children, hoping they'd want to come back and play some more. But when I looked over, I found myself staring into the horror-struck face of another little girl.

She screamed, crying out one word over and over.

Magi.

Both her parents and mine came running, followed by a small crowd. The little girl clung to her mother's leg, cowering away from me as if she was afraid I'd hurt her at any moment.

But as isolating as it felt to watch the other nomads shrink away from me, the agonized expression in my mother's eyes was far worse.

The Dunefox caravan didn't report us, but they demanded we leave by nightfall. Less than an hour later, my parents and I traversed the canyon trails alone by moonlight. Mom cried the whole way, and it had been my fault.

The memory shook me. I blinked back my tears as I watched Mom cry again through the silver bars of her prison cell, my father unable to hold her.

Just then, I heard footsteps approaching from the cavern behind me. Probably Ulf coming to get me as the prison closed for the night.

I hurried to gather the game cards and stack them near Mom's cell. But when I looked up, it wasn't the half-born guard standing in the cavern mouth.

It was a pair of enforcers—silver-clad Mage Hunters.

"We're here to move the prisoner Ivar to his new cell," one said, brushing his hand against the silver whip clipped to his belt. A clear message not to protest.

Dad and I did anyway.

"You can't separate them," I objected.

"What do you mean, new cell?" Dad said, challenge flashing in his eyes. "I can't leave her."

Mom's weeping intensified.

"It's not up to you," the Mage Hunter said. "We're moving you tonight, by order of the new Captain of the Guard."

My blood went cold.

"New Captain of the Guard?" Dad said. "Why in the void would the Captain give a scale what cell I'm in?"

Dad caught my eye, his brow furrowing as he took in my expression. Mom looked up from her hands.

"Who's the new Captain, Meleya?" she asked.

I didn't respond.

"Tell me who it is!" she cried.

The Mage Hunter answered for me. "Zoren of the Dragon Isles. The Ursadon himself."

I didn't need to use the Sight to see Mom's spirit breaking.

The Mage Hunter enforcers pushed past me to open Dad's cell. While one fiddled with the lock, the other turned to me.

"Visiting hours are over."

"Please, just let me stay until the transfer is done."

"I said visiting hours are over."

"But I can't just leave her—"

"Enough," the Mage Hunter snapped. "I have a direct order from the Captain of the Guard. Now leave before I call your commander and get you court martialed."

With that, the Mage Hunter used both hands to shove me backward toward the cave entrance. I scrambled to grab my basket.

Dad's protests echoed through the cavern, mixing with Mom's sobbing as I forced myself to walk away.

Chapter 5: Trials

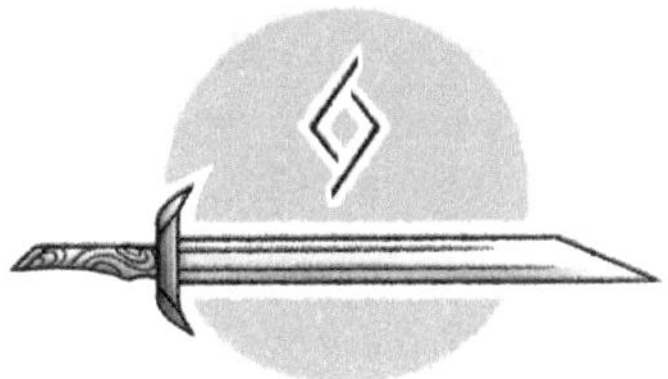

Storm clouds rolled in overnight, blanketing the sky in a layer of dark gray. Thunder rumbled overhead as the first drops of rain fell onto our faces.

Brigan and Solvai were on my left, while the four other members of our new squad stood to my right. Brigan's little chat with the commanders must've worked, because they'd put my two best friends and me together.

But they'd also put me with Edrea.

Splash!

Edrea thrust her boot into the quickly forming puddle. Muddy water splattered all over the hem of my new orange guard's cloak.

I gritted my teeth, casting her a sidelong glance. She glared back out of the corner of her eye, a smirk playing at her lips. In the end, she hadn't bonded a dragon in the chasm. I wasn't about to rub that in her face, but I wasn't above splashing her back.

Beads of reddish mud flicked onto her boot and up her pant leg. She jumped, rounding on me.

"What in the void, Misthaven?" she said. At the mention of my birthplace, everyone in the lineup turned sharply our way.

I bit my tongue, looking straight ahead.

"Edrea, don't," Solvai spoke quietly.

Edrea gestured with her hand as if she were closing Solvai's mouth with it. Solvai recoiled, obliging.

Brigan, on the other hand, stepped out of line. "Don't call her that."

"Brigan, it's fine," I said.

"No, it's not." He folded his arms across his broad chest.

"Why not?" Edrea countered. "It's her name, isn't it? Meleya of Misthaven."

"Not the way you said it."

"Not my fault she was born in the cursed magi city."

"Not mine either," I spat back, standing beside Brigan.

The thick, squarely-built guy who'd been standing beside Edrea took a protective step toward her, shooting Brigan a warning glance. I froze as I took in the sight of him—close cropped blond hair, and a tattoo depicting a hulking drake winding up his neck. He must've done basic training in a neighboring keep, because I definitely would've remembered him.

"Don't mess with my little sister," the guy grumbled.

"Little sister?" I repeated, looking between him and Edrea. There was no resemblance.

"Cam is my stepbrother," Edrea explained smugly. "He just got out of the boot camp run by the prison in Rust Gorge."

Cam cracked his neck and knuckles, and I noticed more tattoos on the backs of his hands, disappearing up his arms under his sleeves.

"What landed you in prison?" Brigan asked, determined not to be intimidated.

Cam's eyebrow twitched. "I beat up the nobleman who messed with my dragon."

Edrea was looking at me with an air of superiority as her terrifying brother stood toe to toe with Brigan. Okay, so maybe her bodyguard looked like he could kill a fully grown man with his pinkie finger, but mine had mad debate skills and monogrammed handkerchiefs, so I could take comfort in that, I guess.

Edrea squinted at Brigan before nudging her brother. "Back off, Cam. They're not worth it." She wrinkled her nose at me once more before stepping back in line, and her menacing stepbrother followed. Thunder boomed.

Brigan and I returned to our places as more rain began to fall. I glanced down toward the little pouch at my belt, feeling glad that the waterproof material was keeping the saltshaker inside from getting waterlogged.

Before long, Commander Gunnar stepped out of the command center at the edge of the training grounds. He crossed the muddy plane to where we stood, looking just as annoyed about the weather as we were.

"New squad," he barked over the pelting rain. "Welcome to your first day as soldiers of Keep Rengard. The seven of you have done well to make it this far."

Commander Gunnar began pacing through the mud in front of us as he went on.

"Now, as for your places within the squad. We'll need to determine which of you'll be front liners and which'll be support. We'll do this through placement trials, run by your squad captain."

Commander Gunnar came to a stop in front of Brigan. My friend squared his shoulders and inclined his chin. Brigan would make the perfect squad captain.

Then Commander Gunnar looked to the end of the line.

"Solvai of Keep Rengard," the commander said. "Or should I say, Captain Solvai."

Solvai's hazel eyes widened to the size of dragon eggs. She took a few steps backward as everyone's attention hit her like a smack to the face.

Brigan stared in disbelief while Edrea audibly scoffed. Even Cam and the two guys I didn't recognize raised eyebrows at Solvai.

"Captain Solvai will run trials in strength, speed, endurance, accuracy, and sparring," Commander Gunnar said. "From there, she'll determine what positions you'll take, as well as lead your squad in combat."

With that, the commander raised a fist to his chest in salute before backing a good distance away and crossing his arms.

We waited in silence for what felt like an eternity, wondering if Commander Gunnar was going to say anything more. Soon, it became very clear that he wasn't. He wanted to see how we handled ourselves from here.

Brigan still looked like he was in shock, and Solvai seemed to be wishing she could sink into the mud and disappear. I nudged her.

Solvai looked up at me, unsure what to do. I nodded to her, trying to be reassuring. She swallowed, then stepped out to face the squad.

"Uh," she began timidly. "I'm Solvai of Keep Rengard. I'm glad…"

A clap of thunder muted whatever Solvai said next.

"…so let's get ready for some trials," she finished.

Rain falling onto our shoulder armor and shields pierced the uncomfortable silence that followed. Edrea gave a curt laugh. Brigan stared straight ahead, his jaw tense. One of the new guys, a young man with a wild mohawk, shook his head with disappointment.

My heart broke as I watched Solvai standing there, the weather plastering her brown hair onto her freckled face. I couldn't be sure if it was rain cutting across her cheeks or tears.

I took a step forward, raising a fist to the opposite side of my chest.

"For Evgard, unite," I called out, my voice strong and confident.

None of my squadmates joined me. But Solvai straightened up, pushing her shoulder blades together as she saluted back.

Only a few minutes into the trials, I was somehow both soaked to the skin with rain and drenched in sweat all at once.

After a rough start, and with no help whatsoever from Commander Gunnar, Solvai led us through a series of fitness tests we'd learned in basic training, keeping careful mental notes of our performances in each trial.

We started with strength, using the huge, stone-carved practice weights they kept near the armory. The trial of strength came down to the mohawk guy, Edrea's tattooed stepbrother, and Brigan. All three put up a good showing, but in the end, the guy with the mohawk was able to heft the heaviest weight.

Brigan scowled as we moved onto the next trial. I knew he was a little off his game, because I'd seen him lift more than that in practice before.

Next came speed. I'd always been pretty fast, but the mud certainly made sprinting a lot more difficult. I came in first of the women, but the mohawk guy beat us all, letting out a loud, whooping holler when he crossed the finish line.

Edrea's stepbrother won in endurance, continuing to run ladders long after the rest of us had all but collapsed. Solvai literally had to stand in front of him like a blockade to get him to stop running.

I was already feeling shaky when Solvai handed me the crossbow. After three years of basic training, I knew targets lined the south perimeter of the grounds. But through the humid, late summer downpour, I felt like I was shooting blind. My squadmates seemed to struggle as well, but Erik, a dark-haired young man with big, nervous black eyes, hit the center with every shot. His accuracy surprised me, since he looked utterly terrified of everything and everyone, especially the mohawked guy and Edrea's brother, Cam.

The final trial was sparring. Commander Gunnar intervened, making sure we exchanged our actual weapons for dulled practice ones. He waved Solvai over, probably to give her a few pointers on what to look for when analyzing our capabilities in single combat.

That left the six of us waiting along the border of a thirty-foot sparring circle lined with stones. Soldiers of Evgard rarely fought against one another, especially with High King Magnus on the throne. They didn't call him 'the Great Uniter' for nothing. Because of that, most of our training focused on getting us in shape to fight dragons. But staring across the circle into Edrea's cold eyes, I felt myself growing determined to prove myself inside the circle today.

Suddenly, the young man with the mohawk materialized at my side. He towered over me, hulking as he passed his long seaxe back and forth between his hands.

"Heard you were from that sooty little cursed town, Misthaven," he said, leaning close to my ear so that only I could hear over the rain. "Bet you're glad you made it out before it disappeared off the map."

"Yeah," I replied. "I am."

I shifted so that I could see his face. As wild as his hair was, his eyes were even more so. The irises sat in the exact center so that I could see white all around them, giving him a manic sort of look.

"Any idea what happened?" he asked. The question came out sounding like a challenge.

I set my jaw. "Nobody knows what happened. My family left long before the camp vanished."

The mohawk guy's face darkened. "Just out of curiosity, what were your parents doing in Misthaven?"

"What are you, a Mage Hunter?" I asked. "They were passing through with a nomad caravan, and my mom went into labor just as they crossed into Misthaven's territory. An unfortunate coincidence."

That was the story my parents and I agreed to tell whenever anyone asked about my having been born in the notorious magi refugee camp. Mom thought I should just lie and call myself Meleya of Red Glen or Meleya of Archdawn, or some other less conspicuous city. But Zoren knew my parents had fled to Misthaven for refuge when my mom was expecting me. As long as he was out there, it was safer to stick with the truth.

"Hmm," my squadmate flared his nostrils as if he'd been hoping for something more incriminating.

From his place a few feet away, I caught sight of Brigan staring intently at my interrogator as he loomed over me. Brigan's fingers flexed and relaxed as they hovered over the hilt of the seaxe sheathed at his side.

"Brigan and Bjorn," Solvai's shaky voice called out as she rejoined our circle, leaving Commander Gunnar to watch from several feet away. "Step into the circle."

My crazy-eyed, mohawk-sporting squadmate gave a low growl like a diamondback wolverine before joining Brigan in the circle.

Brigan didn't look his best as he pulled out his sword and held his round wooden shield in place in front of him. The rain had pulled a few extra curls loose from his ridgeknot, and his eyes were dark with frustration.

"Two marks on the new guy," Edrea appeared beside me, holding out two copper coins.

"Deal," I replied immediately. I knew Brigan fought like he debated—he loved to win.

A maniacal yell from Bjorn made both Edrea and me jump. To our side, Erik let out an involuntary yelp, and all of us took a few cautionary steps backward.

Bjorn charged toward Brigan, eyes wild as he violently slashed with his sword. Brigan raised his seaxe to block Bjorn's turbulent swing.

Clang! Their weapons clashed once, then again in fast succession as each soldier tried to gain the upper hand. Bjorn cried out with each strike, his unnerving yells chilling me to my core.

Then all at once, Bjorn disengaged, darting across the circle. Soot, he was fast. Before I could fully register what was happening, he was streaking toward Brigan, seaxe poised. At the last second, Bjorn leaped like a wild animal pouncing on his prey.

Brigan only just managed to get his shield between himself and our crazy squadmate's sword. Bjorn's weapon hacked at the shield, pressing in on the dragonfire-proof metal.

Brigan looked startled, unsure what to do in such a situation. But Bjorn just kept inching forward, pushing against Brigan's shield. Brigan began to lose his footing on the slick, wet ground. Each second that passed put his feet closer to the edge of the circle.

If Bjorn pushed Brigan out, he'd win. Beside me, Edrea gave a satisfied snort.

"Come on, Brigan," I called out, cupping my hands around my mouth. I knew he was better than this.

Brigan glanced my way, the frustration melting from his face and giving way to determination. With a grunt, he pushed back then ducked to the side, causing Bjorn to stumble as he broke free.

Brigan twirled his sword with a totally unnecessary flourish, then slammed it twice onto the front of his shield. The taunt worked, and Bjorn gave another guttural battle cry.

Bjorn was upon Brigan in a flash with more erratic slashes. Brigan blocked each one, alternating between seaxe and shield. It was a duel between Brigan's excessive finesse and Bjorn's pure insanity. Edrea and I glanced each other's way, neither of us able to tell who would win.

Finally, Brigan feigned to one side, causing Bjorn to stumble. It gave Brigan just enough time to sidestep the menacing soldier. With a superfluous spin, Brigan stepped behind Bjorn and kicked him in the back. Bjorn fell face first into the mud as Brigan trained his sword on him to seal the victory.

Erik started to clap, and I jumped.

"Yes!" I cried, holding out a hand to Edrea. She grumbled and passed over the marks.

Brigan's gaze snapped toward me as I celebrated, a wide, dimpled grin on his face. His hair was messier than I'd ever seen it before, with several strands falling into his eyes. My heart skipped a beat as I realized I liked it that way.

"Meleya and Edrea!" Solvai's voice rose above the rain, and I got the feeling she'd had to repeat herself in order to be heard.

We took our places in the circle, Edrea smirking as she adjusted her grip on her spear. I was aware of her ex-convict brother's eyes on me as he crossed his arms outside the sparring ring.

"Four marks on me," she said.

"You're on," I replied, my face hardening as I pulled out my long, seaxe-style sword.

We circled each other at a distance, trying to time one another's movements. Edrea was a spearwoman, which gave her a distinct advantage in reach. But my weapon was more versatile.

I yelled as I rushed toward her, while she mirrored me as best she could.

She smacked against my strike with her dragonhook spear, tossing it off with ease. Next, she thrust at me and I sidestepped.

I used the time Edrea needed to reposition her weapon to slash at her side. But she pulled back to block with her spear's haft.

"Hey snowhead," Edrea taunted through gritted teeth. "A little dragonfly told me you're a proxy soldier." I frowned as Edrea pulled back her blade and jabbed toward me again.

"Where'd you hear that?" I said, blocking just in time.

"Doesn't matter," Edrea grunted, sidestepping back and tightening her hold on her spear. "But it means I know you don't want to be here."

I came at her with a quick series of blows, making her sweat to keep up.

"Who're you serving for?" Edrea asked, breathing heavily as she tried to throw me off my game. I didn't answer, instead channeling my energy into trying to get inside her guard.

"Parents? Maybe a sibling? What're they in for?" she pressed, growing louder. "Treason? Theft, maybe? You paying off a common thief's sentence?"

With an angry yell, I hacked at the shaft of her spear. She yanked her weapon backward, and I felt my hands, wet with rain, lose their grip on my sword.

My seaxe went flying across the circle, landing with a splash in the muddy sand. Something deep inside me told me to use etherarchy—with rifting, I'd have that sword back instantly.

Stupid, I scolded myself. *I don't need etherarchy. I don't* want *it.*

Edrea used the opportunity to swing toward my head. I dove for the ground, both to dodge and to get at my seaxe. Slick mud splattered onto my uniform and face.

"Come on, Meleya," Edrea was on my heels. "What is it? Poaching? Or are they in for something darker?"

"Shut up," I said as I felt my hand close around the hilt of my blade. Edrea was already stabbing toward me. I rolled out of the way then used my lower position to kick her in the shins and send her down into the mud along with me.

I got to my knees, throwing a sloppy swing Edrea's way. She threw up her spear for a hasty block.

"You don't belong here," Edrea hissed. "The guard is for real soldiers who want to serve the realm. Not desperate proxies."

I swung at her again, and she scrambled backward to get out of range. I was determined not to let her taunting throw me off.

Edrea took a knee herself, reeling back for another thrust. I dodged again, but this time she overextended just a little. Using my off hand, I grabbed hold of her wooden haft and pulled.

That surprised her, and I only kept pulling. I drove the heavy blade of her dragonhook spear straight into the mud, plunging it as deep as I could.

Then, there was nothing she could do to stop me from positioning the tip of my blade just inches from her throat.

"That's four more marks," I said, sticking out my chin.

Edrea's dark eyes stormed more than the sky overhead as I got to my feet, leaving her sitting in the mud.

As I walked toward the circle's edge, I heard Edrea sneer as she stood up.

"This whole squad is a joke anyway," she called, loudly enough that everyone could hear. "How could it not be, with a useless, stuttering weakling for a squad captain?"

I halted mid-step as I took in Solvai's face. She looked completely crushed. Broken. Like she believed every word of Edrea's moronic comment.

That did it.

I dropped my sword and rounded back on Edrea, throwing a wide, arcing punch right toward her jaw. The punch staggered her, then she turned to me with rage flashing in her eyes.

She jumped at me, tackling me into the mud and grabbing for my throat with both hands. I choked as she pinned me down, kicking my feet as I struggled to take a breath.

I vaguely heard Brigan yell my name. He must've made a move toward Edrea, because I heard her intimidating stepbrother, Cam, give a loud grunt. The next thing I knew, Cam was grappling with Brigan.

Solvai's voice barely registered over the pelting rain, mudslinging, and throwing of punches.

"Squad! Stop it—get in line!"

Solvai's pleas were all in vain, and I was running low on air. I dove my hands between Edrea's arms, twisting mine over the top of them to split them apart and get them off my neck. I inhaled sharply the moment my airway was free, wasting no time as I shoved Edrea with all my might.

Her body slammed into Bjorn, who looked like he was just itching to join the brawl. Edrea crashing into him was all the permission he needed. He gave that awful, voidish yell and swung a completely unmerited punch at Erik.

Edrea didn't take long to get back up and rush at me, flinging me into the fight between Brigan and Cam. The three of us toppled into the mud. From there, Edrea leaped onto the pile, clawing to get at me.

Then Bjorn picked up Erik and held the poor guy high over his head before rearing back and tossing him in with the rest of us. Clearly enjoying the violence, he launched himself into the heap as well.

Punches and mud flew in every direction as thunder rolled across the sky.

Solvai called to us desperately, doing her best to dodge the flying sludge.

"Soldiers!" Commander Gunnar's voice bellowed over the chaos. We froze, looking up to see his murderous expression.

We slipped, stumbled, and struggled, but it didn't take long for the seven of us to form a line and stand at attention.

Regret instantly flooded me, along with a sinking feeling. A prayer to the goddesses filled my thudding heart, begging them to not let this get me ejected from the guard.

Commander Gunnar paced the length of our line. Red mud plastered every one us from head to toe.

"Never in all my years have I seen such reckless, insolent behavior from a new squad," he said. "Keep Rengard expects better from its soldiers. Do you understand me?"

"Yes, Commander!" we shouted in unison.

"This is your final warning. The seven of you will run laps every morning this week before sunrise. And you'll spend Keep Rengard's next dragon attack sidelined."

Our faces fell.

"But Commander," Brigan stepped forward. "That's supposed to be our first battle."

"Silence," Commander Gunnar barked. "Would you rather I take it up with Captain Zoren and see if he can come up with a more suitable punishment?"

"No," I cut in, earning looks from the whole lineup as well as the commander.

"Then I suggest," Commander Gunnar glowered at me, "that you don't step out of line again."

Chapter 6: Heartscales

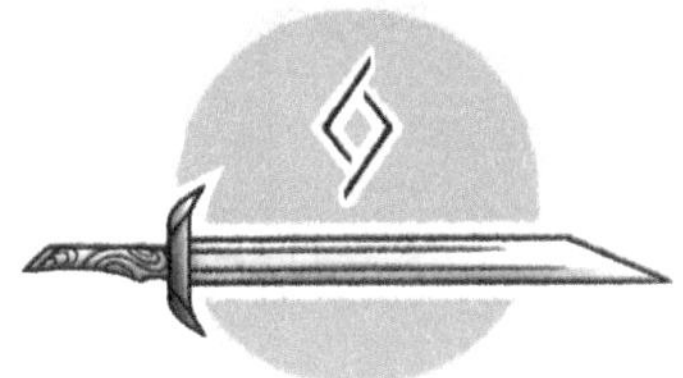

"Gauntlet down: Running laps before sunrise is actually detrimental to your health. Point one—lost sleep. Point two—sore quads. Point three—bad attitude."

Brigan used a monogrammed Keep Solhelm cloth to wipe his forehead. We were all breathing heavily as we left the training grounds, the sun just starting to peek over the rugged red mountains east of the Rise.

"I don't know about the rest of you," Edrea said with heavy, annoyed eyes. "But I'm heading back to the barracks to get an extra half hour of sleep before we have to form up for morning training."

The rest of us mumbled in agreement, though I wasn't planning on hitting the barracks. My head was already in the bunker, planning what to make for breakfast.

We'd just reached the head of the trail when we crossed paths with another group of soldiers. I recognized many of them as those who'd fought beside us in the Dragon Chasm.

"What's going on?" I asked.

"This mornin's trainin', that's what," a cheerful voice with just a hint of a northern accent answered me. I turned around, recognizing the voice as Solvai's mother's.

Lorelai looked like Solvai plus twenty years. She, too, had thick brown hair and a pretty face full of freckles. The only difference was in their eyes—where Solvai's were hazel, Lorelai's embodied a pale, crystal blue.

"All dragon riders, report to the stables for trainin'," Lorelai called. "Troopers, you're free until lunch."

Edrea, Bjorn, and Solvai grinned.

"Bye, riders," Edrea smirked, though I was willing to bet the six marks she'd lost to me that she secretly wished she was a rider as well, even if it meant extra training sessions.

As the head dragon keeper, Lorelai assembled the new riders outside the main entrance to the dragon stables. I looked up at the towering edifice with anticipation.

The stables on the Rise stood just outside the white adobe walls of the Keep Rengard citadel. Outside of the castle itself, the stables were the largest structure on the butte. Crushed dragon egg shells had been mixed in with the adobe clay along the four high walls. Wooden support beams set at intervals lined the walls and up the tall, sloping roof. The roof itself was a mix of ornately-carved wooden panels and patches of gleaming starglass.

The starglass was more evidence of the realm's dependency on ether-archy. Though they scorned magi, Evgard had no qualms employing as-tromancy to create the crystal-like translucent skylights along the stable roof and walls that provided light for the dragons inside. It was a beautiful building, a jewel in Keep Rengard's crown. Even the king himself kept his dragon at the stables.

Lorelai stood before us, hands on her hips. Her strong, low voice carried across the assembled soldiers.

"Welcome, dragon riders, to your first day of trainin'. For those of you who did basic in neighborin' cities, I'm Lorelai, the head dragon keeper here at Keep Rengard. My assistants and I are available to answer any questions or give you any tips on ridin' your new bonds. We have enough experience between us, after all."

Lorelai reached under her tan dust scarf and pulled out a heavy cord necklace laced with at least a dozen dragon heartscales. I smiled as awestruck murmurs rippled through the group. I'd seen Lorelai's impres-sive lineup of heartscales before. Collected over a lifetime of performing in dragon rodeos, Lorelai had more than anyone I'd ever met.

Lorelai laughed, then went on. "So, without further ado..." she gestured toward the enormous set of doors behind us.

Just then, a pair of Lorelai's assistants pulled open the doors to reveal a whole slew of eager dragons. More keepers held them by harnesses attached around the bases of their necks and forearms or forewings.

Though the dragons were clearly thrilled to see their riders, they patiently waited, shuffling as the keepers held to their reins. All, that is, except for a certain bright yellow evren, who gave a little yip when he caught sight of me.

The other new soldiers dove out of the way as my hovering dragon yanked free from the hands of the exhausted-looking keeper holding his reins. Sniff careened toward me, his four wings practically blurs. He slowed just enough to not kill me on impact, though we both went tumbling onto the packed earth ground.

Sniff nuzzled at my neck, his tongue wet against my skin. I laughed, scratching him under the chin and around the ears.

Brrring. Contented music played through our bond.

"Good to see you too, Sniff," I said. Then I looked past the large, lemony dragon in front of me to see the other riders giving me looks.

I cleared my throat, then reached under my collar and clutched my dragon's heartscale.

Hey, I thought through the bond. *Uh... wanna sit, boy?*

Ping!

Sniff backed away, plopping his tail end onto the ground, his four wings folded in half as he used the claws at the hinges like feet to prop himself upright. He panted proudly beside me as I gave Lorelai and the others an apologetic smile.

"Sorry," I said.

Lorelai chuckled. "It's quite alright. All of the new bonds will have a little breakin' in to do. Now, everyone else find your dragon—calmly, please." She cast another amused glance my way.

Once the keepers had gotten all of us situated beside our dragons, Lorelai returned to her place in front of the group. She rubbed a heartscale between her fingers, a look of concentration passing over her face. In a flash, another dragon came swooping out the double doors of the stable. The mossy green-colored wyvern landed obediently at her side.

"Riders," Lorelai said. "I'd like you to meet Comet."

With that, Lorelai threw one leg over the dragon's back. She gave a short command, and the wyvern shot into the air.

Once Lorelai was high above our heads, she gave her wyvern another command. Immediately, the dragon began to thrash, his body twisting and turning this way and that as his hind legs kicked.

We watched with anticipation as Lorelai expertly clung to the dragon's saddle with one hand, the other loose in the air. Most performers chained their bucking dragon to the earth so that they didn't go too high before attempting to ride them in case they fell. Not Lorelai.

After holding on for well over ten seconds, the wyvern gave one last flail, spinning so that for a moment, Lorelai was upside down. The riders around me gasped at the show of skill, and I whooped.

When Lorelai and her wyvern landed, she smoothly slid off the saddle and gave a deep bow. When she came up again, she waved one hand in the air to temper our applause.

"Now," Lorelai laughed as she quieted us. "Don't be attemptin' nothin' like that today unless you wanna end up in medical for a week. In fact, any of y'all with a flyin' dragon, don't go higher'n 'bout twenty or so feet until you and your dragons get used to each other. Take your new dragons for a spin around the Rise or wherever y'all choose. Be back in an hour."

"That's it?" Brigan piped up, raising his hand. "We aren't going to stick around here and drill flight patterns or something?"

"Not with me in charge. Best way to learn to ride is through old fashioned, hands-on experience. Ain't no drills can substitute for that."

Brigan and a few others looked a little nervous about having so much unsupervised freedom. Sniff gave an excited little growl.

Lorelai clapped her hands together twice. "Alright then, dragon riders. Let's saddle up."

Lorelai's assistants distributed saddles and began instructing us on how to properly secure them to our dragons. I was struggling to get Sniff to hold still long enough for me to cinch mine when Lorelai appeared at my side.

"So was that an alright demonstration?" she asked quietly, no longer using her show woman's voice. When she wasn't performing, her demeanor reminded me a lot more of her daughter's.

"Are you kidding?" I smiled. "You were inspiring. I'll be lucky if I can get the saddle on, let alone fly half that well."

Lorelai laughed, reaching up and putting a hand on Sniff's neck. As she did, I caught sight of the well-worn, caramel-colored marriage bracelet around her right wrist. I found it sweet that though Solvai's father had died nearly eighteen years ago, she still wore the band.

Sniff leaned down and put his head on the ground as Lorelai rubbed him, starting at the base of his head just to the side of his spine. Sniff's eyes rolled back, and he stuck out his tongue as he relaxed.

"Well, that's a neat trick," I said, finally able to latch the last buckle of the saddle.

"You pick up a thing or two after bein' in the game as long as I have," Lorelai shrugged.

I cinched the strap tight just as Lorelai stopped rubbing Sniff's neck. He immediately sat up straight, his gaze going slightly cross-eyed.

"Oh no," I said, recognizing what it meant when Sniff made that face. "Look out!"

Brigan and his dragon stood right in front of Sniff, and my friend heeded my warning just in time. He raised his circular shield as my dragon let out one of his ether-charged sneezes. White, spiraling marks spun out over the surface of the shield as Brigan cautiously peeked over the top.

"Sorry," I said. "Sniff kind of does that sometimes."

"That's alright," Brigan gave a little chuckle as Sniff sniffled. "Happens to the best of us, huh, buddy?"

Brigan reached into the pocket of his tunic and pulled out a few strips of dragon jerky. He must've brought it for his drake, but he tossed a big piece toward Sniff.

Sniff leaped upward, catching the treat in his mouth. As he chewed, he gave an excited little snort and his musical voice sounded in my heart with an ascending melody. Sniff liked Brigan.

Brigan went back to securing his own dragon's saddle as Lorelai placed a hand on her hip.

"So you've bonded a mythic dragon," she said. "That puts young Sniff a class ahead of the rest."

Lorelai rubbed the green scale that hung from the cord around her neck. Her wyvern obediently hurried to her side.

"Comet here's an Astromancer as well," Lorelai said with a snap of her fingers. On cue, Comet pointed his face upward and opened his jaws wide.

A jet of white ether shot from his mouth into the sky, and I realized why his name was Comet.

The ether blast was so controlled, so sophisticated. I nudged Sniff, channeling my thoughts to him through our bond.

One day, boy.

Tring! Sniff agreed, his face twisting up in anticipation of another sneeze. Both Lorelai and I shrank back, covering our heads.

Then Sniff's face relaxed, and he gave another sniffle. Lorelai and I breathed easy once again—for now.

"I know it's only been a day," Lorelai said. "But soot if I don't miss havin' you and Solvai 'round the house already."

Lorelai beamed at me, then took hold of my cloak on either side of my shoulders. "My girls, all grown up and wearin' Rengard orange. And Solvai's a squad captain, no less. Like her father once was."

"I'm sure he would've loved the chance to see her like this," I said.

Lorelai got a glassy look in her eyes for a moment before shaking her head. She gave me a winning smile and patted my dragon.

"Well then, Miss Meleya," Lorelai said. "What d'ya say we get you flyin'?"

Dragonflies danced in my stomach as Sniff and I zoomed over the training grounds then out over the city on the Rise. We flew low, Sniff rising and falling along with the shops, cactus gardens, and adobe estates of the Rise's noble class.

I clung to the saddlehorn as the wind cut across my cheeks, my long, white braid streaming out behind me. I felt the rush of flying fill me from my core all the way to the tips of my fingers. A laugh escaped my lips, and Sniff responded with a chortle of his own.

Sniff flew fast, and it wasn't long before we reached the end of the butte. Sniff shot across the gap between the Rise and the rim of the canyon, and my stomach dropped for just a moment before we were back over the land again on the other side.

Careful, buddy, I emoted through the bond. *Not too high, remember?*

As Sniff flew, I felt the air cooling my face. The beautiful expanse of the Canyon Keepdom spread before me like a richly colored painting. Reddish mesas, hoodoos, and the beautiful curve of Sunrise Arch dominated the landscape, with occasional splashes of green from junipers and sagebrush. Spiny cacti and yucca palms sprouted between rocks and across sandy surfaces, toughened by life beneath the scorching desert sun.

From here, I could see down Rengard Canyon for miles, the Ridgeback River winding along with the rock. The canyon meandered endlessly northward, but when I looked to the south, I could see the abrupt end in the distance—a wall of thick, white fog, extending as far as the eye could see from east to west.

The Dragon Mists.

The Mists cut off the southern border of Evgard, spanning miles, all the way from the eastern sea near the Dragon Isles to the western sea south of Evyndale.

I swallowed as I stared out at the Dragon Mists. Gold lightning flashed sporadically within the dense, pale clouds, and the spiraling tendrils of mist seemed to reach along the ground toward Rengard Canyon. Hundreds of years ago, the Mists were miles away from the capital of the Canyon Keepdom. Now, they were only about a half-day's journey from the Rise by riverboat. I wondered how many generations it would take before they came up against the city itself.

Brigan had thrown out several theories—or rather, thrown down several gauntlets—about the ever-encroaching Dragon Mists. Sometimes he hypothesized that maybe the wild dragons who lived in there were running out of food and skystone to feed on within the Mists, so they were somehow expanding their primary hunting grounds. Or perhaps it had something to do with the more frequent skyfalls across the realm. Once Brigan had even declared that maybe it was the fault of secret magi who had an evil plot to overthrow Evgard.

I didn't love that one.

I hadn't noticed how high we'd been flying until suddenly Sniff was diving. Soot, this was *really* high, I realized as I saw the earth nearly a hundred feet below. Suddenly, I became very aware of just how far we were from any help. Was that long crack in the earth below us the Dragon Chasm?

My heart jumped, panic setting in as I felt Sniff's saddlehorn slip from my fingers.

I tried to grab hold of my dragon with my legs, but my feet slid out of the stirrups. Within moments, I was freefalling as my dragon zipped downward without me.

I cried out, the wind ripping my scream from my throat. Sniff immediately stopped his dive, looping around to try and catch me. Frantic notes played in my heart through the bond.

I grunted as I thudded ungracefully onto Sniff's back. The force knocked the wind out of me, and I couldn't hold onto anything before I'd already flopped onto one of Sniff's hindwings. His flapping wing tossed me like a doll back into the air, and once again I was falling.

One idea pierced my thoughts like lightning. I should use my etherarchy.

Time seemed to slow as I fell, my mind racing as a memory flashed before my eyes. I was eleven years old, only two years before the Ursadon captured my parents. I'd fallen behind my parents as we traversed Rengard's desert alone, on our way to a new nomadic caravan. I'd stayed to gather yucca root for a stew I planned to make for dinner that night. When my parents saw me crouched in the distance, they waved for me to hurry along.

Nobody was around, so I'd hastily traced the rifting rune, one of the only two I knew. Within seconds, I'd stepped through a portal and appeared at my parents' side.

Mom hadn't said anything right then. But that night after dinner once we'd set up our tent, she pulled me inside.

"Why did you rift back there?" she asked.

The question had filled me with shame. "I don't know."

"Oh Meli." Mom looked me in the eye. "I need you to remember this: You're so much more than your etherarchy."

The memory swirled before my eyes, giving way to the fast-approaching ground. I was falling straight into the wide, earthen crevice of the Dragon Chasm.

Mom's words stuck with me. *You don't need rifting to be strong and capable.*

The striped chasm walls rushed upward on either side of me. From somewhere above, I heard Sniff let out a worried shriek.

You don't need rifting to be special.

As the sandy canyon bed rose to greet me, I realized that while I may not need rifting to be special, I sure as the void needed it to not splatter against the stone.

My fingers flew faster than Solvai's favorite violet-scaled hummingbird as I traced the rune. The corresponding rune lit up over my forehead in gold, and I felt my ether well drain just a little. The gold-rimmed portal tore itself open over the ground below me.

I fell through, the world going white as I passed through Etheria. Then, in a flash, I was falling through the exit portal.

I'd placed the exit just a few feet away from the entrance, but facing upward. It ejected me, and for a second, I was falling up.

Then my momentum slowed, gravity pulling me back down. Only this time, I was falling from a few feet.

I crashed to the sandy canyon floor in a tangled heap. A layer of reddish dust coated my dragonleather uniform.

Coughing, I rolled onto my back and did a personal inventory. A couple of places on my arm, shoulder, and hip were bruised, but not badly. At least, not as badly as my pride. Not only did I let myself get carried away with flying high despite Lorelai's warning, but I'd also used etherarchy.

I was positive nobody had seen me all the way out here. Sniff and I had strayed much further than the other riders, and the Dragon Chasm was only used once every year for new soldier initiations. They wouldn't be bringing in new dragon eggs until spring so they could hatch them inside the cavern and raise them for the next group of recruits who finished basic training.

No, my secret was safe. That wasn't what bothered me.

As I lay there, I felt a heavy weight settle onto my heart. I guess Mom was wrong—I wasn't as strong as she'd thought.

I knew the thought was useless. Anyone in their right mind would've done whatever it took to save themselves from certain death. In fact, the relief of drawing from my ether well felt good—like a stew pot that'd had its lid on too long finally being allowed to let off steam. Yet, I still felt like I'd let my mother down. I felt like I'd let myself down, too, by depending on my etherarchy.

A cold shudder ran through my body, as if I'd just been hit by an icy canyon breeze. When I turned my head, I frowned as I realized that couldn't have been the case. There was no rustle from the leaves on the nearby weeds. The tumbleweed in the corner was still. Even the flyaway hairs on my braid didn't move.

I sat up, glancing around for the source of the sudden chill, but saw nothing. Dusting myself off, I got to my feet.

Within a split second of standing up, a very energetic yellow evren barreled directly into me. I grunted, falling back to the ground as Sniff licked the side of my face.

Bing-bong-bing! Through the bond, he played a fast-paced ballad, mingling notes of apology with melodies of relief.

"It's okay, it's okay," I tried to reassure him. "Next time, warn me before taking a dive though, alright?"

He yipped, pawing at the ground with the claws on the hinges of his wings.

"What were you looking for, anyway?" I asked.

At that, Sniff began panting eagerly. He tossed his head, beckoning for me to follow him as he took to the air.

His wings beat at high speeds as he zipped across the chasm floor toward the cave mouth on the north side. The heavy metal gate the guard used to blockade the wild dragons in was still wide open. Sniff hovered inside the doorway, waiting.

I hurried toward him, rubbing my bruised arm. Once I got to the gate, Sniff chortled and flew deeper into the rock. I followed, my hand on the hilt of my seaxe in case one of the wild dragons had decided it would rather hang out in the cave than swarm the recruits with the others yesterday morning.

Inside was a warm, stony cavern. The smooth rock walls flowed like waves of a petrified, rust-colored ocean. Small breaks in the rock above worked like skylights, allowing rays from the sun to shine down into the cave.

Then Sniff zipped down a passage, and soon we found ourselves in a much larger cavern. More gaps in the rock above us let in more warm light, which glinted off of what looked like shattered crystal all over the sandy floor.

It took me a moment to realize that the pieces of shattered crystal were actually eggshells. Dragon eggshells.

Some of the pieces looked like shards from quartz or geodes, while others were made up of tiny scales. Among the fragments, I saw more egg pieces that looked like shredded leather. I realized that the dragon keepers must've brought the eggs here and used the cavern as a sort of hatchery. Once the dragons had hatched, they were ready to face the guards in the chasm.

The scene was both disturbing and beautiful all at once. So many creatures found new life here in the cavern, yet they were fated from the start to be captives at Evgard's hand.

I could relate to that.

Sniff let out a vigorous sniffle to get my attention. I saw him crouched protectively over a perfectly round crystal, one half silver and the other half gold.

I joined him, doing my best to sidestep the eggshells. Gently, Sniff nudged the crystalline sphere toward me.

It was a nearly whole fragment of an evren egg. It was badly battered, with several long, deep scratches along the silver half of its gleaming surface.

"What happened to it?" I asked Sniff. He whimpered.

A melancholy set of notes sounded in my heart through the bond, and I got a strong impression that this egg hadn't been properly secured on its way to Keep Rengard.

I felt a lump forming in my throat as I fingered the deep gashes across the egg's crystalline surface. As I gently turned the egg over in my hands, I heard a gentle tinkling noise, followed by a thud.

Looking at the ground, I realized that a single, shimmering scale had slid out from one of the cracks along the egg.

As I reached toward the scale, I suddenly felt a warm, calming feeling flood my body. The feeling bloomed within my chest as my fingers closed around the silver scale.

I stood straight up, looking around. I'd felt that feeling before, yesterday morning. It was as if I was bonding another dragon.

But besides the highly conspicuous yellow evren right in front of me, there wasn't a dragon in sight.

What's going on, boy? I asked Sniff through our bond.

He gave a happy little yip, jumping off of his claws into the air. His wings spread, and he hovered gleefully beside me like a puppy who'd just been thrown a ball.

The faint sound of distant horns pricked my ears, and suddenly my heart leaped into my throat. I knew those horns.

They were alarms—the sentries' way of alerting the guard that they'd spotted wild dragons approaching the keep.

The Rise was under attack.

Chapter 7: Sidelined

Not wanting to raise any suspicion, I put the silver scale on a second, longer cord around my neck. That way, I could pull out Sniff's without anyone seeing I wore two necklaces.

Sniff and I rushed back to Guard Square, and I slid off of my dragon's back. The scene just outside the dragon stables was one of organized chaos as the guard prepared to defend the keep. Some soldiers rolled out massive ballistae while others loaded their scaleslayer crossbows. Squads of seven assembled outside the dragon stables as Lorelai and the other keepers kept order, getting dragons from inside paired up with their riders.

It was impressive, seeing the well-trained squads prepare for battle. Dragon riders from Squad Valor rode out on their mounts while their troopers charged to their post at the citadel gates. Squad Drakesbane stood their ground in front of the command center. These were some of the best, most reliable squads in Keep Rengard, earning strong squad names from the commanders after their first battles. It made me wonder what they'd name our squad.

Brigan rode up to me, looking like the quintessential Evgardian warrior on the back of his rusty orange drake. He swung a leg over his dragon's back and slid down beside me.

"There you are," he said, throwing his strong arms around me for a hug. "Where've you been? I looked for you and Sniff all over the Rise, and when I heard them sound the alarm..."

"I'm fine," I assured him. "Do you know what's going on?"

"A whole horde of flying dragons is coming at us from the south. Probably from the Dragon Mists, but there are so many that the guard posted at the canyon mouth couldn't hold them."

Brigan pointed toward the south skies, and sure enough there was a dark cloud rushing toward us overhead. There had to be at least fifty or more dragons up there.

"Soot," I swore, shielding the sun from my eyes with my hand. "Why so many at once?"

Brigan's brow furrowed. "Not sure."

Erik and his sky blue wyvern appeared next, followed by Cam and his thick-skinned drake. The rest of the squad hurried toward our group as well, huddling together as we tried to stay out of the other soldiers' way as they rushed past.

"So what do we do, then?" Edrea asked what all of us were surely thinking.

Brigan gave a little grimace before he nodded to Solvai. "That's up to the squad captain."

"Um…" Solvai swallowed. "Well, technically we're not supposed to… I mean, we're still uh…"

"I think the word Captain Solvai is looking for is *sidelined*." Commander Gunnar appeared beside us, looming over our squad. "Thanks to your squad's insubordination yesterday morning, you're out of this battle."

"But Commander," Brigan began diplomatically. "New squads are supposed to get their name in their first battle. We were hoping—"

Commander Gunnar held up a hand for silence. "If you don't want me to name you 'Squad Mudslingers,' I'd suggest you put your dragons up in the stables and get to the barracks."

Brigan's mouth formed a tight, frustrated line. None of us talked back as we obeyed the order. The other riders from my squad guided their dragons toward the large stable door, but when I turned around, Sniff was gone.

With scales that bright, it didn't take long to spot him chasing his tail near the far wall of the command center. I darted over and tried to coax him back to the dragon stables. He was so riled up by all the action that I wondered if I'd ever succeed.

That's when I saw a flash of brilliant turquoise standing out against the rusty tans and oranges around me. I looked up to see a young man with unruly black hair wearing a vibrant turquoise dust scarf around his neck.

He was standing in the open window of the third story of the command center. If I wasn't mistaken, that was near where the Captain of the Guard's office was located.

Under his arm, the guy clutched a wooden case with some sort of fire symbol emblazoned on the front.

Before I knew what was happening, the young man jumped from the window.

My breath caught. He wouldn't survive a fall from that high up. Unless…

Suddenly, his eyes flashed gold. His descent abruptly slowed, and he levitated safely into a clump of sagebrush at the base of the building.

My whole body tensed. He was a magi. A magi, and a thief.

I looked down at my new orange cloak. Capturing the bandit who'd been using the chaos of battle to rob the command center would probably go a long way in getting my squad out of hot water.

Sniff, I thought through our bond as I drew my seaxe. *Get back to the stables.*

Ping? Sniff asked.

No, I don't need any help, I thought back. Part of me worried having Sniff along would be a liability. Besides, even if the young man in the turquoise scarf was an Archon, I could handle a common thief.

I followed the thief as he headed around the back wall of the command center. He stood with his pilfered case just around the corner. I held my seaxe ready as I took a deep breath, then rounded the wall.

I caught him off guard, and he stumbled backward as I trained my sword on his throat.

"Stars," he said, blinking at me with bright, dragonfire green eyes. Light glinted off the dark teal scales on the tips of his pointed ears. He was a half-born.

"Don't you know it's rude to sneak up on people like that?" he scolded, an unwarranted twinkle in his eye. "Though I gotta say, excellent technique. Didn't hear you at all."

"What's in the case?" I narrowed my eyes at him, giving his chest a warning tap with the end of my seaxe.

"Whoa," he held tightly to the box. "This is all just a big misunderstanding."

"I think I understand pretty well. I saw you jump from the command center, thief."

"Thief is such a strong word—I prefer to think of myself as an expert repossesser of valuable objects."

"I prefer to think of you as behind bars."

"Hmm," the thief tapped his chin. "Been there, snowhead. It never really works out."

The obnoxious young man took a small step back, raising one hand out to the side as his eyes flashed gold again. Golden etherlight swirled all around his hand, elongating as it solidified. Within moments, the thief was brandishing a cutthroat dragonhook spear made entirely of crystalline, white starglass.

The thief tossed and caught his newly formed weapon. "So, are we gonna do this?"

I lowered my eyebrows. "Absolutely."

We were about to charge toward each other, weapons swinging, when a guy wearing way too much plate armor came flying out of the bushes.

He stood between us, hands outstretched. "Stop. You have to stop right now."

"Why?" the guy in the turquoise scarf asked.

"Because," his companion answered, "if you engage a guard, there's only a thirty-four percent chance we'll make it out of here undetected. And that's only if you uhh... *dispatch* her."

The guy cast me an apologetic look.

"So what's the plan then?" the thief asked. "Kheradok will be here any second to blast us."

"Well," his armored friend answered, exasperated. "I'm still working on it. It'd be really nice if the general of the drakking Drekai army wasn't void-bent on fighting you in an honor duel. So much for a quick trip to Keep Rengard."

"What can I say?" said the thief. "I like surprises."

"Good," I said, suddenly lunging past the armored guy toward him.

My seaxe came within inches of his ribs when another blade caught it. Materializing at the thief's side was a tall girl with dark, wavy hair and a floor-length gown. The dress looked a little worn out from traveling, but it was clearly expensive.

My eyes popped when I saw the white creature that clung to her back and peeked at me from over her shoulder. It was a little white dragon. But with four legs and a folded pair of wings sprouting from its back, this wasn't just any dragon.

It was a true dragon.

I knew from my study in basic training that the only true dragon left in Evgard belonged to High King Magnus himself. Who were these people, and why did they have a baby true dragon with them? Were they somehow behind the wild dragon attack on the keep?

"Nice try," the well-dressed girl said to me, gripping her saber. "But I need my boyfriend alive."

The turquoise scarf guy gave a lopsided grin. "Aww, thanks Elle. But I'm still not quite emotionally ready to—"

"Give it a month," the girl cut him off, rolling her eyes.

I was just considering the risk involved in engaging all three of these strange thieves at once when some sort of compact ball of flaming green dragonfire rolled up right behind the guy in the turquoise scarf.

"Oh soot," he swore.

"Run," the girl said, and the half-born in the turquoise scarf thrust the case into her hands. She and the armored guy darted past me.

Rather than follow his friends, the first thief burned more ether. His eyes blazed gold once more as he formed a starglass dome over the top of the fireball. He turned to run as well, but found himself face-to-face with me.

"What are you still doing here?" he cried.

"What is that thing?" I asked. Without answering, the guy circled back and threw himself onto the starglass shield that contained the fireball.

As he landed, the little green ball exploded.

The bomb sent both of us flying backward along with a hailstorm of etherdust, dirt, and twigs. I landed hard on my back, coughing as I inhaled the smoky dust. The thief fell on top of me, and I grunted at the impact.

He coughed as well, but propped himself up with one arm so that our noses were only a scale's breadth away.

"Are you okay?" he asked, his dragonfire green eyes searching mine.

My breath caught in my dust-coated throat, but I nodded.

From the direction of the exploding fireball came a voice. I didn't recognize it, but he had the same accent as Zoren.

"Asher of Steel Rim," the voice boomed. "Fight me in single combat and prove your worth."

The thief got to his feet, and I joined him soon after. As the smoke cleared, I saw a fierce, armor-clad Drekai. He couldn't have been much older than twenty, but he carried himself like a war-hardened leader. Twin horns sprouted off the back of his head through his helmet, and a pair of red and black scaled wings grew from his back. His battle-worn bronze armor was ornately decorated, with spikes running along the sides of his gauntlets. It was definitely not the armor of an Evgardian soldier.

"Fight me now," the Drekai repeated, holding up a scimitar as he tossed a lock of black and red-streaked hair from his face. "Other urgent matters require my attention. I do not have time for any more games."

"I get that," the thief shrugged. "Which is why you have my full endorsement for canceling this duel to the death. I won't tell any of your friends, I swear."

The red-scaled Drekai growled. "My honor demands that I fight the fool who interrupted my honor duel with the king of Drakfell. My fight is with you."

The thief shook his head. "Everyone wants to fight me today." He looked at me over his shoulder. "Get in line, snowhead. I'll be right with you."

With that, the thief took up a fighting stance, wielding his brilliant, starglass weapon.

His friend with the excessive armor popped out of the sagebrush. "You're not ready to fight him yet. You have a ninety-seven percent chance of failure."

"I can handle those odds."

"Ash—"

Before the fight could officially begin, the sound of footsteps thundered behind us. When I turned around, I saw two commanders and three squads worth of soldiers, all pointing their weapons at the Drekai. At once, the thief dismissed his starglass spear and ducked out of their way.

"Good work soldiers," the thief nodded toward the newcomers. "I'll let you take it from here."

Ignoring the thief's idiotic comment, the commander at the head of the group called to the Drekai. "Call off the attack, General. Starting a war with the Canyonlands would not end well for the Dragon Isles."

The young Drekai glared. "You Evgardians have no idea what you are talking about. The empress wishes to prevent war at all costs."

"You should've thought of that before besieging the Rise with your army of dragons." The commander pounded one side of his chest in the Evgardian salute. "Soldiers, attack!"

The small army rushed toward the Drekai, who launched upward into the air. His wide, draconic wings flapped as he took to the skies.

"After him!" the commander ordered.

As the soldiers rushed after the Drekai General, I realized that the trio of thieves had disappeared amidst the chaos. The sagebrush rustled, and I moved to stop their escape.

I felt a strong hand grab me by the scruff of my cloak, and I stopped in my tracks. When I turned my head, I found myself looking into the angry face of Commander Gunnar.

"Where do you think you're going, Meleya of Misthaven?" he barked.

"I was just—"

"Join your squad in the barracks at once."

"But—"

"At once, soldier!"

Chapter 8: The Stables

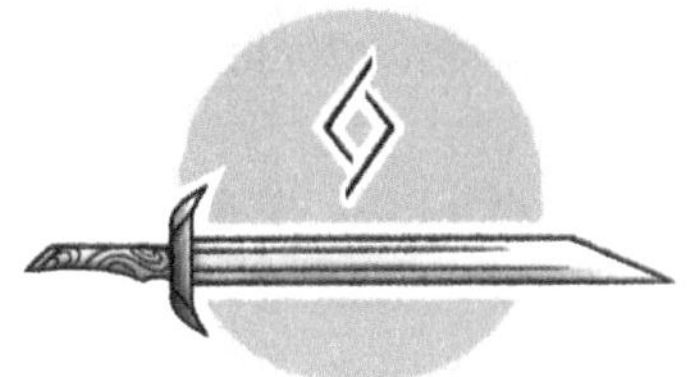

Awkward silence reigned supreme over the barracks.

Each squad had their own set of two rooms in the two-story adobe building. The seven members of mine now sat or stood scattered throughout the common space in the women's room. When I'd first joined them, I'd told them all about the Drekai General and the commanders tracking him down as the source of today's dragon attack. My squadmates had been shocked. We all knew that the Keepdom of Drakfell was on thin ice with the Dragon Isles, but if the Drekai were moving in on Rengard as well... that could mean all-out war.

Though we were certain that the armies of Keep Rengard could handle the Drekai's onslaught of dragons, the news still put everyone on edge. Nobody was happy about being sidelined during what should've been our first real battle.

Well, nobody except maybe Erik. He seemed relieved as he sat at the small wooden desk, sketching in a yellowed notebook.

I didn't tell the squad about the thieves. I wasn't quite sure why, but it felt wrong. I remembered the way the half-born with the turquoise scarf had thrown himself on that explosive in an effort to keep it from blowing me to bits. It seemed only right to not go telling on him—for now, at least.

While Erik drew quietly in the corner, Solvai and I leaned against the wall on either side of the door. Edrea sat on her bunk, feet dangling over the side, while her tattooed brother, Cam, stood protectively beside her. Brigan leaned back in a chair against the wall nearest the desk, while Bjorn sat in the room's second story window.

He crouched inside the window's frame as if he were a diamondback wolverine scanning his domain. Suddenly, his haunting singing voice pierced the silence:

Don't draw the dragons near, keep them far away
Don't draw the dragons near, never let them stay

The hairs on my arms stood straight up as I recognized the song as one the nomads used to sing around campfires at night.

Don't draw the dragons near, or without a doubt
Don't draw the dragons near, we will find you out

Stay away
You magi need to listen
Stay away
The dragons have arisen
Stay away
From every keep and town
Or we will hunt you down
Yes, we will hunt you down.

His last note lingered ominously in the stillness. Absently, I cracked my knuckles, earning me a glance from everyone in the room.

Edrea had just begun humming the magi hunting tune under her breath when Brigan suddenly leaned forward in his chair.

"Gauntlet down," he said, snapping his fingers. "Magi should be allowed to live freely in Evgard."

My gaze shot up toward him as he began laying out his argument.

"Point one—they can't help being born with etherarchy. How can we penalize an entire group of people for something out of their control? Point two—the nobility of Evgard find plenty of use for their high mages, and the other registered magi. The very keeps we live in were built using the geomancy and psionics of magi of old. My own family uses the etherarchy of our lightwielding high mage all the time. I even heard that High King Magnus is looking into new types of etherarchy to try and save his son, High Prince Mason, from the shadow wasting. Perhaps the keepdoms can find use for the other magi as well."

I couldn't believe what I was hearing. Brigan, a nobleman, arguing on behalf of magi? I leaned toward him as he went on.

"Point three—and this is a very important one—think of all the marks Evgard would save if we disbanded the Mage Hunters."

The last words had barely left Brigan's lips when Bjorn leaped from his place in the window. He landed in a crouch, then slowly rose to his feet.

"As long as there are magi around, Evgard needs the Mage Hunters. Drak anyone who says otherwise." Bjorn stalked slowly toward Brigan, a feral scowl on his face.

"Not if we can find a way to help them assimilate peacefully," Brigan said, excited that someone had taken up the debate gauntlet. He seemed to not notice Bjorn's prowling approach. Solvai and I took a step toward our friend, hands on our weapons.

"Peacefully?" Bjorn spit on the ground. "Let me tell you something, you sooty, blind nobleman. In the real world, the outlander town where I come from, we get wild dragon attacks every day. Lose a dozen fighters a year. But still, I'd take a thousand wild dragons over the damage one group of rogue, ethercursed magi wrought on my town."

I cringed at Bjorn's use of the slur, ethercursed. Only those who truly hated magi dared call them something so vulgar.

Bjorn was hovering over Brigan now. But Brigan refused to be intimidated, still relaxed in his chair.

"Magi are dangerous killers," Bjorn went on. "I lost my grandfather and two uncles that day. And you want to just let those people roam free?"

There was a tense moment as Brigan stared up at Bjorn. I felt my palms sweating as I waited on pins and needles for how he was going to respond.

"Of course not," Brigan said, sweeping away the tension with his light tone. "I just like to be able to articulate both sides of an argument. Obviously magi are too dangerous to be allowed in the realm in large numbers. The wild dragons they draw would doom us all."

I did my best to appear indifferent, but Brigan's declaration deflated me inside.

"Although…" Brigan said thoughtfully. "Gauntlet down: All magi should be offered the chance to get the cure before execution."

"So the cure is real?" I jumped at the sound of my own voice. Bjorn cast me a look, and I shrank back against the wall.

"My parents say it is," Brigan said. "They've just finished developing it at the Mage Hunter Academy in Evyndara. If all goes well with the final stages of testing, they'll be able to completely remove a magi's ability to cast. They'll be normal like the rest of us."

I felt my heart beating faster as I pictured it.

That was when I felt the sudden, sinking feeling. A single, terrified note sounded, long and loud through my bond with Sniff.

When I saw the faces of the other dragon riders, I knew they were feeling something similar through their own bonds.

Solvai frowned, catching on to our anxiety. "What's going on?"

"Something is wrong at the stables," Brigan answered for all of us. "The dragons—they're in danger."

I didn't hesitate. Gripping the hilt of my seaxe, I reached for the door handle.

"Where do you think you're going?" Edrea stood. "We're sidelined—we aren't going out there."

She turned to Cam as if she expected him to back her up. But he was a rider too, and looked just as anxious to rush to the stables as I felt. His neck muscles flexed along the drake tattoo there, and I remembered that he'd gone to prison because someone had messed with his dragon.

Another panicked note rang in my heart. Brigan jolted, and Erik inhaled sharply. Cam's knuckles went white as he gripped the haft of his dragonhook spear.

"We aren't disobeying orders, right, *Captain* Solvai?" Edrea rounded on Solvai. My friend looked small, jumping a little as all of the attention shifted to her.

With six sets of expectant eyes on her, Solvai clammed up. Her lips pressed together, and a shiny film formed over her hazel eyes.

She was doing everything in her power not to blink and let the tears spill over. She caught my eye, and I gave her a nod, looking toward the little falcondrake charm around her neck.

She reached for the token, carved for her by the soldier father she admired so much. Her forefinger and thumb rubbed the charm, and she took a deep breath.

"Squad," she started, only the tiniest shake in her voice. "To the dragon stables, on the double."

Lime green flames engulfed the dragon stables.

The swarm of enemy dragons circled the stables overhead like a flock of scale-headed vultures. Every so often, one of them would breathe another jet of emerald flame down onto the massive building's roof, as if the dragons were working together to build an enormous funeral pyre.

The front doors to the stables were nothing more than a pile of rubble, as was a huge portion of the wall. No wonder we'd felt such fear through our bonds—there were still dozens upon dozens of dragons trapped inside.

All around us, squads fought off enemy dragons from the hoard. They fired scaleslayer crossbows and swung long seaxes or dragonhook spears. But this attack was far worse than the ones from the usual wild dragons who came to the keep. According to the commanders, this was a focused assault, led by the Drekai General himself.

Too many orange-cloaked soldiers already lay scattered across the clearing around the stables. Several dragons lay still as well, but I couldn't tell if they were ours or the Drekai's. All of them, including the ones fighting us in the sky, wore protective armor over their chests. The kind of armor a dragon needed when it no longer had a heartscale. That meant they were being commanded by remote riders—probably more Drekai.

A shadespitter evren opened its jaws to shoot a stream of black liquid at a nearby squad. Shadowbinding venom. The acid splattered across the squad's shields and chestplates, eating away at metal or dragonleather and weakening them. Psionic dragons bore gold runes floating over their foreheads as they used telekinesis to rip crossbows from the guards' hands.

The army of Keep Rengard fired mighty ballistae from towers along the citadel wall. We saw those take down a few enemy dragons. Then before our eyes, one mythic dragon began to change.

The brassy wyvern was already huge and menacing, with spines like a horned lizard growing along his back. Probably on his third ascension. Then, angular, Sentinel patterns glowed to life along his hide before a golden cloud of ether encompassed the wyvern. Seconds later, the ether cloud dissipated, and the wyvern reemerged at least nine times larger than it had been before.

Soot.

The wyvern was almost the size of the stables now. I'd seen smaller creatures like stony desert iguanas use geomancy to change their size and intimidate enemies. Dad said it was them using earth etherarchy to take on the aspect of mountains. But I'd certainly never seen that power used on this scale before.

When the guard's next hooked javelin came flying toward it from the ballista, the wyvern simply knocked it aside with its enormous tail. It gave a vicious, earth-shaking roar, then dove toward the ballista launcher, crushing it with its claws.

Some soldiers gave a warrior's yell when they saw someone ride in on a black and amethyst evren. He wore a Captain's helm, modified to accommodate the horns that sprouted from his head. A dusky blue cloak billowed behind him.

Captain Zoren wielded a long, silver chain. He whipped it out toward the gigantic geomancer dragon, and the wyvern's supersized form seemed to falter where the silver touched it. The wyvern rose into the air, ready to meet the Captain of the Guard.

Nearer the command center, a booming tremor drew my attention. Flying away from the explosion was the Drekai General, his red and black wings fanning the heavy smoke.

That's when I saw Lorelai's wyvern, Comet, bolting after him into the air to bravely try and stop his escape. But the Drekai was too well trained. He slashed with his scimitar, sending Comet spiraling to the ground.

From a short distance away, I heard Lorelai scream in anguish. My heart broke for her, but I was just grateful to see that she wasn't inside the burning stables.

"This is insane," Erik muttered from his place at the back of the squad.

"We got a plan?" Cam asked.

A scream made me jump. At the nearest gate along the citadel wall, I saw a man in gleaming brown ascension armor. He had a short beard, dark hair, and an ornate circlet around his head with an orange topaz at its center.

My eyes widened. The king of Rengard rarely left the citadel walls. Now, he struggled to get past his own high guard as they held him back.

I couldn't hear all of what they were saying, but I caught scattered phrases from the high guard.

"Too dangerous, King Axel.... Nobody can get in... lost too many soldiers trying."

I realized the king had come for the same reason as we had—His dragon was trapped inside the burning stables.

"Great move, Captain Solvai," Edrea snapped. "You want us to fry trying to get into the stables now too?"

Another pained melody from Sniff sounded through our bond. Beside me, I saw Brigan fall to his knees, staring helplessly at the stables where his dragon was. The high guard confirmed it—There was nothing any of the soldiers could do.

But maybe there was something I could do.

No, I thought to myself. *I can't use etherarchy. It's reckless. It's wrong.*

From where we stood at the edge of battle, I could hear the agonized roars from the dragons trapped by fire. The flames leaped higher, and I wondered how long the building would last before hot, heavy coals crushed every bonded dragon inside.

Dad's words sprang to the forefront of my mind.

They have souls as refined as yours and mine.

Sniff's frightened song pounded in my heart, each note making me feel like I was bleeding out of my chest. I pictured his face, with short ears always on high alert. The joy in his large eyes every time he saw me. We'd only known each other a short time, but already I knew I had to do everything I could to keep him safe. I knew Brigan felt that way about his bond as well. And Erik, and Cam, and every other rider whose dragon now faced certain death if they didn't escape those stables.

They have souls as refined as yours and mine.

I squeezed my eyes shut and balled my hands into fists. It went against everything I'd ever been taught. The tremendous consequences for what I was about to do loomed before me, but I pushed them to the back of my mind.

I opened my eyes and turned to Solvai. "Do you trust me?" Without hesitation, she nodded.

I swallowed hard. "Then order everyone to follow me."

With that, I took off running toward the burning building. From behind, I heard Solvai give the command.

"You heard her. Everybody, follow Meleya!"

Flames consumed the stables on every side, but we needed to find a way in. The door—or rather, the dense, fiery pile of rubble—was definitely not an option. The enemy dragons had intentionally crushed them all. It dawned on me that the Drekai attackers had done it to try and kill as many of Keep Rengard's dragons as possible, including the king's own wyvern, in order to cripple our guard.

I grit my teeth. The innocent bonded dragons shouldn't have to pay that price.

I spotted a panel of starglass on the wall near where I stood. It wasn't big enough for a dragon, but a human could squeeze through in a pinch.

"Does anybody have any silver?" I called over my shoulder.

Surprising no one, Bjorn whipped out a long silver dagger strapped to a holster on his thigh.

"Here," he said, offering me the weapon. His eyes narrowed with challenge as he carefully anticipated my reaction.

I bit my tongue as the icy silver sent pain rushing through my arm, but kept my face even. It was just like the silver rod test at the gates of Spydra Prison.

I thrust the dagger into the center of the window. The silver reacted with the ether in the starglass, and it shattered into thousands of tiny particles of gold etherdust.

I passed Bjorn his dagger. More green dragonfire partially blocked our way through the opening, but I took a few steps backward to gain some momentum, then darted through the flames. Solvai and Brigan were close behind, followed by the rest of the squad.

Inside the stables was an oven of chaos. The tall wooden beams were charred, surrounded by lime green dragonfire. The feeding troughs and hay scattered across the floor sent blazes high into the air.

Many dragons flew frantically, darting all around the room as they fruitlessly searched for a way out. Others were curled up in the center of the stables where the flames were lowest, almost as if they'd already given up. The air in here was so hot and thin that it was difficult just to breathe.

A bright yellow evren zipped toward me, nearly knocking me to the ground. As Sniff nuzzled my cheek, music flooded my heart—a cacophony of relief, fear, and anticipation. Beside me, Brigan's orange drake, as well as Erik and Cam's dragons, hurried toward their riders.

At the same time, a majestic, third ascension wyvern flew down from the flaming, unstable rafters. Her hide was a rich shade of brown, the green flames from the fire reflecting onto each shining scale. This could only be the king's bond.

Foolish soldiers, the dragon's voice appeared in our minds, startling me. I'd almost forgotten that the further a dragon ascended, the better they could communicate. *Leave now. There's nothing you can do here.*

"Well," Edrea said. "That's good enough for me."

She turned on her heel and began heading back toward the shattered window, but a piece of flaming timber came crashing down from above right between us and the exit. Edrea stopped in her tracks.

Solvai turned to me. "What now, Meleya?"

I breathed in the chaos around me, fixing my gaze on another small starglass window along one wall. Through it, I could just see the clearing outside. I thanked the goddesses—I needed to see where the exit portal would go for this to work.

"On my word," I said. "Get the dragons through."

"Through what?" Brigan asked with a frown, following my line of sight.

I didn't answer. Instead, I took a few steps toward the window and lifted my finger.

Trying to keep my finger steady, I carefully traced the rifting rune in the air. Gold light trailed from my finger, and the rune appeared over my forehead like a jewel in a crown.

I heard Edrea cry out in shock, and a string of swear words from Bjorn. Out of the corner of my eye, I saw something like terror in Solvai's eyes. Brigan's jaw dropped. Both of my closest friends stared at me as if they didn't recognize me.

A tear overflowed onto my cheek as I tuned them all out. I stretched my hands out in front of me, and a golden crack began to form. It started small, then grew, reaching from the packed earth floor all the way up to the rafters.

A sharp jolt sent shivers up my spine as my ether well began to drain. I'd never made a rift this large before. I wasn't even sure I could.

My hands trembled as I made a prying motion with them. Following my movement, the crack slowly ripped apart, revealing the white-tinged spirit world.

In one swift action, I thrust my hands apart to either side. The portal did the same, opening wider until it spanned the length of at least several dragons.

Soot, it was hot in here. Sweat was already dripping off the ends of my hair as I put all my energy into holding the rift open. I could feel my ether well draining fast.

I craned my neck and saw my squad watching in disbelief. My voice ragged, I called out to them.

"Get them through!"

Solvai shook her head, springing into action first. She rushed up to the king's mighty brown wyvern.

"Will you help us?" she asked. The wyvern reared back her head and gave a powerful roar.

The dragons all around the stable responded. They clustered around the king's wyvern, hope returning to their eyes as they looked into the portal. Through the white hue I could just see the clearing outside of the burning stables where my exit portal was.

Solvai began ordering the squad to keep the panicking dragons in line as they began herding them through the rift. Wyverns and evren flew over my head as drakes thundered past me on either side.

The mad rush of dragons seemed endless. My arms were getting tired, and I could feel my ether well becoming dangerously depleted. I'd never attempted to use this much etherarchy before, not even close. I had no idea what would happen to me if I ran out completely.

As one drake clawed its way through the portal, its tail came whipping out behind it. The spiked tip caught me in the arm, sending pain shooting up my shoulder.

I cried out, almost recoiling and letting the portal drop. But with more dragons crowding into it, I bit back the burn. A headache bloomed to life across my brow and over my temples as my vision flickered red.

I fell to my knees, but kept the rift going. Sniff hovered protectively at my side, determined to keep any other dragons from accidentally harming me on their way through the portal.

Soon, I heard Solvai calling to me. "That's all of them! All but the king's wyvern and Sniff."

"Go," I replied hoarsely.

Luckily, she understood. She ordered the squad to flee through the portal, along with the king's dragon.

I just saw the hem of Brigan's cloak disappear when I felt my ether well bottoming out. Sniff must've felt it through the bond, too, because he let out a shriek.

He pressed his head against my back, pushing both him and me through the quickly-shrinking portal. The whiteness of Etheria surrounded us for only a moment before we were stumbling through the other side, onto the hard dirt of the clearing. We were safe.

My portal winked out in a flash of gold, and the sound of splintering wood and shattering starglass filled my ears. With an earth-shaking crash, the roof of the stables collapsed, sending dust and fiery smoke racing across the ground all around it.

Stars filled my vision as my knees buckled. Over the roar of the crumbling stables, I heard Solvai and Brigan saying my name, and felt someone grasp my hand.

The last thing I saw before blacking out was Bjorn's wild, snarling face as he raised his silver dagger over my head.

Fragment - King Axel of Rengard

King Axel watched as the high guard rushed his body through the corridors of the citadel, wondering if they'd make it to the healers in time.

The king felt like he was floating along with them, as if he were being pulled by a tether connecting his soul to his body. He looked down at his hands, not his physical ones, but the odd, spirit ones in front of him. They still looked like his hands, but they were translucent, and a misty sort of aura hung around them in an earthy shade of hickory.

Looking toward his physical body, he realized he didn't look so good. His face was badly bruised and several ribs were definitely broken. Blood dripped onto the polished castle floors.

King Axel remembered the battle at the dragon stables. He'd felt the tug from his wyvern, Lantha, alerting him to the desperate plight of the dragons there.

The high guard had been right to stop him. He'd been so weak since contracting the shadow wasting—it was the reason King Axel rarely left the citadel. But even the high guard hadn't been able to stop the onslaught of enemy dragons that came for the king once they'd spotted him. A mythic dragon had zapped him with a well-placed blast of violet dream energy to the head, at which point Axel felt his spirit separate from his body. If his wyvern, Lantha, hadn't escaped the burning stables when she did, Axel would surely be dead already.

Healers were ready and waiting inside the king's chambers. They laid his body on the regal bed and tore open his shirt. Many fresh wounds covered his chest, along with the jagged gray marks along his skin. The shadow wasting was spreading more each day.

The healers set to work. King Axel's spirit settled into a comfortable place at the edge of the bed to watch.

It wasn't long before the door burst open. Frantic sobs filled the room as Queen Ilona rushed toward her husband's body and threw herself over his chest.

"My queen," a healer said. "If you'll allow us to finish—"

"Oh, Axel," she wept, prying herself away. "My sweet Axel."

Axel frowned. As usual, her tears were perfect. Exactly what everyone would expect from the queen whose husband lay dying. She'd been the perfect queen from the moment he married her last year. From her face to her clothes to her manners.

But as he looked at her through his spirit's eyes, something felt wrong. Her eyes didn't seem quite so large and round. Her hair was missing that ethereal shine, and her skin was no longer flawless. It was still her same face, just less idealized. To be honest, King Axel preferred this more natural look. But the subtle differences still took him aback.

Then Axel noticed it—the rune glowing over the center of the queen's forehead. Axel's eyes widened. Only magi, specifically Mystics, used runes. That had to mean... no. Ilona couldn't be. Surely Axel would've realized if his own wife had been a magi all this time.

But the evidence was right there before Axel's eyes. Well, his odd spirit eyes at least. It dawned on Axel that Ilona must've been cloaking the rune in the physical world using an illusion. That's how nobody had noticed it.

Illusions... Axel thought. *That must be what Ilona's been doing to change her appearance. Tricking everyone—including me—into thinking she's the epitome of beauty.*

But here in this strange world-between-worlds, Axel saw the truth. Ilona had been deceiving him. But why?

The healers worked for hours, Ilona standing by and quietly sobbing. Finally, they'd done all they could do for the day, leaving King Axel alone with his body and his wife.

Hello, Ilona... a voice echoed in Axel's ears. He frowned, turning his head toward the source of the sound. The voice had an air of superiority about it—nothing like Ilona's usual sweet, silky tone.

"Rise, Dasha," Ilona replied to the voice. Axel's spirit stumbled backward when some kind of gray shadow rose up from the floor at Ilona's feet. The being's misty form appeared almost like a woman from the waist up, her legs trailing into smoke. Her face was blank, though a pair of vibrant, lightning blue eyes glowed from the mask.

The king lives, the voice emanated from the gray shadow. *We have failed once more.*

"Don't worry. It's only a matter of time," Ilona replied curtly.

If King Axel's spirit could draw breath, it would've caught in his throat. Ilona looked past the being toward Axel's body and Axel was certain Ilona couldn't see the being the same way Axel could. Though she clearly could hear her.

"Besides," Ilona went on. "The attack on the dragon stables wasn't a total loss. The Captain of the Guard and his commanders are convinced it was the Drekai who sent the dragons. Already they talk of war with the Dragon Isles."

Our Seers were correct then, the being said. *The Drekai General was on the Rise today.*

"Keep Rengard's arrogance will grant the Gray Ones their wish. War is coming to Evgard."

Axel rushed forward to stand beside his wife, automatically trying to put a firm hand on her shoulder. But his spirit hand went right through her.

The gray being seemed to laugh. *Now, if only the king had perished today, all of the pieces would be in place for the Coven to take the Rise.*

"That sooty unregistered magi from the guard slowed things down by freeing the dragons. But they'll execute her soon enough and she can join sweet Axel in the afterlife."

Ilona leaned over the king's body and traced the bridge of his nose with her finger. Axel felt strange as he watched, barely feeling the touch, like the memory of a breeze.

The king was a fool to think he could trick you by secretly meeting with the Farseer. But when you rule the keep, Rengard's alliance will not be with the Knights of the Torch.

The gray shadow spoke of the band of rebels with disdain. Ilona nodded, her face twisting into a dark smile. Despite her sinister expression, Axel still found her face beautiful.

"With the Gray Ones at the helm, magi will finally take their rightful place above the rest." A passionate look flashed across Ilona's face, a look of longing, and perhaps something even more.

"Life to the Soul Reaper," Ilona said, and the gray shadow laughed.

Axel cried out in fury, but his voice was silent. He wanted to scream, lash out—do *something*. But stuck in just his spirit form, he was completely helpless.

Momentarily, Axel froze as a pair of glowing, blue eyes turned from the queen to look his way. It seemed his outburst had drawn the shadow's attention.

Its gray form whooshed across the floor to hover directly in front of Axel's face. Whatever substance flowed through the king's spirit veins ran cold.

Oh dear, it whispered. *It seems that while his body sleeps, our dear Axel's spirit hears our every word.*

"Scorch," Ilona cursed. But the creature laughed once more.

It is well. Quickly, before someone comes. We must wipe his memory.

"Of course," Ilona replied, her gaze darkening. The gray shadow seemed to dissipate into an inky mist as it leaned forward toward the traitorous queen. It almost looked like the creature was leaching into Ilona's body, and for the briefest second, Axel saw her eyes flash bright blue before returning to their natural color.

Ilona smiled as she raised a finger. An eerie blue light followed it as she traced a rune, reaching down to gently touch his temples, and then...

King Axel felt like he was floating. Somehow, he was watching his body below, his beloved queen leaning over him, tenderly caressing his face.

He looked down at his hands, not his physical ones, but the odd, spirit ones in front of him. They still looked like his hands, but they were translucent, and a misty sort of aura hung around them in an earthy shade of hickory.

Looking toward his physical body, he realized he didn't look so good.

Chapter 9: Sentenced

I knew I was in silver manacles before I opened my eyes. Frigid pain shot from my wrists up to my elbows, cutting off my ether flow to my hands so that I wouldn't be able to runetrace. Not that my ether well had refilled enough yet anyway.

Bring-a-ling! A delighted melody filled my heart as Sniff felt through the bond that I was conscious. He hadn't been sure I'd wake up.

As I lay there, I sent back a reassuring thought. *I'm fine.*

A tight knot formed in my stomach, and a lump rose in my throat as I realized that was a lie. I was anything but fine.

My eyelids felt like they weighed a hundred pounds as I forced them slowly open. The tan adobe ceiling of the barracks filled my vision. I was lying in my own bunk. When I turned my head, I saw two silver-clad Mage Hunters in dusky blue cloaks standing defensively in the doorway, ready and waiting.

I was surprised when I saw two more people in the room. Bent over the table near the doorway were Solvai and Brigan. When I saw them, my lower lip began to tremble.

"I know what you must be thinking," I said, my voice coming out groggy. Solvai and Brigan's faces snapped toward me.

"Meleya—" Brigan started, but I pressed on.

"You can't believe you spent three years so close to a magi. That all this time you were near someone so detestable and dangerous."

"Meleya—" Solvai tried to get a word in. The Mage Hunters in the doorway took a step closer, listening to every word, but I didn't care.

"But the fact is, that's who I am." My words came out in a ragged rush, tears forming at the corners of my eyes. "I never asked for it. Soot, I never *wanted* it. That said, I can't blame you for wanting nothing to do with me anymore. I'm sure it took a lot of convincing for them to let you near me, and I appreciate you coming to say goodbye. But I just have to say this: maybe I am a magi, but that's not all that I am. I'm still the same person who found our bunker with you, then spent the next few weeks by your sides clearing spydrawebs and scrubbing dust from the floors. The same one who spent three years with you in basic training. The same one who baked you huckleberry fire-cake for your birthday, Solvai, because it's your favorite—"

"*Meleya*," Solvai tried again as Brigan got up from the table and made his way to my bunk.

"I'm not finished—"

Brigan knelt beside me. His warm, brown eyes were calm and sure, like a familiar blanket on a cold winter evening. As I gazed into them, they seemed to ground me and slow my racing pulse.

I swallowed. "You mean you don't despise me?"

"How shallow do you think we are?" Solvai stood beside Brigan, her dark hair swinging as she shook her head at me. "We're just glad you're finally awake. Three hours is a long time to let your best friends worry—never do that again."

"Bjorn," I said, remembering our squadmate's silver dagger. "He tried to…"

"A certain Heir Duke of Solhelm took care of Bjorn," Solvai nudged Brigan, who still stared softly at me with a calming gaze. "The rest of us had to step in just to stop Brigan from killing that son of a dragonmutt."

"What about the dragons?" I asked. "The battle?"

"Won, for now," Solvai answered. "Though that Drekai General escaped. And now they're talking about war with the Dragon Isles."

"But you don't need to worry about that right now," Brigan said, his voice low and smooth.

"No, she doesn't," one of the Mage Hunters in the doorway spoke up. "She's awake now, so it's time to alert the Captain of the Guard that she's ready to appear before a court martial."

"She needs time to rest," Brigan said.

"What's the point of rest when she's bound for execution?"

"That's assuming the trial finds her guilty."

The Mage Hunter's steely eyes rested on me. "With the Ursadon himself sitting on the judicial council, I'd say we'll see a death by dragon before sundown."

Zoren's office was a magi's worst nightmare.

I'd been to this room once before when Captain Cenrik was still in charge. Gone were Cenrik's colorful tapestries of Evgardian history. The walls now held shelves laden with what looked like spoils of war. A dragon's wing stretched on a wooden frame, the horn of a craghopper. But most of the objects were from conquests of magi. A Seer's wand lay broken in a display case. A small, carved rattledrake fang looked suspiciously like a Wildshaper's totem. I grit my teeth when I recognized a chunk of runemarked onyx. That Rifter's anchor had belonged to my mother.

Rays of late afternoon sunlight streamed in through the room's one window, highlighting the dust particles in the air with an orangish light. The stuffy warmth made sweat bead along my forehead and wrists, where the silver manacles still burned me with their freezing, painful touch. Behind me stood the pair of Mage Hunters, their silver armor so close that I could feel the chilly aura on my back.

In front of me, behind the office's large desk, sat the military judicial council, who would ultimately decide my fate. Commander Gunnar took one chair, with Captain Zoren sitting in the center. A third chair sat empty as we waited for a representative from Evgard's noble class to join us.

My squad stood in a stiff lineup in the back of the room, ready to bear witness as to what I'd done at the dragon stables earlier that morning. I could feel Bjorn's stare boring into the back of my head, even colder than the silver surrounding me.

A clerk sat beside the window, prepared to take notes, while the trial counsel, a bored looking, middle-aged man with a handlebar mustache, meandered around the floor opposite me in front of the desk. Tapping his foot and glancing out the window toward the setting sun, he broke the heavy silence.

"Righty then," he said with a thick northern accent. "I say if that noblewoman judge don't show up in the next coupla minutes, we proceed with this 'ere trial. I've got a nightly routine, ya see, where I watch the sun set from my back porch with my darlin' bloodhusky, Ol' Fuzzy."

Commander Gunnar made a face. "That sounds… difficult to miss."

The prosecutor nodded, grateful the commander understood his plight. Then he leaned over the large, oak desk to grab the gavel set in the center. Three sharp knocks rang out, and both Commander Gunnar and Captain Zoren narrowed their eyes at the man's obvious breach of protocol.

He was oblivious to their annoyance. "Welp, in the name of cozy night-time rituals, let's get this 'ere court martial hurryin' along—"

The door to the office swung open to reveal a petite silhouette in the dusty light. A woman in a long, rose-colored dress glided into the room. My breath caught as I realized it was Ilona, the queen of Rengard herself.

"Forgive me," the queen said in a soft voice. "I know you asked for Lady Aneli to sit in judgment today. But I asked her to step aside so that I might preside as the noble representative for this case." Thick, black eyelashes fluttered over large, round eyes. "I hope that's alright," she added.

For a second, nobody answered. I glanced around the room and realized she held everyone—especially the men—captivated. Even Brigan's mouth hung open a little as he stared at the queen's beauty. I grimaced, unsure why that bothered me.

"Alright?" the prosecutor said, twirling his mustache as he let out a low whistle. "Your highness, if it means we get the privilege of starin' at your lovely face, we don't mind if you done locked up the other noblewoman and threw out the drakkin' key."

Commander Gunnar gave the trial counsel a truly disturbed look. Meanwhile, I could feel my stomach twisting into knots as the queen took her seat behind the desk beside Captain Zoren. What was so special about my case that it would bring the queen of Rengard to the trial? She laced her fingers together delicately over the table in front of her, her face a perfect mask.

Zoren frowned, turning to the queen. "Shouldn't you be with the king during his recovery?"

The Queen pursed her shiny, bow-shaped lips. "If he wakes, they'll send word. For now, I must do what I can to see that justice is served."

She tilted her head my way, and I felt my already twisted stomach drop.

Zoren cleared his throat, pounding the gavel once on the desk. "Now that a full military judicial council is present, we will proceed with the statement by the trial counsel as to the general nature of the charges."

The prosecutor gave Ilona one final wink before stepping back into the middle of the room opposite me.

"Welp," he began. "For starters, my name's Jedidune of Scale Summit, son of the youngest daughter of the old Keeper there too, 'bout three generations back." He waggled his eyebrows at Queen Ilona, as if expecting her to be impressed that he was distantly related to some northern nobility nobody had ever heard of. The queen gave a small smile back.

It was enough to make the man puff out his chest. "All y'all can call me Judge Jed, though."

"You know you're not a judge, right?" Commander Gunnar asked.

"Anywho," not-a-real-Judge Jed went on, gesturing to me. "This 'ere soldier's been accused of bein' a magi. Her squad here witnessed her doin' some kind of mythic shenanigans durin' this mornin's battle. Six of 'em witnessed it, ain't that right?"

Judge Jed turned to my squad in the back of the room. Bjorn nodded eagerly while the rest did so with at least a little less enthusiasm.

Judge Jed continued. "And the punishment for bein' an unregistered magi's the ol' six-axeheads-under treatment, if you know what I mean."

He looked me straight in the eye, and I held my head high as I stared back.

"You do know what I mean, right?" he looked at me as if concerned that my stone face meant I wasn't getting it. "Six axeheads under? Pushin' up smokesage? Payin' a visit to the goddesses? Dead as a doorscale?"

"I understand," I assured him, earning a grateful glance from Commander Gunnar for shutting him up.

"It's a pretty simple case," shrugged Judge Jed. "I move we plan ourselves an execution and have done with it so we can move on with our various evenin' plans. 'Specially seein' as the magi in question ain't got no defense counsel to speak on her behalf—"

"Actually, she does."

I straightened with surprise as Brigan left the back line to join me before the judges.

"Soldier." Commander Gunnar lowered his eyebrows. "Stand down. This is not appropriate."

"What could be more appropriate than the Heir Duke of Keep Solhelm standing in as the defense counsel to the accused?" Brigan replied, effortlessly slipping into the same enthusiastic, self-assured voice he used when he threw down a debate gauntlet.

"Brigan, don't be foolish," Commander Gunnar warned. "What would your father say?"

"Let him speak," Captain Zoren's voice was stoic. I frowned, wondering why Zoren would allow Brigan to say anything on my behalf. Wouldn't the Ursadon want me dead more than anyone?

"Pshaw," Judge Jed waved a limp hand at Brigan and me. "If he can think of anythin' to say that'll support'er."

Despite the looming tension, Brigan gave a confident, charming smile. "I'd like to call Squad Captain Solvai to speak."

From her place hugging the back wall, Solvai's eyes widened. She took a shaky step forward.

"Captain Solvai," Brigan said, beginning to pace the length of the room as if he owned it. "Tell us what happened in the barracks this morning."

"Uh," Solvai began. "Commander Gunnar had sidelined us for disorderly conduct. But then the riders felt their dragons calling out to them that they were in danger. So we left the barracks and went to the stables to check it out."

Brigan stopped pacing and held up a finger. "Was it Meleya who forced us to go to the stables?"

Solvai shook her head. "No, as squad captain I gave the order. It... it seemed like the right thing to do."

Brigan nodded as if this was a fascinating piece of information. "Thank you, Captain Solvai. That is all." Brigan turned back to the judicial council. "So, as just stated by Meleya's squad captain, Meleya was simply obeying orders when she found herself at the dragon stables this morning. How can we fault her for following through with an order from her superior to evaluate the situation at the stables, and from there do all within her power to help the distressed dragons?"

The panel behind the desk watched Brigan's speech with interest, as did the Mage Hunters and the rest of my squad. Judge Jed was even nodding along.

"Furthermore," Brigan continued. "I'd like to point out a few things that we'd be remiss to overlook regarding the future impact Meleya's decision to save the dragons had on the army as a whole. Think about it. Were it not for Meleya's actions at the stables this morning, not only would Keep Rengard have lost hundreds of bonded, battle dragons, but we would have lost so much more."

"How'd'ya reckon?" Judge Jed said, genuinely intrigued.

"I'm so glad you asked." Brigan gave a winning smile, the dimples on either side of his cheeks showing up stronger than ever. I felt my heart lighten.

Brigan continued. "Estimating low, a dragon egg costs what, a gold mark? Maybe two, depending on the type of egg and whether or not it's mythic. Replacing at least a hundred dragons, well, that alone would have significantly hurt the guard's finances."

Commander Gunnar and Captain Zoren exchanged glances, as if realizing Brigan was right. Brigan pressed on.

"Then, consider the impact on the squads. Losing that many dragons would call for significant retraining of almost every squad in the guard. Effectiveness would go down, leaving the Keep vulnerable for years to come."

Judge Jed stroked his mustache, muttering. "That's true."

"Finally, think of the emotional ramifications for every soldier who would have lost their bond that day. I'm sure each one of us has seen what the loss of a bonded dragon can do to a soldier. As a bonded member of the guard myself, I can tell you."

Brigan's eyes got just the tiniest bit glassy as he thought of his drake. When he spoke again, it was with quiet reverence.

"Commander Gunnar, I've watched you and your bond, Flecha, for years while in basic training. Seeing the unity the two of you share—the way she stands protectively behind you during each class, the way she responds immediately when it's time for her to accompany you into battle—it's what I always wanted for myself."

Commander Gunnar looked like he had a lump forming in his throat. Brigan's words made me think of Sniff, and the fear I'd felt this morning at the thought of losing him.

Sniff played notes of comfort in my heart through our bond.

"And Captain Zoren," Brigan went on gently. "I saw you this morning, fighting the enemy dragons with your own valiant evren at your side. The unique connection each dragon rider shares with their bond... it's something irreplaceable."

Brigan looked at the floor. "I hate to picture the agony such a loss would have inflicted on the nearly one hundred soldiers who would've lost their bonds this morning, were it not for Meleya."

Brigan turned his gaze on me, his almond-shaped eyes full of sincerity and gratitude.

Looking at him, I could feel him reassuring me. I didn't want him to look away.

"Soot on a stick and a half," Judge Jed cursed. "Welp, drak if that weren't the most convincing scorchin' argument I ever done heard."

Sure enough, both Captain Zoren and Commander Gunnar seemed to be deeply considering Brigan's points. I dared to picture my parents' faces, and hope that I may not have completely let them down rose in my chest.

"How well you speak, young Heir Duke," Queen Ilona's sweet voice floated across the room. "You'll make a fine ruler one day."

Brigan's cheeks deepened as he inclined his head before the beautiful queen.

"But I must remind my fellow judges," she said, "of the principles of strength and justice that Evgard was built upon."

Her large eyes filled with tears and her lower lip gave the slightest tremble. "How can we deny the justice owed to my husband? Even now he lies dying because of the dragons that stormed our keep. And what draws the dragons near?"

From behind, I heard Bjorn answer, his mouth twisting into a smile. "Magi."

Ilona nodded. "I can't stand by and watch the great Keepdom of Rengard go soft. It's not what my dear Axel would've wanted."

I felt my hopes wither and die as I noted the grim faces of both Captain Zoren and Commander Gunnar. No matter their personal opinions, they couldn't go against the queen of Rengard.

Panic began coursing through my veins as the reality of the situation hit me like a whip to the face. They would most likely set my execution for sunrise. I'd seen magi executions before—the most common way was to tie them to a post on a platform far enough from the Rise that they wouldn't be a danger to anyone else. They'd give you a weapon to make themselves feel better and trick you into thinking you had a fighting chance, then wait for the wild dragons to finish you off. Death by dragon.

I drew a ragged breath. Would they let me see my parents one last time? How long would they let them live in Spydra Prison before executing them too now that their proxy was gone?

I squeezed my eyes shut. I hoped they would just execute Mom quickly, without telling her they'd already killed me first. The pain she'd feel hearing of my death would be worse for her than the death by dragon.

"I see no further need for discussion," Queen Ilona said. "Our ruling is that at sunrise, the magi will suffer death by—"

"Wait," Brigan cut off the queen. My eyes snapped toward him, as did everyone else's. The queen's temperate gaze darkened.

"Brigan," Commander Gunnar's jaw was tense. "I respect what you're trying to do for your friend, but part of being a leader is knowing when there's nothing you can do."

"No," Brigan insisted. "I'd like to call one last witness."

"What witness you talkin' 'bout?" Judge Jed scratched his head.

Brigan lifted his chin confidently. "Lantha, the bonded dragon of King Axel."

It didn't take long for them to call for the king's wyvern. She was on her third ascension, far too large to fit inside the Captain of the Guard's office. Instead, she appeared in the wide third story window, using the claws at the folds of her wings as well as her hind legs to cling to the wall.

Brigan took a knee in front of the window before addressing the wyvern. "Lantha, thank you for being willing to testify before the council today."

Of course, she used her third ascension power to speak to every mind in the room.

"You're aware that King Axel was wounded in battle this very morning. He cannot speak for himself, but as his dragon you are bonded to him, and have been for over ten years. What would you believe the king would say regarding the plight of Meleya of Misthaven?"

The dragon stared nobly down on those of us in the office, as if choosing her words carefully.

This young woman saved my life, Lantha thought. *And the life of every dragon in the stables. I know the king would grant clemency for this, magi or not.*

Queen Ilona opened her mouth to protest, but before she got the chance, Captain Zoren rose to his feet.

"In light of this new information, I propose a compromise," Zoren said. "As the queen has stated, we cannot allow Meleya to remain in Keep Rengard for fear of the wild dragons she would continue to draw to our haven. But I have a solution."

I squared my shoulders as Zoren overlooked the room. He went on.

"As pointed out by her defense counsel, it was the entire squad, led by their squad captain, who disregarded Commander Gunnar's order to remain sidelined during the battle. The Realm of Evgard respects unity above all else; therefore, I find it only fitting that the entire squad assume punishment for this outcome. For their actions at the dragon stables this morning, the squad in question will be given the name 'Squad Reckless.'"

Protests rose from behind me, but Zoren was unfazed as he lifted the gavel.

"Our ruling is that until further notice, Squad Reckless will be stationed at Outcast Outpost."

Zoren banged the gavel onto the desk. Commander Gunnar stood with Zoren in support of his decision.

"Surely nobody can object to such a ruling," Zoren said, giving me a dark look. "The magi won't draw more dragons from the wilds, since she'll practically be *in* the wilds. Additionally, I'll be sending a pair of my best Mage Hunters to the Outpost to keep an eye on her. I trust them more than anyone."

The queen's face flashed with anger for only a split second before she replaced it with a demure nod of acceptance.

If the squad had been upset about the name, Zoren's decision about our reassignment put them over the edge. Edrea swore under her breath while Cam cracked his knuckles. Erik shook his head in disbelief, and even Solvai and Brigan looked horrified.

Right on the edge of the Dragon Mists, everyone knew Outcast Outpost was the most dangerous assignment a soldier of Rengard could receive. Only the most... *disposable* squads got sent to the Outpost. I looked at Brigan. I didn't think they were even allowed to send noble soldiers to the southern border.

Zoren dismissed everyone present, asking me to stay behind. The queen shot me an unreadable look as she floated out the door, pursued closely by not-a-Judge Jed.

"So, exactly how married would you be if King Axel—goddesses possibly rest his soul—were to, you know, bite the o'l Scorchwind dust? Go to the big citadel in the sky? Cash in his scales?"

I stayed put, both Mage Hunters still standing rigidly at my sides, as I watched everyone from my squad filter out. That is, everyone but Bjorn, who lingered at his place near the back wall. He held his silver dagger in one hand, rhythmically slapping the flat of the blade onto his opposite palm.

"May I have a word, Captain Zoren?" he said.

Zoren gave a single nod.

"I wish to transfer to a new squad. I won't serve alongside a *magi*." The way Bjorn said the last word made it sound dirty. Maybe it was.

"Their kind don't belong," Bjorn continued. "Asking me to serve on her squad without killing her is like asking a starving man not to hunt the drakalope in his backyard."

I expected Zoren to tell Bjorn no right away. Zoren's punishment involved all seven of us going to the Outpost. Though Bjorn's threat made me sure I wouldn't get much sleep at night with him nearby.

Zoren was silent for a long moment as he eyed Bjorn's gleaming silver dagger. Finally, he spoke.

"Your transfer will be complete by morning, soldier."

Bjorn gave a self-satisfied smirk before stalking toward the door. As he passed me, he gave one last snarl before spitting directly into my face.

I gasped, trying to wipe my eyes the best I could with my hands still cuffed in silver. Bjorn slammed the door behind him.

I looked back to Zoren as the last light from the setting sun bathed the room in a dim, purplish light. His black Drekai horns contrasted harshly against the tan adobe wall behind him.

"There are two last matters to attend to," Zoren said, pulling open a drawer of his desk. "The first is the matter of your parents."

I swallowed. The last thing I wanted was to discuss my parents with their longtime pursuer and captor, the Ursadon.

"The three years you've already served the guard were under false pretenses," Zoren went on. "Therefore, effective immediately, your proxy service on their behalf will begin anew."

My heart dropped. That meant the three years I'd spent in basic training no longer counted toward my parents' six-year sentence. I'd thought I was halfway to earning their freedom. I felt like Zoren had just snatched the floor from beneath my feet, and I was now falling through empty space.

"Don't worry, your mother will be safe," Zoren said. "I'll make sure of that."

"And my father?"

Zoren's face stayed neutral as he pushed past my question. "If I were you, I'd get used to my place in the guard. You never know if your parents' six-year sentence might need to be extended."

My jaw clenched, and I looked behind me to see if the other two Mage Hunters were hearing this. Neither moved a muscle. And why would they? The Ursadon was the Mage Hunters' infallible champion.

Zoren slid open a drawer in his desk as the Mage Hunters to my left and right each roughly grabbed one of my arms.

"Stand down." Zoren held up a hand for them to release me. He began walking toward me, holding a long, razor-sharp pen and a bottle of shiny, silvery ink.

My blood froze when I saw it. "Are those…" I trailed off.

"Tools for silvermarking," Zoren confirmed, placing the bottle of ink gently on the desk and dipping the knifelike pen into the pool of silver. "They tell me it hurts like the void, so would you prefer to hold still, or would you like my associates to restrain you?"

I set my jaw, taking a defiant step away from the Mage Hunters behind me.

Zoren nodded, then closed the gap. I stood like a statue as he reached to steady my chin. The back of his hand shone with black and dark purple scales.

For a brief moment, Zoren's gaze flicked to the cords around my neck. His eyes narrowed like he was taking a mental note—had he realized I wore two necklaces? He quickly refocused on the task at hand.

Zoren carefully brought the silvermarking pen to the top of my cheekbone. The tip of the knife cut into my flesh, sending icy shivers ripping through my body and a trickle of red blood down the side of my face.

I wanted to scream, but I didn't move a muscle. My hands balled into fists as Zoren carefully made the first incision, then the second.

When he finished, Zoren stepped back to admire his work. I felt another drop of blood slide down my cheek and drip off the point of my chin. It fell onto Zoren's office floor, another token marking his success as a Mage Hunter.

Silently, Zoren pulled out the silver seaxe sheathed at his belt. He offered it to me, holding it in front of my face so that I could see my new scar in its reflective surface.

Etched into my cheek was the ancient Rifter's symbol, matching the one on the vandalized dragon skull in the canyon, as well as the one showing through all the burn marks on my mother's left cheek. A disconnected diamond with elongated points slanting off the top and bottom.

For now, the mark shone red with blood. With time, it would turn silver, untouchable by any form of etherarchy. I slowly brought a manacled hand to my cheek, barely recognizing myself now that I was a branded magi.

My days of hiding were over.

94

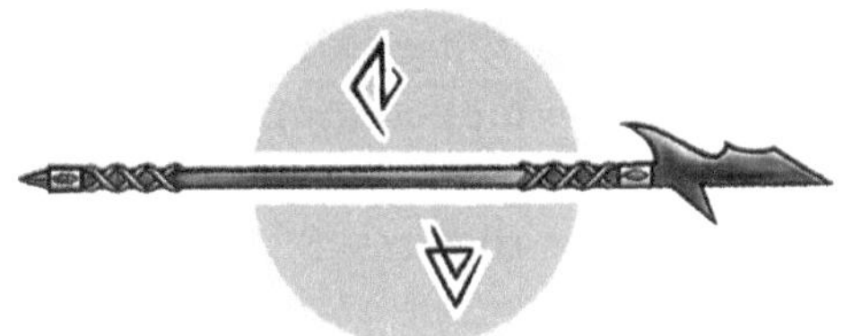

B lack swans circled the outside of the spire as screams echoed from within.

Vidya watched on with fascination. She'd always known Jaira had the grit and determination to be great, but the young Mage Hunter was taking it to a whole new level as she held a length of her silver whip taut between her hands.

"You'll tell me what was in that case," Jaira spoke darkly. "Or suffer."

Cenrik set his jaw. His sage green ascension armor lay on the floor while the Canyon Keepdom's former Captain of the Guard sat in one of Vidya's ornate black chairs. Jaira had roughly bound his hands to the chair's arms using lengths of silver-infused cords that cut into Cenrik's wrists in painful, icy stripes. Blood dripped from his left cheekbone where Jaira had carved the man's Lightwielder's silvermark. Vidya was impressed—for a secret magi, the man had made it far in the ranks of Rengard's army. Hiding his own lightwielding powers behind those of his bonded sunscale wyvern had been a stroke of genius.

"I already told you," Cenrik's voice was even. "I didn't know about the case."

Jaira rolled her eyes, then expertly lashed her whip toward Cenrik like an ashviper's tongue. The sharp, silver blade on the whip's tail hit Cenrik in the chest, and he winced at the touch of the freezing, painful silver.

Vidya shifted on her feet. Jaira wasn't a magi herself, and had never experienced the extra layer of agony that they felt when in contact with silver. Of course, now that Vidya had discovered the key to expanding her own ether well, she was no longer vulnerable to the gleaming metal herself. But she remembered all too well the pain she'd felt the day her family delivered her to the Mage Hunters for silvermarking.

"We know you ascertained the location of the Coven of the Gray Ones in the south," Jaira snapped. "The Mage Hunters need the information in that case."

"No," Cenrik said, and Vidya sensed the slightest tremor in his voice. Then he grit his teeth as Jaira whipped him again, this time at the base of his neck. Vidya frowned.

"You know what I think is in that case?" Jaira's upper lip curled into a snarl. "I think you know the true name of the Liberator. You were saving it to bring to the other Knights of the Torch. Does that sound about right?"

Cenrik stubbornly stuck out his chin. Jaira flicked her whip, sending a few more drops of blood cascading from a new scar on his chin. Cenrik cried out.

"Speak, you scorching Knight," Jaira demanded. "What was in the case?"

Cenrik's voice cracked. "A... a shard."

"Go on," Jaira prompted, fingering her whip.

"A shard of crystal. A skystone, only instead of white, it was a vibrant shade of blue."

Vidya and Jaira exchanged glances.

"This shard," Vidya said, leaning forward in her seat. "There was something written on it. You'll tell us what it said."

"I never saw the shard myself," Cenrik replied. "It was my dragon who found it—hidden in the caves beneath the dragon stables at Keep Rengard. When he shared his discovery through our bond, I could tell it was forged using dark etherarchy. Neither of us dared touch the stone, let alone read it. I wrapped it in cloth and hid it inside the case."

"Liar," Jaira glared. "You saw two names carved into that stone. What were they?"

Vidya frowned, watching Cenrik's eyes water.

"I swear, I never saw what was written on it," he said.

In response, Jaira flashed her whip once more, cutting Cenrik's upper lip. He recoiled at the pain as a line of blood streamed into his mouth.

"You're lying," Jaira seethed.

"No," Cenrik spoke earnestly. Jaira roared, lashing out again with her whip twice in quick succession.

Cenrik screamed as the bladed tip slashed once, then again, in parallel slashes right above and below his eye from his dark eyebrow into his cheekbone. He cried out, insisting he didn't know what names had been scratched onto the shard. He bowed his head, fearing another strike.

Vidya felt the hairs on her arms stand on end as she watched her apprentice. Jaira's eyes were alight with ruthless drive.

"I swear by the light," Cenrik plead. Vidya's jaw tensed.

"Jaira," Vidya said sternly. "That's enough."

Don't be soft, spoke the voice in Vidya's head.

But Vidya stood her ground. "I believe the Knight never read the name on the shard. In fact, I can't help but admire his dedication to the light, even if his belief is misplaced."

Cenrik looked toward Vidya with both surprise and gratitude in his eyes.

"Fine," Jaira growled, folding her arms. "Then I believe it's time we handed him over to the Soul Reaper."

"S-soul Reaper?" Cenrik stuttered.

"You did promise, great Black Valkyrie," Jaira said, challenge in her tone. "That when we were finished with the Lightwielder, that I could have his ether well. I'm ready to become a skymage."

"My ether well?" Cenrik said, fear written all over his face.

Don't be soft, the voice repeated in Vidya's mind. *Jaira will make a powerful skymage. The Gray One who follows her is strong. Don't let that fool Solrac think you're weak.*

"Yes," Vidya agreed. "Jaira, take Cenrik down to the laboratory. Tell the Soul Reaper to prepare him for surgery."

The swans continued circling the spire as screams resumed their echoing from within.

Chapter 10: Reassignment

The sounds of bustling early morning activity rang out across the docking station at the base of the Rise. The Ridgeback River lapped beneath the wooden planks underfoot.

"You're sure you've got everything you'll need once we get to the Outpost?" I asked for the third time.

"Yes, Meleya," Brigan and Solvai replied in unison.

"Have you got your backup weapons?"

"Yes," Brigan answered.

"Are they sharpened?"

"Always," said Solvai.

"Great," I said. "Now, I doubt they're going to feed us on this thing, so I made everyone a lunch last night."

I reached into a large burlap sack and pulled out two smaller sacks, each labeled with a name in black ink.

"Brigan, this one's yours." I handed over the sack. "And don't worry, Solvai, yours doesn't have onions."

My friends peeked into their sacks, and I watched as both their faces lit up at the smell.

"These aren't your bunker-famous sweet dragonpork sandwiches," Brigan grinned.

"Maybe," I shrugged.

"When did you have time to slow cook the meat?" Solvai asked. "Or bake flatbread for that matter?"

"You'd be amazed at the things you get done when you can't sleep," I replied.

"I hear that," Brigan mumbled under his breath.

Meanwhile, I grabbed my enormous burlap bag and walked to where the rest of the squad stood nearer the edge of the dock. Only Bjorn was missing. Captain Zoren's decision to transfer him had ruffled a few feathers from the others, but whatever Zoren's reasoning, I was glad the diamondback wolverine guy and his crazy eyes weren't coming with us this morning.

"Hey," I said, reaching into the sack. "I made everyone a lunch for the journey."

I passed Erik and Cam theirs, which they eagerly took. Then I fished for the one labeled 'Edrea' and held it out to my squadmate.

Without a word, she turned away from me and crossed her arms. For a second, I just stood there with my arm outstretched, holding her sack and waiting to see if she turned back around again.

Of course, she didn't. Seeing his sister's unclaimed sack of food, Cam boldly plucked it from my hand.

"More for me." He grinned and lumbered away.

It wasn't long before they brought our dragons down from the Rise to meet us before we shoved off together. Two dragon keepers helped get the dragons situated on the large deck of the river longboat, among them Lorelai herself. She probably didn't want to miss her last chance to see Solvai off.

It wasn't easy getting Sniff to sit still on the longboat. And getting him to stay in his place opposite Erik's wyvern to try and evenly distribute the weight was near impossible. Finally, with Lorelai's help, we got Sniff to perch atop the carved dragon figurehead at the front of the boat, with Brigan and Cam's drakes opposite each other on the deck and Erik's dragon in the back center. That way, when Sniff inevitably took to the skies, it wouldn't rock the ship too badly.

"That's quite the li'l evren you got there," Lorelai said once we'd gotten Sniff tentatively in place.

"Sniff's one of a kind, for sure," I smiled, fingering his heartscale around my neck. Lorelai watched me do so.

"Astromancer, right?" she asked, and I nodded. "You know, until Sniff came along, my Comet was the only starshard—that is, Astromancy usin'—dragon in the army here at Keep Rengard."

A shadow of sorrow crossed Lorelai's face. I remembered seeing her dragon fall to the Drekai General during the fight at the stables. I couldn't imagine how painful it must be to lose a bond.

Lorelai crossed her arms, looking at my evren with a sad smile. "Now, it's only you, Sniff. You've got quite the legacy to uphold, y'hear?"

She looked like she was about to say something more when Lorelai suddenly pulled me into a hug.

"Soot, if I ain't gonna miss you two," Lorelai muttered.

I squeezed her back. "Thank you Lorelai. For everything you've done for me over the years."

"This drakkin' realm was wrong to force you into the guard for somethin' you can't help. Least I could do was offer you a home. You're special Meleya, and you deserve so much better. You'n Solvai both."

Lorelai leaned back and looked me squarely in the eye. "Now, listen up. I need y'all to be careful out there. You and Solvai look out for each other, alright? I've got an old friend who lives in that ramshackle shanty town down at Outcast Outpost. You tell old Torsten that Lorelai's given 'im strict instructions to keep you two gals safe."

I nodded, then watched as Lorelai bid farewell to Brigan, then gave Solvai an even tighter hug than she'd given me. She and the other dragon keeper stood on the dock, waving as we shoved off down Ridgeback River.

As expected, it didn't take long for Sniff to get bored of his perch. We'd only just rounded the first bend in the canyon when Sniff launched off of the dragon figurehead and began zipping around the outside of the boat.

I listened to him play an adventurous melody through the bond as he skimmed over the surface of the water, dipping the tips of his wings in one at a time. He liked the way they made little ridges of waves as we floated downriver, the light of morning just barely creeping over the high canyon walls.

As I watched Sniff loop around the side of the boat, Erik caught my eye as he sat with his knees to his chest in a corner of the deck. His head was buried in his arms.

Worried, I made my way over to his spot and took a seat next to him. He peeked up at me for a split second and I saw that his eyes were rimmed with red. Erik hastily sat up straight and rubbed his eyes with his sleeve.

"Meleya, hey," he said, his voice cracking just a little. He turned away from me as he spoke, trying to hide his tears.

"It's okay," I said, keeping my voice low so that we wouldn't draw anyone's attention. "We're heading to Outcast Outpost of all places—nobody blames you for feeling uneasy."

"That's the thing," Erik said. "I feel more than uneasy. Not that I blame you, Meleya. You saved the dragons, and I wouldn't trade that for anything. But… I know it's not very manly of me to say, but I was scared enough to be in the guard at all, let alone at the border."

I frowned. "Then why did you join?"

Erik hesitated, turning to look at me with round, black eyes. I backtracked immediately.

"Not trying to pry," I rushed. "You don't have to tell me."

"No," Erik swallowed the lump in his throat. "If and when I die out there, it would be nice for someone to know."

I wanted to reassure him that he'd be fine, but the words stuck in my throat. Erik went on.

"I joined for the stipend. My father was killed in a wild dragon attack a few years ago, and as the oldest of seven kids, we needed the money. It wasn't so bad when I was in basic training in Brackentown, since there wasn't any actual danger. I spent the last three years dreading the day I became a real guard, and now, with this assignment, it's worse than I ever could've imagined."

Erik pulled out his creamy sketchbook from the satchel at his side. He flipped it open to a page near the beginning to show me a charcoal drawing of nine people who must've been his family. I recognized Erik in the group, standing taller than the six children on the page.

Seeing the picture tugged at my heartstrings. While traveling with the nomads, I'd always watched on with longing when I saw others my age playing with their siblings. I'd once overheard my parents talking about what it would be like to have another child, but Mom had dismissed the idea immediately. She didn't want to risk having another magi like me.

I wished I could say something to Erik to make it better. I wanted to send him home to his family with a sack of a hundred gold marks, but all I had were words. Words, and a mental promise to do my best to keep my squadmate from falling on the battlefield.

I looked him in the eye. "You're a brave son and brother."

Erik gave a short, weary laugh. "Brave. I'm over here crying like a baby while the rest of you face the Dragon Mists with weapons held high."

I reached across him to grab the scaleslayer crossbow at his side. Then I held the weapon above my head before taking Erik by the wrist and pulling his hand up to take the crossbow.

"There you go," I said. "Now you've got yours held high as well."

Erik chuckled as he pulled the crossbow back down.

I nudged him with an elbow. "You know what, Erik? The big secret is, we're all as scared as you. The only way any of us have a chance out there is if we have each other's backs."

"For Evgard unite?"

I raised a hand to my opposite shoulder. Erik did the same, giving me a nod. He didn't exactly look any less terrified of the horrors we faced at the Outpost, but if nothing else, we'd both found a friend.

The riverboat continued along the canyon, and soon we passed the awful lineup of dragon skulls, the warning against magi painted in copper behind it. That meant Spydra Prison was getting close.

I checked my sack and saw the last three lunches inside. One for each of my parents, and one for Ulf and his wife. I couldn't wait to ask the prison guard if he was a proud father yet.

Once the cave mouth came into view, I approached the ferryman. It was the same man who'd brought me downriver every week for the past three years.

But when I asked him if we could stop for just a few minutes, he didn't respond. Thinking he may not have heard me, I tried again. This time, he pointedly turned away, refusing to even look me in the eye.

An involuntary lump formed in my throat. Where the orange cloak had earned me respect, the silvermark now deemed me unworthy of a response.

I stood at the edge of the longboat, the sack of food at my feet. I bit my lip as I watched Spydra Prison pass, then fade from view as we continued down the canyon.

I shouldn't have been upset. It wasn't like I'd been planning on seeing my parents, anyway. Ulf would've brought the lunch sacks to them—I was sure he'd understand my desire not to let them see me like this. Not that the scale-tipped ears of a half-born were the same as having a silvermark, but at least he understood something of being an outcast.

I knew seeing me with a freshly-cut Rifter's mark branded into my cheek would be too much for Mom to handle. If there were any goddesses out there, I hoped they'd ensure that Zoren and his guards didn't tell her about that part. Or that I was heading to the Outpost. All she needed to know was that they'd assigned me somewhere outside of the keep proper, and I wouldn't be able to visit the prison anymore.

The lump in my throat grew as I remembered what Captain Zoren had said last night in his office. He'd heavily implied that as long as he lived, I'd never be able to serve out my parents' sentence. I doubted we'd ever reach northern exile, at least not through my proxy service in the guard. And then there was the strange way he'd refused to confirm my father's safety the same way he'd done for my mother's. I'd have to find another way to get them out.

Lantha, the king's wyvern, had vouched for me, assuring everyone present at my court martial that King Axel would've sympathized as well. Maybe if the king woke up, he would be willing to see me. The Queen was strongly opposed to magi, and would be against any action to help me, of course. But if Lantha was right, King Axel might see things differently.

I sighed, absently reaching toward the cold, tender scar on my left cheek. It was a long shot. But with a silvermarked face, long shots were the only kind I had left.

"Beautiful canyon," Brigan appeared at my side, and I quickly pulled my hand away from my face. I gently shook my head, allowing a few loose strands of white hair to fall over the mark.

Brigan was right about the canyon. The natural layers in the redrock flowed in red, orange, and brown patterns along the stony wall. It reminded me of the marbling in a good cut of steak.

"I've never been this far south before," I said.

"Neither have I," Brigan said. "Someday, I'd love to show you the northern end where the river flows from the Scarlet Strait."

"I thought the Ridgeback River flowed out from, oh, you know. The Ridgeback Mountains."

Brigan smiled. "It does. But there's a smaller channel that makes head on the coast of Solhelm. It's one of my favorite places in the realm: Dragonheart palms growing along the banks, the sound of the ocean at your back... Gauntlet down: Keep Solhelm should be the capital of the Canyon Keepdom, not Keep Rengard."

I couldn't help but laugh as I watched him talk about his home. He got this light in his eyes, and those dimples on either side of his mouth came out strong.

"I never got to properly thank you," I said. "For what you did at the trial."

"Anytime," he shrugged as if sticking his neck out for someone like me was nothing. "Gotta put those debate skills I learned while studying with the Sons of Streya to some use."

He leaned one elbow on the side of the ship. I took a deep breath, the spray from the rushing river sprinkling my face with mist.

"I still don't think you should've had to come along," I said, a wave of guilt hitting me. "As a nobleman, I mean. Aren't you too important to serve at Outcast Outpost?"

Brigan shook his head. "My parents were pretty furious. They told the Captain of the Guard to reassign me without delay. It took a lot of convincing to get them to let me go."

"You had the chance to back out but didn't take it?"

"What kind of leader would I be if I held myself above the rules?" Brigan mused. Then he flashed me a grin. "Besides, I couldn't abandon you and Solvai."

"You really don't mind being associated with me?" I asked. "Now that you know the truth?"

"You think I pick my friends solely based on whether or not they're technically allowed to legally live in the realm?" Brigan teased.

"Maybe." I shrugged.

"Trust me, it's going to take a lot more than that to get me to stay away from you."

In that moment, I became aware of just how close Brigan and I were standing. The wind carried his scent toward me, the familiar smell of wood and freshly-pressed clothes. Without my permission, my feet sub-consciously stepped toward him.

Suddenly Brigan went rigid, taking several steps backward.

"Uh…" he muttered, his fingers fumbling for the orange heartscale hanging around his neck. "What was that, Bolt?"

He turned to his dragon who was curled up on the other side of the deck. At the sound of her name, Bolt raised her long, regal neck.

Brigan reached over and gave me an awkward little pat on the shoulder. "Sorry, but Bolt needs me for something. Good talk."

With that, he scurried across the deck to his dragon, leaving me stand-ing alone.

Good talk? I thought. Brigan wasn't usually that inarticulate.

Ping! Sniff trilled in agreement through our bond. My yellow evren appeared beside me over the edge of the ship, his four wings humming as he kept up with the quickly moving longboat. Sniff pointed his nose toward Brigan's retreating back.

Ding dong, Sniff thought.

I chuckled. *Be nice.*

Brrring!

I reached across the side of the boat to scratch Sniff under the chin.

I know. I like him too.

After a while, we rounded another wide curve in the canyon and a large wooden sign came into view. It looked like it had seen better days as it hung crookedly from a thick branch of a scraggly, dead juniper tree. Scrawled into the wood were the words: '5 miles to Outcast Outpost—last chance to turn back.'

With a lurch, the longboat came to a stop as the ferryman pulled it off to the river's edge.

"I don't go further," he said with finality.

We unloaded onto the shore. Us riders mounted our dragons while Solvai and Edrea climbed on behind Brigan and Cam. Sniff and I took to the air, leading the group as our squad continued down the canyon.

As we closed in on the last mile, Sniff zipped ahead. I held on tightly to the saddle to avoid getting thrown.

We soared around the final bend, and my breath caught at the sight before my eyes.

Shabby dwellings were built into the base of the stone, with more rising up along with the steep canyon walls on either side. They were patched together using an odd mix of splintering wood, mud bricks, and crisscrossing support beams. They'd built many buildings into pockets in the canyon wall itself.

What once must've been a strong stone wall spanned the space between the canyon cliffs. The Ridgeback River narrowed as it cut through the center of town, a low arch along the bottom of the wall allowing it to pass through. Many holes and cracks peppered the wall, which blockaded the shanty town from the wonders beyond.

A vast, white wall of fog surged only about a mile or two beyond the wall. It swirled in on itself, shimmering against the bright sunlight. Home to an endless horde of wild dragons, dreklings, and other feral dragonkind, right in my new backyard.

The Dragon Mists.

And from the looks and sounds of things, the Mists had just released a fresh swarm of dragons to attack the Outpost.

Chapter 11: Outcast Outpost

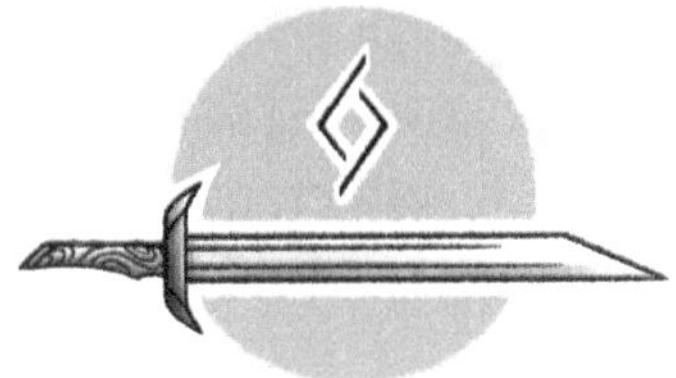

Screams from humans mingled with the shrieks and roars of wild dragons as they came swooping down from the skies. I heard the clang of swords, the twang of crossbows, and the whizzing of harpoons launching from towers as orange-cloaked soldiers fought to defend the wall.

Through the numerous gaps in the crumbling bricks, I saw that the majority of the soldiers defended the canyon from the Dragon Mists' side. Several soldiers, however, darted along the side nearer the town, cutting down any drekling or drake who managed to literally slip through the cracks.

Sniff and I landed as the rest of my squad joined us to gape at the chaos.

The sound of thundering claws grew as a woman wearing a commander's uniform rode up to us on the back of a large drake. She yanked on the reins, and he reared back as he came to a stop.

From the drake's back, the woman called down to us in a grating, annoyed-sounding voice.

"You must be the new squad that Captain Zoren sent." She narrowed her bright, fiery green eyes at us, and I realized she must have Drekai blood in her somewhere.

We looked to Solvai to answer, but she looked completely overwhelmed by the Outpost and didn't respond. Brigan piped up.

"Squad Reckless at your service, Commander."

"Reckless?" the woman scoffed. "You'd better be."

The woman spit on the ground and wiped the grime from fighting dragons off her forehead. She had strawberry hair and a fair complexion, but even with barely detectable eyebrows, her glare was murderous.

"I'm Commander Hildred," she said, the sounds of battle punctuating her words. "Which one of you's the squad captain?"

Solvai took a hesitant step forward.

"Drak," Commander Hildred swore as she looked at Solvai from head to toe. "Of course it's you. Well, soldier, get your squad's sorry scales to the front lines, on the double!"

We all just kind of stood there.

Solvai faltered. "But we uh, we just got here. And we've never uh... don't we need training before...?"

The commander rolled her dragonfire eyes. "Sooty cowards. No better trainer than near-certain death."

"But Commander," Brigan put in. "We're down a squad member."

"I'll be sure to let the wild dragons know to go easy."

Just then, a scream pierced the air from the town as a pair of soldiers fled a wild wyvern who'd swooped over the wall. The dragon was heading straight for one of the shops at the base of the cliffside. The soldiers pressed up against the shop, struggling to reload their crossbows as the wyvern closed in.

In the nick of time, one fired off a shot, taking the beast in the chest. The soldiers dove out of the way as the wyvern's body crashed into the business and lay still. Copper dragon blood splattered across the front door.

Without pausing to celebrate their victory, the soldiers hurried back toward the chaotic battle. After a second, the door to the shop creaked open just enough for a hand to reach out and hang a sign on the knob that read 'closed.'

We all slowly turned back to Commander Hildred, disbelief etched onto our faces. What was this place?

"What are you dragonhens still doing here?" she shouted. "Your new drakking squadmate's already on the field. Go join him."

"How will we know which one is him?" I asked.

"Trust me, he's impossible to miss."

With an otherworldly series of snarls, a terrifying, scaled monster lunged toward the commander from behind. The drekling had a hunched frame with oversized shoulders and arms that dragged along the ground as it ran. A draconic head, clawed hands and feet, and a long tail marked it as one of the monsters that came with the meteors from skyfalls.

I shuddered, my eyes growing wide as it leaped toward Commander Hildred. The nomad caravans had to deal with plenty of rogue dreklings, and I knew how vicious they could be.

Without so much as turning her head, Commander Hildred thrust toward the drekling with her oversized dragonforged warsword. The creature let out one last halting squeal, then fell to the ground behind the commander and her drake.

Commander Hildred yanked back on her warsword and whirled it in front of her, sending a spray of coppery blood into the air. We cringed as it splattered down on us like rain.

"Squad Reckless," Commander Hildred said as she casually wiped a stray lock of bloodied hair from her face. "Welcome to Outcast Outpost."

Within two minutes of joining the battle, I was already falling to my death.

Sniff shrieked and clawed at a wild evren above me, not yet registering that I'd slipped off his back. It was like our first practice flight back at Keep Rengard all over again, when I'd fallen over the Dragon Chasm.

Then, I'd had to resort to using etherarchy to save myself.

Then, I'd been alone.

We'd been flying high above the battle on the Dragon Mists' side of the wall. The wind cut across my cheeks, cold against my raw, silvery scar. I was a known magi now. Did that mean I could use my rifting openly?

There were so many people here. Witnesses everywhere. *Could* I use my etherarchy, even if I wanted to?

I tried to runetrace, but my finger didn't obey, years of hiding my powers bubbling up like some kind of mental block.

The ground was rising fast, a cluster of three or so dreklings waiting hungrily below.

Rift, Meleya, I begged myself. *Just rift.*

Mom's disappointed face appeared in my head, and I couldn't make myself trace the rune.

Then out of nowhere I saw another soldier standing on the back of an emerald green evren just below me in the sky. The soldier ran up the spines of his dragon, then suddenly launched himself into the air, kicking off of his dragon's strong head.

He held an axe high in the air above him, and I did a double take when I saw a golden rune alight over his forehead. It was a rune I recognized—one my father used to use to move things telekinetically as a Psion.

The soldier used his psionic power to push the axe through the air toward me as he held on tight. Before the squabbling dreklings below could snap me up, the flying Psion grabbed me around the waist with one of the most muscular arms I'd ever seen in my life.

I grunted at the impact, but held on for dear life as he continued his path upward, still pushing on the axe.

"Got you," he said gruffly.

Confident that I was no longer falling to my death, I dared to look at the soldier who'd just saved my life as he continued to hold onto the telekinetically-charged axe above his head.

In an effort to accentuate his athletic arms and shoulders, he'd ripped the sleeves off of his guard's uniform. He was probably a few years older than me, and had messy, steely gray hair with a maroon bandana wrapped across his hairline. He looked down at me, midnight blue eyes darting quickly to my silvermark before he met my gaze.

"Uh, thanks..." I said lamely.

"Jax," he replied with a quick nod, sending my heart racing more than it was already.

"Meleya," I managed.

A wyvern roared as it caught sight of us, probably drawn to our ether wells.

Jax smirked at the wild dragon, then looked back at me. "Be right back."

With that, he hurled me into the air like I weighed nothing. Naturally, I screamed.

Jax continued to telekinetically hold himself aloft by his first axe, then reached onto his back to pull out a second one. The rune over his forehead pulsed with life as he chucked the axe toward the wyvern, powering the throw with more psionic ether.

The axe embedded itself into the wild wyvern's chest, sending the dragon spiraling to the ground. Jax reached toward it, psionically pulling back his weapon, now covered in copper blood.

He replaced the axe on his back, then reached out toward me. Once again, his rune glowed more brightly as I felt a tug from my belt and leather armor, stopping my descent.

Then I was rushing upward through the air yet again, his psionic hold on my clothing sending me back into his grip. He held me around the waist as he lowered us to the ground.

We landed on our feet near the swarm of dreklings. Snarling, they dove toward us, eager to devour our ether.

We didn't waste a second. I could feel Jax at my back as he hacked at the monsters with his axe. I swung my blade toward those surrounding us on the other side.

I sliced across the neck of the last drekling just as Jax's axe left a gash across its midsection. The beast slumped to the earth. For a moment, everything was silent except the sound of Jax and me breathing heavily. We turned to each other, each giving a single nod.

Then I remembered the rest of the soldiers. As I looked back toward the rest of the battlefield, I realized the fight was over. Wild dragons and dreklings lay scattered on the ground at the feet of orange-cloaked soldiers, many of whom were staring at Jax and me.

Sniff came zooming down from the sky, that old, apologetic melody ringing through our bond. He nuzzled against my cheek, and I rubbed him behind the ears to assure him I was alright.

Although, we'll have to work on the whole me-not-falling thing, okay buddy?

Sniff let out a little ether sneeze in agreement.

Jax's green evren glided down to join us as well. She was much larger than Sniff, probably on her second ascension. Though rather than emerald ascension armor, Jax wore the same uniform as the rest of us—well, minus the sleeves—so he must've bonded her after her ascension.

Among the soldiers staring was Brigan. Now that the attack from the Dragon Mists had ceased, he slid off his drake's back and ran over. I was surprised when he wrapped his arms around me.

"I saw you fall—glad you're okay," he said.

"Thanks to Jax," I said, pulling back and nodding to the new guy.

Brigan took a step toward him, extending an arm. "You must be our new squadmate. I'm Brigan, Heir Duke of Solhelm."

"Duke-man," Jax said, grasping Brigan's forearm back. "They let fancy nobles like you serve here?"

"Not lightly," Brigan replied, his arm flexing.

"Probably don't have to do much real fighting where you come from."

Brigan seemed taken aback by the accusation. I narrowed my eyes at the newcomer.

"Brigan was top of our group in basic training," I said defensively.

Jax nodded, pretending to be impressed. "Top, huh? We'll have to see if that translates to the field, Duke-man." Then he punched Brigan lightly in the bicep, cocking his head as if evaluating it. "Key is to not go easy on arm day. I can give you a few pointers."

Brigan furrowed his brow but bit his lip. I was about to give this arrogant new guy a piece of my mind when Commander Hildred's booming voice rolled out across the battlefield.

"Soldiers! Line up!"

The other members of the squad joined us, as did the rest of the Outcast Outpost guard. We gathered along the fractured stone wall on the town side, Commander Hildred in front of us.

"Squad Choke!" she barked, and a group of seven soldiers stood at attention. "Squad Retreat! Squad Struggle! Squad Flee! Squad Nothing! Meet Squad Reckless."

As I listened to her rattle off the names of the other squads stationed at the Outpost, I got the sense we weren't exactly among Keep Rengard's most favored.

"This is their first assignment, so by all means, be extra rough on them. Let them know what it's like out here at the border." Hildred paced the length of our line, stopping at Jax and me.

"You two," she said, the fire in her eyes burning bright. "Let's get something clear right away. I don't care if you can spin shadowsilk, read minds, or sprout cactus thorns."

She spoke in a mocking voice. Jax and I glanced at each other. He was a Psion, and I was a Rifter, which meant he could use telekinesis and I could teleport—none of the things the commander had actually listed.

"But I don't give a flying scale about your cute little powers," she continued. "Sure, use them if you really can't find another way to keep up. Just know I won't be thanking you for it."

She spat at our feet, her glare coming to rest on the waterproof pouch clipped at my belt.

"What's that, soldier?" she clipped.

I hurried to undo the clasp on the little leather bag and held up my saltshaker.

"Some kind of ether dust?" Commander Hildred narrowed her eyes to slits.

"No, Commander," I fought an involuntary smile. "It's salt."

"Right. Hand over the magi powder or whatever it is."

"It really is salt, Commander," Brigan piped up from his place beside me.

"Why in Streya's name would a soldier carry salt?"

"I like to cook," I replied.

Hildred scoffed. Then she muttered under her breath, something about cooking being a stupid hobby for a soldier.

"Either way," she went on. "You two are the only magi ridgerats they've stuck me with in this void. Don't you dare breed more. Got it, soldiers?""Yes, Commander," Jax and I answered in unison, though I wasn't entirely sure what the order was.

"Soldiers!" Commander Hildred took a few steps backward as she addressed the group again. "Get yourselves to the barracks for some rest before the sentries call us back to the battlefield. And for Solei's sake, please wash up in the river before you do."

The other soldiers quickly scattered, leaving our squad standing alone by the wall. Jax stepped out and faced the group.

"Name's Jax of Blackfjord. I arrived a few days ago after they transferred me from Keep Drakfell. When Drakfell went traitor, some of us still loyal to Evgard got evacuated and placed on different squads throughout the realm. If you were to ask the Captains in the keeps along Rengard's northwest border, you'd see my story definitely checks out. I have family in the shanty town, so there's no reason to question the guard assigning me to the Outpost here."

Jax spoke as if he were reciting some kind of memorized speech. Solvai, Brigan, and I exchanged glances, and my friends shrugged. Maybe Jax was just a little awkward.

"I think that's everything you need to know about me," he said, tugging at the collar of his uniform. "Soot. Anyone else could use a drink?"

There were a few murmurs of agreement.

"Come on." Jax waved for us to follow him toward the cliffside shanty town. "You can all meet my father."

Chapter 12: The Broughkin Arms

On our way into town, Jax gave us the grand tour of Outcast Outpost.

It was a very short tour.

The ramshackle buildings on the west canyon wall belonged to the guard. Grayish brown adobe walls full of cracks made up the barracks, armory, Commander Hildred's personal office, and a sorry excuse for a mess hall. I certainly hoped I'd find better culinary facilities somewhere in this goddess-forsaken place.

The dragon stables here were more like a cavern. The entrance opened up to a large cave with plenty of natural gaps in the rock to let in the sunlight. I saw a single keeper shoveling dung just inside.

Stacked shacks rose high up on the east canyon wall. The lowest tier of irregular structures appeared to be various businesses—a trading post, a general store, a butchery. Already a few grunt workers were carting over dragon corpses from today's battle and dropping them off just outside the butcher's shop. Nobody would ever dream of eating the meat from a bonded dragon, but even the bonded dragons themselves didn't mind taking a bite out of the wild ones.

The unfortunate people who dwelt at the outpost lived in splintering shacks on stilts above the shops and up the side of the canyon. Narrow staircases crudely carved into the rock allowed them to get from one place to another. Already, townspeople were peeking their heads out of their doors and hesitantly beginning to go about their day's business once more.

It must've been hard, living each day knowing that, at any moment, more dragons would be back. Having the Dragon Mists themselves in your backyard, always looming over you. Only the truly desperate or those exiled from regular society would ever choose to live at Outcast Outpost.

I grimaced as I realized that I now fell into both those categories.

Along the bottom row of buildings stood a weather-worn tavern hugging the rock. Jax led the way toward the tavern's rickety front porch, where a scraggly-haired man lounged in an oversized rocking chair, fast asleep. He held an empty bottle in his hand, and it was a good thing the chair was wide because the man's girth filled the seat.

The man didn't stir, even when the door to the tavern swung open and two people in dusky blue cloaks walked out, silver chain whips hanging from their belts.

Mage Hunters. My blood froze as I remembered what Zoren had said about sending them to keep me out of trouble.

My hand automatically went to my sword, and without thinking, I drew it.

"Whoa," one Mage Hunter said, putting both her hands up. "No need for an altercation. It's barely noon."

She laughed, tiny crinkles forming at the corners of her eyes. She had a thick auburn braid and a light eastern accent.

The other Mage Hunter was an older guy with a tan-colored patch over one eye. His skin was riddled with scratches and scars, and I did a double take when I realized he was missing at least three fingers on one hand.

"You can call me Trickshot," the auburn-haired Mage Hunter said. Then she gestured toward her partner. "This here's Mute. At least, that's what we call him on account of a drekling slicing off his tongue. Not actually sure what his real name is, and he sure as scales can't tell us."

We all cringed as Mute opened his mouth. Sure enough, his tongue was nothing more than a nub.

"Why do they call you Trickshot?" Brigan asked. The question had barely escaped his lips when Trickshot whipped back the flap of her dusky blue cloak. Quick as a flash, she pulled a miniature crossbow from a holster on her thigh and shot from the hip.

The bolt whizzed past Brigan's leg, so close that the bolt's breeze ruffled his cloak. A hiss and a rattling noise sounded from behind him, and we all spun to see what the Mage Hunter had hit.

Writhing on the ground was a rattledrake with a crossbow bolt sprouting from its neck.

We all looked back at Trickshot, impressed.

"That answer your question?" she said, holstering her miniature cross-bow.

The rattledrake hissed, and that was when I noticed its coloring—while most rattledrakes I'd seen were brown and tan, this one was pure gray, with bright, lightning blue eyes.

As we watched, the rattledrake's body began dissolving into ashy, gray mist, starting with the tail. But before it fully vanished into the breeze, it shot toward Solvai's calf. She yelped as the creature's fangs pierced through her pant leg.

The rest of the slithering gray monster dissipated until only those haunting blue eyes were left. Last of all, those too curled into nothingness as a tiny, pinkie nail-sized chunk of crystal clinked to the ground where the creature's heart had been.

"Solvai!" I cried out.

"I'm fine," she said, rolling up her pant leg. "It wasn't... *there* enough to do any real damage."

Trickshot strode over to my friend. "How does it feel?"

"Really strange," Solvai replied, staring at the two small, reddish marks on her leg where the thing's fangs had nearly pierced her skin. Surrounding the marks were odd, dry-looking gray patches.

"Feels sort of empty, doesn't it? Almost blank," Trickshot said, reaching for a medium-sized bag at her hip. "Scorch those umbral creatures. They're everywhere down here this close to the Dragon Mists. Hold still."

Trickshot produced a little crystal vial filled with some kind of golden liquid. She carefully knelt over Solvai and poured a single drop onto her leg. The grayness fled immediately, followed by the marks from the fangs.

"That's liquid light, isn't it?" Brigan said, pointing to the tiny bottle. "My family's high mage is a Lightwielder."

"Sure is." Trickshot replaced the cork on the vial. "Best thing for stopping the shadow wasting from spreading—if you can get it on you in time. Be careful—they'll decommission any soldier who gets the shadow wasting. But I studied healing at the Mage Hunter Academy, so if any of you get bit, you come to me right away."

I frowned. Was this Mage Hunter being... cool? I tried to process that concept.

A long creak and a groan drew our attention back to the tavern's porch. The hearty man who'd been lounging in the chair stretched out both arms as he woke up, and more stringy hair fell into his face. He seemed pleasantly surprised when he noticed the bottle still clutched in his hand, then disappointed when he realized it was empty.

When he saw our squad watching him, the man gave a sleepy grin.

"Well, well, well, looks like a bit of fresh meat. Ain't that a pleasure. Welcome to the Broughkin Arms," he said, his northern accent strong as he tipped his hat. Well, he acted like he was tipping a hat, though he didn't actually have one.

"Broken arms?" Brigan said. "Seriously?"

"I thought it had to be pronounced 'Braugh-kin' or something," Erik said, pointing to the peeling sign over the door.

The man laughed heartily, as if Erik had just told the greatest joke he'd ever heard in his life. I wondered what had been in that bottle.

"Woo-wee," he said. "Have I got a tale for you."

"Here we go again," I heard Jax mutter.

"It started years ago," the man began. "Right near when Outcast Outpost were just bein' established, the Brough family were banished by the nobility of Keep Rengard."

"The *Brough* family?" I interjected.

"That's right, little lady. See in those days, them drakkin' Mage Hunters—no offense to y'all, of course," the man nodded to Trickshot and Mute, "were out enactin' orders from High Queen Frida to execute all the Rifters. I reckon y'all know all about the Rifter Purge of forty-eight. Dark times, them. I weren't no more'n ten. Spent three years in a bunker up north."

The man shook his head, remembering. As he did, tangled locks of hair fell away from his face, and I caught a glimpse of the silvery scar beneath his left eye.

He had a Rifter's silvermark like mine.

"Anyway," he said. "This family of Broughs got caught helpin' out some of them Rifters on the run. Brought shame to the Brough name. They ended up gettin' banished to the Outpost, but weren't too keen on bein' associated with the disgraced Brough family, so they pretended to only be distantly related kin to 'em. Named the tavern the Brough-*kin* Arms."

The man burst into more uproarious laughter, and Brigan, Solvai and I exchanged amused looks. That's when Jax's expression caught my eye. He was grimacing, as if the drunk man's display had made him uncomfortable.

"What're we doin' just standin' out here?" The man slapped his knee, and the motion sent ripples through his entire gut. "Let's get your new squad inside for a couple of drinks, Jax, my boy."

"My boy?" Brigan said.

Jax sighed, as if he'd been dreading this moment. "Yeah." The muscular young man stepped onto the porch beside the grinning drunk.

"Squad Reckless," Jax said. "Meet Torsten. My uh... my dad."

The man gave a little bow from his rocking chair, more hair falling over his face.

Dad? *Dad?*

I searched for any family resemblance as I looked from father to son, wondering if this was the future in store for the toned, ruggedly handsome Jax.

Then, like a little flame flickering in the back of my mind, I remembered what Lorelai had said right before sending us off.

You tell old Torsten that Lorelai's given 'im strict orders to keep you two gals safe.

Torsten winced in the bright light of the sun, probably still hungover after downing that bottle. *This* was Lorelai's old friend? I seriously doubted this man would be mentally—or physically—capable of keeping Solvai or me safe. I wondered how long it had been since Lorelai had seen him.

Brigan seemed to take the revelation that Torsten was Jax's father in stride. "Well, in that case, Torsten, it's a pleasure to meet you. We're excited to have your son on the squad."

"Not near so excited as I am," Torsten beamed. "Been rough havin' Jax away in Drakfell for so long. Ain't glad the keepdom went traitor, of course. Them Knights of the Torch're a dangerous bunch. 'Specially that Farseer."

A look passed between Jax and his father. I wasn't sure what it meant, but both their faces looked intense, challenging.

"Right," Jax said. Then he turned to us. "Anybody up for a drink?"

Torsten raised his hand, and Jax motioned for the rest of us to follow him into the tavern. The two Mage Hunters, Trickshot and Mute, said goodbye as we headed inside.

The first thing that caught my eye were the redrock hoodoos that stood scattered across the tavern floor. The stump-like stones were being used as chairs, with wobbly wooden tables set up wherever they grew through the floorboards. Dozens of bottles sat on shelves lining the back wall, which was the vertical redrock of the canyon itself.

The tavern's other three walls were covered with brightly colored, handmade blankets. Each blanket had a unique pattern and color, and many bore angular designs that looked suspiciously like Mystic runes.

Behind the bar, gold light cut through the air. The light pulled itself apart, revealing the black interior of an exit portal. I did a double take as Torsten appeared, chair and all.

The rift winked out, and without missing a beat, Jax's father reached for a cluster of glasses beneath the bar. The glasses clinked as he set them on the counter in front of him.

"Nothin' alcoholic for the guard, I'm afraid," he said, looking at us with genuine pity. "Might get called into battle any minute out here. 'Specially nothin' tipsy-makin' for you 'n' you."

Torsten pointed first to Jax and then to me.

Jax put up his hands. "Never touch the stuff."

"Why?" I asked.

"Alcohol clouds a Mystic's mind," Torsten explained. "Makes it drak-near impossible to runetrace."

With that, Torsten took a swig from a flask of something undoubtedly alcoholic. Draquila, maybe? The Rifter's silvermark on Torsten's cheek was a clear sign that he was a Mystic as well. I looked at Jax and raised an eyebrow. He shrugged.

Torsten lifted a finger and began tracing. Gold light trailed as he drew, but instead of clean lines, they appeared blurred and a little shaky. The matching rune glowed to life over his forehead, and soon, a hand-sized tear split the space in front of him. The other end of the portal tore open high above our heads along the shelves of endless bottles.

Torsten reached through, his hand vanishing, then materializing through the other end of the portal as he grabbed a couple of the bottles. He pulled them through and held them close as both the portals and the rune dissolved into etherdust.

The squad was staring at him, open-mouthed at the display. Admittedly, I was transfixed too. I'd never seen anyone use rifting for something so mundane. It was like when I watched Jax's psionics during the battle—I was both impressed with their power, and incredibly jealous that using etherarchy came so naturally to them.

"What?" Torsten said. "Done said it was drak-*near* impossible to rune-trace."

Jax leaned over to me, gesturing to the squad. "You'd think they just saw him raise the dead rather than just grab a few bottles."

I gave a half smile, then whispered back. "Wait until we tell them about the Sight."

"Or when they see what a Psion can do."

We laughed together, and I was surprised to feel a slight weight lift from my shoulders. For the first time, I felt like someone could really understand me.

Torsten was just pouring his mix into the last glass when he traced another, more complicated version of the Rifting rune I knew. Almost subconsciously, I took mental notes on the way he traced the lines. The rune came out just as blurry as his first, clear evidence of his intoxication. The rune appeared at his forehead and a small portal bloomed to life in front of him.

Not a moment later, seven small portals tore open, one for each of us. One by one, Torsten passed through our drinks. Edrea hesitated before accepting hers, eying the gold-rimmed exit portal with suspicion.

"No need to hire a wait staff, eh?" Torsten laughed heartily once more, sounding only a little hysterical.

I looked into my glass. Deep purple liquid streaked with white swirled inside.

"'S'called a Dragonberry Sour." Torsten took another swig from his personal canteen. "Black dragonberry 'n lemon, with a couple'a squirts of Evyndellian coconut milk."

I took a sip, and bright flavors bloomed to life in my mouth. Not bad.

Torsten raised his canteen. "Welcome to Outcast Outpost."

We all drank.

About two seconds later, we heard a long, rugged horn pierce the air.

"That's not..." Edrea said.

"That's the sentries' alarm," Jax confirmed. "We've got more dragons."

"Already?" Brigan sounded indignant. "But we just came off of a battle."

Jax gulped down the rest of his drink and reached for one of the axes strapped to his back.

"Like Tor—Dad said. Welcome to Outcast Outpost."

"Please don't tell me this many attacks is normal," Erik said, hands shaking as he held his crossbow.

Torsten shrugged. "Usually we get 'bout one a day. We'll skip a day every now and again if we're lucky'n Streya's in a good mood."

Erik's dark skin seemed to lose all its color and his eyes went wide. He made eye contact with me and I gave him a reassuring nod, which seemed to help somewhat.

"I wonder what could be drawing extra dragons near," Edrea muttered, her eyes flashing to me as her lip curled. A wave of guilt washed over me.

As we filed out of the Broughkin Arms to prepare for battle, I heard Edrea humming. It was a tune I recognized all too well, the same song Bjorn had been singing in the window of the barracks the day everything went wrong. That already felt like a lifetime ago.

My mind couldn't help but fill in the lyrics as Edrea hummed.

Stay away
You magi need to listen
Stay away
The dragons have arisen
Stay away
From every keep and town
Or we will hunt you down
Yes, we will hunt you down...

Fragment - Zoren

Z oren's breathing was shaky as he walked the long, winding tunnels of Spydra Prison toward her cell. He knew he had to get it together, but the thought of seeing her filled him with both elation and dread. The last time they'd spoken hadn't exactly been pleasant.

It had been three years since he'd apprehended Freya. He'd recklessly leaped after Freya and her family as they fled, despite the quickly-closing portal. The rift had shut before he'd fully made it through, ejecting him out the exit end with a new painful ether scar spiraling up his jaw. But he hadn't cared—the Ursadon had finally attained his prize.

Zoren had been all too happy to toss that good-for-nothing thief Freya called a husband in jail at long last. But he felt awful about consigning Freya's daughter, Meleya, to serving in the guard. There hadn't been a way around it, though. Without Meleya's service, the drakking Evgardians would've executed Freya.

He'd known for a while that the girl was a magi, possibly even before Freya and Ivar did themselves. Magi had a certain spark in their eyes, a glint of gold when they caught the light the right way. Not everyone could spot it the way Zoren could, which was why he'd done so well as a Mage Hunter. Zoren had always been too observant for his own good.

Zoren shoved down his emotion as he turned down the final curve in the tunnel. There it was—Freya's cell. She sat inside, her head buried in her arms atop her knees as tangled hair spilled over her shoulders. It took Zoren only seconds to glean a thousand clues from what he saw.

Her hair may have been messy, but the woven marriage bracelet around her wrist was clean and well cared for, the gem woven into it polished to shining. That meant Freya still valued her relationship with Ivar and, by extension, her family, above all else, even her own well-being.

Zoren kept his pace even as his footsteps echoed down the cavern. It wasn't until he was directly in front of the silver bars that Freya finally looked up.

Her large, brown eyes were rimmed in red that seemed to have a permanent place there. Her face was every bit as beautiful as the day she'd first found Zoren in the Mirror Forest, though now its left side was mangled and burned. Despite Freya's many attempts to rid herself of her silvermark, the Mage Hunters' ink ran deep, and the Rifter's symbol still showed through all of it.

"You," she whispered the word as if it weighed more than all the silver in her cell.

"Freya," Zoren breathed her name, doing his best to keep his voice even, emotionless. "I have news about—"

"You," Freya's eyes went wide, and she clambered backward in her cell all the way to the back wall, as far away from Zoren as possible.

"As I was saying, I bring news—"

"They told me you're the Captain of the Guard here now," Freya said, terror still evident on her face. "Why hang up the blue cloak?" She glanced down at Zoren's long, dusky blue Mage Hunter's cloak. "Though I can see you haven't. Why have you come, Zoren? Ivar's already been moved at your command. There's nothing more you can take away from me."

Zoren frowned, second guessing his decision to come here personally. He could've easily sent a messenger in his stead. Deep down, he knew it was because he *had* to see Freya. He'd protested the Black Valkyrie's order to come to Rengard, but now that he was here, he couldn't stay away. He'd just been waiting for an excuse.

"I'm here on official business. I have news concerning your daughter."

Freya immediately stopped clinging to the back wall of her cell, instead rushing to the front. She barely reacted to the silver as she gripped the bars.

"What have you done with Meleya?" Freya seethed.

"I saved her life," Zoren's tone was smooth as scales. "When she revealed her etherarchy in battle, I kept her from execution."

Freya's expression crumbled at Zoren's every word. Her breathing became rapid and irregular.

Zoren couldn't stand to see her this way. He reached through the bars, but Freya recoiled at his touch.

"Streya please, let it not be true," she said haltingly, then turned to Zoren. "Where is she?"

"She... she couldn't remain in the keep. I had no choice but to transfer her to Outcast Outpost."

"The border guard at the edge of the Dragon Mists?" Freya sank to the floor, unable to speak. She gulped frantically as if she couldn't draw a full breath.

Zoren felt helpless, fear rising in his chest. He hated to admit it, but Ivar was fairly effective when it came to bringing Freya back from the brink. Although, Zoren blamed Ivar for Freya's anxiety in the first place. She'd been so different before meeting him and having Meleya.

"Don't worry," Zoren said. "I promise you she'll be safe. I've sent the best healer among all the Mage Hunters to the Outpost with her."

"You have to get me out of here," Freya said suddenly. "I can protect her—you know I can. I did well at the Academy."

"Freya—"

"You have to, Zoren. If you ever loved me, free me now so I can help her. Ivar as well. We'll leave the keepdom—the realm if we have to. We'll go north—you'll never have to see us again."

At the thought of Freya leaving with Ivar, Zoren felt a numb darkness growing within him. The same darkness that had followed him ever since he'd left the Dragon Isles and entered the Mirror Forest at the Drekai empress's command. It had been nearly two decades since she'd given him his mission, and Zoren had sworn not to return to the Dragon Isles without what he'd come for. But if Freya agreed to come with him, Zoren just might break that oath.

"You know I'll never let that happen," Zoren said, stone-faced. "But if you swear to leave Evgard with me, I'll set you free. We can take Meleya if you want, run away to the Dragon Isles where they won't punish you or her for being what you are."

"I'll never leave without Ivar."

"Then you'll never leave at all."

Zoren turned to leave the tunnel, but only made it one step before stopping in his tracks. Slowly, he turned back around.

"You spent some time in Misthaven about seventeen years ago," Zoren said darkly. "Before its disappearance, Misthaven was a camp run by the Coven of the Gray Ones."

Freya looked up at Zoren with tear-filled eyes. Only the numbness kept Zoren from melting under her gaze.

"Did you ever know someone called the Liberator?"

Freya shook her head, but Zoren noticed the way her bottom eyelids squinted slightly at the sound of the title. Freya knew more than she let on.

"I need to know who this person is—their true identity. You'll tell me what you know." Zoren spoke without emotion.

"I don't know who the Liberator is," Freya insisted.

"Fine," Zoren said coldly, swishing his cloak as he turned on his heel, heading for the end of the tunnel. "Perhaps Ivar will be more forthcoming with the information."

"Stay away from him," Freya's voice rose.

Zoren continued down the tunnel, ignoring Freya's desperate protests. It was easy when he surrendered control to the darkness.

But a single, sharp pang in his heart cut through the void. Before Zoren turned the corner to head toward Ivar's cell, he took one last look into Freya's beautiful brown eyes.

Chapter 13: The North Tower

The next two weeks proved Torsten right about how often dragons besieged the Outpost. At least once a day, the guard rode into battle.

Some days were better than others, with only a small pod of dreklings rushing toward the town wall from the Dragon Mists. For attacks like that, Commander Hildred didn't even call in the whole platoon. But both my logic and my aching muscles told me she didn't like giving Squad Reckless a break nearly as often as the others, and it had everything to do with us having two magi on the team.

One day, we hobbled back to the barracks after a long afternoon fighting dreklings out beyond the wall. We'd seen the skyfall—the shower of green, dragonfire-tailed meteors—land in the Mists last night. The skyfall must've been what brought so many dreklings this morning. It seemed the rumors about increased skyfalls across the realm were true.

The constant battle had made me come to loathe the sound of the Outpost's ragged alarm horn. I'd started hearing it in my dreams, setting my teeth constantly on edge. The strain was clearly taking a toll on the rest of the squad as well as we headed in after the long afternoon battle.

Jax was all but yelling at Brigan. "The reason I didn't have your back was, oh, I don't know, maybe the fact that I was fighting two dreklings solo out there?"

"That's the problem," Brigan glared right back. "You keep trying to take on the enemy alone. The point of the Evgardian army is that we're unified."

"For Evgard, unite!" Jax mockingly pounded his fist against his chest. "Thanks for the advice, Duke-man."

"While we're on the subject," Edrea threw her usual disparaging hat into the ring. "Erik, where in the void were you out there today?"

Erik looked down. "I was there."

"No, you were *up* there," Edrea accused, pointing to the blue sky above. "*Way* up there, hiding out and doing nothing."

"I was looking for an opportunity to snipe."

"Back off Edrea," I snapped.

She ignored me as she glared Erik's way. "More like waiting for one of us to get killed instead of you."

"Soldiers!" Solvai tried to bark the same way our commanding officers always did, but it came out more like a chirp. "You're way out of line. We'll do a battle evaluation once we're back at the barracks—"

"Like you and Meleya don't deserve any heat either," Edrea remarked, breezing past Solvai's order.

"Hey!" I said. "Solvai did twice as much as you out there."

"Guys, please—" Solvai attempted to cool the situation, but we were far past cooling.

"Are you kidding me?" Edrea plowed on. "You and your sooty yellow dragon were probably drawing all the dragonfire to us for miles."

"At least I didn't spend the entire battle on a single drekling," I seethed.

"At least I'm not a branded little piece of Misthaven soot!"

"Hey!" Jax butted in. "Our *captain* gave us the order to shut the void up."

Edrea and I looked away from each other. I didn't know why I let her get under my skin. Void, I didn't know why she hated me so much. Ever since we'd gotten here, she'd been hiding behind the excuse that she despised me for my etherarchy. But Edrea had been throwing scales at me long before Captain Zoren sent us to Outcast Outpost.

We never ended up having that battle evaluation back at the barracks. In fact, none of us spoke to each other for the rest of the afternoon.

Just as night began to fall, we silently packed our gear and began trekking a short way north up the canyon. Tonight, it was our squad's turn on watch duty at the Outpost's North Tower.

We'd passed the tower on our way in two weeks ago, not long after the ferryman had dropped us off, though I hadn't paid much attention at the time. Like everything at Outcast Outpost, the North Tower was in awful disrepair. The adobe bricks were crumbling, and so much dirt had blown through the canyon throughout the years that a large pile completely blocked the front door. At this point, the tower was more of a landmark than a fortification soldiers could effectively use.

The post was meant to guard the way into the main canyon by way of a thin canyon passage called the Narrows. The passage let out somewhere near the Dragon Mists to the east, bypassing the main outpost, which meant the occasional wild dragon could slip through and head north to the Rise. Because of that, Commander Hildred liked to have a squad on watch at the North Tower when things were slow at the border.

The squad settled in a small clearing around the tower's base. Scattered juniper trees formed a loose semicircle, and a gigantic, smooth redrock four times my height sat nearby.

Erik and his pale blue wyvern climbed onto the rock, probably to avoid human contact for a while. He pulled a pad of paper out of his pack and started sketching before we lost the daylight. Edrea and Cam went off into a corner of their own, Cam's drake lying down between them and the rest of us. Solvai had brought tools for carving, as well as a block of cindercone pine. She pulled up a juniper log to sit on and began to carve, the tension she'd been holding in her brow slowly melting away.

Jax stood in the clearing, picking up a couple of smallish rocks and lifting them one at a time to do bicep curls. He had a gold rune aglow over his forehead, though I wasn't sure why.

Solvai noticed Jax's impromptu workout at the same time I did. We made eye contact from across the clearing and both held in a laugh. If Jax's bulging muscles came from lifting weights that small, it was a wonder he looked as good as he did.

Sniff nuzzled my face with his head, playing a sleepy melody in my heart through our bond.

"Go on, buddy," I said, sliding a hand across his scaly head. "You've earned some rest."

Sniff let out a grateful little chortle, then flitted toward a large juniper tree growing on the far side of the tower. Using the claws on the hinges of his wings, he grabbed onto a high, sturdy branch and perched there for just a second before swinging so that he hung upside down like a bat. Then he wrapped himself up in his wings and closed his massive eyes.

I did a quick scan of my surroundings before choosing a large, flat rock near the edge of the clearing. If I knelt down, the rock came up to just above my elbows—the perfect height for a wilderness countertop.

Brigan helped me unload a few supplies I'd swiped from the sorry mess hall at the Outpost. I carefully laid out a large metal pot, a cutting board and knife, as well as a sack of vegetables and a few other ingredients I needed for tonight's meal.

A little rush of excitement ran through me as I looked over my preparations. I hadn't had the chance to cook a proper meal for anyone since arriving at the Outpost. We were always so exhausted between battles, not to mention the grumbling cook at the mess hall was both passionless and territorial. He'd quickly shut down my request to help out there the first week. But with Brigan's help, I'd managed to convince the man to let me borrow these tools and ingredients tonight.

I smiled for the first time in days as I placed stones in a tight circle in the middle of the clearing. I needed to start the campfire right away, because if the others were half as hungry as I was after our long day, I'd need to get dinner ready fast.

"Brigan, would you mind gathering some firewood while I get started?" I asked, returning to kneel at my countertop rock.

"Of course," he said, heading into the canyon away from the group.

As I chopped potatoes in the low light, I heard footsteps behind me. A glint of gold appeared, brightening my surface.

When I looked up, I saw Jax, a golden psionic rune alight in the center of his forehead. He was still exercising with his fist-sized rocks, grunting as if he were lifting hundred pound weights.

"Really?" I said, using my knife to gesture at the puny rocks. "That's all you got?"

Jax grinned, as if he'd wandered over here just so he could get me to comment on his workout. "Oh, you wanna try?"

He offered me a rock, his muscles inexplicably straining.

"Sure." I rolled my eyes before setting down my knife. Then I got to my feet, holding out a confident hand toward him.

"Might wanna use two hands, M."

I stubbornly pulled back my dominant right hand and extended my left instead.

Jax smirked. "Okay then."

Jax grunted again as he hefted the rock, dropping it into my hand. The shocking weight of that diminutive stone dropped me like a ton of bricks.

Jax laughed as I sat there in the dirt. "You're lucky I didn't let it crush your hand."

I glared, dusting myself off. "What did you do to it?"

He pointed to the glowing gold rune still floating in front of his forehead. "Psion, remember? I'm telekinetically pushing down on the stones to add the extra weight. Gotta push myself somehow."

With great effort, he heaved, throwing the other rock to the ground behind him. Then he walked over to me and brushed some dirt off of my shoulder.

"Thanks," I said, looking down. When I turned back toward Jax, we were practically nose to nose.

"Um… hi," I said cleverly, looking straight into his midnight blue eyes.

"Hey," he bit his lower lip as he smiled down at me.

My eyes flashed to his lips for a split second before I ducked back toward my countertop. I grabbed my knife and started intensely chopping more potatoes.

Jax plopped down beside me, hovering over my shoulder as I worked.

"Do you mind?" I asked.

"Nah," he replied, getting comfortable. "So tell me, M. Why'd you send Duke-man out to get firewood when you could've used your etherarchy to gather as much as you wanted within seconds?"

The question took me aback. "Um," I stumbled. "I guess the thought didn't cross my mind. Rifting doesn't exactly come naturally to me. I only know two runes."

"Only two? Really?" Jax frowned. "The guys told me what you did at the dragon stables in Keep Rengard. You're telling me you've never read a Mystic runebook? Never had a mentor?"

Mom's crying, burned face appeared in my mind. I winced as I replied.

"No. Where I grew up, etherarchy was a big no-no."

Jax folded his arms, using his hands to push out his muscles so they bulged even more. I fought an eye roll and lost.

"So that's why you won't rift in battles," Jax said.

I chopped more earnestly. "Maybe."

"You should get over that."

"Stars, what a great idea." I roughly dropped the diced potatoes into the pot and reached for the carrots.

"Seriously," Jax went on, ignoring my sarcasm. "You could do a lot more good out there on the field."

"What if my rifts alert more wild dragons? The light from the portals might draw them in more than my ether well's very existence does already."

"That sounds like another stupid excuse not to use your power."

"Does it?" I whipped my knife onto the cutting board, decapitating a carrot.

"I think you're just afraid of what you can do," Jax said, his tone infuriatingly calm.

Slamming my knife onto the rock, I turned to Jax.

"I *am* afraid! I don't have a drakking clue how to use my etherarchy. What if I mess it up out there and someone gets hurt? Anyway, shouldn't I be enough without it?"

I didn't mean to raise my voice, but my little outburst was enough to get Solvai to look up from her carving on the other side of the clearing. She glanced from Jax to my frustrated face, then pointed to her spear as she gave me an inquisitive look.

I shook my head at her to let her know I was fine. She didn't need to run our new squadmate through, though I was honored to know she was willing. Solvai shrugged and went back to her block of wood, keeping an eye on me just in case.

Jax was staring at me, looking pretty uncomfortable himself. I wished I could disappear into the sandy canyon floor. Then his gaze darted away, and he absently runetraced. Probably just to have something to do other than look at me in all my awkward glory.

He made a raising motion with his hand, psionically lifting a smooth, round pebble into the air. Slowly, he moved the rock toward me, turning it over and over before my eyes.

"You don't need your etherarchy to be enough, M," Jax said cautiously, still not relaxed enough to look me in the eye. "But your power is a part of you, whether you want it to be or not."

Jax flipped his hand so his palm faced down, and likewise, the pebble dropped. I automatically reached out and caught it. The speckled red and gray stone fit perfectly in the indent beside the base of my thumb.

As I studied the pebble, suddenly I felt my hand slam to the earth from its weight. I looked up at Jax, my dark brown eyes furious.

He let out a loud, aggravating laugh. Aggravating, but contagious. I found myself chuckling as I struggled to lift the psionically weighted pebble.

Just then, a loud clattering noise pulled my attention. Standing in the clearing was Brigan, dropping a pile of dry juniper wood beside the fire pit.

"Got the firewood," he announced. Brigan's face was neutral as he watched me laughing with Jax, but I noticed the way his neck muscles tensed. "Anything else you need?"

"I think that's everything," I muttered, letting the pebble roll into the dirt. Jax gave me one last look as he got up, brushing off his pants before returning to his workout. He traced another rune to psionically float his twin axes, using the long handles together as a bar. He hung from it by his knees and began doing upside-down sit-ups, his tight abs flexing through his tunic each time he crunched up. I pointedly didn't watch.

Brigan was still looking at me expectantly, almost as if he was hoping I'd give him another chore.

"Would you mind getting the fire started while I finish up the prep?" I asked.

"Anything for you." Brigan answered.

Before long, the smells of simmering stew filled the chilly evening air. The light of the roaring fire glinted off of the pot and drew the members of my squad ever closer. Erik had slid down from his perch and now sat on a log near Solvai as she carved. Cam's gaze was fixed on the food as well, and even Edrea had chosen a stone to sit on around the blaze.

Brigan leaned back against the stump of a dead tree as I pulled the little shaker of salt from the pouch at my belt and sprinkled some into the pot. For a second, the desert scene melted away, and it was just Solvai, Brigan, and me back in our bunker on the Rise.

Brigan must've sensed the familiar mood as well, because as he looked around the circle, he tried to strike up a heated conversation.

"Gauntlet down," he started. "Soldiers should adhere to the dress code."

"Dress code?" Solvai repeated, not looking up from her wood.

"Our uniforms," Brigan clarified. "They're designed the way that they are for a reason. Point one—protection in battle. From the dragonleather chest piece, bracers, pauldron, and shin guards, down to the scale mail tunic, each piece keeps us safe from enemy dragons."

"Obviously," Edrea agreed, the firelight catching in her eyes as she watched Brigan speak.

Brigan went on. "Point two—cost effectiveness. The uniforms are simple, easy for the keepdom to produce since they've been doing so for years. And finally..." Brigan's gaze flashed to Jax as he stretched to cool down after his workout.

"...Point three—wearing the uniform properly promotes unity among the soldiers. So no one thinks they're somehow better than anyone else."

I eyed the ripped seams along Jax's shoulders where he'd torn the sleeves off of his uniform. Jax straightened.

"You got something to say to me, Duke-man?" Jax asked.

Brigan shrugged, moving onto a new debate topic. "Gauntlet down: Basic training in Keep Rengard is superior to those in any of the Western Keepdoms."

Jax scoffed. "By 'Westen Keepdoms,' I'm assuming you mean Drakfell?"

"Skygard's in the west as well," Brigan said flatly.

Jax stood, making his way toward Brigan. "I'll have you know, they didn't bother putting me through basic training in Drakfell. Went straight to the guard."

"Sounds like you're making my point for me," Brigan stood. He was taller than Jax, but while Brigan was plenty toned and athletic, Jax's physique was on a whole other level.

"Sounds like you want a fight."

"Gauntlet down," Brigan prefaced, then confirmed. "Gauntlet down."

I startled everyone in the circle when I banged on my stew pot with a spoon. The clanging sound rang throughout the canyon and echoed off the walls. Everyone turned to me, including Brigan and Jax.

"Dinner's ready," I announced.

Gauntlets forgotten, soon the sounds of spoons scraping against bowls dominated the night. Nobody spoke—everyone was too busy relishing the warm tastes of tender dragonbeef, robust vegetables, and thick, savory broth.

That kind of silence was one of my favorite sounds.

It wasn't until we'd all had second and third—and, in Cam's case, fourth—helpings that Erik finally said something.

"Skyfall."

We followed the trajectory of his finger as he pointed toward the sky.

Sure enough, there was a small army of fiery, green-tailed meteors. At least seven or so of them shot across the dark sky to the south, probably landing in the Dragon Mists. With any luck, they'd have landed deep in the Mists so that the dreklings they carried would never make it to the Outpost.

"Where do the skyfalls come from?" Erik mused aloud.

"Etheria, of course," Edrea replied.

"Not Etheria," I corrected. "Etheria's here, all around us."

"So you think when we die, our souls just… hang around?" Edrea crossed her arms.

"Well, I don't know for sure, I guess," I said. "I've never seen the soul of someone who's passed."

"You've seen souls?" Erik's eyes widened with interest. "Is that a Rifter power?"

Erik gestured to my silvermark, and I felt my cheeks grow warm in spite of the icy scar. I hadn't meant to bring up my etherarchy.

"Yeah," I spoke slowly. "I'm not sure exactly how it works, but I can use what's called the Sight to see Etheria."

"I thought Rifters were teleporters," Brigan said. "Like what you did at the dragon stables."

"They are—I mean, I am," I explained. "Using the Sight is basically like opening a portal for my vision. At least, that's the way it feels to me. All rifts use Etheria for instant travel, so the Sight is kind of like just, *not* opening an exit portal."

"Well, that's nice and vague," Edrea said sarcastically.

"What does Etheria look like?" Erik asked, ignoring Edrea as he gestured to the canyon all around us. "What do you see right now?"

"Nothing right now," I replied quickly. "I can't see Etheria unless I trace the right rune."

Erik looked at me with eager anticipation. The rest of my squadmates were waiting with interest as well.

I felt panic welling up inside me. They wanted me to use etherarchy openly, right in front of them! I could hear a lifetime of Mom's warnings to never let anyone see me use my power reverberating inside my head.

Across the circle, Jax caught my eye. He gave the slightest incline of his head, and the encouragement was enough.

My hand only trembling slightly, I raised my finger to runetrace. Gold light shone down from my forehead as the symbol for the Sight glowed to life.

I blinked hard, and before my eyes, a thousand colors blossomed over the drab canyon. Tiny, teal and pink auras winked in and out as little smokeflies buzzed around our fire. The fire itself had an aura surrounding it—a dynamic, cinnamon-colored cloud dancing along with the orange flames of reality. This was a cooking fire, so it glowed differently from destructive ones like dragonfire or forest fires.

Everything surged with life and color, from the sage green mist around the plants to the bright auras of the bonded dragons sleeping near the North Tower. When I looked hard, I could even detect the peach-colored light of our conversation flowing from person to person around the fire. I had everyone's attention at the moment, so each thread streamed toward me.

But all the vibrance and patterns paled in comparison to the auras of my squadmates themselves. I did my best to describe it to them while Erik took careful notes on a sheet from his sketchbook.

I started to my left with Solvai, whose aura gathered around her core in bright clouds of deep, velvety cerulean. The glowing blue burst from all around her like thousands of sharp, intricate feathers. It was gorgeous and powerful—the aura of a mighty warrior. Erik's pencil flew across the page as I described it.

Erik himself was next, his aura shining with a soft, flaxen yellow. The wisps were dense all along his shoulders in a shape that almost looked like heavy armor. Around his wrist was a band of misty light blue, signifying his bond with his wyvern, Eris.

Edrea's was a rich, majestic shade of purple. It was so heavily concentrated around her head that the color there appeared almost black.

I thought Cam's aura would be rough and intimidating like his physical appearance. But gentle, spring green clouds calmly rolled all around him. It was a sweet, inviting aura that reminded me of a happy family picnic. His bond with his drake shone like a dark, reddish brown cuff around his wrist that matched his dragon's scales.

I'd expected Jax's aura to be some sort of maroon, like the bandana he always wore across his forehead. But it was several shades brighter, with vibrant, tangerine clouds. You couldn't help but look at it. A jewel-toned green band wrapped around his wrist for his bond with his evren, Jade. When I squinted, I thought I could almost make out the crystalline outline of his ether well floating up near his head.

Finally, Brigan's aura filled my vision. Vibrant red mists concentrated tightly above his head, then poured down around his body like a waterfall. The flow of his aura churned with turbulence all around his chest, the royal red mist swirling like rapids. I wondered what that meant, but I knew next to nothing about aura interpretation. Like the rest of the riders, Brigan had a band around his wrist from his bond with Bolt, only his was orange to match her scales.

"Fascinating," Erik muttered as he continued scribbling. "And yours, Meleya?"

I held out my arms in front of me to get a better look as I described the tangled, spiraling strands of indigo light and mist clinging to me.

I trailed off, however, as something caught my eye beyond the group. Behind the North Tower, almost invisible amidst all the bright colors before my eyes, was a cloudy, gray shape. In the middle of the shape, what looked like a pair of bright blue eyes was staring directly at me. A strange, dark feeling rushed through me like being splashed with cold water. I gave a sharp inhale as I jumped in my seat.

"Meleya?" Brigan put a hand on my arm, the red of his aura mixing with the blue-violet of mine. "Are you alright?"

When I looked back toward the North Tower, the gray aura was gone.

I frowned, wondering if I'd imagined it. Still, I blinked hard and deactivated the rune for the Sight, and the world around me returned to its normal shades of reddish-brown, gray, and tan.

My squadmates laughed as they talked about their auras, trying to decide whose sounded the most intelligent or the most interesting. I wanted to join in the conversation, but I still couldn't shake the feeling that the blue-eyed gray being was still out there, watching me.

Chapter 14: Blink

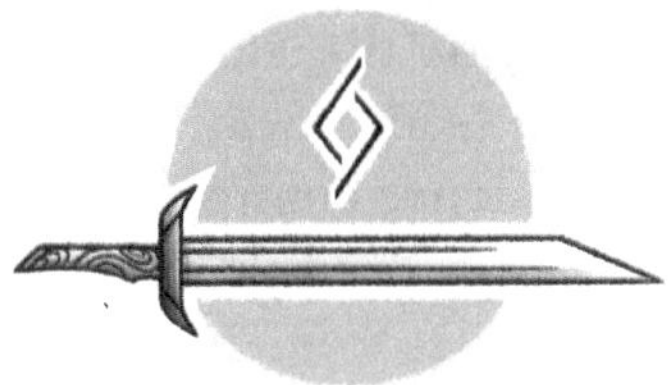

I stared up at the night sky, starry constellations blinking down at me. At least, I assumed they were. I was never very good at finding patterns up there among the celestial lights. Some nights back when we traveled with the nomadic caravans, Mom would point out the spydra constellation—the star sign for the month I was born.

Mom used to tell me that people born under the spydra were smart and purposeful, brave and unyielding. In hindsight, it felt more like a bad omen, warning me about the Rengardian prison where my parents would spend indefinite years of their lives. I couldn't stop thinking about what Zoren had said about getting used to my place in the guard, because he was never planning to let my parents free. My service kept them from execution, but so long as Zoren lived, we would always be trapped.

I shivered a little as I pulled off my thick, aldraka wool blanket and sat up. The fire was down to embers, the rest of the squad sleeping soundly in their bedrolls surrounding it. All but Solvai, whose brown hair and orange cloak I could just see over the top of the high, smooth redrock near the clearing.

Being careful not to wake the squad, I climbed the rock to join her.

"Hey," I spoke quietly, sitting on the rock beside her. "You've been on watch for hours. Let me take over while you get some rest."

Solvai didn't answer as she used her thumb and forefinger to rub the wooden falcondrake charm around her neck. We sat in silence for a moment, looking out across the starlit canyon. Chilly night wind rustled the juniper leaves, and we could hear the low rush of the Ridgeback River across the canyon floor. Dragonowls hooted in the distance, and I could see the glowing, green abdomens of a few dragonfire-flies near our rock.

"I shouldn't be squad captain." Solvai's voice was barely audible.

"Says who?" I teasingly grabbed the hilt of my seaxe. "I'll fight them."

"I'm serious," Solvai said. "You pretending otherwise won't change the fact that I'm no leader. Nobody on the squad respects me or even listens to me. Brigan's a natural born leader; why didn't they make him squad captain? Or Jax, who has confidence coming out of his ears? Or you, who was not only brave and powerful enough to single-handedly save every dragon in the Keep Rengard stables from death, but is meticulous enough to make sure everyone's always prepared, all the way down to sharpening our backup weapons?" Solvai buried her face in her hands, continuing without giving me the chance to respond. "My father was a squad captain back when he was alive. My whole life I've wanted to be like him, but soot, I'm not cut out for this. I... I'm like a baby snow dove with broken wings that somebody dropped out of a tree, somehow expecting it to fly."

Her shoulders shook a little as she cried. The chirping sounds of dragon crickets filled the air as I gently rubbed circles along her back.

"Remember what I said about your aura?" I said after a while.

Solvai sniffed, lifting her head to answer. "Yeah. It's light blue."

"The thing about auras," I explained, "is that they're more than just interesting colors. Each one means something. Your aura is like the expression of your soul, you know?"

"So my soul is blue. How appropriate."

"Hey," I scratched at her back a little harder. "I'm no expert at interpreting auras, but I can tell you what it feels like to look at yours. Your shade of blue shows strength and wisdom. The way it centers around your core means you have good instincts, and you should trust them. Like your call for our squad to save the dragons at the stables."

"That call landed us at Outcast Outpost."

"And saved nearly a hundred bonded dragons' lives! Your aura takes the shape of feathers along your back. You're not some little snow dove with broken wings. Your wings are sharp and strong like the wings of a falcondrake. Whether you know it or not, Solvai, you're meant to fly."

Solvai sat up a little straighter. "You're not just saying that to make me feel better?"

"I'm just telling you the truth." I shrugged, looking at the charm around her neck once more. "Your dad would've been so proud of you."

My friend looked at me with shiny, hazel eyes.

"Now, Squad Captain," I said, clapping her on the arm. "I suggest you order yourself to get some rest while Meleya takes the next watch."

Solvai gave a small smile, getting ready to climb down the rock. Before disappearing over the side, she turned back to me.

"Thanks, Meleya."

I nodded, waving her onward.

It wasn't long before a bright yellow snout and a pair of shiny, green eyes appeared over the edge of the rock.

Ping? Sniff's note sounded through our bond as he panted with anticipation.

"I can't go out flying right now, boy," I whispered. "I'm on watch duty."

Trill? Sniff gestured toward the top of the nearby North Tower.

"You want to go up there?" I pointed. Sniff panted harder, a draconic smile on his face.

I thought for a moment. The North Tower *was* the original lookout point, after all. Smiling as I shook my head, I climbed onto my evren's back.

He landed atop the reddish tan adobe tower, and I alighted. Like everything at Outcast Outpost, the tower wasn't in the best of shape, with several of the surrounding turrets either crumbling or broken. Weeds flourished in the spaces between bricks, and a family of ridgerats had built quite the lavish nest in one corner.

From here, I had the perfect view of both the main canyon as well as the Narrows that led back to the Dragon Mists. After making sure there was no oncoming threat, I turned to my dragon.

"Alright, Sniff," I started. "Why did you bring me—"

Then I felt it.

A warm, calm feeling rushed through my body, accompanied by a sharp, thrumming sound. *Ba-dum, ba-dum, ba-dum,* like a drumbeat resounding in my heart.

I instantly reached for my heartscale necklace, where Sniff's golden yellow scale hung. But with all the chaos of coming to the Outpost, I'd nearly forgotten about the other scale I'd tied there on its own, longer cord—the silver scale Sniff had brought me from that cracked egg in the Dragon Chasm.

Boom, the drumlike sound played in my heart once more. Where Sniff's communication always sounded like high, trilling notes from a flute, this one was low, thunderous, and rhythmic.

I nearly whipped myself in the face with my braid as I looked around, searching for another dragon. But Sniff was the only one I could see.

That is, the only one I could see with these eyes.

My finger flew as I traced the rune for the Sight. Gold light cut the air, the corresponding rune glowing to life over my forehead.

Then I blinked.

I stumbled backward when I saw her. Mere feet in front of me, hovering majestically before where I stood at the edge of the tower, was a semi-transparent, glowing, silvery evren.

She looked nearly identical to Sniff, but the horns on her head were longer, spiraling at the ends. Her large, dragonfire green eyes stood out against her silvery scales. A misty, silver aura hung all around her, trailing through the dark night as she beat her four wide wings.

I reached toward her, noticing for the first time the silver cuff around my wrist beside the gold one that signified my bond with Sniff. Did that mean I'd bonded this one too?

The misty evren flew closer toward my outstretched arm. But when I tried to close the distance, my hand went right through her as if she were no more than a cloud.

She was a spirit. Not a spirit tethered to a physical body, but the spirit of a dragon who'd passed on into Etheria. Then I remembered the silver and gold egg Sniff had shown me back in the Dragon Chasm. The silver half of the egg had been battered, hurt during its journey to Keep Rengard.

Sniff trilled through our bond as he launched from the tower toward the silver spirit evren.

The sound of drums answered as the two evren flew upward. They spun circles around each other, their gold and silver auras painting stunning patterns against the starry night sky.

I channeled my thoughts through the bond. *Are you two... twins?*

A musical duet between flute and drum answered my question. Both Sniff and his twin sister flew one last loop together before returning to hover in front of me at the side of the tower. A laugh bubbled up in my throat as I looked into the silvery spirit evren's large, blinking eyes.

"Welcome to the family," I smiled at her, and I could swear the rolling drumbeats she sent back sounded almost like purring. "Blink."

Ba doom doom, the evren answered, approving her new name.

I was so focused on my bonds that I nearly missed the feral growling.

In the narrow slot canyon just past where Blink and Sniff hovered, I saw a shadowy, gray mass. Gray fur bristled along the backs of a band of wild dragon coyotes.

My heart dropped as I realized these weren't just any dragon coyotes. Each cloudy, gray beast had a pair of glowing, lightning blue eyes.

Umbral creatures.

In my panic, I let the rune over my forehead go out. Blink vanished from my view, as did the gray auras from the umbral coyotes. They all but turned invisible against the darkness of the Narrows.

Sniff sensed my distress through the bond and yelped when he realized what was going on. Leaping onto Sniff's back, I steered him back toward the clearing where the squad still slept.

"Wake up!" I yelled, sliding off of Sniff's back and drawing my sword. "Umbral dragon coyotes at the head of the Narrows!"

Within moments, the entire squad was armed and facing the slot canyon. We waited, but saw nothing but the dark, moonlit slot canyon mouth.

"Where?" Edrea asked, squinting into the dark.

A second later, we heard a sharp, guttural growl. A pair of lightning blue eyes prowled closer, but the darkness camouflaged its shadowy gray body.

"Drak," Jax swore. "More umbrals from the Dragon Mists." He held his axe ready to strike, and I got the feeling he'd fought umbral creatures before.

"Remember what Trickshot said," I warned. "Don't let them bite you, or you risk getting the shadow wasting."

"It's too dark," Cam muttered as he narrowed his eyes toward the band of umbral coyotes.

"He's right," Brigan agreed. "How are we supposed to fight these things when we can barely see them?"

The band of shadowy dragon coyotes emitted sharp, terrifying growls. A few yipped, and one howled as they closed in on us. My stomach leaped as even more pairs of eerie, bright blue eyes poured in from the Narrows.

We were about to charge when Solvai threw up a hand. "Hold your attack."

"Are you crazy?" Edrea hissed, her knuckles white as she gripped her spear.

"Hold," Solvai ordered again as she dove toward the dying coals of our campfire. Immediately, she began throwing more wood onto it.

"What in the void are you doing?" Edrea said. "Now is not the time to worry about being warm and cozy."

"Wait for my word," Solvai said. "Brigan, get Bolt to stoke the flame."

Brigan didn't hesitate as he obeyed our Squad Captain. Almost instantly, his orange Lightwielder drake opened her mouth toward the campfire, blasting it with a crackle of gold lightning.

The blaze roared to life, shining firelight onto the prowling umbral creatures. In the light, we could see the nearest eight or nine umbral coyotes prowling through the brush, their teeth bared and mouths foaming. The fire glinted off their gray fur as wispy, gray mist curled off the ridges down their backs. The coyotes only shrunk back for a second as the flames burned high, but now at least we wouldn't be fighting a nearly invisible enemy.

I couldn't help but smile, proud of my friend. My excitement died quickly as more coyotes barked, the nearest ones leaping toward us with open jaws.

Solvai called out with determination, "Squad Reckless, attack!"

We gave battle cries as we rushed to meet the monsters.

My longsword slashed against a set of raking dragon coyote claws. The creature reeled back, but another was close behind. With a rasping bark, it darted toward my leg, its gray jaws poised to clamp down on my flesh.

I stumbled back to avoid getting bitten, but tripped over a third coyote, catching myself just in time to avoid falling to the ground.

Just as all three beasts turned toward me, Sniff swooped in with an evren shriek. He narrowed his eyes at the beasts, rearing back and letting out a massive sneeze.

Sniff's sneeze sent a dart of ether cutting through the air like a comet. He hit the nearest coyote in the thick mass of gray fur around its neck. That slowed it down enough to let me jab it through its chest from below.

The coyote let out a whine as it fell to the ground.

When it hit the dirt, the coyote's shadowy gray form began to dissolve, just like the rattledrake Trickshot had taken out on our first day at the Outpost. Its body vanished into the whistling canyon wind until only its vivid, blue eyes were left, as well as a glowing blue crystal where its heart had once been. Then in a flash, the blue eyes winked out, while the crystal fell to the ground and turned white.

It wasn't a skystone—it was too plain. The raw gem must've been a mere quartz, but by the faint glow, I could tell there were a few drops of lingering ether inside it. It was as if the shadow wasting had gone so far as to crystalize the beast's heart.

Sniff and I continued fighting off the umbral coyotes, doing all we could to avoid getting bitten. But there were so many.

I glanced around me and realized my squad was struggling. Thank the goddesses, none of us had gotten bit just yet, but it was clear we'd never fought these things. Edrea and Solvai were using their spears to try and herd the vicious shadow creatures away. Cam, Brigan, and Jax clung to the light of the fire as they slashed and hacked, stopping a group of coyotes on their way toward where I stood beside the campfire. Erik sat astride his wyvern, downing as many as he could with his crossbow. Each time one fell, it dissolved, dropping another small crystal to the earth. But more of the demonic, blue-eyed monsters kept coming.

But they weren't just filtering into the canyon and attacking our squad as if we were just another group of meaningless prey. As I fought side by side with my dragon, I couldn't help but feel like they were targeting me.

I knew that was crazy—umbrals weren't like dragons, drawn by the ether wells of magi. Besides, the ones Jax fought didn't seem to be interested in him more than the others. In fact, several were skirting around Jax's range and heading straight for me.

Sniff was sneezing up a storm as I slit the nearest umbral coyote's throat. The monster vanished into smoky, gray clouds, which parted to reveal at least four more feral beasts prowling my way.

Panic began to set in as they worked as a team to push me further and further from Sniff. My seaxe was everywhere at once as I put all my energy into keeping them at bay.

Suddenly, I felt something cool and flat against my back—the large rock bordering our campsite. The coyotes had me cornered. Looking out over the clearing, I realized my squadmates were far too busy fighting umbrals of their own to assist me.

Rifting, I thought. Frustration and resentment rose in my chest at the idea that I couldn't handle this without my powers. But I was out of options.

I raised a finger to runetrace. Halfway through drawing the rifting rune in the air, two umbral dragon coyotes came at me from either side with wide, canine jaws.

My unfinished rune dissolved into etherdust as the first coyote raked its paws across my upper torso. My dragonleather armor protected me well enough, but my relief was short-lived as the other coyotes' cold, umbral jaw clamped down onto my forearm, puncturing my bracers.

A strange, empty sensation bloomed across my skin. I felt the stinging pain from the bite, but it was as if the umbral had bitten into my very soul, leaving blank nothingness behind.

The coyote shook its head, wrenching my arm along with it. Red blood soaked into my sleeve.

I cried out as I tried to slash at it with my sword arm, but my seaxe slipped from my hand as another coyote swiped toward me. Fear gripped my heart.

Sniff sent panicked, discordant notes to me through our bond. I heard a set of fast, frightened drum beats from Blink as well.

With the coyote still clinging to my forearm, I was about to resort to kicking at it with my feet when out of nowhere, a curved, flat piece of metal came whipping toward the coyote.

I did a double take—I'd seen a weapon like that before. A refugee from the Dragon Isles who'd traveled with us for a while with the Copperhead caravan had wielded one. He'd called the bladed boomerang a Drekai *kalaata*.

The *kalaata* took the coyote in the head as it flew, sending its smoky form disappearing into the canyon winds. The eyes lingered on me for a second more before dissolving as well, then it dropped its crystal core to the ground.

Before the other umbral coyotes surrounding me had the chance to pounce, a scraping sound came from over my head. A woman with sharp, tan horns on her head and a long, lashing tail came sliding down the side of the redrock.

She landed between the coyotes and me just in time to catch the boomerang as it came flying back through the air. She wore minimal armor over her wrap tunic and loose pants that tightened at the ankles, and the beige-colored scales along her hairline and shoulders gleamed in the firelight.

The edge of her *kalaata* glowed with golden etherlight as she arced the weapon across the nearest line of umbral beasts. They whined as their shadowy forms vanished into nothingness.

From atop the rock, two more Drekai appeared, joining the first. One wielded a long-handled scimitar in each hand, the other a heavy warbow.

The band of umbral coyotes didn't stand a chance against the Drekai warriors. The first flung her *kalaata* boomerang, the golden edge slicing the umbrals into oblivion, while her companion sent them into Etheria one-by-one with his bow. Meanwhile, the last Drekai used each of his light-edged scimitars to slash at the creatures using graceful, flowing motions so quick that I could barely keep track. Although, maybe I was a little dizzy from my wound. I undid my bracer and pulled up the sleeve on my left arm to reveal an inky gray mark creeping its way along my arm beneath the bloody bite.

I shoved down the pain, shakily grabbing my fallen seaxe to rejoin the fight. With minimal help from our squad, the Drekai silenced the umbral coyotes until before we knew it, only one whimpering monster remained.

The shadowy, gray coyote whined, knowing it didn't stand a chance. Jax lunged for it, his psionically-charged axe ready to hack it to pieces.

"*Ziita khiini!*" The Drekai woman held up a hand to Jax, then repeated in an accented voice. "Wait!"

Jax froze, and the umbral coyote barked once before turning on its heel and fleeing back down the slot canyon.

"Should we go after it?" Edrea asked, ready to pursue.

"No," the Drekai woman snapped at Edrea. "Leave the *umbraali* alive. Stay out of this, Evgardians, if you know what's good for you."

Then she turned to her companions. "Pursue it back into the Mists. *Karaaza ku tolkuua ra kun umbraali.*"

The other two nodded in agreement before joining her as they took off after the coyote.

Wait, I thought in disbelief. *Did she just command them to follow the coyote* into *the Dragon Mists?* I couldn't believe it. Going into the Mists was suicide.

We just stood there for a long moment as we watched the Drekai disappear into the Narrows, our heavy breaths echoing off the canyon walls.

"Is everyone okay?" I asked shakily, relieved to see no gray marks on anyone but me.

Brigan yelped when he noticed the blood running down my arm. I rolled up my sleeve, looking down to see that the inky gray splotches had already spread up to my elbow. A pit formed in my stomach as I stared at the strange, vacant-feeling mark, my knees growing wobbly.

"Oh soot," Jax swore. "We need to get liquid light on you before the shadow wasting gets to your heart and sets in. Who has a vial?"

Nobody did. Brigan hurried to my side, grabbing hold of my elbow to steady me.

Nerves bubbled up in my throat as I realized what this could mean. "They won't decommission me, will they?" I asked, fear creeping into my voice as I thought of what that would mean for my parents. If they didn't have a soldier in the guard serving their sentence...

"They decommission every soldier who gets the shadow wasting," Edrea mumbled, her eyes wide as she took in the sight of my wound.

"A drakking decommission is the least of your worries right now," Jax said sharply.

Solvai took charge, nodding to my dragon who hovered nervously nearby. "Sniff, fly Meleya back to the Outpost as quickly as possible. Get her to Trickshot—she'll know what to do."

Sniff gave an urgent roar of approval. Brigan took my trembling hand, helping me onto Sniff's back.

"You'll be okay," he looked me in the eye and spoke in an even, soothing voice. I knew he couldn't know that for sure, but his tone slightly calmed my racing pulse.

As we flew, I watched the inky gray patch leeching along my forearm as that awful, blank feeling slowly crept its way closer to my heart.

CHAPTER 15: PSION

JAX

Jax couldn't sleep.

He sat up in his bunk in the barracks where he shared a room with the other men of Squad Reckless. Erik slept soundly in the bunk above him while Cam snored in the one across the room. Brigan's bunk was empty—no surprise there. Insomniac Duke-man was probably out at the stables with his dragon or reading by candlelight in the hallway to try and get himself tired enough to sleep.

After their encounter with the umbrals, the squad had rushed back to the main outpost to report the skirmish to Commander Hildred. The commander hadn't seemed too concerned about the incident, since apparently her sentries had spotted Drekai chasing umbrals around the edge of the Dragon Mists a few times before. She'd cursed them for waking her and slammed the door in their faces.

Normally, Jax slept like a rock. But he'd tossed and turned all night, worrying about Meleya. She'd gone to Trickshot for healing last night, but he hadn't yet heard if she'd made it back in time.

Through the window, Jax could tell the sun was about to rise. How early was too early to check in and see how she was doing?

Jax remembered months ago when he was crossing the Scar with his Knights of the Torch team. They'd run into a shiver of umbral sandsharks out there, and Valla had been bitten. Solrac had been so worried that they wouldn't get her to Ghost Lake for some liquid light in time. Now Jax was getting a small taste of that same worry.

A rustling sound from the table in the corner drew Jax from his bed. He crept over, taking a seat beside the table's centerpiece: a small starglass terrarium.

Inside the transparent haven was a tiny mirror gecko with enormous shining eyes.

She stared up at Jax from atop the chunk of dried juniper wood she used as a perch. Kai had said the dream mirror copy of his original ethereal familiar, Glint, would survive indefinitely without draining his ether as long as it got plenty of sunlight. Kari had heard that, and hurried to build the little gecko this terrarium, specially made to capture the sun's rays using little reflective panels on the top. So far, this Glint copy had thrived off of sunlight streaming in from the barracks window, so Kari's invention must've been working.

Thinking of Kari still made Jax's chest feel tight. Per Solrac's advice, he thought about her less these days—Kari had made the choice to break up with Jax months ago, and he had to respect her decision.

But soot if it didn't still hurt.

Jax hated that he'd let himself be so vulnerable with her. He'd told Kari that while he tried to appear strong and indifferent on the outside, on the inside, he was terrified of being left behind by those who pretended to care about him.

In the end, she'd moved on too, just like all the rest.

Jax shoved down the stupid lump forming in his throat as he watched the little gecko. The sun was just beginning to creep over the east canyon wall, washing the room in low morning light. The gecko was still staring up at Jax, and as he watched, she slowly stuck out the tip of her tongue and ran it deliberately over her lips.

"What?" Jax whispered to the gecko. "Are you hungry or something?"

The mirror gecko blinked twice.

"I'm guessing that's a yes," Jax muttered, scanning the room for any sign of food. A leftover crust of bread from the dry, brick-like loaf they'd served at yesterday's breakfast caught his eye.

Jax picked up the rock solid crust and gingerly lowered it into the terrarium. The mirror gecko crawled down to it, tapped it briefly with one foot, then turned up her nose and crawled away.

"Well, it's all I've got, you slimy little lizard," Jax shrugged. From the other side of the room, Jax heard Cam's voice.

"You up, Jax?" Cam asked as he sat in bed, rubbing sleep from his eyes.

"Yeah," Jax replied.

Cam stretched his heavily tattooed arms. "Give me a minute and we can squeeze in some reps before morning muster."

"I'm in."

Cam nodded to the terrarium. "What's the gecko's name?"

"Uh… Three, I think." Jax knew Kai had numbered and color coded his dream mirror gecko army. This one had tiny yellow scales.

"Three?" Cam repeated. "Strange name for a pet."

Jax grinned. "You should meet His Majesty the bloodhusky."

Just thinking of the loyal, fun-loving mass of red fur filled some of the cracks in Jax's heart. Through everything, His Majesty had always been there for him. Even during the darkest times when Jax was living above the Naga's Head tavern, His Majesty and Solrac's visits a couple of times a week were bright spots in his routine. Solrac would take Jax and the dog out to the nearby fields to both play fetch and practice psionics all at once. Jax would telekinetically throw the ball as far as he could, and still His Majesty would gleefully come trotting back each time.

The memories reminded Jax what Solrac would say if he were here: That Jax should fill his extra crystals with ether, just in case he needed the extra boost in battle today. Jax pulled two palm-sized chunks of white quartz from where they hung at his belt.

Solrac had taught Jax how to mark the crystals with some kind of ancient symbol from the Guardian era. Jax held one crystal to his forehead, focusing on transferring ether from his well into the quartz.

Within a few moments, the marked crystal glowed white with fresh ether. Jax did the same with the second stone before tying the rocks back to their place at his belt. Jax's ether well would refill itself over the next hour or so, but the stones would leave Jax with extra ether at his fingertips should the need arise. The crystals would drain after three days, so if he didn't want to waste it, he'd have to make sure to use their ether before then.

Solrac would've been proud of Jax for remembering to save the extra ether. If only he'd have been proud of how Jax was fulfilling his assignment here at Outcast Outpost.

Just thinking about the assignment set Jax's teeth on edge. Solrac knew how Jax felt about his selfish, chronically drunk father. Why would he send Jax here undercover to get information from him about the Coven of the Gray Ones? Couldn't someone else spy on the dark, Gray Ones-worshiping cult? Jax was better with the more hands-on, labor intensive tasks anyway. He was no good at sneaking around and tricking people into giving up information. Solrac should've picked Asher. Asher was Solrac's favorite new protégé anyway. They were so alike.

As usual, that left Jax on the outside.

Just then, some kind of cold feeling crept into Jax's chest, spreading like frost on a winter lake. Jax shuddered. He'd felt this strange sensation before, almost like something was watching him. Ever since his and Boone's operation in Ghost Lake, he couldn't shake the feeling that he wasn't quite alone.

Three the mirror gecko shrunk behind her chunk of wood. She must've felt it too.

Resisting the impulse to put on a tunic with sleeves, Jax set his jaw and shoved the feeling to the back of his mind.

He had to show Solrac he could do this. Maybe Jax hadn't been able to get Torsten to open up about the Coven of the Gray Ones—every time Jax tried to bring it up, his father shut him down and took another swig of draquila. But maybe someone else could get Torsten to talk.

Jax smiled. He had just the candidate in mind.

His smile quickly turned to a worried frown. He just wished he knew if that candidate was going to recover from her umbral wound. And not just because he needed her help to make his newly forming plan to get information from his father to work. Meleya... well, she'd just better be okay.

"What?" Jax said accusingly at the mirror gecko's wide-eyed stare.

Three narrowed her eyes before she stuck out her tongue at him and scurried off behind the juniper.

Relief flooded Jax when he saw a stark white braid a few soldiers in front of him in line at morning muster in the mess hall.

Meleya stood at parade rest between Duke-man and the squad captain during Commander Hildred's short, lackluster speech about how she sure hoped most of us stayed alive today. When she dismissed the platoon, Jax immediately made his way over to Meleya.

"There you are, M," Jax said, folding his arms and putting on an indifferent face. "Guess you were just being dramatic last night about that umbral bite."

She narrowed her dark brown eyes at Jax, and he smirked. He liked it when she glared at him.

"Trickshot was able to stop the shadow wasting from setting in," Meleya said as she rolled up her sleeve. Jax had to stop himself from grimacing as he took in the sight of her healing bite mark. At least the gray splotches from the umbral poison had shrunk down to only one small patch in the center.

"She says I'll need a few follow up doses of liquid light, but that within a few days the gray should be gone," Meleya explained as she replaced her sleeve.

The whole thing made Jax sick. He should've been there to stop the coyote from getting to her. None of the other guys in the barracks last night had realized that the umbral monsters had been targeting her, but Jax certainly had. He just couldn't figure out why—usually umbrals were like any other wild animal, attacking without thought, or at the very least going for the weakest link. But nobody who'd seen Meleya wield her seaxe could ever think she was weak.

"Breakfast, anyone?" Solvai asked. "We'll need our strength if we get called into battle today."

"You mean *when* we get called into battle today," Meleya said. She made a face as she turned toward the row of soldiers lined up to get this morning's pile of slop.

Jax couldn't hide his grin. Time to enact his plan.

"You two go ahead," Jax nodded to Brigan and Solvai. "I have something I want to show M."

Meleya infused so much skepticism into raising her eyebrow that Jax couldn't help but chuckle.

Brigan took an almost subconscious, defensive half-step between Meleya and Jax. "What is it?" he asked.

"Wouldn't you like to know, Duke-man?" Jax stood a little straighter. He'd grown up in a bar, which meant he was always ready for a fight.

"Relax," Meleya put up both her hands, wincing at the pain in her forearm. Brigan automatically put a protective hand on her upper back. That made Jax cringe inside. But Meleya's next words more than made up for it.

"I'll be right back," Meleya said to Brigan and Solvai.

Jax couldn't help but flash Brigan a smug look as he led Meleya out of the mess hall.

Jax and Meleya had to sneak past Torsten, who snored loudly from his chair on the porch. He had a pile of colorful blankets at his feet that must've fallen off of him during his rest. Meleya made them stop and quietly replace the blankets before going in—it was a chilly morning.

Jax would've just as soon let Torsten stay cold, or better still, waited for him to get his lazy scales out of that rocking chair and get the fallen blankets himself. He watched as Meleya tucked the blankets under the arms of the chair, careful not to wake the passed-out drunk.

Afterwards, Jax led Meleya around the hoodoo rock spires to the tavern's north wall. The wall was covered in more of Torsten's colorful, intricately woven blankets.

"What's with all the blankets anyway?" Meleya asked.

"One of Torsten's hobbies," Jax replied. "Says he weaves them to look like people's auras."

Meleya's eyes lit up as she gazed with new understanding at the walls draped in Torsten's aura blankets, each with its own unique color and pattern. Jax smiled, remembering the way Meleya had come alive when telling the squad about each of their auras around the campfire. She'd described Jax's aura as a bright, bold shade of tangerine. Something that stood out and added vibrance and strength to everything around it.

Torsten had only ever told Jax his aura was 'some kind of orange.'

Meleya's smile faded instantly when she noticed a light blue blanket with a feather-like pattern. She pointed to it, turning to Jax.

"Why does he have this one? Who's it for, I mean?"

Jax shrugged. "Ask him if you want, I guess. Ready to see why I brought you here?"

Meleya studied the light blue blanket one more time before nodding, a hint of skepticism still evident on her face.

Jax made a big show of pulling back an extra large, sage green aura blanket to reveal a hidden door. Then he turned the handle and slowly pushed the creaky door open.

He and Meleya stepped inside an incredibly cluttered, cobweb-filled room. A couple more thick hoodoos rose through the floorboards up to the height of Jax's shoulder. Someone had draped the redrock spires with dirty dishcloths. A window lit up a dusty countertop, mud brick oven, and a set of battered old pots and pans.

Meleya's mouth flew open, but no words came out. She gingerly took a few steps further into the messy, dusty kitchen.

Jax felt a twisted clump of dragonflies jump into his stomach. Maybe he'd misjudged what she'd like, and giving her the tavern's dirty old kitchen had been presumptuous and aggravating. He rushed to speak.

"You don't have to use it—I was just talking to the others and someone brought up how you used to cook a lot during basic training. And since nobody was using this—well, clearly nobody's used it in years, I figured you might, I don't know. Don't feel like I'm trying to get you to spend your extra time in the kitchen—"

"I love it," Meleya cut Jax off.

Jax relaxed. "Yeah?"

"It's perfect." A wide grin spread across her face as she reached for an empty wooden crate. She immediately began filling it with the grimy, empty alcohol bottles strewn around the kitchen.

Jax laughed under his breath as she tidied, and he'd no sooner rested one shoulder against the wall to watch when she gestured to the scalemead barrels dominating the countertop.

"Don't just stand there," she said. "Get those barrels off the counter and stack them in the corner. Then you can start sweeping—I think I see a broom over there."

Meleya said it so eagerly that Jax couldn't help but get started. He thought about lighting up a psionic rune over his forehead and moving the barrels with telekinesis, but he didn't do all those push ups for nothing.

Jax grunted as he hefted the first large, drink-filled barrel, his muscles bulging under its weight. Jax pretended not to notice when Meleya pretended not to notice.

It took them a little over an hour to get the tavern kitchen clean enough to satisfy Meleya. Together, she and Jax surveyed their work, admiring the gleaming countertop, immaculate dishes, and spotless floors.

Meleya leaned back against one of the hoodoos and sank to the ground with a happy sigh. Jax joined her, sitting with one leg up, his arm draped casually over his knee. He couldn't help but notice the way her dragonleather tunic fit her tall, graceful body, or how her long, white hair shone in the light from the window.

"I can't thank you enough," Meleya said.

"I'll bet you can," Jax replied, his voice low and rough. He leaned closer to her, casually flexing his biceps as his eyes flashed not-so-subtly toward her lips.

Meleya's big brown eyes, as well as her carefully guarded expression, seemed to melt for just a second as Jax closed in.

Then, at the same moment, both Jax and Meleya pulled back and looked away.

What am I doing? Jax thought. *I've never hesitated when it comes to girls.*

But ever since Kari had broken things off, Jax felt like he was floundering. Now, whenever emotions were involved, it was as if the old Jax—the confident, fearless Jax—was nowhere to be found.

Besides, Jax and Meleya were squadmates, which meant they were stuck together for the foreseeable future. Before Kari, Jax had only ever gone for girls he knew he'd never see again. It was a lot easier knowing the girl wouldn't be around to actually get to know him. If they did, Jax was sure they'd leave him behind without a second thought. Like Kari had.

"Uh," Meleya said, breaking the awkward silence. "Yeah. Thanks again for this. I grew up in so many different nomadic caravans that I only really feel at home when I'm cooking."

"It was purely for selfish reasons," said Jax. "I can't stop thinking about that stew you made while we were on watch at the North Tower."

Also, he thought, *I need you to like me so you'll want to help me out.*

Suddenly, Jax felt a powerful rumble in his chest.

Careful, Jax heard Jade's thought through their bond. His green evren had already been on her second ascension when she'd bonded Jax, which meant she could project her thoughts using simple words and phrases.

Don't use her, Jade warned, sending Jax another rumbling sensation like a storm brewing in his heart. Jade sent a cautionary impression through the bond as she reminded Jax about the time she'd been trapped in a forced bond. Her rider had taken her heartscale against her will, trapping her into doing his will rather than letting her choose for herself.

Meleya deserves better, Jade thought, and Jax knew she was right. After all, he couldn't stand it when people tried to use him for their own selfish purposes either. He needed to be allowed to make his own choices. The last thing he wanted to do was coerce Meleya into helping him without first telling her the truth.

That left only one course of action: honesty.

"I'm not who you think I am," Jax blurted out. Those pesky dragonflies began buzzing in his stomach again, and his palms began to sweat. Opening up like this made him feel so stupid and vulnerable. What if Meleya thought he was crazy?

Jax swallowed as Meleya raised an eyebrow. It was too late to turn back now.

"Who do you think I think you are?" Meleya questioned.

"Oh, you know. Some good-looking stranger from Drakfell who's really good with an axe." Jax thought for a second. "Well, I guess I am those things."

Meleya rolled her eyes, then flashed her gaze toward the door. "Maybe we should get back—"

"No, M. Please wait," Jax said, grabbing onto her arm. Meleya's eyebrows lowered, her arm tensing.

Jax went on. "I... I need your help."

Somehow, that seemed to work. Meleya's expression softened as she looked expectantly at Jax.

"What do you need?" she asked gently.

Jax spoke slowly, deliberately. "Have you ever heard of the Knights of the Torch?"

Meleya cocked her head. "I've heard as much as the next soldier. Old legends about a band of renegades sworn to protect the realm." She laughed, and Jax sensed a note of bitterness. "Their patron, the great Farseer, who supposedly shows up to help worthy magi in dire need."

"What if I told you they're not just a myth? I'm a Knight."

"Are you serious?"

"Completely. There are actually more of us than you think, all across Rengard and the entire realm."

Meleya frowned, trying to make sense of Jax's admission. "Before we came to the Outpost, Brigan mentioned something about the Knights of the Torch being the ones to turn Drakfell against Evgard," she said.

"Yeah, that was us. Almost failed, too. It's where I got this."

Jax pointed to the Psion's silvermark on his left cheek. The lines where the pen had cut him were still cold to the touch.

"Anyway," Jax continued, speaking as quickly as he could so he wouldn't lose his nerve. "I'm here undercover, trying to get information from Torsten—I mean, my father. He's part of a group called the Coven of the Gray Ones. It's this cult that worships these ethereal beings and stuff. But I can't get him to let me in—says it's too dangerous for me, whatever that means. That someone called the Liberator would never allow it. But I know it's just because Torsten doesn't trust me. I told him I left the Knights, but he's not buying it."

"Whoa, whoa, whoa," Meleya held up her hands. "This is a lot of information."

"I know," Jax rushed. "But other Knights have lost everything trying to infiltrate the Coven—the Knights of the Torch need to know what they're up to. More especially, they need to know if they're working alone, or if a certain... uh... leader of the Mage Hunters is involved."

Meleya's eyes went wide. "You mean the Black Valkyrie?"

Jax bit his lip, nodding. Evgardians across the realm knew the Black Valkyrie as the ruthless, powerful woman who led the fight against unregistered magi.

Jax knew her as something else.

Mom.

Jax pushed down his feelings about the woman who'd abandoned him when he was six, leaving him alone for years with his miserable, chronically intoxicated father. The last thing he wanted to do right now in front of Meleya was get emotional.

"Until I can get that information about the Coven, I'm stuck here," Jax said. "I've never run an op alone before, but I won't disappoint... the other Knights."

Jax had been about to say he wouldn't disappoint Solrac. He was the real reason Jax was in the Knights of the Torch in the first place. Solrac believed Jax could do this, and Jax couldn't let him down.

Meleya leaned back against the redrock spire sprouting through the wooden floor. For a long moment, she didn't say anything.

Finally, her eyes met Jax's. "Give me one good reason why I should trust you."

Inside, Jax's heart sank. She probably shouldn't trust him.

On the outside, Jax folded his arms and brazenly flexed his biceps.

"I'm a good-looking stranger from Drakfell who's really good with an axe?"

Meleya chuckled and punched him in his rock-solid arm. "I said a *good* reason."

Jax sighed, running his fingers through his wild, steely hair. "To be honest, M, I don't have one other than this: The Farseer himself said I could do this—that it had to be me. The Knights are building a better world for people like us, M. I genuinely believe that, and I'd be honored to have you be a part of that too."

Meleya mulled that over for a second. She looked down at her hands, a dark shadow passing over her face.

When she looked up, she didn't look Jax in the eye. Were those tears she was hiding?

"You said... you said you know the Farseer?" she stumbled. "The one who saves magi in trouble?"

"He was the one who sent me here."

"I'll make you a deal," Meleya said, her voice still shaky. "If you can get me an audience with the Farseer, I'll... I'll ask Torsten to be my mentor. You said yourself you were surprised I never had one. If he agrees, I'll see if I can learn anything about this Coven of the Gray Ones."

As if to punctuate her words, a long blast from an alarm horn sounded across Outcast Outpost. The sentries must've spotted more dragons coming in from the Mists.

Jax and Meleya got to their feet and hurried to the door. Before Meleya slipped back into the tavern, Jax put a hand on her back, and she turned to him with something like hope in her eyes.

Jax nodded to her. "You've got yourself a deal."

The battle went long into the afternoon, and it wasn't until late evening that Jax finally found himself alone in the barracks. The rest of the squad was either cleaning up by the river or sharpening their weapons just outside the barracks after the fight with a pod of dreklings.

That gave Jax the window he needed.

He scooped the unsuspecting mirror gecko out of her terrarium. Three let out a surprised little clicking sound as Jax held her carefully in his palm so that she was in contact with his skin.

Then he focused his thoughts, channeling them through the gecko.

Kai, Jax thought. *You there?*

For a second, Jax heard nothing. Then he felt the mindlink solidify, Kai's voice echoing inside his head.

Jax? It is you, isn't it?

In the flesh... wait. Not in the flesh. In the... brain.

Kai ignored Jax's idiotic thought, instead channeling a joyful, celebratory noise. *Yes! I can't believe the mindlink still works from such a far distance. You're the first to try it. I'm assuming you're still at Rengard's southern border?*

Yeah, Jax thought, and he could swear he was getting the impression of Kai taking notes, even through the mindlink.

Kai thought on, *And we're about to cross into Evyndara, hundreds of miles away! That is, if all goes according to backup plan five—Asher, don't touch your illusory nose.* Kai paused. *I know it's an ugly nose, but it's nondescript and that's the whole point. Ugh. Anyway, Jax, what do you need?*

Can you put me through to Solrac?

Jax could practically feel Kai's excitement, as well as the vibe that he was flipping through pages in a book. *Of course. Let's see, I left Solrac with Glint One. If I trace... this rune, that should get her to glow. If Solrac is near her, he'll know to put her in contact with his skin, and the mindlink will extend to him as well.*

They only had to wait a few minutes. Jax couldn't help but smile at Solrac's familiar voice.

I was just about to sit down to dinner with the queen of Behrfell when my pocket started glowing. I figured I had better step out and see what was the matter. Is everything alright?

Soot. I didn't mean to interrupt dinner with the drakking queen, Jax thought through the mindlink.

Jax! Solrac thought gleefully, and Jax could practically feel Solrac clapping his hands together. *Well, if I'd known you were going to be on the mindlink, I'd have left dinner with an extra skip in my step. I'm sure Valla can handle being charming on her own.* Solrac hesitated. *Well, at least for a few minutes... On second thought, we had better keep this brief.*

I'll think fast, Jax assured him. *I need to ask a favor.*

Anything.

I've found someone who can help me get the intel I need here at Outcast Outpost. But in return, she wants to speak with the Farseer. I know that's a big ask, but I figured there was no harm in... I don't know, petitioning him or whatever.

Jax could feel Solrac's mind reeling as he took in the request. *Who is this accomplice you've recruited?* Solrac thought.

Jax stood, carrying his Glint out the barracks door. He spotted Meleya sitting a short distance away from the rest of their squad, her white hair falling around her face as she sharpened her long seaxe.

Jax played what he was seeing over the mindlink so the others could get a look at Meleya. He didn't expect the abrupt mental gasp from Solrac at the sight of her.

Stars above, Solrac thought.

What is it? Jax thought back.

Nothing, Solrac rushed to reassure him. *Kai, Asher is with you, right?*

Is he ever, Kai thought, sounding concerned. *And about to hover-jump off the edge of a cliff—Elle, can you get him to stop? I'm almost finished here. Impatient son of a dragonmutt...*

Good, Solrac's tone relaxed. *Jax, I'll speak with the Farseer. He won't be able to come right away, but tell the snowhead girl I'll arrange a meeting. May I ask her name?*

Jax watched as Meleya finished running the whetstone along the bladed edge of her sword. She gave the weapon a practice twirl, ending in a fierce fighting pose.

Meleya, Jax thought over the mindlink. *Meleya of Misthaven.*

Chapter 16: Bonds

"Hold still, Meleya," Trickshot said, gently placing a hand on my shoulder to stop me from turning around. "I swear, girl. You're as distractible as my little sister."

"Sorry." I winced as she dabbed a cleansing solution onto the bite marks on my forearm. The gray, blank-feeling patch was almost completely gone.

I'd met Trickshot for my daily wound tending in the Broughkin Arms. My whole squad had accompanied me—after this morning's skirmish with a couple of wild drakes, we all thought we could use a drink.

Trickshot had been enjoying a glass with Commander Hildred. When our squad walked in, Hildred had given Jax and me her usual disgusted glare before stepping out.

When I'd woken Trickshot the other night to get her help, I'd asked her about the strange behavior I'd seen from the umbral coyotes. While she'd cleaned my fresh gray wound, I'd mentioned that it seemed like the beasts were targeting me specifically, though I knew that sounded crazy. She'd frowned, assuring me that umbral coyotes wouldn't have had any reason to prey on one of us over the others.

"Unless," Trickshot had said with a frown. "Some kind of mind control etherarchy was at play. At the Academy, they drilled us on clues to recognize when something was being controlled by a Seer."

The idea that someone was trying to hurt me by controlling the minds of umbral monsters filled me with dread. It also confused me—Why would someone go through all that trouble?

"""

Erik drew in his sketchbook at a nearby table while Brigan sipped a golden boltbrew as he leaned against an orange stone hoodoo. Solvai, Edrea, and Cam drank theirs while listening—or rather, watching—as the Mage Hunter, Mute, acted out the story of how he'd lost his eye. I couldn't be sure, but it seemed pretty brutal.

Jax was working out again. Once more, he'd lit up a psionic rune to telekinetically hold his axes aloft in the air above him. He held the handles as if they were a bar in order to do chin ups.

"Eyes over here, Meleya," Trickshot reminded me as she held my injured arm in place.

"Why are you doing this?" I asked as she applied the ointment to my forearm.

"Tincture of scale will help you heal faster," she replied.

"No. I mean why are you helping a magi?"

Trickshot gave a little exhale through her nose. "That's a stupid question."

"But you're a Mage Hunter. It's your job to capture us, then either kill us or bring us to Evyndara."

"You know that little sister I mentioned?" Trickshot said. "Shadowbinder. You think I want to see Shaya executed?"

I blinked back at her. "Of course not."

"Not everyone becomes a Mage Hunter out of loathing for magi. Some of us simply believe the Hunters do more good than harm. How would you suggest Evgard keeps the magi from drawing dragons to the keeps?"

"Um," I started. "I don't know. Maybe the magi themselves can help defend them?"

"Not everyone's cut out to be a soldier. Too many more innocent lives would be lost. I agree that getting rid of all but the registered magi isn't a perfect solution, but for now, it's the best we've got."

"Is your sister registered?" I asked.

"A family friend offered to get her special registered status if she joins the Mage Hunters next season."

The idea of having to become a Mage Hunter just to survive appalled me. Then again, I'd become a guard just to save my parents.

"I saw you out there on the field this morning," Trickshot changed the subject. "That drake almost got your squadmate, Erik. I had to dress a pretty bad scrape on his chest."

"Yeah," I muttered, remembering the pit in my stomach as I'd watched the attack. "Lucky his dragon got to him in time."

"I bet if you'd used a portal, *you* could've gotten to him in time."

Trickshot's statement took me off guard. "I guess that's true," I said.

"I'm just saying. You're already wearing that mark," Trickshot pointed at my left cheek. "Why continue to hide your etherarchy?"

"I don't need it to be a good soldier," I said automatically.

"No, you don't," Trickshot said forcefully, putting my arm down and looking me dead in the eye. "But next time, don't let your pride get you or your team killed. Not when you can do something about it."

I found myself getting defensive, my voice raising slightly. "It's not pride."

"Fear then," Trickshot said matter-of-factly. Then she sighed, whispering so that we wouldn't draw the rest of the tavern's attention.

"My first day in the field as a Mage Hunter, several pairs of us ended up in an altercation with some pretty dangerous magi criminals. They wounded my partner badly, and I had to heal him on the spot before we'd captured the magi. I was terrified they'd kill me before I could finish stabilizing him."

Trickshot closed her eyes as she told her story. "We made it out, but even now, years later, I still get scared every time I have to rush out onto a battlefield to save someone's life. What if I get hurt while my back is turned? What if I'm too late to save them? Or worse, what if I'm not skilled enough?"

"So what made you decide to become a healer in the first place?" I asked.

"Because I'm good at it." Trickshot didn't say it like she was bragging, but rather like she was stating a fact. "I won't let fear keep me from using my gift."

I pondered that as she poured a single drop of liquid light from her crystal vial. The shimmering, golden substance cascaded onto my forearm, consuming the last patch of inky grayness from the umbral's bite.

"There," Trickshot said, admiring her handiwork. "That should be the last dose you need. Check back with me in a couple of days and we'll make sure there's no lingering umbral venom."

Trickshot was right. She *was* good at this. I thanked her as the bar's front door swung open and another squad of soldiers poured in. They looked beat, and a couple of them sported new cuts or grazes from battling dragons. They must've just come in from the battlegrounds beyond the Outpost wall.

They sat at the table nearest the one where my squad sat as Mute finished acting out his tale. Moments after they settled down, a gold rimmed portal ripped open behind the bar. Torsten, rocking chair and all, appeared there, his red-tinted eyes glassy.

"Welcome in, soldiers," he gave a sloppy salute to the newly arrived squad. "One round coming up."

Torsten set to work, using Rifting to pull bottles from the high shelves. He mixed and poured, then delivered the squad a round of golden bolt-brew via portal. When he was done, he wiped his brow as if he'd just put in a hard day's work, then took a swig from his canteen of draquila.

The soldiers instantly began guzzling. After downing his glass, their squad captain wiped his lip with the back of his hand. He was a taller guy, probably in his early twenties, with sharp eyebrows that always looked angry. His nose looked a little swollen, probably from the battle.

He turned to our table, narrowing his eyes. Then he got up and walked behind Erik, hovering over his shoulder to peer at his drawing.

Erik sensed someone behind him and tensed, his pencil stopping mid stroke.

"Um... hello," Erik said quietly.

The soldier scoffed and snatched the sketchbook out of Erik's hands. Erik halfheartedly tried to grab it back, but the taller guy held it high and out of reach.

"Is this supposed to be your squad?" the other soldier's voice was nasally and harsh.

"Give it back," Erik said.

"Guys, take a look at this." He brought the sketchbook over to his own squad's table. The others quickly huddled around the page.

I sprang to my feet, anger rising in my chest. The rest of Squad Reckless eyed the other squad with apprehension as well.

"You must be joking!" one of the women from the other squad giggled. "I mean, their Drakfell transfer's biceps are basically potatoes, so that's accurate, but look at this pose."

Another of their squadmates chimed in. "Look at the big guy. He looks just as dumb on the page as he does in reality."

Cam frowned, hurt evident in his face. Edrea's hands balled into fists.

"Aww, in the picture, their squad captain *actually* looks like a leader."

"They all look so fierce in the drawing. Too bad it's nothing like reality."

"Right? And the snowhead's battle face is more like..."

The other soldier made a mocking face. Okay, someone was asking for a punch to the throat.

"The biggest problem I see is the artist himself," their squad captain added. "In the drawing, he's down there with his squad, fighting at their side. Now, I may be wrong, but I've never seen that puny guy anywhere near a battle. He's always up hiding in the clouds like a scorching coward."

That was it.

I was at the other squad captain's throat in an instant, throwing a wild swing at him as high as I could reach. He reeled back as my fist smashed against his jaw.

The rest of my squad was close behind me, Edrea kneeing the gut of the guy who'd taken a jab at Cam. The other soldier doubled over.

Meanwhile, the squad captain turned to me with fire in his pale eyes. He cracked his knuckles, and I prepared to duck.

It turned out my defensive move was unnecessary, as both Brigan and Jax appeared between me and the tall guy. Jax caught his hand before it could get to me, roughly shoving it aside. Both guys looked ready to rip the other squad captain's head off.

Suddenly, multiple flashes of gold light ripped across the space between us and the bullying squad captain. Two of the small golden tears opened just in front of my hands before moving to encircle my wrists. My hands disappeared into the whiteness of Etheria as the gold rims of the small portals tightened around me like manacles. My skin tingled slightly as the gold light touched it, the first sign of a coming ether burn.

All around me, I saw the same thing was happening to the other soldiers, both of Squad Reckless and the other squad. It was a strange—yet impressive—sight, all of our arms ending in shining, gold-rimmed portals. Rather than break anyone's jaw, any fist that had been about to fly had vanished harmlessly into Etheria. I'd never seen such a unique use of rifting.

"Soldiers! That's enough!" Torsten's voice thundered from behind the bar. He had a complicated rune aglow over his forehead, his portals effectively stopping the fight.

Maybe it was the fact that I'd never heard Torsten speak so forcefully, or even so clearly for that matter. I hadn't been able to picture it before, but for a split second, I actually saw the soldier of Evgard still inside him.

Protests resounded as Torsten tightened his portal shackles around our wrists. That burning sensation flared a little, but as I moved to try and pull out of Torsten's rifts, the portals followed my hands.

Torsten held us captive for another few seconds, just to make sure he'd sufficiently subdued us. Then he let the rune over his forehead go out, and all of the portals vanished into etherdust. I rubbed my wrists. Though Torsten hadn't left an ether mark, I could still feel the tingling sensation. I had no idea Rifters were capable of power that precise, and I found myself wondering where Torsten had learned those runes.

Meanwhile, a few of the soldiers muttered under their breath, shooting Torsten dirty looks after his display of etherarchy. I heard one of them call him ethercursed. But Torsten didn't seem fazed as he continued giving us warning looks.

Jax growled, and both Edrea and I gave final glares at the other squad before returning to our own table. Brigan swiped the sketchbook back and passed it to Erik. I caught a glimpse of the drawing before Erik hurriedly closed the book. It depicted the seven members of Squad Reckless, forming an epic tableau as we prepared to fight the enemy. We looked fearsome, strong, and united.

For the first time since our squad was formed, I felt like we were just that.

"Soot and scales be upon all y'all," Torsten muttered, seeming a little winded from his generous use of etherarchy. "Drakkin' drinks done spilt everywhere."

He reached under the bar and pulled out a towel. He wadded it up and tossed it at the other squad captain's face.

"Squad Choke ain't allowed in the Broughkin Arms again unless y'all clean up this mess, y'hear?"

The angry squad captain cursed under his breath as he unfolded the towel. He began wiping the table with one hand while the other rubbed at his jaw.

Torsten nodded with satisfaction as he poured a couple extra drops of dragon's blood into his flask. He added more splashes from a couple of unknown bottles, then closed it up.

"Meleya," Torsten said, shaking up his freshly-mixed draquila. "You 'bout ready?"

I shot Jax a look and found him staring back at me with gratitude. Last night, I'd finally gotten up the courage to ask Torsten if he would mentor me in etherarchy. He was a Rifter, like me, after all, even if every rune he ever traced came out blurry and smudged.

At first, I hadn't been sure what to think of Jax's confession about being a Knight of the Torch. But last I heard, King Axel still hadn't woken up from his coma, so relying on him to wake and pardon my parents as an act of gratitude for my saving his dragon would be foolish.

But over the past few days as I'd mulled over what Jax had said, I'd realized that this could be exactly the chance that I'd been hoping for.

If Zoren wouldn't let my service get my parents out of Spydra Prison, maybe the Farseer could.

Besides, I was ready to learn how to really use my etherarchy. Trickshot was right—by neglecting my Rifting, I was putting my squadmates in danger.

Torsten held up his canteen toward me in a salute. "Meet ya 'round back near the wall."

With that, he opened another portal. Using his hands to guide it, he pulled the portal around him and his chair before he disappeared into Etheria.

As I made my way toward the tavern's front door, Jax took hold of my arm. Then he leaned in close to whisper in my ear.

"Good luck, M."

His breath on my cheek made my pulse race. He raised his eyebrows twice at me as I closed the door behind me.

Boom-boom, boom-boom. I felt Blink reach out to me through our bond, her drumlike communication mimicking my thudding heartbeat.

Hey, I thought back. *Jax isn't my type, okay?*

Boom-boom, Blink replied, and I got the feeling she wouldn't be mad if I changed my mind about that assessment.

Brrring-a-ling! Sniff's flute appeared alongside Blink's drumming, and an image of Brigan's face came to mind.

Sniff! I scolded, my cheeks reddening as I walked. *Brigan only thinks of me as a friend.*

A string of unconvinced notes sounded through the bond, followed by more contradictory drumbeats from Blink.

Enough, I ordered through the bond. Both Sniff and Blink played one last chord before obliging, leaving me alone inside my mind and heart once more.

I shook my head. I didn't have time to worry about my feelings, or my dragons' feelings about my feelings. Now, I needed to focus—I was about to go and learn to do the one thing Mom had always taught me to avoid:

Etherarchy.

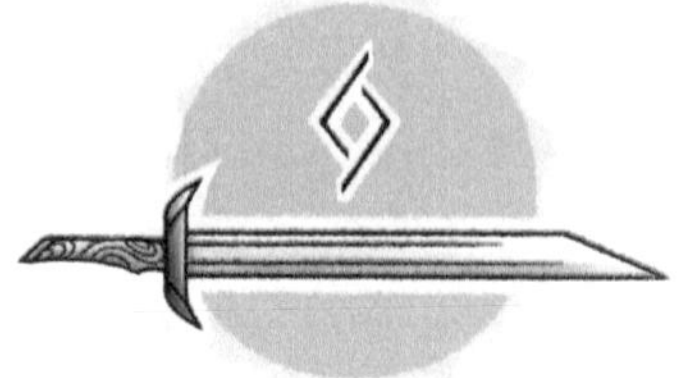

Torsten was waiting for me right where he said he'd be, on the shanty town side of Outcast Outpost's long, broken-down wall. He looked very out of place there, still sitting in that rocking chair in the middle of a patch of dirt. I began jogging over to meet him.

I was still several yards away when Torsten held up a hand and shouted. "Hold up, little lady. That there's close enough."

Stopping in my tracks, I cocked my head and yelled back. "Why?"

Torsten popped the cap of his canteen and took a long swig. When he finished, he exhaled with contentment before putting it away somewhere amidst his folds of clothing and... belly.

"How many runes ya know?" he asked.

"Two," I admitted.

Torsten stuck out his lower lip, nodding. "That should be enough."

"Enough for wh—"

Before I could finish, Torsten was runetracing faster than lightning. Two smallish portals, an entry and an exit, burst to life.

The exit portal startled me, ripping open just a few feet in front of me. Torsten drew his weapon, thrusting it through the entrance portal at his side. Suddenly, his rusty, old long seaxe was right in my face.

I yelped, my training kicking in. I drew my own blade, blocking the seaxe before it slashed my head off.

Leaning to the left, I looked past the hand-sized portal to see that Torsten hadn't left his chair. He lounged comfortably beside the wall as he engaged my blade from afar.

One look at my bewildered expression, and Torsten began laughing hysterically.

"Go on then," Torsten said between snorts. "Let's see what ya got."

I lowered my brows, my eyes darkening at the challenge. How hard could it be to take down one overweight drunk guy who wouldn't—probably *couldn't*—lift himself out of a grandmotherly rocking chair?

With a grunt, I swung at Torsten's blade. His exit portal moved along with his arm to block, and the duel began.

Clangs and swipes filled the air as I battled the floating blade, Torsten directing the portal to dart all around me. Torsten was shockingly quick, and I had no trouble believing he was once a force to be reckoned with as a soldier.

"I could do this all day," Torsten said casually, relaxing more deeply into his chair as he fought.

Sweat was already beading at my hairline. Torsten's rifting swordarm was far too agile, allowing him to get inside my guard without the usual consequence of opening himself up for a counterstrike. It was taking all my energy just to keep him from landing a hit on me.

If I wanted to win this, I needed to get inside his guard. The trouble was, his guard was about three drake lengths away.

I spun away from the portal, then started running at Torsten, my sword poised.

With a borderline maniacal chuckle, Torsten traced a follow up rune. It joined the first over his forehead, and within a half a second, another exit portal had opened between Torsten and me. His dirty blade retreated into the first portal, then popped out of the second one, slashing toward me once again.

With a frustrated yell, he forced me to skid to a stop and block. I swung hard at the rusty seaxe, trying to push him to the side so that I could try skirting around the portal again. But by that point, the original exit portal had caught up. Torsten's sword bounced in and out of both exit portals, making me work twice as hard to keep him at bay.

I did my best to get away, but Torsten's seaxe was everywhere at once. Whether I faked right but went left, maneuvered backward and to the side, or even when I tried ducking under, Torsten's portals followed.

Then Torsten had the audacity to use his off hand to take a swig of draquila.

I ground my teeth. I knew what I had to do.

The next time I blocked Torsten's blade, I pushed in on it, stalling his sword to buy myself some time.

With my other hand, I traced the basic rifting rune. I felt a comfortable release inside my head as I accessed my ether well.

Torsten wrenched free from my sword's hold. He was halfway through a swing when I threw up a portal of my own directly in front of the one where his hand and weapon stuck out.

His sword disappeared into Etheria.

It shot out of my exit portal, which I'd placed right next to Torsten's face.

Torsten couldn't stop the momentum from his jab. His eyes widened as his rusty blade clipped his stringy hair right before lodging into the high back of his rocking chair.

It was a strange sight: Torsten stuck in his chair with one arm disappearing into a portal, that same arm involuntarily sticking out of yet another portal where his own sword had nearly taken him out.

I couldn't stop the half-smile from appearing on my face as I traced the same rune again, stepping through the new, me-sized portal.

I reappeared instantly in front of Torsten. I wasn't entirely sure what came over me as I reached over and gave his rocking chair a victory push. It creaked, and the backward motion pulled Torsten's sword arm as it still grasped his weapon, which in turn pulled Torsten forward, making him jolt awkwardly in his chair. I could barely wrap my head around it, but either way, I proudly sheathed my weapon.

If Torsten's snickering before had been hysterical, his next bout of laughter brought it to a whole new level.

"Drak an' a half, little lady," Torsten howled. "That's what I'm talkin' 'bout. Maybe y'are cut out to be a decent etherarchist after all. Now all we's gots'ta do is get some of that into your instincts. Your gut reaction's usin' that there sword, but never forget you've got a whole 'nother tool in yer arsenal—riftin'. And soot if you ain't got a knack for it."

He let go of his sword hilt and pulled his hand back through the portals to slap his knee. The impact sent a tidal wave of ripples across his beer belly as he let his runes go out. I let my own rune dissolve into etherdust, then helped Torsten yank his sword out of the back of his rocking chair. I'd left a pretty deep gash in the wood, but the chair was already so battered it hardly mattered.

"The way you stopped the bar fight with all those small portals on our wrists," I said. "That was incredible. Can you teach me how to do that?"

Torsten's laughter continued in full force. "Took me years to figure out how to split my focus like that. Let's learn you how to walk 'fore you start sprintin.' First thing you need is to memorize yerself a few more runes. That way, you'll have more wiggle room with them portals'n such. Be able to move 'em, grow 'em, shrink 'em, 'n multiply 'em a lot more easily. Not to mention puttin' up false rifts to confuse yer enemies. Why, I remember once when I was in the guard, we were facin' down a whole row of wild ridgerunners…"

Torsten went on to tell an epic tale of when he, a fearless squad captain, led his team into battle against the feral dragonwolves. He seemed to embellish more than a few details, but despite that, it all sounded pretty impressive.

Still, I frowned as I listened to his story. There was something about it that seemed familiar, though I couldn't put my finger on it.

"Anyway, this'll help with all them runes," Torsten said, grunting as he shifted his weight to reach into a pocket. He produced a small, dark brown leather book. It had an ornate cover with hundreds of tiny runes etched into it. The book looked worn, with each of its corners rounded and discolored.

Torsten tossed me the book, and I sat down on a nearby fallen stone from the crumbling wall to get a look inside.

Each page featured a different rune that Rifters could access to maximize their ability to use teleportation. It even looked like several pages toward the back went over dreamweave runes—the shared power between all three types of Mystics.

I gripped the little book in my hands, excitement filling me. I'd never been allowed to so much as look at runes before. Now I had all the knowledge I could possibly want at my fingertips.

"Thank you, Torsten," I said, closing the book and fingering the spine. The book's title was written along it. *Noy Ryfna Odya e Runa.*

"S'called 'The Rifter's Guide to Runes,' in the ancient Guardian tongue," Torsten said. "Belonged to my own mentor back in Behrfell. Maybe one day you can pass it on'ta the next."

"I'll take good care of it," I promised.

Torsten looked at me, a half smile on his face. For just a second, his hazel eyes didn't seem so glassy and disconnected.

"Torsten," I started. "Jax said you wove all of those blankets in the tavern, and patterned them after people's auras."

"Aww, my son's goin' 'round braggin' 'bout me, is he?" Torsten laughed, only this time it sounded the tiniest bit bitter.

"May I ask about one of the blankets?"

"Sure thing, little lady."

"There was a light blue one near the door to the kitchen. It had a pattern like hundreds of intricate feathers on it.""I know the one. Know it well."

"Whose aura did you make it for?" I asked, holding my breath.

Torsten let out a long, sad sigh. "Made that one for someone special. Someone I never got to meet."

He took a long swig from his canteen of draquila. Suddenly, I remembered where I'd heard that story about Torsten leading his squad against a pack of wild ridgerunners before.

I let out my breath, putting the pieces together.

"Torsten," I said hesitantly. "Did you ever know a woman named Lorelai?"

Torsten lurched forward in his chair, spitting a mouthful of draquila all over the dirt. I cringed as some of the spray misted onto me.

"Wha… what makes ya ask a scorchin' question like that?" Torsten sputtered, looking at me with wide, searching eyes. I wasn't sure I should answer truthfully—Lorelai undoubtedly had her reasons for hiding the truth from both Torsten and Solvai. I pressed my lips into a line.

"I'm gonna need ya to answer me, little lady," Torsten's gaze darkened.

I shrank back a little. "Uh… she's the head dragon keeper on the Rise. She might've mentioned your name—that's all."

Torsten narrowed his eyes at me. "That's all?"

I nodded, fiddling with the hem of my cloak to avoid his gaze.

Torsten pressed on. "Anyone ever tell ya yer a terrible liar? Why'n the void ya bringin' her up now?"

I realized I was trapped. Then again, right before we'd left the Rise, Lorelai had specifically told me to tell Torsten to keep an eye on Solvai to make sure nothing happened to her. That had to mean Lorelai intended for him and Solvai to have *some* kind of relationship, right?

I swallowed. "Lorelai is Solvai's mother."

"Solvai… y'all's squad captain?"

I nodded. Torsten sat back in his chair, looking deeply shocked.

Jax's father... and, I guess Solvai's too, slowly took another swig of his drink as he processed the information. We sat in silence for a long while, listening to the distant chirping of dragoncrickets. Finally, Torsten began absently rubbing at his wrist. As he moved his sleeve, I noticed for the first time a woven black band around his wrist. It was in pretty shabby condition, but I was certain it was a marriage bracelet.

After a while, Torsten put the cap on his canteen. He mumbled incoherently, running his fingers through his stringy hair, then looking at his hand with distaste.

Suddenly, I remembered why I'd asked Torsten to mentor me in the first place. This could be a good time to get him talking.

"Torsten?" I asked, trying to sound nonchalant. "Have you ever heard of the Gray Ones?" Torsten's gaze snapped onto me. "Why you askin'?"

I answered carefully, surprised by the truth leaving my mouth as I spoke. "I've been getting these strange, cold impressions lately. Then the other night at the North Tower I saw something while I was using the Sight. A gray shadow with bright blue eyes."

Torsten's demeanor changed as he nodded with understanding. "I see. Sounds to me like one of the Gray Ones is thinkin' 'bout choosin' you."

"Choosing me?" I repeated, nerves appearing in my stomach.

"The Gray Ones are the ethereal servants of the goddesses," Torsten explained, his tone serious. "The reason us magi have our etherarchy in the first place. 'Twere bestowed upon us by the Gray Ones, their chosen vessels. Some Rifters can see 'em usin' the Sight."

To emphasize his point, Torsten runetraced, the Sight rune appearing over his forehead. When he blinked, I could just see the faintest gold rim around his irises that reminded me of the edge of our portals.

"Well, hello there," he said, waving to what looked like nobody. He held up his canteen, offering it to the open air. "Any spirits for my spirits? No? More for me I guess."

He took a long swig, and I wasn't sure whether Torsten was actually seeing ethereal beings, or if it was the alcohol talking. No wonder Mystics weren't supposed to drink.

I thought about using the Sight myself to see if I could see anything. But then I remembered the icy stare of those vibrant blue eyes the other night, and I couldn't bring myself to do it.

"The Gray Ones can make us far more powerful than we are alone," Torsten went on, his words slurring slightly. "Even have the ability to make us immune to silver, like the Guardians of old, ain't that right, my friends?"

With that, Torsten toasted nobody.

Immune to silver? I thought. That intrigued me. It would render Mage Hunters all but useless.

"What are Guardians exactly?" I asked.

"Ancient magi who could access all nine types of etherarchy."

"Like true dragons?"

Torsten nodded, his eyes glazing. "Some say true dragons are the only livin' Guardians now. But the Gray Ones tell us there are still other ways to wield that kind of power... for the good of Evgard."

I leaned forward on my rock. We had to be getting closer to the information Jax needed—I just needed to keep Torsten talking.

"How might one learn more about... that power?" I said, feeling the clumsiness of my words as they left my lips.

Despite his increasingly drunken state, Torsten looked at me with skepticism. My cheeks flushed.

Drak. I was good with a sword and great in the kitchen, but I couldn't lie to save my life.

Torsten let out a dark chuckle. "You ain't ready for that kind of information, little lady. Perhaps another time."

"But—" I tried.

"I said that's enough," Torsten's voice came out harsh and commanding, like when he'd intervened to stop the fight between our squad and Squad Choke.

I fell silent as a cold feeling seemed to surround me, the same way it had back in the Dragon Chasm after I fell from Sniff's back, and again at the North Tower.

I shuddered, again considering putting up a Sight rune of my own. But if Torsten was right about the Gray Ones being so close, I wasn't sure I wanted to see what was happening in the spirit world.

Torsten tried to take another drink, but his canteen was empty. He swore.

"For now," he said with finality, "we best be gettin' back to the ol' Broughkin Arms. Never know when they'll need you at the front."

FRAGMENT - TRICKSHOT

Trickshot carefully stowed her crystal vial of liquid light inside her medical kit. It was getting a little low, but she wasn't worried. The bottle they'd given her at the Mage Hunter Academy was enchanted using skystone, set to refill itself as long as it got enough sunlight.

Warm rays streamed through the window of the Captain of the Guard's office. She'd have plenty of time to let it replenish during the journey downriver on her way back to Outcast Outpost.

"I should get back." Trickshot slung her bag over her shoulder. "One of Commander Hildred's lieutenants took an umbral bite in the foot yesterday. No risk of the shadow wasting, but I'd like to give him one more treatment tonight just to be safe."

"Of course," Zoren replied, standing up to see her out. Trickshot's old Mage Hunter partner laid a hand on the doorknob, but stopped before opening the door.

Zoren turned to Trickshot. "Before you go, did you do as I asked? Regarding Meleya, I mean?"

Trickshot nodded. "It wasn't easy to find a natural way to fulfill your request. But she came to me late the other night with a nasty umbral bite along her forearm."

"What?" Zoren's dragonfire green eyes flashed. His Drekai tail twitched the way it always did when he was stressed. "What happened?"

"Relax, she's fine. Just finished her last treatment a few days ago. But when she came seeking healing, she was badly shaken. Less careful and guarded than usual, and I got a better look at the cords hanging from her neck. You were right—she wears two."

"Yes?" Zoren leaned forward.

"One holds the golden yellow heartscale for her evren," Trickshot explained. "As for the other cord, I only just glimpsed it, but I'm sure it holds a second heartscale. A silver one, from an evren as well, if I had to guess."

"But Sniff is the only dragon you've seen with her, correct?" Zoren asked.

As Trickshot nodded, a grave look settled over Zoren's face.

Trickshot crossed her arms. "Why? What does it mean?"

"*Khaviila ji Zolehi,*" Zoren replied, keeping his voice low even though they were alone. Trickshot didn't recognize the Drekai words. Zoren didn't often speak his native language—as far as Trickshot knew, he hadn't been to his homeland in nearly two decades. She waited for him to translate.

Zoren sighed. "My people's legends speak of ethereal protectors sent by the ancient Guardians. They're spirits who have passed on into Etheria, yet linger near this world by using some sort of physical anchor—like the heartscale—to be close to those they're bound to defend. We call them *khaviila.*"

"*Khaviila,*" Trickshot repeated the word. "It sounds like a good thing. If it's true, Freya's daughter is more likely to stay safe."

But Zoren didn't look reassured. Tensely, he cracked the door open to let Trickshot out of the office. But before she started down the hall, Zoren put a hand on her shoulder.

"Look after her," he said, lines of worry creasing his brow. "If a *khaviila* truly follows Meleya, I fear for her future. These protectors are more than a simple bond."

Trickshot frowned as Zoren finished.

"They are an omen of grave peril to come."

Chapter 18: Onions

In one corner of my new tavern kitchen, Solvai sat at an impromptu table made from beer barrels. Atop the barrels was a half-carved block of wood, Solvai's carving knife held carefully in her hand as she worked with it.

In the other corner, Brigan leaned back in his chair against the wall near the window. Meanwhile, I stood at the countertop wielding a kitchen knife as I chopped the crusty bread left over from yesterday's meal into crumbs for today's.

I couldn't stop smiling. This was the most at home I'd felt since our last day in the bunker on the Rise. The only thing we were missing was an obnoxious, thieving draccoon living in the rafters. I hadn't seen my father's ethereal familiar, Dusty, since coming to the Outpost. I imagined he was still relaxing in the bunker, probably stealing all of the ingredients I'd left behind.

"Gauntlet down," Brigan said, and I could tell he was just as thrilled at the familiarity of having the three of us in a kitchen together again as I was. "Rengard should incentivise its citizens to evacuate along the southern border now, before the Dragon Mists continue their path north and flood them out."

"People won't want to leave their homes," Solvai said, not looking up from her carving.

Brigan nodded. "True, which is why I don't think the keepdom should force anyone out. But if Rengard could somehow encourage them to move, perhaps with a stipend or by building affordable new keeps elsewhere, maybe some would. That would help prevent mass emergency evacuations later."

"That is, *if* the Dragon Mists really end up pushing them out. They've lasted this long."

"The problem is," I put in, gathering my breadcrumbs into a pan. "Whether Rengard wants to admit it or not, a huge number of the towns along the southern border are magi refugee camps. They'd never want to fund them or build them new homes. They'd just as soon let the Mists devour them."

Brigan frowned. "That's a point I hadn't considered."

"Is that what happened to Misthaven?" Solvai asked gently.

For whatever reason, Solvai's question gave me pause. I'd never spoken honestly about my family's time in Misthaven before, but I couldn't think of a reason to hide the truth from my best friends any longer.

As I thought about how to respond, I carefully raised a finger. My friends watched in fascination as gold light trailed after it through the air, a new rune glowing to life over my forehead.

A little horizontal crack appeared before me, brightening the room further with more golden etherlight. Following the motion of my hand, the crack tore itself open to reveal a small white space, like a pocket in Etheria. This portal had no exit. From what I understood from the rune-book Torsten had given me, this little ethereal compartment followed my soul wherever I went, allowing me to store whatever objects I wanted inside. The book had called it a 'rift hold.'

This style of etherarchy was still new to me, so I couldn't make a very large rift hold, but it was the perfect place to store some of my favorite spices. A little jar of paprika, another of cornflour for thickening sauces, a basil sprig, and a couple of long, dark Evyndellian vanilla beans Torsten had given me out of the tavern's stock.

I still kept my saltshaker in its pouch at my belt. I didn't want to have to rely on etherarchy to get at that.

My friends seemed impressed as I sprinkled a few shakes of paprika onto my pan of crumbs before replacing the jar and closing my rift hold.

"What?" I said, my cheeks going slightly red. I knew I needed to get more comfortable with using rifting, but even in front of my best friends, it wasn't easy. Part of me still worried they'd respond with fear or repulsion.

"Nothing," Solvai said with a reassuring smile. "That was just awesome."

I let out a breath I didn't know I'd been holding as I hefted the pan of crumbs to place them in the oven.

"You were asking about Misthaven," I said. "I was only a baby when my parents lived there, so I don't remember when the camp disappeared. But my mom, dad, and I were there that day."

My friends leaned forward in their seats, Solvai's carving set aside. Nobody in Evgard knew what my parents knew about the cursed magi city's disappearance. As far as I could tell, my family and I had been the only survivors.

I went on. "They don't talk about it much, but they told me one day the town was fine, the next, a group of Drekai showed up near the spring in the town square. Without warning, they all traced rifting runes, working together to create this colossal portal."

I took a deep breath before continuing. "The portal started pulling in the whole town. Misthaven wasn't all that big—it was the smallest of the southern magi refugee camps. My parents fled along with some of the others, but nobody else was... um... fast enough."

I stumbled over the end of my sentence, unsure whether or not I could mention my mother's rifting. It was the only reason we'd made it out before the Drekai had rifted the entire camp to only the goddesses knew where.

"But why?" Brigan's brow furrowed. "What did the Drekai have against Misthaven?"

I shrugged. "I was too young to remember anything, and my parents, well, at least my mom, didn't like talking about our time there. She still doesn't like talking about anything to do with etherarchy."

Solvai and Brigan looked thoughtful as I pulled out butter, milk, eggs, wyvernhog sausage, and onion from their places on shelves under the countertop. Torsten and Jax had helped me stock my kitchen with everything I could possibly want.

Solvai chewed her lip. "Your parents are magi too, aren't they? That's why they're in Spydra Prison, and why you're in the guard at all."

I froze. Sure, I knew my friends would put it together eventually, but it still felt strange after so many years of hiding. Solvai and Brigan had long since known that I was serving as Mom and Dad's proxy, but until recently, I'd done my best to make them assume they'd been incarcerated for something petty like theft. Now, the truth was obvious.

"Yeah." I shoved down the unwelcome tears that were fighting to flee my eyes. "Best case scenario, I serve out their sentences and we get exiled to some wasteland somewhere."

And that's only if Captain Zoren ever lets them out, I thought. I was getting anxious. It had been weeks since Jax promised me a meeting with the Farseer. I wasn't sure what the Farseer's schedule looked like, but Jax assured me he would come as soon as he was able.

"It's not fair for the realm to imprison people for something they can't change," Solvai said.

"Gauntlet down," Brigan said. "Things will be better once they've perfected the magi cure."

Brigan cast me what was meant to be a reassuring look, but I found myself recoiling at his comment. Not long ago, I would've jumped at the chance to receive a cure, to be freed from the burden that was my etherarchy.

But the past couple of weeks, as I'd been training with Torsten and studying my book of runes, I wasn't sure what I wanted anymore.

Just then, a loud knock sounded at the door. Solvai answered and found Erik there bearing a message from Commander Hildred. She'd called for all squad captains to meet in the mess hall to discuss new formations and strategy.

Solvai quickly put away her carving before rushing out the door. She didn't want to be late and risk angering the already rage-prone commander.

I watched her close the door behind her before going back to my cooking. The hot oven warmed my face as I removed the perfectly-toasted breadcrumbs.

I'd been planning to tell Solvai my suspicions about Torsten, but I hadn't found the right time. She so admired the perfect father she'd created inside her head. If I was right about Torsten, it would crush her.

I was surprised when I turned back to the countertop to find Brigan no longer in his chair. Instead, he was standing on the other side of the counter facing me. He gave a winning, dimpled smile. "Gauntlet down: I think it's time you taught me your top secret recipe for dragon fritters."

I raised an eyebrow. "The Heir Duke of Solhelm wants to learn to cook?"

"I'm always interested in learning new things."

I thought for a second. Even from my childhood in the canyons, I'd always cooked alone. With Mom too exhausted from the anxiety of keeping us safe and Dad putting so much energy into fighting off canyon dragons and being there for Mom, meals had generally ended up low on their list of priorities. They'd always made sure I was fed, but it wasn't long before I took over breakfast, lunch, and dinner duties to try and ease their load. I'd spent hours watching nomadic women and men stew pots, roast drakalope, and bake bread in makeshift campfire ovens, collecting and modifying their recipes over the years.

Brigan was still looking at me expectantly, that familiar smile still in place on his warm, russet face. His little curl caught the light from the window, glinting with the same brown as his eyes.

"Alright," I agreed, moving aside so that Brigan could stand beside me at the countertop. "I'll get started on the mix while you chop up the onion."

Brigan joined me as I shoved a cutting board and knife his way. Then I tossed him an onion, which he caught and placed on the board. He flourished the knife before hacking into the onion.

"Whoa," I caught him around the wrist before he could make another chop. "You can't leave the skin on."

"I can't?"

"Not unless you want to find papery onion skin in the fritters," I laughed, removing the onion's outer layer.

"Oh."

"Also," I pointed to the knife he wielded at shoulder height. "This is not a sword, and the onion isn't a wild drekling. You've got to be gentle, deliberate. Here."

Placing my small, beige hands around Brigan's large, deep brown ones, I guided his knife's movements. I could feel his warmth on the back of my shoulder as I reached across the cutting board, and felt myself relax as his woody, fresh smell reached my nose.

"You see?" I said, not quite ready to lift my hands off his, but doing so anyway out of obligation.

Brigan's hand took mine before I got far, and my breath caught.

"Almost," Brigan said quietly. "Could you show me one more time?"

"Sure," I breathed. Together, we cut into the onion a couple more times. I became aware of the rhythm of his breathing, the steady rise and fall of his broad chest so close to me.

The moment lingered until all at once I felt every muscle in Brigan's body tense. I quickly pulled my hands back, and he stepped away.

"Drakking onion," he said, looking away from me as he rubbed a tear from one eye.

He bent over the cutting board, carefully chopping. As I pulled out a mixing bowl, a playful set of notes rang through my heart.

Prrring! Sniff sang, letting me know how thrilled he was about whatever I'd just been feeling for Brigan.

I poured a cup of milk into the bowl, my cheeks reddening slightly.

Give me a break, Sniff, I thought through the bond. *He's obviously not interested. I need to stop thinking about him like that, starting right now.*

Ba doom doom, Blink's impression came through as well, putting an image of Jax into my mind. Something told me Jax wouldn't be as withholding as Brigan.

My cheeks deepened even more as I realized what Blink was getting at.

Ting-a-ling, Sniff argued for Brigan.

Boom, Blink projected a solid drumbeat in favor of Jax.

I can't believe this, I thought to my warring dragons. *Do both of you mind?*

Together, they played one last discordant chord before retreating from my head. I gave Brigan a sideways glance as he worked diligently over the onion. Another little curl had escaped his ridgeknot hairstyle, carelessly falling over his face. I got the urge to pull the loop from his hair and mess up all his curls just to see what he'd look like that way. I got the feeling I'd like it.

I cut butter into my mixing bowl, reminding myself that it didn't matter, since clearly Brigan wasn't looking to be anything more than friends.

I'd just pulled the last dragonfritter out of the pan when I heard the commotion. The sound of glass shattering and a large thud got Brigan and me rushing out of the kitchen door to see what was the matter.

Inside the tavern, I saw a disheveled Commander Hildred standing angrily beside a fallen table and the shards of at least three or four broken glasses. She was breathing heavily, a look of murder on her face as she pursued...

I did a double take.

Commander Hildred faced down a squat, ring-tailed draccoon. My jaw dropped—I would recognize those mischievous, beady black eyes anywhere.

Dusty.

I guess he wasn't relaxing at the bunker back home after all.

"That drakking vermin stole my things!" Commander Hildred roared.

Dusty chittered back, clearly taking offense at the commander's insult as he clutched something shiny closer to his chest.

Behind Hildred, Solvai and some of the other squad captains crowded into the bar to get a better look at the scene. Dusty must've interrupted their meeting.

With a violent roar, Commander Hildred lunged toward the draccoon.

Dusty squealed, darting onto one of the tavern tables. He leapt from table to table across the room, just out of the commander's reach.

Finally, with a final wild leap, Dusty flung himself toward me. I automatically caught his furry body, and he buried his little face into my shoulder.

"Hand over the draccoon," Commander Hildred barked, looming over me.

"He didn't mean any harm," I said, shielding Dusty protectively against the threat.

"Now, soldier!" she ordered.

"He'll return your things. Just give me a minute—"

"Scorch you, drakking ethercursed," Hildred swore, her hand reaching for the oversized blade sheathed on her back. I shrank at her use of the dirty word for magi. "You probably sent the sooty little thing in the first place. You thought it would be funny, didn't you?"

Dusty clung to me on one side while, almost unconsciously, my other hand grabbed hold of the hilt of my seaxe.

"Alright, alright," Brigan stepped between us, a charming smile on his face. "No need to make a scene. Meleya will get Dusty to return the commander's things. And Commander, I can't tell you how right you are to be upset. This little draccoon is a notorious thief. But if I were you, I'd take it as a compliment. Dusty only ever steals from people with class."

Hildred was still staring me down with disgust in her fiery green eyes. Admittedly, I was eyeing her with skepticism myself. But ultimately, we both stood down.

"Meleya," Brigan prompted. "The commander's property?"

Dusty looked up at me. With an innocent squeak, he handed over a delicately-woven band with a single, gleaming emerald in its center.

I recognized it instantly as a marriage bracelet. But I'd never seen it before on Commander Hildred's wrist, nor had I heard anything about her having a husband or betrothed.

Based on the fuming expression on her face as the rest of the room and I stared at the marriage bracelet, things hadn't worked out.

"Drakking magi," Hildred said as she snatched the bracelet from my hands and tucked it away. Then she stormed toward the door of the tavern past all of the squad captains.

"What are you staring at?" she thundered. "Meeting adjourned—now get lost."

In an effort to obey her order, the squad captains and even the other patrons at the tavern immediately did their best to resume normal activity. Mugs clinked and chatter picked back up. The only one who still seemed rooted to the spot was Torsten, and not just because his rear end remained all but glued to his rocking chair.

He sat inconspicuously behind the bar, the rune for the Sight alight over his forehead. He was staring at the group of dispersing squad captains with a look of agonized longing.

Then I realized that he wasn't staring at the group. Rather, he was taking in the aura of Captain Solvai.

A pained expression on his face, Torsten reached automatically for his canteen. But as he watched Solvai, he stopped just before bringing the flask to his lips. He glanced at it, clearly conflicted, before replacing the stopper and setting it down on the counter.

Chapter 19: Grunt Crew

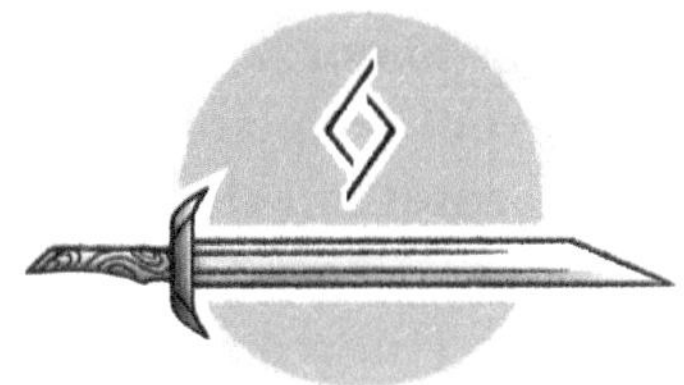

"**S**quads Choke, Retreat, Flee, Struggle, Nothing, and Reckless."

Commander Hildred's voice echoed across the battlegrounds as we stood lined up on the Dragon Mist side of the wall. I could've sworn she just liked calling out our squad names to remind us that we were the Rise's rejects.

We were bruised, bloodied, and bone-tired after a long battle with wild dragonkind. Commander Hildred had already dismissed our bonded dragons, who were either washing themselves in the Ridgeback River or back at the dragon cavern resting.

Commander Hildred paced menacingly in front of her platoon. It had been a week since the incident with Dusty. I'd set my father's ethereal familiar up with a cozy tower of old whiskey crates in a corner of the tavern kitchen. He'd made himself quite comfortable there, staying out of the commander's way.

But Commander Hildred had spent the week even more on edge than usual.

"I've received some sooty news from the Rise," Hildred began. "The Canyon Keepdom has declared war on the Dragon Isles."

Murmurs rose from among our ranks as Hildred went on.

"The Queen of Rengard has taken over as regent while King Axel remains incapacitated. The war means a couple of changes for us down here."

"Are they sending us to the Dragon Isles?" one soldier asked.

"You think the great drakking army of Rengard would send a squad called 'Retreat' to the front lines?" Hildred bit back. "No. We're still stuck here defending the canyon. What the war means for us is that Captain Zoren's recalling our grunt crew. That means the sorry saps who usually haul in the mess you drakpats leave after a battle are gone. So, I need a couple of you to take on cleanup duty this afternoon. Don't want to? Well, I don't care."

My squad did all in our power to not make eye contact with our commander, and I could feel the rest of the platoon doing the same.

"There are a lot of dragon corpses out there ready to rot. Do you want the stink to invite more live ones?"

More shuffling. More silence. Hildred's pacing feet came to a sandy stop.

"No volunteers? I suppose I'll have to choose a few of you at random." She paused for only a moment before choosing two soldiers 'at random.'

"Magi," she pointed to me and Jax. "Hit the field. Pile up the remains outside the butcher's shop. The rest of you, hit the river. You all reek."

The rest of the platoon dispersed while Squad Reckless lingered, unsure whether or not they should stay to help Jax and me. Cleaning up the battlefield after a skirmish usually took the grunt crew at least a few hours, and that was with twelve or more people working together. It was definitely not a job for only two.

"And no helping them, either," Commander Hildred clarified, her fiery eyes narrowing at the rest of the squad. "Let the magi do it alone."

Solvai, Brigan, and the others muttered their sympathy for Jax and me. Cam looked especially disappointed, probably because he knew that if I was stuck here all afternoon, that meant I wouldn't be there to make dinner for the squad tonight. That made me sad, too. I'd been planning on sending Sniff out to catch a few dragonbass from the river, then serve the fish with buttered vegetables.

Jax and I watched the squad follow Commander Hildred and the rest of the platoon through the wall to the town side. I couldn't help but wonder what had made the commander so bitter against magi, and whether it had anything to do with that unused marriage bracelet.

Jax and I surveyed the field. The carcasses of about forty dreklings, wild dragons, and a few torradons and ridgerunners stared back with blank eyes. My stomach churned.

When I turned to see how Jax was feeling about our impossible task, I was surprised to find him grinning from ear to ear.

He folded his arms across his chest, tilting up his chin at me. "Bet I can bring in more than you."

Something about the way he said it triggered a deeply competitive nerve. I raised an eyebrow.

"Doubt it."

"It's on," Jax said. "Psion versus Rifter."

"You mean, you want us to use our etherarchy?" I asked.

"Want to be done by sundown or not?"

Jax had a point.

I felt a bundle of nerves fill my stomach at the thought of using my powers out here in the open like this. Since I'd started training with Torsten, I'd only dared to incorporate the occasional small rift on the battlefield. I'd spent every spare moment poring over the runebook, memorizing ones I thought could be useful.

Seeing the challenge in Jax's midnight blue eyes, I figured this was the perfect opportunity to try them out.

Rather than answer Jax with words, I took off running toward the battlefield, my finger flying through the air to runetrace.

Behind me, Jax gave a whoop as he followed.

A variation of the rifting rune appeared over my forehead as I came to a stop in front of the dragonmoose-sized corpse of a wild drake. I planted my feet wide on the ground, then raised both hands as the gold crack ripped vertically in front of me.

Jax watched, still grinning as I pulled my hands apart to tear the rift open. With a pushing motion, I directed the portal toward the drake.

I couldn't help but break into a grin myself. I'd never been able to move my portals before.

Momentarily, the gold-rimmed, white rift encompassed the drake's body as the beast slowly disappeared into Etheria.

I placed the other end of the portal facing down beside the cracking Outpost wall. With a heavy thud, the dragon carcass fell to the ground to form the beginnings of a pile. I made a bold swiping motion with my hands, already moving my portal toward the next fallen wild dragon.

Meanwhile, Jax wasn't about to let me win that easily. He lit up a psionic rune over his forehead, then flexed his dense arm muscles as he telekinetically lifted one of the biggest torradon bodies on the field into the air.

He grunted as he made a shoving movement, sending the hefty hunk of dragonbull flying toward where my drake already lay, landing atop mine with a satisfying thud.

We found our stride, neither of us letting up as we used our etherarchy to add more and more fallen beasts onto the pile. Jax strained as he telekinetically lifted carcass after carcass, launching them further each time across the field.

After I'd moved all the ones closest to me, I traced my usual rifting rune, which showed up in gold over my forehead alongside the first. My ether well drained a little more as I used my second portal to teleport myself to different parts of the field to move more dead dragons at better angles and without overexerting myself.

I appeared and disappeared rapidly, like a flurry all along the battlefield. A laugh escaped my throat—despite the morbid nature of the task, I couldn't remember having this much fun.

Jax laughed too as he watched me, whistling. Seeing me bring in more fallen creatures only made him work faster.

Before long, I saw sweat dripping down the side of his face as Jax drained more of his ether. He'd already used a lot on the battlefield today, and I was starting to worry he was using too much. But he didn't let up.

Our pile of dragon, drekling, and torradon bodies was comically enormous, and there was only one last drekling corpse still on the field. Jax and I looked at each other, our eyebrows lowering.

We dashed toward the final prize. Jax pulled ahead in our race, reaching out toward the drekling.

The beast lifted into the air as Jax pushed upward on it. But it didn't take long for me to vanish through a portal, appearing at the drekling's side.

I thrust my hands upward, putting up a portal directly above it. Before Jax could stop his telekinetic momentum, he'd lifted the drekling through the rift for me.

I dropped it through the exit portal onto the tip top of the pile. Jax whirled around to watch, then spun back toward me with an indignant expression on his face.

"You sneak!" he shouted, running toward me.

I doubled over laughing as I let the runes over my forehead go out.

Jax, on the other hand, still had plans for his psionic powers. He skidded to a stop, reaching out toward me.

Suddenly, I felt a sharp tug from my belt as I went shooting through the air in his direction.

"Hey!' I called out, trying uselessly to stop myself. I slammed into Jax, the momentum sending us both to the ground.

I got to my feet and glared at Jax beside me. Now, he was the one laughing hysterically.

He sat up, and I gave him a shove. He responded by telekinetically pushing upward on my boots.

"Whoa!" I called out, arms flailing as I tried to balance myself. But Jax was in control of my feet. He pushed me higher as he stood up, positioning himself below me.

"Put me down," I insisted.

"Done."

Jax snapped, and his psionic rune went out. I yelped as I fell—right into Jax's arms.

He caught me effortlessly, one strong arm under my knees and the other around my back. His grin was still teasing, though there was something intense in his midnight blue eyes that instantly sent my pulse racing.

I tried to open my mouth to speak, but no words came out. Jax raised an eyebrow as if he knew he was leaving me speechless and he liked it.

A series of drumlike thumps played through my dragon bond, and I could tell that Blink was all for it as well.

He's too arrogant, I argued with Blink.

Boom-ba-doom, Blink replied, and I could somehow tell she was correcting my word choice to 'confident.'

"Um," I started. "So, I won, right?"

"You wish," he laughed.

"We still have to get these to the butcher's."

"Right," Jax said. "You rift, I'll lift."

He roughly dropped my legs to set me back on the ground, holding fast around my waist for an extra second so I wouldn't fall.

I positioned myself beside a large fissure in the wall so I could see the pile of dragon carcasses on one side and the town on the other. From here, I could just make out the large, fenced-off space beside the butcher's shop at the base of the canyon wall.

I traced one last rune, pushing the entry portal open and placing the other over the top of the pen beside the butcher's. It was a good distance away, and I could feel my ether well draining fast, sapping my strength as I made the rifts wide enough.

My fingers trembled a little as I held the portal open for Jax as he telekinetically pushed the dragons and dreklings from the pile through my rift. I watched them drop one by one through the exit portal in the distance.

Sweat was beading along my hairline, and I could feel my head starting to throb as my ether supply got lower and lower. Finally, Jax pushed the last limp monster through.

With a gasp, I let my runes and portals go out. I pressed my fingers into my temples as a headache bloomed across my forehead.

"Hey," Jax said. "M, you alright?"

"Headache," I cringed.

"Drak. Ether overuse—I know what that's like."

I squeezed my eyes shut, lowering myself into a crouch. It didn't seem fair—Jax had burned at least as much ether as I had. More, actually, since he'd been using psionics during the battle earlier. Years of neglecting my ether well must've made it smaller. I'd have to keep practicing in order to expand it back to its proper size.

"I'm gonna give you one of these." Jax tossed back his cloak and fiddled with something attached to his belt. Soon he handed me a raw, white chunk of crystal about the length of my thumb, which he told me to tie to my belt beside my saltshaker.

"It's a quartz," he explained. "You can fill it with ether each morning at sunrise. Your well will replenish, and this'll hold the extra ether for about three days. I wish it could refill your well now, but only the magi who fills the crystal can access the ether inside it."

I nodded with gratitude, my head still pounding.

"For now, let's get you to the tavern," Jax said, putting a hand on my back. "You need water and some rest. Wouldn't be bad to splash a little water on your face, too. That always helps me."

I struggled to my feet, and with Jax's help, we began making our way back to the Broughkin Arms.

Jax was right. After chugging a few mugs of water and relaxing with my head in my hands for several minutes, I felt recovered enough to start dinner.

Before long, the seven members of Squad Reckless sat around our regular table in the tavern, enjoying crispy, flaky dragonbass and warm, buttery carrots, yellow scalesquash, and string beans. I was sure if I traced the Sight rune and watched them eat using my ethereal eyes, I'd see a contented aura running throughout the table as tender, savory bites melted in their mouths.

We were just putting down our forks after our second helpings when one of Commander Hildred's messengers opened the creaky tavern door. When she spotted our squad, she made her way over.

"Parcel just arrived for you, Heir Duke of Solhelm," she said, handing Brigan a small bag and a thick, creamy envelope with an orange seal bearing Keep Solhelm's insignia.

"What is it?" Edrea leaned closer to Brigan, her arm brushing against his as she peered at the bag.

Brigan didn't respond as he untied the string cinched around the top. He carefully pulled open the bag, and brilliant white light shone from within. Brigan reached inside to pull out a chunk of glowing crystal.

"Is that a skystone?" Edrea's eyes widened.

Brigan nodded, his face shining in the light from the stone. It was a fairly large crystal, about the size of a plum, which made it by far the most valuable object I'd ever seen in my life.

"What's it for?" Erik asked.

Brigan frowned, replacing the skystone inside the bag and retying the string with a double knot. "I'm not sure," he said it flippantly, and I didn't quite believe him. "I'm sure the letter explains it."

Brigan hastily reached for the envelope and peeled off the seal before anyone could press him about the skystone. He pulled out a fancy piece of stationary and began to read.

My friend's frown deepened as he scanned the letter's contents. The rest of us watched on with curiosity as the sounds of Cam licking his plate filled the silence.

Finally, Brigan looked up again, worry churning behind his warm, brown eyes.

"Brigan?" Solvai asked, cocking her head. "What's going on?""It's a letter from my father," he gulped, his tumultuous gaze coming to rest on me. "It appears my fiancée has been kidnapped."

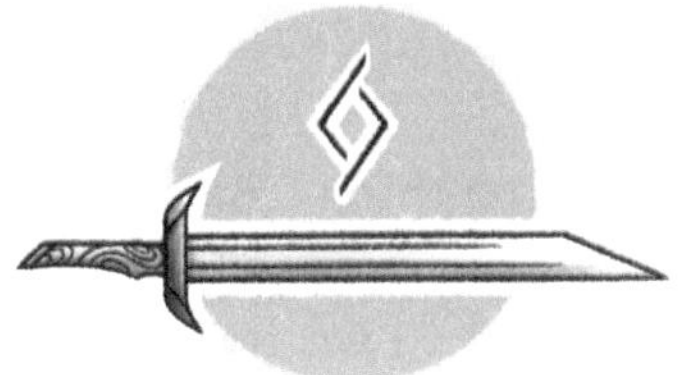

The squad uproared all around me, but I felt frozen in my seat at the tavern table. All this time, I thought I'd known Brigan pretty well. I'd found so much comfort, reassurance, even safety in his presence. Now, I wasn't sure what to think.

The skystone all but forgotten, the squad bombarded Brigan with questions. I looked away, not knowing what to say.

"How long have you been betrothed?" Edrea's question rose above the rest.

"Since I was a kid," Brigan said, the slightest waver in his usually confident voice. "I've only seen her three times in my life. We were supposed to meet again a few months ago just before we joined the guard, but they ended up having to change the date of their royal gala so I couldn't make it. I actually haven't seen her since we were fourteen."

I recalled how Brigan had been so strange and withholding with me whenever we were alone. Now I knew why.

Across the table, Edrea was staring at me, a darkly satisfied look on her face.

"She's been kidnapped?" Solvai said. "Is she alright?"

"I'm not sure," Brigan replied. "My father writes that her parents are telling their people that she's being held hostage by a pair of thieves from Drakfell's western outlands. Last they heard, they'd fled the Badlands Keepdom to only the goddesses know where."

Jax frowned from his place beside me. "What's the name of your fiancée?" He took a swig of water from his drinking horn.

Brigan's voice sounded formal as he answered. "Eliana, Princess of Drakfell."

Jax choked on his drink and began coughing uncontrollably. He took so long to compose himself that I was worried for a moment. Then he cleared his throat, leaning on the table and looking at us as if nothing out of the ordinary had happened.

"What?" Jax asked.

"We were wondering the same thing," Brigan said. We all stared at Jax, waiting for an explanation for his intense reaction.

"Uh…" Jax fumbled. "It's just, I… I was transferred from Drakfell, is all. Not that I've ever met the Princess. I mean, I've seen her once or twice from a distance I think, possibly. Possibly not, though—maybe she uses a body double. Heard she's a decent singer."

Jax's halting outburst earned him strange looks from the rest of the table. I couldn't help but wonder if, as a Knight of the Torch, Jax knew something more. Jax had confirmed to me that the rumor flying around the realm was true—that the Knights of the Torch had been behind Drakfell's decision to betray Evgard. Could that have something to do with Jax's odd response?

I nudged Jax with my elbow, raising an eyebrow. He looked at me with a sharp 'we'll talk later' kind of face.

"Anyway," Brigan said, scanning the letter once more. "With all that's been happening in Drakfell lately, my father says this kidnapping is the last scale."

"So are you engaged or not?" Edrea asked, subtly scooting closer to Brigan in a way that set my teeth on edge.

Brigan looked up from the letter, his eyes darting between my face and the intense way Jax was still looking at me.

"I wish I knew," Brigan answered, his words mirroring my thoughts exactly.

The next few weeks were filled with battling draconic creatures from the Mists and more practice sessions with Torsten. He'd laughed hysterically when he found out that I was using my rift hold as a spice cabinet, but was otherwise proud of my progress. I'd been diligently studying the runes whenever I got the chance, usually with the book open on the countertop while I was cooking dinner.

Solvai had been spending more time with Torsten as well. The other day, I'd caught a glimpse of her carving a block of wood on the tavern steps while Torsten offered her pointers from his rocking chair. She'd seemed at ease chatting with him, and I hadn't spied a bottle or draquila canteen anywhere near Torsten.

Brigan and I never really got the chance to talk about his tentative betrothal to the Princess of Drakfell—not that there was really much to say, anyway. I hoped at the very least that things would go back to normal between us soon. He seemed to be keeping his distance, but maybe he was just tired from all the battles.

The sun was high in the sky, and I was on my way to the dragon stables. Jax had agreed to meet me there to give me an update on when the Farseer would grant me an audience. I was starting to feel anxious about my half-baked plan to try and convince the legendary, red-robed Seer to break my parents out of prison.

I found Sniff inside the cavern, hanging upside down near a fissure in the ceiling. He must've sensed my presence too, because I'd no sooner set foot inside than he was spreading his wings and zipping toward me.

With an energetic yelp, Sniff tackled me in his usual way, licking my face as I lay in the dirt. I laughed and scratched him under the chin and behind the ears.

There were only a few other dragons in the cavern since most were out hunting or drinking from the river. The few who were still here slept soundly in nooks or crannies along the cavern walls.

I fed Sniff his favorite snack—ground peanut paste. He licked at the plate I'd brought him until it was sparkling. Then he settled down on the ground beside me while I leaned against his side and waited for Jax to arrive.

The sound of drums in my heart brought a smile to my face. I traced the rune for the Sight, and sure enough, I found Blink's spirit curled up beside me as well. Her shimmering, silvery body shone with the wisping clouds of her aura as she blinked up at me with large, dragonfire green eyes. I reached out to her and, of course, my physical hand fell right through her. But still, she gave me a contented, draconic smile as the rolling drumbeat through our bond made me think of a dragoncat's purr.

A pang of longing hit my heart. I wished Mom and Dad could meet my dragons. Dad and Dusty would get along well with Sniff—I could easily picture them throwing a ball together around the desert. Dad would love the thrill of soaring over the canyons on evrenback.

And Mom would love Blink's calm, proud personality. In another world, I imagined them spending hours together in companionable silence, Mom reading with Blink curled up at her feet.

I felt a lump rise in my throat as I realized that Mom would only be able to meet Blink if she used the Sight. Would she ever allow herself to use her power so informally?

If the Farseer truly could free them, perhaps we could flee to Northern exile ourselves. Or, better yet, maybe he could get my family to freedom in Skygard. If anyone could get us past the heavily guarded borders, it was the Farseer.

Just then, the sound of wings filled the cave as a second ascension green evren flew through the wide cavern mouth. With the rune for the Sight glowing over my forehead, her emerald aura fluttered behind her like swirling clouds. A vibrant orange aura clung to the dragon's rider, pulling my attention as if it were a magnet.

Jax alighted from his dragon Jade's back, then walked toward me. The low light in the cavern cast strong shadows along his jaw and shoulder muscles. Beside me, Blink played a couple of approving drumbeats through our bond in response to my quickening pulse.

I shot her a glare before I dismissed my rune, the bright colors all around me dulling to the normal shades of reality.

"Hey," I said, getting to my feet.

"Hey M," Jax looked around, making sure we were alone. Besides Sniff and Jade, the few other dragons in the cave remained fast asleep.

Still, Jax directed Sniff and Jade to lie on their stomachs, curving their large, scaly bodies around the two of us to create an extra barrier. Both dragons extended their four wings in order to create a sort of shell around Jax and me. The light shone through the translucent skin between their wingbones, shining onto us with yellow-and-green-tinted glows. The brisk, late autumn air couldn't reach us inside the warm cocoon.

Jax's voice was low as he spoke. "What have you found out from Torsten?"

"First," I said. "I've been meaning to ask you something."

Jax raised an eyebrow expectantly.

"The other day at dinner—I saw the way you responded to Brigan's announcement about his... uh... about the Princess of Drakfell. You know her, don't you?"

Jax chewed his lip. "Eliana. Yeah, I know her. Not as well as a few other Knights I could mention, but yeah."

"So? Who is she?" I asked, feeling a little embarrassed. For some reason, I felt like I was spying on Brigan just by asking.

"She's one of us," Jax said confidently. "A Knight of the Torch. That story about her being kidnapped is just a cover. Last I heard, she was actually making her way to the Mirror Forest in the Ridgeback Mountains to be trained as a true dragon rider."

I gaped. "She bonded a true dragon? But I thought the High King had the only true dragon left in Evgard."

But even as I said the words, I realized they weren't true. I'd seen another true dragon in Evgard myself—back on the Rise during the attack on the stables, just before everything had gone wrong.

I looked up at Jax, my eyes narrowing as I tried putting the pieces together. "The Princess... Was she traveling with two others?"

Jax frowned. "Yeah, why?"

"One wears way too much armor."

Jax looked at me with surprise. "That's Kai."

"And the other's a half-born in a turquoise scarf."

"Asher."

The way Jax spoke his name made me think they had a complicated history.

"So that was his name," I mumbled, blushing as I remembered sticking a seaxe in his face. Then I thought about the way he'd jumped on that explosive to try and keep his friends—and me—from getting hurt. So, this Asher was a Knight as well.

I told Jax what I'd seen outside of the command center. It felt good to get the story off my chest, since reporting the incident to the commanders hadn't seemed right. Now knowing that the thief, Asher, and his companions were Jax's fellow Knights of the Torch, I was relieved I hadn't run him through.

"Asher," I said, half under my breath.

Jax's jaw muscles tensed as he watched me say the thief's name. He hurriedly changed the subject.

"Enough about him—Tell me what you've learned from Torsten."

"Right," I shook myself out of the memory. "I already told you about the Gray Ones. How Torsten thinks they choose certain magi to be their vessels."

"Yeah. Whatever that's supposed to mean."

"And he believes they follow him. Like they've chosen him for something." I didn't say anything about how Torsten had mentioned the Gray Ones wanting to choose me as well.

"Yeah," Jax said, sounding impatient. "But what about the Coven? What's their plan, and who are they working with?"

"I'm still not sure," I admitted. "Torsten clams up every time I ask for more information."

"Drak," Jax swore.

"Yesterday he mentioned something about the Gray Ones following someone called the Liberator."

"Yes?" Jax's eyes lit up.

"But when I asked who the Liberator was, he made me practice tracing the false portal rune ten times with each finger."

Jax's face fell. "M, that's not enough. I need you to give me more."

"Or what?" I said, getting defensive. "Or you'll tell the Farseer not to see me? Back out on our deal?"

"Our deal was that you help me and I'll help you. I still can't tell the Knights what the Coven is planning."

"Great," I said sarcastically, raising my voice. "So it's only fair that you hold the Farseer over my head until I do."

"I don't control the Farseer," Jax's tone matched mine. "I can't drakking control anything about this whole stupid assignment, especially... especially..."

"Especially when you're working with someone as incompetent as me?" I said angrily. "Is that what you were going to say?"

"No," Jax snapped back. "I'm not blaming you. Calm down."

"I'm calm!" I practically shouted.

"Is that what you call this?" Jax gestured to me.

Sniff growled from his place behind my back and I could sense warning notes through our bond letting me know Jax was walking on thin ice. If Jax got me more upset, Sniff wouldn't sit idly by.

I took a deep breath, trying to relax myself the way Dad always tried to help Mom do. Again, I felt a lump rising in my throat when I remembered how Captain Zoren had forced them into cells nowhere near each other.

How was Mom managing without Dad? She was probably a mess, and I had to go and get myself sent to Outcast Outpost right when she needed me most.

I bit my lower lip to keep it from trembling. Jax's gaze softened, and he took a couple of steps closer.

"Look, I'm sorry," he said. "I realize I never asked why you wanted to see the Farseer in the first place."

I hesitated for a moment, but the earnestness in his midnight blue eyes opened the floodgates. The story of my parents' plight spilled out of me, from the day the Ursadon finally tracked us down just outside Keep Rengard to the day he all but assured me he'd never release them from Spydra Prison.

"So that's why I have to see the Farseer," I explained. "He's my only shot at getting them out of there. If he doesn't have the power, nobody does."

"Oh, he has the power," Jax said, nodding as I finished my tale. I felt my face growing warm inside our makeshift dragon wing tent.

"I hope so," I said quietly.

"And M," Jax said, his voice serious. "Even if the Farseer won't help your parents, I will. That's a promise."

My mouth fell open just a little as I turned to look him in the eye.

"What if I can't get the information you need about the Coven of the Gray Ones?" I whispered.

"Drak the Coven. Drak the Knights. Choosing light is part of the Knights' code, anyway. I can't think of a better way to do that than helping you save them." Jax moved a little closer, and I found myself subconsciously doing the same.

"Hello?" a voice called out from the dragon cavern entrance.

Sniff made an excited little noise, sticking his head up to get a better look at the newcomer. He and Jade pulled back their wings, tucking them in at their sides to reveal Jax and me standing nose to nose. Silhouetted in the mouth of the cave was Brigan, his orange drake, Bolt, at his side.

With a happy yelp, Sniff zipped over to Brigan, his dragon tongue hanging out of his mouth as he panted gleefully. Brigan gave Sniff a little rub on the nose before pulling a piece of dragon jerky out of his pocket and tossing it into my evren's mouth.

"Just here to drop off Bolt after her hunt," Brigan called, eyeing Jax and me. "I'll be gone in a moment."

I took a deliberate step away from Jax. "This isn't what you… uh… Jax and I were just discussing…"

I trailed off, feeling incredibly stupid. Brigan pressed his lips into a line as he came deeper into the cavern, leading Bolt to her usual place. About a week ago, Bolt had ascended, shedding her scales and becoming larger and stronger. Bolt's slender horns had more points on them now, and the ridges along her back were thicker. She was more powerful now, too, able to send a pulse of gold light across her scales to shield herself and Brigan against enemy attacks.

"Honestly, I don't really want to know what you two were discussing," Brigan pretended to be very busy with his dragon.

I hated seeing Brigan closed off like this. It wasn't like him.

"Brigan," I started, then faltered. I'd been about to tell him that his fiancée, the Princess of Drakfell, was going to be alright, hoping that might put him at ease. But then I realized that to reveal such information would be a breach of Jax's trust, and that was one thing I couldn't do.

Besides, something inside me didn't want to bring up Brigan's betrothed to him. The idea of him being with the dark-haired, sophisticated true dragon rider I'd seen behind the command center made me feel uneasy. Even defensive somehow.

"Yes?" Brigan turned around to look me in the eye. I was aware of Jax staring at me too, waiting to hear what I had to say.

Despite the cool air, with both Brigan and Jax's intense gazes on me, I suddenly felt overheated.

"Umm…" I said cleverly. I cast a sideways glance toward the cavern entrance, gauging just how humiliating it would be if I made a break for it with zero explanation.

I swallowed, looking back and forth between the two of them. I could've sworn I heard musical laughter, both flute and drum, inside my heart through my respective bonds with Sniff and Blink.

"Shut up," I said, my cheeks blooming when I realized I'd said it out loud. From where Sniff stood near Brigan, he gave a little draconic chortle.

"What?" Brigan cocked his head.

"Nothing," I rushed. "Just… Did I leave the oven fire lit? I'd better…"

I slowly shuffled toward the cavern entrance for a few steps. Then, my face ablaze, I made the most awkward exit of my life as I turned and fled the cave.

Chapter 21: Warning

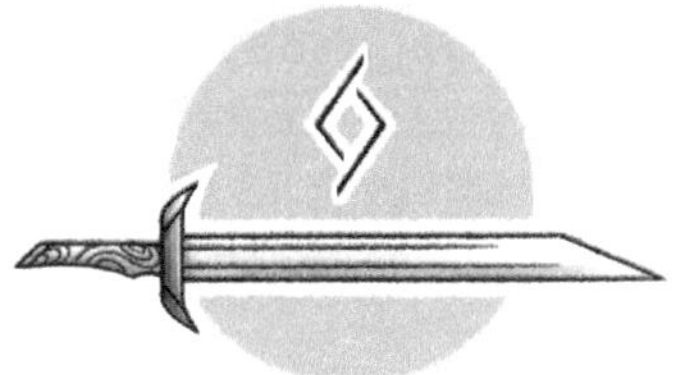

Not long after sunset, the rest of the squad headed to the barracks for the night. Meanwhile, I went across the canyon toward the Broughkin Arms. A quick skirmish with a wild starspitter wyvern that afternoon had kept me from my usual training session with Torsten, and I wanted to see if he had any time for one before bed.

I expected to find him outside in his wooden rocking chair. But when I arrived, the porch was empty.

The door creaked as I slowly pushed it open. Low torchlight lit the room, dancing ominously off of the orange hoodoos sprouting through the tavern floor. No patrons sat at the tables, leaving everything eerily silent.

I was about to shut the door and head back to the barracks when a single, empty bottle rolled out from behind the bar, clinking as it skipped across the floor. A low groan followed.

Worried, I hurried across the tavern. I found Torsten sitting sprawled on the floor, leaned up against the back side of the bar. More empty bottles surrounded him, and his eyes were glazed over and bloodshot, as if he'd been crying.

"Are you alright?" I knelt beside his feet, unsure what to do. A twinge of sadness ran through me as I took in the scene. Torsten had been doing so much better lately, turning down alcohol in favor of spending real, present time with Solvai.

"Meleya?" Torsten slurred. "Drak an' a half, what're you still doin' here?"

"We missed our training session today. I came to see—"

"No, no, no, no, no," Torsten threw his head back, pounding his fist against the wooden floor. "You can't be here. None of yous can."

I jumped backward a little. "Why?"

Torsten didn't answer. Instead, a low chuckle began in his throat, growing louder and more desperate until eventually he was doubled over with agonized, frightening laughter. I felt myself growing uneasy, almost wishing I hadn't come. But I was concerned about Torsten.

"S-see this?" Torsten stuttered, fumbling shaky fingers around his collar. He eventually managed to pull out a small wooden falcondrake charm, identical to the one that Solvai always wore around her neck. Though hers was worn smoother along the back and front from all the times she'd rubbed it while nervous or thinking.

"Made one'a these for my baby 'fore she were born," Torsten said, his eyes filling with fresh tears. "Thought she'd like it—were s'posed to be born in the month of the falcondrake star sign, y'see. But her mama done told me she buried her with it instead. Everythin'—my whole life—were s'posed to be different." Torsten let out a long sniff.

I spoke slowly and carefully. "You may have missed a lot with Solvai, but she's here now. And you still have Jax."

At the mention of Jax, Torsten's expression twisted. More of that wretched laughter filled the empty tavern as he fumbled for the nearest bottle. He tried to take a drink, but when he found it empty, he swore and flung it against the back wall. I scrambled back, covering my face as the bottle shattered into a thousand tiny shards.

Meanwhile, Torsten went back to crying. I carefully got to my feet. Making my way through the sea of broken glass, I retreated to the tavern kitchen where I kept a broom. I returned a short moment later and began meticulously sweeping fragments away from the area immediately around Torsten. As I cleaned, Torsten wept.

It took a while, but eventually I got every piece of broken bottle into a pile. I disposed of them in a waste barrel in the kitchen where I knew Torsten wasn't likely to go anytime soon. Then I started gathering the many other empty bottles surrounding him, lining them up carefully under the bar where he couldn't get to them without effort.

For a moment, I thought Torsten had fallen asleep. Then he suddenly sat straight up and pointed to the empty air.

"Oh, get the void outta here an' leave me alone for once, will you? Can't exactly seem to get myself to choose light right now, but I still choose nothin' over y'all," Torsten cried out. "An' tell your drakkin' friend to leave Jax alone, too. He don't want this."

Watching Torsten's outburst reminded me of what he'd said about the Gray Ones following him. Carefully, I took my place sitting in front of him, making sure to stay out of arm's reach. I took a shallow breath—I had to know what he was seeing.

Swallowing my fear, I lifted a finger to runetrace. The symbol for the Sight glowed in gold from my forehead, adding a little more light to the dim room.

Then I blinked.

I gasped at what I saw. Misty gray shadows—at least a dozen of them—hovered all around Torsten. Most were small, about the length of my forearm, lurking just beyond the churning clouds of his caramel-colored aura. Each little shadow had a pair of vivid, lightning blue eyes.

But one gray being stood out from all the rest. This one was larger, its cloudy gray mass taking the form of a man from the waist up. A blank face stared out over Torsten's shoulder, vivid blue eyes watching him.

"Gray Ones," I muttered, stumbling backward on my hands. Then I froze as I took in the rows and rows of bottles along the tavern wall. More, even smaller gray wisps clung to the bottles, concentrating most heavily around the ones still filled with alcohol. Their glowing blue eyes were narrowed, as if the creatures were just waiting to latch onto an unsuspecting patron.

I shivered, rubbing my arms. How had it suddenly gotten so cold in here?

Torsten shook his fist toward the largest Gray One, his voice cracking as he spoke. "I can't lose 'em both. I won't. The drakkin' Coven of the Gray Ones won't take 'em away from me."

At the mention of the Coven, my eyes widened. Shoving down the rising chill inside my chest, I leaned forward, waiting to see if Torsten would go on. When he didn't elaborate, I tried to push.

"What about the Coven?" I asked, doing my best to sound casual as I ignored the attention from the multitude of gray shadows.

Torsten turned his watery eyes my way, the red around them making the hazel color stand out. They were nearly the exact same shade as Solvai's eyes.

"Still a terrible liar, ya know," Torsten said with an affectionate guffaw. Despite everything, I stuck out my chin.

"Jus' promise me, Meleya," he said, his expression earnest. "You'll get yourself, Solvai, and Jax outta here by dawn. Head north back toward the Rise, or east toward the dunes. Jus' get out before sunrise."

"Why?" I said, a pit springing to life inside my stomach.

"That's when the Coven'll launch their attack on Outcast Outpost," Torsten's voice was grave. "I don't drakkin' care where you go, but I won't see the three of you in danger. Get the void outta here while you still can. The Coven will attack at dawn, an' they'll be comin' outta the Dragon Mists."

I didn't waste a second. I shut off the rune for the Sight, relief flooding me as I no longer had to see those cold, blue-eyed shadows, then raced from the tavern. It was very late, but I knew I needed to warn Jax—now.

A little out of breath from my sprint from the town side of the canyon back to the barracks, I flung open the door to the men's side.

The men of Squad Reckless stirred in their bunks as I rushed into their room. Brigan was already sitting up in his bed when I got there, but when he saw me walk in, a look of worry and confusion appeared on his face. Erik jumped a mile when he saw me, and Cam gave me an annoyed grunt before rolling over and shutting his eyes as if I were an obnoxious dream.

"M?" Jax said, rubbing sleep from his eyes as he propped himself up on one elbow. His blanket slid off his broad shoulder and fell around his waist, revealing a ridiculously toned chest and tight set of abs. My mouth fell open slightly, and an embarrassing, rosy blush spread across my cheeks. I was never more grateful for the low moonlight.

"What's going on?" Jax asked.

"Uh…" I started, shaking my head to focus. "It's your father. He told me what the Coven's planning."

Jax went on high alert, throwing off his blanket and hurrying to my side. I was relieved when I saw that he was wearing pants, but a thousand dragonflies raced into my chest as shirtless Jax came close.

"Shh," he put a finger to my lips. "Not with everyone here."

"This affects everyone!" I pushed his finger away. "We're all in danger. The Outpost—they're coming for it at dawn. They're coming to wipe us out and take it."

Jax's face went ashen. "Soot. That's not enough time to bring in rein-forcements."

I shook my head.

"I have to tell Solrac," Jax muttered, crossing the room in a few strides. I did a double take as Jax reached into a glass box with sand and a little juniper log at the bottom. When his hand emerged, it was holding a small, yellow gecko.

"What's that?" I asked.

"Three," Jax replied in a hurry. As if that was a sufficient explanation, Jax grabbed a sleeveless tunic and headed from the room with the little gecko in tow.

There was a short, stunned silence after Jax left, but within moments Brigan was at my side, his strong hand wrapping around my forearm.

"What's going on?" Anxiety colored his tone, and there were dark circles under his eyes.

His touch calmed my racing heart and cleared my head. "A dark magi coven will attack the Outpost at first light. I... I need to warn Commander Hildred."

Without hesitation, Brigan nodded. "I'm coming with you."

The commander was not pleased about being woken up by a magi. Having Brigan along certainly helped, and once he'd reasoned with her, Commander Hildred begrudgingly called an emergency meeting. Within ten minutes, the lieutenants, squad captains, and even the Mage Hunters, Trickshot and Mute, stood gathered together in the torchlit mess hall.

"And I'm just supposed to believe this drakking pseudo threat?" Commander Hildred snapped, folding her arms. "How do I know you're not in this sooty coven yourself, Misthaven?"

She said my birthplace like it was a dirty word. Brigan came to my defense.

"If she was, she wouldn't have gone out of her way to warn you of the threat," Brigan reasoned. Hildred narrowed her eyes at me, but otherwise kept silent.

"Her information checks out," Trickshot stood up as the attention shifted to her. "The Mage Hunters have been doing what we can to keep tabs on the Coven of the Gray Ones for years. Though we lost track of them a while back, their last known location was in one of their magi camps along Rengard's southern border. If they're somehow hiding in the Dragon Mists, it would make sense for them to be somewhere near here."

Hildred was still all but shooting dragonfire at me with her eyes. Trickshot took a step between the commander and me.

"Besides," Trickshot said. "I'm sure Mute would be happy to let you know what happens when you don't take threats seriously."

Trickshot gestured to her hunting partner, who waved a three-fingered hand at Commander Hildred.

Trickshot spoke earnestly. "If she's wrong and we're ready, we lose one night's sleep. If she's right and we're not ready, we lose everything."

Commander Hildred growled in her throat as she took in Trickshot's words. Then she stepped out in front of the lieutenants and squad captains.

"Wake the Outpost," she commanded. "Get the townspeople to start evacuating northward, up the canyon toward the Rise."

The lieutenants nodded, already making their way toward the doors as Commander Hildred gave her final order.

"Tell the soldiers to prepare for battle at dawn."

Chapter 22: The Coven of the Gray Ones

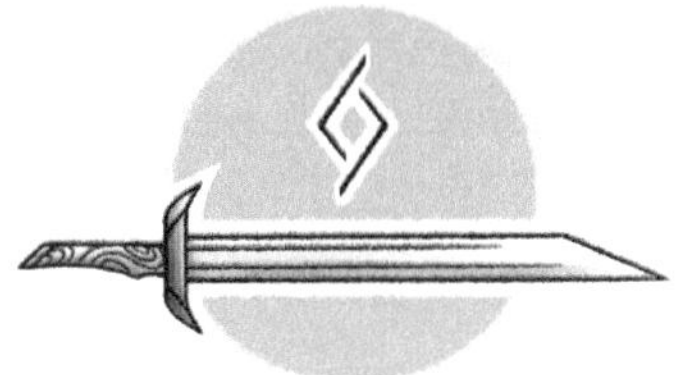

S quad Reckless had just stepped out of the armory and into the moon-lit night. All of us wore full battle armor, from our thick, drag-onleather chest pieces and shoulder pauldrons to the bracers and shin guards over our boots. I didn't normally like to fight with a helmet, but today all seven of us wore black helmets with shallow cheek and nose guards.

"Does everyone have their primary weapons?" I asked, looking every-one over.

The six soldiers nodded.

"Backup weapons?" I asked. Everyone nodded again, except Cam and Erik.

"That's okay, I snagged these while we were in the armory." I produced a tomahawk for Cam and a pouch filled with long iron darts for Erik. They were called flechettes, perfect for dropping on enemies from above.

"Now we've all got backup weapons," I continued. "Are they sharp-ened?"

The squad nodded once more.

"That leaves only one thing…" I held up a large sack filled with smaller sacks, each labeled with the names of my squadmates.

"What's this?" Jax asked, taking his sack.

"Breakfast," I replied. "And lunch, too. I'd suggest trying to get yourself to eat at least a little now before the battle—you never know how long it'll go. Then I thought the riders could put the rest in our dragons' saddlebags, Bolt's should have a little extra room for Solvai's and Chonk should for Edrea's—that way, we can make sure to keep our strength up no matter what happens out there today."

I finished my speech as I held out the last sack to Edrea. She eyed it and me with uncertainty.

"Your sandwich has extra cheese," I said, my arm still outstretched.

Edrea flashed one last look at my silvermarked cheek before gingerly taking the sack and looking away. I felt my heart grow warm. This was Edrea here—she might as well have just gushed about how grateful she was.

The squad dispersed to eat their breakfast and do their final preparations. Solvai, Brigan and I lingered behind.

We didn't say anything—we didn't need to. We just wrapped our arms around each other in a long embrace. I pressed my helmet into each of theirs.

When we finished, I saw Jax standing alone. He looked nervously toward the eastern canyon wall where the sun would soon be rising. I walked over to him.

"I couldn't get in contact with Solrac," Jax said, sounding forlorn. "I left a message for him, but even if it gets to him, there's no way the Knights can send backup by dawn. I'm on my own here."

I slipped my hand into his. "No you're not."

He looked down at me, his midnight blue eyes appearing black in the low moonlight. He squeezed my hand back, not letting go.

"I thought of a name for the battle we're about to fight," he said.

"A name?" I cocked my head.

"Something a Knight I know likes to do. He names all of our operations."

"Well?" I asked, and Jax smiled.

"M," he said. "Get ready for the one-time-only performance of 'The Outcasts Cast You Out.'"

The gray wash of the moments just before sunrise loomed over the Outpost. Our platoon of soldiers and dragons stood in formation atop the sorry wall, facing the Dragon Mists. It was a heavily clouded morning, with only a few breaks in the gray blanket that covered the sky.

Though the Outpost wall was no longer in the best shape, Commander Hildred and her lieutenants planned to use it to the fullest to keep the enemy at bay. Almost the entire platoon held scaleslayer crossbows as they stood lined up along the top of the wall, avoiding the places where the mud bricks had crumbled away. I leaned over, noting where Solvai and Edrea were stationed among them. Some soldiers perched on towers set at intervals, ballistae trained on the swirling white wall of mist.

The commander had ordered most of the drake riders to join the wall guard, with their mounts waiting below. At Commander Hildred's word, they'd hurry down the wall to their wingless dragons to act as cavalry should the need arise. Brigan and Cam were among these, their drakes at the gate on the ground. I hoped my squadmates wouldn't need to cross the wall onto the Dragon Mists side, but I wasn't counting on it. None of us knew what to expect when the sun rose.

I sat astride Sniff, in position with the rest of the aerial team. We stood atop the large launch platform on the far west side of the wall, ready to fly at any moment. I spotted Jax and his evren, Jade, near Sniff and me, while Erik and his wyvern, Eris, waited near the back of the group. We shifted nervously as the warm breath of our mounts turned white in the chilly morning air.

Nobody spoke, the silence thick across Outcast Outpost as we awaited the arrival of our enemy.

Before long, a single, clear voice pierced the air. From her place with the crossbow wielders, Trickshot sang into the silence, a war song I recognized as one the nomads used to sing on long, lonely nights in the canyons. It was an old song—they said it was older than Evgard itself, sung from the perspective of the three primal goddesses:

The dawn of battle comes
And with it strains of thunder
Take heart, dear soldier, we are with thee
Though realms be torn asunder

I joined Trickshot on the next verse, my voice harmonizing with hers:

Calm your troubled mind
Take up your sword, my brave one
For on the other side are with thee

Solvai, Edrea, and the rest of the female soldiers took up the song as well, while the men hummed a powerful note beneath our melody. Our voices rolled out across the battlefield as the first rays of sunlight threatened to stream over the canyon wall:

The creatures wail and cry
The ground below you trembles
The trees reach out to hold you, soldier
As friends and foes assemble

Though dark has been the night
The light of morning rising
Reach out, dear soldier, fill your heart now
With hope and love surviving

The last note lingered as we all held our breath. The sun rose over the cliffside, its light reflecting off the misty white wall for only a moment before dense clouds hid its face.

"For Evgard, unite!" Commander Hildred called out from drakeback as she paced the wall behind the crossbow wielders. She pounded one fist against her chest. As one, the platoon echoed the rallying cry.

"For Evgard, unite!"

The Mist answered us with a heavy, lone *thud.*

We shifted in our positions. This was it. Commander Hildred shot me a glance, acknowledging that I'd been right about the coming attack.

Another *thud* followed, then another, each one closer than the last. The loose pieces of brick around our feet shook with each *thud.*

A dark shadow appeared along the base of the Mists. We gripped our weapons tightly.

"Hold fire." Commander Hildred's order was tense.

Thud. The sounds drew closer.

Sniff let out a little whimper. I stroked the back of his neck, but how could I calm him down when I was just as terrified as he was of whatever lay just inside those mists?

A chitter sounded from behind me. I whipped my head around to see a little draccoon standing on his back paws, his beady black eyes wide as they watched the threat emerging from the Dragon Mists.

"Dusty," I whispered sharply. "Get out of here!"

The draccoon gave another squeak as another, much closer *thud* resounded. Dusty launched his furry little body toward me, latching onto my leg.

"You sooty little monster," I muttered, hurriedly stuffing him into one of Sniff's saddlebags. "Don't you dare get yourself killed."

Dusty squealed in agreement. He was an ethereal beast, which meant that even if he was killed, my father could remake him. But with Dad in prison, I didn't want to risk putting the little guy through any pain or danger.

With one last ground-shaking *thud*, the shadow was upon us. A dark line lay just beyond the last thin film of mist.

"Hold fire!" Commander Hildred called out once more.

We held our breath as the first enemy broke through the Mists into the cloudy, low morning light. The hairs on my arms stood on end as I peered over the wall to see a person dressed in a loose, hooded gray robe step out. They wore an ornate gray mask over their face, with sharp, black eye holes cut out of it. While I was too far away to read what it said, a word scrawled in white paint had been scratched across the mask. Sharp, terrifyingly beautiful, black dragon horns sprouted from their head.

They held no weapon, which was somehow more chilling than if they'd been wielding the largest, most menacing dragonforged blade in the realm. Suddenly, the person looked up at our platoon along the wall, and the eye holes in their mask glowed to life with otherworldly lightning blue light. The same light I'd seen before in the eyes of umbral creatures.

The person lifted both hands, gently holding them out to either side.

Then, all at once, the enemy army emerged from the Dragon Mists.

More hooded, gray-masked people came charging out from the white wall, wielding a variety of weapons from halberds to long seaxes to magi staffs. Some had words scratched into their masks, while others' masks were plain. Those with words had those same glowing, bright blue eyes.

Accompanying the masked army were dozens and dozens of umbral creatures. Smoky, gray dragon bears, ridgerunners, and all three kinds of dragons roared and howled as they raced across the battlefield toward the wall. More masked enemies rode the umbral dragons.

We saw the source of that heavy, ominous thudding sound as well. An umbral dragonelk as tall as the Outpost wall we stood on thundered through the Mists, shaking its wide, twisting set of antlers and sending wispy gray smoke trailing through the sky around its head. I remembered the unnaturally gigantic dragon Captain Zoren had fought the day the dragon stables burned. It had grown itself to giant size using geomancy. I had the feeling this nearly canyon wall-sized elk had done the same, taking on the aspect of a mountain. It opened its mouth and let out a high-pitched, bloodcurdling wail.

Several soldiers around me clapped their hands over their ears, and our dragons shifted nervously beneath us. Sniff shrank back as well, sending warning notes through our bond. I felt a strong, encouraging thrumming from Blink, helping to calm him down.

With a violent yell, Commander Hildred gave the order. "Fire!"

We cried out with all the courage we could muster as we showered crossbow bolts down on the masked, shadowy, gray and lightning blue army. One or two went down, but many raised shields to protect them-selves. Still, most of the bolts made sharp turns as enemy Psions stopped them all at once, sending our bolts harmlessly into the dirt.

"Next round, fire!" Commander Hildred barked, and more of our sol-diers stepped in with their readied crossbows while the first group re-loaded. The enemy kept coming, and there was nothing to stop their Psions from stopping the next volley as well. Meanwhile, a few of the gray-hooded magi stretched out arms or weapons toward the wall, blast-ing it with bolts of lightning. The lightwielding blasts shook the wall beneath our feet, and several soldiers had to brace themselves to keep from falling through the cracks.

My heart sank. We were trained to fight dragons, not a standing army of magi like this.

In addition to the force coming at us from below, there was the cluster of flying dragon riders swooping our way from above.

"Don't let their flyers breach the wall!" Commander Hildred bellowed.

In response, I heard our flight leader call out over the din, "Wyvern and evren riders! Attack formation!"

Sniff's wings hummed as we rose into the air alongside the other aerial dragon riders. As a unit, we took off from the wall's launch pad and shot toward the approaching enemy.

We were far less trained in fighting as a unit, since we'd always fought as teams of seven within our squads. The variety of weapons and positions in a squad was more effective against the sporadic attacks from wild dragonkind. But the consequence of peace between the Keepdoms was that it had been years since soldiers of Rengard had gone up against another army of people.

While the rest of the platoon defended the wall, we met the hooded gray army of flyers in the air. They just about matched us in number, with many riders wielding long, bladed, runemarked staffs. Those blank masks stared back at us as the riders trained their staffs on us, each one glowing with the same lightning blue energy as the runes over their foreheads.

Soot. There were so many magi.

That blue energy concentrated at the bladed ends of their staffs—then they opened fire.

Arcs of blue energy shot toward us like a meteor shower, hitting many of our front line's dragons. The dragons didn't roar in pain, but rather wavered mid-flight, unstable. It was as if the Mystic's mini meteors somehow made them more tired. I wracked my brain, remembering something from Torsten's runebook that now sat in my tunic pocket—were they called dream darts? Though, those were supposed to be purple, not this strange, umbral blue. Just what were these magi, anyway?

Our flight leader raised his shield to block one headed for his face, but dream darts weren't affected by physical objects. The dart soared straight through his shield, blasting him in the forehead. He slumped forward in his saddle, eyes closed.

With a panicked roar, the soldier's wyvern dove out of formation to try and get him to safety, leaving us without a leader.

As more glowing blue dream darts shot at our flight, riders and dragons alike fought to stay in the air. The enemy trained their staffs on us, preparing for their next volley.

Without thinking, I urged Sniff forward, weaving between our fellow flyers until we reached the front of the pack.

By the time we got there, I'd already traced one of the many new runes Torsten had been drilling into my head. It glowed with golden light over my forehead as I focused to access my ether well.

I spread my arms wide, leaving myself open to oncoming dream darts as nine small, gold-rimmed portals ripped to life between the masked dragon riders and my fellow soldiers.

I positioned the portals to intercept the entire round of blue dream darts. There may have been nine entry portals, but I'd only formed one exit, aimed straight back at the Coven of the Gray Ones' lead flyer.

All the blue darts merged into one as they blasted the masked magi. The magi's head lolled, and they dropped their staff as they slipped from their dragon's back, their robes fluttering as they fell to the earth far below. The magi's umbral dragon didn't seem to care enough to even try to catch them, a sure sign that they'd been bonded to the magi by force.

A loud whoop pulled my attention to Jax flying nearby. He cupped his hands around either side of his mouth and called out.

"That's the M I'm talking about!"

I couldn't help but smile, but there wasn't time to celebrate. Our crossbow-wielding flyers were opening fire back at the Coven. One inky gray dragon roared as it took a bolt directly in the vulnerable place where its heartscale once grew, sending both dragon and rider spiraling downward. I traced the bolt's trajectory back to Erik, and I felt a small rush of pride.

As the two aerial battalions met in the cloudy sky, the real battle began. Spears and long seaxes clashed with bladed staffs and the Coven's other weapons as we fought from dragonback. I bit back emotion as orange cloaks fell to gray hoods.

Sniff moved fast as he and I zipped from enemy to enemy, trying to land a solid hit. Out of the corner of my eye, I caught a flash of green from Jax's dragon, Jade. Jax had his usual gold psionic rune alight over his forehead as his axes telekinetically spun through the air. His hands made yanking motions as he wrenched Coven members' staffs from their hands and flung them away.

I saw Erik as well, his pale dragon nearly invisible against the clouds as they flew high to drop flechettes down onto the Coven. Erik's aim was precise, and the sharp, heavy projectiles showered the enemy.

I looked down when I heard a cry from the ground. A masked magi directly below me had fallen, while from my saddlebag came a maniacal chitter.

Dusty must've stolen a bag of flechettes of his own. Every so often, he peeked out from his place in Sniff's saddlebag to fling another down on the gray hoods.

"Good draccoon," I said right before coming face to mask with a new foe. He flew just above us so that he could get a good angle on me without our dragons' wings tangling.

I raised my sword to block his spiked halberd. From here, I was close enough to read the white writing etched onto his mask. A shudder ran through me as I read the moniker: *The Ghost.*

I pressed back on the halberd, rapidly slashing straight through the masked person's middle. They didn't even bother blocking or dodging my strike, and I quickly realized why.

My blade passed right through them as if they were incorporeal. I cursed—was this some kind of shadowbinding etherarchy? Suddenly, the title 'Ghost' made sense.

I sliced toward the Ghost a few more times to no avail. Each strike went through them as if I were hacking at a fog bank. They relaxed during my offensive swings while I had to expend energy blocking all of theirs.

In the air downward and to my left, I caught sight of another Coven magi about to blast one of my flight mates with another blue dream dart. That gave me an idea. Acting quickly, I threw up a large rift between the Ghost and me.

I pushed the portal toward the Ghost, trapping him inside my portal against his will. He came out, dragon and all, at the other end, which I'd placed directly in front of that freshly-charged dream dart.

The other magi's dream dart took the Ghost in the chest at point blank range. The Shadowbinder slumped in his saddle. Even a ghost isn't immune to powers affecting his spirit.

As I scanned the battle, both in the air and back at the wall, I realized things were not playing out in our favor. That enormous shadow elk had used its wide, rock-solid antlers to take out a section of our wall. Several soldiers had fallen, with little chance of surviving a drop like that. Tension appeared in my jaw when I couldn't spot Solvai or Edrea right away.

Meanwhile, Commander Hildred had already called in the cavalry. I spotted Brigan and Cam amidst the drake riders thundering through the Outpost wall gate. They greeted the Coven on the ground as the enemy worked to break through the wall near the arch where the river passed under. The Coven turned on them, and I watched in horror as Outcast Outpost guards took psionically-charged daggers to the chest or had eerie blue lightwielding bolts shock them off the backs of their dragons. I felt my stomach drop as an enemy Woodweaver brutally strangled one of our soldiers in tangled, thorny vines. That soldier had been right next to Cam.

We were in way over our heads. We were the dragon guard, not Mage Hunters.

Just then, I heard a yelp from high above my head. When I looked up, I saw a Coven magi had found the sharpshooter who was taking down so many of their fellow flyers. A masked Astromancer had a blue-tinged starglass sword trained on Erik as they held him by the scruff of his cloak. Erik's dragon snapped at the magi, but more starglass materialized along Eris's jaw, holding the wyvern's mouth shut.

I'd opened a new portal in less than a second, leaping off of Sniff's back to jump through it. I reappeared—much to the Astromancer's surprise—atop their wyvern directly behind them in the saddle. They dropped Erik as I held my seaxe at their throat. I'd have dispatched them then and there, but they tucked their chin downward, blocking my blade with the bottom of their metallic mask.

It was hard to tell under the loose robes, but the Astromancer was probably a man, and had no trouble using his superior strength to wrench my sword arm away. He twisted in the saddle to face me, and I read the title written in white on his gray mask: *The Shardmaker.*

He reeled back his fist for a punch, and I saw more of that blue-tinged starglass sprouting from each of his knuckles to form sharp blades. I doubted I could runetrace fast enough to stop his blow.

I ducked, and at the same time, the dragon below us jerked. The Shardmaker's fist went awry, missing my face but scraping across my pauldron and down my arm. I cried out as his blades cut along my upper arm and blood soaked into my sleeve.

The dragon twisted violently in the air again, and I realized it had taken a perfect shot from a crossbow to the eye. My distraction had given Erik time to reload.

As the Shardmaker and his dragon fell, I bit back my pain and rapidly got to my feet. I launched myself off of the saddle and into the air, my next rift swallowing me. It dropped me into place right behind Erik, straddling his wyvern, Eris.

"Meleya!" Erik said, surprised. "Your arm—Are you okay?"

"Barely felt it," I replied, the battle adrenaline coursing through me making my claim almost true. "Are *you* okay?" I asked.

"I think so," Erik nodded. "I didn't know how to engage them."

"Here," I said, reaching into my boot. I pulled out my father's antler-handled dagger and passed it to him. "Sometimes you need a backup backup weapon."

Erik took the dagger, then gave me the guard's salute. I saluted him back before rifting myself back into Sniff's saddle.

So many orange cloaks lay still across the battlefield in the shadow of the Dragon Mists.

Hardly any soldiers remained on the wall, either having fallen because of the antlers of the giant elk, or else having joined the ground troops in trying to stop the Coven from breaking through. I watched the elk tear through another section of the bricks right near where Commander Hildred still stood giving orders. She and her drake leaped from the wall even as that section crumbled, her dragon using its lizard-like claws to race straight down the side while Hildred clung on for dear life.

Many of our fallen had gray splotches from umbral bites crawling along their skin. The gray hoods swarmed our meager platoon, outnumbering us three to one, not even counting the umbral creatures who fought alongside the faceless army.

I caught sight of Trickshot and Mute's dusky blue Mage Hunter's cloaks below. Mute fought off Coven magi as Trickshot hurried from soldier to soldier, searching for any it wasn't too late to save. She was bent over a struggling guard when a masked magi wielding a blue-tinged starglass mace swung toward her. Mute was busy engaging a different gray-hooded warrior, but Trickshot was fast, stopping the mace with her silver Mage Hunter's sword.

My eyes widened as her silver blade blocked as it would any other weapon. That shouldn't have been possible—the starglass should've shattered on impact. Silver always stopped etherarchy. But then I remembered what Torsten had said during our first training session:

Gray Ones even have the ability to make us immune to silver, like the Guardians of old.

Was this what he was talking about? The Coven of the Gray Ones' strange blue etherarchy?

Trickshot may not've been able to shatter the magi's starglass, but she was still the fastest shot in the south. She whipped out the mini crossbow at her hip and downed the magi with a bolt to the neck.

The guards on the towers had already shot the last of the Outpost's scant supply of chained harpoons at the giant dragonelk. The creature shook its head, the long chains slipping from its antlers to crash on the ground at its hooves.

The umbral elk gave another one of those heinous, bloodchilling wails as it thrashed its enormous, rock solid antlers against the Outpost wall again. The stones gave way, sending most of the wall, as well as the soldiers on the towers, falling. Cheers erupted from the Coven's fighters below.

I gripped the hilt of my blade, unsure what to do next. The dragonelk was doing too much damage. As long as that monster was alive, we didn't stand a chance.

Apparently, I wasn't the only one who thought so. With a flash of orange scales, Brigan and Bolt charged toward the back hoof of the enormous dragonelk.

Bolt leaped, her powerful second ascension claws latching onto the creature's leg. She bit down hard, sending crackles of golden lightning up the scaly surface of the elk's skin. The giant beast seemed mildly annoyed, but not badly hurt. It shook its hind leg and Brigan and his dragon flopped onto the ground between its stomping cloven hooves.

I screamed, runetracing as fast as I could. I had to get him out of there.

Sniff and I shot through our exit portal beneath the scaly super elk just as Brigan and Bolt got back on their feet. Before another massive, heavy hoof had the chance to smash us to a pulp, Brigan and I rode our dragons through my next portal.

We came out in a small clearing on the battlefield between the elk and the bulk of the fighting. Brigan took one look at my bloodied sleeve and blanched.

"Meleya," he said, his brows knitting.

"I'm fine," I assured him.

Solvai was running up to us, and I breathed a sigh of relief to see her alright. Edrea was close behind her, followed by Cam riding up on his thick-skinned drake. My scream must've alerted my fellow flyers, because within moments Jax and Erik were landing at our side as well. I was both shocked and thrilled that all of Squad Reckless was still in one piece. Battle bruised, but alive.

"The ranks are falling apart," Brigan said, observing the field.

"We don't stand a chance," Edrea added.

Solvai's voice was firm and grounded. "If we can take out the giant dragonelk, we might."

"Impossible," Edrea declared.

"Maybe," Solvai agreed. Then our squad captain set her jaw and started barking out orders.

Chapter 23: The Dragonelk

"Cam and Edrea," Solvai's tone was determined as she addressed our squad. "Take Chonk and get to those harpoon chains on the ground over there. See if you can get them tied around the elk's legs so we can topple it."

Solvai turned to Jax and Erik next. "You two are our best shots. Wait for Cam and Edrea to slow the elk down, then head underneath its body. See if you can take it in the chest or stomach where it's most vulnerable."

My squadmates nodded, hurrying to obey Solvai's orders. My heart swelled as I watched her lead.

"What about the three of us?" Brigan asked.

Solvai's hazel eyes stormed. "We're gonna give it the void from above."

Solvai explained her plan, and we nodded. Brigan, Solvai and I exchanged determined looks, trying not to dwell on the very real possibility that this thing might kill us.

"Ready?" Solvai asked. In response, I runetraced, tearing a wide portal in the air.

Gold glowed from my forehead as together, Solvai, Brigan, and I charged through the portal.

We came out on top of the gigantic umbral elk's head, right between its antlers. Brigan and Bolt clung to its face, Brigan's seaxe poised, while Sniff and I flew to get a better angle on its neck. Meanwhile, Solvai climbed up to the lowest rung of the creature's antlers, holding onto it with one hand for balance. With her dark hair streaming out behind her as she brandished her dragonhook spear, Solvai looked like a war hero from the old legends.

With the leverage from her higher position, Solvai stabbed her spear downward into the dragonelk's head. The beast raged, thrashing from the pain. From the place her spear stuck, shadowy gray smoke poured upward. But the creature's skull was so thick that Solvai's strike hadn't killed it.

Below, Cam and Edrea worked together. Solvai had been wise to send Edrea as well, because from her place behind Cam on Chonk's saddle, I could tell she was the one strategizing and giving orders while Cam executed them. Using a harpoon chain with one end already pinned beneath heavy fallen stone from the wall, they carefully timed their attempts to wind the other end around the umbral monster's front legs. Cam and Chonk pulled tight, stopping the elk in its tracks.

That gave Jax and Erik clear shots at its underbelly. From my position at the elk's side, I could tell their arrows and axes were doing some damage. Not enough to send the umbral creature wisping away into the breeze, but from the streams of smoke seeping upward from below, I could see that they'd at least started the process.

Meanwhile, Sniff was sneezing up a storm, sending ether darts flying at the dragonelk's thick neck. White, spiraling ether marks burst across its gray scales, and I could tell by its forthcoming wail that the creature was in serious pain. I put up another portal and shoved my hand through, my blade slashing across its neck at close range. The elk huffed, and the wound smoked with umbral mist, but still, my blow didn't down the giant.

A moment later, I heard a strange noise, like crystal shattering. When I looked up, I saw Brigan had thrust his seaxe directly into the umbral elk's lightning blue eye as Bolt clung to its giant cheek. Chunks of what looked like blue crystal exploded from the site before wisping into the wind all around Brigan.

The dragonelk howled with more rage than I'd seen from it thus far. It thrashed its whole body violently, and my heart leaped as I saw the force throw Brigan from his dragon's back. Runes glowed from my forehead, draining my ether well more than I would've liked as I reached toward Brigan. My portal caught him as he fell, the other end spitting him out safely—if a little ungracefully—on the ground.

At the same time, the rattle of chains tipped me off that Cam and Edrea had lost their hold on the giant umbral beast. Hearing Edrea scream, Sniff and I zipped down the creature's side to see that she'd somehow gotten caught beneath the creature's enormous, stomping, cloven hooves.

Sweat beading along my hairline, I threw up another portal and launched off of Sniff's back to get through it. Time seemed to slow as I emerged through the exit portal at Edrea's side, right as the elk's massive front hoof was coming down toward our heads.

My second entrance portal was only a few feet away. I tackled Edrea through it, just avoiding getting smashed.

We stepped out of Etheria right beside Brigan. Bolt was with him—she must've come down to make sure he was alright. Without thinking, I shoved Edrea to safety in Brigan's arms. I just caught the way her cheeks flushed at his touch before I jumped through my next portal. As I landed back in Sniff's saddle, I could feel a headache blooming along my temples and forehead. Soot, my ether well was getting low.

"Meleya!" Solvai's voice sent Sniff and me flying back to where my friend was clinging to the elk's antler with all her might. A splintered half of her dragonhook spear stuck out of the elk's head, the other half nowhere in sight. This wasn't working—It was time for me to get her out of there.

I tried to get close enough to pull her onto Sniff's back behind me, but between the bright yellow wings and thrashing dragonelk antlers, I couldn't close the distance quick enough. I'd have to rift again.

"Wait," Solvai called as I lifted a finger to runetrace. "Get to the side so you can see its feet!" She yelled out the rest of her plan.

I didn't like it. With my ether well so low, I didn't know if I'd be able to pull her out in time.

"Go!" Solvai ordered.

There was no time to analyze better options. Sniff and I zipped to the umbral dragonelk's side. My headache intensifying, I opened a giant, hoof-sized portal right below the dragonelk's front hoof as it prepared to stomp down.

My hands shook as power coursed through me. Seeing stars, I put the other end of the rift directly above the elk's thick neck.

Its hoof came crashing down through the portal, and a sickening crack echoed across the battlefield as the creature snapped its own neck.

The umbral elk's shadowy body began to dissolve as it fell. Already, I could see through its chest enough to catch a glimpse of an enormous, glowing, crystal core. Soot, the blue gem that was once the beast's heart was nearly as big as I was. From her place atop its head, I saw Solvai holding on with all her might.

Panic rose within me—I could sense my ether well was down to dregs. I doubted I had enough for even one more portal.

Then I remembered the quartz Jax had tied to my belt to hang beside my saltshaker pouch. At his instruction, I'd been refilling it with ether every few days.

Clasping the quartz, I felt a surge as the ether inside it flowed through my body and up to my head. The golden rune hovering just above my eyes pulsed with renewed life.

The portal opened before Sniff and me, and we didn't waste a second before launching through.

We shot out the other end, surrounded by the curling, gray shadow that was once the elk's head. Solvai flailed about, struggling to cling to the vanishing wisps. With a light thud, she landed behind me on Sniff's back. I reached behind and grabbed onto her cloak to keep her from slipping off.

We landed beside where Jax, Erik, and Cam had joined Brigan and Edrea. Our whole reckless squad watched in awe as the beast's enormous, blue gemstone core fell to the earth with a heavy thud, then faded to white before our eyes. All around it, the last remnants of the shadowy gray giant disintegrated into the rushing wind.

For a moment, everything was still. We'd just done the impossible—maybe the Outpost had a chance.

But with the umbral elk's body gone, we could see the rest of the battle, and I realized just how wrong I was. Everywhere I looked, I saw orange cloaks lying still at the feet of gray hoods.

The remainder of our forces were gathered by the crumbling wall near us, giving the fight their all. Commander Hildred swung her massive dragonforged warsword relentlessly from her drake's back as she downed another gray-hooded enemy.

Across the field, the masked warrior with the draconic horns sprouting from their head seemed to spot us. It was the first gray hood to come through the Dragon Mists. Perhaps they recognized us as the ones who'd just taken down their giant umbral monster. I swore I could feel their gaze.

It quickly became clear why the warrior fought with no weapon. They crouched low, placing a hand on the ground. Lightning blue Sentinel patterns flowed up their hand and arm, glowing strongly enough to shine through their gray clothing. A blue mist surrounded them as they transformed into a vicious, pitch black wyvern.

Wildshaper.

The magi used their wyvern form to breathe blue-tinged dragonfire in a circle all around them. I drew a sharp, horrified breath as the dragonfire charred and downed every soldier within range.

The wildshaping wyvern gave a ferocious roar, then took off into the air, flying straight toward our squad. On their way, they used their hind claws to seize more orange-cloaked soldiers and throw them violently back to the earth.

Our squad scrambled as the wyvern approached. I leaped between it and my team, prepared to use my last bit of ether to defend them. Not to my surprise, Solvai stood by my side. Though she no longer held her dragonhook spear, she bravely wielded her backup tomahawk against the Wildshaper.

As the wyvern landed, more bluish mist engulfed it as it transformed back into its gray hooded, human form. From this close, I got a better look at the white writing on their mask.

The Liberator.

So this was the Coven's leader. The one Torsten had spoken of with both fear and reverence.

The Liberator stalked closer to Solvai and me, their weaponless presence filling my heart with dread. If they'd wielded a spear or a seaxe, I'd know how to fight them. Not knowing what they planned to do sent my pulse racing with terror.

The Liberator slowly turned their masked face toward me, then Solvai, as uncanny shivers made the hairs on my arms stand on end.

Then, all at once, more blue clouds encompassed the Liberator. When the clouds dispersed, they'd shifted into a terrifying, spiny black drake.

Solvai and I prepared to swing, but rather than leap at us, the drake dove toward the wall.

The beast was on Commander Hildred in seconds. The Liberator raked their draconic claws toward the commander, nearly catching her across the chest.

But Commander Hildred's own drake wasn't about to let the Liberator get to his rider. He reared back, sending Commander Hildred rolling to the ground as he engaged with the Wildshaper.

The two drakes roared, snapping at each other and swiping with their sharp, clawed forelegs. After a violent tangle, the Liberator opened their jaws to breathe a hot gust of dragonfire into the commander's dragon's face. The Liberator used the painful distraction to thrust their claw into the other drake's chest.

Without another sound, Commander Hildred's drake thudded lifelessly to the ground.

The commander cried out, her dragonfire green eyes filling with tears of agony and rage. She got to her feet, and her heart seemed to break as she took in the sight of the battlefield. Nearly no orange-cloaked soldiers still stood.

One look told her the battle was lost. That left only one option.

"Retreat!" Commander Hildred yelled.

After the Coven broke through the Outpost wall, an army of umbral creatures had rushed in, blocking us from retreating back toward the canyon by way of the shanty town. Because of that, Commander Hildred led the survivors east.

To everyone's shock, the Coven of the Gray Ones didn't pursue us in our escape. A few gray hoods tried, leveling crossbows or dream energy-charged staffs toward our backs. But as we fled, the Liberator stood between us and them, raising a gloved hand to stop their pursuit. That should've been a relief, but the way the Liberator and the others silently watched us disappear around the edge of the canyon filled me with a growing sense of dread.

The survivors trekked eastward toward a secluded southern entrance to the Narrows. The slot canyon mouth stood dangerously near the Dragon Mists, and I remembered from our squad's turn on duty at the North Tower that the other end let out further along the main canyon. Hopefully, we could hike through the Narrows in order to retreat back to the Rise.

Once we'd reached the mouth of the Narrows, I realized just how few of us had survived the battle. Besides the commander and her lieutenants, I was relieved to see Trickshot and Mute. But as I looked at the twenty-something soldiers left, I saw that Squad Reckless was the only squad still completely intact.

I remembered the way the Coven leader, the Liberator, had stopped before destroying us. I had no doubt they could have. It didn't make sense.

The weight of what had just happened hung over the group, heavier than the gray clouds in the sky overhead. We'd lost Outcast Outpost.

Without the border guard, the Rise was vulnerable. We'd failed to protect our post. What would happen to Keep Rengard now? Or to us?

Commander Hildred breathed heavily, one hand on a large boulder near the slot canyon entrance. Her choppy, short hair fell all around her face as she looked at the ground.

"Drak you," she muttered. "Drak you, ethercursed."

When she looked up, her green eyes were rimmed with red, her face set in rage.

"I saw the way that scorching Coven leader left you unscathed," Commander Hildred pointed an accusing finger at me. Then she gestured toward all of Squad Reckless. "They left all of you alone because two of you are their own. Sooty magi." Hildred spat on the ground.

"Meleya and Jax aren't—" Trickshot spoke weakly, nursing a bad wound on her arm as she advanced toward the Commander. But after losing her drake, Commander Hildred was in a frenzy. She used her height and bulk to shove Trickshot to the ground, whipping out her oversized dragonforged warsword. Mute knelt beside Trickshot, looking her over to make sure she was alright.

"Not today, Mage Hunter," the commander snapped. "It's up to me to do your job for you."

Commander Hildred took a menacing step closer to Jax and me. "Lieutenants," she barked. "Strip them of their uniforms. They are no longer soldiers of Rengard."

For one brief moment, the lieutenants paused, and I wondered if they'd defy the commander like Trickshot had. Then, slowly, one lieutenant walked toward us, singing that old, chilling magi hunting song. The other lieutenant joined in the song, followed by several other survivors, though none from Squad Reckless, not even Edrea.

Neither Jax nor I protested as the lieutenants obeyed the order, singing in chorus with the others. They took our orange cloaks, dragonleather armor, and even our weapons, leaving us in just our tunics, pants, and boots. The air felt cold through the cloth. Without the rush of battle, I could suddenly feel the hot pain in my upper arm from my wound from the Shardmaker.

I felt a small wave of relief when the soldiers didn't take my belt, where both my saltshaker and empty quartz crystal still hung. But my relief was nothing compared to the panic rising in my chest. If the commander kicked me out of the army, what did that mean for my parents?

Then, without warning, the lieutenant's song got louder as he grabbed hold of the heartscale that hung at my collarbone. He was so focused on the bright yellow scale that he didn't notice that I wore a second, longer cord around my neck, and I felt another ounce of gratitude knowing I wasn't about to lose Blink as well. The lieutenant used a dagger to cut the cord, taking Sniff's golden heartscale from me. Almost immediately, I felt my bond with Sniff dull to almost nothing.

From where he stood behind me, Sniff let out a roar in protest. He reached out his forewing.

"Restrain him!" Commander Hildred snarled, and the other soldiers obeyed, pinning Sniff's four wings to the earth.

"Don't hurt him!" I cried. Beside me, Jax looked just as horrified as they confiscated Jade's heartscale from him as well.

"Jax of Blackfjord and Meleya of Misthaven," Commander Hildred barked, her words punctuated by the magi hunting song the other survivors still sang. She stalked toward us with her warsword, which was soaked in both copper and red blood from battle. "You are hereby ejected from the guard of the Canyon Keepdom. Furthermore, as magi, you're banished from the realm."

She set her angry jaw, then used her sword to gesture toward the wall of white mist that rose up only a short distance away.

"No," Jax said, realizing what the commander was ordering us to do. "We can't—nobody can survive in there."

"Soldiers," Commander Hildred seethed. "If the ethercursed don't flee, I order you to dispatch them." To my horror, many soldiers unsheathed their seaxes and loaded their crossbows as Commander Hildred went on. "If you don't, I will."

She held up her bloodied warsword, ready to strike. I had no doubt she wouldn't hesitate to use it.

Jax must've thought so too, because he grabbed me by the hand. He yanked me along with him toward the Dragon Mists as we fled the still singing survivors.

I cast one last look over my shoulder at Brigan and Solvai's stunned, terrified faces. Near the commander, Trickshot struggled to her feet, taking aim at Jax and me with her crossbow.

"Meleya!" she cried out, pulling the trigger.

Jax yelped, but I understood. I didn't have much ether left, but I rune-traced quickly enough to catch her bolt in a small portal, dropping it through the exit end into my hand.

Grimacing, I gripped the bolt that would be our only weapon against the danger that awaited us.

Then, hand in hand, Jax and I disappeared through the white wall and into the Dragon Mists.

REFLECTION 3

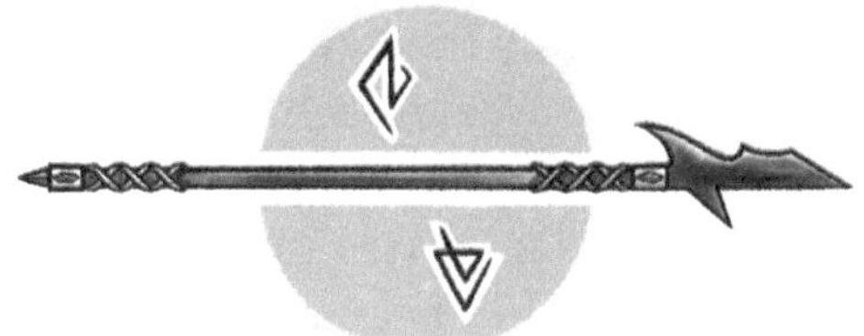

V idya stared into the smudged, scratched surface of a small wooden hand mirror. In the mirror, she saw her own face—proud and strong.

But the longer she stared, the less strong that face appeared. Just beneath the surface, Vidya saw her own doubt chipping away at the powerful facade.

Vidya hurriedly set the diamond-shaped mirror face down on the desk in Swan Spire. She knew she should've destroyed the mirror long ago. She wasn't much for keepsakes from the past.

But try as she might, she couldn't let this one go. It reminded her of the person she once was—a wide-eyed girl with dreams of a life as a performer. A girl in love.

Looking down, she couldn't help but read the words carefully etched into the mirror's wooden back.

Look to each skyfall that flares through the night

And know that my love burns even more bright

Vidya felt her heart clench as she remembered watching Solrac carve those lines.

They'd been young and impulsive—Solrac had just turned twenty, while Vidya had been only nineteen. They'd been traveling with their circus and rodeo troupe, *Marelda's Mythica,* for years at that point, spending every minute together. When the troupe leaders had asked for a few volunteers to travel to the Waterfall Keepdom for a private show, Vidya and Solrac had jumped at the chance.

A few others had planned to go with them, but had to change their plans last minute, leaving Solrac and Vidya on their own. By the time they reached their destination, all thoughts of the show had fled their minds. All they could think about was each other.

They'd found a small Sanctuary and asked one of the Sons of Streya to perform their marriage ceremony then and there. They hadn't thought it through enough even to buy or weave each other marriage bracelets.

They married in secret—mostly out of love, but Vidya was certain a big part of it had been rebellion. Solrac was in line for an important title in the north, and young Vidya hadn't been able to think of a better way to get back at her own family for their resentment of her etherarchy. Not that she ever planned to see them again to tell them.

They spent the night in a run-down inn built beneath one of the keepdom's famed waterfalls. The waterfall inn had been a little grimy, understaffed, and too cold. But Vidya hadn't minded at all.

Solrac had snuck out early the next morning and bought the little mirror off a street vendor. Vidya had woken to the sounds of him carving the poem into the back.

Solrac is a frivolous, foolish man, the voice in Vidya's head declared. *You're better off without him.*

Vidya squeezed her eyes shut, placing a hand on her abdomen. The voice was right. Thinking about those perfect days made her sick now. Everything had changed since then. Solrac had made his choice, and Vidya had made hers. Hers was the one that was going to save Evgard.

Staunchly refusing to shed any more tears over the likes of Solrac, Vidya moved to hide the old mirror in a drawer. In her haste, she accidentally knocked over a bottle of silvermarking ink she kept inside.

The silver-infused ink spread toward the mirror, and Vidya did a double take. Where the ink touched the mirror's wooden frame, the mirror flickered, momentarily vanishing from view.

Rapidly, she grabbed hold of the mirror, dumping the rest of the silvermarking ink onto it. On contact with the silver, the entire mirror disappeared to reveal a tiny chunk of skystone sitting in Vidya's palm.

Illusion.

Vidya ground her teeth. Had it always been an illusion? That couldn't be—She'd have noticed by now. Besides, Solrac was a terrible illusionist. Someone else must have replaced the real mirror more recently with this complex illusion, crafted to fool both sight and touch.

But who? And why?

At that moment, a flash of blue light caught Vidya's eye. She dropped the skystone, thoughts of the mirror fleeing her mind as a small, rune-marked rift anchor began to glow.

Vidya straightened up, pushing her memories to the side and replacing her hardened, aloof expression.

She knew *he* was about to appear. He'd been quicker than she'd expected.

Vidya hated owing people favors—especially people she feared—but she hadn't seen any other way. Her entourage was strong, but they still didn't have a Rifter. That meant they had to rely on the Soul Reaper himself for all their teleportation needs.

Within seconds, the Soul Reaper's rift anchor sent a long, lightning blue tear shooting upward. The portal ripped open, revealing a black interior. In the darkness, Vidya could just make out the shape of a tavern behind two silhouettes. Both men came through the rift into Vidya's tower.

The Soul Reaper wore loose, gray robes that tattered into threads at the ends of its long, hanging sleeves and trailing hem. He said the look mirrored that of the Gray Ones themselves. His face was ghostly pale, with ashy hair slicked back over his head. His eyes looked gaunt, with heavy black circles beneath them. He seemed oddly ageless, and though he was only about as tall as Vidya herself, his presence struck fear into her heart.

Behind the Soul Reaper was the man she'd needed him to bring to her. Vidya wrinkled her nose as she took in the sorry state of him, his overweight frame draped over a rickety rocking chair. His stringy hair fell over his eyes, and he clutched a canteen in his hands as if it were a lifeline.

"Torsten," Vidya said. "It's been too long."

"Not long enough if you ask me," Torsten replied, his speech slow and muddled. It was hard to believe this was the same smooth-talking, handsome soldier she'd met long ago in the Glacier Keepdom. Still, even back then, his drinking habits made him easy to trick.

"I'll only need him for a few minutes, then you can return him to that pitiful bar of his back in Rengard once more," the Black Valkyrie said to the Soul Reaper.

"Perfect," The Soul Reaper's echoey voice sounded as if it were doubled, sending chills down Vidya's spine. "Will that be all, sweet Black Valkyrie?"

"Yes, thank you," she replied, eager for him to leave.

"Of course," a small smile played over his pale, dry lips. "We are certain you will soon repay our kindness."

With that, he traced a rifting rune and disappeared through another blue-rimmed portal, leaving Vidya alone with Torsten in Swan Spire.

"Well, ain't he a piece of work," Torsten commented, looking at the space around his head as if he could see something Vidya couldn't. "What d'ya mean you like him? He could scare the scales off a fully grown drake!"

Torsten shook his head and took a long swig from his canteen.

"Enough," Vidya said as she took a step toward Torsten's chair. "Wouldn't you like to know why I summoned you here?"

"Figured it were 'cause you missed me," Torsten shrugged.

"Hardly. No, Torsten. I know you still follow the Coven of the Gray Ones."

"What's it to you? Them Gray One's're my only consistent company these days. Ain't y'all?" Torsten gave a little wave to the space on either side of his chair.

Vidya's skin crawled as she watched Torsten interact with whatever spirits he was communing with in Etheria. Rather than dwell on it, she plowed ahead. "I seek the leader of the Coven, the one who promises an end to magi captivity. I seek the Liberator."

Torsten froze. He narrowed his eyes to unfocused slits as he stared up at Vidya.

"I don't know nothin' 'bout no Liberator," he said darkly.

"I think you do." Vidya cocked her head. "I've sent the Ursadon to the Rise to search for them, but I fear he may have become... distracted."

Vidya had contacted Zoren only a few days ago, but the legendary Hunter hadn't impressed her with any useful information. He claimed he'd gotten a strong lead from one of the prisoners at Spydra, but that he needed more time to follow up on it. The Ursadon said his investigation of a particular member of the court would require great caution. Besides, his work as Captain of the Guard was demanding since things were so unstable with the pending war against the Dragon Isles. Vidya was growing impatient with the Ursadon's excuses.

Vidya went on. "I hope you can find it in you to speak freely, lest I'm forced to resort to less civilized methods." She made a show of dragging her finger along the length of the silver whip coiled at her belt.

"Less civilized?" Torsten scoffed. "I ain't afraid of you'n your demon, Vidya. Y'all may have this big bad Black Valkyrie thing down to scales, but I can't see you as nothin' but the lady who done ruined my life."

"I ruined your life?" Vidya said, keeping her voice silky smooth.

"Sure as the void," Torsten said, a strange sort of bleary, drunken fire appearing in his eyes. "I could'a been happy if it weren't for you. Livin' a simple life with the woman I loved and the drakkin' daughter she kept from me 'cause of you." Torsten's eyes filled with tears, but they didn't douse the flames. His hands began shaking as his anger rose. "That special little girl's all growed up now without a clue who I am. And drak it, look at me. Can't tell her now—would break her heart."

"You had the chance to raise a child," Vidya said, darkness creeping into her tone as well.

"Don't you go there," Torsten's voice thundered. "I loved Jax as best I could, but I ain't no fool."

"Tell me what you know about the Liberator," Vidya snapped, changing the subject back before things got out of hand. She lit up a psionic rune and telekinetically pulled her dragonhook spear from its place leaning against the wall.

"I spent years pretendin' not to know the truth about that kid, and for what?" Torsten went on, ignoring Vidya's demand.

"The Liberator's true identity," Vidya said threateningly, pointing the tip of her spear toward Torsten's gut.

But Torsten wouldn't be swayed. "No more—not now I know I could'a been with my real daughter all this time if I hadn't been stuck with a boy that weren't even mine."

Vidya's eyes blazed lightning blue as she lit the blade of her spear with black shadowfire. Torsten barely flinched.

"You want the drakkin' Liberator?" Torsten seethed. "Think about the facts right before your eyes. You're usin' the Ursadon as a spy on the Rise, but he ain't bringin' you the information quick enough. The Ursadon's a Drekai, come from the Isles seekin' out information on them Gray Ones in the first place. You know they cling to him, whisper to him. I seen 'em myself usin' the Sight."

Vidya's eyes widened as she realized what Torsten was implying. Frustration rose in her chest—How had she missed it before?

She held Torsten at spearpoint for a moment longer before flourishing her weapon to hold it back at her side.

"You've been most helpful, Torsten," Vidya said demurely. "If you'll just wait here, the Soul Reaper will return momentarily to see you out."

"Great." Torsten set his jaw.

Vidya turned on her heel and headed for the door that led to her personal sleeping quarters. She needed to pack a few things before heading to the Canyonlands. With a pang, she realized this was the first time she wouldn't be packing the diamond-shaped hand mirror.

Before slipping out, Vidya softly called out to Torsten still sitting in his dilapidated rocking chair.

"And of course Jax is your son," she said, laying on the sweetness. She swallowed the lump in her throat as she remembered her time at the waterfall inn. "Whom else's could he be?"

Fragment - Solrac

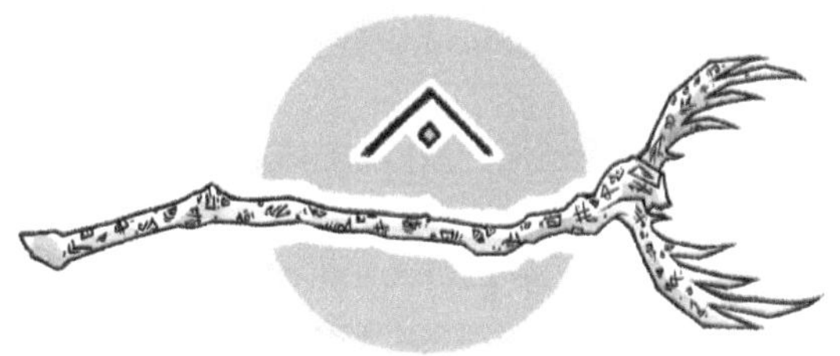

S olrac knew Jax was in trouble.

Frantically, Solrac scrambled around the lavish chamber, throwing the few things he'd need for the journey into a pack. Two tailored jackets, an extra pair of boots...

Solrac hesitated as he realized he was about to pack a diamond-shaped, wooden hand mirror. Unable to help himself, he slid the mirror carefully amidst the folds of his shirts, not daring to fully look into the reflective surface.

Nobody had noticed him taking the mirror from Vidya's chamber in Keep Drakfell last summer. Asher had been too distracted to notice. Stars, *Solrac* had practically been too distracted to notice what he was doing. Still, he knew the mirror held secrets the Knights of the Torch needed to know. He just hadn't been able to bring himself to look for those secrets just yet. Perhaps Solrac would find the courage soon, but for now, the memories were too painful.

Besides, now, Jax needed him.

Solrac felt like a fool for not acting on his premonitions earlier. When Jax first contacted him about needing the Farseer to pay a visit, Solrac had known that murky darkness lay ahead for the young Psion.

Solrac had considered potential ways he could've fulfilled his promise to send the Farseer to Outcast Outpost without having to go in person. It was rare that Solrac actually wore the Farseer illusion himself—It kept people off his scent when they saw him standing in awe before the mythical figure alongside everyone else.

But there was only one way Solrac could think of to instantly project the Farseer illusion all the way down at the southern tip of the Canyonlands. If he could use Kai's ethereal familiar, the illusion would be possible. The dream mirror copy of Kai's gecko, Glint, that Jax kept there could project the illusion. Then Solrac would've been able to have the 'Farseer' meet with the snowhead girl, Meleya.

But it was *Kai's* ethereal familiar, so Kai would have had to be the one to cast the illusion. Solrac knew Kai was more than capable of the etherarchy since he'd already convincingly projected the image of the Farseer once before. But the omens told Solrac that Kai wasn't ready for the burden of Solrac's secret. Not yet.

Solrac had felt so overwhelmed already. His quest in the North required finesse as he and the queen discussed Behrfell's possible future with the Knights of the Torch. An alliance with Behrfell was key for the future of Evgard, and his presence as the Duke of Glacia was their best chance of securing the northerners' loyalty.

In addition to all that, Solrac was worried about the other leaders of the Knights. There was trouble brewing in Skygard, and Solrac didn't like being so far away while the others made important decisions without him.

With so much on his mind, Solrac hadn't been paying as much attention as usual to omens regarding Jax and the others. He felt like kicking himself—all this time, the Coven of the Gray Ones had been plotting their assault on Outcast Outpost.

When Jax had tried to contact Solrac using the mirror gecko mindlink, he'd left a message with Kai, saying the Coven would attack the next morning. A vision of Jax's future had hit Solrac like a blast of dragonfire to the face, showing the young man enshrouded in an unmistakable swirling mist. Chaotic, snarling monsters had surrounded him, followed by a flash of lightning blue.

Solrac hadn't been sure exactly what it had meant. Drakking omens and their symbolism. But he knew one thing—Jax needed him.

Solrac had immediately sent the mythraven ahead with a rift anchor—He could travel faster than Solrac by using the Astral realm and following etheric ley lines. That was nearly two nights ago. Solrac pleaded with the goddesses that the mythraven would get to Jax soon, before it was too late.

He might already be too late.

Meanwhile, Solrac was back at his citadel in Glacia, pulling all sorts of favors and making all manner of promises in order to gather as much skystone as he could. He'd need it to make this big of a jump.

In the doorway to Solrac's chambers, an enormous red bloodhusky whined.

"I'm trying, His Majesty," Solrac said, gesturing toward the brilliant white crystals laid out on the bed beside his pack. Absently, Solrac reached toward the door to telekinetically close it behind the dog. Solrac had been using the ornate bracers on his forearms to perform psionics for so long, he'd nearly forgotten the psionic power came from the relics and not his natural Seer etherarchy.

His Majesty padded over to the bed, dropping a small shard of glowing skystone onto it beside the others.

"Good boy," Solrac said, scratching him on the head. His Majesty barked. He'd do anything to save Jax as well.

Wanting to check the omens one last time to see if they had any new insights regarding Jax, Solrac made his way to the fireplace. His finger flew to trace a complicated Seer rune, and gold flames burst to life as he knelt before the hearth.

A Seer rune glowed over Solrac's forehead as he gazed into the fire.

He saw the towering, redrock butte that was Keep Rengard's Rise. A Mage Hunter with dark auburn hair holding a vial of liquid light. The woman looked vaguely familiar, but he couldn't put his finger on it. Either way, Solrac understood what the omen was saying: He'd need to tell the mythraven to leave another rift anchor with this woman. It wasn't yet clear why. Solrac didn't like it, since it meant it would take more time for the mythraven to get to Jax, but he knew better than to defy the omens.

Meanwhile, the flames weren't finished. They showed more of those ever-present gray mists, punctuated by vivid blue lightning. Then, a once-flaming torch turned cold and gray, followed by that same turbulent snowstorm Solrac had seen before. As always, the vision ended with a single, black swan feather floating on the wind.

"Drak," Solrac cursed. The visions were growing even more vague as the future became more uncertain. So much hinged on decisions the players didn't yet know they'd have to make.

A sharp knock sounded just seconds before the door began to creak open. Solrac hurried to douse the fire using another Mystic rune, the golden light just vanishing from over his forehead as the newcomer entered.

"Boone and I are almost ready to depart," Valla said, frowning as she took in the sight of Solrac kneeling before an empty fireplace. Solrac mentally chided himself. He was letting his emotions make him sloppy.

Then again... if anyone could handle the truth, it was Valla.

Valla had stood loyally by his side for years now. While Solrac's time with Vidya had been filled with highs and lows with very little in between, Valla had always been constant. He knew he could trust her with his life.

But was he ready to trust her with his secret?

No. Solrac had never told another living soul that he was the Farseer. He and Vidya had once been married, and he'd still kept that side of his life from her. If he hadn't even been able to tell his wife, how could he tell someone who wasn't? Even someone as special to him as Valla?

"Solrac?" Valla cocked her head, her dark, almond-shaped eyes curious, concerned, and beautiful. For a second, Solrac got lost looking at her. He loved the way her dozens of silver scars from her encounters with the Mage Hunters told a story.

Solrac shook his head to clear it. Swallowing his guilt, Solrac hurried to his feet. He ignored Valla's skeptical gaze and slightly red cheeks as he rummaged through a cabinet full of elixirs. He knew one of these contained the remedy the King of Rengard would need if all went well. Soot, there was a lot to remember.

"Everything is going to be excellent," Solrac said, trying to summon his usual optimism. "Head south toward Skygard. I'll give you more instructions if I arrive."

"*If* you arrive?" Valla's eyebrows lowered. "Not *when*? You still haven't told us where you're going—where Jax is."

Solrac sighed, casting one last glance at the cold, vacant hearth. "Where I'm going, there are only 'ifs.' Valla, prepare for what is hopefully not my final performance as I star in *The Daring Debacle: Dancing with Death in the Dragon Mists*."

CHAPTER 24: FALCONDRAKE

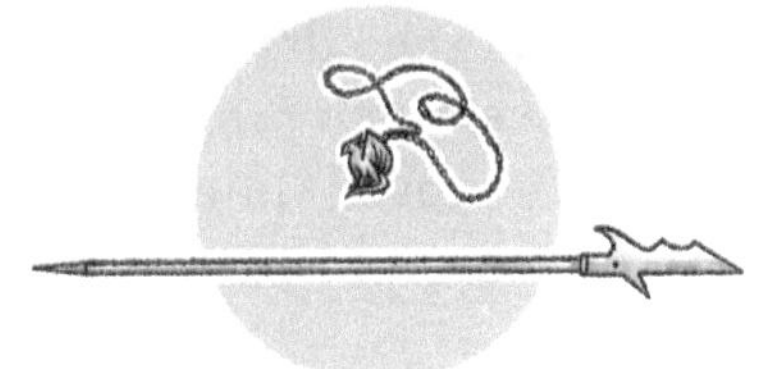

SOLVAI

S olvai led what was left of Squad Reckless through the narrow slot canyon. They naturally fell behind the other survivors, and before long, they couldn't even see the rest of the group. It was almost as if Solvai and the rest of her squad were going slow in hopes that their banished squadmates would emerge from the Dragon Mists and catch up.

Of course, that wasn't going to happen. Solvai knew the Mists were wild and unpredictable. One step in and you may never find your way out again.

But Meleya was smart, and both she and Jax were powerful magi. Maybe there was a chance they'd survive the Dragon Mists long enough to escape. Solvai ignored the fact that both Meleya and Jax had already expended almost all of their ether during the battle. She clung to that shred of optimism like it was a lifeline.

The Narrows were exactly that. Compressed redrock canyons so tight Solvai felt almost like she couldn't breathe as they hiked through them in single file. They'd had to send their squad's dragons, Bolt, Chonk, and Eris climbing the walls up to the top of the ravine. They'd reconvene with their riders where the slot canyon let out into the main one at the North Tower. Eris struggled to climb the cliff face since one of her wings had been badly scratched during the battle, but with Erik's encouragement and a little push from Bolt, she made it to the top where she could walk safely.

Solvai hoped the lieutenants were being good to Meleya and Jax's drag-ons, Sniff and Jade. Commander Hildred had ordered her lackeys to make sure the two evren didn't follow their old riders. Since the lieutenants possessed their heartscales, the dragons had no choice but to obey.

Solvai ducked and climbed around the smooth slot canyon formations. Each footstep echoed a little, and the flowing, horizontal patterns along the rock reminded Solvai of wood grain. Everything smelled damp, as if this place often filled with water then drained again.

They reached the North Tower, then pressed on carefully up the main canyon toward the Rise. They moved quietly, not wanting to give the Coven of the Gray Ones any reason to pursue in case they had sentries on watch nearby.

Squad Reckless followed the river north until sundown when they made camp near the base of the canyon wall. Commander Hildred and the other survivors were still nowhere in sight, most likely settling down for the night somewhere further up the canyon. Even without Meleya and Jax to spark the commander's ire, Solvai felt it best that their entire squad give her a little distance. They'd meet up with the others back at the Rise.

Besides, as they journeyed north through the canyon, they continued to see small groups of Outcast Outpost refugees making their way to Keep Rengard proper. Solvai figured it was best if they acted as a rearguard, in case any of the refugees needed help.

Nobody had said a word since they'd started their hike up the Narrows, a silence that held as the squad settled in for the night. It was hard enough coming to grips with the loss of Outcast Outpost. On top of that, now they were dealing with the loss of their friends. For Solvai, the closest friend she'd ever had.

Solvai shoved down her bitterness toward Commander Hildred, but bits of it kept bubbling up. Hadn't the platoon lost enough soldiers already during the battle against the Coven of the Gray Ones? It was just wrong.

They hadn't escaped Outcast Outpost with any supplies like bedrolls, but when Brigan, Cam, and Erik checked their dragons' saddlebags they found the labeled burlap sacks with each of their names on them. The lunches Meleya had packed for them before the battle.

Solvai and the others silently sat around their small campfire, eating their gourmet dragonhog ham and soft, white cheese sandwiches. Solvai felt a lump in her throat as she swallowed. As always, Meleya had skipped the onions on her sandwich, just the way she liked it.

Everyone was in a somber mood as they ate the delicious meal. Strong, menacing Cam shed a tear with each bite, probably realizing he'd now have to go back to eating the plain rations the rest of the army got. Erik's eyes were rimmed with red, and Solvai frowned as she watched him fiddle with a dagger she'd never noticed him carrying before. She recognized it, from the angular blade to the handle carved from antler. That was Meleya's dagger.

Edrea finished her sandwich, then sat beside Brigan on a juniper log. Brigan was holding his lunch sack, staring despondently at his handwritten name on the front of it.

"For what it's worth," Edrea said, cautiously nudging Brigan, "the bread was a little dry."

Without looking Edrea in the eye, Brigan stood, tightly clutching the sack. He hurriedly strode across the campsite to where Bolt lay curled up, then sat with his back against his dragon and his head in his hands.

Edrea scowled after him. Then she noticed Solvai watching her.

"What? I was just trying to lighten the mood."

Solvai joined Edrea on the log, speaking quietly so the rest of the squad wouldn't overhear. "He'll never like you more for being rough on Meleya."

"Wha... what? Why would I care if he...? No way."

Solvai shrugged. "Don't worry, Brigan has no idea."

Edrea frowned, then gave a resigned sigh. "Tell me about it. He has no idea I exist. He can't see past that drakking snowhead."

"That snowhead who stayed up all night to make us food? The one who saved both our lives on the battlefield today?"

"Yeah, but she's so... ugh."

"Sure, she can get riled up and let her emotions cloud her judgment. She struggles to trust anyone, even those closest to her. She's a terrible liar. Meleya's a lot of things, but one thing she's not is a bad person."

Edrea grumbled, kicking a loose pebble across the dirt.

"But what's the point?" Edrea asked. "He knows nobility can't be with magi." She grit her teeth and crossed her arms.

Solvai spoke softly. "You can't control the way Brigan feels. All you can do is focus on being the best version of yourself, then let the scales fall where they may."

"But what if that version still isn't enough?"

"It will be for the right one."

Solvai sat with Edrea a little longer as they watched the campfire's translucent flames. The canyon night air was brisk, and Solvai found herself leaning forward toward the heat.

"Thanks, Solvai," Edrea mumbled, as if it was hard for her to say the words. "Maybe you're not a terrible squad captain."

Solvai gave a small smile, then absently reached toward her neck where her carved falcondrake charm normally hung. For a moment, she panicked when she felt nothing there, then remembered how the chain had snapped while she'd battled the gray-hooded magi that morning.

She reached into the pocket of her tunic and pulled out the charm and its broken chain. As usual, the tiny metal links felt cold to the touch. It was strange not feeling the gentle, chilly weight around her neck. Ever since she could remember, Solvai's mother had encouraged her daughter to wear the necklace as a reminder of the father she never got to meet. The man Solvai's mother had once loved.

Solvai kept the charm safely in her pocket, but let the silvery chain slip from her hand and into the dirt below. She'd have to get a new one once they got back to the Rise.

At first light, Squad Reckless continued their path north along the winding river. It wasn't until mid-afternoon that they passed the hole in the rock that was the entrance to Spydra Prison.

Not long after passing the prison, a scream brought Solvai and the others to a halt.

There, tight against the cliff face, was a little adobe cottage. Ropes sagged between sparse fence posts, serving as a little corral for a couple of fleecy aldrakas. A woman stood outside, pointing upward as she cried out.

Had flyers from the Coven already made it this far up the canyon?

Solvai followed the line of her finger to see the stark black underside of a giant, scaly condor. Solvai recognized the species of bird by the white feathers that formed a triangle on each of its wide wings. It had a featherless, pinkish head covered in rough, gnarled scales. They were well known in the canyons for being aggressive, often fighting wild dragons to feed off abandoned animal carcasses.

To Solvai's horror, it was no animal clutched in the condor's enormous clawed feet.

Swaddled in a woven beige blanket, trapped in the cage formed by the giant bird's talons, was a helpless human baby. Solvai could hear its wails mingling with the woman's.

"Soldiers," the woman cried, spotting their squad. "Please—this creature has been plaguing us, snatching up our livestock for weeks. I was preparing a meal for some of the Outpost refugees and turned my back for only a second..."

The woman trailed off, making a strangled sound in her throat as the condor rose higher.

Solvai felt her stomach drop. They had to do something. But as she glanced at the stunned faces of the rest of her squad, she realized they couldn't. Without Jax and Meleya's dragons and with Erik's wyvern badly wounded, none of them could fly.

"Don't just stand there, Erik," Edrea shouted. "Shoot it down!"

Erik's eyes went round as he aimed his crossbow upward, his hands shaking just a little. After a second, he lowered the weapon.

"I... it's just..." Erik stammered.

Edrea threw up her hands. "What?"

"He can't get a clear shot without hurting the baby. Or making it fall," Solvai muttered. Erik nodded.

Panic welled up inside Solvai's heart and she felt herself shutting down. Resigning herself to cower on the sidelines as fear cycled through her to the core.

She shut her eyes tightly, unsure. She'd always been unsure. Solvai had been trying to step up and lead her squad, but it was all a mask. She told her friends the great war stories of her brave, deceased father, longing to be like him. But in the end, Meleya and Brigan were the brave, fearless ones, not Solvai. She would only ever be their quiet, awkward friend—a little snow dove with broken wings whom everyone expected to fall.

Solvai thrust her hands into her pockets, feeling the falcondrake charm stowed there. As she held it between her fingers, she felt something deep inside her snap into place.

Solvai stopped thinking. She shoved down her doubt and ignored logic as she dashed toward the midday shadow directly below the condor.

She heard her squadmates calling after her and felt their eyes on her back. She fought the urge to cower under their gazes, still sprinting to that spot, though completely at a loss for a plan.

Suddenly, a sharp tug like an ocean wave pulled at her gut. Her instincts took over, and it felt like every bone in her body was on fire.

Clouds of gold light overtook her vision as she ran. Solvai felt something warm, powerful, and primal fill her soul.

When the clouds cleared, it was as if Solvai was seeing clearly for the first time. The stone along the canyon wall had sharpened into focus, and Solvai could make out each individual feather along the giant condor's wings even as it circled so high above her. The baby's cries resonated with perfect clarity in her ears.

Solvai let go of every remnant of rational thought or debilitating fear. She abandoned that voice in the back of her mind that always told her she wasn't enough. Everything was swallowed up in her instincts.

And then Solvai was flying.

Solvai felt the rush of wind cutting across her face and shoulders as she soared through the air. She was vaguely aware of dark chestnut wings, the same shade as her hair, unfolding at her sides. A slim, black beak extended down from what had once been her nose. Instead of arms and legs, Solvai had a scaly, drake-like body and claws. Solvai would know those features anywhere.

She had become a falcondrake.

She let out a piercing shriek as she jetted toward the condor. The other bird cawed ferociously as Solvai clashed with it in the air.

They were evenly matched in size and strength. They tangled, Solvai's strong foreclaws raking across the condor's sharp, black wings.

It must've realized Solvai in falcondrake form would knock it out of the sky. With another squawk and a mighty flap of its wings, the scaly condor disengaged from Solvai, releasing the baby from its talons as it retreated upward.

The condor forgotten, Solvai's instincts propelled her downward toward that precious bundle. Using her foreclaws, Solvai carefully caught and cradled the screaming child.

Solvai swooped back toward the canyon bed, smoothly landing on her hindclaws before the weeping woman. A man had come running out of the house to join her, and Solvai gently laid the baby at the couple's feet.

Immediately afterward, Solvai felt a wrenching sensation in her gut. It was almost as if she'd drained herself of power by transforming. More gold smoke surrounded her until suddenly Solvai felt very small.

Dazed by what had just happened, Solvai reached into her tunic pocket and pulled out the falcondrake charm from her father. The worn charm burned with glowing, angular patterns for another second before going dark.

Brigan and the rest of the squad appeared beside Solvai, the couple, and the bawling baby. Their eyes were wide with both shock and fear.

"The charm," Brigan said, pointing to the little carved falcondrake in Solvai's hand. "Those were Sentinel marks."

"Magi," the man said, holding his wife as she clutched the baby to her chest. "She... she's a Wildshaper, isn't she?"

Solvai got her first look at the little baby's face. It was so small and fragile, with curly wisps of hair and enormous, dragonfire green eyes. Looking at the child's father, Solvai saw those same eyes, along with a pair of scale-tipped ears. The man wore the same orange cloak as Solvai and the squad.

"Thank you," the half-born man said, extending a hand toward Solvai. "My name's Ulf. I owe you a debt of gratitude."

Solvai grasped his forearm. "There's... no need."

She still felt sick to her stomach and wobbly on her feet. Brigan took a step closer, offering an arm for support.

"Did you know?" Edrea asked. Brigan shook his head.

"Not you," Edrea said to Brigan, then gave Solvai a look.

Solvai shook her head. She wasn't sure how this was possible. How could she be a Wildshaper? Besides, while Solvai didn't know much about magi, she knew they almost always manifested their powers before the age of nine. How had it taken Solvai this long?

Instinctively, her fingers flew to her neck. Ever since she could remember, Solvai had worn that strangely cold chain. Had the alloy of metal in the links included silver all along?

Edrea straightened up, giving each member of the squad one of her trademark scowls.

"None of us are going to say a word about Solvai being a magi," Edrea said. "Not to Commander Hildred, Captain Zoren, or anyone else."

To Solvai's surprise, every one of them nodded in agreement.

CHAPTER 25: THE DRAGON MISTS

E ternal dusk.

I had no idea how long we'd been in the Dragon Mists. A couple
of days maybe? It felt like a lifetime.

The sun was nothing but a memory—a distant dream lost beyond the
thick, constantly churning fog. The mists themselves put out a faint,
ethereal glow as they ebbed and flowed all around us. Sometimes, I felt
like I could see for miles across the wild prairie grasses and muddy,
reddish landscape. Then the mist would circle back so that I could barely
see my hand in front of my face.

At first, we thought we could navigate the Mists by way of the Ridgeback River. Surely if we could stick close to the bank, we could follow it
north and escape this void.

But wild magic was at play here. Somehow, the more we followed the
river, the more lost we became.

Within a few hours of running into the Mists, Jax and I had needed to
wash our battle wounds. While traveling with the nomads, my father had
taught me how important it was to clean deep cuts right away, and how to
bind them with the right kind of moss to prevent infection. The cut on my
arm from the Shardmaker's starglass knuckle blades stung as I used the
rushing water to rinse out dirt and even a couple pieces of my tunic sleeve.
Jax helped me wrap it, and I helped him with a scrape on the shoulder he'd
gotten during the battle at the Outpost as well.

But we quickly learned that strangers were not welcome near the
river—That belonged to the wild dragons and dragonkind, all of whom

wanted a taste of our ether wells. They'd chased us off, and we hadn't dared venture back since.

Consequently, we found ourselves in a never-ending loop of running, hiding, then running again. We hadn't slept a wink since before our defeat at Outcast Outpost. However, the greatest weight on my mind wasn't any of the danger lurking in the Dragon Mists.

It was the crushing feeling of having failed my parents.

Without my service in the guard, I knew it was only a matter of time before Rengard executed them. The Farseer hadn't come through. I'd been foolish to think I could depend on outside help. I had to believe there was a chance they would hold off on executing them—maybe Zoren would find it in his heart to pull a few strings? He'd had the chance to kill us once before, after all, but had instead sent me to the Outpost and preserved Mom and Dad's lives. Maybe he'd do the same again, though I still worried about his apparent resentment of my father. Either way, my only real hope now was to live long enough to find a way out of the Mists and break my parents out myself.

But I was still sane enough to know that was a fantasy. If the wild dragons didn't get us, it wouldn't be long before pure exhaustion did. Nobody who went into the Mists ever came out.

There was no conquering the Dragon Mists.

There was only survival.

"On your left, M!" Jax's voice was ragged as he traced a psionic rune quicker than lightning. Then he telekinetically threw our only weapon—Trickshot's crossbow bolt.

The bolt zoomed past my head, sinking straight into the gut of a feral dragonbat. It had been seconds away from draining my blood for its breakfast. Or maybe it was closer to dinnertime.

Thoughts of warm dragonbeef stew with tender vegetables filled my mind. That would be perfect with freshly baked and buttered rolls, with crackling, golden crusts and soft, pillowy insides. I could even use the leftover rolls for the next meal by toasting them and frying up eggs with cheese… My mouth began to water.

I banished the thoughts from my mind. Jax and I were fighting for our lives here. Now was not the time to make a meal plan. Still, as Jax psionically pulled the crossbow bolt from the beast's body, I couldn't help but wonder what roasted dragonbat might taste like.

The sound of terrified chittering ripped me from my culinary fantasies. Clinging to my leg, Dusty the draccoon let me know he was just as unhappy about the Dragon Mists as I was.

"Hey. You're an ethereal familiar," I chided. "If you die in here, Dad could just remake you. It's not that simple for humans."

Dusty gave an indignant squeak.

I shrugged. "Well then, maybe you shouldn't have run in after us."

An angry buzzing sound ended the brief reprieve. Approaching fast from the swirling mists above was a massive, black cloud made up of thousands of thumb-sized, fanged dragon wasps.

Their buzzing raised in pitch, and I knew they'd spotted Jax and me. Like everything else in here, they were hungry for our ether.

We took off, but the dense prairie grasses slowed us down. I yelped as the first dragonwasp sank its fangs into the back of my arm. My tricep seized up as its venom injected into my skin.

There was no outrunning them. Jax must've realized that too, because he grabbed me roughly by the hand and pulled me to the ground, trying in vain to shield me from the wasps. Dusty curled up into a furry gray ball at my side.

Jax's cries grew more intense as the dragonwasps assaulted us wherever they could find flesh. It felt like being stabbed with a hundred searing, venomous needles.

Jax writhed next to me, and I desperately traced the rifting rune. My chronically low ether well drained some of its precious contents, and a portal appeared to the side of the swarm.

My hands shaking, I guided the portal to encompass the wasps. To my surprise, it was as if I were trying to hold water with a sieve. The wasps didn't disappear into Etheria the way they should have.

I frowned, looking down at what should've been my swollen, bite-covered arms. But other than various scrapes and bruises from the battle at the Outpost and others from the past couple of days in the Dragon Mists, I saw nothing out of the ordinary.

Ba boom, Blink's drumbeat played through our bond, confirming that things were not as they seemed. For the umpteenth time, I was grateful that the soldier who'd taken Sniff's golden heartscale from me hadn't noticed Blink's silver one as well. Since arriving in the Dragon Mists, I could feel Blink by my side nonstop, doing her best to warn me of danger through our bond. Her drumbeats felt pained as my spirit dragon longed to be better equipped to protect me.

Needing to get a look at what Blink was seeing, I hastily traced the rune for the Sight. The drab colors of the physical world gave way to Jax's vibrant tangerine aura beside my indigo one.

I'd expected to see a thousand pesky little wasp auras descending on us. But using my ethereal eyes, I saw nothing. Nothing except a single, vicious, little red aura like a tight ball of spikes hovering a few feet above us. The wasp attached to the aura was half the size of the others. It had no fangs, and I could just make out a tiny ring of mystic runes along its forehead.

I didn't have to whip out Torsten's runebook to realize that this was no swarm of dragonwasps. It was one wasp projecting an illusion. A multilayered illusion that involved visual, auditory, and sensory elements, to give us the illusion of pain.

My awareness of the illusion dulled its power over me to nothing. My arms, legs, and face no longer felt like they were on fire. I blinked hard, dissolving the rune over my forehead so that I wouldn't waste any more ether than I had to. The world returned to drab, normal colors once again.

"Jax," I called over the illusory buzzing sound. "Jax, you have to relax."

But his screams only intensified. I felt panic rising in my chest. The agony he felt may've only been an illusion, but the way his muscles were tensing and seizing... the phantom pain could actually be enough to kill him.

Without thinking, I sat beside him, then leaned over to wrap my arms around his broad, incredibly muscular shoulders. His automatic response was to thrash more to try and get me off of him, and I had to strain just to get ahold of him again. Doing so made my arm wound throb, but I bit back the pain.

I slowly began running my hands up and down his arms, trying to soothe Jax and let him know there were no bites there. I laid my head against his chest until the sound of his galloping heartbeat filled my ears.

"Jax..." I said his name over and over, trying to calm him down. At long last, his breathing evened out, his tense muscles relaxing.

"Illusion?" he asked, his voice even more thrashed than before after all the yelling.

"Yeah," I responded.

Then out of nowhere, Jax chuckled.

"What?" I asked.

"Nothing," Jax said as his rough hands slipped over my sides, coming to rest on my back.

Despite everything, I felt my heart begin to race almost as fast as Jax's had been a moment earlier. I froze, wishing this moment of respite and safety could last forever.

But, as always, the Dragon Mists had other plans.

Suddenly, everything went eerily still. The wind vanished. The Mist's constantly swirling white clouds seemed to hold their breath.

Dusty poked his fuzzy gray head up to look skyward. He let out a series of panicked warning chitters.

Then came the thunder.

It sounded like the roar of a hundred dragons, but more primal. Deeper, as if it came from the sky goddesses themselves.

Suddenly, a bright, lime green light pierced the misty haze. The noise got louder as the approaching light became so big it filled the sky.

Jax's eyes grew wide as he scrambled to his feet, pulling me up along with him. Once again, Dusty clung to my leg.

"What is it?" I called over the sound.

"Skyfall," he yelled back.

I realized he was right, remembering all those times we'd watched the Dragon Mists swallow up the falling stars. I'd never seen one up close before.

Now, I was about to see one far *too* close.

The falling meteor was about the size of a kitchen table, and coming up on us fast. It was about to squash us.

Jax seemed to realize this as well. Faster than lightning, we lit up our runes.

Jax threw out his arms toward the falling star, trying to psionically push against it. No amount of working out could've possibly produced the strength necessary to stop the meteor's celestial momentum, but Jax did all he could, his muscles bulging and veins standing out along his biceps and forearms.

He slowed the green-tailed comet just long enough for me to get a portal going. My rift tore open in front of us, the gold rim widening in tandem with my outstretched arms.

My head began to throb as I got the portal open wide enough to consume the large meteor. My fingers trembled as the rock, then the tail disappeared inside.

I could only rift something to a place I could see, and the thick, white mists made it impossible to see very far. Consequently, my exit portal sent the comet careening into the prairie grass-covered earth only a short distance from us.

The impact shook the ground, setting the grasses around the newly-forming crater ablaze with green dragonfire. Jax and I clung together with Dusty the draccoon at my feet as the flames raced toward us. Thinking fast, I put up another portal in front of us to catch the oncoming fire. I placed the exit at our backs so that the spot we stood was the only place not charred by the meteor's blaze.

For a second, the world was still. The only sounds were our heavy breathing and the licking flames. The flickering dragonfire lent the white mists a greenish, alien glow.

Hesitantly, Jax and I peered into the crater. The meteor was disturbingly beautiful. Rough, otherworldly black rocks covered the surface, broken up by the occasional glowing white chunk of crystal. Skystones at their original source.

But while the space rock held about three fist-sized skystones, several rugged oblongs lay encrusted into the side of it as well. With a sickly shattering sound, many of those shell-like structures began to crack.

"Drekling eggs," Jax breathed as the first clawed hand broke the surface. The uncanny, garbled snarling of drekling chatter filled the air as the hulking, draconic monsters broke out of the eggs. Sticky, stringy goop stretched between six of the creatures' too-long arms, dripping off of their draconic faces and tails.

The eggs themselves had only been about the size of their heads, but the dreklings that crawled out were fully grown, almost my height. As with dragon eggs, the creatures must've used some kind of etherarchy to fit inside—maybe something like a rift hold.

But the science behind drekling eggs somehow didn't seem that important as the six ravenous monsters caught sight of Jax and me.

"Jax?" I whispered, pulling closer to him and wishing I still had my seaxe.

"This is nothing," he muttered. "I once faced a skyfall with ten times this many dreklings. Of course, then I fought alongside two very powerful Astromancers and my mom in disguise."

"What?"

"I also passed out halfway through. Didn't exactly see how we made it out."

"Well, I feel a lot better now," I said sarcastically as the dreklings garbled at one another with their aggressive, grating snarls. They seemed to agree that Jax and I would make a delicious, welcome-to-Evgard, celebratory meal. At least someone might get to eat today.

Jax jumped between me and the dreklings as they scrambled up the side of the crater. Though I knew he was just as low on ether as I was, he telekinetically sent our crossbow bolt zipping through the air. The bolt went right through the nearest hunched monster, dropping him at our feet. Jax kept the bolt going, redirecting it toward the next drekling.

This one had brought a large, jagged shard from its broken eggshell. The shell must've been hard as scales, because the drekling used it like a shield to deflect Jax's bolt. The bolt went flying into the misty haze.

Soot. Jax couldn't psionically push something he couldn't see. So much for our only weapon.

That didn't stop Jax, though. When the drekling leaped toward him, jaws wide, Jax slammed the beast to the ground and began wrestling with it.

I knew we wouldn't last long against the dreklings. There were too many, and Jax and I were so low on both ether and energy that it was a wonder we were still standing. That left outrunning them off the table, too.

Our only choice now was to stand and fight—Maybe we could even get ahold of one of those skystones and use it to replenish our wells.

Dusty, for his part, hid bravely behind my boots.

I tore open a new portal, guiding it over the next closest drekling. Its top half vanished into Etheria, reappearing as far away as I could see by the green dragonfire light. Next, I tried shutting the portal around its middle.

The drekling wailed as the portal ejected it out of the exit end. A spiraling, white ethermark bloomed along its torso, a scar from the closing portal.

Before the next monsters had a chance to get too close, I opened another rift in front of me, this one the size of my hand. That drekling's impromptu shield had given me an idea.

I reached through the portal, my hand coming through right at the base of the meteor. I grabbed a fallen shard of drekling shell that somewhat resembled a dagger.

Rapidly, I moved my exit portal up along the fallen star to the site of the nearest glowing, white skystone.

I tried to pull it from the rock to no avail. Then I tried chipping at it with my drekling shell dagger, but the skystone was stuck fast and I was out of time.

I yanked my hand back just in time to slash at the next drekling. Copper blood dripped from my shell dagger as I engaged the monster.

I took a nasty slash across the shoulder from the drekling's raking claws. The edges of my makeshift weapon dug into my hand as I wielded it.

Then a sickening crack pierced the air, one drekling's garbling coming to an abrupt stop as Jax snapped its neck. He didn't have time to relish his victory before three more dreklings clambered on top of him.

Meanwhile, my own drekling swiped at my arm so hard that the shell dagger clattered to the ground. Weaponless once again, I pulled back my fist and threw a hard punch at the drekling's throat.

It made a strangled, coughing noise as I sent saliva flying from its mouth. Before I had the chance to make another attack, it went for my throat as payback.

I tried to dodge, but the thing's arms were almost as long as I was tall. In half a second, the drekling grabbed me by the throat and hoisted me high into the air.

My legs flailed as I tried to rip its hand away. But there was a reason I fought with a long seaxe and not hand-to-hand.

As I struggled for air, I cast a pleading look at Jax. But three of the draconic monsters had pinned the steely-haired Psion to the ground. If I was going to get out of this, I would have to do it myself.

Blurry darkness played at the edges of my vision. Completely out of good ideas, I traced the rune to access my rift hold.

The tiny portal ripped to life, revealing the ethereal pocket I'd been using as a spice cabinet. I felt around inside, my hand closing around my little shaker of paprika.

I desperately whipped my hand toward the drekling, sprinkling the dried red pepper spice into the monster's eyes. The beast roared, stumbling backward and releasing its hold on me. I gasped as I went crashing to the ground.

There wasn't time to celebrate my unconventional success. Off to the side, the mists had cleared just enough that I spotted Trickshot's crossbow bolt lying at the edge of a patch of prairie grass. I rapidly stowed my paprika and dove for the bolt before stumbling toward where the other dreklings wrestled Jax.

When I turned around, I was shocked to see that someone else had beaten me to it.

With a warrior's cry, the newcomer lodged a bladed boomerang, a Drekai *kalaata,* into one of the dreklings grappling Jax.

The *kalaata*'s edge shone with golden etherlight. The Drekai woman who wielded it had tan horns sweeping off her head and a long, spiked tail lashing from under her wrap tunic.

I did a double take—it was the same Drekai woman who'd fought off the band of umbral coyotes those months ago in the canyon.

Her blow downed the drekling, and it was enough to let Jax crawl out from beneath the other two.

"Follow me, Evgardians," the Drekai woman said as she yanked her *kalaata* from the fallen drekling's back. "More dreklings come—too many to fight."

More cracking sounds from the crater assured me she was right. Already another round of the otherworldly monsters were hatching from their eggs, hungry eyes locked onto us.

"*Akaviitzi,*" the woman said. Then she translated. "Quickly."

With that, she darted into the swirling white wall of mist. Out of options, Jax and I dragged ourselves after her, Dusty the draccoon following close behind.

The dreklings weren't about to lose their magi meal as they pursued us into the fog. Jax and I could barely keep up with the Drekai woman as she held up her glowing boomerang like a beacon.

"*Zelkiin kholem,*" she yelled over her shoulder. "Almost there."

The turbulent mists cleared just enough for us to see the gaping mouth of a cave. As we raced toward it, the snarls from the dreklings behind us turned into whines and whimpers.

"The dreklings..." Jax said. "They're falling behind."

"*Akaviitzi*," the Drekai beckoned for us to hurry once more.

The woman skidded to a stop inside the cavern, then stood her ground in the opening. Jax, Dusty, and I darted behind her and watched the whimpering dreklings give chase just a moment longer, howling as they got to within a few feet of the cave. Then, to my surprise, the monsters turned around and disappeared back into the swirling white mists.

Relief flooded me, and with it my knees buckled. Jax barely caught me, but his exhaustion must've caught up to him too as we both slumped to the ground within the cave.

Chapter 26: The Cave

The cave was a small sanctuary from the threats within the Dragon Mists. Here, no wild dragons or other monsters reared their ugly heads at Jax and me for the longest stretch of time since our banishment. No unpredictable ethereal forces muddled our directions or played tricks on our minds. For the first time in days, I felt almost safe.

The cave was actually an old lava tube that had cooled over thousands of years, with rough, black, igneous walls. Odd, glowing orange moss grew in sporadic patches along the ceiling, giving the cavern a warm glow. It was clear that the Drekai woman had been living in the cave for some time. A small circle of stones and some charred logs indicated a cooking fire, and around a stalagmite down a small side tunnel was an alcove she'd been using to sleep. A little further down the cave was a stream—probably a tributary of the Ridgeback River—that the Drekai woman had been using to hydrate and wash.

Once we'd caught our breath, I turned to the woman. "What's your name?"

"Zyri," she answered in her accented voice.

"Thank you, Zyri. We owe you our lives."

"You are welcome, Evgardians."

"I'm Meleya, and this is Jax."

A miffed chitter sounded from beside me.

"Oh, and this is Dusty." The draccoon gave a satisfied twitch of his nose as I brought a hand to my still-throbbing head.

"You're Mystics," Zyri observed, gesturing to the silvermarks on our left cheekbones. "Here."

She brought us a skin of water from the stream, and Jax and I each drank in turn. I felt the pressure in my head ease slightly.

"Rest," Zyri said. "Regain your strength. You're gonna need it if you want to keep surviving."

Jax cleared his throat. "Why don't the dragons and dreklings touch us here?"

Zyri cast a sideways glance into the blackness of the tunnel beyond. "It's because even they fear what lies at the end of the cave."

We followed Zryi's line of sight, and I felt an ominous chill sweep through my body. Maybe my ether overuse headache was playing with my vision, but I could swear I saw the tiniest pinprick of blue light at the center of the cave's darkness.

"What's at the end of the cave?" Jax asked, picking up on the eerie energy as well.

Zyri took no pleasure in her response.

"*Kuakiina*," she breathed, then she translated. "Death."

I woke up with my eyes still closed and my legs curled up, my body trying to keep itself warm against the cave's chilly air. Heat flowed through my back, and I found myself shifting backward toward the source.

My eyes flew open as I realized that the source of the warmth was Jax. I sat straight up as I realized I'd been sleeping against the curve made by his torso and knees.

My unexpected movement didn't rouse him. As I watched him sleeping in the low, orangish light from the cave moss, I couldn't help but notice the differences in his face from when he was awake. The tension and pressure to hold himself a certain way was gone. The lines along his forehead beneath his maroon bandana had faded, the corners of his mouth curved slightly downward, and I saw a little white scar on his bottom lip that I'd never noticed before. His steely, dark eyebrows were relaxed as he took slow, even breaths. I suddenly wished I hadn't sat up so soon.

Boom-boom, Blink sent a knowing drumbeat through our bond.

"You and your Psion are very protective over each other," Zyri spoke softly when she saw I was up.

I was careful not to wake Jax as I quietly crept over to where Zyri sat guarding the mouth of the cave.

"That happens when you're each others' only lifeline in the Mists," I said, staring out into the roiling white fog. "And we were squadmates before that for months at Outcast Outpost."

"My *khiirakaai* back home and I were that way. We worked together long before we became something more."

"Oh," I stumbled, my cheeks deepening. "Jax and I aren't... uh..."

Zyri chuckled lightly. "I understand. Perhaps it is too soon for the two of you. But remember to never hold back when it comes to your heart. You never know which mission will be your last."

With that, Zyri cast another forlorn look down the dark tunnel.

Another shudder ran through me. "Zyri, why did you save us from the dreklings at the skyfall? That's the second time you saved us—I thought Drekai hated Evgardians."

"We aren't the ones who shun half-borns," she said quietly, and with what sounded to me like a hint of resentment. "We didn't start the Dragon Wars. The Drekai live by strict codes of honor. That's why I saved you, both from the skyfall and the *umbraali* coyotes in the canyon."

"The others who fought with you then," I asked. "Are they...?" "*Kuakiin*. Dead, in the darkness that lies at the end of the lava tube." She straightened her back. "I'm Empress Khaisa's last hope now."

"Hope for what? If I'm allowed to ask."

"I suppose there's no need for secrecy here," Zyri gave me a small smile. "Besides, as a magi, I doubt you'd be too keen on running back to Evgard's anti-magi nobility and sharing our secrets. And even if you did, they'd call you mad."

Zyri continued staring into the cold abyss down the lava tube as she went on.

"Have you heard of someone called the Soul Reaper?"

The hairs on my arms stood on end as she said the title. I shook my head.

"The Soul Reaper is a servant of those ethereal spirits your people call the Gray Ones. We call them *khaamu*, or wraiths."

At the word, a strange stillness settled over us. I shifted uncomfortably, getting the feeling that we were being watched.

"The Soul Reaper is a dangerous person the *khaamu* have weaponized against all of us in the land, though the Evgardians do not yet know it.

Many follow the Soul Reaper in one form or another—or at least they follow the wraith that has bonded him."

I frowned. "Someone told me the Gray Ones were behind magi receiving their powers. That magi were their 'chosen vessels.'"

Zyri laughed, but there was no humor in it. "Undoubtedly someone from the Coven of the Gray Ones. Their Liberator preaches that lie and others, all in service of the Soul Reaper and the *khaamu*. My companions and I were spying on the Coven's camp along the mist's edge right before they attacked. I assume they were successful in taking Outcast Outpost?"

"They were," I said somberly.

"The Outpost is just the beginning," Zyri forewarned. "They plan to launch a coup on all of Rengard by storming the Rise the night of the Winter Solstice—they have spies of their own in the citadel—including the Liberator."

My stomach twisted into knots. Last I'd heard, the king of Rengard was still on death's door and the queen was declaring war on the Dragon Isles. This was not the time to have traitors amongst the court.

"Soot," I swore. "We have to get out of here and warn someone."

"No," Zyri spoke sharply. "Our best chance of victory is to stop the Soul Reaper. I will not abandon the Dragon Mists until I've retrieved his voidshard and delivered it to Empress Khaisa."

"Voidshard?" I asked.

"Yes. Voidshards are the key to accessing voidarchy—dark ether. The same bright blue power the *umbraali* draw upon. The dark forces your Evgard's sky-forsaken Mage Hunters have been dabbling in as well."

This was a lot to process, and that cold feeling was still growing within me. My stomach felt like a hollow pit.

Although, that might've been because I hadn't eaten since the morning of the battle.

With Zyri's permission, I stoked the campfire with sticks from her woodpile while she retreated to her offshoot cavern to get some sleep herself. I used the longest branch to hang Zyri's single piece of cooking equipment—a metal canister with a thin handle—over the fire.

While the fire heated the canister, I gathered cindershrooms from crevices in the cave walls. I recognized the plump mushrooms as the same ones a woman from the Stormcharger Caravan used to gather for stews and sauces.

I crumbled the mushrooms into the canister, then added a little water from the stream. Next, I added a few shakes of salt from the shaker clipped to my belt, never more grateful for my emergency supply. The sleep I'd gotten had replenished my ether well enough that I traced the rune to access my small rift hold spice cabinet.

Maybe I should start keeping a real backup weapon in here, I thought. Although, the paprika had worked surprisingly well in a pinch.

I added a few shakes of cornflour to try and thicken my makeshift mushroom soup, then sprinkled in some paprika and continued to simmer, adding more water little by little.

Jax awoke to the savory smell of my bare bones cave mushroom soup. His hair was even more tousled than usual, all smashed to one side.

"Good morning, sleepyscales," I teased him as I stirred the little pot. "I mean, I knew you always slept like a rock, but this is taking it to the next level." I chuckled, pointing to the pattern of the stone he'd been using as a pillow imprinted into his cheek. Jax felt at his face, then shot me a look.

"I'd say you don't look all that nice yourself, but that wouldn't be true." Jax grinned as he looked me up and down.

Soot. There was that blush again. I blamed the cooking fire.

"Food'll be ready in a few more minutes," I said, glancing away.

Jax nodded, then leaned back against the cave wall. A few moments passed in silence before Jax opened his mouth once more.

The Dragon Mists' dark forces are as deadly as they say.
We almost died a thousand times but made it out okay.

My jaw fell open as Jax sang. His voice was raspy from all the screaming we'd done since running into the Mists, but it was also low and rich. I settled in to listen, though while Jax's voice was surprisingly good, I couldn't exactly say the same for his lyrics.

A single bolt from Trickshot became our only blade
We ran into the Mists as old companions watched and sang
Then M saw through that swarm of wasps, and got me to relax
Turns out when you're as hot as her, it's quite a simple task

And I took out that dragonbat, with just one shot, it's true
But we had still seen nothing yet, weren't even halfway through

Because a massive skyfall... fell, and almost crushed us flat
But M and I, we found a way to make it not do that

Then in the crater that it left, hatched dreklings to attack
And though those things outnumbered us, we still did push them back
Still in the end, 'twere Zyri who showed up and saved the day
Or maybe just prolonged our deaths here in this... lava cave?

What battle must we clash with next? What daring must we do?
We'll see if we can make it through M's funky mushroom stew

His last note lingered in the stillness until I couldn't hold back my snort any longer.

"M's funky mushroom stew?" I repeated, and Jax shrugged. Then I used the stick holding up the little can to take it off the heat. I brought it over to where Jax was sitting, then dragged over the rock he'd been using for a pillow to use as a table. As I took my seat beside him, Jax immediately reached for the can.

"Ah ah—Gotta wait for it to cool," I warned. Jax pulled back his hand. I was sure he was at least as hungry as I was.

"Why didn't you tell me you could sing?" I asked.

"Didn't want you to fall in love with me." Jax gave a sly smile. I raised an eyebrow.

"Arrogant much?" I asked, lightly punching him in his rock hard abs.

"Temper much?" He teasingly shoved me back hard enough to throw me off balance.

"What temper?" I said indignantly.

Once the stew had cooled, we took turns drinking from the canister. I made sure we left enough for Zyri when she woke up, and promised Jax I'd make more in a few hours. We didn't want to overdo it and eat more than our stomachs could handle after going so long without food.

Next, Jax and I drank our fill from the stream. I knelt down along the bank, the low orange light from the cave moss glowing from above my head as I cupped water in my hands.

From there, we cleaned and redressed our wounds. The cut on my arm was finally starting to heal.

I also wanted to wash up a little—I was covered in days' worth of sweat and grime from both the battle at the Outpost and the Dragon Mists —so

I carefully reached into the slow-moving water to try and splash some on my face.

Jax thought it would be the perfect time to light up a psionic rune and give me a telekinetic push on the back, using my tunic. I got a face full of water, gasping as I came back up for air.

"Oh," I sputtered, anger rising in my chest. "You did *not* just do that."

Jax doubled over laughing as my runetracing finger flew. A rift appeared in front of him and I guided it to encompass his whole body before he could dart away. Then I dropped him out the other end, which I'd positioned horizontally above the stream.

Jax splashed into the water, limbs thrashing as he struggled to get to his feet. He stood, the water coming up to his middle as he pointed to my furious face.

"There," he said with a smirk. "There's that temper."

Jax used the telekinesis rune still aglow over his forehead to pull me by my belt. This time, he sent me flying straight into the water, pulling me toward him.

I roughly slammed into him, and Jax wrapped a muscular arm around my waist. The water was chilly, but Jax's body was warm.

As he looked down at me with those dark, midnight blue eyes, I couldn't help but remember that this was how he'd held me when we met. Time seemed to slow down as we stared at each other, challenge ablaze in our eyes. For a long moment, the only sounds were the lapping of the stream and our slow, steady breathing. It struck me that the glow from the cave moss was a similar shade to the one I remembered from Jax's tangerine-colored aura.

The way Jax studied my face sent a shiver up my spine. He examined the black fringe of my eyelashes around my round, dark brown eyes. Then his gaze worked its way down to the tip of my nose, finally coming to rest on my mouth for just a second before returning to my eyes. My own gaze flashed to that little white scar on Jax's bottom lip.

Suddenly, my rage gave way to the urge to close the distance between us and press my lips against his. He must've gotten the same feeling, because all at once our mouths were only centimeters apart.

"Wait," I whispered, immediately wanting to kick myself.

"What?" Jax muttered, still holding me close.

"It's just... I've never kissed anyone before. What if I do it wrong?" Jax gave a low, light laugh, lifting a hand to my chin. "Relax. I'll teach you."

He tilted my chin upward and started moving in again. I pulled back.

"Sounds like you have a lot of experience," I said as an army of insecurities bubbled up inside my chest. "How many girls have you kissed?"

"Doesn't matter." Jax shook his head.

"How many?" I insisted.

Jax hesitated, and I could swear his cheeks were turning red. I gave him another look to let him know he wasn't going to get away without answering.

He looked away, almost as if ashamed. "You'd be number seventy-one."

My heart sank faster than a scale in a stream. I ducked out of his arms and splashed toward the bank before clambering back onto the stony cave floor.

"M, wait!" Jax called after me.

I kept walking.

Days passed inside the cave. Zyri was right—no wild creatures from the Dragon Mists bothered us. Whatever darkness lay at the end of the tunnel was quite effective at keeping them out.

On the same scale, every time I looked into the blackness I got that same cold, still feeling. Like frosty emptiness, and the impression that I was being watched. I shoved down the feeling, trying to ignore it as we made plans.

I filled Jax in on what Zyri had told me about the Coven of the Gray Ones. Jax and I knew we had to get out of the Mists so we could warn both the leaders of Rengard and the Knights of the Torch of the Coven's plans. But Zyri refused to leave the cave until she'd ventured down the tunnel to try and retrieve the voidshard she was sure was down there. Without her and her lightwielding-infused boomerang, I doubted we stood a chance of navigating the Mists.

I cooked up more cave-mushroom stews and sauces, adding in some drakefish I caught from the stream. Using small, fish-sized portals, I was able to catch them off guard in a rift then drop them at my feet on the bank. Zyri said my cooking was a vast improvement over the meager lichenroots she'd been subsisting on before we arrived.

Dusty was an ethereal familiar, which meant he didn't technically need to eat as long as he was getting enough direct sunlight. He certainly wasn't getting enough of that here, so when I caught him getting at the last scrapings from the bottom of the can, I didn't mind. Each time I cooked, Dusty took his share back to the little alcove he'd claimed above the fire near the lava tube's ceiling. He was surprisingly good at clinging to the craggy formations above our heads.

Torsten's runebook was still in my tunic pocket. I was glad it hadn't fallen out throughout everything we'd been through in the Dragon Mists. When I got the chance, I'd pull it out and study more runes by orange moss light. Every few days, I made sure to replenish the ether in the crystal Jax had given me. I never knew when I'd need the ether to make a couple of extra portals.

I'd lost track of the days, but it must've been a little over a week since Zyri brought Jax and me to the lava tube. We were just finishing up a meal when we heard the snarl. Zyri, Jax, Dusty and I all looked toward the cave entrance.

My heart leaped into my throat when I saw a hulking, long-armed creature standing calmly, eerily backlit by the softly glowing wall of white mist. A garbled growl reverberated from the drekling's throat as a pair of lightning blue eyes stared out from its completely gray form.

"*Umbraali,*" Zyri muttered, drawing her lightbladed *kalaata*. "They do not fear the void beyond."

Jax pulled out Trickshot's crossbow bolt, carefully runetracing and psionically lifting the bolt to hover in the air at his side, ready for action.

I stared at my empty hands and, for the thousandth time since coming here, wished for my seaxe. I felt my breathing becoming more rapid and shallow as two more umbral dreklings joined the first.

"I don't have a weapon," I muttered, panic rising in my chest. "I don't even have a backup weapon."

"M," Jax put a hand on my back. "You *are* the backup weapon."

I swallowed, lifting my finger to runetrace as the first umbral drekling stepped into the cave.

Chapter 27: Umbral

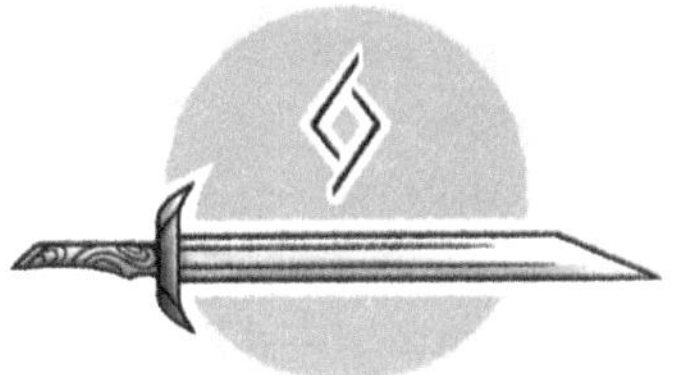

The umbral drekling had only just lunged forward when Zyri shot toward it, slashing with her *kalaata.* The lightwielding infused into her weapon worked effectively against the umbral's gray, shadowy form, and it vanished into misty nothingness without another sound. A blue, crystal core dropped to the ground, then faded to white.

Meanwhile, the drekling's two companions roared, charging in after us with their long claws poised. Jax sent Trickshot's crossbow bolt psionically whizzing through the air toward one, nailing it in the head and sending it into the breeze. I took on the other one, waiting for it to get closer before I threw up a portal, dashing through and coming out the other end to land on the umbral drekling's slick, scaly back.

The drekling snarled and reared back with surprise, but I clung to it with my legs, reaching my arms around its neck. Gritting my teeth, I tightened my grip to cut off the drekling's airways.

From the ground below, I heard Dusty chittering at me. It almost felt like he was stepping in as my instructor or squad captain, encouraging me from the sidelines.

The drekling made a stilted choking noise, thrashing to try and get me off. But I held fast with all four of my limbs until at last the drekling dissolved into smoke, its lightning blue eyes lingering for a moment longer than the rest.

I fell through the smoke to land somewhat smoothly on the ground beside the beast's crystal core. When I looked up, Zyri gave me a nod of respect, and Jax was smiling.

"Remind me never to get on your bad side." Jax extended a hand to help me up.

"*Zaavu*," Zyri said the word as if she were swearing.

Jax and I followed her line of sight to see more umbral dreklings swarming the entrance of the cave. Dozens emerged from the mist, and those were only the ones we could see as they slowly approached, snarling at us in quiet, otherworldly tones.

"Soot," Jax echoed Zyri's sentiment.

"There are too many to face," Zyri said. "We have to run."

I glanced down the lava tube into the darkness beyond. "But—"

My protest died on my lips as the veritable army of dreklings charged. Together, Zyri, Jax, Dusty and I ran for our lives down the lava tube.

We were faster than the dreklings as we darted past the stream and into the unknown. Their long, uncoordinated arms made it difficult for them to duck under low-hanging stalactites or scale the uneven terrain underfoot. Their eerie mutterings and roars fell further behind.

The tunnel became colder as we went, and the glowing orange moss became so sparse I could only just see the white puffs from my breath in front of my face. Then we rounded one final twist in the tunnel to emerge in a wide cavern.

The chilly cavern had a low, craggy ceiling. Where orange moss had lit the section of cave we'd made our home for the past week, here, lightning blue crystals grew along the rocks, washing everything in their sapphire light.

Gray umbral dragonbats hung from the ceiling, their bright blue eyes trained on us. Umbral spydra clung to their shadowsilk webs, filling corners and the spaces between stalactites. Beside me, Jax muttered a curse directed at the spydra.

The stream must've gone underground to feed into the large, eerily-still pool of water that filled most of the cavern. We stood on a bank about the length of a drake, and that bank extended in a circle all around the pool's edge. The sound of slowly dripping water echoed here, and everything smelled icy and damp.

My heart jumped when I saw what looked like blue lightning crackling within the pool. Barely disturbing the surface of the glassy water, the heads of several dozen naga—giant, electric dragon eels—emerged from below. Like the dragonbats and spydra, the eels had typical umbral gray scales and vibrant, glowing blue eyes. In their midst, I saw the long neck of an aquadon sprout from the pool, its fangs bared as its front flippers sent the lightest ripples across the water's surface.

I wondered how we could've survived in the cave mouth for so long without these monsters coming for us. Then I watched as the aquadon and the naga formed up, eyeing us with defensive rage as we stood on the bank of their territory. All of the umbrals here seemed to lock into position, almost as if they were guarding something.

Zyri pointed across the underground lake. "There it is—the Soul Reaper's voidshard. The *umbraali* protect it."

Squinting, I saw a shard of bright blue skystone as long as my finger. It hung suspended over the center of the pool, probably via some kind of psionic etherarchy. I couldn't quite tell from here, but it looked like white writing had been scratched onto the crystal. It immediately made me think of the masks that the Coven of the Gray Ones had worn into battle.

Remembering Zyri had said the Drekai needed that shard to stop the Soul Reaper, I instantly began runetracing. I could easily grab it using a portal, then, if we somehow managed to make it out alive, Zyri would be able to bring it back to the empress.

"Stop," Zyri caught my hand as the first trail of etherlight cut across the air. "Using etherarchy will wake him."

My hand froze, the gold light dissolving into shimmering dust. "Him?"

Before Zyri could explain what she meant, Jax yelped as he nearly tripped over the body of a Drekai man.

It was one of Zyri's companions whom I'd seen that night while on watch at the North Tower. Only now, his eyes were closed and his cold skin was completely gray, from his face to his arms and legs. Dual-pronged bites from what looked like the umbral dragonbats punctured his body everywhere. I noticed several small, raw chunks of white crystal cores scattered all around him—evidence that he'd slain quite a few umbrals before they overpowered him.

"*Zolehi khelaaza,*" Zyri muttered what could've been a prayer or a curse. Then she turned her gaze toward the edge of the water, where her other companion lay dead as well. His body was similarly grayed out, though judging by the oblong bite marks along his arms, it was the naga that had gotten him. I narrowed my eyes at both of the Drekai's bodies, my hopes falling when I didn't see any weapons on them.

The blue lightning from the naga crackled across the still water as they slowly began swimming toward the bank where we stood, their heads peering out over the surface. The aquadon growled, stretching out its neck toward us. While we hadn't been a threat to their prize before, our time of relative peace inside the cave mouth was over.

From the tunnel behind, I could hear the snarls of the dreklings coming closer. We were surrounded with nowhere to run. Unless we could think of something fast, we'd soon join Zyri's fallen companions.

Zyri gave a mighty cry. "*Valiiza kun Zariit Lokiika!*" Then she dashed fearlessly toward the water, leaping from the bank onto the head of the nearest naga.

The umbral dragon eel hissed and snapped at her feet, but Zyri was quick and agile. She bounded from naga head to naga head, using them like stepping stones as she headed for the voidshard suspended over the center of the pool.

I stared in awe as her fingers reached out to clasp the blue crystal—She was going to make it!

But just then, a swift gray force shot from the pool, its shadowy form bursting to life between Zyri and the voidshard, taking the shape of a man made entirely of curling, gray mist. His legs turned to mist at the knees, his face was cloudy and indistinct, and like the umbrals, he had glowing, lightning blue eyes.

Zyri nearly slipped as she choked on a single word: "*Khaamu.*" I remembered it as the word she'd used to describe what the Gray Ones' truly were.

Wraiths.

A wave of icy terror rolled through me as I watched the ghostly being pull together wisps of gray clouds from his murky arm to form a weapon. His arm extended into a deadly, smoky blade—a jagged sword with a shadowy edge so sharp it looked like it could cut to someone's very core.

Zyri was already hurling her *kalaata* toward the wraith. For a moment, it looked like the lightwielding etherarchy within the blade was burning away at the gray shadow, but too quickly the weapon passed right through it. The gray being hissed as the light touched him.

Then the wraith made his move. As he lunged toward Zyri, his misty body seemed to solidify somewhat, becoming corporeal for a split second while he struck his blow.

His sword thrust straight into Zyri's chest, cutting short her fierce battle cry. Then the wraith yanked back on his weapon, returning to his wispy, untouchable form. Zyri's body dropped, barely making any ripples as she sank into the pool. I nearly screamed in horror.

Meanwhile, Zyri's bladed boomerang landed with a soft thud along the shallow bank on the side opposite us. The wraith's cold, blue eyes stared across the water at Jax and me in silent warning.

A lump of fear rose in my throat. As the wraith lingered in the background, the umbral naga swam ever closer. The snarls of the umbral dreklings echoed in the mouth of the tunnel. Above us, more umbral bats and spydra lurked, ready to fly into the fray at any moment.

Jax and I didn't stand a chance.

Still, I took a battle stance, not about to go down without a fight. To my surprise, Jax handed me the crossbow bolt. Then I saw Zyri's fallen *kalaata* shooting toward us from where it had fallen across the pool. Jax had a rune aglow over his forehead as he telekinetically pulled her weapon, then suspended it at the ready in the air in front of him.

At my feet, Dusty let out something between a squeal and a whimper, then shot me a thoroughly annoyed look before darting up the cave wall into a shaded crevice on the ceiling. I hoped he'd be safe there, though at least as an ethereal familiar, there was a chance he wouldn't permanently die in here.

Jax and I went back-to-back, wielding our wildly insufficient weapons as the fight began.

Jax chucked his boomerang at an approaching umbral drekling, but he was clearly not well practiced with something of that shape. He sent it flying through the air the same way he would one of his axes, and it took him several telekinetic hacks before the lightbladed boomerang downed the drekling. It dissolved it into a shadowy haze, then dropped its crystal core to the ground at Jax's feet.

On the other side, a bold naga shot its head from the water onto our outcropping on the bank, its gray maw ready to pierce my legs. Using Trickshot's bolt, I managed to stab it in the head, though in the time it took to dissipate, the umbral naga's teeth sank into my calf, and I felt the numb, empty feeling bloom as blood soaked into my pants and boot.

I bit back the pain, runetracing to throw up two entrance portals the size of round, Evgardian-style shields. I put both of their corresponding exit portals right below the entrances, facing outward toward the umbral army. Then, using every ounce of concentration I could muster, I directed the two gold-rimmed entrance rifts, using them the same way I would a regular shield to protect both Jax and myself. Every time an umbral clawed or snapped at us, I blocked with a portal and turned their attack against them.

That worked for a while as drekling claws meant for Jax swept through one portal to take out the naga gunning for me. Dragon eels shot through the shield on one end only to come out with their jaws sinking into the dreklings on the other side, sending the draconic monsters wisping away into nothingness.

Unfortunately, it didn't take long for the umbral forces to catch on. Little by little, my ether well drained as I tried to keep my shields blocking their attacks. But the swarm only continued to grow, and I couldn't split my attention well enough. Jax cried out as a drekling's fangs closed around his thigh.

He stabbed at the thing with Zyri's boomerang and it vanished. I tried to move my shield portal more effectively to block the next blow against him, but that left me vulnerable to another attack from a naga throwing itself toward the bank. Its mouth was cold as it clamped onto my upper arm.

I screamed, skewering it multiple times with the crossbow bolt until it dissolved. The empty feeling spread down my arm and up to my collarbone, and I lost focus on my shield rifts. Both portals winked out.

The slew of umbral dreklings didn't hesitate. They descended on us, and the bats above took that as their cue as well. I felt their fangs puncturing my legs and neck. From somewhere at my side, I could hear Jax yelling as well. The umbrals didn't seem interested in eating us; rather, it was as if they all wanted a quick bite, to release their strange, numbing venom into us until our bodies went as still and gray as Zyri's Drekai companions before us. Once the shadow wasting flowed into our hearts, it would leave us so numb that we couldn't fight back anymore. Before long, we'd succumb to our wounds.

I kept fighting, desperate to get another portal up to try and stop the frenzy. But the numb feeling running up and down my arms made rune-tracing all but impossible. Battling these beasts was pointless, I realized. I found myself slowly sinking to the ground as a rush of indifference washed over me.

Nothing mattered. I'd already failed my parents, my brief service in the guard amounting to absolutely nothing in the end, thanks to Captain Zoren. Then Commander Hildred had ejected me from the guard, taking away the one thing that was keeping Mom and Dad from execution. They were most likely already dead anyway. By continuing to try, I was beating my head against a stone wall.

The numbness spread across my limbs as I lay down on the ground, letting more umbral creatures leech at my flesh. I could barely feel them anymore. Beside me, I saw Jax on the ground as well, giving in to the gray. As I looked at his strong profile, I wished I had just let him kiss me back in the stream.

I reached out through the frenzy, my hand closing around his. At the touch of his skin, a surge of warmth flowed into me. As if the mere touch of another human had the power to combat the numbness.

Ba doom doom! I suddenly felt Blink's frantic drumbeats pulsing through our bond. It was like she'd been trying to get through to me, but had been unable to pierce my haze of hopelessness.

Blink's thrumming continued, a desperate rhythm that begged me to not give up. Though I felt like my arm weighed a thousand pounds, I lifted a finger to runetrace.

The Sight blossomed before my eyes. Though the umbral creatures' auras appeared just as murky and gray as they had in the physical plane, I saw a glowing, silvery dragon fighting back against them.

Blink flapped her four ethereal wings at the naga, keeping a few at bay. Her jaws snapped at the dreklings, and though she had no physical form, she was still somehow able to send a few of them dissolving into shadowy nothingness. It seemed even a spirit could affect the umbral monsters. It was clear she was the reason we weren't already dead.

Seeing Blink fight back gave me the faintest shred of hope. If I was going to die today, I wanted to go down fighting as well.

I pushed through the numbness, sitting up and racking my brain to remember a particular variation on the rifting rune I'd seen in Torsten's book. More umbral bites sent streams of blood down my arm as I traced. Did the curved flourish go on the rune's right or left?

The trailing gold light didn't result in a portal, so it must've been the left. I tried again, and this time, the corresponding rune glowed to life over my forehead as the rift began tearing itself open above me.

I clawed my way to where Jax still lay. Kneeling beside him, I used my hands to guide the new portal in an arc, forming a protective, translucent bubble around us so that the umbral creatures couldn't reach us. I glanced toward the pool of water, placing my exit portal just above it, facing down.

It worked. Every creature that clawed or dove at us ended up falling through the portal and landing with a splash. A spark of satisfaction rushed through me.

I felt my ether well draining fast, so this time I accessed the small supply of extra ether from the crystal hanging at my belt. When that ran too low, I started pulling from the tiny drops of ether left in the crystal cores dropped by the slain umbral creatures. I could only use the few that were near enough, and each crystal held barely any ether. There was no way I could keep this up for long, but soot if I wasn't going to try.

I looked down at Jax and realized I still had the rune for the Sight going as well. His aura billowed around him in dynamic, tangerine clouds, contrasting with his dark blue eyes as he looked up into mine.

I quickly shut off the Sight rune, not wanting to waste a drop of ether. Jax's skin was as bad as mine was, with splotches of inky gray creeping up his shoulders and jaw. We'd taken so many bites. Even if we somehow survived the umbrals, without a substantial supply of liquid light, the shadow-wasting venom would reach our hearts and kill us within the hour. Tears pricked the backs of my eyes.

As Jax's gaze met mine, I saw the tiniest fleck of that umbral blue flickering within his irises.

"Don't you dare go void on me," I said, my voice hoarse as the first tear cascaded down my cheek.

Jax gave the tiniest ghost of a smile. His voice came out so low that I could barely hear him over the snarls of the umbral monsters surrounding us.

"I wish I'd gotten the chance to become the kind of man you deserve."

I could feel my hands trembling. I wasn't sure how much longer I could hold the rift.

Then I heard a long, loud cawing sound. I looked up, and through the whitish haze of my portal, I saw the flutter of large, black wings. Raven's wings, covered in starry, golden runes.

The oversized raven dropped a smooth, black stone from its talons onto the ground near my rift bubble. I could just make out a glowing, golden runemark along the stone's surface.

I frowned as I recognized the rune that marked the stone. If I wasn't mistaken, that was the symbol for a rift anchor's exit.

Sure enough, a golden tear sprouted from the portal to rip the air above it. A moment later, a man in flowing, dark red robes stepped out of the rift.

He looked just like the stories described, wielding a long, runemarked staff with a pair of dragonstag antlers sprouting from the top. Vibrant red dragonscale gauntlets covered his hands, with an angular symbol on the back of them. His hood was up, and all I could see within it were a pair of glowing eyes and a brilliant white skystone hovering between them over his forehead.

The Farseer.

Chapter 28: The Wraith

With a flourishing twirl of his staff, the Farseer let out a blast of dream energy that shot across the ground everywhere but where Jax and I huddled, somehow skirting around us. The army of umbral dreklings cowered backward as the blast drained them of their stamina. The naga hissed, and they retreated into the pool. Afraid, the umbral bats shrieked and shot back toward the craggy ceiling.

The immediate threat gone, I let my portal dissolve into etherdust. Jax sat up like a shot, pulling me closer to him as the Farseer faced his true foe—the wraith that hovered protectively over the pool in front of the voidshard.

The umbral creatures hung back, both dazed from the Farseer's blast and anxious to see what would happen in this clash of power.

At the same moment, the wraith and the Farseer charged.

The wraith glided across the water, his misty lower half trailing as he left the voidshard he guarded behind. He and the Farseer met at the water's edge, sword against staff. As their weapons hit, the wraith flashed corporeal the same way he'd done while attacking Zyri. Runes lit up along the Farseer's staff, and the man raised a red-robed arm to telekinetically hurl a volley of loose lava rocks at the wraith.

Wait... had the Farseer just used psionic etherarchy? I'd been certain that the Farseer was... well, a Seer. Add to that his using the rift anchor to get here, and that meant the Farseer was employing all three Mystic types of etherarchy.

That shouldn't have been possible. Unless...

I remembered what Torsten had said so long ago it felt like another lifetime. He'd mentioned the Gray Ones being able to grant magi the ability to wield multiple types of etherarchy, like true dragons did, or the ancient Guardians once could.

My heart leaped into my throat. Had the Farseer—as Torsten put it—been chosen by the Gray Ones?

But as I watched him fight the wraith with the ferocity of a father dragon protecting his young, it definitely didn't seem like he and the Gray Ones were exactly friends.

The lava rocks shot through the air like bolts from a crossbow, but when the wraith pulled back his sword-arm, his form went airy and immaterial once more, each jagged chunk of stone whizzing right through his body. He then stretched out his shadowy fingers, a lightning blue rune appearing over his forehead as he used dreamweave energy to level a series of blasts toward the Farseer. Instead of their usual violet, the dream darts were the same shade of blue as his icy eyes.

The Farseer spun his staff as gold runes lit up along its length. Purple dreamweave energy whirled along with the staff to produce a shield that absorbed the wraith's blasts.

Next, the Farseer used his staff to gesture toward the body of the fallen Drekai near the bank. Twin scimitars, both edged with light like Zyri's boomerang, rose from the water.

The Farseer psionically guided the scimitars toward the wraith, slashing across its chest. The lightwielding etherarchy within the blades seemed to burn at the wraith's misty gray body, and he let out a sinister, bone-chilling hiss. It made me want to clap my hands over my ears, and I found myself scooting closer to Jax. He wrapped his arms more tightly around me.

The wraith engaged the Farseer's scimitars, the red-robed man using his staff to control the swords' movements. Both combatants were equally matched, the wraith moving faster than shadow as he tried to skirt around the scimitars to get at the Farseer himself. The wraith surrounded itself with a trio of jagged shields made from blue dreamweave energy. The shields rapidly darted back and forth around one another to block each of the Farseer's attacks.

Meanwhile, the umbral creatures began daring to venture out into the open. A growl from behind forced Jax and me to our feet to face the horde of gray-skinned dreklings and their void blue eyes.

My whole body shook as I gripped Trickshot's crossbow bolt. I felt so numb, and my ether well was so low I didn't know if I could runetrace without passing out. Jax, normally so strong and determined, looked like he was on his last leg as well as he gripped Zyri's *kalaata*.

The Farseer saw our pathetic attempt to stand against the oncoming umbral monsters. In response, he sent both scimitars clattering to the ground and put out both his arms, as if taunting the wraith to come at him.

The wraith obliged, leaving behind its shields to skate toward him like a gray comet. His sword was poised, the wraith's body going corporeal just before the strike.

The Farseer saw it coming, and at the last second, he blasted the wraith full in the face with dream energy. The wraith was stunned for only a second, but that was all the Farseer needed. He psionically seized one of the light-edged scimitars and thrust it into the wraith's corporeal, gray back.

With another awful, shrieking hiss, the wraith's body trembled. Only instead of dissolving into shadow like his umbral followers had, his body suddenly compressed into a cloudy gray ball. Everything went silent. The small cloud crackled with blue light for a split second before bursting, sending a resounding wave of voidish energy rushing across the cavern as it disappeared. The icy blue ripple blew my hair back from my face and chilled me to the bone.

From the place the wraith had hovered, a chunk of crystal about half the size of my fist dropped onto the bank. The void blue stone pulsed once before changing color, the blue giving way to glowing white. While the other slain umbral creatures left behind near-empty quartz crystals, this gem had that telltale otherworldly shimmer, and it was brimming with ethereal light.

A skystone.

Not wasting any time relishing his victory over the wraith, the Farseer telekinetically pushed himself to quickly take the crystal. As he reached for it, he seemed more lethargic than before, but I watched him pull some of the white, raw ether out of the skystone. The ether swirled around his head and disappeared, seeming to give the Farseer a slight boost of energy.

He sent another blast of dream energy toward the umbral creatures as he rushed toward Jax and me. Then he pulled another rift anchor stone from within his robes. As he held it, a gold rune lit up across its surface and another portal sprouted to life before us.

"Go," the Farseer ordered. He didn't need to ask twice. Jax and I leaped through as the Farseer's raven swooped in from above our heads. At the last second, I heard a frantic chitter from a small, ring-tailed draccoon who scurried along the jagged cave ceiling from above the pool, clinging to the stalactites. I'd nearly forgotten about Dusty, but I was too distracted to wonder what in the void my father's ethereal familiar had been up to. Dusty flung himself into the portal after us, the rift closing just as the first drekling tried to follow.

I was surprised when we didn't tumble out the other end of a portal right away. Instead, I found myself in a strange, cloudy white room, the occasional flash of bright color winking in and out around me. It seemed sort of familiar.

I quickly realized why—This was a rift hold, just like the one I used as a spice cabinet. Only mine was infinitely smaller than the Farseer's. I didn't even know rift holds could be as large as an entire room.

"We don't have much time," the Farseer's voice rumbled majestically as he stood before Jax, Dusty and me. The black raven perched atop the antlers on his staff as the Farseer continued. "The omens told me you would need healing, and fast. When we leave this place, you will find yourselves with the Mage Hunter called Trickshot. She will tend to your wounds to prevent the shadow wasting from setting in."

"Great Farseer," said Jax, who looked and sounded like he was on the brink of passing out. "I have... information. Information about the Coven of the Gray Ones—they're planning a coup on Keep Rengard on the Winter Solstice."

Hurriedly, Jax told the Farseer what we'd learned from Zyri. The Farseer nodded.

"You've done well, Jax of Blackfjord." Jax perked up a little at those words. Then the Farseer turned to me.

"You, Meleya of Misthaven," he said, his glowing eyes seeming to penetrate my very soul. "You have desired an audience with me."

"Um, yeah," I said cleverly. "It's my parents. They're magi, locked up in Spydra Prison near the Rise. Please, all I want is for them to go free."

I felt a lump rising in my throat as I spoke. I tried to swallow it down—I didn't really want to start bawling in front of a literal folk hero—but the corners of my eyes kept filling up until finally they spilled over.

I could almost see sympathy in the Farseer's strange, glowing gaze. "The omens have spoken. Your best chance to free your parents is by waking Axel, King of Rengard. He is the answer to both your parents' plight as well as that of all of Rengard against the Coven's attack."

With that, the Farseer reached into his robes to produce a little crystal bottle with a long neck and amethyst stopper. Inside was a shimmering violet liquid.

"This remedy will wake the king from the dream realm and release Astra's hold over him. He must drink it within the next four days, or it will be too late. Jax and Meleya, see to it that the king takes this by your own hand. Trust nobody in the citadel but King Axel himself. If the Canyon Keepdom, and perhaps all of Evgard, is to survive the Coven's coup, it will need Axel at the helm. Do you understand?"

Jax and I nodded as we accepted the tiny bottle. I felt my legs starting to buckle, and I leaned on Jax for support. But it was like leaning on a wobbly pile of stones, about to fall over at any moment.

"I must go. There is much to discuss with the leaders of the Knights in Skygard. Trouble is brewing in Orothion, and I fear your information about the Coven, and especially the things we witnessed in that cavern, will only bring more unrest," the Farseer said, seeming a little shaken himself. He must've expended a lot of ether to get to us. I still wasn't sure how exactly he'd done it—or even more importantly, why he felt Jax and I were worth saving.

"Solrac will be in contact soon," the Farseer said. "But Jax, do not hesitate to reach out to him should the need arise. He will always be there for you."

The Farseer gave Jax one last solemn look before swirling his staff once more. Another gold-rimmed portal appeared amidst the clouded white walls of the rift hold, and Jax and I stumbled through, Dusty hot on our heels.

Just as the Farseer had promised, the exit rift anchor led us straight to Trickshot. She seemed completely shocked by our sudden appearance, her face blanching as she took in the bloody, gray sight of Jax and myself.

"Stars," she was on her feet in an instant as the portal winked out behind us. "You're alive. In a manner of speaking."

She rushed toward us, leaving behind a man with a distinct ether scar on his chin which led to a shock of white in his dark hair. Black horns swept off the back of his head, and he wore an oversized silver pauldron bearing both the symbol of the Mage Hunters and the insignia of the Captain of the Guard.

The Ursadon, Captain Zoren, had a sleeve rolled up, revealing a gray patch of skin just like the ones covering Jax and me. Despite everything, I gasped a little. Trickshot was treating the Ursadon for the shadow wasting. When he saw me looking, he roughly pulled his sleeve down to cover the marks.

Suddenly, I realized that the Farseer's rift anchor had dropped us inside Captain Zoren's office. The sun had long since set, the nearby torchlight casting strange shadows along the walls from all of Zoren's keepsakes from his Mage Hunter conquests. Had the Farseer's omens really told him that Jax and I would be safest coming out here of all places?

At that moment, I didn't care. My legs gave out, and though he tried to catch me, Jax went sprawling to the floor as well.

Chapter 29: Remedy

After nearly three days under Trickshot's constant care, Jax and I were almost completely healed. The gray patches on our skin had retreated, and the bloody bites from the dreklings and naga were down to pink marks. Even the cut I'd gotten from the Shardmaker during the battle of Outcast Outpost was practically gone. The liquid light was doing its job better than I ever could've hoped.

Yes, our bodies were recovering nicely. But I was constantly on edge, every little sound making my heart thunder in my chest as I raised a finger to runetrace. I wasn't sure how long it would take for that side effect to wear off.

They'd put Jax and me in a room inside the medical wing of the Rise's Sanctuary of Streya. They had either a commander or an entire squad watching us at all times, but even still, I knew Captain Zoren was having a void of a time keeping the other Mage Hunters at bay, since many of them felt Jax and I should be held in Spydra Prison while they decided what to do with us. I wasn't sure how much longer Captain Zoren could hold out.

It surprised me even more that he was willing to stick his neck out for us at all. We'd heard through the bramblevine that Captain Zoren had confronted Commander Hildred about her rash decision to banish us, demoting her from commander and suspending her from the guard for the time being. Likewise, he'd kept my parents from execution while I was gone by telling the judges that until they could confirm my death, I was still considered a proxy soldier serving under his command. He hadn't been sure how long that would've held up, but none of it mattered now that I was back.

Consequently, Captain Zoren's finagling had brought a lot of internal conflict within the guard. All because the Ursadon wasn't willing to let them execute us.

It didn't make sense to me. The Ursadon was the reason my parents were in Spydra Prison in the first place, yet now, he was the only thing standing between me and its silver bars.

So, until further notice, Jax and I were under hospital arrest.

Unfortunately, that made obeying the Farseer's order to personally deliver the remedy to the king of Rengard an impossible task. He'd said we had to get the remedy to Axel within four days, which meant we only had one left. I was worried that if they didn't let us go to the king soon, Jax would resort to breaking out and forcing his way into the citadel.

"I don't think you're listening to me," Jax was saying through gritted teeth. "We have to see the king. We have vital information about the Coven of the Gray Ones, the cult who attacked Outcast Outpost."

"Is that so?" said the commander watching us from his place near the room's locked door. They'd even installed bars on the room's one window.

Out of all the commanders rotating shifts to keep an eye on us, Commander Leif was by far the worst. The others simply dismissed us when we asked to see the king. Commander Leif actively snubbed us at every opportunity.

Commander Leif scoffed, wrinkling his large nose. "The cult who attacked the Outpost. You mean that puny little group of magi rebels you cowards at the border couldn't handle? The king's high guard swung by the Outpost last week and wiped them all out."

"I don't believe that for a second," Jax got to his feet, muscles bulging.

"Whoa there, Psion," the commander tapped the handle of the seaxe at his side. "Get back in that bed and have a lie down. Aren't you supposed to be in recovery?"

"I'll put you in recovery," Jax growled.

"Jax," I said sharply, and he reluctantly sat back down. Somehow, I didn't think Jax beating a commander of Rengard to a pulp would bode well for our eventual release.

"If we can't see the king," I began. "Then please, send for the Captain of the Guard."

"What makes you think the Ursadon will come just because some ethercursed wants him to?" Commander Leif folded his arms.

I thought about what Zyri had told me that first night in the cave. She'd said that her mission to retrieve the voidshard was worth risking everything. It was the reason she'd come from the Dragon Isles in the first place. Long ago, Mom had told me that Zoren had come to Evgard to spy on the Mage Hunter Academy for the Drekai. I had a crazy hunch, but we were out of options now.

I tried to speak with confidence, but my voice shook. "Tell... tell him we know where to find a voidshard."

"Voidshard?" the commander sneered. "What in the stars is that?"

"Just swear you'll tell him," I said.

"Hmm," Commander Leif leaned back in his chair. "When I feel like getting up, maybe I'll think about it."

There was a knock from the door. Rolling his eyes, Commander Leif got to his feet and cracked the door open. From beyond, I heard a familiar voice, though it was muffled slightly by a helmet.

"Replacement squad's here to relieve you of watch duty over the magi, Commander."

Commander Leif seemed taken aback. "Thought I was supposed to watch them until sundown."

"They felt you could use a break. Can't be easy, guarding two magi at once."

"That's true," the commander muttered nobly.

"Take the afternoon off," the convincing, masculine voice said. "Get yourself a drink down at the Dry Dragonstag."

That was enough for Commander Leif. Without so much as a second glance toward Jax and me, he strode out the door.

I smiled so wide my face almost split as the 'replacement squad' filed in and shut the door behind them.

"Reckless!" I laughed as they removed their helmets. In a flash, Brigan and Solvai were at either side of where I sat up in my recovery bed. They threw their arms around me, only slightly straining my bruised muscles and lingering injuries.

"Meleya of Misthaven," Solvai whispered, her voice cracking. "Never do that to us again, you got it?"

"Do what?" I felt a couple of tears welling up in my eyes. "Get banished and sent to my death?"

"Exactly."

I squeezed my friends harder. "I'll do my best."

Finally, Solvai, Brigan and I released each other, but Solvai immediately made herself comfortable on the bed right beside me while Brigan sat near my feet. The rest of the squad stood close as well, between my bed and Jax's. They all looked relieved to see the two of us still alive—even Edrea.

"Hey Jax," Cam said, carefully reaching into a pack at his side. I did a double take when Cam pulled out a tiny, yellow gecko with enormous, reflective eyes. I vaguely remembered Jax removing the gecko from a terrarium back at Outcast Outpost, but still, I raised an eyebrow.

Jax, on the other hand, looked elated. "Three!" he called out the gecko's strange name, reaching for it. The little lizard gave a small, delighted croaking noise as it crawled from Cam's hand to Jax's.

"Found her in Jade's saddlebag after the battle," Cam explained. "Kept her safe. Didn't know when you'd be back, but we couldn't leave Three behind. Been feeding her. Her favorite food is—"

"Spiny crickets," Jax finished, nuzzling the gecko against his cheek. I stifled a laugh. I'd never seen this side of Jax.

"Exactly," Cam said proudly. He and Jax exchanged understanding, brotherly nods.

"I still can't believe you're okay." Solvai gave my arm another squeeze, then leaned forward to see Jax. "Both of you."

"Nah." Jax waved a hand. "I know all you guys really missed was Meleya's cooking."

Everyone laughed as Brigan spoke up.

"How did you two... you know. Escape the Dragon Mists?" From where he sat near my feet, Brigan looked at me with warm, searching brown eyes. Just looking at them made me feel more relaxed and at ease.

Jax and I exchanged glances. We doubted we were supposed to run around telling everyone that the Farseer himself had rescued us from an army of umbral creatures, not to mention an actual wraith. But this wasn't just anyone. This was our squad.

We shared our tale of our time in the Dragon Mists, making sure not to reveal anything specific about Jax's involvement with the Knights of the Torch. While Jax and I eagerly shared about the epic battles we fought against a skyfall of dreklings and the umbral naga, we couldn't bring ourselves to talk much about Zyri. And we definitely skipped over some of the more... personal details. I could feel a blush blooming across my cheeks as I remembered the way Jax had held me as we stood in the dimly-glowing lava tube stream, his face just a breath away from mine. I shot Jax a glance, wondering if he recalled what he'd said to me right before the Farseer's mythraven had appeared—when we thought we were going to die. The words were burned into my mind.

I wish I'd gotten the chance to become the kind of man you deserve.

A light pressure from a hand on my calf pulled my attention back to Brigan as Jax continued telling our wide-eyed squad about the way the Farseer had battled the wraith. Brigan tilted his head as if to ask what was on my mind. My blush deepened, and I shook my head.

For a second, what looked like a pang of hurt crossed Brigan's face. But he recovered so quickly I wondered if I'd imagined it.

Jax wrapped up our story, finishing with the Farseer's instructions to get the remedy to King Axel. He cast an irritated look toward the door, as if he was considering making a break for it now that Commander Leif wasn't watching us like a dragonhawk. But Jax must've known he wouldn't have made it past the guards at the door to the palace. Besides, if he left, that would undoubtedly get Squad Reckless in trouble, and I wasn't about to let Jax do that.

Solvai leaned over and nudged Brigan. "I guess this means you were right. There *is* some mystical, red-robed man running around, popping up to save magi in need like in the old stories."

"Gauntlet down," Brigan said with a smile not quite wide enough to show his dimples. "You should listen to me more."

"What about our dragons?" I said suddenly. "Is Sniff alright?"

"Sniff and Jade are fine," Solvai assured me. "They brought them to the new dragon stables first thing. They're still finishing the final repairs on the stables, but your dragons are in good hands with my mom and the other dragon keepers."

I leaned back against my propped up pillow, a weight lifting from my heart. A little drumline from Blink played through our bond in response, and I longed for a trilling melody to accompany it. I hoped Lorelai and the others were giving Sniff lots of attention, and scratching him behind his ears the way he liked.

"What's new with you guys?" I asked. "Have the commanders replaced us on the squad yet?"

Brigan chimed in. "They've been waiting to reform understaffed squads until things are more solid regarding the war. It's been a little hectic, especially with King Axel still out of commission. The queen's acting as regent, but she's been getting a lot of pushback from some of Axel's advisors and higher-ups in the guard."

Jax and I gave each other another look. We had to get the Farseer's remedy to the king, and fast.

"And as far as what's new with us," Solvai said slyly, "I kind of have a surprise."

"What is it?" I cocked my head. My friend had a new, confident light in her hazel eyes.

Solvai slipped off my hospital bed, taking a few steps backward. But before she could tell me anything, Edrea leaped between us, getting right up in my face.

"Wait." Edrea narrowed her eyes, flashing them between Jax and me. "First, the two of you have to swear you'll keep the secret."

Solvai piped up. "Edrea, Meleya wouldn't—"

"Swear it," Edrea cut in. "Nobody outside this room knows. Never tell another soul what you're about to see, you understand?"

"Uh... okay," I said, solemnly raising a fist to my chest in the guard's salute. Jax did the same.

Solvai smiled as she pulled out the falcondrake charm she always wore around her neck. Only now, instead of a shiny chain, it hung from a leather cord.

My eyebrows furrowed as an angular gold symbol began glowing from the charm. Suddenly, golden clouds of ether billowed all around Solvai's back. My jaw dropped as the clouds dissipated to reveal an enormous, folded set of rich, brown wings sprouting between Solvai's shoulder blades.

Solvai spun a little, showing off her magnificent falcondrake wings. Edrea and the others looked to Jax and me for our reactions.

"You're a Wildshaper," Jax concluded, the shock on his face matching mine. Solvai nodded excitedly.

"Since when?" I stammered.

"Not sure," Solvai said. "It turns out the chain I'd worn my whole life had silver in it, suppressing my etherarchy for years. I showed my powers for the first time just after we left Outcast Outpost. It was like, out of nowhere, suddenly I'd gone full falcondrake."

"It was kind of epic," Erik said, holding out his sketchbook. The page depicted a majestic falcondrake in flight, battling another bird amidst the canyon rocks. I pointed to the drawing.

"This is Solvai?" I asked, and Erik nodded. I looked back to Solvai now, her demeanor confident and bright as her wings caught the sunlight. A wave of pride washed over me—she was always meant to fly.

"That's enough," Edrea said as she glanced nervously toward the window. "Shift back before anyone comes in." More gold clouds engulfed Solvai's back as her wings disappeared. She returned to her place at my bedside, and Edrea finally seemed to relax. Since when did she feel so protective over Solvai?

We sat in silence for only a moment before Brigan felt it was time to strike up one of his heated debates.

"Gauntlet down," Brigan started. "The skystone debt crisis will only get worse as more skyfalls hit Evgard."

Edrea put a hand on her hip. "But the skyfalls are what bring skystones in the first place. Why would more of them be a bad thing?"

I could see the fire sparking in Brigan's eyes. "Because while the skyfalls bring skystone, they also bring dreklings. And with more keeps sending soldiers to war as the Dragon Isles threat grows, there are fewer people left to guard the cities against the skyfall's dreklings. That means more places are falling to invading dreklings, who take the skystone for themselves and become even more powerful. It's not as big a thing when the skyfalls hit near a big city, but refugees from smaller towns are flooding the larger keeps."

"That's true," Jax nodded. "Keep Drakfell's struggling to stay on top of it." The rest of the squad nodded as if it all made sense.

Brigan looked a little disappointed when nobody contradicted him further. Then he snapped his fingers.

"How about this instead? Gauntlet down: Spineapple doesn't belong on cheesy tomato flatbread."

The squad erupted with both protests and defenses. Brigan smiled, his dimples coming in strong as he prepared to state his points.

I was about to inform Brigan that he was dead wrong when I felt a little tug on my sleeve. Looking down, I saw Dusty sneaking out from underneath the bed.

"There you are, little guy," I whispered to him under the din of conversation. "Where have you been hiding?"

I was glad to see my dad's ethereal draccoon. I hadn't seen him since returning from the Mists when he'd immediately snuck out Captain Zoren's office window after coming through the Farseer's portal.

Dusty squeaked, narrowing his eyes and using his tail to gesture toward the door. I didn't speak draccoon, but I got the feeling he'd been steering clear of the commanders keeping watch on me for the past three days. Like my dad, Dusty didn't mix well with authority.

Dusty gave a sly chitter, holding something shiny in his ratlike fists. I raised an eyebrow and held out my hand.

If I hadn't already been sitting down, I might've passed out. Glowing up from my palm was a long, thin crystal, pulsing with lightning blue energy. Scratched in white along both its top face as well as the face on the opposite side were words—or rather, two names.

On one side was the name *Kjell*.

On the other, *Agnai*.

As I read the names in my mind, a cold, even violent shudder shot through me. My blood ran with ice at the sound of a shrill scream inside my head, and for a moment, my vision flashed bright blue.

Then, as quickly as the terrifying feeling had come, it was gone.

I didn't dare think the names again. The second one puzzled me, since it wasn't an Evgardian name. It sounded much older. I had no idea what the names written on the crystal meant, but already I knew I didn't want to find out.

"Anyone who puts fruit on flatbread should be banished from the realm," Edrea was saying.

Jax came to spineapple's passionate defense. "Tomatoes are a fruit, and you let them stay."

"You could put literally anything on cheesy tomato flatbread and I'd be in," Cam reasoned. He jabbed Jax with an elbow, and the two guys exchanged united glances.

The squad continued arguing as Dusty beamed up at me. I remembered how good he'd been at climbing along the craggy cave ceiling back in the lava tube. He must've snuck across the stillwater pond while the Farseer had distracted the wraith. That's why I'd seen Dusty make a flying leap from the stalactites above in order to make it through the Farseer's escape rift in time.

Soot, I thought as I clutched the blue voidshard in my hand. People had died trying to get this thing. And its dark power was unmistakable.

Suddenly, I heard the door slowly creaking open, and Dusty darted back beneath the bed. Unsure what else to do, I ducked my head and rapidly runetraced to open my spice cabinet rift hold. I shoved the deadly, realm-shattering blue crystal inside the tiny space, right between the paprika and vanilla bean.

I had no sooner dismissed my rune and closed the rift when the door swung open. I was surprised to see Commander Leif in the doorway, huffing as if he'd run all the way here.

My squad scrambled to their feet, pretending they hadn't just been laughing with the prisoners.

"Commander," Brigan started. "We were just—"

Commander Leif cut him off. "Captain Zoren requests the magi report to him at once to be brought before the king."

"The king of Rengard?" Brigan was taken aback. Admittedly, so was I.

"Thank the goddesses," Jax muttered, getting to his feet. I did the same.

We were just about to leave with Commander Leif when Brigan joined us in the doorway.

"I'd better come along, Commander," Brigan patted the hilt of his seaxe. "For supervision purposes."

Commander Leif gave a distracted nod of agreement as the four of us started toward the citadel.

Chapter 30: The King

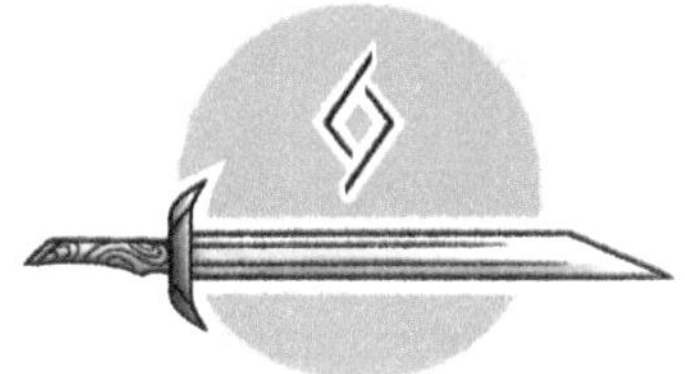

The citadel hallways reminded me of traveling down the canyons. They made you feel small and insignificant as you walked their endless trails. Intricate tapestries lined the halls, as well as portraits of past queens and kings of the Canyon Keepdom.

They'd given Jax and me new, clean guard's uniforms for our visit before the king. They still hadn't decided whether they'd reinstate us or not, but this way we'd raise less suspicion. It felt right to once again have the orange cloak falling over my shoulder, though I wished they'd given us back our weapons as well. I felt too vulnerable without my seaxe.

Captain Zoren led Jax, Brigan, and me at a brisk pace. Brigan seemed giddy at the idea of meeting the king himself, even if his highness wasn't going to be conscious when we got there. Jax seemed just as overwhelmed as I was by the finery and grandeur of the citadel.

As we hurried toward the king's chambers, Zoren spoke with urgency. "The voidshard—What did it look like?"

"Like a sharp fragment of skystone," Jax replied. "Only bright blue."

"Did you see anything else?" Zoren asked. "Any... writing on it?"

"It was too far away in the cavern," Jax answered. Zoren cast me a glance over his shoulder as we walked.

I didn't speak up. The thought of saying the names written in the crystal out loud filled me with a sense of icy dread. Besides, I still wasn't sure what side Zoren was on. He was one of the most famed Mage Hunters in the realm, and Zyri had mentioned something about the Hunters being among those dabbling in the darkness. What if Zoren wanted to use the shard to bring more darkness to Evgard?

"In the cavern, Meleya," Captain Zoren pressed, his tone flat and foreboding. "Did you get the chance to see what was written on the voidshard?"

I swallowed. "No."

It technically wasn't a lie. I hadn't been able to read the shard until my thieving pet draccoon had dropped it into my palm *after* leaving the cavern.

Zoren cast me a dark, skeptical look. But we'd just arrived at a set of ornately-carved double doors, a pair of guards standing in front of each side. As members of the king's high guard, they wore long, black cloaks with Rengard orange trim.

Zoren took another step closer, but the high guards didn't move.

"Step aside," Captain Zoren said. "We need to see the king."

One of the soldiers narrowed his eyes at Zoren's sharp black horns.

"Step aside, by order of the Captain of the Guard," Zoren repeated more forcefully, turning so that the guard could get a better look at the Captain's symbol on his oversized pauldron. His dragonfire green eyes were glittering. I realized with a pang of sympathy that, as a Drekai, he must've been used to dealing with pushback like this constantly.

The guard stuck out his chin, but moved out of the way. Zoren reached for the handle, flinging the door open himself. Both high guards gave distasteful looks directed at our silvermarks as Jax and I followed. At least Brigan made it through without any negative reactions.

The king's chamber was even more grand than the hallways. It was spacious, with high ceilings and long windows that would've let in a lot of light if the elegant, dark orange drapes hadn't been shut tight over them. The room seemed to go on and on, black and white pillars carved with flying dragons separating the different sections. There was a personal banquet table and chairs to one side, and a large desk covered in papers and books on the other. A lush dragon buffalo hide rug sat in front of a stately fireplace, and more orange drapes swept from the canopy of the largest bed I'd ever seen.

A cluster of healers huddled around the bed, as well as Queen Ilona herself. She looked just as lovely as she had on the day of my trial, her long, white and orange gown draped over the edge of the bed where she sat. Her long hair was curled to perfection, and a single tear graced her large, dewy eyes.

The rest of the king's high guard stood by as well, and I couldn't help but size them up as we entered the room. They were the ones who had supposedly single-handedly taken out the entire Coven of the Gray Ones. They certainly looked capable, but I was still sure no squad of seven would stand a chance against so many magi. Some sort of treachery was definitely at play.

Both the high guard and the healers gave Jax and me more disapproving looks as we approached. Jax held the crystal bottle filled with the Farseer's purple remedy in his hands.

The healers parted just enough for me to catch my first glimpse of a real king. King Axel looked ghostly pale as he lay on his silky pillow, his eyelids tense even in slumber.

Suddenly, one healer stepped between us and the king.

"We're sorry, Captain Zoren," he said in a snobbish voice. "As Captain of the Guard, we had no choice but to agree to your request to come before the king. But we can't allow the administration of this strange medicine."

"The remedy my soldiers bring comes from the Farseer himself," Zoren countered, not losing his cool.

"A mere legend," one of the other healers hissed.

"A rebel," seethed another.

"I trust my soldiers," Zoren stated.

"Well, isn't that reassuring," the first healer raised an eyebrow. "A *Drekai* trusts a couple of illegal *ethercursed.*"

A couple of people seemed shocked by the use of the word, especially in the presence of the noble family. But the rest seemed to feel the derogatory term was appropriate.

From his place at my side, Brigan confidently stepped in front of the healers. Without hesitation, he launched into a speech.

"You're absolutely right. Trusting the magi would be a mistake," Brigan said. On my other side, I could see Jax getting ready to protest. I shot him a look to tell him to hold off and let Brigan work his own kind of magic.

"Who's this?" the head healer asked pompously.

"Brigan, Heir Duke of Solhelm, fourth house of the Canyonlands," my friend responded proudly, and the healers seemed to accept this as grounds for allowing him to go on.

"Your desire to protect our great king comes first and foremost, as it should. I can't help but admire that," Brigan continued, and the healers brightened a little at his praise. "And that's why I'm sure you'll be among the first to admit, none of the standard cures seem to be working."

The healers glanced toward the dying king. Brigan went on.

"At this rate, King Axel has what? A few days?" The healers grimaced, looking at their feet.

Brigan raised his eyebrows. "Perhaps not even that. Now, by trying this new remedy, we lose very little in the grand scheme of things, no matter how things play out. Worst case scenario, it fails to revive the king. But think of what we would gain if it were to work."

Brigan began pacing in front of the healers, making his way closer to where King Axel lay.

"We'd have our great leader back, and you would be the reason. Your decision to take this chance to save the king's life would prove your wisdom as healers. It would be the source of so much good, especially in these dark times as we face imminent war with the Dragon Isles. What greater gift could be bestowed upon the keepdom than the chance at life?"

A couple of healers nodded as Brigan gave his impassioned closing argument. I found myself nodding as well—Brigan's points made a lot of sense. The king was going to die unless they tried something drastic, and it looked like deep down, the healers knew that as well.

The head healer looked at the tiny crystal bottle in Jax's hands. Then he gave a reluctant wave, ushering Jax forward.

"No," a soft voice rose from the king's bedside. Queen Ilona looked at us, her large eyes shining in the low light.

The head healer spoke up. "But as the young Heir Duke said, we have no—"

"Please." The queen's shiny lower lip quivered. "I will not allow anyone to disturb my husband's last moments. If he must pass into Etheria, he will do so in peace."

A low growl erupted from deeper within the chamber. My eyes widened as a large, third ascension wyvern with gleaming brown scales emerged from the shadows.

"Lantha," I muttered, automatically inclining my head with reverence toward the dragon. She'd saved my life once already with her testimony at my trial.

Axel wishes to have the remedy administered, Lantha projected her thoughts to everyone in the room. *My spirit is still connected with his, and can feel him through the bond. His emotions are difficult to detect, but they are clear. He trusts the magi who saved my life during the attack on the dragon stables. Let her pass.*

Even Ilona couldn't argue with Lantha's declaration. The queen stepped aside, her beautiful face screwing up as I took the Farseer's remedy from Jax and made my way to the king's bedside.

He didn't look peaceful as he slept. The light wrinkles around his mouth and along his forehead were strained and deeper than they should've been. The king couldn't have been more than thirty-five or so, but the dark circles beneath his eyes made it look like he'd lived a long, difficult life.

Steadying myself against the edge of the bed, I tried to keep my hands from shaking as I felt everyone's eyes on me. When I pulled out the stopper from the crystal bottle, a smell like sweet lavender wafted from within.

I reached behind the king's head, tilting it backward so that his mouth opened at just the right angle. Then I carefully poured the elixir down his throat.

The entire room held their breath, eyes locked onto King Axel. Nothing happened for over a minute.

Then, with a sudden, sharp inhale, the king's eyes flew open. Gasps and mutters reverberated throughout the room, and immediately the head healer rushed forward, grabbing me by the scruff of my cloak and shoving me away.

Competing with the head healer for the prime place at King Axel's bedside was Queen Ilona, her eyes bright with more tears.

"My sweet Axel," she sidestepped the head healer to melodramatically throw herself over her husband's chest. The king winced.

"Ilona?" King Axel murmured.

"They said you wouldn't wake—I was so worried. Months, Axel. Months you've been so far from me, but I never lost hope. Not once."

The king narrowed his eyes at the queen as a deeply confused look crossed his face. He looked like he wanted to say something to his wife, but he seemed to notice for the first time the small army of healers and strangers gathered around his bed. Everyone in the room immediately knelt before the King of Rengard. I took a knee alongside Brigan and Jax.

With a measure of difficulty, King Axel got the queen to pull back enough to allow him to sit up. He rubbed his head, trembling with the effort. Lantha made a low, rumbling sound in her throat as she lowered her head toward her rider.

"Lantha," King Axel said, putting a hand on her head. The tiniest bit of tension released from his brow at his dragon's touch.

"My king," Captain Zoren began, still down on one knee. "Much has happened since the dream realm claimed you. I understand if you need time to rest before—"

"Absolutely he needs time to rest," the head healer snapped. "A few days at least before you pester his majesty with your petty matters."

"Petty matters?" Captain Zoren got to his feet. "Is that what you call our Keepdom's situation?"

"Enough. We don't want to overwhelm our poor king. Not in his current state."

But before Captain Zoren could respond, King Axel cleared his throat. "If I may, I'll be the judge of my own state. How does that sound?"

The head healer grit his teeth. "Of course, your majesty."

The king nodded calmly before turning to Captain Zoren. "Please, Captain. Tell me what's happened."

Captain Zoren explained everything with surprising efficiency. He told the king of the events after the attack on the stables, and how the queen, acting as his regent, had called for war with the Dragon Isles. King Axel cast his wife a measured, unreadable look.

Zoren went on to tell Axel of the Coven of the Gray Ones' assault on Outcast Outpost, and the high guard jumped in to assure the king that they'd taken care of the threat. Zoren narrowed his eyes at the high guard, but didn't contradict them.

"Whatever the case," Zoren said, his voice even, "I have it on good authority that the Coven's intention is to launch an attack on the Rise on the night of the Winter Solstice two days from now."

One of the members of the king's high guard scoffed. King Axel frowned as he spoke.

"And what authority might that be, Captain?"

Without hesitation, Captain Zoren nodded to Jax and me. "Two of my soldiers, Meleya of Misthaven and Jax of Blackfjord, your majesty."

A few from the high guard muttered the word 'magi,' under their breath. One was bold enough to call us 'ethercursed,' earning a look from the king.

The king cleared his throat. "If you trust your informants, Captain Zoren, then that's enough for me. We must prepare for the worst." Beside him, Queen Ilona made a little noise of mock shock.

The king winced again, bringing both hands to his head.

"What did I tell you?" the head healer said. "He needs some time to recover."

"A little time, perhaps," King Axel managed. "Captain Zoren and I will talk in private once I can clear my head. But in the meantime, Captain, you'll fulfill my order to…"

The king trailed off as another wave of dizziness hit him. His breathing was ragged as the healer quickly produced some kind of ointment, waving it in front of King Axel's nose. It didn't seem to help.

"Yes, your majesty?" Captain Zoren prompted.

The king closed his eyes, trying to regain his bearings. "Go, Captain Zoren. As of this moment, I want you to prepare the troops. When and if the Coven of the Gray Ones attacks the Rise on the night of the Solstice, we will be ready."

FRAGMENT - SNIFF

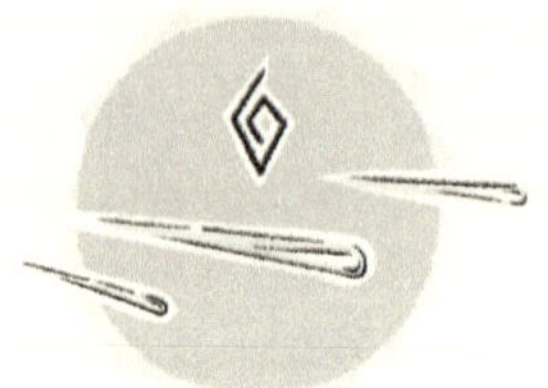

C hains.

Meleya's bond hadn't felt like chains.

Sniff wrapped his wings more tightly around him. It was dark down here. Dark and quiet, despite the eight other dragons huddled in the cage with him. He didn't know where he was, only that he was afraid.

Whoever had kidnapped Sniff had been subtle. One moment, he was being taken to the newly-rebuilt stables on the Rise, and the next, someone was shoving him into this dark cave. They'd used one of those lightning blue dream darts to make him too tired to fight back.

Not that Sniff had had a choice. After all, they had Sniff's heartscale.

When Meleya had worn Sniff's heartscale, it had made him feel stronger. Empowered and connected. But the person who wore it now wasn't someone Sniff had chosen. This bond felt hollow. Cold.

Like chains.

Chapter 31: Rescue

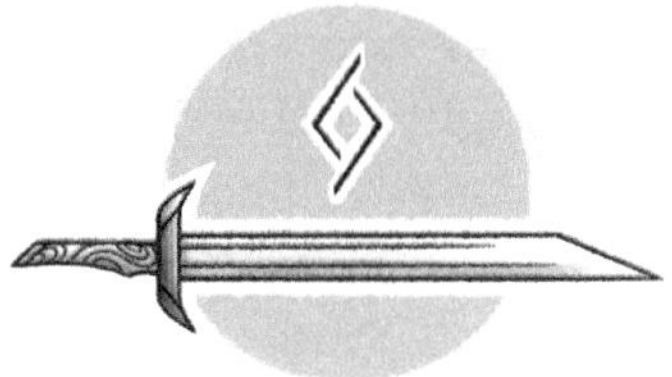

The deep orange sunlight streamed through the window, shining onto the bunker's tan adobe walls. The feel of flour on my hands, the smell of fire from inside the oven, and the comfort of being surrounded by people I cared about meant that for the first time in a while, I truly felt at home.

Solvai sat in her usual place at the end of the table, a block of wood ready to take shape in front of her. Brigan sat opposite Solvai, leaning back in his chair against the wall. Even Dusty was happily snoring from his old spot above the rafters.

The bunker was small, but the others had managed to find places of their own. Edrea sat at the table as well, Cam at her side. Erik was on the floor near the door, hunched contentedly over his sketchbook. And Jax... well, Jax seemed to have recovered from the fatigue of the Dragon Mists. He'd swiped my heavy iron tea kettle, psionically adding extra weight to it as he lifted while doing squats near the window.

As for me, I was right where I belonged behind the countertop, rolling out circles of dough and putting together toppings for tonight's dinner—cheesy tomato flatbread. I assured Brigan, Edrea, and Erik that I'd refrain from putting spineapple on half of it.

I'd been elated when, at Captain Zoren's request and with Lantha backing him up, the king granted Jax and me temporary magi registration status. The war had restationed a few of the keep's nine registered magi in places closer to the Dragon Isles anyway, which left room for us—for now.

At King Axel's order, Captain Zoren was doing what he could to prepare the troops on the Rise for battle. Many of the commanders were hesitant to halt their efforts toward the Dragon Isles war, especially for a threat they saw as baseless. So many seemed to genuinely believe that the king's high guard had eradicated the Coven of the Gray Ones from Outcast Outpost. They thought the Coven had been so weakened that imagining them attacking the Rise the night of the Winter Solstice in three days was laughable. The other soldiers who'd been there with us didn't believe it either, but after a while, we'd stopped arguing back. Who'd believe a soldier from Squad Choke, Squad Struggle, or Squad Reckless over the high guard?

Still, King Axel insisted that they take every precaution, just to be safe. However, his waking had created even more conflict within both the court and the guard, since many of his advisors felt he was still too unstable to make rational decisions. Captain Zoren was getting pressured from all sides, but he was determined to do all he could to fulfill the king's wishes.

Meanwhile, the Rise was bustling with activity, preparing for the annual Winter Solstice Ball at the citadel. Every year, nobility came from all across the Canyon Keepdom to eat and dance and play their political games. Captain Zoren had strongly suggested they cancel the ball this year due to the Coven's threat, but Queen Ilona had refused, stating how important it was to keep up the keepdom's spirits during this time of fear. King Axel had given in to the queen's demand, though I was willing to bet he privately agreed with Captain Zoren.

Zoren had ordered the guard to practice battle formations the next morning at sunrise. Our temporary magi registration earned Jax and me places in the guard, which meant we were expected at morning muster along with the rest of Squad Reckless.

We'd just finished dinner when the sun was beginning to set. Solvai suggested we all return to the barracks to get some sleep before the following day's drills. As we started down the path back, Brigan pulled me aside.

"Can you stay for a minute?" he asked.

"Of course." I glanced down the dirt road at the retreating forms of our squadmates. Jax immediately noticed I'd fallen behind and turned around to check on me. When he saw me with Brigan, his eyebrows furrowed slightly and he took a step back toward us.

I waved him along the path, then held up a finger to let him know I'd be along soon. He didn't seem thrilled about it, but he nodded.

Once Brigan and I were alone, he started walking down another path toward the little juniper glen near the northern edge of the butte. I fell into step beside him, the light of the setting sun casting long shadows of the two of us.

"It's good to be back on the Rise," I said after a lengthy silence.

Brigan didn't respond, so I kept talking.

"Beautiful evening." I gestured to the light shining against the twisted branches of the juniper trees. Still, Brigan said nothing. It was so unlike him—Brigan always had something to say.

"Thanks for helping clean up after dinner," I said again, trying to fill the silence. "I really appreciate—"

Brigan suddenly stopped walking to throw his arms around me. He cupped his hand gently around the back of my head, pulling me into the crook between his shoulder and neck. I hugged him back, my voice muffled by his cloak.

"Are you okay?"

"Not really," he answered, not letting me go.

"Talk to me," I prompted.

He inhaled deeply, breathing in the scent of my hair. "I thought I lost you. I thought I'd never see you again, and I'd missed my chance."

"Chance for what?" I gently pushed back on Brigan's chest to look him in the eyes. They were as warm as ever, but lines of worry ran along the edges. He reluctantly released me from his embrace.

"I... I've never been at liberty to tell you... well, to tell you how I feel before." Brigan rubbed his palms together and I could tell they were sweating. I felt my cheeks starting to burn a little—where was Brigan going with this?

He plowed on, less articulate than I'd ever seen him before. "My whole life I've been engaged to another girl, which meant I had to be careful to keep my feelings in check. But when I met you, scorch, you didn't make it easy. You're brilliant and compassionate. You always put others' needs ahead of your own, and you're skilled, both in combat and in the kitchen. And on top of it all, you just had to have these gorgeous brown eyes that make me melt every time I see them."

I felt like my face was on fire as I looked down at my feet. I wasn't sure what to say. Not that Brigan was about to give me the chance. He was barely pausing long enough to breathe.

"Then the second I got that letter from my parents all but releasing me from my engagement, I felt like I was too late. I saw the way you laughed with Jax when he teased you. I've never seen you so relaxed, so free and happy."

Relaxed? I thought about telling Brigan about how often Jax and I argued, but thought better of it.

"It about killed me when I had to watch you running into the Dragon Mists with him," Brigan went on, hurt flashing across his face. "I felt so powerless and weak, and so stupid for letting you go without telling you how I felt."

I felt an army of dragonflies aflutter in my stomach. "Brigan, I—"

"Please. I have to say this." Brigan looked desperate as he took a deep breath. When he exhaled, his heart came out along with his breath. "I love you, Meleya of Misthaven. Whatever happens, I need you to know that."

My mouth fell open, but no words came out. The best I could achieve was a couple of awkward, stuttering noises.

Brigan took my silence as a signal to plow forward. "I want you to accompany me to the Winter Solstice Ball at the citadel. Not as my squadmate, but as my guest as the Heir Duke of Solhelm. Don't worry if you don't have a ballgown—My family is coming into town tomorrow and I'm sure we can find you something of my sister's that fits."

"No." My voice came out as barely a whisper.

Brigan frowned. "Of course. We can absolutely get a tailor to make you a new gown—"

"Not that," I said. "I mean, I can't accompany you to the ball. It wouldn't be right."

Brigan's face fell. "Because of Jax?"

"That's part of it, I guess." I wrung my hands, cracking my knuckles just to have something to do. "Though I'd be lying if I said I never wished there could be something more between me and you. But Brigan, look at me. I'm a silvermarked magi. I doubt your parents and the other nobles would exactly be thrilled to see me on your arm."

"I've thought of that," Brigan swallowed. "If we could just tell them you were working on getting shortlisted for the magi cure, they might accept it."

My heart dropped into my stomach. "You still want me to get cured?"

"Of course," Brigan said. "Isn't that what you want? To be allowed to live freely in the realm? Be with whomever you want? Your parents—I could get them on the list as well, I'm sure of it."

A thousand thoughts churned inside my head. Brigan was right—or at least he would've been just a few months ago. Before going to Outcast Outpost, I longed for the cure and the chance to be like everyone else. But now… I couldn't exactly explain it, but I'd found a new purpose as a Rifter. I loved the rush of channeling my etherarchy. I loved feeling strong and capable when it came to protecting those I cared about.

Jax understood that. It hurt me to realize that Brigan didn't. Maybe he never could.

"I'm sorry," I felt tears well up in my eyes. Not wanting him to see me cry, I took a few steps backward along the path before turning and hurrying away.

Behind me, Brigan's voice broke as he called my name, but I couldn't bring myself to go back. The first tear cascaded across my left cheek, sliding smoothly over the ridges of my silvermark.

Blue lightning crackled all around me as the storm raged. Only I wasn't on the ground—I was falling through endless gray clouds. Below me were the gaping jaws of an enormous, bloodthirsty dragon.

Blink's silvery evren wings flapped between me and the beast. She roared, as if preparing to battle the gigantic monster, but I knew she couldn't win against such a foe.

Suddenly, I came face to face with a pair of glowing blue eyes. The man was pale, and his oddly ageless face seemed hollow. Shreds from his tattered gray robes swirled in the air around him as he brandished a jagged starglass dagger.

I tried to scream, but no sound came out as I fell through the emptiness.

When I finally managed to force myself to wake from the nightmare, I was sweating. My breathing was ragged, and my whole body trembled.

On the pillow beside me, a vivid blue light pulsed. The Soul Reaper's voidshard lay only inches away from my face, one of the names I didn't want to think about again staring at me, taunting me.

I hurried to close my fist around the crystal. I was sure I'd left it in my rift hold—How had it gotten here?

If Solvai or Edrea woke up and saw the shard, they'd have questions. Just knowing about this thing could put them in danger. Unsure what else to do, I shakily traced the rune to reopen my rift hold and replaced the voidshard inside it.

I'd no sooner closed the ethereal pocket when a long, pleading note rang out so sharply I was almost positive the others had heard it as well.

I narrowed my eyes at my squadmates' bunks, but Edrea and Solvai still slept soundly.

I clutched at my heart. That note had felt an awful lot like Sniff's high-pitched, musical communication. Blink's heartscale hung securely around my neck, but Sniff's was still gone. So why did I get the feeling my little yellow evren was in danger?

My feet landed on the cold adobe floor with a soft thud. Edrea didn't stir, but Solvai rolled over in her bunk, her eyes fluttering open. When she saw the look on my face, she frowned.

"Meleya?" she whispered, rubbing the sleep from her eyes. "What's wrong?"

"Sniff," I said quietly. "I think he needs help."

"You can still feel him?"

I nodded.

Solvai flipped her blanket aside and got to her feet. Already, she was reaching for her boots.

"What are you doing?" I asked.

Without hesitation, Solvai responded. "I'm coming with you."

Solvai and I left our orange cloaks behind, not wanting to look too conspicuous as we snuck into the barrack's shared hallway. We were surprised to find Brigan there, sitting against the wall, reading a thick book by candlelight.

Based on the dark circles under his eyes, he hadn't slept since our conversation. Guilt pricked my heart.

When he saw Solvai and me, he immediately shut his book. Solvai explained the situation, and Brigan stood.

"I'm coming too," he said. "If Sniff's in trouble, I want to help."

He looked at me, pain still etched in his eyes. But there was also determination there. He'd always been a rock to me, a source of peace and calm amidst so much chaos. That was the kind of man Brigan was. I felt a sudden, rushing wave of regret—Had I been wrong to turn him down?

Both Solvai and Brigan knew we were risking a lot by going out. But they also probably knew I wouldn't just stand by and do nothing, not when my dragon was afraid and possibly in danger. Anger filled my heart at the very thought of someone hurting him.

I set my jaw. "Do you have your primary weapons?"

Solvai gripped the shaft of her dragonhook spear while Brigan patted the hilt of his seaxe. A long seaxe of my own hung satisfyingly at my belt, right alongside my saltshaker pouch and the quartz crystal Jax had given me. I'd filled it this morning, the extra ether ready for use in a pinch.

"Backup weapons? And are they sharpened?" I asked, and my friends nodded. Solvai's tomahawk was strapped to her belt and Brigan gestured to the jeweled dagger at his.

A sinking feeling hit me as I realized I was the only one without a backup weapon. I'd given Erik my father's dagger back at Outcast Outpost. Since returning to the Rise, Erik had offered to give it back, but I told him to keep it until he got his hands on another that was to his liking.

Then I remembered what Jax had said back at the Dragon Mists:

M, you are *the backup weapon.*

I looked between my two best friends, giving them a reassuring nod as we quietly headed down the hallway.

There was no time to waste. Though my bond with Sniff was dull and unpredictable, I could feel that he wasn't too far—though I didn't think he was on the Rise. We snuck through the city all the way to the narrow, geomancy-powered land bridge that connected the butte to the eastern rim of the canyon.

Somehow, we didn't think the guard on duty there would look upon three soldiers crossing in the dead of night without suspicion. Brigan was sure he could convince the guard to keep quiet about it, but I had a simpler solution. We hid ourselves behind a cluster of bramblevines where I could still see the other side of the canyon. I locked my gaze on a stony hoodoo across the gap, then runetraced.

The gold light was brighter than I wanted it to be in the darkness, but the vines covered us pretty well. Solvai, Brigan and I stepped through the rift to emerge beside the hoodoo. I felt my ether well drain a little, but it still felt fairly full. Just a few months ago, a jump that far would've used up half my ether.

Faint traces of flute-like notes pulled me further east. I felt a little ridiculous, guiding my friends across the varied landscape by literally following my heart. We traveled further and further into the craggy, juniper and sagebrush-covered wilderness until finally, another tiny tug from Sniff caused me to stop.

My friends and I looked around at the wind-smoothed sandstone formations beneath our feet. There were a couple of squat, spiny cacti nearby, but not much else. As if to emphasize my thoughts, a single tumbleweed rolled across the ground in front of us.

"Where now?" Solvai asked, absently assuming a battle stance with her spear, as if something might come at us at any moment.

"I'm not sure," I muttered, closing my eyes to focus. The dim melody from Sniff didn't compel me forward, backward, left, or right. That left...

I looked down at the sandstone beneath my feet. Frowning, I raised a finger to trace the rune for the Sight.

When I blinked, the dim world burst into vibrant color. Solvai's cerulean aura and Brigan's red one burned brightly at my sides, but I was surprised by the large, silvery spirit dragon that hovered along with them.

Blink, I thought through our bond. *Have you been following us this whole time?*

Drrrum-ba-bum, Blink confirmed, and I could tell she was worried about Sniff too. I got the feeling she'd been having about as much trouble connecting with him lately as I was.

Suddenly, a distant musical note that felt almost like a scream directed both my gaze and Blink's downward. I did a double take when I realized I could see faint traces of what looked like auras through the stone. During our training sessions, Torsten had assured me that as I got more experienced with the Sight, physical barriers like walls would stop mattering as much to my ethereal eyes.

As if reading my thoughts, Blink's spirit suddenly dove straight downward through the stone as if it were air. Her silvery aura joined the others I saw down there. My eyes narrowed as I tracked her movement beneath the stone, her clouded, shining form coming to a stop a short distance from the rest of the other, dimmer auras.

I felt a solid thud through our bond, as if Blink were inviting me to join her down there. My brows furrowed. Could I do that?

"What's going on?" Solvai asked.

I still hadn't told anyone about Blink, but I explained that I could see some faint auras through the solid rock. Looking around, I picked up a smooth, solid piece of redrock just smaller than the size of my palm. I'd practiced the rune for rift anchors enough with Torsten that I had it memorized. I used my finger to trace it now, gold light burning the symbol into the stone.

"What's that?" Brigan pointed to the little rock as I set it on the ground at our feet.

"Rift anchor," I replied, already tracing the standard portalling rune in the air. "So I can get back here without physically seeing this spot. I'm going to try rifting down to those auras under the ground," I said. "I know that's insane, so don't feel obligated to come along."

Both Brigan and Solvai stood staunchly to my left and right as I focused on Blink's aura through the ground beneath our feet. I wasn't sure it would work, rifting to an aura rather than a place I could see with my physical eyes, but still, the gold tear ripped open before us. Together, Solvai, Brigan, and I stepped through the portal and into the unknown.

Chapter 32: Underground

When we came out the other side, I felt like I'd stepped into my nightmare.

I bit back a scream as I took in the dark tunnel lit by lightning blue crystals. The cold, still air sent dragonbumps up my arms, and the hairs on the back of my neck stood on end.

I stumbled backward, barely catching myself on my hands as I fell to the ground. Without thinking, I began looking around for Jax, terrified that I'd see umbral monsters or a wraith about to slit his throat. Then, for a horrifying instant, I irrationally feared that I'd see that pale, gray-robed man from my dream stepping out of the shadows.

I started taking in rapid, shallow breaths. Within a second, Brigan was kneeling at my side, a hand on my arm.

"Breathe, Meleya," he whispered. "Just focus on breathing."

With the Sight still activated, I could see his strong, red aura interacting with my indigo one. The red mist flowed like water, calming the wild blue-violet spirals. I felt my pulse slow, and my breathing evened out.

As I relaxed, I let my rune dissolve. The Sight fled my eyes, leaving only the eerie, bright blue crystals to light the tunnel.

"It's so much like the cavern I saw in the Dragon Mists," I shuddered.

"It's like the light in the eyes of umbral creatures, too," Solvai observed. "And the etherarchy the Coven of the Gray Ones used."

"I think that's exactly who's using it now," Brigan said. "Look."

Brigan pointed further down the tunnel, where something was written on the wall. There was a depiction of a bright red moon with blue lines running through it, right beside the words: *The Gray Ones will rise.* On the ground beneath the writing was a mask like the ones the Coven had worn into battle.

I felt like a frigid hand had closed around my heart. Did the Coven have Sniff?

"Listen," Solvai said, taking a few more steps down the tunnel.

Then I heard it too. The all-too-familiar sound of otherworldly, draconic snarls.

"Dreklings," I confirmed, realizing that those must've been the other auras I'd seen through the rock. Just as I said it, I felt another faint, musical tug from Sniff coming from further down the tunnel, right past the snarling dreklings.

Of course.

"This way," I said, keeping my hand at the ready on the hilt of my seaxe. Cautiously, the three of us headed down the blue-lit tunnel.

It wasn't long before we came across the first alcove carved into the rock. Iron bars blocked it off from the rest of the winding tunnel, and pressing up against those bars were at least ten angry dreklings. Umbral ones, just like those Jax and I had battled in the wraith's cavern.

We hugged the opposite side of the cave wall, avoiding their long, clawed hands as the gray monsters tried to get at us. They were probably extra hungry for my ether well—and Solvai's.

More garbled noises and the clanging of scales against iron alerted us to another similar pen of umbral dreklings a little further down the tunnel. As we continued walking, we saw more and more of these alcoves filled with the rabid, umbral creatures.

"These must be the ones the Coven of the Gray Ones is planning to use in their assault on Keep Rengard," Solvai said, dodging a swipe from a gnarled, gray claw. "Where in the void did they get so many dreklings?"

"Probably skyfalls in the Mists," I replied. "They must be luring them in with skystone, or maybe their own magi's ether wells, then turning them all umbral."

I shuddered at the thought. Brigan started mumbling numbers under his breath.

"What are you doing?" Solvai cocked her head.

"Thirty-six, thirty seven..." Brigan mumbled before turning toward us. "Getting an estimate of their numbers so we can tell the king and Captain of the Guard what to expect."

Brigan continued counting as we came to the end of the tunnel. We cautiously peeked out from behind a jutting sandstone, staring into the wider space before us.

My breath caught as I took in an enormous cage that reached from ceiling to floor. Inside the cage were nine dragons—among them a terrified evren crouching in the corner, his bright yellow scales standing out from all the rest.

I felt a tiny ping of sadness through our ghost of a bond. The bars in the cage shone in the dim blue light from more crystals, and I was certain the bars were forged with silver. They glinted in the same way as the ones on my parents' cells in Spydra Prison. The cage was vast, but not quite big enough for nine full-sized dragons, which meant every once in a while a wing or tail would brush against the silver, causing a dragon to roar or whimper in pain. Did that mean all of the dragons in the cage were mythic?

"Stars above," Solvai muttered under her breath, jabbing me with an elbow.

I followed her gaze to see a man seated in a creaky wooden rocking chair not far from the cage of dragons. He snored lightly as his enormous girth slumped in the chair, an empty bottle clutched in his hand.

There was no mistaking Torsten.

"He's alive," Solvai whispered, relief coloring her tone. "I worried what would happen to him and the others in the shanty town when the Coven took the Outpost."

"It looks like your worry was unnecessary," Brigan said darkly. "Torsten must've been in the Coven the whole time."

Brigan was right, of course, and seeing him here as some sort of guard for these dragons dispelled any doubt my friends might have had. Solvai pressed her lips into a tight line.

"Drakking traitor," she muttered. I cringed. This was probably not the right time to tell my friend that Torsten was almost definitely her father.

"I can see Sniff over there," Brigan said quietly. "Torsten's a pretty heavy sleeper..."

"You think we can sneak past him?" I finished the thought.

I was about to leave our relatively hidden position behind the sandstone ridge when the sound of footsteps froze me in place. Brigan, Solvai, and I sank back behind the rock, just daring to peek over the edge to see who was coming.

A figure in loose, hooded gray robes stalked proudly across the space in front of the caged dragons. I felt my blood run cold as I recognized the ornate, marked mask with sweeping draconic horns molded into the crown.

The Liberator.

Brigan and Solvai tensed as they recognized the Coven leader as well. Following close behind the Liberator were two more gray-robed figures, both wearing marked masks. I wasn't quite close enough to make out what the writing on their masks said.

The Liberator and their companions came to a stop in front of Torsten's wooden rocking chair. They waited for a few moments, clearly expecting him to wake up. Instead, Torsten let out a long, echoing snore.

Even in the low light, and despite the masks, I got the vibe that the more masculine of the Liberator's hooded followers was rolling his eyes. Angular gold patterns glowed from the skin on the back of his hands as he held them over a strange, rope-like belt wrapped around his waist.

The belt trembled a little as it began snaking around his body and onto the ground. I realized that it wasn't a rope at all, but a growing vine. By the sharp, steely-looking thorns running along its length, I guessed it was a cutting from an ironclaw plant. Etherarchy like that could only mean this Coven member was a Woodweaver.

The vine wound its way up the leg and along the back of Torsten's chair. One sharp thorn grew longer, its tip just centimeters away from Torsten's nose.

A split second before it stabbed him, Torsten's eyes flew open in alarm. His arms flailed as he rocked so far backward in his chair that I was shocked when it didn't fall over and dump him onto the ground.

"Drakes alive," Torsten sputtered. "An' a good mornin' to the likes of y'all as well."

The Woodweaver gave a gruff, sinister chuckle. Torsten heard him and promptly burst into uproarious laughter himself, a couple of tears streaming down his face. The Woodweaver stopped laughing immediately, as if Torsten enjoying his prank had ruined the fun.

Then the Liberator spoke, their voice sounding so strange and distorted that I couldn't tell whether the voice belonged to a man or a woman. Some kind of auditory illusion etherarchy was clearly at play.

"We've come for an update regarding our forces at Outcast Outpost," the Liberator said. "Have the new soldiers arrived from our camps along the mist's edge?"

"Ain't that a question," Torsten observed, slurring as badly as ever. "Lemme just pop over there an' check."

With that, Torsten traced a blurry, drunken portaling rune. He clumsily directed it over himself and his rocking chair as he vanished into Etheria. He returned mere moments later, laughing hysterically, a new, full bottle of dark mystery liquid in his hands.

"Woo," he wheezed as if he were still talking to someone not present here under the rock. "Take care of yourself, Jormund! See you at the coup!" Torsten doubled over with laughter as he fumbled to undo the stopper on the bottle.

The Liberator silently watched Torsten's display, but the shorter, more feminine of their masked followers folded her arms impatiently. When the woman spoke, her voice was muffled by her mask.

"We don't have time for this soot and nonsense. People will notice our absence—particularly *my* absence, soon. Speak, drunk. Have our new soldiers arrived at the Outpost?"

Torsten stuttered in response, "Sure as the void, them soldiers've arrived. Swarmin' the Broughkin Arms tavern, too. Glad I checked on 'em—snagged this lil' darlin' 'fore it were too late!"

He caressed the bottle for a second before returning to the task of opening it. His face turned red as he struggled with the cork. With a final grunt and a popping noise, Torsten sent the cork whizzing into the air, through the silver bars of the dragon cage to smack a wyvern in the flank. The dragon hissed, but Torsten was too busy taking a gulp to apologize.

The Liberator's distorted voice filled the underground. "Our army is nearly complete. Two nights hence, we'll launch our attack and take the keepdom."

"But what about the king?" the female Coven member said with bitterness. "Already he grows in strength from that scorching remedy."

"I know," the Liberator said. "He and the Captain of the Guard also know we plan to strike on the Solstice. But we won't let this frustrate our plans. Our numbers are strong, our power even stronger. And now that I've obtained the heartscales of all nine types of mythic dragon, the power of the ancient Guardians will make me unstoppable."

The Liberator stalked toward the cage of dragons, using their gloved hand to pull out a cord from under the collar of their robes. Nine shining heartscales to match the hides of the dragons in the cage hung from it. My eyes widened.

The Woodweaver clasped his hands together gleefully. "You were able to find a replacement for the Astromancer dragon we lost?"

I felt my pulse race like rapids as the Liberator singled out a bright yellow heartscale on their necklace. They closed a hand around it, and I saw Sniff's body go rigid as he obediently made his way past the other dragons to the front of the cage. His fiery green eyes were round with fear, but with his heartscale in the hands of the Liberator, he had no choice but to serve their whims. Another faint pang swelled in my heart and my blood began to boil.

I hadn't realized I'd been getting to my feet until Solvai put a strong hand on my arm to pull me quietly back down. She was right—taking action now wouldn't help Sniff. It would only put my friends and me in danger. We needed a rescue plan with finesse, not brash aggression.

I bit my tongue to avoid gasping while blue mist encompassed the Liberator's arm. Within moments, they'd grown a row of dark brown feathers along their forearm, hand, and fingers.

That's right, I thought. *The Liberator is a Wildshaper.*

They stretched their arm into the cage, waving the tips of their feathers under Sniff's nose. Sniff's face screwed up, his eyes crossing as he prepared to sneeze.

Just as Sniff was about to blast their faces, the Liberator morphed their hand and arm back to normal, squeezing Sniff's yellow scale. Obediently, Sniff threw his head upward, directing the ether blast accompanying his sneeze toward the cage roof. Since it was made from silver, the ether did nothing to affect it.

The Woodweaver smirked. "Impressive. Not the most sophisticated dragon, I'll admit."

"But he'll serve our purpose," the Liberator concluded.

"Where did you find him?"

"He was the only starshot dragon in the guard at the Rise. I'd been working to remove his rider from the picture for months before the commander at the southern border did our job for us, leaving the dragon ripe for the picking. The omens have favored us."

My stomach turned as I recalled what Trickshot had suggested about the umbral coyotes who'd attacked me at the North Tower. Had the Liberator been the one mind controlling them? All in an effort to get me killed—or at least decommissioned—so they could take my dragon?

The Liberator continued. "With the power of the Guardians at our disposal, the people of Evgard will soon bow before the Gray Ones."

When the Liberator spoke of the Gray Ones, a surge of cold washed over me so strongly it felt like a mighty canyon wind, though the air was perfectly still. This time, it wasn't just the feeling—I heard a voice as well.

Meleya.

The voice was quiet and raspy, chilling me to my bones. Without thinking, I took a step backward, as if I could flee the voice.

My foot scraped against the stony ground, echoing throughout the tunnel behind me. I froze as Solvai and Brigan cast me horrified looks. We ducked behind the sandstone, huddling together.

The Liberator and their followers went silent. They'd definitely heard me. I cursed myself.

Then Torsten broke the silence with an enormous burp.

"Did you hear that?" the masked woman asked.

Torsten cleared his throat. "Oh sorry, y'all. That was me."

"Not that," she snapped.

"Someone's here," the Liberator assured her. Then there was silence for a moment before I heard the low growl of a dragon. It sounded closer than the ones in the cage, and I wondered if the Liberator had wildshaped once more.

I pressed myself even closer against the sandstone ridge, clinging to Brigan and Solvai as I tried not to tremble. This was all my fault. If the Liberator found us—*when* the Liberator found us—there was no telling what they'd do.

The three of us held our breath as the sound of clawed feet approached our hiding place. In the dim blue light, I saw the shadow of a mighty dragon spill onto the tunnel wall.

I wanted to close my eyes and wait until this was over, but something gave me pause. It was hard to tell against the craggy walls of the tunnel, but I could've sworn that the shadow had four legs and a set of large, tucked wings. Only drakes had four legs, but they couldn't fly. Did that mean I was looking at the shadow of a true dragon? But I knew those were all but extinct in Evgard. Other than the young, white true dragon I'd briefly encountered behind the command center, I'd never seen one.

Until now, possibly.

Suddenly, the draconic footsteps came to a stop. I could hear the wild-shaping Liberator's draconic breath right above our heads. Brigan, Solvai, and I didn't move a muscle. I felt the urge to runetrace to rift us out of there, but on the slight chance the Liberator hadn't seen us, the last thing I wanted to do was light up a glowing, gold-rimmed portal in the darkness. Still, I held my finger ready.

Then I saw wisps of that blue Wildshaping mist curling around the edges of our hiding spot. The true dragon shadow disappeared as human footsteps retreated toward where Torsten and the others waited.

"Nobody," I heard the Liberator's distorted voice.

"Are you sure?" The Woodweaver sounded indignant. "I definitely heard something—"

"You were mistaken," the Liberator cut in. "We must go. The three of us must return to the citadel before anyone gets suspicious."

Shocked, and more than a little confused, Solvai, Brigan, and I waited as we heard the last sound of footsteps disappearing in the same direction they'd come. We could still hear Torsten finishing off that bottle, satisfied exhales piercing the silence every once in a while along with the shifting of the caged dragons.

After what felt like an eternity, we heard Torsten give one final belch. A few minutes later, he began to snore once more.

I counted the snores, and once I was sure he was deeply asleep, I stood up. My legs felt like a million needles were gently pricking into them over and over, and I had to grab onto the sandstone ridge to keep from crashing back to the ground.

I rubbed them quickly, and the second I regained enough balance, I strode right out into the open toward the dragon cage.

"Meleya," Solvai sharply whispered after me. "Are you crazy?"

"Yeah," I confirmed.

Casting a few more nervous glances toward Torsten, both Solvai and Brigan got up and followed me.

When Sniff saw me approaching the cage, his eyes lit up. He rushed toward the bars as if he wanted to barrel into me and lick my face like he always used to.

But the silver bars stopped him. He whimpered a little as they touched his hide and he backed up as I arrived.

"It's okay, buddy," I said, carefully reaching through the bars, avoiding contact with the silver myself. Sniff began panting gleefully as I rubbed him behind the ears.

"I'm going to get you out of here," I muttered. Then I took a step back, tracing a rifting rune. The gold-rimmed entrance portal ripped to life before me.

But when I tried to step through it, it felt like I'd just slammed my body into a solid stone wall. Sure enough, the silver in the dragon cage had prevented my exit portal from glowing to life inside.

I tried again, this time draining even more ether as I tried to channel enough to overcome the silver. I grunted in exasperation as my second attempt failed, then my third.

"Meleya, it's no use," Solvai said gently.

"I'm not leaving him." I stubbornly reached between the silver bars toward Sniff once more.

Just as my fingers came to rest on his nose, something in Sniff's eyes changed. His dragonfire green irises flashed, turning lightning blue. His round, puppy-like eyes narrowed to slits.

Sniff growled ferociously, then snapped his jaws toward my hand. I was stunned, and didn't think to move.

Luckily, Brigan stepped in, yanking me back from the cage just in time. Sniff gave another angry roar and, despite the silver, pressed his face up against the bars of the cage to try and get at me again.

I was vaguely aware of Torsten stirring not far from where we stood as Sniff barked and thrashed inside the cage.

"Meleya, we have to go," Solvai insisted.

"No," I said, still dazed. "Sniff, this isn't you."

Brigan continued to hold me back as I lifted a finger to trace the rune for the Sight. As the spirit plane exploded to life before my eyes, Sniff's brilliant, golden yellow aura filled my vision.

I focused on the small cavity in his chest where he'd scratched off his heartscale to give to me back in the Dragon Chasm. That day, I'd seen that space fill with indigo light from my aura.

Now, that piece of me was gone. Replacing it was black essence, surrounded by more of that cold, awful void blue.

I held up my wrist where a strong, golden yellow cuff once marked my bond with Sniff. It had faded to barely a wisp.

Sniff gave a long, feral roar. Behind me, I heard Torsten wake.

"What in the void," he slurred. "It can't be—What're you three doin' here?"

None of us knew how to respond. I was too busy staring at the dragon that was once my dear friend as he harmed himself on silver bars trying to kill me. Brigan tightened his grip around my waist—I must've still been fighting to get to Sniff.

"Drak," Torsten cursed. "Get the void outta here before the scorchin' Liberator or one of the others sees y'all."

Solvai and Brigan looked at me, but I couldn't think straight.

"Go. *Now*," Torsten ordered desperately.

With one last look at Sniff's wild, angry blue eyes, I lifted a finger, concentrating on the redrock rift anchor I'd left above. My vision bleary with tears, I let Solvai and Brigan drag me through the portal. We had to get back and warn the guard about just how real the Coven's threat truly was. Numbly, I wondered how high a number Brigan had managed to count up to.

Chapter 33: Strategy

I stood at parade rest alongside my squad, still feeling raw after seeing Sniff last night. As I looked around Captain Zoren's office, I couldn't help but remember how I'd once stood trial for my life here. Now, I was among the few soldiers and others invited to an elite strategy meeting with the king of Rengard.

The room was even more crowded than it had been on the day of my trial. Squad Reckless lined the back wall behind two of Captain Zoren's hand-picked, trusted squads of seven. We were without a doubt the least important people here, and we'd only been invited in the first place just in case Jax and I could answer any questions about the Coven. We'd already told Zoren everything we knew, though—well, everything but the fact that I was secretly keeping the Soul Reaper's personal voidshard in my ethereal spice cabinet.

When Solvai, Brigan, and I had returned to the Rise before dawn this morning, we'd gone to Captain Zoren right away. Brigan had explained everything we'd learned, from the Liberator's indifference to Keep Rengard's knowledge of their coup, to their satisfaction with the reinforcements that had arrived at Outcast Outpost.

Zoren had been both grateful for the information and frustrated by it, since most of the commanders and lieutenants still insisted that the king's high guard had reclaimed Outcast Outpost. They refused to consider any alternative.

A handful of leaders, including Commander Gunnar and the rude Commander Leif, stood together to one side of Zoren's long desk, with Solvai's mother, Lorelai, among them as head dragon keeper to the guard. To the other side were a cluster of Mage Hunters including Trickshot and Mute. Through the sea of heads, Trickshot gave me a reassuring smile.

Behind the desk stood Captain Zoren, and to his right was King Axel of Rengard himself. He looked pretty good for having just spent the past several months in an etherarchy-induced coma, his short dark beard well-trimmed and his skin much warmer than when he'd spoken to Captain Zoren in his chambers.

The king's voice was quiet and controlled, yet somehow still commanding. After so many years under the barking Commander Gunnar and months at the Outpost under Commander Hildred, I wasn't used to that style of leadership. It was both refreshing and reassuring.

"Those of you in this room are among the few I can undoubtedly trust," the king began, gently placing his fingertips on the desk. "I fear certain members of my court and even those... closest to me may be rebel spies. They will be dealt with, but we must proceed with caution lest we provoke the Coven of the Gray Ones."

Murmurs rippled throughout the room. I lowered my eyebrows, my mind reeling as I recalled the troubled look the king had given his wife upon waking. What if by 'those closest to me,' the king meant Queen Ilona herself?

I thought of the way the queen had spoken at my trial, her gentle tears arguing for my execution. Suddenly, I remembered what Solvai, Brigan, and I had overheard the Liberator say to her followers last night in their underground hold.

The three of us must to return to the citadel before anyone gets suspicious.

A sinking feeling pricked my heart and chills ran up my arms. The gray-hooded figures had spoken of the king with contempt, as if they wished he'd have died during the attack on the dragon stables. Was it possible that Queen Ilona herself was part of the Coven of the Gray Ones? All three of the coven members' masks had muffled their voices, and the Liberator's had been so distorted I couldn't even tell if they'd been a man or a woman at all. Soot... could the queen herself be the Liberator?

That would explain why the queen had been so against administering the Farseer's remedy to the king. Without King Axel, Ilona would be free to all but let the Coven in through the citadel's front door. And if the king's high guard was in her pocket as well, it would justify how they were so easily able to 'eradicate' the threat at Outcast Outpost. Pieces began to fall into place

"We must take extra care and caution as we prepare to defend the Rise," the king went on. "Thanks to the valiant efforts of a few of our soldiers, we know when the Coven will strike. We'll have all of our squads on high alert tomorrow night in and around the mesa, including squads from our satellite cities, Rust Gorge, Brackentown, and Archdawn. Against the full army of Rengard Capital, the Coven of the Gray Ones won't stand a chance."

"But my king," Commander Gunnar spoke up. "What about the war? A large portion of our soldiers, both from Keep Rengard and across the Canyonlands, have been gathering to prepare to march on the Dragon Isles."

"Forget the war with the Isles," the king said firmly. "I want all our forces guarding the mesa tomorrow night."

"We'll want our healers at the ready as well."

I nearly jumped at the sound of Brigan's voice beside me. The room full of authorities turned to the back to see what low-tier soldier had made it his business to speak at the king's elite meeting.

"Oh…?" the king said, eyeing Brigan with amusement.

"That's Brigan, Heir Duke of Solhelm, your highness," Captain Zoren muttered from his place beside the king.

"Speak, Heir Duke," King Axel gently gestured toward Brigan.

Brigan stepped forward, out of line. "As my squadmates and I have already reported to Captain Zoren, we infiltrated one of the Coven's underground strongholds last night. They have at least a hundred umbral dreklings at their disposal, assuming they aren't keeping more elsewhere."

That put everyone on edge as murmurs rippled throughout the room. Brigan continued.

"The Coven also fought with many umbral creatures by their sides in the battle for Outcast Outpost, controlling them using some kind of telepathic etherarchy. I would suggest having as many healers at the ready as possible alongside the soldiers, each equipped with as much liquid light as we can spare."

King Axel nodded. "Very good, Heir Duke. Commander Gunnar, please speak with the Sisters of Streya and see what they have in their stores. If it's not enough, reach out to the sanctuaries in the lower town, then send riders out to collect any from the neighboring keeps—anyone who can get back here before tomorrow night."

Commander Gunnar agreed. The king went on, along with Captain Zoren, about specific strategies to enact during the Winter Solstice Ball. The two of them explained formations and other details to the commanders and squads present, and gave Lorelai instructions to tell her assistant keepers to have all the guard's mounts battle ready. Next, they went over which siege weapons needed to be primed, such as the ballistae and harpoons.

It wasn't until later on in the meeting that King Axel said something that focused my attention faster than a dragonhawk zeroing in on its prey.

"...it has come to my attention that the queen has given the order that all the magi from Spydra Prison are to be executed tomorrow night at the ball. It is to be the crowning event of the evening, a signal to the rebel magi who attacked our Outpost that Rengard won't stand for such magi violence in the future."

My heart dropped into my stomach. If Queen Ilona really was a follower of the Gray Ones, I doubted the execution was a warning for her fellow cultists. More likely, she wanted to show the Coven and the people of the Canyonlands firsthand the cruelty of Evgard's practices toward magi to rile them up before the attack.

"I disagree strongly with this decision," the king said, and I breathed a sigh of relief. At the king's side, it looked like Zoren had done the same.

King Axel continued. "Rather than execute the magi prisoners as a show of dominion, I plan to free them as a symbol of mercy."

Elation rushed through my body from my very core. My parents... tomorrow, the king was going to free them. Was this what the Farseer had foreseen?

I felt a strong hand against my back, and turned to see Jax giving me a knowing look. He must've been thinking the same thing.

Next, Captain Zoren and the king went over strategies for how to best protect the Rise. The bulk of the guard would be just outside the citadel itself, ready to respond to any issues that might arise at the party within. Meanwhile, the high guard squads of the king and other nobles would be inside the ballroom and adjacent outdoor courtyard to take care of any immediate threats. If anything serious were to happen at the ball, our dragon riders would easily be able to provide backup.

The king gave one final warning about keeping our plans as secret as possible. Then he adjourned the meeting.

I was about to file out of the office alongside the rest of my squad when the king's demure yet strong voice rose up from behind Captain Zoren's desk.

"Squad Reckless, I would like you to stay behind a moment."

The seven of us turned to the king, surprise evident on our faces. The king of Rengard knew our squad's name?

We recovered quickly, lining up at attention before King Axel. Captain Zoren closed the door after the last Commander exited, leaving only us, the Captain of the Guard, and the king of the Canyonlands.

Still, King Axel spoke quietly. "Your squad is the only one here who fought the Coven of the Gray Ones at Outcast Outpost. The only one still intact, anyway." The king looked down in reverence for the fallen soldiers. Then he went on.

"Not only that, but my bond, Lantha, tells me you were the ones who saved her and the others in the burning dragon stables. Additionally, it was members of this squad who brought the remedy from the Farseer and somehow convinced my healers to let you administer it."

Jax, Brigan, and I exchanged glances.

"Only the nobility's defensive squads will be allowed in the citadel during the ball itself. I'd like Squad Reckless to be among them as my personal high guard."

My eyes widened, and I could see the others were just as taken aback as I was. Brigan stood up even straighter at the honor.

"Some would call you too young and inexperienced for the task," King Axel said. "But the way I see it, the seven of you have more practical experience against this particular threat than any other squad at my disposal. And with the doubts I harbor concerning my current high guard's true loyalties, I'd feel better having you at my side tomorrow night. So, Squad Reckless, what say you?"

We all looked at our squad captain. Solvai blushed from her ears to the tip of her nose, but cleared her throat and straightened up.

"It would be our honor, King Axel."

The king gave a warm, kind smile. Captain Zoren explained that we'd get our modified, high guard uniforms before tomorrow night. He also told us that in order to minimize scrutiny on this decision, we'd be protecting the king alongside his current high guard. During such perilous times as these, nobody would question the king wanting to double his security.

The king nodded to us once more as we prepared to leave. "Some may find your squad's name, Reckless, worrisome." The king's expression turned grave. "Yet I fear that tomorrow night, that is exactly what you'll need to be. Although, I'm hoping you won't find yourselves in harm's way. I didn't tell the others, but I've sent for someone who should be arriving in time to aid us against the Coven. Someone with a great deal of experience in stopping rogue magi."

Captain Zoren frowned. "Who?"

King Axel inclined his chin. "The leader of the Mage Hunters herself has promised to join us."

To my side, I heard Jax's breath catch as King Axel finished.

"Tomorrow night, the Black Valkyrie is coming to Rengard."

Chapter 34: The Dry Dragonstag

After a long day of drilling formations and running battle scenarios with the rest of the guard, I was grateful for the chance to head back to the barracks for some much needed rest. Although, part of me was terrified to sleep—What if I had more nightmares? I remembered waking up to find the Soul Reaper's voidshard lying on my pillow next to me. It must've somehow burned through my rift hold.

I shuddered. Even thinking about the voidshard made me feel cold.

The sun had just set and Solvai, Edrea, and I had just climbed the stairs to get to our second story room when we heard a small clicking noise from the windowsill.

All three of us turned toward the open window, our senses on high alert. We waited, narrowing our eyes when another pebble came flying through, landing with another perfect click on the sill.

I grabbed my seaxe while Edrea and Solvai brandished their dragonhook spears. Slowly, we approached the window and peered out.

Standing on the ground several feet below our window was Jax. He had a psionic rune glowing over his forehead as he chucked one more pebble, telekinetically guiding it so that it gently bopped me on the forehead before falling onto the floor.

"Hey," I whispered with irritation. "What was that for?"

I could see Jax looking up at me in the dark. He cupped his hands around his mouth and called out.

"Come down, M."

"Why?" I asked, suddenly worried. "Is something wrong? Are you okay?"

Jax chuckled, putting his hands in the pockets of his tunic as he casually kicked up dirt with his foot. "Relax, nothing's wrong. I just want to take you somewhere."

I furrowed my brow and ducked back into the room. Edrea and Solvai were giving me amused, knowing looks.

"What?" I whispered, feeling my cheeks grow hot.

Solvai's mouth quirked into a smile. "So, are you going to go?"

"I... um," I stammered. "I don't know."

"Do you *want* to go?"

"Yes," I answered without thinking.

"Then go," Solvai said with a small giggle. "We'll cover for you, right, Edrea?"

Edrea rolled her eyes, but I noticed a ghost of a smile playing at her lips as well. "You want to sneak out with Jax? Absolutely I'll cover for you."

I felt my heartbeat pick up as I returned to the window. Jax stood expectantly below, his midnight blue eyes shining.

"I'll be right down," I whispered to him as I lifted my finger to trace the portalling rune.

Jax led me down the path from the guard's quadrant of the Rise toward the center of town. There were a decent number of people still milling about, laughing and walking by the light from metal posts topped with ornate bowls of flames.

We saw a few orange-cloaked guards escorting a small group of raggedly dressed people away from the town square. They were likely refugees seeking somewhere safe to live after losing their homes to skyfalls. According to Brigan, the skyfalls were driving more and more people to the larger keeps, and the Rise was no exception. Though from the looks of things, the elite Rengardians on top of the mesa didn't want such riffraff cluttering up their perfect city. Especially since it looked like a few of the refugees' skin bore inky gray splotches from the shadow wasting.

Only the wealthy lived on top of the butte, so everything here was clean and fine, from the white adobe shops to the elegant statues of dragons or the goddesses.

Ironically, Jax took me straight to the worst kept building on the street. The torch on the tavern door lit up a sign that read: 'The Dry Dragonstag.'

Though the wintery night air was brisk, the inside of the tavern was stuffy and overcrowded. Drunk men and women laughed and clinked their glasses while a bard yowled loudly from atop a small stage in the corner. The floor was a little grimy, and a man's sweaty arm bumped against my shoulder as he hurried past me to meet his friends.

"This is where you wanted to take me?" I asked Jax over the din.

He gave me a cocky smile. "Not quite." Then he grabbed me by the hand, pulling me along as he wove through the crowd toward the bar.

The bartender looked a little frazzled as she passed out drinks to impatient patrons. Jax leaned against the end of the bar, waiting for her to notice us.

"What are we doing here?" I put a hand on my hip.

Jax raised an eyebrow, clearly enjoying keeping me in suspense. "You'll see."

Finally, the barkeep got around to asking what we wanted. Rather than order drinks, Jax leaned further over the bar and spoke in a voice so low that I could barely hear him.

"The Hunter's torch is lit again."

I had no idea what he meant, but the bartender squared her shoulders at the phrase. "Right this way," she said.

She led us out of the crowded space down a deserted hallway. A row of antlered dragonstag heads were mounted along the wall.

Eventually, she stopped at the head of a reddish stag with gold horns. With a nod, she took hold of one golden antler and pulled down on it like a lever.

I jumped as a large section of the wall jolted forward with a creak. It rotated, opening to reveal a dimly-lit set of stairs behind the wall. Jax grinned smugly when he saw the surprise on my face. He held out a hand toward me.

I hesitated for a split second, not completely positive I should follow the roguish, sleeveless spy down a dark set of stairs into some unknown, underground place beneath a stuffy tavern. But as I slipped my small hand into his large, rough one, my reluctance gave way to shivers that ran up and down my spine.

Once we were on the staircase, the barkeep closed the door behind us, cutting off the bustling sounds of the tavern. In the silence, I thought I could make out a few soft, melodic notes from a lyre. I glanced down the stairs, then cocked my head. Jax gave a low chuckle as he led me down toward the source of the music.

The staircase opened up to another tavern, this one completely different from the one above. Thick, lush dragon buffalo rugs spread before a lavish fireplace. The fire kept the room warm against the winter chill, but there weren't so many people down here to overheat the place. A long, elegant bar ran along the back wall, and a small stage occupied one corner.

A duo of musicians stood atop the stage. A man strumming the lyre we'd heard on the staircase stood beside a woman in a shimmering dress. She opened her mouth to sing, and her rich, low voice filled the space without being overpowering or drawing too much attention. Her voice echoed somehow, and I noticed a small crystal pendant glowing around her neck. A glowing gold rune was etched onto its surface, and I was willing to bet it was providing her voice with some kind of reverberation illusion.

The pendant wasn't the only evidence of etherarchy at play in the underground tavern. Glowing orbs filled with some kind of liquid lit the large room, some radiating gold light and others red. The orbs varied in size from as small as a bean to as large as a pumpkin as they psionically floated around the room.

When Jax and I found seats at the bar, the man tending it held up a finger to let us know he'd be with us shortly.

Jax pointed behind the bar. "May I?" he asked the bartender.

The man nodded, gesturing to the space behind the bar as if to say 'be my guest.'

Jax gave my hand one more squeeze before hopping onto the bar and swinging his legs over to the other side. Then he smoothly slipped off, leaning over the short counter toward me.

"What'll it be, M? An Evyndellian paloma? Golden boltbrew?"

I just kind of looked at him, a couple of stammering, incoherent sounds escaping my lips.

Jax raised both eyebrows twice in quick succession. "A surprise then."

With that, Jax lit up a psionic rune over his forehead and began telekinetically pulling drinks off of shelves like he'd been doing it his whole life. He poured this and that into a couple of glasses, expertly mixing our drinks.

"Where did you learn to do this?" I asked once I'd found my voice again.

"You pick up a thing or two when you grow up in a bar." Jax shrugged as he worked. "Some good, some not so good."

"I'm guessing the Broughkin Arms wasn't the first tavern Torsten's worked in?"

"Unfortunately, no," Jax said. "The Naga's Head in southern Skygard was where I lived from age six until I was old enough to join the Knights and leave that goddess-forsaken place. I spent a lot of time sitting under the bar playing with the empty bottles. Practicing psionics mostly."

"Where did you live before that?" I asked, leaning forward onto my elbows as I watched him mix.

"With my mom. Things were actually pretty good for me when I was with her. But she... she felt like I was getting in her way, so she handed me off to my father. She thought she was doing it to protect me or something. Mom had a lot going on back then... still does, to be honest. She's always said she'd come back for me one day, but..."

Jax glanced off to the side. It wasn't like him to get nervous. But I didn't want him to stop talking. Suddenly, I wanted to know everything about him. I scooted closer, waiting for him to go on.

Jax closed his eyes and took a deep breath. He slid one glass toward me and another to his place. Then he walked around the edge of the bar to sit beside me, leaning in so close that I could breathe in his earthy, metallic scent.

"I guess I'd better tell you about my mom before you meet her tomorrow night," he said, sounding nervous.

A wave of nerves washed over me as well. "I'm meeting your mom tomorrow?"

Jax swallowed. "Uh, yeah, if all goes according to the king's plan. See, my mom is kind of... well, my mom is the Black Valkyrie."

My jaw might've fallen onto the floor. So many questions flooded my mind, I wasn't sure where to begin.

"But..." I started. "Wouldn't that mean she and Torsten..."

I trailed off, and Jax nodded. "Back then my father was a lot less...""Sloppy?" I supplied.

"I was gonna say a scorching mess, but yeah. Less of a drunk, selfish drakbag." That made sense, especially considering the stories of the war hero father Solvai always talked about. Soot, Torsten had once had quite the busy life!

I felt my heart start to ache as I studied Jax's face, picturing his mom dropping him off for the last time at Torsten's bar. I remembered the night I'd found Torsten drunk on the floor when he'd warned me about the Coven's coming attack on the Outpost. He'd scared me, shattering that bottle against the wall.

My eyes flicked to Jax's lower lip. Hesitantly, I reached toward his face, gently touching the little white scar there with my thumb.

I didn't have to ask where he'd gotten it—His eyes told me all I needed to know.

My hand seemed to have a mind of its own, slipping around his jaw to cup his cheek. Jax's eyes searched mine, and I could tell it wasn't easy for him to open up like this.

"Things got better after a while," Jax continued, speaking slowly, as if he was worried any sudden movement would get me to pull my hand away. "Solrac started coming once a week—he told Torsten it was to train me as a Psion—but I knew it was mostly just to make sure I was okay. Solrac and His Majesty were like a lifeline."

"Solrac and who?" I asked.

Jax laughed, looking lost in memory for a moment. "His Majesty is the name of Solrac's bloodhusky. Drak, I'd love for you to meet them."

"I can't wait," I said.

Jax looked at me with eager anticipation. "Does that mean... I mean, after all this is over, I'm going to have to go back to Skygard to get my next assignment from the Farseer. I wonder... I guess I was sort of hoping you'd come with me."

"Come with you?" I asked anxiously, suddenly pulling my hand back to where I could wring it in my lap. "Become a Knight of the Torch?"

Jax's face flushed. "Yeah."

"Oh. To be honest, I've never thought about what I'd like to do after Mom and Dad finally went free," I confessed. "It's never really mattered what I wanted, since I know they'll need me to take care of them. Mom especially. She's, um... her mind is..."

I trailed off as my voice broke. Suddenly, I couldn't look Jax in the eye and admit that my mom was unstable, and that it was because of me.

Desperate for something to do, I reached for the bubbly, whitish drink Jax had mixed up and took a swig. It sparkled in my mouth, sweet and sour blending in a refreshing, harmonious way.

"Soot," I said. "This is actually amazing."

Jax took a drink from his own glass. "Lime, mint, just a little bit of cream, and completely alcohol free. I call it the 'M.'"

I finished my second gulp. Setting down my glass, I looked at him and raised an eyebrow, speaking softly.

"M for mint, right?"

"Right. For mint."

The tension between Jax and me was so strong I could practically hear it buzzing in my ears. The way his dark blue eyes searched mine filled me with fire from my chest to my fingertips.

At the same moment, both Jax and I closed the distance between us, our foreheads pressing into each other. I wanted to kiss him so much I could taste it.

"Wait," he said suddenly, his mouth a mere breath away from mine as he spoke.

"What is it?" I whispered.

We lingered that way for several more seconds. Then, as if doing so were harder than lifting a psionic ton of bricks, Jax pulled away. I felt my heart plummet.

"What's wrong?" I asked. "I know I didn't want to kiss you back in the cave before, but—"

"Meleya," Jax spoke my full name, and it sent warmth flowing from my core. "I've never wanted to kiss someone so badly in all my life. And that's why... that's why I can't." I tilted my head to the side as he continued.

"I've never held back when it comes to that side of things. But before I go there with you, I want to prove just how much I care about you. I don't ever want you to doubt. So, even though it's literally killing me, I'm not going to kiss you tonight."

If Jax saying my name warmed my heart, his speech made my whole soul glow. Any apprehension I'd felt about him before melted away.

Jax and I talked late into the night. He shared tales of fighting off an umbral dragon in Ghost Lake, and of infiltrating the guard at Keep Drakfell to help his team of Knights steal a true dragon egg. Jax had ended up in prison the night of their heist, barely getting out thanks to the valiant efforts of his friends. In turn, he'd fought alongside the other Knights of the Torch against his own mother, the Black Valkyrie, in order to keep her and her entourage from capturing the Farseer.

He'd lived such an exciting life compared to me, but I reluctantly opened up about what it was like growing up in the canyons. I told him about how we'd moved caravans fifteen times before I was ten years old because my mom was so worried about them finding out we were magi. I shared about the many times I'd watched women and men stir stew pots or bake bread over the campfire, memorizing their recipes so I could feed my family. Until meeting Solvai and Brigan at basic training, I'd never been in one place long enough to have any real friends.

I wasn't sure how much time had passed before we finally left the underground bar. The tavern above was nearly deserted as we headed through it and back up the path toward the guards' quadrant in the dark.

We were just outside the barracks when Jax looked down at his tunic pocket. I was surprised when he reached into the pocket to pull out Three, his mirror gecko. Her tiny scales were aglow, pulsing with a soft yellow light.

"I've got to take this," Jax said apologetically.

I raised an eyebrow. "Take what?"

"The other Knights are trying to contact me," Jax said, then gave me a meaningful look. "Want to listen in on the mindlink?"

Jax held out a hand, and with only a little apprehension, I took it. He guided my fingers to gently rest on the gecko's bumpy back.

As soon as I touched the little reptile's skin, I felt my mind suddenly expand. A vaguely familiar male voice echoed inside my head.

Jax, are you there? the voice said. Or thought, I guess.

Talk to me, Kai, I heard Jax's voice, but not out loud. He was speaking inside my mind, too. Was this some kind of telepathic Seer power channeled through Three, the mirror gecko?

The name Kai rang a bell, and I remembered when I'd told Jax about the Knights of the Torch I'd run into outside the command center. He'd called the one wearing excessive plate armor Kai. This had to be him.

Wait a second, Kai thought. *There's someone listening in. I can sense it.*

Don't worry, Jax thought back. *That's Meleya. She's with me—she's cool. Say hi, M.*

Uh... hi, I thought, feeling like an idiot.

She's a Knight? Kai thought skeptically.

Basically, Jax replied. *She's already helped me and the Farseer on a job.*

Well, as long as the Farseer knows, I guess it's fine. Although, I really should develop some stronger mental security measures... maybe a passphrase or something.

Jax gave something like a mental chuckle, as if he were used to musings like that from Kai. *So what's up?*

I don't have a lot of time, Kai thought. *But Solrac told me to reach out to you and let you know he's planning on sending aid against the Coven of the Gray Ones' attack on Keep Rengard. Not much, I'm afraid, since it's such short notice. But from the way he spoke, I'm worried there's something more going on with him. He said he wanted to get in contact with other Knights of the Torch closer to your location on the Rise, but the other two heads over the Knights stopped him.*

Why would they do that? Jax asked.

Kai seemed to mentally sigh. *I wish I knew more. From what I've gathered from the rest of the team, there's a major conflict brewing between Solrac and the other leaders. They make it sound like Orothion is verging on a schism.*

Well, that's sooty news, Jax thought.

I could be wrong, Kai replied. *This is all conjecture. But Solrac did tell me to warn you about trying to rally any Knights yourself—He's not sure who's on his side and who isn't. But the bottom line is that while Solrac is tied up right now, some help is on the way.*

Okay, Jax thought. *Did he say who's coming?*

Instead of a coherent response, I heard something like mental cursing over the mindlink.

What is it? Jax asked.

Drakking Asher, Kai's thoughts sounded a million miles away.

What did Dragon-boy do this time?

Improvising again, trying to be a hero or something. Left a scorching note—he's not even here. Drak, drak, drak. Listen, Jax. I've got to go.

I understand.

Good luck tomorrow night. Trust me, some of our best will be fighting at your side.

With that, the gecko stopped glowing, and I felt the mindlink go out. Jax gave Three an affectionate pat on the head with his finger, then reached into his pocket and pulled out a dead cricket to give her.

"Good job, girl," Jax said in a fond, yet ridiculous voice. It was kind of endearing. He waited for the mirror gecko to finish eating her cricket, then slipped her carefully back into his pocket before turning back to me.

Standing outside the barracks, I could tell Jax wasn't quite ready to go in yet. To be honest, neither was I. But tomorrow, a dark Coven was planning to storm the Rise.

"We'd better get some rest so we're ready for battle tomorrow," I said, shivering in the chilly night air.

Jax nodded, looking determined. "We're gonna give that Coven the void."

I took a step toward the barracks door, turning back to Jax with one final, vital question:

"Got any requests for tomorrow's breakfast?"

REFLECTION 4

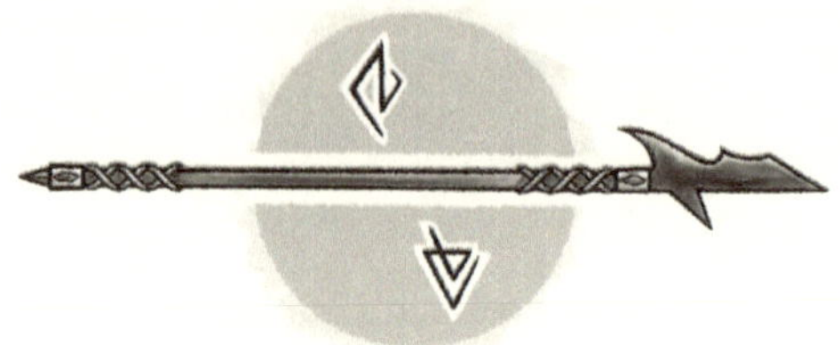

Vidya slipped into the office of the Captain of the Guard, closing the door softly behind her. The Ursadon was looking over battle plans from his place behind the desk, but when he heard the gentle click from the door, his dragonfire green eyes snapped to where she stood.

"King Axel said he'd sent for you," the Ursadon's tone was even.

"How could I deny a personal invitation from the king of Rengard himself?" Vidya replied, sauntering toward his desk.

"I'm glad you came," the Ursadon said, casting another glance over the pages on his desk. "I fear the Coven's numbers are greater than we'd realized. Having the Black Valkyrie and her entourage at our sides could tip the scales."

"You're very clever, you know," Vidya's voice dripped with sweetness.

The Ursadon frowned, his gaze returning to Vidya's face. He was studying her, gleaning information the way he did when trying to solve a case.

Vidya mused. "The Great Ursadon, legendary Drekai Mage Hunter. Never fails to hunt down his prey. Could there, perhaps, be more to his title than meets the eye?"

"What are you implying?" the Ursadon asked.

"Oh, I just wonder why such a skilled detective would've taken so long to succeed in an assignment as simple as uncovering the identity of a prominent cult leader. The Coven of the Gray Ones just so happened to decide to launch a coup on Keep Rengard mere months after I assigned you to be Captain of the Guard. With such a perfect position, I suppose you just couldn't help yourself."

Understanding dawned in the Ursadon's eyes. "You think *I'm* the Liberator?"

"You played me well, Zoren of the Dragon Isles. All that talk of not wanting to become a skymage, as if you were above our methods of etherarchy. Yet you were already one of us, tapping into the power of the Gray Ones all along."

The Ursadon launched to his feet, slamming a hand on the desk.

"Lies," he hissed.

"Oh?" Vidya said coyly.

"You dare question my loyalty? Have I not served you well these past years?"

Vidya shrugged.

The Ursadon went on. "I'm no wildshaping Liberator. But my contact in Spydra Prison was very forthcoming with some key clues once I'd made the appropriate threats. He spent a few years in Misthaven about eighteen years ago, and while he'd never seen the Liberator in human form, he knew a lot about dragons from so many years spent in the canyon wilds."

"So what?" Vidya narrowed her eyes.

"The Liberator's preferred Wildshaper totems are from dragons. The prisoner told me that while in Misthaven, there was a time when the Liberator visited. They took the form of a black drake with a thin snout and slender horns." Zoren looked at Vidya as if this information were somehow telling. When she didn't react, he continued.

"When a Wildshaper takes an animal form, they shift into that creature's version of themselves. Female dragons have more slender snouts and horns than males, which means—"

"The Liberator is a woman," Vidya concluded.

"Correct. Additionally, dragons' hide reflects the color of their ethereal aura."

"So, according to your source, the Liberator's aura would be black." Vidya's mind was racing.

"Precisely," the Ursadon said. "Luckily, I know someone who can use the Sight."

Vidya raised an eyebrow. "Freya was willing to help you?"

"Not at first," Zoren looked away. "I had to promise her something in return."

"What was her request, if I may ask?"

Zoren looked Vidya dead in the eye. "She wants to speak with you. She… wouldn't tell me why."

"Oh?"

"She was insistent. But the point is, I now know the identity of the Liberator."

Vidya leaned over the desk as Zoren continued.

"She was right in front of our eyes this whole time, wielding her power with subtlety and cunning."

Vidya's eyes were bright.

The Ursadon spoke flatly. "Tomorrow night, you'll have your chance. You'll get your sooty Wildshaper's ether well and become the great agent of the void you've always wished to be."

"Agent of the void? No, Ursadon. I will control the void. I will be the only thing standing between Evgard and total annihilation."

Vidya squared her shoulders. The voice in her head began to laugh.

BRIGAN

Brigan usually loved a good party. There was nothing quite like seeing a citadel decked out in fine curtains and carpets, long tables heaped with dainty finger foods, and goblets upon goblets of drinks. Black and white braziers carved to look like dragons in flight lit both the vast ballroom and the open courtyard through the large double doors. Brigan loved seeing people dressed in their finest suits and ballgowns as they swirled around the dance floor.

Tonight, Brigan wore a crisp new uniform, complete with special additions made from the rusty orange scales Bolt had shed during her ascension. Brigan had known exactly what to do back at the Outpost when his parents sent him that parcel containing a skystone. He'd waited until nobody else was around, then fed it to Bolt, the highly-concentrated ether from the skystone prompting her to ascend.

The scales adorned Brigan's dragonleather chest armor, and a few had been embedded into the hilt of his seaxe, as well as the thin iron crown across his brow. They would allow Brigan to access some of Bolt's lightwielding etherarchy, though he hadn't learned how to wield it yet. Brigan had also taken extra care to smooth his hair into a tidy ridgeknot, with a single curl falling over his forehead just the way he liked it. But despite the grand surroundings and his impeccable appearance, Brigan just couldn't seem to find his usual smile.

Brigan spun and clapped in time to the music with a lovely noblewoman on his arm, his high guard cloak flaring out behind him. Each royal family present tonight had their own high guard squads with them at the ball, standing by while their noble charges mingled and danced. While Brigan was still a part of King Axel's elite defense squad tonight, as a nobleman, he was expected to be involved in the festivities while the rest of Squad Reckless took point on protecting the king.

Brigan's eyes never strayed far from the young woman standing with Squad Reckless and the rest of the king's high guard in a defensive formation. The king sat behind them on his rusty red throne while the queen sat at his side. She kept glancing toward the double doors that led to the vast, outdoor courtyard as if she were waiting for something.

They'd ordered the squad to take special care of their appearances tonight as well, in order to look their best at the ball. Their uniforms had been buffed and polished, their weapons gleaming at their sides or on their backs. As newly-minted members of the king's high guard, Meleya and the others wore new black cloaks with rusty orange trim to set them apart from the other soldiers.

Not that Meleya needed the cloak to stand out. Her stark white hair wasn't in its usual long braid down her back, but had been tightly braided up the left side of her scalp with the rest long and flowing over her opposite shoulder. With her hair like that, it was impossible to miss the glinting silvermark on her left cheek.

Gauntlet down, Brigan thought. *Ballgown or not, Meleya of Misthaven is the most beautiful girl here.*

He twirled his dance partner twice in time to the music, his thoughts still miles away. He couldn't stop thinking about the look of betrayal Meleya had worn the evening she'd turned him down, right after he'd suggested she get the magi cure.

Brigan had been beating himself up about being so tactless ever since. He hadn't meant to offend her—not when all he ever wanted to do was make her happy.

Muscle memory kicked in as Brigan and his dance partner clasped hands. Brigan noted just how empty the girl's touch felt—not like the jolt of heat that had flooded him when Meleya had taught him to chop an onion. The way her delicate fingers rested on Brigan's knuckles, and the beautiful contrast between her suntanned beige skin and Brigan's darker reddish brown.

Stop thinking about that drakking onion, Brigan chided himself. *You know she has.* Now, onions made Brigan cry for a whole new reason.

Brigan circled his partner, but his eyes and ears zeroed in on Meleya again as a tiny gasp sounded from her place near the king's throne.

Jax had stepped out of formation to flirtatiously jab Meleya in the side. She whirled on him, large brown eyes alight with fire. She gave Jax a quick scolding, and he got back in line. But Brigan couldn't help but notice that when Meleya returned to her position facing forward, she had a wide, sparkling smile on her face.

Somehow, that smile felt like a dagger driving into Brigan's chest. A blunt wooden dagger, splintering as an invisible hand twisted it.

Brigan knew he was being dramatic, but scorch. Jax may've been arrogant and unsophisticated, but in that moment, Brigan would've given almost anything to be him—to be the one making her smile like that.

The song ended and Brigan thanked his partner before ducking away into the crowd. He fled toward the food table, just to have somewhere to go. But when he tried the mini honey fry bread canapes, all he could think about was how much better Meleya's were.

This was getting ridiculous. Was there nothing in this world that didn't remind him of her?

"What do you think you're doing?" Brigan's father, Duke Brodrik of Solhelm, appeared behind him.

"Eating unnecessarily small finger foods," Brigan replied.

And dying inside, he couldn't help but mentally add.

"I mean, why aren't you asking Lady Teagana for a second dance? You know who she is, I assume? Firstborn grandchild of the Duke and Duchess of Keep Gray Fen. That means she's a likely heir to the second house of the Canyonlands."

"Ah," Brigan said absently.

Duke Brodrik's lips pressed into a frustrated line. "As heir to only the fourth keep, you'd do well to not cast her aside so easily."

"Gauntlet down," Brigan replied boldly. "Being born noble doesn't fundamentally make someone a better ruler. "

Brigan raised his eyebrows expectantly. His father had been born to the youngest child of the brother of a Baron over a small outlander town in eastern Rengard. The more powerful houses of the Keepdom had barely recognized him as nobility at all until he'd married the Heir Duchess of Solhelm.

"I did well for myself by marrying up," Duke Brodrik replied. "It's not wrong to want the best for my only son and heir."

"But what if what's best for me is to be with someone who makes me happy? Wouldn't a content duke in Solhelm make a better ruler than a miserable one in Gray Fen?"

Brigan's father's eyes narrowed, and Brigan instantly regretted speaking from his heart. Normally, he loved getting others heated since it made for a much more engaging debate. But Brigan didn't want to argue with his father. Not tonight.

"There's someone else," Brigan's father stated suspiciously.

Brigan tried to backtrack. "Of course there's not. I know better than to—"

"One of your squadmates?" Duke Brodrik's gaze snapped toward where Squad Reckless stood around the king's throne. He looked over Edrea and Solvai with scrutiny, his eyes widening when they found Meleya.

"Stars," Duke Brodrik said. "It's the snowhead, isn't it? That's why you've been so tight-lipped—You have feelings for a magi."

Scorch. It was as if Brigan's father had an extra sense for these things. He'd been playing political games for so long, he knew exactly what signs to look for. There was no use hiding the truth any longer.

"So what if I do?" Brigan replied. "Magi or not, she's intelligent and caring. Both qualities any keep would be lucky to have in a ruler."

"Drak, Brigan," his dad quietly seethed, though on the outside, he provided a perfectly calm veneer for the other guests. "If you'd wanted a commoner, that would be one thing. But a scorching magi? They're the lowest of the low. Their very presence threatens the safety of our keeps. You couldn't have made a worse choice, though I'm sure she's played quite the cunning seductress."

"What?" Brigan's voice rose, drawing the attention of a few nearby nobles. "She doesn't have a guileful bone in her body. Besides..." Brigan swallowed, lowering his voice to almost nothing. "...she already turned me down."

"You asked her—" his father closed his eyes and put up both hands in disbelief. "Brigan, you know better than to play around with one of the most important decisions you'll ever have to make. I wish to the goddesses the Keepdom of Drakfell hadn't turned traitor. Then, you'd have married Princess Eliana, and all would've been as it should be. Perhaps I'll need to make your selection for you once again."

Duke Brodrik took a couple of steps backward toward the crowd, as if he planned to hunt down Brigan's future duchess right then and there.

"One more thing," Brigan's father said, turning back to his son. "Chin up. The magi did you a favor by rejecting you. I know you won't squander the opportunity."

With that, Duke Brodrik turned on his heel, leaving Brigan once again feeling utterly alone.

He exhaled, and a strange, cold feeling bloomed inside him. It was almost as if some dark presence was glad Brigan was feeling this way and wanted to push him further down that lonely path.

Then, as quickly as it had come, the feeling fled as a refreshing, cool pulse of sympathy rolled through Brigan's heart like a wave. Gentle ripples of comfort lapped at the fringes of his soul as his drake, Bolt, let him know he wasn't alone. Brigan took the heartscale around his neck and held it between his thumb and the knuckle of his forefinger.

The way Bolt spoke with Brigan through the bond reminded him of the way the ocean interacted with the shore at his home in Keep Solhelm. Homesickness filled Brigan as he thought of the salty, humid air that blew in from the Scarlet Strait. The citadel there was built atop a small hill just off the beach, and Brigan's room had the perfect view of the ocean. Brigan let his heavy eyelids close as he imagined the rhythmic crashing of waves. Without that sound to help him drift off, Brigan rarely found sleep these days.

"Nice party," a voice wrenched Brigan from his thoughts. "I've never been to a ball before."

Edrea stepped up to Brigan, a nervous smile on her face as she gestured to their grand surroundings. Brigan looked away, not wanting her or any of the nobility here to see the Heir Duke of Solhelm cry.

"They're not all they're cracked up to be," Brigan mumbled in answer to Edrea's attempt at small talk. He knew she'd probably only come over to see if she could cheer him up, but he couldn't bring himself to look her in the eye as he rushed out of the ballroom and onto the outdoor courtyard.

Tiny, delicate snowflakes fell in sporadic flurries from the sparse storm clouds above. More braziers carved with dragons lit the citadel courtyard, but they offered little warmth, which meant there were very few guests gathered outside. That left Brigan with some space to compose himself before squaring his shoulders and returning to the party where he'd spend the rest of the evening pretending he was fine.

Brigan wandered across the enormous space toward the west side of the courtyard where a long wall, just higher than Brigan's waist, ran along the edge. Not just the courtyard edge, but the edge of the Rise itself. When he leaned against the top of the wall to look over the side, Brigan could just make out the tiny, faint lights of the lower town hundreds of feet below.

He got a slight rush of dizziness as he realized just how high up they were. Maybe it was a good thing Brigan had bonded a wingless drake instead of a flying dragon.

Brigan stood at the balcony for a long time, staring up through the scattered cloud cover at the starry night sky. He'd studied a little about the constellations and their meanings with the Sons of Streya before starting basic training here at Keep Rengard. Brigan thought he spotted the brightest star in the great True Dragon constellation near the horizon. Each year, the Dragon got closer to its predicted alignment with the Phoenix and the Dire Wolf networks. The Sisters and Sons of Streya spoke of the convergence with reverence and a little fear, though Brigan never cared much for the stars. Not when there was so much to focus on down here.

A flash of fiery green streaked across the Dragon's chest before plummeting toward the earth. The skyfall, carrying both valuable skystone and deadly dreklings, probably landed somewhere near Red Glen or the Lost Dunes. Brigan hoped the border guards in those keeps would be able to contain the threat. So many outlander towns were falling to dreklings, leaving hundreds of Rengardians without homes. The larger cities with stronger guards could offer protection, but there just wasn't enough food and shelter to go around.

"I worry about the increasing skyfalls as well," a soft voice from behind startled Brigan.

When Brigan turned around, he immediately inclined his head. "King Axel."

The king's earth-colored wyvern, Lantha, stood protectively behind her bond as he approached. Brigan couldn't help but admire how right they looked together. Many high nobles, particularly kings and queens of keepdoms, often went out of their way to ensure they bonded dragons who were capable of etherarchy. Even Brigan himself had been drawn to Bolt's lightwielding abilities back in the Dragon Chasm. But even though Lantha wasn't mythic, Brigan could see that by accepting the wyvern's bond, Axel had made the proper choice.

King Axel smiled. "Relax, Heir Duke. Is it alright if I call you Brigan?"

"Of course," Brigan replied. "Shouldn't you be inside where the rest of the squad can protect you?"

"I needed some fresh air," the king said. "Besides, you're part of my high guard, so I'm sure I'll be fine for a few minutes."

The king joined Brigan at the balcony's edge. Together, they took in the starlit silhouettes of the rocky mesas and irregular spires of the Canyon Keepdom.

"I can tell you care about the people of this land the way I do," King Axel said. "The way you spoke at the meeting showed me you put much thought into the betterment of our great Keepdom."

Brigan spoke without thinking. "Unfortunately, many among our class are so bent on keeping things the way they are that they can't see the flaws in our current system. Evgard is a mighty realm, but, for example, the way we handle magi is barbaric and illogical." Brigan surprised himself with his own boldness.

"I'm inclined to agree," the king said gently. "Once I repair the damage done by prematurely declaring war on the Dragon Isles, I had hoped to consider alternative solutions for the magi plight. Although, recent experience has shown me firsthand the darkness etherarchy can achieve when wielded by the wrong hands."

"You could say the same about a seaxe," Brigan contested.

"But a seaxe can't fool the senses through illusions. It can't transform its shape at will or become impenetrable like a mountain. It can't turn invisible or cut with an edge of pure light."

"But I've seen the good etherarchy can do as well," Brigan said, becoming animated. "The tremendous healing liquid light achieves, or the battle prowess of a Psion. The salvation from danger one Rifter's portal can offer."

"So do you believe King Rodan of Drakfell was right to align himself with the Knights of the Torch? Despite the pushback from the High King's forces?" King Axel sounded genuinely curious.

Brigan nodded confidently. "I do. At least, I think trying something new in order to make things better was a good move. I can't speak to the cause of the Knights of the Torch specifically, since I haven't studied it. Most writing I've found on the Knights is more in the vein of epic literature than factual texts."

The king tilted his head, looking at Brigan as if he were somehow evaluating him. "Would you be interested in borrowing a book of mine?"

Brigan's eyes lit up. "Absolutely."

The king smiled, then turned toward the door to the ballroom and raised a hand. Several of the king's attendants stood on call nearby, and the king asked for one by name. He gave them instructions and sent them back into the citadel in search of the book.

"If I may ask," King Axel said while they waited for the servant to return. "What makes you so interested in the cause of the magi?"

"I used to not care much at all," Brigan admitted. "But as you know, I spent a lot of time serving at Outcast Outpost with magi squadmates. They deserve to make lives for themselves wherever they choose, just like the rest of us."

"And yet, the fact remains, magi draw the dragons near," the king sighed.

"I've been thinking about that. I think many magi would be fit and willing to serve for a season in the guard, defending the keeps against the dragons they bring. But that solution is incomplete, especially considering the steep learning curve of training that many soldiers. I've been wondering if the anti-ether elements of silver could do something to block the magi's ethereal signature that alerts the wild dragons in the first place. But I don't want to force the magi to wear anything that would bring them constant pain—maybe there's a way to work it into the keep walls? I know silver is costly and fairly rare throughout the realm, so we'd have to find the right balance by diluting the metal with something else while still allowing it to be effective. Though, I'm no alchemist or inventor, so we'd have to find somebody who knows far more than me on that subject..."

Brigan could've probably gone on for hours, but King Axel began to laugh. Brigan gave a light chuckle.

"Sorry," Brigan said. "It's not easy to come by someone who's willing to listen to my musings. Least of all one who might actually be able to implement any of them."

"It's more than alright, Brigan," the king said with a smile. "I admire your desire to consider the possibilities. You'll make a great leader one day."

The king's servant returned, hurrying toward them with a thin book in their hand. The volume had a well-worn, dark red cover, with gold lettering that read: 'The Knight's Code.' King Axel looked over the book before passing it to Brigan.

"I hope you will find it as enlightening as I have," the king said.

"I'm sure I will." The book felt heavier in Brigan's hands than he would've expected. "Thank you, my king."

"If I might offer one piece of advice as you continue your path of learning," King Axel said, notes of sadness coloring his tone. "Open your eyes to see clearly, your heart to feel with compassion, and your mind to discern with wisdom. Don't neglect any one of them, lest you find yourself deceived by those who claim to have your best interests at heart. You… you never want to find yourself loving a mere illusion."

As he watched the king looking out into the night, it was almost as if Brigan could see the heavy burden of caring for the entire keepdom on his shoulders. Brigan's gaze flicked to the king's right wrist as he fiddled with the jeweled, woven marriage bracelet there. Brigan recalled the way Queen Ilona had spoken at Meleya's trial. It was clear that the king and his wife differed greatly in their beliefs.

Once again, Brigan found himself thinking of Meleya. While his father was wrong about the qualities that Brigan should care about in a future Duchess of Solhelm, he'd been right about one thing: Brigan knew better than to play around with one of the most important decisions he'd ever have to make.

Brigan felt the chilly winter wind through his jacket as he set his jaw with determination. Maybe Meleya only saw him as a friend for now, but he wasn't willing to give up on her without a fight. He sighed, once again looking upward toward the stars.

Chapter 36: Reunion

I stood at the ballroom door with the rest of Squad Reckless. The king's wyvern, Lantha, had assured us that she was keeping a close watch on our noble charge, but Solvai was making sure we always had eyes on King Axel anyway. From here, we could see the king leaning against the courtyard balcony while he spoke with Brigan. They seemed deep in conversation, and I could tell by the way Brigan's face lit up that he was passionate about the subject. The corner of my mouth quirked into a small smile.

"But Mama, I want to go outside," a child's voice spoke from just inside the ballroom. I turned to see a well-dressed little girl, maybe seven or eight years old, tugging on the full skirt of her mother's ballgown.

I startled when I caught sight of the mother's face. Her lip was curled into a snarl, her eyebrows furrowed as she stared directly at me. Or rather, at the mark on my left cheek.

"Come away from the door," the noblewoman took her child by the shoulders, pulling her closer.

The child protested. "But—"

"I said come," the woman snapped as she dragged her daughter away toward the safety of her noble house's personal high guard.

A surge of shame filled my stomach. All night, my presence had shocked and horrified the noblemen and women of the Canyon Keepdom. They'd cast me dirty looks and edged away, as if putting slightly more distance between us would keep them safe from the wild dragons I might otherwise draw to their party.

Looking down at my boots, I was more sure than ever that I'd been right to turn down Brigan's invitation. It would've only made things difficult for him.

Watching the noblewoman lead her child away brought me back to the Dunefox Caravan, all the other children shrinking back from me as they clung to their parents. As if I were something vile, dangerous, and undesirable.

The memory of Mom's crying echoed inside my head, louder than the din of music and conversation surrounding me.

Automatically, I put a hand to my cheek, concealing my silvermark from view. The scar was still slightly cold against my hand, though it had been with me for months.

Back at Outcast Outpost, things hadn't been so bad. Sure, some of the other soldiers had blamed me for the extra time they'd spent on the battlefield, and Commander Hildred had literally sent me to my death in the Dragon Mists. But somehow, being at this party among people who stared down their noses at me purely because of the mark their system had carved onto my face felt even worse.

"Still no sign of the other Knights. Or the Coven," Jax whispered, appearing between me and the noblewoman's retreating back. When he saw me cupping my hand over my cheek, he frowned.

"What happened? Did someone try to hurt you?" he looked around as if he were planning to beat up the first person who dared look him in the eye.

"No, I'm fine," I insisted. It wasn't exactly a lie—physically, I was fine.

Suddenly, a commotion from out in the courtyard caught my eye. I recognized Captain Zoren's large pauldron with the insignia of the Captain of the Guard emblazoned on it above the Mage Hunters' triangle mark. Four pairs of silver-clad, blue-cloaked Mage Hunters accompanied him, and interspersed amongst the Hunters were about eighteen bedraggled-looking people. The people were silvermarked magi wearing simple brown tunics and heavy silver cuffs around their wrists. I winced, remembering the way silver manacles had once sent freezing pain up my own arms.

I felt my heart leap into my throat as I spotted Dad right away, his shock of white snowhead hair standing out amongst the lineup. I was relieved to see Mom standing at his side, their arms brushing up against each other as they walked.

She looked utterly exhausted, with her long, tangled hair, and heavy dark circles beneath her brown eyes. Her posture was like that of someone twice her age, and the angry, red burn on her left cheek highlighted her Rifter's silvermark.

Captain Zoren led the prisoners past where King Axel and Brigan stood along the balcony that blocked the courtyard from the sheer drop off the edge of the Rise.

"Soot," Jax muttered as he watched the lineup. "It's her drakking entourage."

I barely heard him—I was already running.

Before anyone could think about stopping me, I'd crossed the courtyard and flung my arms around my parents. I nearly knocked them down with the force, but they didn't seem to care as they squeezed me back, clutching me as closely as they could despite their manacles. It was the first time we'd been able to hold each other in almost four years.

"Meli," Mom breathed as she buried her face in my hair. We were the same height now. I could feel my whole body trembling, and I almost didn't dare let go.

"Tonight's the night," I said. "Tonight, the king promised to release all the magi prisoners as a show of mercy. You'll finally be free."

"After all these years," Mom said. "We'll be safe, together at last. We'll be a real family again."

Dad pulled back first. "Woowee! Look at you," he said with a proud smile. "Last time we saw you, you'd only just gotten your orange cloak. Now you mean to tell us you're in the king's scorchin' high guard?"

"It's a long story," I said with a smile, not bothering to stop the tears from spilling out the corners of my eyes.

As I stepped away to allow my parents some room to breathe, my mom's hand flew to her mouth as pain flashed across her eyes. My body tensed—She'd noticed my left cheek.

"Freya," Dad said soothingly. "We knew she'd been silvermarked."

"Still," Mom choked, reaching out to pull a section of my long white hair over the mark.

Guilt flooded me as I took in the pain on her face from seeing me like this. I didn't brush the hair away.

"M, you've got to be more careful," Jax materialized at my side, putting a strong, protective hand on my back. "The Mage Hunters here are—"

"Hello, Jax," a young woman with short, black hair in a low draketail approached. She had intense eyebrows lowered over a cold gaze, and a Mage Hunter's cloak trailing behind her.

"Jaira." Jax automatically reached behind his back to pull out one of the twin axes he kept there. Before he got to the weapons, Jax did a double take as the Mage Hunter turned her face to reveal what looked like a fairly fresh Lightwielder's silvermark on her left side.

"For reasons she won't disclose, the Black Valkyrie has given us strict instructions not to gut you like a drakefish tonight," the young woman said. "But watch yourself, Jax. Sometimes things happen on the battle-field…"

I felt my blood rise instantly as the Mage Hunter threatened Jax. Stepping between them, I gripped the hilt of my seaxe in warning.

My quick movement caught her off guard, and she jumped backward, putting a hand on the silver whip looped at her belt.

"Stay away from him," I growled.

"Yikes," Jaira replied, wrinkling her nose at me. "Get yourself a new girlfriend, did you? Shame."

To the side, I saw my dad raise his dark eyebrows at the word 'girl-friend.' He looked from me to Jax, cocking his head with curiosity. Despite everything, I felt my cheeks burn.

"That's enough, Lightbane," a new voice cut into our conversation.

My eyes widened as a harshly beautiful woman in black armor strode up to where we stood. The oversized pauldron on her shoulder had a silver swan in flight etched into it, and the long black cloak flowing behind her was adorned with black feathers. She had steely gray hair and midnight blue eyes, the same shade as the ones I'd lost myself in just last night.

"Black Valkyrie," the Mage Hunter, Jaira, replied.

"Keep an eye on the other prisoners, won't you?" the Black Valkyrie ordered. Without hesitation, Jaira ducked her head and walked away. Somewhat reluctantly, I let my hand fall from the hilt of my seaxe.

Once Jaira was out of earshot, the Black Valkyrie turned to me with a brilliant smile. "Jax, I don't believe I've met your friend."

"Uh…" Jax started, looking nervously from me to his mother.

To my utter humiliation, Dad chimed in. "Was just about to say the same thing. Mels, who's this strappin' young gent, and whatever hap-pened to his sleeves?"

Dad winked, and my already warm cheeks blazed.

Jax's mom turned to my dad, extending a hand in greeting. "I'm Jax's mother, but you can call me the Black Valkyrie."

"I'm Ivar, Meleya's father," Dad grasped the Black Valkyrie's forearm. "And this here's my wife, Freya."

"Hello," Mom said quietly.

"Of course," the Black Valkyrie said, understanding dawning in her eyes. "The Ursadon mentioned the two of you recently helped him on an important case. In exchange for your help, Freya, you wanted to speak with me."

"That's right," Mom nodded. Dad frowned as if he didn't know what the Black Valkyrie was alluding to.

"Come see me after you're freed."

"I will," Mom replied.

"A Rifter like your daughter, I see." The Black Valkyrie gestured to the silvermark on Mom's cheek, ignoring the gnarled skin of her burn. "Don't see many magi like you these days."

"Not since the late High Queen's Rifter Purge," Mom answered.

"Indeed."

"So," Dad said boldly. "You're in the business of huntin' magi? Can't be easy, not when you're a Psion yourself. Or are you a Shadowbinder? I see two marks there on your cheek."

I took a closer look and realized Dad was right. The same psionic mark Jax wore shone from the Black Valkyrie's high left cheekbone, but just to the side and upward from that mark was another, following the angle of her eye.

Jax's gaze darkened when he saw the mark, but he didn't look surprised.

"Jax and Meleya," the Black Valkyrie said, changing the subject as she turned to us. "How did the two of you meet then?"

"Uh…" Jax mumbled again.

Lucky for us, they chose that moment to blow the horn to announce the end of the dance. Jax and I breathed a sigh of relief in unison.

"The king's about to speak," I rushed.

"Of course," the Black Valkyrie flashed us another winning smile. "But don't think this conversation is over. Maybe we can chat over dinner sometime."

"Absolutely," Dad jumped in. "Mels makes the most amazin' fry bread—you've got to try it."

"I'd be delighted." The Black Valkyrie nodded to my fearless father. "I'll be in touch. In the meantime, please keep my relationship with Jax to yourselves. I wouldn't want to put him in any more danger than necessary. I'm sure you understand."

"Completely," Mom whispered.

The Black Valkyrie offered a gracious smile and took a step backward. "It's been a pleasure. Now, if you'll excuse me, I've got to prepare for the siege."

With a dramatic flourish of her cloak, the Black Valkyrie walked away.

"Siege?" Panic creased Mom's forehead.

I swallowed. I guess they hadn't told the prisoners everything.

I had just opened my mouth to explain when nobility began pouring through the ballroom doors and flooding the courtyard. They wore light wraps or jackets, which they pulled more tightly around their shoulders as they commented on the sporadic flurries of lightly falling snow.

King Axel was already in place in front of the line of prisoners, preparing to speak while his wyvern stood regally close by. The rest of Squad Reckless already stood in formation around the king, while Solvai gave Jax and me a meaningful look.

"We've gotta go," Jax muttered, replacing his hand against my back. His touch made my heart skip a beat.

"Just…" I flashed my parents one final, desperate glance. "Be careful. I love you."

"We love you too," Dad gave me a reassuring nod, and I knew he'd do everything he could to protect Mom. As Jax and I were about to step away, Dad leaned forward to loudly whisper, "But you've got to tell me—How serious are things with this Jax guy? He seems nice, but then again, I'm partial to Psions."

"*Dad*," I hissed. I shot him one last glare before hurrying off to join the rest of our squad.

Solvai directed Jax and me to our places behind the king and the others. She gave me an apologetic look—They must've asked her to hide the two of us as best she could since we were silvermarked. I gave her a small shrug to let her know I understood.

"Noble houses of Rengard," the king began, his voice remaining gentle while still carrying across the spacious courtyard. "Tonight, I welcome you into my home."

The crowd applauded the king. Then he continued his speech, addressing the great need to come together as a keepdom during this time of war and uncertainty.

Jax bent toward me, speaking quietly out of the corner of his mouth. "Sorry about that. I wasn't planning on turning it into a whole meet-the-parents thing."

"That's okay," I whispered back. "Your mom seems pretty nice, actually."

"Hard to believe she's void-bent on destroying the Farseer and the Knights, huh? Your parents are cool, though."

"But it's not hard to believe that Dad's void-bent on embarrassing me."

Jax stifled a laugh, and Brigan turned his head toward us. Jax and I straightened.

As the king continued his speech, I noticed Queen Ilona and some of the original high guard standing beside our group. The queen looked as perfectly beautiful as ever, though I noted an edge of harshness staining her otherwise innocent features. Her gaze kept darting westward toward the edge of the balcony as if she were expecting something.

Nerves returned to my stomach in full force. If my suspicions about Queen Ilona were correct, she was probably watching for her army of fellow worshippers of the Gray Ones.

I knew that Captain Zoren had every soldier in the keep ready to defend the Rise. A platoon blockaded the land bridge that led onto the butte, and squads guarded every entrance to the castle itself. Flying dragon riders were supposed to be ready to swoop in at the Captain's word. But despite knowing the plan, I couldn't shake the feeling that something was off. I knew that was stupid—I was probably just nervous because my parents were here.

"Traditionally," the king held the attention of the crowd, "unregistered magi are executed for the danger they pose to our realm. But tonight, I wish to set a new precedent..."

Suddenly, every brazier in the courtyard went out. It was as if a great wind had swept through, dousing each one, but I felt no breeze on my cheek. Rather, that dreaded icy stillness settled over the darkened courtyard. The king's speech came to a stop, as did the general bustle of the crowd.

I furrowed my brow, looking westward to see if the Liberator's army had somehow come to cause the cold, dark eeriness. I was startled when

I saw the dark glimmer in Queen Ilona's perfect eyes. Behind the king, Lantha growled.

Suddenly, each of the braziers burst to life again, but no longer with their warm, orange fire. Now each one flickered with a single lightning blue flame.

My stomach dropped. I knew that color all too well.

The Coven's coup had officially begun.

CHAPTER 37: COUP

A proud laugh echoed across the stillness of the courtyard, sending chills up my spine. I whipped my head around to see one of the fully-armored members of the old high guard toss a chunk of black onyx toward the western edge of the spacious balcony. The rock skidded to a stop against the wall, and I saw the glowing gold rune on one face pulsing.

I recognized the rune—that was a rift anchor.

I wasted no time, breaking formation to dart toward that stone. Who knew what void would unleash through that portal once it ripped to life. Jax and Brigan were hot on my heels.

Captain Zoren must've understood the significance of the anchor as well. Behind me, I heard him give the order.

"Call in the rest of the guard!" he barked urgently.

Before I could reach the anchor, the high guard who'd thrown it casually sidestepped into my path. He didn't bother pulling out a weapon to block; rather, he thrust both hands toward me.

Suddenly, tangled ironthorn vines shot from his sleeves. They twisted around me, halting my momentum and pinning my arms to my sides as their sharp spines dug into my skin. More vines grew from the first, winding around Jax and Brigan as well. The plants constricted, holding us in place. The crowd gasped at the display of woodweaving etherarchy.

Out of the corner of my eye, I saw the line of Mage Hunters guarding the prisoners tense. But the Lightwielder who'd threatened Jax earlier, Jaira, held up a hand.

"Hold your attack until the Liberator shows their face!" she said.

Next, I heard one of Zoren's commanders breathing heavily as he reported to the Captain. "The doors to the ballroom and all the other exits have been sealed shut—some kind of geomancy."

My mind raced as I struggled against the vines. That meant the majority of our army was trapped outside.

The high guard laughed again, ripping off his helmet and dropping it to the stone floor with a clank. A few of the nobility screamed at the sight of his Woodweaver's silvermark. This had to be the same man who'd been with the Liberator in their underground hold. I struggled against my ironthorn bonds, but I couldn't get free. Jax and Brigan grunted to my left and right, in a similar bind. I thought I heard the rest of the squad hurrying our way.

"Call in the drakking flyers then," Captain Zoren roared.

The Woodweaver gave one sharp laugh before turning to the Captain of the Guard. "Your precious dragon riders won't be coming. We knew all of your 'secret' plans—someone slipped a few drops of astralock into the dragons' food. By the time they wake, the Rise and all of the Canyon Keepdom will belong to the Coven of the Gray Ones. Victory to the Liberator!"

I glanced toward Queen Ilona, who wore a well-practiced look of shock on her angelic face. If she was in on the coup, she was doing a good job of hiding it.

From the row of Mage Hunters, I heard Jaira speak again. "I said hold until the Liberator—"

Apparently, Trickshot was fed up with waiting. The auburn-haired Mage Hunter whipped out her miniature crossbow, aiming to kill the Woodweaver.

Her shot was perfect, but some kind of wooden armor rippled to life across the man's chest. The armor looked like the rock solid bark of a diamondoak, and Trickshot's bolt glanced off uselessly.

But Trickshot was the fastest shooter in the southern keepdoms. Her next shot took the Woodweaver straight in the arm he was using to channel etherarchy. Instantly, the vines trapping Jax, Brigan, and me stopped squeezing, allowing the three of us to disentangle ourselves.

Brigan charged toward the rift anchor on foot while Jax and I runetraced faster than lightning. Jax had just begun psionically lifting the anchor when my entrance portal appeared beside it. I placed the exit portal off the edge of the Rise.

Jax was a split second away from launching the black anchor through my portal when the pulsing rune on the onyx bloomed with gold light as bright as the sun. A long crack formed, running vertically through the air and stopping Jax and me from disposing of the anchor through my rift.

We were too late. The Coven's portal burst to life, opening along the balcony edge as wide as three sets of extended wyvern's wings.

Chaos spilled through the portal. A gray army of umbral dreklings and dragons mingled with more than double the number of gray-robed, masked magi as had been at the Outpost. The magi instantly displayed their power, some levitating a head above the crowd while others brandished long, runemarked staffs pulsing with that unnatural blue light. The blue reflected against the gently falling snowflakes.

Above the sounds of nobility screaming and shrinking away from the neverending gray army, I heard Captain Zoren's voice.

"High guards of the Canyonlands, to arms!"

Fear gripped my heart as I realized Zoren was right. With the rest of the guard unable to get to us, Squad Reckless and the other high guards of the keepdom's nobility were the only defense the Rise had.

Well, us, and the Mage Hunters.

The Coven must've known that, because the first thing they did was target the Hunters in their dusky blue cloaks. Before any of us could react, a masked Astromancer blasted both Trickshot and Mute with bolts of blue-tinged ether. White streaks immediately grew amidst their dark hair as the pair fell to the ground. They lay still, and I couldn't tell if Trickshot was alive or dead.

Meanwhile, a burly Mage Hunter with a Geomancer's silvermark took three crossbow bolts in the chest, falling to his knees. His partner had a Seer's mark on his face and a long, silver snake draped over his shoulders. The snake hissed as an enemy Psion's tomahawk went flying through the air to hack at the Mage Hunter's hand. The Seer cried out in pain as the axe took out the index and middle fingers on his right hand—That would make runetracing difficult.

Only Jaira was able to react in time. Using her Lightwielding powers, she reinforced her silver shield with a layer of light to reflect the oncoming bolts of dream energy. She protected both herself and her redheaded partner, whose jaw dropped with relief. My eyes grew even wider as I realized her lightwielding was bright blue, just like the power the Coven used. Was the Mage Hunter using the same dark etherarchy?

More psionics sent the two enforcers clad in silver armor rising into the air. More gasps rang out from the crowd—silver was supposed to be impervious to etherarchy. But I knew from experience that silver meant nothing against the strange, bright blue power of the Coven.

The enforcers, trapped by the very armor that should've protected them, shot upward. Another masked magi blasted blue-tinged pieces of starglass toward the Mage Hunters, shards jabbing into their underarms and everywhere else there were gaps in their armor.

The dramatic display achieved its purpose of shocking the noble crowd. The nobility cowered away from the Coven, banging uselessly on the geomantically-sealed ballroom doors. Dreklings snarled, chomping at the bit to attack the nobles, yet holding back as if they were waiting for something. The black-and-orange-cloaked high guards shakily stood their ground.

"First, death to those who hunt us!" the Woodweaver man shouted through the pain of his crossbow wound. "Next, death to those who oppress us!"

As the Coven's portal finally closed, we heard an earth-shaking roar from the west. For a few tense seconds, everything was still.

Then a set of wide, magnificent wings unfurled, backlit by the bright white moon. Four claws caught the light as a full-sized true dragon soared toward the courtyard.

Its scales were inky black, which meant it wasn't the true dragon of High King Magnus. It wasn't the young, pearlescent white true dragon I'd seen with the thieves behind the command center those months ago either.

I remembered the true dragon's shadow I'd seen with Brigan and Solvai in the Coven's underground hold.

My gaze shot toward Queen Ilona as she stood surrounded by half the high guard. The queen's enormous eyes were even wider than usual, a look of perfect shock on her pretty face. I frowned.

The menacing true dragon landed on the edge of the balcony. Within moments, nine other dragons—wyverns, evren, and drakes—flanked the true dragon, those with wings flying in behind while the drakes walked up, having come through the portal with the rest of the army. Among the evren beside the true dragon, I caught sight of one with bright yellow scales. It broke my heart to see Sniff growling alongside the rest, his normally bright eyes blue with voidfire.

Instantly, the gray-robed, masked coven members stopped what they were doing to bow before the great, black true dragon. Even the umbral dreklings fell to their knees and hushed their snarls. It was as if the true dragon could somehow control them the way they'd controlled Sniff back in the cage. This must've been whom they'd been waiting for.

The true dragon stood proudly, waiting until it had the attention of every soul in the courtyard.

Then, an enormous cloud of shimmering blue swirled around the true dragon. I gripped my seaxe—My instinct had been right. This was the wildshaping leader of the Coven.

When the smoke cleared, a figure in loose gray robes stood before the crowd. They wore that same menacing, horned mask as before, and wielded no weapon in their hands.

"Nobility of the Canyon Keepdom," the Liberator said in that same distorted voice I'd heard before. "I have come to usher in the Gray Age: The Age of Ether. To free magi, and to put them in their rightful place as rulers over Evgard. I am the Liberator."

The gray-hooded figure took a step forward, and though they held no blade, the crowd cringed backward in fear.

One brave soldier from a noble family's high guard gave a warrior's yell, charging toward the Liberator with his long seaxe raised. The Coven leader didn't even flinch as one of the many masked magi nearby stepped toward the high guard, holding a spear made from crystalline starglass.

The starglass spear grew longer as the Coven magi attacked, the blade piercing the soldier's side. He fell without another sound.

No one else dared approach as the Liberator continued their speech.

"For too long, the noble houses of Evgard have silenced our kind. Executed us simply for being born. Yet now, rather than shed your blood in payment, we offer you the chance to surrender. Allow the Coven of the Gray Ones to claim the Rise, and we will leave you unharmed. To fight us would be foolish, as we are blessed by the Gray Ones with power beyond your comprehension."

To emphasize their point, the Liberator accessed their Wildshaping etherarchy. Each of the nine heartscales hanging from their neck glowed blue, wildshaper markings flowing across them. Sentinel markings burned beneath their robes as another cloud engulfed them. The crowd whimpered as the Liberator reappeared as a true dragon once more.

I jumped as the Liberator's voice appeared in my mind. One look around told me everyone else in the courtyard could hear them as well.

The Gray Ones have chosen me, shared with me the secrets of their power. In this form, I can achieve all nine types of etherarchy, as did the Guardians of old. The choice is yours, noblemen and women of the Canyonlands. Life in your rightful place below magi, or death in the name of justice.

For what felt like an eternity, silence reigned over the courtyard. Then the king of Rengard stepped forward, each footstep echoing in the quiet.

Seeing the king approach, Solvai nodded to each member of our squad. I could tell she was terrified, but still, she led us toward the king.

"No," King Axel said, holding up a hand toward us. "Stay back, Squad Reckless. You too, Lantha." He turned sternly to his wyvern as she made a low, rumbling noise in her throat.

"But, my king—" Solvai started.

"No," the king repeated.

It seemed the entire realm was holding its breath as King Axel stepped out into the open space before the true dragon.

"Liberator," the king said, his voice as gentle as the quietly cascading snowflakes. "I do not wish for this night to end in bloodshed."

Then submit, former king of the Canyonlands, the Liberator's voice rolled throughout our minds.

"Call off your gray army, and meet with me personally inside the citadel. I promise to hear your concerns and do what I can to meet your needs."

Laughter echoed inside my skull. It seemed the Liberator was less than satisfied with King Axel's proposal.

You nobles are all alike. Think you hold all the power. For years, we magi were forced to hide and cower before you, always living in fear. Praying that our children wouldn't be born with gifts. Yet tonight, those very gifts will end your breed, unless you submit.

"Evgard has wronged you," the king said, keeping his voice calm and even. "However, a strike in response to a strike leaves both sides crippled. Tonight can be a new beginning for the magi of Keep Rengard. Let us come together as an example to the rest of the realm that peace and safety can be achieved. The magi prisoners who stand along the back wall deserve a chance to serve Evgard as full citizens."

I found myself nodding as the king spoke. Even a few of the gray-hooded magi seemed to find reason in the king's words. The true dragon gave pause before speaking again.

You say these things only now, as your keepdom stands on the precipice of ruin.

"I say these things because they are true," King Axel said. "Call off this attack, Liberator."

The Liberator in true dragon form breathed heavily through their nostrils, considering the king's plea.

King Axel put out both hands to his sides in a gesture of peace. "Please. To harm the innocent would not serve your goals."

At that, the Liberator's pupils narrowed. Instantly, Lantha gave a roar and lunged toward her bond, the king. The true dragon reared back, and must've spoken to the minds of their nine bonded dragons, because Sniff and a few others rushed to stop Lantha, pinning her wings to the ground with their claws.

The Liberator stretched out their neck in anger, their voice thundering in the minds of everyone present.

You dare call these the innocent? When Keep Gray Fen sacrifices innocent magi to wild dragons out on its bog each day? When Keeps Mesa and Scarlet Shore compete to see which can slaughter more of our kind? Even here, in the illustrious capital of the Canyonlands, you nobility ensnare magi in silver before brutally tossing them from the heights of this very butte. These noblemen and women are not innocent. It is for the true innocents that I fight, Axel of Rengard. Submit, or die.

"Please," the king said, the first hint of desperation appearing in his tone. "I swear we'll find a solution—"

Last chance, your highness.

"Wait—"

The Liberator shot their neck forward, eerie, void-blue dragonfire spraying from their mouth.

Chapter 38: Battle Begins

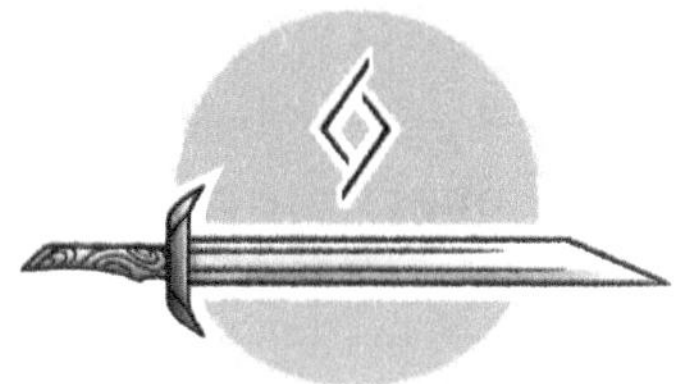

For an awful moment, flames engulfed the king.

Our squad sprang toward the fire, but when the flames sputtered out, we saw King Axel lying on the stone courtyard floor.

Lantha roared, overpowering the dragons that held her down for only a moment before an ether blast from Sniff stopped her. The other dragons struggled, but held the king's wyvern down once more.

A scream ripped from my throat as my squad surrounded King Axel, followed closely by Captain Zoren and many of his commanders.

Solvai arrived first, tears of horror and shame welling in her hazel eyes. The king's body was badly burned, his limbs limp and his face still. Brigan cradled King Axel's head as the rest of us hovered around. Brigan looked up at us, his face confirming the worst.

I stood dumbfounded, a thousand questions racing through my head as a solid lump formed in my throat. Our king lay dead at the hands of the Coven's Liberator. A good man who'd planned to free my parents tonight, but didn't get the chance.

Captain Zoren turned toward the true dragon, his green eyes bright with fury. He drew his silver Mage Hunter's blade, extending the tip toward the leader of the Coven of the Gray Ones.

The Liberator's voice resounded in every mind once again.

So be it. Let the slaughter begin.

Then, chaos.

Immediately, the Coven's hordes of umbral dreklings sprang into action as if someone had released them from a cage. They gave their awful, otherworldly snarls as they charged wildly toward the nobility. The barricade of high guards bore arms against the monsters to protect their charges.

But at the dreklings' sides were the Coven magi themselves. Their void-blue etherarchy manifested in glowing eyes behind their masks, in runes hovering over their foreheads, or in the patterns shining beneath their gray, hooded robes.

My stomach flipped as I realized the dreklings and magi weren't only going for the nobility. Two dreklings were charging straight for the lineup of silver-cuffed prisoners, led by a Coven magi wielding a heavy spiked mace.

Solvai saw the look of horror on my face and didn't waste another moment grieving. Squaring her shoulders, she gave us our orders.

"Cam, get the king's body away from the action. Everyone else, defend the magi prisoners."

We darted back to where the eighteen prisoners shrunk away from the approaching dreklings and gray-hooded figures.

"Which of you prisoners will join the Coven of the Gray Ones?" the masked magi yelled over the discord.

"Your Liberator slew the king who would see us freed!" one brave prisoner yelled back.

"Very well," the Coven magi said, raising his mace. The dreklings howled eagerly as they waited for the magi to make the first strike.

My squadmates and I were a split second from reaching the magi when two white blasts of ether shot toward him. One blast hit him squarely in the chest while the other sent white marks spiraling across his masked face. The magi choked, dropping his mace a split second before going limp and crashing onto the courtyard floor.

The two dreklings, as well as the six of us, turned to see what powerful Astromancer could've managed hits like that.

Standing atop the courtyard wall, his legs apart in a battle stance, was a wiry man holding a smoking, forward-curved starglass dagger in each hand. He had dark scruff on his chin, a shock of white snowhead hair, and his skin was tan and leathery, as if he'd spent a lifetime outside without ever setting foot indoors.

The man had a fierce expression on his face as he surveyed the battle. He blew on the smoking wisps of ether rising from each of his daggers, then expertly twirled them in his hands before taking aim at the duo of umbral dreklings and firing off two more blasts. The umbral dreklings wailed as the shots turned them into curling gray smoke that disappeared into the wind. Two blue crystal cores clattered to the stone below and turned white.

A black dragonhawk screeched as it landed at the man's side. The second it touched ground, a column of gold clouds billowed around it, and when they cleared, the dragonhawk had wildshaped into a woman with dark hair. She had scars running along her body everywhere I saw skin. Her expression was hard, as if she'd kill you at the drop of a scale.

A hulking bloodhusky with thick, red fur leaped off the balcony wall from his place beside the man. With a thunderous, joyful bark, the dog charged toward where our squad stood beside the fallen drekling cores.

"His Majesty!" Jax cried, dropping his axe and holding out both arms. The bloodhusky slammed into him, nuzzling against his neck and face as Jax roughly wove his hands into the creature's fur.

The snowheaded Astromancer and scarred Wildshaper hurried toward Jax as well.

"Well, drak an' a half, Jax," the wiry man said. His voice was gruff, and his northern accent stronger than any I'd ever heard before. "Leave it to you to get into more trouble'n'a dragonowl in a viperdrake pit."

"I swear," the woman added seriously. "Can't leave you alone for five minutes."

"Boone, Valla," Jax couldn't keep the grin off his face.

"Ain't got time for one of them sappy reunions," Boone said, pulling out his starglass daggers once again as he surveyed the courtyard's chaos. "Y'all might wanna duck."

Our squad obeyed, and Boone sent three rapid shots of ether from his curved daggers blasting straight over our ducked heads. Two took out more umbral dreklings while the other hit one of the gray-robed magi in the arm. He dropped the oversized warsword he'd been about to swing at Edrea.

"You got that there silver-eatin' spydra spit, Valla?" Boone asked, narrowing his already squinting eyes in search of his next victim.

"You mean silverbane?" Valla grumbled in response. Then she pulled out a starglass vial filled with some kind of greenish-gold liquid.

"Get it to them chained up pris'ners yonder," Boone ordered. "Free them Solei-forsaken sons'a dragonmutts 'fore somethin' gets 'em killed."

"You're going to free the prisoners?" I blurted, hope rising inside my chest.

Boone nodded. "Sure as the void. See, Jax, Solrac ain't sent us on no rescue mission. This here's a recruitment." Boone turned to the prisoners. "How's a bit of freedom sound to y'all?"

Several prisoners cheered, including my dad. Behind him, Mom's eyes were round with worry.

"Every last one of y'all's a magi—means you can fight. First thing we's gotta do is fight off this drakkin' Coven. That done, I'm offerin' each one'a yous a place with the Knights of the Torch. But the choice is yours. Either way, Valla here'll get y'all outta them drakkin' cuffs." Boone turned toward our squad. "Meanwhile, y'all and I's gonna keep them ghost-'nfused dreklin's from shadow wastin' the livin' daylights out of 'em. Y'all with me?"

Jax grinned, holding a battleaxe in each hand. "Let's bring the void."

"Them Gray Ones done beat you to it, but I like the energy."

With that, our squad sprang into action. Between our squad's weapons, Boone's Astromancy, and His Majesty's fangs, the dreklings didn't stand a chance. We managed to defend our little corner of the balcony long enough for Valla to administer that strange, greenish liquid to the magi prisoners.

Out of the corner of my eye, I watched as she poured just a couple of drops onto each prisoner's manacles. On contact, the substance began eating away at the silver, producing little clouds of orange smoke. It surprised me when it didn't burn the prisoners' wrists, as if the solution was instantly healing the flesh as it finished working through the silver.

Boone's speech had worked. Once they were free, many of the prisoners joined the fight. Dad gave a whoop as his finger trailed gold light through the air, and for the first time in years, a golden rune appeared over his forehead.

He reached out, telekinetically pulling weapons off of fallen soldiers or straight out of Coven members' hands.

"Alright everybody," Dad addressed his fellow prisoners. "I've got seaxes, I've got dragonhook spears and a couple of hand axes. Looks like I've even got a flail here, if that's your thing. Take your pick."

I reduced an umbral drekling to smoke and a crystal core as Dad armed the other prisoners. Soon Boone had a small army at his flank.

"Alrighty y'all," Boone said, rallying the prisoners. "For freedom, for light, and for kickin' the sooty hiney of every drakkin' ghost dares show its face!"

Surprisingly, Boone's strange battle cry got the prisoners calling back with warrior's yells as they joined us against the dreklings. I caught a glimpse of Mom gripping the hilt of a long seaxe, her brows forming a hard line on her determined face. I did a double take as I took in her perfect battle stance—She knew exactly how to wield that sword.

Beside me, Jax leaned over to Boone and Valla as they fought.

"I should warn you," Jax said. "*She's* here."

Boone's gaze darkened. Valla ground her teeth as she brandished a sharp, long seaxe in each hand. She took out her rage on a duo of umbral dreklings, stabbing one in the gut with one hand while using the other to slit the second drekling's throat. I reminded myself not to get on her bad side.

"By *she*," Valla said, a look of murder in her eyes. "I assume you mean…"

Valla trailed off as a group of black swans swooped low, narrowly missing Valla's head. The wedge of six birds shot toward the westernmost edge of the courtyard where the Liberator stood, back in hooded human form, overlooking the battle.

Within moments, the swans were circling the Liberator, their wings scattering the falling snow. The Liberator swatted at the swans as if they were nothing more than mildly annoying dragonflies.

Then, out of nowhere, the Liberator went sprawling to the ground as if something had kicked them in the chest. The swans landed in a V formation, the peak of their V an empty space at the Liberator's feet. The Liberator lay on their back, supporting themselves on their elbows as they looked around for the source of the attack.

Suddenly, the attacker materialized. Out of thin air, the Black Valkyrie appeared at the point of the swan's V formation, her eyes glowing with Archonic power. But rather than the typical gold, the Black Valkyrie's eyes flashed with the same lightning blue the Coven and Jaira fought with. She'd been using invisibility—a Shadowbinding trick.

Before the Liberator had time to react, the Black Valkyrie used the tip of her spear to flip the Liberator's horned mask off of their face, their gray hood slipping off their head.

I audibly gasped as I recognized the Liberator's face. Suddenly, I understood why the Liberator hadn't killed us—both on the battlefield at Outcast Outpost and in the Coven's underground hold.

Wavy brown hair fell around her shoulders. She had sparkling eyes and a face full of freckles, just like her daughter.

I whipped around to where Solvai stood, her eyes wide with shock as she took in the sight of her gray-robed mother getting to her feet before the Black Valkyrie. One look told me my friend hadn't known either.

"Lorelai," the Black Valkyrie's lips curled into a dark smile. "We meet again."

Chapter 39: Reckless

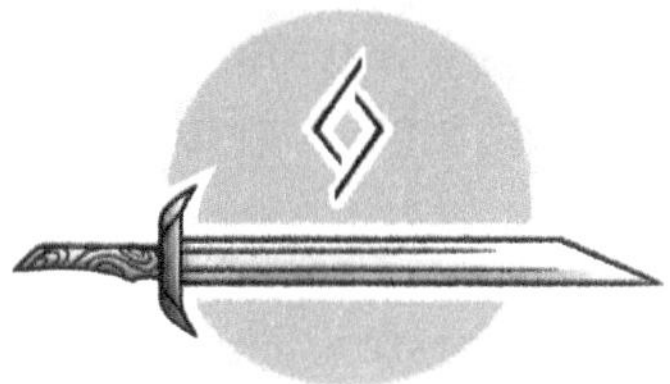

"Vidya," Lorelai said, her voice no longer distorted. "Have you come to finish the work we started years ago? Or are you here to further ruin my life?"

"The second one, naturally." The Black Valkyrie's voice was sweet.

I wanted to stop the raging battle so I could watch the scene unfolding before me. But the umbral creatures and the Coven magi weren't about to let up, and neither could we. Solvai still looked dumbfounded, her spear clutched limply at her side.

I gave a small yell, lunging toward my friend to stop the drekling about to swing a claw at her. Solvai shook her head, trying to process things enough to get back on the defensive. But she still seemed rooted to the spot as she watched the interaction between the Black Valkyrie and her mother—the Liberator. I defended my friend against the umbrals, straining to hear what was happening myself.

"We still want the same thing," Lorelai said as she and the Black Valkyrie began to slowly circle one another at a distance. "A safe Evgard for our children and all magi. When will you realize the law ain't gonna get you there?"

"The law is what keeps us safe. Your way breeds chaos and destruction."

"Yet we both follow the Gray Ones."

The Black Valkyrie narrowed her eyes. "The Gray Ones follow me."

Lorelai laughed. "You keep tellin' yourself that as long as you can, Vidya."

Just then, a gold-rimmed rift tore open, depositing Torsten, rocking chair and all, between the two women. As usual, his stringy hair fell over his eyes and he clutched a bottle in his hand.

Both the Black Valkyrie and the Liberator wrinkled their noses at him.

"Ladies, ladies," Torsten said, his hands gesturing along with his words. "Glad to see the two of you on speakin' terms again. I was thinkin'—maybe instead of this whole coup, the three of us could all go out for—"

The Black Valkyrie rapidly traced a psionic rune and sent the Liberator's fallen mask flying toward Torsten. The mask slammed, upside down, into his face, effectively shutting him up. At the same moment, Lorelai accessed her wildshaping to sprout a long drake's tail, which she used to shove Torsten's rocking chair away.

The Black Valkyrie sneered. "I see you still keep *him* around."

"What's it to you?" Lorelai raised an eyebrow. "You want to 'borrow' him again for the night? Maybe it'll still make Solrac jealous."

"Don't start, Lorelai," the Black Valkyrie's jaw tensed.

"Who knows?" the Liberator taunted. "Last time you even got a souvenir."

"Shut your mouth," the Black Valkyrie snapped, and for the briefest second, her eyes flashed to Jax.

Lorelai must've noticed too. Slowly, she straightened, her head turning toward where Squad Reckless fought. Her gaze locked onto the steely-haired, midnight blue-eyed young man throwing axes beside me.

"Of course," Lorelai muttered under her breath. Then her eyes filled with that same fiery competitiveness I'd seen before whenever she performed on dragonback.

Sentinel patterns lit up along Lorelai's skin, shining with blue energy. My heart leaped into my throat as her pupils changed from round to vertical slits like those of a dragon. The rest of Lorelai remained human as she opened her mouth to spit a jet of void blue dragonfire... this time at Jax. I hadn't reacted in time to save King Axel, but I wasn't about to let that happen again.

I leaped between Jax and the fire, my finger flying to runetrace faster than ever before. I thrust one hand toward the blue flames, a rift appearing to catch them before they could get to us.

I extended my other hand skyward, the exit portal bursting to life at my fingertips as Lorelai's strange, blue dragonfire spouted harmlessly into the air.

The Black Valkyrie gave a furious yell as she dove toward the Liberator. A line of black shadowfire blazed along the edge of her dragonhook spear.

Lorelai turned to the Black Valkyrie, rage still alight in her draconic eyes. She raised a hand to block the spear, her thin fingers morphing into draconic claws as more Sentinel patterns glowed along her skin. Claws and spear clashed as the two women engaged.

"Let them drakscallions have at it," Boone muttered, wiping sweat from his brow and blowing more ether smoke from his daggers. "If I were you, Jax, I'd make myself scarcer'na scaleworm durin' a bloodeagle's mornin' feed."

I raised an eyebrow, but Jax didn't seem fazed by Boone's odd choice of phrasing.

"No!" Brigan's voice rose above the sound of battle. Without another word, my friend took off running, his black and orange cloak disappearing in the chaos.

"The nobility," Solvai said, still sounding shaken by the Liberator's unmasking. "Their high guards are falling."

I turned to see that Solvai was right. Already several men and women in black and orange cloaks lay dead at the gray hoods' feet. The unarmed nobility were next, screaming as the rebel magi moved in for the slaughter.

Brigan rushed toward a trio of well-dressed nobles, each of whom had dark, corkscrew curls like him. His parents looked frantic, clinging to their teenage daughter as a masked magi wielding a heavy warsword approached. The Solhelm high guard had already fallen, and it looked like Brigan wasn't going to make it in time. Even if he did, who knew what etherarchy the gray hood may've had up their sleeve.

I set my jaw. Maybe Brigan couldn't get there fast enough, but I could.

My finger tingled as I rapidly traced the portalling rune. In a flash, I was gone, dashing for a millisecond through the whiteness of Etheria.

I emerged with my seaxe held high to block the Coven magi's warsword as they swung at Brigan's family. I grunted, my limbs shaking as I struggled to hold back the enemy blade—this masked magi was clearly a man about twice my size. White writing on his mask read 'The Granite Giant,' tipping me off that he was all but certainly using Geomancy to enhance his strength. Wonderful.

The magi quickly grew tired of our meaningless standoff, using his superior strength to shove me to the ground. I collapsed as he raised his arm to make another strike toward the nobility.

I threw up my next set of rifts just in time. When he swung, the Granite Giant's blade vanished into my gold-rimmed portal, reappearing to hack into his own back.

The Granite Giant made a choking sound, then fell to the courtyard floor.

I looked into the faces of Brigan's family to see relief from both his mother and sister. But Brigan's father's eyes were narrowed, staring at me as if I were just as guilty as the Geomancer who'd just tried to kill him. As if he'd rather have died at a magi's hand than have been saved by one.

Brigan arrived within seconds, throwing himself at his family in an embrace. He turned to me, gratitude glistening in his warm brown eyes.

But there wasn't time for words. Already, more umbral creatures and gray hoods were stalking toward the nobility. Everywhere I looked, bodies draped in flowing ball gowns or decorative jackets littered the ground. The Coven was taking a few losses as well, but most of those were umbral dreklings, their fodder. If we couldn't come up with a plan, the Canyon Keepdom would be leaderless by the end of the night, just like the Coven of the Gray Ones wanted.

Soon, the rest of Squad Reckless joined us, protectively surrounding Keep Solhelm's royal family. A few dreklings tried to come for them, but Jax's axes and Cam's spear sent them wisping into oblivion.

Out of nowhere, a gray-hooded magi appeared behind our line, standing directly beside Brigan's sister. They'd gone invisible using shadow-binding etherarchy, the same kind the Black Valkyrie had used to sneak up on the Liberator.

Brigan's sister screamed as the Shadowbinder moved to stab her with a blade edged in black fire. The magi laughed, enjoying the girl's reaction to their sudden appearance.

Then abruptly, the masked magi made a wet coughing sound. A second later, they slumped to the floor to reveal Erik standing behind them. Erik held my father's antler-handled dagger—the backup weapon I'd given him during the battle at Outcast Outpost. It was now dripping with blood.

Erik looked completely shocked by his own daring rescue. Brigan's sister looked at Erik, impressed and grateful. I could've sworn I saw Erik's cheeks blazing under her gaze as he squared his shoulders.

Solvai surveyed the scene of carnage surrounding us, as if realizing how hopeless our situation was.

"There are too many gray hoods," she said. "We have to get the nobility out of here."

"Gee, why didn't any of them think of that?" Edrea replied sarcastically. "Hey nobility, why don't you just, you know, leave?"

Solvai ignored Edrea's retort, turning to me. There was a look of determination in her greenish-brown eyes.

A nervous lump formed in my stomach as it dawned on me what she was asking.

"I can't," I said, my gaze flashing toward Brigan's father. He was still glaring at me like I was his true enemy. "I... I don't have an anchor anywhere, and there's nowhere I can see that's safe."

"How long do you need to make an anchor?" Solvai asked.

My mind spun as I recalled the rune. "Not long, but—"

"We'll hold off the Coven. Make one, now."

My squad captain gave the order with such confidence, I didn't question her again. I looked around, searching for any sort of small stone or gem I could use to make the anchor.

Unfortunately, the first one I spotted was on the thin iron crown circling the Duke of Solhelm's head. Every minute more people were dying, so I swallowed my nerves.

"Um, excuse me," I pointed to the quartz embedded in the circlet over Brigan's father's angry eyes. "I wonder if I could... borrow that."

"You'd like the crown, wouldn't you? You ethercursed."

The derogatory word sent my heart plummeting. Luckily, Brigan came to my rescue, taking my hand and placing a red gem he'd pried from his own ornamental sword hilt into my palm.

"Here," Brigan said. "Use this."

"Thanks," I muttered, my face still burning with shame. Brigan gave his father a stern, frustrated look before rejoining the others in battle.

I used a finger to etch golden lines into the flattest plane on Brigan's stone. The exit anchor rune glowed to life.

"Solvai," I called over the din of fighting, holding up the anchor. My friend was at my side in a flash.

I held up the runemarked gem. "It won't do any good unless we can get it away from the action."

Solvai looked more determined than I'd ever seen her before. "Don't worry about that." She must've noticed the skepticism on my face, because she put a firm hand on my shoulder. "You were right about me, Meleya. I was meant to fly—and so are you."

Solvai took the rift anchor, clutching it in her hand. She gave me one last confident nod. "Give me two minutes."

With that, I saw gold markings light up along the wooden charm on a cord around her neck. Similar patterns flowed along Solvai's arms, neck, and cheeks.

I took a step back as gold mist surrounded her. When it dissipated, Solvai was a mighty, chestnut brown falcondrake.

She let out a shriek, then took off into the air with the rift anchor. Erik stood by with his crossbow, ready to take out any aerial attackers who may've challenged her, but the Coven most likely assumed the Wildshaper was one of their own.

Soon Solvai was out of sight, disappearing somewhere over the Rise. After two agonizing minutes, I knew it was my turn.

I stood behind Squad Reckless as they battled the Coven's forces, knowing they'd cover me.

I closed my eyes, breathing in the chaos around me. A scream from a nearby noblewoman echoed in my ears, sending a shiver down my spine. My eyes flew open, going round as the scream sent me jolting back to a memory from my past.

I was seven years old again, standing in the doorway of our family's tent. I watched in horror as my mother screamed while pressing the hot coal into the left side of her face. Her silvermark was so abhorrent to her, she'd rather live with a distorted burn on her face than see it again. She hated what she was—what we both were.

I felt like the world was moving in slow motion as I whipped my head toward the balcony's edge, where we'd left Boone and his prisoner army. It was as if the sea of gray and bloodshed had parted for just one moment, giving me a clear view of Mom.

She still held her sword with shaking hands, but she was watching me. Her once beautiful face was stricken with fear, and I could've sworn she mouthed my name.

Anxiety bloomed inside my chest. Using etherarchy like this would make me a target for every gray hood in the courtyard. I remembered her reaction to seeing me silvermarked, and I felt a wave of fear wash over me as well. I didn't need to be a mind reader to know it would break Mom's heart to ever see me like that.

I looked down at my hand, the skin still bearing its discolored scar from wrenching the coal from Mom's hands all those years ago. My legs shook, and I shrank down to my knees.

Guilt flooded through me. Guilt for the danger my presence posed to my friends each day. Guilt for causing my parents so much pain.

The sounds of battle disappeared as the hunting song my old squad-mate, Bjorn, once sang sprang to the forefront of my thoughts. His voice, along with those of the survivors after the battle at Outcast Outpost, echoed within the walls of my mind:

Stay away
You magi need to listen

I felt the weight from years of hiding my etherarchy crushing me. My chest felt like it was growing tighter as I struggled to get a full breath.

Stay away
From every keep and town
Or we will hunt you down

As the notes thundered inside my head, I almost let the fear swallow me.

I cast one last desperate look at the battlefield. What if I didn't have it in me to save these people—these people who hated me?

Yes, we will hunt you down

Amidst the pandemonium, I caught sight of a flash of dark auburn hair, newly streaked with white. Trickshot was alive after all, rushing as quickly as she could to tend to the wounded and get them out of harm's way. Despite her own injuries and scars, she was still doing everything she could.

I won't let fear keep me from using my gift, Trickshot had said at the Outpost.

Though it felt like I was lifting the weight of worlds, I got to my feet.

Like a flickering candle on a moonless night, golden etherlight trailed from my finger. I tuned out the protests from the Duke of Solhelm and the cries of terror from the other nobility staring at me. I didn't look back to where I knew Mom was still watching.

I stretched my hands out in front of me, and a golden crack began to form. It started small, then grew, reaching from the courtyard floor all the way up to the snowy winter sky.

A sharp jolt sent shivers up my spine as my ether well began to drain. But I wasn't worried. I knew I could make a rift this big—I'd done it before.

My hands were steady as I made a prying motion with them. Following my movement, the crack slowly ripped apart, revealing the whiteness of the spirit world.

With a yell, I thrust my hands apart to either side. The portal and I moved in tandem as it split apart wider and wider.

I craned my neck, spotting Brigan, Jax, and the others struggling to defend the nobility against the gray hoods.

"Get them through!" I yelled.

Squad Reckless turned to see me holding my rift open. They'd hesitated back in the burning dragon stables so long ago, but not this time.

Brigan took point on rallying the nobility, encouraging them to dash through the gold-rimmed portal. He was just the man for the job, since it took a lot of coaxing to get the first skeptical nobles to make the leap. Most of the magi in the courtyard tonight had been trying to kill the nobility, but Brigan was able to convince them that my rift wasn't their doom, but their salvation.

I caught sight of Edrea half-dragging Queen Ilona toward my rift. The delicate queen wrenched her arm free, looking back toward the battle.

"I can't go through there," Queen Ilona's lower lip trembled. "My husband... our people."

But there was something odd about the way she spoke, as if she were desperately searching for a good reason to stay on that balcony. But I was certain there was genuine fear in her perfectly round, shining eyes. Perhaps I was wrong to have been suspicious of her.

"Your safety is our priority now, your highness," Edrea spoke with confidence as she led the queen closer.

In the end, Ilona cast one last desperate look toward the gray army wreaking havoc on the courtyard before vanishing through the portal with the others.

In spite of the cold, sweat began beading along my forehead as I strained to keep the rift going. Cloaks and ballgowns vanished before my eyes, and I could feel my ether well draining lower and lower. Keeping a rift that jumped this far open for so long would've completely sapped me of my power just a few months ago. Not this time.

A group of masked magi saw what was going on and immediately began dashing my way to try and take me out. My gut screamed at me to go for my sword and defend myself, but this was about more than just me. There were still nobility hurrying through my rift—I couldn't drop it now.

Jax materialized behind me, his back to mine and his axes at the ready. I was aware of him psionically catching every blade headed my way, then sending them swinging back toward their original wielders. His axes zipped left and right, hacking at anyone who would do me harm.

Out of the corner of my eye, I saw a gray hood twirling a long, gnarled staff. Void blue dream energy built up at the top before they took aim and fired the dense dream dart straight at Jax.

He tried to block the dart by psionically raising a fallen soldier's shield, but physical objects meant nothing against dream energy. The dart passed through the shield, blasting Jax along his collarbone. He stumbled forward.

I called out his name, my portal wavering for a split second as my focus turned away from it. I quickly honed my thoughts in on the portal to keep it active, though it pained me to do nothing as Jax fell.

Jax groaned as he struggled to lift his head. His movements were lethargic, his eyelids heavy.

Taking advantage of my bodyguard's state, the Coven magi prepared another dream energy dart, pointing their staff my way. Noble guests were still dashing past me, which meant I had no way to defend myself if I wanted to see them safely through. I held my ground, bracing for the pending blast.

But when the ball of stamina-draining energy came, another black-and-orange-cloaked soldier leaped between it and me.

Edrea took the dart in the shoulder. The force was enough to send her to the ground, barely conscious.

I gaped, half worried about her and half completely shocked that she'd intentionally taken the blast for me. She must've weighed the options, figuring it was more important overall for me to stay on my feet right now than her.

Edrea struggled to keep her eyes open as Cam stepped in to battle the Coven magi who'd shot the dart, his strength quickly snapping their staff in half.

"Edrea," I managed, holding open my portal as the final noble stragglers still filtered past. "Are you okay?"

"Mm," she mumbled, shakily rubbing her eyes. "Drak, snowhead. Look what you did."

My heart swelled as I gave Edrea a grateful smile. And for the briefest of seconds, I thought she might've almost smiled back.

Then I heard it—an angry, guttural roar. All heads turned toward where the Liberator still dueled the Black Valkyrie. Though by the looks of things, the Liberator had just caught sight of my portal and realized I'd been evacuating all of the Rengardian nobles she'd planned to slaughter tonight.

With another roar and cloud of void blue mist, Lorelai once again shifted into a mighty true dragon. Her pitch black scales shone in the blue light the braziers still cast.

Enough of this opening act, the Liberator's voice echoed proudly inside our minds. *On to the main event.*

She puffed out her draconic chest and reared back her head. Then, she blasted the courtyard with a spray of lightning blue dragonfire.

CHAPTER 40: SNOWSTORM

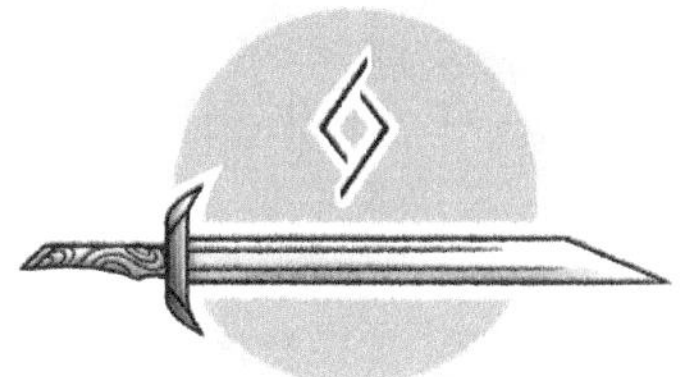

I screamed as the flames headed straight for where the prisoners still fought alongside Boone, Valla, and His Majesty.

Boone, looking extremely frustrated as his eyes flashed gold, threw out his hands before the oncoming jet of blue fire. A thick wall of white, crystalline starglass sprouted from the ground to shield him and his prisoner army.

Boone gave a long, loud whoop as the flames licked at his barrier. Once Lorelai in true dragon form ran out of breath, Boone reeled back and fell to the ground as his starglass wall shattered. He winced, clutching at his chest.

"That'll drain an ether well faster'na drunk drains a flask of draquila." I could just make out Boone's words.

Valla took a turn next, racing toward the inky black true dragon. As she ran, gold mist encircled her.

When she leaped from the cloud, Valla was no longer a scarred, dual seaxe-wielding woman. Rather, she was a drake-sized, pure white polar wolf.

She barked, her teeth clamping onto the true dragon's foreleg. The Liberator reared up onto her hind legs to shake Valla off, but the Wildshaping woman held fast with her forepaws.

That's when a cluster of three brightly-colored dragons with void blue eyes raced from where they'd been battling the king's wyvern, Lantha. Six of Lorelai's dragons remained, while Sniff and two others zipped toward Valla's polar wolf form.

A drake and a wyvern stood by while Sniff reeled back, his eyes crossing. There was nothing I could do to warn Valla of what was coming.

Sniff sneezed, sending a series of ether darts blasting toward Valla's powerful polar wolf forelegs. The ether hit, causing Valla to lose her grip.

With a whine, the polar wolf fell to the courtyard floor. She looked fiercely annoyed as the three dragons stood before her, ready for a fight. Though her odds weren't great, Valla didn't hesitate as she engaged all three dragons simultaneously.

Meanwhile, the Black Valkyrie stepped toward the true dragon, the blade of her dragonhook spear alight with black shadowfire. Her hair was mussed and her face contemplative, as if she were strategizing as she went. The Liberator had kept her occupied for practically the entire battle so far, neither woman gaining the upper hand. And that was before the Liberator had shifted into her true dragon form. It was as if the Black Valkyrie were playing out the fight inside her mind, and was realizing that her chances of defeating the Liberator alone were slim.

"Lightbane," the Black Valkyrie called across the courtyard. The Mage Hunter with the Lightwielder's mark, Jaira, finished off the gray hood she'd been fighting with a stab from her silver sword. Then she turned toward her leader, deep loyalty in her intense gaze.

"Join me," the Black Valkyrie ordered, and Jaira began hurrying to her side.

The Black Valkyrie scanned the battlefield once more, her eyes finally coming to rest on me as the last of the nobility scurried through my rift.

"Meleya," the Black Valkyrie called my name, gesturing for me to join her as well. "We have to stop her."

I scanned the courtyard, confirming that all of the nobility had finished evacuating, and were now safe with Solvai on the other side of my portal. With a grunt, I pulled my arms back toward my body, allowing my rift to dissolve into etherdust. I checked on my ether well and was relieved to find it only about halfway drained.

The Liberator flapped her great wings, rising a short distance into the air. Her chest expanded again as she prepared to send off another blast of dragonfire down on the rebel prisoners who resisted her gray hoods.

I rapidly raised my finger to trace out the rune to form another portal. Without hesitation, I stepped through, reappearing between the true dragon's fire and Boone's impromptu army. My next portal was up in a flash, catching the Liberator's blast and sending it through the exit aimed straight at the dragon's right wing.

The dragon roared with pain and anger as her own fire scorched her, then retreated to the ground to nurse her wound. Sentinel patterns flowed out across her burned wing as she focused on it, already beginning to regenerate the delicate skin there.

The Black Valkyrie was right—we couldn't let Lorelai continue her rampage of death and destruction. I made another quick rift, dashing through to reappear opposite Jaira at the Black Valkyrie's side. Meanwhile, I heard the Black Valkyrie order another one of her Hunters to stand by and distract the Liberator if she finished healing herself before the Black Valkyrie finished speaking with Jaira and me.

The black-clad leader of the Mage Hunters looked between Jaira and me and gave a confident smile.

"The three of us can stop her if we work together," the Black Valkyrie began. "But we'll need to fight smart. In this form, Lorelai has access to all nine types of etherarchy, while between us, we only have four. But she's unpracticed with many of those types, lacking our deeper skill and finesse. Do you understand?"

"Yes, Black Valkyrie," Jaira said without hesitation. The Black Valkyrie looked at me with determination, and I nodded.

"Take this, Meleya," she reached into her boot to pull out a tiny, silver snake. It looked like a miniature version of the longer one I'd seen draped over one of the Mage Hunter's shoulders before the battle.

"Seers can create copies of their own ethereal familiars to allow a group mindlink. Keep in contact with it, and you'll be able to communicate with the rest of us. It's a little trick I recently learned."

I remembered Three, Jax's yellow mirror gecko, so I understood the concept. The snake hissed as it slithered from her palm onto mine, then sent a little shiver up my leg as I transferred it to my boot. The second its slick scales touched my ankle, I felt the mindlink bloom to life.

Can you hear me, Meleya? the Black Valkyrie's voice appeared inside my head.

Yeah, I replied.

Who's this? a male voice I didn't recognize resounded between my ears.

Before me, the Black Valkyrie smiled again. Over the mindlink, she replied:

Our missing piece.

With a growl, the true dragon turned on us, ready for her next attack.

The Black Valkyrie gripped her spear. "Follow my lead, and we'll take this dangerous magi rebel down."

The Black Valkyrie gave concise orders to Jaira and me through our mindlink. Our first strategy: overpower the Liberator with well-placed strikes to the chinks in her scaly, draconic armor.

Lightbane, strike at her underbelly, the Black Valkyrie commanded. *Meleya, see if you can land a hit along her neck.*

I was runetracing in a flash, stepping through my portal and coming out atop Lorelai's draconic back. I grabbed hold of the black spines at the base of her neck, swinging around to get an angle on the softer scales at the front. The Liberator roared as I slashed at her with my seaxe.

But my blow wasn't enough to take her down. Though my sword drew her red, still human blood, more Sentinel markings appeared as she began to instantly regenerate.

At the same time, the true dragon reared back to shake me off. I went flying into the air, but my next rift was right there to catch me.

I reappeared once again, this time on top of the true dragon's head. I got to my knees, gripping tightly to a horn with one hand while the other took a stab at her head.

The Liberator reacted just in time. As my sword hit the scales between her horns, her hide grew and thickened, becoming hard as stone.

Soot, I swore mentally, communicating my frustration over the mindlink. *Looks like she's got some skill in geomancy, as well.*

Very good, the Black Valkyrie thought approvingly. *We have to learn where her talents lie and where she's weak.* Below, I saw her in a fierce battle stance, her ethereal black swans protectively surrounding her. She telekinetically pulled all kinds of weapons off of fallen soldiers or Coven magi, then one by one, she sent them flying toward the Liberator. The true dragon kept up with her, stopping each one with rudimentary psionics of her own.

She has some proficiency in psionics, the Black Valkyrie thought, *though she can't seem to use it offensively very well. It's all about blocking my attacks rather than making her own.*

Lightning, Jaira added. *She's got lightning down.* Inside my head, I got a clear picture of what was going on from Jaira's perspective. She was kneeling beside the true dragon's flank, her silver whip lashing out toward the Liberator's underside. As the whip made contact, void blue lightning crackled along the scales there, sending sparks racing down the whip toward Jaira.

Drak, Jaira cursed. *It's taking all of my own Lightwielding ether just to keep hers from frying me.*

Get another angle, the Black Valkyrie ordered. Jaira's point of view vanished from my mind as she moved on.

Ilyan, the Black Valkyrie thought. *Try to get inside her head. Get a read on what moves she plans to make so we can interrupt her.*

I'm far better with illusions than I am with all that, but I'm trying, the same male voice from before replied. Over the mindlink, Ilyan showed us an image of his own hand. Both his pointer and middle fingers were missing—a result of the Coven's initial targeting of the Mage Hunters.

Hard to runetrace correctly when you're missing a couple digits, he said.

You have another hand, you know, Jaira thought incredulously.

Easy for you to say.

Meanwhile, I was doing my best to get at the Liberator from as many sides as possible. I darted through portal after portal, appearing on the true dragon's back, then resurfacing near her right foreleg. One second I was swinging toward a wing, the next I was slashing across her chest. The Liberator nearly caught me with lightning once, but I vanished through a portal in the nick of time.

I was moving so fast it became impossible for the Liberator to keep track of me, especially when I started throwing up false portals to keep her guessing. She stopped being able to geomantically strengthen her scales in the right places at the right times. She roared as my blade left a long gash across her scaled chest.

Over the mindlink, I heard the Black Valkyrie laugh.

What is it? Jaira asked.

Oh, the Black Valkyrie replied. *I just thought of something. A title for our young, talented Rifter.*

The Black Valkyrie sent an image of me over the mindlink, my sword arcing, my white hair flying out behind me as I rifted in and out of portals. The flurries from the thickening clouds above caught the gold light from my rifts. I was surprised by the way she saw me—so confident and strong. Through the mindlink, I could feel that the other members of the Black Valkyrie's entourage saw me like that as well.

The Snowstorm, the Black Valkyrie thought.

With a rapid series of strikes, I landed another hit on the Liberator's flank. She seethed, but the pain lasted only a moment before her Sentinel etherarchy kicked in. She regenerated the damaged hide, but this time much more slowly than before. With any luck, that meant she was running low on ether.

I checked in on my own ether levels. My well was only about a quarter full now, not counting the extra held within the crystal at my belt. I needed to be careful.

As I battled the true dragon alongside the Black Valkyrie and Lightbane, I subconsciously looked over the rest of the battlefield. I caught sight of Mom and Dad fighting off more gray-hooded magi. Clinging onto Dad's shoulder and chittering up a storm was a certain ring-tailed draccoon. Dusty psionically chucked loose daggers and splintering pieces of wood from broken spears at the gray-hooded magi, all the while shaking his tiny fists in rage. Dad looked thrilled to have his ethereal familiar back.

I did a double take when I saw Captain Zoren standing between my Mom and Dad, his sword slashing. The three of them fought together, Mom's long seaxe arcing with precision to take down a masked enemy. She swung like she'd done it a thousand times before.

I furrowed my brow. Where had Mom learned to fight like that?

As the prisoners worked against the Coven magi, I caught sight of Squad Reckless. I breathed a sigh of relief when I saw that Solvai had safely returned, and was wielding her spear in human form once again. That meant she must've gotten the nobility to safety on the other end of my portal.

They'd moved Edrea to a safe corner, and it looked like she was just getting over the dream blast enough to shakily sit up. Jax was back on his feet as well, biceps flexing as he gripped his twin axes.

The squad banded together, and I could tell Solvai was calling out orders. I followed the trajectory of her pointing finger toward Lorelai's nine mythic dragons. Two still fought Valla as a polar wolf, but one she'd killed lay dead at her feet. I was grateful it wasn't Sniff. Three more of Lorelai's dragons still struggled to keep Lantha from entering the fight. The final three dragons narrowed their eyes toward where the Black Valkyrie, Lightbane, and I battled their bond, the Liberator.

Sniff looked up from his fight with Valla to bare his teeth as well. Through their bonds, the Liberator must've given the dragons the order to take us out.

Solvai must've realized that too, and knew that the best chance of taking her mother down was to keep those dragons from interfering in the fight between the Liberator and the Black Valkyrie, Lightbane, and me, the Snowstorm. As a team, Squad Reckless charged toward Lorelai's bonds. I said a silent prayer that the goddesses would keep them from hurting Sniff.

I was so distracted by the action across the courtyard, I nearly missed the Liberator's wild tail swing. I flung myself through a portal just in time to not get the wind knocked out of me.

This isn't working, Ilyan's thoughts came through the mindlink once more. *Even when I get the rune right, I can't get a read on the Liberator's thoughts. She's blocking me somehow.*

Drak, the Black Valkyrie cursed, sounding distracted as she fought. *She must know some Seer etherarchy as well. Guarding her mind.*

She's not running out of ether fast enough either, Jaira thought. *She must be getting an extra supply from somewhere.*

Or multiple somewheres, the Black Valkyrie thought. *She has a mythic dragon of each of the nine types—perhaps they're lending her more power. But they're not the real problem.*

Who is? Ilyan asked.

Then I heard a small, eerie sound coming from the mindlink. It sounded like faint, self-satisfied laughter. It felt like it was coming from the Black Valkyrie's mind, but it didn't sound like her voice.

Her wraith. The Black Valkyrie's voice sounded grim inside my head. A cold, still feeling settled over me, and I shuddered as I tried to shake it off.

The way the Black Valkyrie's thought came across made it seem like Lorelai had somehow found a way to use a specific Gray One to enhance her power. Almost like the way a rider bonded a dragon, and could then access a little of their power through their heartscale.

That's exactly right, the Black Valkyrie replied to my thoughts. I felt a twinge of embarrassment—I didn't realize my thoughts could sneak onto the mindlink like that.

The Black Valkyrie continued. *But Lorelai grants her bonded wraith too much dominion. That's the reason she's more powerful than I am—She's given up her control.*

As if to emphasize the Black Valkyrie's point, the Liberator slashed wildly with her foreclaws. Jaira went rolling across the courtyard, and I only just managed to dodge through another portal to avoid taking the hit. One of the Black Valkyrie's swan's fell to the courtyard floor in a flurry of feathers.

Wait! a new male voice jumped onto the mindlink, sounding eager to help. *What if we're going about this all wrong? We're attacking the* dragon, *when we really should be attacking the* wraith.

There was an awkward moment of mental silence, then several voices chorused over the mindlink in unison.

Shut up, Lothar.

But—

Weapons can't fight something that's not of this world, Lothar. Jaira did the mental equivalent of rolling her eyes as she audibly groaned and got back to her feet. A couple of others agreed.

Sorry. Shutting up now, Lothar thought back. Clearly, he was used to being disregarded.

But Lothar's idea got me thinking—I'd seen a wraith before back in the Soul Reaper's cavern in the Dragon Mists. Maybe they weren't of this world, but that didn't mean they couldn't affect it when they were powerful enough. I'd seen the Farseer hurt and even kill that wraith, so I was certain we could do the same now. It was just a matter of knowing where to strike.

Actually, I thought. *Maybe Lothar's on to something. The Gray Ones are native to the spirit plane, Etheria, right?*

That's right, the Black Valkyrie thought, intrigued.

As a Rifter, I can see the spirit plane using the Sight. Maybe I can project what I see to the Black Valkyrie and Lightbane.

That's cute, Lightbane thought back. *But it still doesn't help us actually kill it.*

Archonic power, Lothar mentally muttered.

What do you mean? Ilyan asked.

Oh, Lothar thought, almost as if he were embarrassed. *Just... earlier this year, someone gave me some insight. I've been meditating in stages each* morning, *trying to connect with the higher powers that direct the three types of etherarchy.*

Shut up, Loth— Jaira started.

Let him finish, the Black Valkyrie ordered.

Lothar went on. *My meditation has led me to study more from ancient texts about the distinctions between the three types—Mystic, Sentinel, and Archon. Each one is strongest in the plane they're born to. While all affect us here in the physical plane, Sentinel power interacts with us physically the most strongly. Mystic power has the greatest effect on the mind and the mental plane. And Archonic etherarchy, while powerful here, is most effective in the—*

Spirit plane, the Black Valkyrie finished. *This is why we keep you around, Lothar.*

What does all that drivel mean? Jaira sounded annoyed. Her strength was probably waning against the Liberator's attacks. I was starting to tire myself as I tried to distract the true dragon long enough for one of the others to land a hit. My ether was draining faster than I liked; it wouldn't be long before I'd need to dip into the extra reservoir held in my crystal.

It means that we should try Snowstorm's idea, the Black Valkyrie said. *She can use the Sight to show us where Lorelai's wraith is, then we'll hit it with something Archonic. Lightbane's lightwielding or my shadowbinding, perhaps.*

I realized she was right. The weapons Zyri and her companions had wielded against the wraith in the cavern had been edged with golden lightwielding etherarchy. When the Archonic light touched the wraith, it had burned it.

We have to stop fighting her separately, I added. *Face her head-on as a united front.*

For Evgard, unite, the Black Valkyrie agreed.

I dashed through another portal, reappearing at the Black Valkyrie's side in front of the true dragon. Jaira joined us as well, using her levitation to run across the courtyard faster than should've been possible.

The Black Valkyrie's dragonhook spear blazed with Archonic shadow-fire as she pointed the tip toward my seaxe. When her blade touched mine, her irises pulsed with blue light and the black and blue flames leaped onto my weapon to line the edge.

I gaped at my flaming sword, and the Black Valkyrie smiled. Now, I'd be just as effective against the wraith as she was.

Jaira and the Black Valkyrie continued targeting the Liberator, Jaira sending flashes of lightning while the Black Valkyrie used psionics to hurl a fallen long seaxe toward her. They covered me as my finger flew to trace the rune for the Sight. The symbol glowed to life over my forehead and I blinked hard, the world blooming to life with ethereal color.

The mixing array of auras across the courtyard-turned-battlefield clashed like violent ocean waves.

Beside me, I saw the auras of Lightbane and the Black Valkyrie emanating misty clouds off of their bodies. Jaira's was a harsh shade of magenta while the Black Valkyrie's shone with rays of pale lavender. I startled when I saw a cloud of semi-formless gray hovering over each of their shoulders. Within each gray nebula, a pair of lightning blue eyes stared out.

The Gray Ones clung to the auras of my companions, gray threads of mist weaving into their natural magenta and lavender. Did these wraith bonds explain why the Black Valkyrie and Lightbane channeled blue etherarchy instead of gold?

I could just make out the faint outline of the Black Valkyrie's ether well hovering near her head. But my eyes widened when I noticed another one tethered to the area around her heart, appearing to have an aura of its own. While the Black Valkyrie radiated lavender, this ether well pulsed with a vibrant shade of deep turquoise.

"The Liberator, Snowstorm," the Black Valkyrie prompted. She was right—There wasn't time to get distracted.

I turned my gaze toward the true dragon before us and transmitted what I saw over the group mindlink. Lorelai's aura matched the scales of her dragon form—a powerful inky black. She emitted clouds of unwavering charcoal conviction.

Then I saw it. A misty, gray wraith in a vaguely-humanoid form, sitting astride the true dragon's back. The wraith wielded a shadowy, gray sword in a style unlike any I'd seen in Evgard. Like the wraith the Farseer had fought, a jagged blade sprouted from its arm as void blue eyes glittered from its otherwise blank face.

There you are, the Black Valkyrie thought.

The Liberator gave another mighty roar, planting her four clawed feet as she faced us. I could practically see a smile play over her draconic features, as if she were glad for the chance to kill us all at once. She opened her mouth, and I saw a ball of blue fire sparking in the back of her throat.

"Now!" the Black Valkyrie yelled, her voice carrying over the sounds of battle and the crackle of dragonfire.

At the same time, the Black Valkyrie, Lightbane, and I charged.

Chapter 41: For Evgard, Unite

Lightbane's eyes flashed blue as she accessed her levitation power to leap extra high over the flames. I runetraced, diving through an entrance portal. The Black Valkyrie's blue psionic rune glowed from her forehead as she summoned about seven round shields from fallen soldiers and Coven magi.

The flames from the Liberator's voidfire licked at the Black Valkyrie's heels as she ran up the shields like a set of stairs. Her eyes went blue as well as she levitated between the shields, running diagonally through the air toward the true dragon's head.

I dropped from my exit portal, landing on the true dragon's back at the same moment the Black Valkyrie stepped onto her head. Jaira wasn't far behind, using an extra boost from her levitation powers to throw herself onto the Liberator's back. She grabbed hold of one of the many black ridges running along the dragon's spine between her wings.

Using the Sight, I saw the wraith between us, her misty sword held high. Her bright blue eyes locked onto the Black Valkyrie's shadowspear, my flaming seaxe, and the crackling lightning running along Lightbane's silver whip. She knew what we planned to do.

Before she could react, the Black Valkyrie stabbed the wraith, the archonic power in her spear eating away at her shadowy chest.

When the Black Valkyrie yanked back her spear, the wraith slashed back, her sword and her body going corporeal as she attacked, just like the wraith from the cavern.

The Black Valkyrie threw up her weapon faster than lightning, blocking the wraith's blow.

At that moment, the Liberator must've caught on to our strategy. With a flap of her great wings, she launched into the air. Lightbane and I clung to her black spines, but the Black Valkyrie lost her footing, falling backwards.

Draining more of my precious ether supply, I threw up a portal at her back to catch her. I placed the exit on the dragon's back, and she landed safely beside us.

Thanks, the Black Valkyrie thought.

We held fast as the Liberator flew higher and higher, trying to shake us from her back. Jaira saw the wraith through my eyes and flicked her whip toward it, lightning arcing along the chain.

The wraith reeled at the archonic power, the light burning at its gray form and weakening it. In all the places where Jaira's etherarchy hit, shadowy holes ripped through its body. Strands of gray slowly began trying to pull the creature's ethereal form back together. But still, the archonic strikes weren't enough.

I remembered the way the Farseer had fought the wraith back in the void cavern. The only attacks that hadn't seemed stifled somehow were the ones he'd made *while* the wraith himself was attacking. The most lasting damage occurred during the brief second it turned corporeal.

I was about to convey my thoughts through the mindlink when the Liberator turned upside down mid-air. Her large wings caught air as she hung there, and there was no way any of us could hold on.

My hands were the last to slip from the spines on the Liberator's back as the three of us plummeted toward the courtyard below. The flurries of snow had become squalls as the white flakes swirled around me.

The Black Valkyrie used telekinesis on her dragonhook spear, clinging to it to keep herself from crashing onto the hard stone. Jaira's eyes flashed as she activated her levitation in the nick of time.

Aware that I was practically running on ether fumes, I made myself a portal flush with the ground below. When the courtyard floor rose to greet me, I kept falling straight into Etheria.

My momentum flung me through the exit portal upward into the air, but I managed to land on my feet. I was getting used to the rapid ins and outs of portalling.

I stood before the stark black true dragon, ready for her next blow.

What I wasn't ready for was the bright yellow evren careening toward me at high speed.

Sniff barrelled into me, but this time it wasn't playful or loving. The Liberator's hold over him was strong, and I caught sight of his feral blue eyes as his jaw clamped onto my shoulder.

We went tumbling across the courtyard, white hot pain spreading down my arm and across my collar. Sniff didn't let go, but I heard an agonized whine from deep in his throat, and I could tell by the churning of his golden aura that he hated what he was doing to me. Somehow, knowing the Liberator was controlling my dragon, forcing him to do awful things against his will, hurt more than the bite to the shoulder.

Although, the bite still hurt like the void.

I screamed as Sniff finally let go. Red blood poured over my chest armor from punctures made by his fangs. I was vaguely aware of a silvery aura clashing with Sniff's golden one in Etheria.

Blink. Her spirit was struggling with Sniff's, trying to keep him from hurting me. I could tell Sniff's spirit wanted his twin to succeed. But the Liberator's hold over his actions remained too strong.

Before me, Sniff reared back, his nostrils flaring as he went slightly cross-eyed. I knew what came next.

My hand trembling, I bit back the pain and gripped my fiery seaxe. But I couldn't bring myself to strike at my own bond, even if he was lost to me now.

Then suddenly the Black Valkyrie was standing between me and Sniff's feral face. When his ether bolt came, she raised her hands and a large, black swan rose from a small pool of water on the ground. The Black Valkyrie's ethereal swan spread its black feathers wide like a shield as the bolt hit it straight in the chest.

White, spiraling marks appeared from the point of impact for a split second before the blow took it out. The swan vanished back into Etheria. With the Sight still activated, I saw the swan's physical form disappear, leaving a misty lavender swan in its place. It would take some time for the Black Valkyrie to resummon her ethereal familiar back into the physical plane.

The Black Valkyrie gripped her spear, preparing to plunge its tip into Sniff's heart.

"No!" I shouted. Over the mindlink, I sent feelings of love for the yellow evren, hoping it would make her understand before it was too late.

The Black Valkyrie stopped her spear mid-thrust. Instead, she spun it around so that the butt end faced Sniff. I watched as a ball of churning dream energy formed at the head, then flew through the air toward Sniff. Instantly, the dream energy drained him of his stamina and dropped him, sleeping, onto the courtyard floor. Gratitude from the bottom of my heart filled the mindlink.

The Black Valkyrie slumped forward, her breathing heavy. She was using so much ether.

She knelt beside me, worry etched onto her face as she took in my shoulder wound.

"Are you alright?" she asked.

I didn't get the chance to answer. Within a second, the Liberator was taking advantage of the Black Valkyrie's momentary distraction. The true dragon's foreclaw pinned the black-clad warrior, sending her spear skittering away and ensnaring her on the courtyard's stone floor.

The Liberator reared back, a blast of dragonfire in her throat ready to end the Black Valkyrie for good.

"Mom!" I heard the shout from across the courtyard. Jax, worn out from the battle, reached out one arm toward the Black Valkyrie. He wore a desperate expression on his face, and his tangerine aura was bright with helpless terror.

In that moment, I saw not the Black Valkyrie lying trapped, but my own mother.

Adrenaline coursed through my body as I tapped into the crystal at my belt, draining most of its ether supply. My portal burst to life over the Black Valkyrie to swallow the jet of deadly blue voidfire.

I placed the other end beside the first, but facing the opposite direction. A column of fire blasted the Liberator full in her draconic face.

She reared back in anger, but I was already dashing through my next rift, using the last of the extra ether contained inside my crystal. A split second later, I was falling through the air directly above the true dragon's back.

Falling with me, I saw Blink's silvery spirit form. I knew she couldn't interact with me physically, but for one moment, I felt like my spirit was riding her as we shot together toward the wraith.

I could see the wraith below me now, and though its face had no nose or mouth, anger was still evident in its glittering blue eyes. It raised its misty, gray sword and I raised my flaming blade as I descended through the snowstorm.

I landed on my feet on the dragon's back, roaring at the pain in my shoulder on impact. Blink's spirit shot out from under me, racing toward the wraith. As my dragon's spirit snapped at hers, the wraith burned with pain and rage. I held my swing, waiting for the wraith to make the first move.

The wraith's weapon arced toward me, her misty form flashing corporeal for only an instant. I let her blade hack into my side, sacrificing my body in order to land a counterstrike—I needed to make this one count.

My seaxe struck true, stabbing deep into the wraith's shadowy gray chest. I cried out, channeling all of my strength into that one blow.

As I did, I felt something dark burst to life inside me. With the Sight activated, I could see void blue sparks of energy crackling all along my body, flowing down my arm and into my shadowfire blade. I could feel that my eyes glowed with flecks of that same color as well. I'd never felt more powerful, and I realized with a degree of terror that it was coming from the Soul Reaper's voidshard. It was lending me its dark strength.

The wraith seemed to scream as its essence burned. All at once, its body compressed into a tight ball of gray clouds and void blue lightning, and I felt the gray blade withdraw from where it had been partially-embedded into my side. The whole world seemed to go silent.

Then the ball exploded, sending a wave of sapphire energy rippling through the air. It nearly blew me backward as blood spilled from the wound in my side. Lightheadedness caused patches of black to frame my vision.

But destroying the wraith must've worked. Beneath my feet, I felt the black scales of the true dragon give way as Lorelai defaulted back into her human form.

The ground approached so fast I had no time to runetrace. Not that I had enough ether in me anyway.

Still, beneath me, I saw a white tear rimmed with golden light. Whose portal was this?

I fell into Etheria, letting unconsciousness wash over me.

Fragment - The Liberator

Without the Gray One to fuel her power, Lorelai fell.

Her weak human body crashed onto the stone courtyard floor. Lorelai could feel her ether well draining faster than a rushing river now that her Gray One could no longer give her the extra boost. In fact, the Wildshaping clouds that surrounded her as she shifted back into human form were no longer coursing with vivid blue energy. They were gold, her etherarchy as mundane as it had been before she'd bonded the Gray One.

Lorelai felt her abdomen constricting with pain. It had been a while since ether overuse had made her sick to her stomach.

Within moments, the Black Valkyrie and her lackey, Lightbane, had Lorelai in chains. For the first time in years, the silver in their whips sent icy agony coursing through her body.

That confirmed it. Skapa was gone—her form broken, banished to the voids of Etheria. It would be a long time before the shreds of her spirit gathered back together, reforming enough to speak to Lorelai again. The powerful Gray One had been destroyed at the hands of none other than Meleya of Misthaven.

Lorelai still wasn't entirely sure how Meleya had managed it. Was Meleya the one who'd found and stolen Lorelai's voidshard? That was the only way she could've destroyed Skapa—that is, unless the young Rifter somehow had access to an even higher form of voidarchy. But that was impossible.

It all puzzled Lorelai. Last she checked, her daughter's friend had been so afraid of her own power that she'd barely known how to use it. Lorelai had been a fool to underestimate her.

This wouldn't have happened if I'd listened to Skapa, Lorelai thought as she lay tangled in the silver chains, *and killed the girl when I had the chance.*

Lorelai's Gray One had chided her for being too soft in the canyons near Outcast Outpost. Using the totem from her Seer drake to mind control the umbral coyotes, she'd sent them after Meleya. Solvai and the others in Squad Reckless were never really in danger then. Lorelai had been certain the Coven could succeed if they could only get Meleya decommissioned from the guard—then they could take Sniff's heartscale and the Liberator's true dragon totem would be complete.

But Skapa hadn't wanted to take any chances, diving deeper into Lorelai's consciousness to assert her control over the umbrals, usurping Lorelai's will. If it hadn't been for those Drekai jumping in and taking out the coyotes, Skapa might've gotten her wish.

But Lorelai never wanted to hurt the young Rifter. Not when magi like her and Solvai were the very reason Lorelai fought. They deserved a better Evgard—one that honored them for their gifts rather than see them executed for their 'curse.' Lorelai had suspected Meleya was a magi from the moment they met, even before she'd revealed her powers at the dragon stables. It was part of why Lorelai had been eager to take her in.

Likewise, Lorelai had been sure Solvai was going to be a magi before she was born. With a Wildshaper for a mother and a Rifter for a father, her odds had always been high. In a better world, Lorelai and Torsten could've happily raised their daughter and taught her the intricacies of her etherarchy.

But the world was cruel.

A tear slipped down Lorelai's cheek. For the first time, she'd seen Solvai spread her rich, brown falcondrake wings tonight. Solvai hadn't told Lorelai she'd discovered her powers. The silver chain had stifled Solvai's etherarchy for so long, but Lorelai had known it was the only way to keep her daughter safe for as long as possible.

"It's straight to the Soul Reaper for you, great Liberator," Lightbane spoke with satisfaction. She pulled more tightly on the silver chains, and Lorelai inhaled sharply at the pain.

"We're wasting time," Lightbane said. "Ilyan has the anchor—let's get out of here." Lightbane turned to the Black Valkyrie. Though, to Lorelai, her old circus friend would always just be 'Vidya.'

Lorelai struggled to turn her head. Solvai... there she was. Standing with her squad near where Meleya had gone down—alongside a proud, third ascension wyvern. Lantha, the king's bond. Or at least she was before Lorelai... before the Liberator had killed the king of Rengard.

Lorelai had been hesitant to slay the king. After all, he'd been far from Rengard's worst ruler. But the price of Queen Ilona's loyalty had been the promise to kill her husband, and Skapa was only too happy to oblige. Although, Lorelai wasn't entirely sure who'd been in control when she'd blasted King Axel with blue voidfire. Why did it bother her so much to realize she might've been the one to do it?

But it needed to be done. Like Lorelai, Ilona felt that a magi deserved the throne.

Lorelai grit her teeth as she remembered watching the nobility escape via Meleya's rift. They were supposed to fall tonight. At least the queen had fled through the portal alongside the others—that meant her cover was still intact. As the sole ruler of Rengard, Lorelai knew Ilona would continue the Gray Ones' work. Eventually, all of the Canyonlands' noble class had to go if they were to make a better Rengard for a future generation of magi.

Lorelai tried to reach out toward her daughter, but silver chains held her fast.

"Please," Lorelai looked into Vidya's cold eyes, as dark blue as the night sky. "Let me at least say goodbye."

Vidya looked down her nose at Lorelai, and Lorelai could practically hear the denial on her lips already.

"You'd want to speak with your son one last time," Lorelai said.

That got a reaction out of Vidya, as Lorelai knew it would. They may have disagreed on tactics, but deep down, they both simply loved their children.

Vidya gave a curt nod, but wouldn't let Lorelai out of her and the Mage Hunters' hands. Two Mage Hunters held Lorelai roughly as she sat between them, still wrapped in chains. To one side was Lightbane, and to the other, Vidya's stocky Geomancer. Strange, Lorelai had thought for sure he'd taken three arrows to the chest at the beginning of the fight, yet now he stood as if he hadn't been mortally wounded only a short time ago. Vidya's other Hunters stood by, ready to intervene should Lorelai try anything. Lorelai knew it was all unnecessary. She was powerless.

Lorelai called for Solvai, whose gaze shot toward her mother instantly. Solvai approached with caution.

"My girl," Lorelai said, tears already filling her eyes. "My brilliant, talented Solvai. I am so proud of you."

Solvai's hazel eyes glistened as well, and when she spoke, her voice shook.

"Mom?"

The questioning word felt like a stab to the gut. Solvai spoke it as if she were speaking with a stranger.

"I'm right here, Mini-me," Lorelai's voice cracked when she used the old nickname. "Lovin' you just as much as ever."

Solvai swallowed. "All this time, I had no idea. All those late night meetings with the other dragon keepers..."

"Yes, it was all for the Coven."

Solvai's tears spilled over as she knelt opposite her mother. "So many lies."

As if on cue, a gold-rimmed portal ripped open beside the two of them. When the etherlight winked out, Torsten was there sitting in his rocking chair.

"I thought 'bout stayin' away," Torsten began, eyeing the lurking Mage Hunters with suspicion. "But I didn't know if we'd ever get another chance for all three of us to be together."

Lorelai was all too aware of the reason her family had been torn apart, especially as she knelt on the courtyard floor, Vidya's blade ready to stab her in the back. This time, literally.

But Vidya kept silent, allowing Solvai to process what was happening. Lorelai's daughter's brow was furrowed over hazel eyes the same color as Torsten's.

"What do you mean?" she asked. "What are you doing here, Torsten?"

Torsten sighed, tucking his stringy hair behind an ear. "Oh darlin.'" He glanced toward Lorelai, who nodded. "Darlin.' I... I'm your father."

Solvai looked like someone had punched her in the stomach. She looked between her parents as if she didn't recognize either one.

"No," she said, her voice just above a whisper. "My father died in battle."

But Lorelai knew Solvai saw the truth before her. She looked down at Lorelai's right arm, where the woven marriage bracelet encircled her wrist, the caramel color perfectly matching Torsten's aura. Torsten still wore the one that matched Lorelai's black aura as well. Solvai squeezed her eyes shut, then got to her feet.

Then she turned on her heel and began to walk away.

"Darlin' wait," Torsten said, an edge of desperation in his tone. When Solvai didn't turn back, Torsten grunted loudly as he pushed himself up and out of his chair.

Standing for what may've been the first time in years, Torsten reached out toward his child. Solvai stopped, looking just as surprised as Lorelai to see Torsten on his feet.

"Please, Solvai," he said. "I never got the chance to love you growin' up. Let me start now."

Solvai sniffled as more tears flowed over her freckled cheeks. She stared at Torsten, then turned her gaze back on Lorelai. Her voice trembling, she finally looked up toward the Black Valkyrie.

"What will you do with her?"

Vidya spoke smoothly. "The Liberator is too dangerous. We'll take her to Evyndara for the cure and remove her powers for good."

Lorelai watched as Solvai mulled this over for a moment. Then her daughter's face hardened.

"Good."

Lorelai felt her heart bleed as she watched Solvai walk away, this time without looking back.

"Time to go," Vidya said, and her Mage Hunters pulled Lorelai to her feet. The icy silver chains dug into her skin. Then Vidya turned to Torsten. "Don't think you're getting away. You'll join us in Evyndara as well, Torsten."

The Mage Hunters who weren't holding Lorelai moved to seize the overweight man, but Torsten made them jump when he started laughing hysterically. Lorelai couldn't tell whether he was laughing to throw the Hunters off, or if it was purely out of broken grief. Probably both.

Tears running down his face, Torsten had bought himself enough time to throw up a portal. He stepped through, disappearing before the Mage Hunters could grab hold of him. Only Torsten's rickety rocking chair remained, a still-full canteen of draquila left behind on the seat. Only the goddesses knew where he'd gone.

Lorelai stared at the items the man she still loved had left behind, wondering if this was his way of taking the first step toward change. Despite everything, Lorelai couldn't stop the small smile from appearing on her lips.

CHAPTER 42: THE INVITATION

A gentle hand stroked white strands along my hairline. The smell of herbs filled the air. After the clangs and roars of battle, the soft singing in the relative silence seemed out of place.

Hold on to my hand
As we soar through the sky
And wander the stars, so free

And then understand
As you look to the light
Constellations that call out and plea

As you soar on
alone
Know you're not
on your own
I'll watch over you
as you fly

And though it's been grand
Exploring all night...
Now it's time to ride a skyfall, right back to me

Mom's voice pulled me from sleep, giving me the energy to open my heavy eyelids. The edges of my vision were still a little blurry as I took in the loving, protective face of my mother leaning over me.

"Meli," she whispered, relief evident in her large brown eyes. A tear caught on the twisted skin of her burn.

They must've gotten the ballroom doors open again, because I lay on a blanket in a relatively private corner of the grand dance floor. Several other wounded soldiers sat or lay nearby, healers treating their battle wounds. Trickshot seemed to be running the makeshift medical zone, and I was grateful to see Mute at her side. The shock of white hair from his new ether scar fit right in with the laundry list of battle injuries he couldn't tell anyone about.

I looked down and found white bandages under my tunic, wrapped tightly around both my shoulder and torso. Both places still throbbed, but clearly someone had treated me with some kind of soothing salve to take the edge off.

"Mom," I mumbled, my voice coming out groggy and ragged. "You... I saw you fighting. Incredible. How?"

"Hush," Mom put a soft finger to my lips, pushing past my semi-coherent statement. "What matters now is that you're safe."

"Dad?" I asked.

"He's not here," Mom said, her voice lowering even more. "After the Liberator went down, the Coven retreated. That left the Black Valkyrie and the Mage Hunters, so Dad fled with Boone and the other prisoners before they could capture them. I all but forced your father to go with them. They'll be on their way to Skygard now, but I promised Dad I'd be in touch soon."

I frowned. "You should've gone with them."

Mom shook her head. "I've chosen another path."

"What path?"

Mom hesitated. "Whatever happens, Meli, know that I love you. I love you with my whole soul."

My brow furrowed. I struggled to sit up, ready to confront my mother, but I gasped as I strained my wounds.

Footsteps approached, and Mom got to her feet. "Things will be better soon. I promise."

"Mom—"

"Meleya!" Solvai rushed to my side, carefully wrapping her arms around me for a hug. Brigan was close behind her, his tense shoulders relaxing the moment he saw me alive and somewhat well.

I craned my neck around Solvai to see Mom looking back at me as she slowly walked away along the edge of the ballroom. What had she meant? What path did she mean to take? Had she been waiting for me to wake, but now that she knew I was safe felt she needed to leave before the Mage Hunters tried to arrest her?

Solvai spoke so fast it was hard to keep up. "Didn't I tell you never to do that again? Three hours is a long time to let your best friends worry, remember?"

"I'll keep that in mind next time," I gave a light chuckle, which sent pain screeching through my torso and shoulder once again.

Behind Solvai and Brigan came the rest of Squad Reckless, crowding around me in my corner of the ballroom. I found myself relaxing as I realized they'd made it through the battle alive as well. All of them had bruises and bandages of their own, but for now, my squad was safe and together.

They seemed glad too as they sat beside me, speaking with animated reverence about the battle we'd just survived. Solvai shared how she'd guided the nobility through my exit rift to safety in Guard Square where the bulk of Keep Rengard's army was stuck outside the citadel. The other soldiers had corralled the noble families of the Canyonlands, ready to defend them should the need have arisen.

Brigan hurried to comfort me by letting me know they'd brought Sniff and the other dragons abused by the Liberator back to the dragon stables. They were recovering there along with the other drakes, wyverns, and evren of the guard whom the Coven had sedated with astralock before the battle.

The others talked of their skirmish with the rest of the Liberator's dragons. How they'd freed Lantha, and the great third ascension wyvern had fought bravely at their side.

They told me of the awe they'd felt watching me battle alongside the Black Valkyrie and Lightbane, and how worried they'd been when they'd seen me fall.

"What about the Liberator?" I said, my eyes flashing to Solvai. "I mean Lorelai."

"She's with the Mage Hunters now," Solvai said, reservation appearing on her freckled face. I could practically see the lump form in my friend's throat. Edrea must've noticed too, because she took over.

"Once the Liberator was out of true dragon form, silver worked against her again," Edrea explained. "That lightwielding Mage Hunter ensnared her with her whip. They'll be taking her to Evyndara in the morning."

My friend stuck out her chin, determined to be strong. Finding out that her mother was secretly the magi leader of a rebel cult couldn't have been easy.

"Hey," I said, looking around at the members of my squad. "Where's Jax?"

"Haven't seen him since the battle ended and they took the Liberator away," Brigan replied. "I'm... we're getting a little worried."

The rest of the squad nodded in agreement.

"We were hoping you knew where he was," Cam said, his neck muscles tensing under his dragon tattoo as I shook my head.

A pit instantly formed inside my stomach. What if Jax had left with Boone and the other Knights of the Torch? The night before the solstice, he'd asked if I'd come with him back to Skygard. I knew he'd been upset with his assignment to go undercover here in Rengard—Now that his job was done, maybe he'd seen an opportunity to get out and he'd taken it.

The thought sent my heart dropping like a psionically-weighted stone.

"So, Meleya," Cam had a hopeful look on his face. "The sun's about to rise, but I'm guessing you're not up to cooking breakfast this morning?"

The squad laughed, and I cracked a smile.

"How do crispy potatoes and eggs sound?"

Trickshot vehemently forbade me from running down to the bunker to make breakfast in my current state, so unfortunately Cam and the others had to settle for whatever rations the mess hall had to offer that morning. But I promised them that the second I was allowed to go, I'd even throw in some dragonhog bacon along with those potatoes and eggs.

The wraith's blade had sent inky gray splotches blooming along my side, but Trickshot had thoroughly applied enough liquid light to stop the shadow wasting from spreading to my heart. A jagged gray line still ran along the lower left side of my ribcage. Trickshot assured me that it wasn't the shadow wasting, but said the scar might never heal. Like my silvermark, it felt strangely cold to the touch.

Brigan had been right to suggest bringing in as much liquid light as possible before the battle. Even with the extra supply, the number of umbral injuries among the nobles and high guard was so great they didn't have enough to heal my bite wound from Sniff. That meant I needed more time to recover.

They soon moved me to a hospital bed at the Sanctuary of Streya, though not under lock and key this time. Apparently the Black Valkyrie had spoken up on my behalf, and as the leader of the Mage Hunters, they couldn't exactly call in the Mage Hunters to bring me in against her wishes. Even Queen Ilona had submitted to her request.

Not long after arriving at the sanctuary, I heard a timid knock at my door.

"Come in," I said, my voice still a little hoarse from battle. Was Trickshot back already to change my bandages?

I was surprised to see a redheaded young man not much older than me shuffle into the room.

Thanks to the shortage of liquid light, his arm was in a sling. He wore a slightly askew Mage Hunter's uniform underneath it. I vaguely recognized him as Jaira's Hunting partner.

"Hello," he said with an awkward wave. "I'm Lothar."

"That's right," I said. "I recognize your voice from the mindlink." My toes curled up as I remembered the feeling of that miniature ethereal snake clinging to my ankle inside my boot. It hadn't been there when I'd woken up, so I assumed it had slithered back to its creator.

"I wanted to thank you for standing up for me," Lothar began, producing a desert marigold from behind his back. As he held up the slightly-crumpled flower, a petal dropped to the floor.

"Oops," Lothar said, watching it fall. "It was supposed to be a get-well gesture."

"It's perfect," I chuckled, reaching for the flower's dilapidated remains.

Lothar placed them in my hand. "And thank you even more for your aid against the Liberator. Capturing her was imperative to our quest."

"Your quest to capture the Farseer?" I spoke without thinking.

Lothar seemed taken aback. "Yes," he replied. "The Farseer is necessary for… well…" Lothar trailed off, as if debating whether or not to go on with his explanation.

Finally, he exhaled. "I suppose it's for the best if I speak openly with you. You're practically one of us, after all. Or at least, you will be."

I raised an eyebrow, about to ask what in the void he meant by that when Lothar plowed on.

"You see, the Farseer's ether well is the only thing that can save my lord from the shadow wasting."

I frowned. "Your lord?" I repeated.

Lothar went on. "Before he fell ill, I was the personal servant to High Prince Mason."

My eyes popped. "You mean Mason Drakeslayer? The son of the High King over the entire realm?"

"Indeed." Genuine sadness settled over Lothar's features. I could tell he really cared for his noble charge.

"I was skeptical of Mason's quest northward to slay the frostdrake from the start," Lothar said. "But he was adamant—He *had* to go. See, I'd been reading from the high citadel's library—they have dozens of texts as old as the realm itself. From Eltosira to Fjordan to Odra the Sage… they even have some books by Theok! Can you believe that?"

"Uh, no?" I answered in what I hoped was the way he wanted.

Lothar's eyes lit up as he continued. "Anyway, that's where I first learned about skymages—ancient magi able to access multiple types of etherarchy and enhance their own ether wells. Mason wasn't much of a reader himself, but he was very interested when I told him about my reading of the great northern frostdrake."

Lothar briefly paused, so I gave a little hmph of acknowledgement. Clearly, Lothar was just thrilled that someone was letting him speak for so long.

"Mason took the book before I got the chance to finish. Next thing I knew, he was preparing to embark on a quest to the northern wilds where the drake lived. Said he was after something that could change Evgard forever, but wouldn't say more. I told him to be careful, but that scorched fool just had to take on the wilds alone."

Lothar sighed mournfully. "When they first brought him back, they were sure it was too late for him. His whole body was gray, down to his hair, and no amount of liquid light seemed to make a difference. But

Mason's father, High King Magnus, wouldn't accept that. He sought out physicians from all across the realm."

Lothar was completely lost in his tale, and I wondered if he even remembered I was here. I listened intently as he went on.

"With Mason in such a state, I joined the Mage Hunters. If he ever woke, I wanted to be able to better protect him from ethereal forces in the future. That's when I ran into the Black Valkyrie and the others. When she found out I was Mason's servant, she invited me to join her team. The Black Valkyrie is a wise and powerful woman, who clearly had deep insight regarding skymages, though she claims I am not yet ready for such weighty secrets."

Lothar's eyes glazed over. "Though, my meditation is doing wonders to prepare me. Perhaps if I can become worthy of skymage powers, I can better serve Evgard, and even help Mason myself. But for now, our best course of action is to apprehend the Farseer."

"Why?" I asked.

Lothar shook himself out of his reverie. "The High King learned from one of the new physicians that the Farseer may have the power to save his son. I'm not sure exactly how, but my reading is clear about one thing: The Farseer possesses the most powerful ether well in the history of Evgard. If anyone can save Mason, he can."

I found myself nodding; I'd seen the Farseer's great power firsthand back in the Dragon Mists. And it was his remedy that saved King Axel, so why not High Prince Mason as well?

Lothar spoke earnestly. "I'm only grateful the Black Valkyrie would allow me to join her on her noble quest. And I'm excited to work more with you, great Snowstorm."

Again, I was puzzled by Lothar's words. "What do you mean?"

"I'll take it from here, Lothar." The Black Valkyrie herself appeared in the doorway.

"Great Black Valkyrie." Lothar inclined his head.

"I wonder if Snowstorm and I might speak privately."

"Of course." Lothar gave me one last grateful nod, his eyes both earnest and sincere.

The Black Valkyrie shut the door behind Lothar and took a seat at the foot of my hospital bed.

"I'll cut right to the chase," the Black Valkyrie said. "I'm heading back to Evyndara in the morning, and I'd like you to join me there."

That took me aback. "Evyndara?"

"I want you and your entire squad to come to the Academy there to train as Mage Hunters."

It was as if my voice had gotten lost somewhere in my throat. My mouth fell open as I stared on in disbelief.

Mage Hunters. The very thing I'd grown up fearing above all else. Now, this woman wanted me to become one?

"You can take a few days to think it over. The next cycle doesn't start for several weeks, but the seven of you will have to travel there, so don't take too long to make up your mind. You fought well, Snowstorm. You have a gift. I'd love to see how far it can take you."

I felt a touch of pride at those words, especially since my mom had only ever seen my etherarchy as a curse. But I still couldn't make myself respond.

"I'd like for all seven of you to come," the Black Valkyrie said, leaning closer. "But I need you and my son in particular."

"Jax?" I managed. "But he's... I don't control Jax."

The Black Valkyrie laughed. "How little you know about men."

She winked, and a rosy blush spread across my cheeks.

"Think about it." The Black Valkyrie got to her feet. "There aren't a lot of magi like you, Snowstorm. You may have the power to change the tides."

With that, the Black Valkyrie turned to leave. Halfway to the door, she stopped in her tracks.

"I almost forgot," she said, fishing an envelope from a satchel at her side. The envelope was large and thick, bulging at the bottom.

The Black Valkyrie passed me the envelope and flashed me one of her winningest smiles before closing the door behind her.

I flipped it open and found a note. I instantly recognized the handwriting as my mother's.

Dear Meli,

First off, I need you to know I'm safe.

I want you to be safe as well, which is why I must ask you not to follow me. I spoke with the Black Valkyrie after the battle and asked her if I could travel to Evyndara to receive the magi cure.

My breath caught in my throat as I kept reading.

This is my choice. Once I'm free from this curse, I'll find you and Dad. I love you with all my heart, my darling little girl.
Love always,
Mom

My insides twisting up, I pulled out a well-worn deck of cards from the envelope. The starry-robed Mystic card lay face up on the top of the pile, and I recognized the dust-encrusted crease on the top right corner.

I had no doubt the Black Valkyrie had read the note. Mom specifically asked me not to go to Evyndara. If the Black Valkyrie wanted me to join her at the Academy there, why would she have given me the letter?

It dawned on me that the Black Valkyrie knew that, once I found out where my mother was, that would be the first place I'd go, whether Mom wanted me there or not.

I was so distracted, I was only vaguely aware of more knocking at my door, followed by the creak of it opening. When I saw the Ursadon standing silently in the doorframe, I nearly jumped out of my skin.

"Captain Zoren," I said, hurriedly laying aside the envelope and sliding out of the bed to stand at attention.

"Please, Meleya, don't get up. Trickshot tells me you need all the rest you can get in order to recover, but I needed to speak with you as soon as possible. Though I'm sure you're tired of visitors by now."

He spoke with a quiet sort of concern that took me off guard. Still, I gingerly took a seat on the edge of the bed, only slightly nervous as the Captain made his way closer. At least he left the door open.

When he opened his mouth again, he spoke so quietly I could barely hear, though his dragonfire green eyes burned with intensity.

"I know you know something more about the Soul Reaper's voidshard. With so much going on before the battle, I didn't press you before, but decisions must be made. I need you to tell me what was written on that stone."

My voice stuck in my throat. Of course I wanted to tell someone about the shard and hopefully lift the weight pressing ever downward on my soul from within my rift hold. But this was the Ursadon. Besides, I still didn't know if he'd take the information and go running straight to the other Mage Hunters with it. I knew Zyri wouldn't have wanted that. She wanted the information for the empress of the Dragon Isles.

As I stared into Zoren's sincere, almost pleading eyes, I once again wondered what had really brought him to Evgard from the Dragon Isles in the first place. Mom had always told me he'd come to spy on the Mage Hunter Academy before turning his back on the other Drekai and becoming a Hunter himself. But what if there was more to it? I knew my next question was reckless, but I bit back my fear.

"Who do you really work for, Zoren?"

The Captain seemed taken aback, a rare occurrence for him. He always seemed to know exactly what everyone around him was thinking and feeling, yet for just a moment, he was stunned.

Then he squared his shoulders and headed toward the open door. At first, I thought he was going to simply walk away. Instead, he shut the door, then pulled over a stool and sat in front of me so we were on the same level.

"What I'm about to tell you cannot leave this room. *Ever.* Do you understand?"

Slowly, I gave a solemn nod.

"Twenty years ago, I was sent to Evgard by the empress of the Dragon Isles. My purpose was to retrieve the very voidshard you saw in that cave in the Dragon Mists. At the time, our spies had learned the shard was being held in the Mirror Forest of Evyndara, near the Mage Hunter Academy."

He hesitated, and I found myself subconsciously leaning forward with anticipation.

Zoren went on. "Obviously, I was unsuccessful. Since then, I've been an undercover agent of the empress. It's taken years to gain the Mage Hunters' trust, but now even the Black Valkyrie herself believes I am her loyal servant. The empress needs to know how deeply the Hunters have dived into the same voidarchy that made the Soul Reaper's shard. Other Drekai agents have been pursuing that stone ever since, and if you, Meleya, know something of what was written on it, that could be crucial in the war we're waging against the Gray Ones."

My eyes were as round as dragon eggs. I couldn't believe Zoren was telling me this—all along, he'd been a Drekai spy? Part of me wondered if he was lying, but he looked so sincere. My head was spinning.

"I cannot impress on your mind enough just how vital this information is." Zoren's voice was so quiet I had to strain to hear him.

I opened my mouth, still unsure if I should divulge what I knew. The Soul Reaper's voidshard was only one rune away. I could get rid of it once and for all. It was as easy as handing it over.

As I considered the possibility, a sudden, cold stillness flooded me. In my mind, a face appeared—that same gaunt face I'd seen in my nightmare the night I'd woken to find the voidshard beside me on my pillow. Out of nowhere, my head reeled with thoughts of that pale man driving his blue-tinged starglass dagger into my chest. My breath caught, and I wanted to scream.

It was like I was frozen where I sat. Like invisible hands held me back to keep me from runetracing. Memories of the Ursadon from my childhood swam in my head. The way he'd relentlessly pursued us across the Canyonlands, forcing us to abandon so many nomadic caravans. His triumphant face the day he'd finally captured us and sent my parents to Spydra Prison.

How could I trust this man?

"But... for so long you were void-bent on arresting us," I said, my voice cracking. "Why?"

Zoren's whole body went rigid. He ground his teeth together, his lips forming a tight line, and I could tell he wasn't going to answer my question.

For a moment that seemed to stretch into eternity, neither of us spoke. On the stool before me, Zoren's eyes narrowed as he sensed my extreme reluctance. I wondered if he'd force me to talk—torture the information out of me or something.

But then he finally stood. Once again, he asked me to tell no one of his true purpose in Evgard, then made his way to the door.

Just as he was about to pull it open, I called out.

"Kjell." Then, before any unseen force could stop me, I blurted out the other name as well. "And Agnai."

As I said the names out loud, more ice poured into my veins, spreading from my core to my fingertips. A sense of dread filled me, and once again I felt like I couldn't move.

Zoren turned back toward me, his face full of both somberness and earnest gratitude.

"Thank you, Meleya. Now I know what I must do." There was a twinge of deep sorrow in his voice. He gave me one final nod before slipping into the hallway and shutting the door behind him.

For a long time, I just sat there. I could feel the heaviness of the voidshard inside my rift hold, and I still felt unbelievably cold. Shivering, I reached for a blanket folded at the foot of my bed.

As I wrapped it around me, I caught sight of the envelope the Black Valkyrie had given me. It still bulged at the bottom. I reached for it, then tipped it on its side, letting the last item inside slip into my open hand.

I gasped as a shining yellow scale thudded gently into my palm. It was a little scuffed around where the Liberator had etched Sentinel markings to create her true dragon totem. It seemed my scale had received battle scars of its own.

The second the heartscale touched my skin, I felt my bond with Sniff bloom to life stronger than ever before. The dark feeling from the void-shard vanished.

Ping-a-ling! Joyful notes played an ascending arpeggio in my heart. Through the bond, Sniff sent an apologetic melody for what he'd done to me in the courtyard, and I rushed to assure him I didn't blame him in the slightest.

He sent a high-pitched trill of relief. My laughter put extra pressure on my still-tender wounds, but at that moment, I didn't care.

CHAPTER 43: SUNRISE

Two days later, I was soaring over the Rise on the back of my bright yellow evren once again. The sun hadn't yet risen, and the winter air was frigid against my face despite my heavy winter cloak. My shoulder and side were still sore as I flew, and it looked like I wasn't going to get away without a couple of nasty scars. But in spite of everything, it felt great to be back in the dragon saddle on the back of my energetic, puppy-like evren.

Silhouetted against the starlight, I took in the rugged landscape, from the towering Sunrise Arch to the wide canyon cutting across the land below. In the distance to the south, I saw the churning, faintly glowing Dragon Mists.

The rune for the Sight glowed over my forehead so that I could see my other bond, Blink. My spirit evren soared alongside us, her misty silvery aura trailing behind her like a comet alongside Sniff's gold one and mine of indigo.

Blink twirled in the air. Not wanting to be outdone, Sniff spun a happy loop himself. I clung to the saddle with all I had to keep from slipping off. My long braid whipped around to hit me in the face, and I chuckled.

I had until tomorrow to decide what I wanted to do about the Black Valkyrie's offer to train with the Mage Hunters. Apparently, she'd spoken with the rest of Squad Reckless after stopping by my room at the Sanctuary and extended her invitation to the others. Solvai, Brigan, Edrea, Cam, and Erik had agreed without hesitation. An invitation from the realm-wide legend herself, plus the chance to learn to fight enemy magi was too good to pass up after what we'd been through with the Coven of the Gray Ones.

But part of me was still hesitant. Maybe it was because nobody had seen Jax since the battle, and it didn't feel right going without him. And not just because the Black Valkyrie had all but ordered me to bring him along.

I felt a sharp pang in my chest, still unable to come to grips with the facts staring me in the face. Jax had returned to Skygard, leaving me behind.

Boom boom, Blink sent a despondent set of drumbeats through our bond.

Brrring, Sniff chimed in. He may not have been Jax's biggest fan, but he still felt sad that I was hurting.

The first inklings of dawn were just beginning to appear over the varied landscape, washing the sky in violet. That meant it was time for me to get back to the bunker and start breakfast before my squadmates woke up.

I dropped Sniff off at the stables, then hurried down the slightly overgrown path toward the hidden bunker. My mind flipped through different breakfast options, weighing them against what ingredients I had access to and how much time there was before morning muster. I'd already made Cam's favorite meal of dragonhog bacon, crispy potatoes, and eggs. We still had some leftover potatoes—maybe I'd try throwing them into a hash.

Ducking around the juniper tree growing right beside the bunker, I reached toward the door. But before my fist closed around the handle, I nearly fell over at the sight of a muscular young man with a maroon bandana wrapped across steely gray hair as he leaned against the wall.

"About time you showed up, M. I've been waiting for almost an hour."

"Jax!" I squeaked, throwing myself at him. Despite the temperature, he still insisted on ripping the sleeves off his tunic.

He wrapped his arms around me and I buried my face in his warm chest. I felt like a weight had been lifted off of my heart and tossed over the edge of the Rise. At his touch, my pulse instantly began racing.

"Relax," he said. "It's only been a couple of days."

"Shut up," I replied. "It felt like a lifetime."

"Yeah, it did," Jax agreed, his voice soft and low. I breathed him in, his metallic scent warming me to my core.

I dragged him into the bunker and quickly got the oven going. It didn't take long for the fire to heat up the small space.

"So, are you going to tell me where in the void you've been?" I asked, chopping up some ember peppers to add to the potatoes.

"Hiding out with Jade in the lower town," Jax replied, his elbows resting on the countertop. "Waiting for my mom to bail."

"Could've told me."

"How? After the way you fought with her against the Liberator, I knew she wouldn't leave you alone until she skipped town."

He had a point—both the Black Valkyrie and Lothar had visited me in the hospital.

I tossed the potatoes and ember peppers into a skillet, then splashed them with a little oil and salt from the shaker clipped to my belt.

Without thinking, I traced the rune to access my rift hold spice cabinet. As I reached for the paprika, I froze when I saw the blue light from the Soul Reaper's voidshard pulsing. I couldn't help but read that strange name etched in white on the surface facing me.

Agnai.

Ice rushed through my veins as I grit my teeth. Twice in the past few days I'd woken up sweating and trembling from gray and lightning blue nightmares. They always featured fearsome dragons and that same shadowy, pale man holding a starglass dagger over my head. Each time, I found the voidshard lying eerily on my pillow next to me. My rift hold couldn't contain it for long.

But I knew this thing was too dangerous to leave somewhere anyone could find it. For the hundredth time since our conversation, I wished I'd been able to give the voidshard to Zoren. I'd gone to his office later, only to be informed that the Captain of the Guard was not on the Rise. They wouldn't tell me more. I wondered where he'd gone—Back to the Dragon Isles to speak with the empress? But that would raise so much suspicion, and I doubted Zoren would want to blow his many years undercover with one trip.

I stared at the voidshard as a shudder ran through me. Once again, it was as if the crystal were begging me to let it out.

"You okay?" Jax cocked his head.

Looking into his eyes, I wanted to tell him everything. But I couldn't shake the feeling that anyone who knew what I had stowed in my rift hold would be in grave danger. I had to keep Jax safe.

"Fine," I muttered as I hurriedly withdrew the paprika and sprinkled some onto the food. Then I replaced the canister and closed my rift hold. The cold feeling subsided a little, but didn't completely leave me.

As I cooked, I looked over my shoulder at Jax, eager to talk about something that would get my mind off of the voidshard.

"Why avoid your mom? I think she really cares about you."

"Right. Cares about me enough to ditch me with Torsten as a kid, then dedicate her life to trying to kill the only group of people who've ever given a scale about whether I lived or died."

His tone was intense, and I lowered my brows. Maybe it was spurred by the icy feeling still lingering in my chest, but I found myself raising my voice slightly as I stirred the hash over the stovetop.

"You know, like it or not, the Knights aren't the only people who care about you now."

"Oh yeah?" Jax stood up straighter, his hands holding to the edge of the counter.

"Our squad does, Jax. All of us."

"Pretty sure Duke-man would love to see me suffer death by dragon."

"Even Brigan, okay?" I dropped my wooden spoon onto the countertop to give Jax a glare. "Don't be so stubborn."

"So what then? Doesn't my mom want me to come crawling to her Academy to join her sooty Hunters?"

"Uh—well…" I stammered.

"I knew it," Jax threw up his hands. "I drakking knew it."

"I think you should come with us," I said.

Jax laughed bitterly. "I shouldn't have stayed. I should've left with Boone and the rest."

"Maybe you should've," I struggled to keep from shouting. Suddenly, I felt the oven was doing its job too well. It was too hot in here.

"Why are you going to her Academy? What could possibly tempt you to become a Mage Hunter?" Jax said, taking a step around the counter toward me.

"Because…" I faltered.

"Because isn't a great reason," Jax pressed.

"Because it's where my mother is!" I exploded. "She's on her way there right now to get that goddess-forsaken cure, and I'm going to drakking find her whether you come or not."

I slammed my hand down onto the countertop, which set off my shoulder wound again. I inhaled sharply, cringing at the pain.

Jax's whole demeanor changed instantly. He rushed to stand in front of me, his midnight blue eyes dancing in the low, early morning light coming through the window.

"I'm sorry, M," he whispered. "I didn't know."

I swallowed, looking down over my injury. Slowly, Jax moved to place a careful hand on the outside of my still tender shoulder. Jax's fingers traveled along the seam of my tunic toward my neck. I held perfectly still as he took hold of the edge of my shirt collar and delicately pulled down to reveal the angry evren bite on my collarbone.

A million dragonflies spun inside my heart and stomach. I could feel Jax inching closer, and I realized I was doing the same.

"Why didn't you leave with the Knights?" I asked, my voice soft.

Jax carefully replaced my tunic collar to look me in the eyes. "I think you know."

We just stood there for a moment, breathing. My chin tilted up slightly as his tilted down.

"Okay," Jax said.

"What?" I asked.

"I'm coming with you to the Academy."

"I don't want you to if you don't—"

"I made you a promise that I'd help your parents. I'm coming, M."

Tears shone in my eyes, and any remaining coldness from the voidshard evaporated. In one quick motion, I removed the skillet of potatoes from the heat—I didn't want them to burn. Then I grabbed Jax's hand and yanked him toward the bunker door.

"Where are we going?" he asked, letting me drag him along.

Now it was my turn to keep him in suspense. "You'll see."

I led Jax away from the bunker to a spot where I could get a clear view of the orange sky through Sunrise Arch. Then I lifted a hand, gold light trailing from my finger. A portal just taller than Jax ripped to life in front of us.

Jax raised an eyebrow at me as I pulled him through the rift.

We emerged directly on top of Sunrise Arch, the brilliant sunlight ready to break over the edge of the land at any moment. We stood in the center of the narrow redrock band, the craggy rocks and smokesage plants about a fifty foot drop below. The breeze tossed my hair and sent a couple shivers down my spine. Jax looked at me in surprise.

"What are we doing here?" he asked.

"You told me once that you'd kissed seventy different girls," I said.

Jax looked down, his cheeks turning a faint red.

I went on, "But I'm willing to bet you've never kissed one in a place like this."

Jax's eyes locked on mine, and he broke into a smile. His finger flew as he traced a psionic rune.

Suddenly, I felt a tug at my waist as Jax telekinetically pulled me by my belt. He yanked me toward him, closing the distance between us and encircling me with his arms.

I felt my pulse fly when, all at once, he was pressing his mouth against mine. I wrapped a hand around the back of his neck, losing my fingers in his hair.

The first rays of sunlight rose over the horizon, their warm beams shining onto the two of us.

Fragment - Edrea

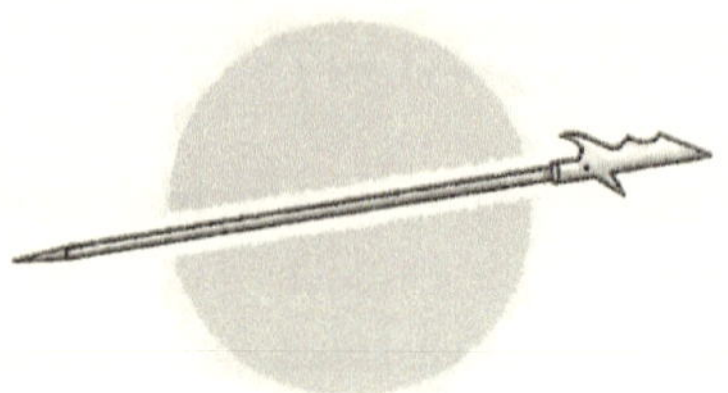

Edrea arrived at the bunker with the others, the smell of fried potatoes and vegetables making her mouth water. Edrea sighed, both with contentment and annoyance. Meleya was an infuriatingly good cook.

When Solvai swung open the bunker door, Edrea caught sight of Meleya at the stove. She was surprised to see Jax there, standing remarkably close to her, with a hand on her back. When Meleya heard the door, she hurriedly stepped away from him.

"Jax!" Cam called out, pushing past the rest of the squad.

Jax broke into a grin as he met Edrea's stepbrother just inside the bunker. The two guys clasped hands in front of them, leaning over to slap each other on the back in some kind of manly embrace. Edrea chuckled.

"Where've you been, man?" Cam asked, shoving Jax roughly on the shoulder.

Jax shoved right back, then haltingly explained that he'd been lying low, waiting for the anti-magi hate to die down after the battle. Edrea didn't totally buy it, but she and the others were just glad to see Jax was back. Squad Reckless simply wasn't complete without him.

Cam took the opportunity to show the group his brand new tattoo—an artistic, angular letter 'R' on the inside of his wrist. Erik had designed it, immortalizing Squad Reckless in ink. Edrea felt a swell of warmth in her chest as the group gathered around to admire the tattoo. She knew how much these people meant to her brother, and what a difference they'd made in his life these past few months. He finally felt like he was doing something good. Cam's grin was wide as his favorite squadmate, Jax, thumped him on the back once more.

Edrea was particularly glad to see the sleeveless wonder or, as Edrea liked to think of him, Meleya's weakness. The more time Meleya spent with Jax, the less she spent with Brigan.

Edrea turned to Brigan now, admiring the sure way he carried himself. She liked everything about him, from his broad shoulders to his heart-melting, dimpled smile. Though at that moment, his smile seemed conflicted. Edrea was sure he was as happy to see Jax as the rest of them, but Edrea got the feeling he'd seen the way Jax's hand was touching Meleya's back when they'd first walked in. Meleya had tried to hide it, but Brigan was observant. At least, he was observant when it came to Meleya. Edrea had known Brigan since they'd met at basic training, but she wondered if he'd be able to recall her eye color if someone held him at spearpoint.

Then again, Edrea wasn't entirely sure if she could name the eye colors of anyone in the squad *but* Brigan's. Erik's were brown, right? Edrea checked—soot, they were more black than brown. Jax's were definitely brown through... soot again.

Meleya interrupted Edrea's musings when she half-dragged Jax back to the counter and ordered him to start serving up the breakfast hash. Then, as the squad took their places around the table, Meleya asked Brigan for a quick word outside.

Edrea was instantly on high alert. The others playfully interrogated Jax about his recent absence, but Edrea couldn't help but casually lean against the wall near the doorframe. The door was slightly ajar, so she could just hear Brigan and Meleya talking on the other side.

"...just wanted to let you know first," Meleya said, her voice sounding apologetic and a little regretful.

Brigan replied dejectedly. "I understand. And I really appreciate the... forewarning."

Edrea frowned. What were they talking about?

She startled when the door swung open again and Brigan and Meleya stepped back inside. Brigan cocked his head when he saw her standing there, and Edrea's cheeks burned as she scurried to take a seat at the table.

They dug in, and as usual, the food was delicious. Perfectly spiced, savory flavors burst inside her mouth, and for a few minutes, everyone was quiet as they enjoyed the meal.

After a while, Meleya cleared her throat.

"Um, so…" she began, clearly uncomfortable as she glanced at Jax sitting beside her. "There's something I—I mean, *we* should tell you guys. Uh… it's just, I'd rather just have it out so nobody has to like, be weird about it… uh…"

As Meleya stuttered, Jax gave a small snort and shook his head.

"What are we, twelve?" Then he pulled his hand out from underneath the table to reveal it was holding Meleya's.

The squad erupted with responses.

"Whoa!" Cam said, snapping his fingers.

"Aww," cooed Solvai.

"I totally called it," Erik laughed. He reached across the table to hold his hand open in front of Cam. Edrea rolled her eyes as her brother passed Erik a copper mark. Under his breath, only Edrea heard Cam mutter.

"Definitely thought it'd be Brigan."

In his place beside Edrea, Brigan remained silent. One look at his carefully guarded expression told Edrea he'd known this was coming—that's what Meleya had pulled him outside to tell him. Edrea had to hand it to Meleya. If she had to break his heart, at least she'd been woman enough to be honest with him first.

While the others teased Meleya and Jax—Edrea wasn't sure if she'd ever seen anyone blush more deeply than Meleya at that moment—Edrea laid a cautious hand on the table beside Brigan's. She held her breath, summoning her courage as she gently bumped her fist against the back of Brigan's hand.

He turned to her, rich brown eyes vulnerable and questioning. Edrea's breath caught, but she recovered quickly enough to give him a reassuring smile.

When he smiled back, it was sincere. Most of the others may've been oblivious to the way Brigan was feeling, but Edrea knew. She was always aware of him.

"Check it out," Erik said, pulling out a sheet of paper from his sketchbook and laying it on the table. "Drew this months ago."

The squad laughed heartily at Erik's drawing. It depicted a stylized sketch of Meleya and Jax standing close, her hand on his muscular chest while his arm wrapped around her narrow waist. It was a good likeness, though Edrea thought the way the two of them were looking at each other in the picture was a little more ardent than the way they looked at each other in reality. As much as Edrea wanted Meleya and Jax to stay together, she could tell Meleya had doubts. Even if Meleya didn't want to admit it to herself.

Erik offered to let them keep the drawing, and while Jax pretended not to care, Edrea rolled her eyes as he carefully refolded the paper and slid it inside his tunic pocket.

After the meal, Squad Reckless began filtering out of the bunker to head back to the barracks. They'd be shipping out to Evyndara tomorrow, and the commanders had given them the day to pack their things and see their families one more time. Edrea and Cam planned to head down the Rise to the lower town to say goodbye to their parents later that afternoon.

Edrea was about to follow the last soldier out when she noticed Meleya remained behind. While the others left to gather their belongings for the journey, Meleya rummaged through cupboards and shelves, gathering ingredients. Edrea watched as she pulled out a small pile of burlap sacks.

It dawned on Edrea that Meleya was preparing meals for the group—probably to bring on their travels the next day.

Edrea cast one last look at the orange cloaks of her retreating squad-mates. Then she shut the door behind them and headed over to the countertop where Meleya stood.

"Edrea?" Meleya raised a suspicious eyebrow. "What're you—"

"What can I do to help?" Edrea cut her off.

Meleya looked dumbfounded as she searched in vain for a response.

"You don't have to act so surprised, snowhead," Edrea said, fighting a scowl.

Meleya stared at Edrea for a moment longer before breaking into a smile. She scooted over to make room for Edrea at the counter and pushed a sack of flour her way.

"You can start on the bread," Meleya said. "We're going to need a lot—it's a long way to the Mage Hunter Academy."

Chapter 44: The Academy

Growing up in the desert canyons, I thought I knew what it meant to be cold. Flying into the Ridgeback Mountains in the dead of winter took it to a whole new level.

Even with my gloves on, I could barely feel my fingers as I gripped Sniff's saddle, and my breath came out in dense, white puffs that got sucked away in the breeze. It took a little coaxing, but I even managed to get Jax to put on a coat.

We'd been traveling for a while now, crossing into Evyndara and the Ridgeback Mountains on our way to the Mage Hunter Academy. While the winter air was numbing my toes, the views took my breath away. I was glad I rode a flying dragon—my squadmates riding wingless drakes on the path below were missing out.

Snowcapped peaks glinted in the brilliant sunlight as far as I could see, stretching endlessly northward. Smattered patches of rich, velvety green spilled down the mountains wherever cindercone pines or skyspruce grew, more white snow blanketing their branches. The snow here stuck in dense piles, nothing like the light dusting we got each winter in the Canyonlands. Luckily, Cam's mount, Chonk, made for a great snowplow.

Every once in a while, I'd glimpse the wide antlers of a dragonmoose or the golden-yellow scales of a cougardrake among the trees. When they saw our squad of dragon riders traveling along the path, the wild animals would scatter.

Solvai spent part of the journey in falcondrake form, soaring alongside those of us who rode flying dragons. When her ether ran low, she rode behind Brigan. Meanwhile, Edrea held on behind Cam atop his drake, casting somewhat jealous glances at us riders every once in a while. Still, throughout the entire journey, she'd only made a handful of snarky remarks, and almost none directed at me. Something had changed between us since the solstice, and I could honestly say I was glad the two of us were squadmates.

According to the Black Valkyrie's instructions, we'd see the spires of the Academy any moment now. Sure enough, as we crested the next peak, the valley came into view.

Spreading across the dip between mountains was the thick foliage of the Mirror Forest. Frozen lakes scattered throughout the forest reflected the sky above, and I understood where the forest got its name.

From our high vantage point, we could see an imposing, slate gray structure laid out like an enormous triangle pointing North. There was a central courtyard inside the triangle, and towers on each of the three points. Cutting through the center of the triangle and extending through the southern line was a long, fortified passage connected to what looked to be a gatehouse and a silver-plated drawbridge beyond the main walls. It didn't take long for me to realize the building was shaped like the Mage Hunters' symbol: A sword stabbing through the ethereal triad.

More buildings that must've been part of the Academy rose in tiers along the mountain's incline. One in particular stood out among the gray stone—a tall, black tower near the mountain's peak.

"Swan Spire," Jax muttered from his place on Jade's back as he flew by my side. As we prepared to descend into the valley, Jax and I locked eyes. Swirling behind his midnight blue irises, I saw turbulence and a hint of fear. This was his last chance to turn back. For a second, I thought he was going to order Jade to turn around and not stop until they were out of Evyndara.

But Jax seemed to find resolve in my eyes, his jaw setting as his neck muscles flexed. I relaxed, trusting that despite the struggle that lay ahead, he was going to help me find my mother.

We alighted at the imposing gatehouse at the Academy's front entrance. Sniff sniffled, intimidated by the heavy-looking, silvery drawbridge. I rubbed his nose.

"Who goes there?" a gruff male voice called down from a perch near the top of the gate. We looked up to see an elderly man bundled up in the thick white pelt of a polar wolf.

"Squad Reckless," Brigan called back with confidence. "We're new recruits, sent by the Black Valkyrie."

"New recruits, eh?" The man narrowed his eyes as he leaned over the side of his perch. "Awful lot of magi among you, I see. Sure you ain't here as targets for the Hunters to practice on?"

The man gave a bitter laugh. Jax, Solvai, and I exchanged glances as Solvai brought a hand to her freshly silvermarked cheek. After her display during the battle on the Rise, she'd had no choice but to accept her mark when the Mage Hunters had approached her. Trickshot had done the job herself, making sure to do so as painlessly as possible and to administer a healing salve the moment she'd finished carving the Wildshaper's symbol.

"Quite sure," Brigan confirmed, not missing a beat.

"We'll see 'bout that," the man muttered, suddenly lifting up a crossbow and resting it on the ledge. Without another word, the man fired off a shot toward Jax.

Jax reacted quickly, a rune glowing to life over his forehead. He telekinetically caught the bolt, stopping it long before it came too close, but all seven of us glared at the man in horror.

The old man cracked up. "Relax, it's a blank. Watch yourselves, though. My eyesight ain't what it used to be. Next time, I might just load one of my silver-tipped sharp ones."

I was just considering giving the old man a piece of my mind when a familiar voice sounded from above.

"Reckless, is that you?" Trickshot's face appeared over the side. Her long hair hung down, the new streak of white woven among the strands of auburn.

We waved up at Trickshot, glad to see she'd arrived safely. After the battle in Keep Rengard, she'd decided to return to the Academy for a few months to take a break from field work. She'd be teaching healing courses here for a while.

"Drak, Jakob," Trickshot chastised the old man. "These seven are on the list. Let them in already."

"Magi on the list," Jakob replied under his breath. "Scorchin' Academy ain't what it used to be." But he disappeared behind the wall. Soon, a sharp creak sounded as the enormous drawbridge lowered.

As we walked across, I realized the drawbridge really was made entirely of silver. While most of my squadmates walked across without a second thought, Solvai, Jax, and I had to bite our tongues to keep from crying out in pain. Being on the drawbridge felt like diving into a pool of bitterly cold lightning.

We hurried to cross, and I noticed Sniff and the other dragons' clear distress as well. I let out a breath as we reached the stone walkway on the other side.

We passed under an archway that led through a passage then into the central courtyard. Trickshot met us below, then directed us through the wide, open space to another door opposite the one we'd entered. She pointed to one of the long, stone buildings built partway up the cliffside.

"Those're the dragon stables," Trickshot explained. "Drop off your mounts with the keeper there and get them settled. I'll tell the heads of your divisions that you've arrived."

We made our way up the cliff on dragonback, finding the dragon stables easily. They were tiny compared to the enormous building at Keep Rengard, but they looked clean and stocked with plenty of equipment and snacks for the dragons.

Solvai accompanied Brigan and I as we found stalls next to each other for our dragons near the back. Bolt curled up in the soft hay right away while Sniff used the claws at the hinges of his wings to hang upside down from a rafter. Both closed their eyes, eager for some well-deserved rest.

As Brigan said goodnight to his drake, Solvai leaned against a wooden support beam and looked over the squad as they got to know the stables. Her expression was pensive.

I took my place at my friend's side, thinking about how impressed I was with the way she was taking so much change in stride. From discovering her etherarchy to finding out her mother was the Liberator, not to mention learning Torsten was her father. It was a lot.

"How are you holding up?" I asked quietly so the others wouldn't hear.

Solvai was silent for a moment as she rubbed her falcondrake charm—or rather, her Wildshaper's totem—between her thumb and index finger. The old metal chain it used to hang on was gone, replaced with a leather cord.

Finally, she spoke. "You told me once that my aura centers around my core, and that it has something to do with having good instincts."

I shrugged. "You do have good instincts."

Solvai went on. "Well, my instincts are telling me that things are going to work out. Maybe my father didn't turn out to be the hero I thought he was, but that doesn't mean I can't become that hero myself. I want to protect the realm, but I want to do it my own way. Not the way my father or mother tried to. I'm not sure where the next few months will take us, but my gut says I'll recognize the right path when it comes. You know?"

I nodded, reaching around Solvai's shoulders and squeezing her from the side. She smiled.

"I'll be right there at your side on that path," I assured her, and Solvai nudged me softly.

Suddenly, Jax appeared behind me.

"We need to talk," he whispered, his breath warm against my ear. A shiver ran down my neck.

Then I remembered we weren't alone. My cheeks reddened as Solvai conspiratorially raised her eyebrows at the two of us.

"Be good to her, half-brother," Solvai said.

"Still not used to that," Jax muttered, shaking his head.

"Never will be," Solvai agreed.

"That makes three of us," I put in.

Jax led me out of the stables and to the nearby treeline. We stood in a somewhat secluded spot on the edge of the Mirror Forest behind the thick trunk of a cindercone pine. Faint smoke trailed upward from the black pine cones growing in its branches.

"What is it?" I asked, my brows knitting with concern.

"First things first," he murmured, then suddenly he pressed me into the tree trunk, his lips warm against mine. For a second, I forgot where we were as I kissed him back.

"Careful," I said, pulling away after a moment. My head was spinning. "What if someone comes?"

"Then they'd see how much I care about you," Jax said as he rested his forehead against mine. I let him kiss me once more, and suddenly the snowy mountains didn't seem so cold.

"I got another message from Solrac." He reluctantly pulled back, though he kept his strong arms wrapped around me as he spoke. "I've been waiting for the chance to talk to you about it, but it looks like things aren't going well."

"What's going on?" I asked.

"The disagreement between the three heads of the Knights of the Torch. Kai was right—There's been a schism."

"A schism?" I frowned.

Jax spoke quickly. "Vesta wants to go to war with Evgard over their treatment of magi. Says we should strike while they're vulnerable, what with High King Magnus so worried about his son dying from the shadow wasting."

I thought about what Lothar had told me about Mason needing the Farseer in order to recover. I hadn't told Jax about my conversation with the High Prince's former servant, but Jax's words got me thinking. With the Farseer being the patron of the Knights, maybe the brewing war had something to do with why he wouldn't help the High Prince?

I felt a knot growing in my stomach as Jax rushed on. "Solrac felt war was the wrong approach, but in the end, Zel sided with Vesta, and that messed up the alliance with Behrfell Solrac was working on too. Things even got bad enough that Solrac and those loyal to him were branded rebels and had to flee Orothion. Even Valla and Boone couldn't get back in with those who left with them after the battle on the Rise, since the forces there knew they'd side with Solrac."

"Wait—" I held up my hands as the knot in my gut grew. "There were a lot of names and things in there I don't recognize, but let me get this straight: Solrac and the rest of the Knights who don't want war are on the run."

"Yeah."

"Including the prisoners from Spydra who followed Boone."

"Probably. But Solrac couldn't tell me where they went. Says it's not safe—yet."

I swallowed. That meant my father wasn't in Skygard kicking up his feet like I'd hoped. Only the goddesses knew where he and the other rebel Knights were hiding now.

"I told Solrac I've gone to the Academy," Jax continued. "He said—and I quote: 'This was the greatest thing that could've possibly happened right now.' Thinks I can spy from the inside, learn what the Black Valkyrie and her lackeys are planning. I told him she'll want to convince me to join her—I mean join her for real—but Solrac's sure I'll make the right choice. Says my intel will be especially valuable now that she'll have to help Evgard prepare for war with the Knights."

"Soot," I muttered. First Keep Drakfell went traitor, then Rengard declared war on the Dragon Isles. Now the Knights of the Torch were preparing to march on Evgard? It seemed the whole realm was falling apart.

Yes.

I jumped as a raspy voice sounded in my head, an icy feeling filling me to my core. My blood ran cold—it was the same voice I'd heard whisper my name when the Liberator had mentioned the Gray Ones in the Coven's underground hold.

I sense the void within your soul, Meleya of Misthaven.

Suddenly, I could feel the heaviness of the Soul Reaper's voidshard within my rift hold once more. The strangest, almost painful feeling pricked at the back of my mind. It felt like the shard was trying to burn through my rift hold right then and there as it reached toward the voice.

Flashes from my recurring nightmare about the man in the tattered gray robes dominated my mind. I'd hoped the dreams would subside during our travels, but I woke up shaking and staring at the voidshard most nights now. Every time, I fearfully shoved it back into my rift hold, unsure what else to do.

My eyes went wide as I looked around for the source of the voice, though I was sure I wouldn't see anything. Not with these eyes, anyway. Though part of me fought it, terrified of what I might see, I raised a finger to runetrace.

"What is it?" Jax said, noting my sudden distress. He held me more tightly, scanning the treeline.

I didn't answer as the Sight bloomed before my eyes. The dull russet auras of the cindercone pines shot upward as the faintly glowing greens of the mossy, muddy ground sprang to life underfoot.

Jax's vibrant tangerine aura mixed with the strands of light from my indigo one. Where the two auras met, they made a sort of fiery cloud between us. I could've stared at it much longer, were it not for my focus on the task at hand.

I jumped when I saw it. Hovering behind me just to the side was a gray, semi-formless being with bright, void blue eyes. Her face lacked detail, but I could just make out shoulders, a feminine torso, and shadowy arms.

"Wraith," I breathed, whirling out of Jax's embrace to draw my sword. The wraith didn't flinch as my weapon passed right through it.

Jax couldn't see what I saw, but within half a second, he brandished both axes in his hands and took a defensive stance at my side.

I jumped again when I glanced Jax's way and saw a second shadowy gray figure standing only a short distance behind him. The other wraith was hulking and masculine, and its bright blue eyes narrowed with hate when they saw me.

"Soot," I swore, not sure where to point my useless seaxe. My breathing became ragged and uneven as my gaze darted between the two eerily calm ethereal shadows.

"M, what's going on?" Jax's volume increased.

I was sure the first was the same Gray One I'd seen so long ago while on watch at the North Tower with my squad. She had been following me for a while.

Sounds to me like one of the Gray Ones is thinkin' 'bout choosin' you, Torsten had said during our first training session.

"Go," I whispered, staring at the wraith nearest me. "I... I don't want to be chosen."

At my words, the shadow seemed to recoil. She reached a wispy, gray hand toward me, and I felt that same icy stillness shoot through me.

I cried out and fell to my knees. I was trained to fight using a seaxe, but I had no idea how to counter an attack on my very spirit.

"Drak, M," Jax was practically yelling as he knelt beside me. "Tell me what's going on!"

I couldn't answer as I struggled to draw a full, normal breath. How could I tell him what was going on when I didn't understand it myself? A wave of hopeless insecurity washed over me as I sunk lower toward the earth. I was worthless against this thing. All my etherarchy, my skill as a soldier—none of it mattered. At that moment, I felt like *I* didn't matter.

Jax chucked his axes to the ground where they embedded into the dirt. His brows lowered over angry eyes as he clasped me by the shoulders. "This isn't fair, M. You don't just get to shut down or whatever this is."

Behind Jax, I saw the second wraith hovering over him. Suddenly, I remembered Torsten's anger the day before the attack on the Outpost. For the first time, I saw the tiniest hint of Torsten in his son.

As I lost focus, the Sight began to fade. Both Gray Ones vanished from my vision as tears filled my eyes.

Jax squeezed my shoulders and pain from my battle wound there resurfaced. I felt a couple of the scabs crack as a few drops of blood soaked into my undertunic.

"Say something, scorch it!" Jax said through gritted teeth. I was still having trouble breathing.

"What's going on?" another voice called out. Through a watery film, I saw Brigan quickly striding toward where Jax and I knelt at the treeline.

"Void if I know," Jax spat, letting go of me and getting to his feet.

Brigan was on his knees beside me in a flash.

"Breathe, Meleya," he said, his voice calm and even.

I locked onto his familiar, warm brown eyes. He inhaled deeply, then exhaled, again and again. I did my best to match his rhythm, my racing pulse slowing little by little.

"You're okay," Brigan assured me. He held out a hand, and I shakily took it as he helped me to my feet. "Can you tell me what happened?"

"Gray Ones," I swallowed. Then I did my best to describe what I'd seen. I didn't mention that I thought the wraith behind me was the same one who'd been following me for months, or that I could hear it speak inside my mind. I wanted to tell them about the nightmares and the Soul Reaper's voidshard, but the last thing I wanted to do was put Brigan or Jax in any danger. Jax wouldn't look me in the eye as I spoke.

"I'm sorry," I said as I finished. "I don't know what came over me."

"No need to apologize," Brigan said with a soft, dimpled smile. "Just remember, you're safe with us. Maybe we can find someone at the Academy who knows about the Gray Ones. Get some answers."

I nodded. Then I leaned past Brigan to get a look at Jax, who was staring off into the cindercones.

Brigan followed my gaze, the sharp muscles in his jaw tightening. It seemed like he had something more to say, but he bit his tongue.

"I'd better check on Bolt again," Brigan mumbled, taking a few steps back toward the stables. Halfway there, he turned back to look me in the eye.

"Let me know if you need anything, Meleya. I'll be right here."

I watched Brigan round the corner, feeling the weight of his last words. My hands started fiddling with the clasps on my coat as I focused on keeping my breathing even. I suddenly felt very tired.

Turning around, I saw Jax still looking off into the forest. I took a few steps toward him.

"Um…" I started. "I'm sorry."

"No." He turned back to me and pulled me into his arms. "I am. I don't know what came over me either."

I settled into his embrace, but my dark brows knit as I leaned my head against his chest. Frowning, I wondered if I *did* know exactly what had come over him—what had come over both of us.

The Gray Ones were clearly not going to leave me alone. I needed to find some answers.

Chapter 45: Mage Hunter

After we finished at the dragon stables, Jaira and Lothar came for us. Well, not all of us, apparently—Just Jax, Brigan, Solvai, and me. The other three members of our squad followed another pair of Hunters I'd never met before.

"Where are they going?" I asked as I watched Edrea, Cam, and Erik's retreating orange cloaks disappear around a bend in the hallway.

"They're about to meet the rest of their division," Lothar replied.

"Same as you four," Jaira added with a smug smile.

That smile was all it took to get Jax to narrow his eyes.

"Wait—" he started. "Why are we in separate divisions?"

Jaira made an odd, snort-like scoff, and it took me a moment to realize it was meant to be a laugh. Neither she nor Lothar offered further explanation as they led us down the hall.

Jax and I exchanged perplexed looks, and he subtly slipped his hand into mine as we trailed after Brigan and Solvai.

Despite the sporadic fireplaces warming the stony corridors, I felt colder inside the Academy than I had outside. Everywhere I looked, I saw silver. Silver-framed paintings of blue-cloaked Hunters lined the walls while silver-encrusted tables held silver statuettes of the three goddesses. Based on the shiny flecks in the mortar between stones, it seemed like they'd even gone so far as to mix silver into the mortar. It was as if the Hunters wanted to ensure that any magi who dared set foot here would remember they weren't welcome.

Checking in with my ether well, I could feel that the silver was stifling it. Not quite enough to stop me from channeling etherarchy if I really wanted to, but plenty to make it so I could never quite relax within these walls. Looking at Jax and Solvai, I could tell they felt the same. Only Brigan seemed physically unaffected by the anti-ether metal. Though based on the deep frown he wore as he walked, something about it definitely disturbed him.

"Wasteful…" he muttered. "Unnecessary and pretentious."

We climbed a few sets of stairs until finally Jaira and Lothar came to a stop in front of a plain wooden door. I caught sight of a small black swan wing insignia engraved into the metal on the door handle.

Jaira faced us. "Welcome to the dorm. You'll meet the rest of our division inside."

"*Our* division?" I asked. "As in, you two are part of it?"

Lothar nodded eagerly. "That's right, great Snowstorm. See, the Black Valkyrie requested—"

Jaira took over. "The Black Valkyrie wants you four to join us in her personal entourage. Congratulations."

I felt a flight of dragonflies rush to my stomach at her words. Looking over, I saw that Jax had gone pale while Solvai and Brigan just seemed surprised. I'd been hesitant about becoming a Mage Hunter in the first place—Now we were meant to be part of the Black Valkyrie's elite team? I didn't know what to think.

Jaira pressed on, clearly enjoying our reactions. "Be grateful—the Black Valkyrie only takes those with real potential. Jax and Meleya, you'll be partners, as will you two, Solvai and Brigan."

Jaira turned to the door, gripping the swan wing-marked handle. "Now, to meet the final pair of new trainees, also hand-chosen by the Black Valkyrie."

Jaira pushed open the door to reveal a vast triangular room. It must've been an entire floor in one of the Academy's corner towers. Unlike the rest of the building, this room wasn't decked in silver, though it looked like that was a fairly recent development. Almost nothing adorned the dark stone walls, leaving the place feeling impersonal and bare. Although, there was nothing to be done about the silver in the mortar, so the room still put off a cold, uncomfortable aura.

Light from outside streamed through a small balcony off of the furthest corner, and a roaring fire warmed the room. On opposite walls, I spotted two doors that Jaira explained led to the men and women's separate sleeping quarters. All at once, the door of the women's side flew open.

"Solei's blade!" squealed a girl with a light eastern accent. "My sister told me you'd be arriving soon!"

She bounded over to us, long dark red hair trailing out behind her and excitement bubbling into her every step. She had a Shadowbinder's silvermark on her left cheek.

"Your sister?" I asked as it dawned on me that this girl looked a lot like Trickshot. I remembered Trickshot mentioning something about her sister starting at the Academy as well. Apparently, she was special enough to have caught the Black Valkyrie's attention.

The young woman nodded. "Torya's just the best. Good at literally everything she does—amazing healer, amazing Hunter, and just *fantastic* with a crossbow." The girl sighed. "One day, maybe I'll be half that incredible. Anyway, my name is Shaya."

That's when I noticed Jax's response to seeing the new girl. His hand had gone slack in mine and he looked like he'd just seen a ghost. His dark blue eyes were as wide as dragon eggs.

I frowned, nudging him. He shook his head and blinked a few times, as if trying to see if the girl would disappear the next time he looked.

Just then, the door to the men's side creaked open. Standing in the doorframe was a tall, bulky silhouette with an untamed mohawk.

No... I thought. It can't be—

"Meet Bjorn of Skullheim." Jaira gave a self-satisfied harumph as she crossed her arms. "Bjorn's one of the most... *enthusiastic* new Mage Hunters to come through the Academy in a while. Though from what I've gathered, some of you already know each other."

Bjorn stalked toward us like a bloodthirsty diamondback wolverine. My old squadmate's eyes were as wild as ever, his fingers twitching as if he were just itching to start a fight.

"Long time, Misthaven." Bjorn's upper lip pulled up on one side in what I could only describe as a mildly feral snarl.

I squared my shoulders as he approached. Bjorn locked eyes with Brigan, who didn't flinch under his gaze. Then, with a sudden, predator-like movement, Bjorn fake-lunged toward Solvai, making her jump backward.

Bjorn smirked. "Still as fearsome a Squad Captain as ever, I see," he mumbled. My jaw flexed. Of all the people I didn't want as a division-mate here at the Academy, Bjorn of Skullheim was extremely high on the list.

Jaira piped up again. "Now, with Ilyan and Shaw out on special assignment, this is all of us. The Black Valkyrie wants the whole entourage together so she can kick off your training and give you your new cloaks. We'll meet her in Swan Spire in an hour."

Jaira gestured toward the balcony. Following her gaze, I caught sight of a tall, black tower standing proudly atop a nearby hill. Six black specks seemed to be circling it, and I realized those were the Black Valkyrie's ethereal swan familiars, guarding the tower.

"In the meantime," Jaira went on, "she's asked me to show you around the Academy. So come on, rookies. It's time for a tour."

Jaira guided us all over the Mage Hunter Academy's main building. There were training rooms, a massive library, a silverforge, a medical wing, and dozens of lecture halls.

But I was hardly focusing on any of it as Jaira chattered on. Rather, Jax and I lagged behind the group.

"You know that redheaded girl," I whispered.

Jax swallowed. "Shaya. She was uh... she was my mom."

That statement earned Jax the most confused look I'd ever made in my life. He shook his head and rushed to explain.

"Not my real mom—I mean, my mom borrowed her face to infiltrate the Knights of the Torch last summer. This girl, the *real* Shaya, she's never set eyes on me. But when my mom was tricking us... none of us knew the truth at first and... Shaya and I..."

Jax trailed off as he stared at the red hair swinging in front of us. Looking at the girl's peppy walk and stunning figure, I suddenly realized Jax had been interested in her romantically.

I grimaced. "She wasn't kiss number seventy, was she?"

"Void, no," Jax said, abruptly coming to a stop. "Though not for my lack of trying, if I'm being honest."

Jax looked down at his feet. I could feel his hand beginning to sweat in mine, as if he were afraid I was seconds away from letting go.

I squeezed tighter. Then I took him carefully by the chin and lifted it so he was looking me in the eye.

"No doubts, remember?" I asked. Jax's face melted, and for a second, so did our surroundings. We leaned closer...

"Hey!"

Jaira's harsh voice snapped me back to the present, and Jax and I dropped hands. I suddenly realized the entire group was staring at us. My cheeks blazing, Jax and I rejoined the tour.

The chilly, silver-infused Academy halls seemed endless, until finally Jaira led us through a set of double doors. Blindingly bright daylight reflected off of the snowy ground and we all had to shield our eyes as we entered the Academy's central outdoor courtyard. Jaira launched into an explanation of how this was where most cadets came to study during the spring and summer months.

I didn't realize I was still lagging behind the rest of the group—even Jax was standing up ahead, listening—until I heard a pair of footsteps prowl up to me from the side.

"How was Outcast Outpost, magi scum?" Bjorn's growling whisper set me instantly on edge. "Obviously not as much a death sentence as I was hoping for."

I grit my teeth, determined not to be intimidated as I replied. "What are you doing here, Bjorn? I thought you got transferred to another squad in the city."

"I did. But when the Hunters came through Archdawn on their way to the Rise, I met Jaira. She saw me tangle with an unregistered Sentinel I found and immediately spotted my talent."

"You mean your thirst for magi blood?" I mumbled under my breath.

My words didn't slip past Bjorn's sharp ears. He must've been waiting for the chance to get a reaction out of me, and I balled my hands into fists as he whipped out his old silver dagger.

"Put that away, Bjorn," I said quietly.

"Why would I do that," he started, "when I've already been learning so much about magi here at the Academy? For example, did you know a Mystic's ether well is near their forehead like some kind of freak third eye? That means it'll hurt you most if I put this here."

Suddenly, Bjorn was pressing the flat of his blade against my forehead. A rush of freezing pain exploded in my head on contact, and I gasped as I rapidly leaped backward out of his reach. The others were still so focused on Jaira, they didn't notice.

Frustration filled me, but I held my head high and bit my tongue as I moved to rejoin the group. Bjorn wasn't worth my attention.

But as I took a step forward, he moved to block me with his hulking frame. I tried to sidestep him, but he shuffled to block me once more.

"Move, please," I grumbled.

Bjorn scoffed. "Why don't you just use a portal to get by, you dirty ethercursed? Or are you still too afraid of your powers?"

Bjorn snarled and prepared to spit at me the same way he'd done so long ago back in Captain Zoren's office. This time, I wasn't going to let that happen.

I had a portal up and going instantly. I caught Bjorn's spit in it, sending it straight back so it hit him directly between the eyes.

Bjorn stumbled back, wiping his face with the back of his hand. When I saw his irises again, they were burning with rage.

Then he gave one of his spine-chilling, maniacal yells as he reached for my throat.

I struck a defensive stance, ready to expand my portal and take him on.

But before I got the chance, both Bjorn and his yell came to an abrupt stop. Jax yanked back on Bjorn's cloak and whirled him around to face him.

Then, in a moment I'll never forget, Jax threw a punch right to Bjorn's face.

Bjorn reeled backward from the impact, but recovered faster than Jax had anticipated. Bjorn dove at Jax and both young men went rolling across the cold, wintery earth of the courtyard. Soon, they were all-out brawling on the ground.

"Jax!" I cried. Glancing around me, I saw that the rest of the division was completely enthralled with the fight, most too stunned or afraid to get involved. Jaira, who, as our leader, should've been jumping in to stop it, seemed to be very much enjoying the display.

I was about to intervene with a portal of some kind when a pair of crossbow bolts stopped the brawl for me. The two bolts pinned both Jax's and Bjorn's orange cloaks to the ground.

"That's enough!" Trickshot's voice rang out across the courtyard. At her emphatic command, both Jax and Bjorn stopped, though they were still glaring at each other, their breathing heavy. Bjorn's jaw was already blooming an angry shade of red, and I saw Jax sporting an injury of his own: A cut bleeding along his forearm. It didn't look deep, but I pressed my lips together with anger as I realized it must've come from Bjorn's silver dagger.

Trickshot scolded the two, then informed Jaira that she'd be taking both of them to the medical wing. She'd send them back when she was finished.

As Jax followed Trickshot out of the courtyard, he cast me an apologetic look. I gave him a proud nod back to let him know he had no reason to be sorry—Someone had finally given Bjorn the punch to the face he deserved.

From there, Jaira continued the tour as if nothing had happened. The others followed her back inside the main building, but I found myself rooted to the spot. Bjorn had just reminded me of why many new Hunters came to this place.

All those lecture halls and training rooms were built for one purpose: Training cadets to hunt down and murder people like me.

With that in mind, the last thing I felt like doing was rejoining Jaira's little tour. I found myself looking around, not sure what to do. I wondered how much time we had before we were supposed to meet with the Black Valkyrie at Swan Spire.

I glanced northward above the Academy walls toward the tall black tower atop the hill. It looked just as majestic and imposing as before, with the black ethereal swans circling the top.

Then I did a double take when I saw a tiny figure racing straight up the side of the tower. A faint trail of gold light seemed to warp the air behind him as he leaped into the window, looking around to make sure he hadn't been seen.

I frowned. Someone was trying to break into Swan Spire.

I shook my head, certain my eyes were deceiving me. Was that a turquoise dust scarf around the intruder's neck? There was no way...

Without a second thought, I focused my sights on that window and opened a portal.

Sure enough, rummaging through the Black Valkyrie's personal things was an unforgettable young man wearing a bright turquoise bandana around his neck. He had messy, jet black hair that looked like it wouldn't stay in its warrior's fangknot if you offered it a hundred gold marks. The short-cropped hair on the sides of his head showed off the dark teal scales on the half-born's pointed ears.

There was no doubt about it—This was the same thief whom I'd caught robbing the command center back on the Rise.

"Asher." I recalled the name Jax had used when speaking of his fellow Knight of the Torch.

I didn't realize I'd spoken out loud until the thief jumped, whirling on me.

"That's me," he replied brazenly.

The thief casually continued rifling through the chest he'd been looking in before my arrival as he spoke. "About time you showed up. You gonna help me out, or just continue standing epically in the window like some kind of needlessly majestic weather vane?"

I cocked my head, feeling inexplicably self conscious as I stepped into the room. "Excuse me?"

"You mean you're not the second representative from the local tower inspection society? Stars, that woman is taking her dear sweet time, isn't she? You certain you're not Frida of Frontier Falls? You definitely look like a Frida."

I frowned with annoyance. "You really don't remember me?"

Asher closed the chest, then glanced up at me for a brief moment on his way to check the desk drawer.

"Sure, sure, I remember you," he said absently, thumbing his way through a stack of papers. "You're that girl who worked the food cart in Naga Bay. Most delicious fried dragoneel west of the Scar, by the way. Ten out of ten."

"No," I growled, taking a step closer. I didn't like his casual tone, or the way he was so flippantly searching the Black Valkyrie's things. He wasn't being very careful—and I *highly* doubted there was such a thing as a local tower inspection society.

"Hmm." The thief scratched his chin. "Then you must've been the girl running the bridge near Longhorn Hill—I knew I'd made quite the impression on you!"

"Enough of this stupid game, thief," I replied. Asher disrespectfully tossed a book over his shoulder, and I drew my seaxe, leveling it at him.

"Oh!" He bonked himself on the forehead. "That's right!"

Suddenly, his face turned serious, his whole joking demeanor vanishing as he looked me straight in the eye. "You're that snowheaded guard who tried to run me through back on the Rise."

We stared each other down for a few more seconds, my brown eyes narrowed as they met his bright dragonfire green ones.

Finally, I spoke. "What are you really doing here?"

His gaze flicked to my sword. "Oh, you know. Normal things. Enjoying the mountain views, getting some cool winter air... robbing the Black Valkyrie."

It all happened so subtly, I didn't realize until that moment that the two of us had begun circling each other. Asher's fingers twitched and he cocked his head.

"But tell me, snowhead. What are *you* doing here?" he asked.

The truth was out of my mouth before I could think it through. "I'm a new member of the Black Valkyrie's entourage."

That did it.

Instantly, Asher's irises flashed gold, and a long, cutthroat dragonhook spear formed in his hands. It was the same one I'd seen him wield before, with a slightly oversized blade and made entirely out of white, crystalline starglass.

My natural response was to runetrace and access ether of my own. A medium-sized, circular portal ripped to life before me, tethered to my forearm so I could maneuver it like a shield.

"Huh," Asher said, eyes widening at the sight of my rift. "That's new."

The rune over my forehead pulsed with golden light. "So, are we gonna do this?"

He lowered his eyebrows. "Absolutely."

We locked eyes one last time, each gripping our weapons as we faced each other. Then, we charged.

Reflection 5

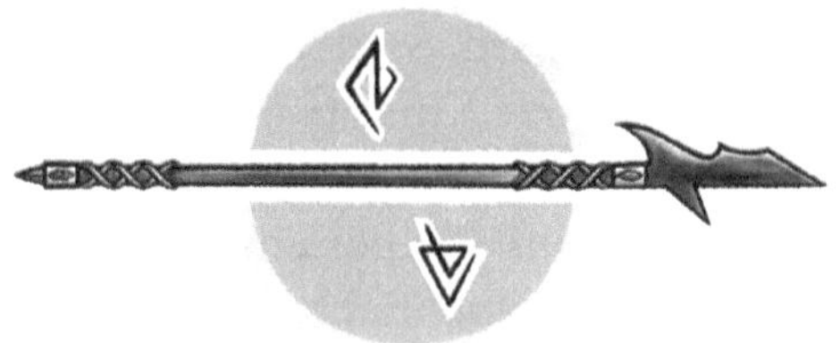

Vidya's calm exterior was cracking. But she knew she couldn't fly off the handle now—Not with the High King in the room.

"But did you not say yourself that the Farseer's ether well was the only one strong enough?" Vidya's jaw clenched.

"We did," the Soul Reaper replied, his odd, doubled voice as chilling as ever. "Only a very powerful well can restore our dear High Prince Mason to full health." As he spoke, he looked down his nose at the young man lying still upon the royal blue bedspread. Everything in the Prince's chambers radiated wealth and excess, from his ornately carved four-poster bed to the jeweled mirrors on every wall.

"But alas, sweet Black Valkyrie," the Soul Reaper continued, "you already had your chance to capture the Farseer for our High King."

Vidya tossed her hair. "Give me one month," she said. "I'll deliver the great Farseer to you on his knees."

"Mason doesn't have a month," High King Magnus piped up. His voice broke as he sat beside his son, clutching the High Prince's cool gray hand. Vidya swallowed. Mason Drakeslayer looked far worse than the last time she'd seen him. His skin, hair, and even his nails were gray, and he looked like he might wither into nothingness at any moment.

High King Magnus was right—Mason would be lucky if he lasted a few more days. Vidya had never seen such a strange case of the shadow wasting. Normally, its victims merely lost all sense of emotion as their skin turned more and more gray, but Mason... Mason hadn't opened his eyes in months. Vidya, like everyone else, wondered what had really happened to him when he'd gone after that frostdrake in the north.

When Vidya had discovered that the Mage Hunter, Lothar, had been the personal servant to the Prince, she'd interrogated him about Mason's recent quest. Long ago, Vidya had read old texts and myths regarding the frostdrake. Most of the writing was vague, but she'd been able to glean one thing for certain: The snow-white drake guarded something far more powerful than any magi in Evgard. Something even more powerful than the Farseer and Solrac's precious Knights of the Torch.

And Mason had slain it.

At the foot of the bed, the Soul Reaper unrolled a pouch to reveal a row of neatly organized surgeon's tools. Each delicate instrument was made from sharply cut, softly glowing crystal. Starglass. Or rather, as the Soul Reaper had called the vivid blue version, voidglass.

The sapphire-colored tools made Vidya shudder. She'd seen them twice before, each time the Soul Reaper had given her a new ether well. Vidya could still feel the chilly tingle in her gut from when he'd carefully stitched the Liberator's well to her soul only last week.

Next, the Soul Reaper produced a clear glass jar. Inside, what looked like an elongated crystal about the size of Vidya's thumb hovered in the center. The ether well was brimming with white light, and little tendrils of pale, red-violet mist danced all around it. Remnants of the previous owner's aura.

"This ether well is small and weak compared to that of the Farseer," the Soul Reaper said as he thoughtfully selected one of his voidglass tools. "We fear it will not be potent enough to save Mason permanently. But as long as we replace it with another before its power fully fades..."

"My son will wake again," High King Magnus finished desperately. "Do what you must, soul surgeon. Anything to save my only child."

The Soul Reaper gave a cold, empty smile. "Then let the surgery begin."

As the Soul Reaper leaned over Mason with his sharp voidglass knife, Vidya swallowed hard. The voice in her head began to laugh, filling her veins with icy stillness.

End of Book 2

Earlier in the Skystone Chronicles...

On the night of Keep Rengard's Winter Solstice Ball, Meleya and the rest of Squad Reckless helped the Black Valkyrie defeat the leader of a dark magi coven. Because of their bravery, the Black Valkyrie invited Meleya, Jax, and the others to enroll at the Mage Hunter Academy in Evyndara. When Meleya learned that her mother had gone to Evyndara to receive the magi cure, she felt she had no choice but to accept.

As a Knight of the Torch and sworn enemy of the Hunters, Jax had his doubts about going to the Academy. But his desire to help Meleya and prove himself to Solrac convinced him to don the dusky blue cloak.

Back at the Knights of the Torch's headquarters in Orothion, there is discord amongst the leadership. Vesta's faction prepares for war with Evgard over their mistreatment of magi, while Solrac and the minority of others who oppose her have been labeled Rebels and forced to flee Orothion.

Elsewhere, the Drekai find themselves engaged in an unwanted conflict with the Canyonlands. Empress Khaisa still struggles to quell the attacks while her thoughts are occupied with the brewing darkness in the spirit plane, Etheria.

Meanwhile, Asher, Kai, and Elle have made their way across Evgard in order to get Elle to one of the realm's last surviving trainers for true dragon riders. The Mirror Forest of the Ridgeback Mountains makes for the perfect training grounds... both for dragon riders and for Mage Hunters.

With danger rising from all sides, the Rebel Knights are growing nervous. But the Farseer fears the Drekai may be right—the greatest threat to the realm may not come from the physical plane. It seems that voidarchy has crept its way into the souls of some of Evgard's most elite, and the Gray Ones are preparing to make their move.

Dragon Hunter – Memory I

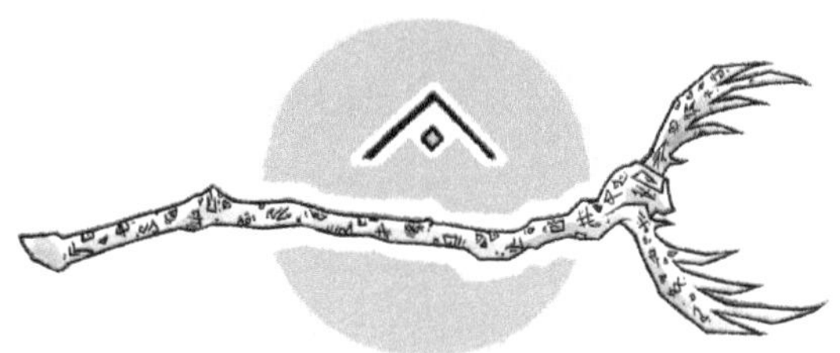

P ure ether.

Solrac knew that an iced-over river at the base of a frozen waterfall wasn't the ideal spot to set up a tent. Especially this high in the Ridgeback Mountains where the wind was so strong.

But the omens had led him there because of its high concentration of ether. Even without using the Sight to see into the ethereal plane, Solrac noted the white layer of faintly glowing ether cascading over the frozen surface of Veil Falls. The raw power source flowed into his tent to fuel his blazing omenfire.

Golden runes pulsed over Solrac's forehead, and he wore the rich, deep red robes of the Farseer as he sat before the golden flames. The flames weren't hot, so at least he didn't have to worry about them melting the icy river below.

All he had to worry about were the terrifying, life-shattering omens that foresaw the imminent doom of the entire realm.

Set on the ground between Solrac and the fire were three objects: a snow white drake's talon, a Drekai scimitar, and a diamond-shaped, wooden hand mirror.

The last was the one Solrac feared the most.

"Let's start with something easier, shall we?" Solrac muttered to himself, turning away from the mirror and reaching for the drake's talon.

The moment his fingers closed around the talon, a vision of the past played within the omenfire.

A blizzard raged around the mouth of a cave. Solrac heard the sounds of rushing wind mingling with low, protective growls. A mighty frostdrake appeared within the mouth of the cave, its icy white jaws opening skyward with an earth-shaking roar.

Facing the drake was a man in his mid-twenties. He donned elegant blue-scaled armor and wielded a jeweled greataxe as he tossed his fair curls.

"Mason Drakeslayer," Solrac said when he recognized the High Prince over all of Evgard.

Flashes of an epic fight between the drake and the High Prince played within the omenfire. Claws clashed against armor until at last, coppery dragon's blood dripped from Mason's greataxe.

Through the powerful memory, Solrac could feel the drake's agony as it lay dying. Feelings of failure pierced through the pain as the wounded High Prince moved to get past the dying drake and into the cave it guarded.

Woosh!

With one final burst of strength, the drake clamped its jaws onto Mason's leg. The young man cried out, falling to the cave floor alongside the frostdrake.

As the drake closed its eyes for the last time, the last thing it saw was a mass of strange, gray shadows descending on the High Prince.

Then, just as swiftly as it had appeared, the vision vanished from the flames.

"Yikes," Solrac said as he gingerly set down the drake's talon. Typically, Solrac sought out omens of the future, or they simply came to him unexpectedly. But memories... memories were far clearer, since the past was much more certain than the future. Still, Solrac was uncertain about whether or not those gray shadows were meant to be literal or symbolic.

Solrac wiped sweat from his brow. Omen reading always left him feeling drained, but on the bright side, since he was out here alone, he didn't have to keep up the epic Farseer presentation side of things too. He needed to focus all his energy—and all of this raw ether—on discovering what was in store for the land of Evgard.

"Perhaps this next one will be a little less ominous," Solrac mused, trying to stay positive as he reached for the Drekai scimitar.

As soon as his fingers wrapped around its long, teal handle, a new vision unfolded within the golden flames. Solrac saw this very blade in action, moving faster than lightning as it clashed against another of similar build.

Two fierce warriors dueled in a clearing surrounded by enormous, gnarled cedar trees covered in thick, green moss. Though he'd never been to the Dragon Isles himself, Solrac spotted the Drekai palace in the background, and it looked like the entire nation of part-dragon people had gathered to watch the fight.

Of course, Solrac knew firsthand that this was no mere fight. This was a Drekai honor duel to the death.

The two female sword fighters dueled ferociously. Solrac wasn't surprised to see that one of them, the woman wielding the teal-handled scimitar, was none other than his old friend, Zerana. Her husband, Akayto, had hesitated at Solrac's request to take his late wife's sword, but Akayto trusted Solrac. At least, he trusted the Farseer, which—though nobody knew it—was essentially the same thing.

This vision showed Zerana at no more than eighteen or nineteen years old, wearing fine Drekai clothing with light chest armor and loose pants that tightened at the ankles. A fine turquoise scarf stood out around her neck, contrasting with the green robes of her opponent.

"Empress Khaisa," Solrac murmured as he recognized the other fighter. He'd seen the empress of the Dragon Isles before in vision, though he knew that currently, the empress was around twenty years older. This memory must've been long before she'd ascended the throne.

"*Ehta nii ikaata!*" Khaisa cried. One of the runes over Solrac's forehead pulsed as he expended a little more ether to make the translation from Drekai to Evgardian play over the vision.

"Don't hold back!" the vision translated. "Use your powers, Zerana!"

"Not until you use yours, true dragon rider," Zerana shot back, weaving her way through Khaisa's guard and knocking her weapon out of her hand.

As the duel continued, the throng of Drekai watching the fight were stomping their feet. Some shouted in support of Zerana, while others favored Khaisa. Zerana's dragonfire green eyes stormed.

Overlaying the vision, the fight seemed to take on a sort of glow—purple light seemed to dance around the warriors while sparks of black frustration and deep green rivalry accented each strike.

"Thank you, symbolism," Solrac mumbled to his omenfire.

Finally, with a cry, Zerana pushed in on Khaisa. A second later, Zerana had her opponent pinned to the ground, scimitar over her neck. Zerana was the superior warrior. The crowd roared.

Khaisa set her jaw, bravely bracing for the killing blow.

"End it," she said.

Zerana froze. From the sidelines, a booming male voice called, "You must finish this, Zerana!"

The vision flashed to the man's pained face. He wore an ornate crown with blue and green jewels that matched the scales along his hairline, cheekbones, and shoulders. It was immediately clear to Solrac that he was looking at the Drekai Emperor, who didn't want to see Khaisa dead, but accepted that their customs demanded an honor duel to the death.

The flames burned brighter as the vision closed in on Zerana and Khaisa's faces. Zerana's betrayed a thousand emotions, ranging from fear to indecision to guilt.

Zerana closed her eyes, slowly raising her blade over Khaisa. Too slowly. Solrac frowned.

In the time it took Zerana to prepare her fatal strike, Khaisa whipped out her emerald heartscale from a cord around her neck. Khaisa moved like an ashviper, eyes glowing gold as she accessed the power of her bonded true dragon.

A golden rune appeared over Khaisa's forehead as she telekinetically threw Zerana backward.

Zerana landed with a thud, but she was smiling. This was more like it.

Zerana dodged a blast of emerald green dragonfire from Khaisa's hand, her own eyes glowing gold as Zerana hover-dashed to close the distance between them. The crowd roared, as did Khaisa's vibrant green true dragon who was watching from the sidelines.

Khaisa reached out a hand to telekinetically pull her fallen blade to her, and the real battle began.

Zerana lashed out with her blades, drawing blood on Khaisa's arm. Golden patterns traced along Khaisa's skin to heal the wound as she responded with a series of slashes of her own. But Zerana's body took on the element of shadow, and Khaisa's blades passed straight through her with no effect.

Zerana was untouchable as the battle wore on, and both the crowd and Solrac could tell that she was toying with her opponent. Despite Khaisa's ability to access many kinds of etherarchy through her true dragon's heartscale, Zerana was still the better warrior.

The odd, symbolic colors from the omenfire still swirled around the duel as it played out in the flames. Frowning, Solrac noted yellow clouds forming around Zerana. He wasn't quite sure what that meant... hesitancy? Perhaps fear? But Zerana was clearly going to win the fight, so what could she be afraid of? Suddenly, the cautious yellow changed to stiff, iron-gray resolve.

Meanwhile, frustration mounted on Khaisa's face. Zerana took a step backward as if to catch her breath, leaving herself vulnerable for only a split second. Solrac's brows furrowed.

At once, Khaisa gathered a massive torrent of emerald green dragonfire all around her. Zerana gasped as Khaisa thrust her hands forward, completely engulfing her in the flames.

The fire blast seemed to continue into eternity. When Khaisa finally pulled back, the crowd was silent as they stared at the pile of ash where Zerana once stood.

For a few moments, there was nothing. Then cheers for Khaisa erupted, echoing throughout the lush forest empire.

The Drekai people swarmed Khaisa to congratulate her on her epic victory, but all Solrac saw were swirling sparks of pale orange confusion surrounding Khaisa's troubled face.

Solrac's expression matched Khaisa's. He'd known Zerana many years after this vision had occurred, which meant that despite what he'd just seen, Zerana had not died that day in the Dragon Isles.

"More of that drakking symbolism, perhaps," Solrac muttered. But what did it mean?

Still reeling from his vision of the Dragon Isles, Solrac turned to the wooden hand mirror lying in wait in the final place on the floor.

He wasn't yet touching the mirror to learn what dark secrets it held, but still, memories filled Solrac's mind at the mere sight of it. He remembered too well the day he'd given the mirror to his new wife after carving the original poem into the back. He knew the lines by heart:

Look to each skyfall that flares through the night
And know that my love burns even more bright

Everything had changed since then. Solrac had become the Farseer. Vidya had become the Farseer's bane, the Black Valkyrie. It was ironic, especially since Vidya had no idea why Solrac had been forced to leave her so soon after their ill-conceived wedding day—as far as she knew, the Farseer was an almighty legend, while Solrac was nothing more than the man who'd broken her heart.

Solrac sighed, turning away from the mirror. Even after all these years, Vidya still possessed a dangerous amount of Solrac's heart.

He couldn't touch the mirror to see what vital memory it held. Not yet.

Suddenly, a surge of ether from the ley lines caused the omenfires to burn higher. Solrac faced the flames and saw a vast, yellowed map of Evgard within them.

Two symbols hung above the map. One he knew well: the fiery beacon of the Knights of the Torch. As for the other... it could only be the triangular icon of the ethereal triad, the symbol of etherarchy.

But wait—A silver sword materialized to stab the triad, causing bright red blood to drip from its center. Screams echoed from within the flames, and Solrac shuddered as he comprehended the symbolism. That was the mark of the Mage Hunters.

Both symbols suddenly came together, bursting with pearlescent white light before ending in a flaming explosion. From that explosion was born an image that made Solrac jump.

An enormous, shadowy dragon seemed to leap out of the omenfire, jaws wide as they clamped around Solrac's head. As the dragon's maw closed, the beast vanished into smoke and the omenfires returned to their neutral golden color.

For a second, Solrac just sat there, frozen in place.

Solrac swallowed hard—He was fairly certain the flames had shown him this strange dragon before. Though, to be fair, this was the first time an omen had tried to bite his head off.

But what does it mean? Solrac wondered. *More wild dragons coming in from the Dragon Mists? Perhaps it represents the Drekai, or even the Gray Ones?* Whatever the symbolism of the marks and the dragon, Solrac feared for the future of the realm. He'd need to consult the omens further, but first, he could use a rest.

Solrac sighed, letting his runes go out. It had been a long, lonely journey into the High Ridgebacks, and it appeared that he wasn't going home anytime soon.

"It's alright," Solrac said to himself. "Some alone time in a dismal, wintery forest with nothing but mysterious symbolism and heatless golden fires just might be the greatest thing that could've possibly happened."

Solrac chuckled, then sat up straighter before accessing his illusion powers to change his regular, lightly accented voice to the deep, excessively grandiose voice of the Farseer.

"Focus, Solrac, Duke of Glacia," he told himself. "There is no time to waste. You must discern the meaning of these omens, and quickly. The future of Evgard depends on it."

ASHER

Even I'd had doubts about stealth-diving into the Mage Hunter Academy in broad daylight.

But as my bonded dragon, Thorn, and I cut through the sunny winter skies above the Mirror Forest, I couldn't help but feel that same rush of adrenaline that always accompanies a risky heist.

Thorn made a low, rumbling roar of agreement. He tossed back his scaly black and bronze head, and I had to duck to avoid getting hit by his majestic, staglike antlers. Through our bond, he sent me a fiery feeling like a blazing bonfire—Thorn loved adventure as much as I did.

I laughed, leaning forward to encourage my dragon to fly faster.

Much faster, Thorn replied through our bond as he obliged.

"Asher! Slow down!" Kai called out. "We're about to come into view of the Academy and I haven't got the illusions up on our dragons yet."

Not far behind Thorn and me, my ever-cautious best friend soared atop his own dragon bond. Kai's stone-colored four-winged evren, Flint, was smaller than my wyvern, but that hadn't stopped Kai from wearing about every piece of heavy plate armor he could. From helmet to chestplate to leg-guarding tassets, Kai was—as always—prepared for the worst.

Against my nature, I urged Thorn to slow down. Kai's finger moved through the air, light trailing behind it. Within moments, a detailed golden rune glowed to life over Kai's forehead. As he completed the rune, the air ahead of and below us seemed to shimmer, then blur ever so slightly. The blur stayed a consistent distance ahead of us as we flew.

"There," Kai said over the rushing wind. "That illusion should mask us from below. Anyone who looks up will only see clear skies. Still, try not to stay in one place too long, since I'm not sure how consistent it will be. The angle should technically be constantly changing relative to our position—"

I didn't *stop* listening to Kai's explanation at that point... My brain just *started* focusing on something else. Anything but Kai's long-winded explanation of the intricacies of his etherarchy. He was a Mystic, the most intellectual of the three magi types. I was never more grateful to be an Archon—When I wanted to use my powers, I didn't have to trace intricate runes I'd memorized beforehand. All I had to do was will it.

Suddenly, I spotted something nestled in the foothills over the next ridge.

"There it is!" I called, pointing.

Sure enough, the Mage Hunter Academy had just come into view. Even from here, I could tell magi like Kai and me weren't welcome there. Three gleaming silver towers shot into the sky, their silver plating accenting the gray stone like a warning. Silver was costly, but I had no doubt they'd spared no expense when it came to showing magi just how much of the anti-ether metal they had at their disposal. The Academy itself was shaped like an enormous triangle with a sword cutting through it—the iconic symbol every Mage Hunter wore on their silver pauldron.

More structures stood imposingly along the mountain to the north, ending with a sharp, black tower proudly overlooking the valley. The tower was tall and thin, with an ornamental design on top that curved elegantly to one side before coming to a sharp, upward-facing point. The shape reminded me of a pair of dark swan wings.

I knew instantly that I was looking at our target. Our enemy sure liked to stick with a theme.

"There's Swan Spire," I called back to Kai.

"That's where we need to go," Kai confirmed. "But we need to be cautious in our approach. Don't stray from the plan, okay Asher?"

"Who, me? When have I ever strayed from a plan?"

Below me, Thorn let out a wyvern chuckle. Silence emitted from Kai's helmet, and I could tell he wasn't about to dignify my comment with a response. That was fair. In fact, I found myself struggling to recall a time where I *hadn't* strayed from my best friend's meticulously laid out plans.

Kai and I shot toward the distinct black tower, closing the distance fast. I noticed a few other glowing golden runes had joined Kai's initial one, forming a row across his forehead.

Asher, can you hear me? This time, Kai's voice didn't come from beside me. Rather, I heard him inside my head, a clear signal that it was time to switch from talking in person to communicating over the mindlink.

On cue, I felt a little wiggle from inside my boot. Kai's ethereal pet mirror gecko, Glint, or at least one of Kai's many copies of her, was hiding in there. Through her, Kai was able to connect with my mind.

Clear as crystal, I thought back. *Then again, I've seen a lot of crystals that aren't clear at all. They're more clouded, you know? Hmm... that phrase is pretty flawed. How about 'clear as water'?*

Asher... Kai started.

You're right, same problem, I cut in. *Maybe 'clear as glass?'*

Thorn chimed in through our bond, *'Clear as air?'*

Chuckling, I relayed his suggestion over the mindlink, then continued, *How about 'clear as my flawless skin?'*

Asher... Even in my head, I could practically feel Kai rolling his eyes.

Right again, Kai, I thought. *But to be fair, that pimple has been gone for days now. You don't have to keep bringing it up.*

ASHER.

Sorry. Focusing now.

If only, Kai's thought was resigned, but I could tell he was smiling. On the inside.

We were now close enough to make out six terrifying black starswans circling Swan Spire. They didn't seem to notice us, which meant that Kai's illusion was working. So far, so good. We were almost within striking distance of that sinister gaggle.

I knew those swans all too well. They belonged to the woman whom I'd hated above all others for nearly five years.

The Black Valkyrie.

I shuddered as we approached her tower. When I'd learned our mission was to rob the Black Valkyrie herself, I'd jumped at the chance—higher than most, since, as an Archon, I could levitate.

Step one, Kai thought over the mindlink. *Take out the starswans. I've got this one.*

Beside me, I saw Kai point a finger at the nearest black swan. Purple energy swirled together into a focused point at his fingertip before he sent it shooting through the air, straight at the starswan's head. As the energy hit, I noticed a subtle shift in the watchbird's flight pattern. Its wingbeats became more rhythmic, its eyes glazing over and glowing purple.

I could sense Kai's satisfaction in my mind. *There. Now, all it will see is the same repeated visual of the forest. You could fly right in front of its beak and it wouldn't see you.*

So, you're saying I—

Kai mentally cut me off. *No, Asher, that doesn't mean you* should *fly right in front of its beak.*

Stars, you're no fun.

I have to balance you out somehow. Plus, we don't know how good a starswan's sense of smell is. This mission is already high-risk enough.

Kai shot more purple energy at the remaining five starswans, complained about how much more efficient his channeling would be if he used a device like a wand or staff, then gave me the go-ahead to move on to step two.

Ready, Thorn? I asked, giving my dragon a pat on the neck.

Hatched ready, he replied eagerly.

Then, I jumped from his back.

The chilly air rushed in my ears, less harsh against the small, dark teal scales along the tips of them. As a half-born, my scaled, pointed ears were one of my most distinct features, and despite the disapproving looks I often got for my Drekai ancestry, I liked to show them off. It was why I kept my jet black hair short on the sides but longer on the top.

As I fell, I could feel my hair coming loose from its fangknot hairstyle. The icy wind contrasted with the warm rays of sunlight on my golden brown skin.

I enjoyed the freefall for slightly longer than I probably should have as the ground rose to greet me. Long enough that Kai sent a panicked warning over the mindlink.

Asher!

I grinned, my eyes flashing from their regular dragonfire green to gold as I burned ether. My archonic levitation abilities kicked in, and all at once, the air stopped rushing around me so quickly.

My hair whipped into my face. Barely resisting the urge to let out a whoop, I threw in a double flip before landing in a crouch on the ground.

I channeled my thoughts through the mindlink. *That. Was. Awesome! Kai, did you see that? Tell me that wasn't the single most epic thing you've ever seen!*

Through my bond with Thorn, I felt a flame of agreement, along with a single word: *Epic!*

Kai was less enthused. *Did you have to add the flip? There must be a lot of silver in Swan Spire, so my illusion was weakened. That stupid flip increased the likelihood that you were seen by nearly fifteen percent!*

Thorn is so much more supportive than you, I mentally grumbled. *Nobody's trained a crossbow on me, so it looks like that fifteen percent can eat soot.*

Moving on, I turned to face the black stone of the building towering before me. I spotted one open window beneath the swan wing-like top of the tower. That would be the simplest way in.

I took a few steps back for extra momentum. Then, I burned more ether, my eyes flashing gold once more as I hover-dashed straight at the wall.

My levitation powers sent me running straight up, my feet all but flying over the stony surface. Again, I fought the urge to whoop as I landed perfectly on the window sill.

Careful, Kai warned, though his voice sounded faint. He must've been right about the silver in the tower stifling his powers.

Relax, I thought back. *I was fast. There's no way anybody saw that.* Still, I did a quick check to my left and right, just in case.

Now hurry, Kai thought, his voice phasing in and out, loud to quiet, in my head. *Next step: Find that key, and fast. I'd estimate that the Black Valkyrie will be back in her tower somewhere in the realm of twenty-one to thirty-five minutes.*

How in the void do you know when that woman will be back? I questioned.

Kai's reply felt strained. *Do you really want me to explain? Because I could tell you every last detail of what combination of runes allows me to run a low ether-signature reverse mindreading hack via contact between her astral familiars—*

No no, I rushed to stop him. *Don't trouble yourself. I beg you.*

Anyway, the bottom line is you should have plenty of time to find the key. It will be the one with the crystal on it. I want you out of there in ten minutes just to be safe.

I only need nine.

With that, I stepped inside the tower.

I hadn't been rummaging through the Black Valkyrie's stuff for long when I found myself staring at a strange, white-haired young woman in an orange cloak who—for the second time in our lives—had drawn her seaxe-style longsword on me.

I was annoyed with her for interrupting my search for the key, but also kind of intrigued. The last time I'd seen her had been miles and miles south in Keep Rengard. She was the last person I'd have expected to find here at the Academy.

There must've been a decent amount of silver in the room, because I hadn't heard Kai through the mindlink at all since coming inside. Even my bond with Thorn felt weak in here. I was on my own.

I'd been trying to stall the snowhead girl, engaging her in somewhat useless banter for the past few minutes while I looked through some of the Black Valkyrie's endless drawers and trunks. No key—so far. First, I'd claimed to be from the 'local tower inspection society,' and when that hadn't worked, I'd pretended not to remember her at all. Her cheeks had grown red with frustration, and she'd only gotten more and more annoyed with every word.

Soot. I'd been hoping to charm this girl into cutting me some slack, but that was clearly not going to work this time.

"Enough of this stupid game, thief," the girl said. She leveled her seaxe my way as I tossed aside a book in my search for the crystal key. Stars, was she always this uptight? I needed to let her know I remembered exactly who she was.

I put a hand to my forehead. "Oh! That's right!" Then I looked her dead in the eye. "You're that snowheaded guard who tried to run me through back on the Rise."

The tension between us was thicker than dragonhide as she narrowed her dark brown eyes. "What are you really doing here?"

My fingers twitched as I glanced at her sword. Was she really going to use it?

"Oh, you know. Normal things," I replied as the two of us slowly began circling each other. "Enjoying the mountain views, getting some cool winter air... robbing the Black Valkyrie."

If Kai's mindlink had been working, I was certain I'd have heard him yelling at me for flat out telling the truth. But I still wasn't certain if this girl was my enemy or not.

Time to find out.

"But tell me, snowhead," I went on. "What are *you* doing here?"

Her response came fast. "I'm a new member of the Black Valkyrie's entourage."

Time froze as her words echoed inside my head. The Black Valkyrie's entourage. For the better part of last summer, that group of good-for-nothing Mage Hunters had relentlessly pursued my friends and me. That confirmed it.

She was *definitely* my enemy.

Without another moment's hesitation, I dug deep to access more ether.

My eyes burned gold as I summoned a weapon of my own. Misty ether coalesced around my hands, turning from glowing, wispy white essence into a solid, super-crystal form. Within moments, I was holding my long, double-bladed dragonhook spear.

In response to my etherarchy, the young woman raised a finger to runetrace. All at once, a round, gold-rimmed portal spun to life just over her arm. Soot—she was a Rifter, a teleportation-based magi. She wielded the portal like a shield as she assumed a perfect battle stance.

For the first time, I noticed the gleaming Rifter's silvermark on her left cheekbone. A symbol carved with silver ink to brand known magi, which certainly hadn't been there the last time we'd encountered each other.

"Huh," I said. "That's new."

The snowhead set her jaw. "So, are we gonna do this?"

I matched her determination. "Absolutely."

Then, we raced to meet each other in the middle of the room, weapons clashing.

My starglass spear didn't shatter on impact with her seaxe-style longsword. That was good. That meant that this would-be Mage Hunter wasn't fighting with a silver weapon. I wouldn't need to resort to fighting with my dad's old skyseeker dagger, or bring out my small stash of silverbane.

We both tried a few more swipes, testing each other out. The snowhead was quick, and clearly well-trained with that sword. She knew exactly how to block, even against my longer weapon.

She kept her eyes fixed on me, but mine wandered to the nearest bookshelf. Would the Black Valkyrie have stashed the key somewhere in there?

"I know who you are," she said, her tone serious. She made a quick offensive swing toward my side, and I jumped backward, both to avoid a hit and to get closer to that shelf.

"Aww, don't tell me I have another stalker." I rolled my eyes. "Helga won't be happy about that—she likes feeling unique."

I jabbed toward her with my spear, but she intercepted it with her arm-portal. Before I knew it, my spear's blade materialized out of a new portal at my side, and I was barely able to hover-dodge out of the way of my own stab.

"Impressive," I said.

"Thanks," she replied.

"Oh, sorry—I meant that was an impressive stab I just made." I winked, which made her frown deepen.

Leaning into her rifting, I dropped my spear with one hand, then yanked it the rest of the way through her exit portal with my off-hand. She hadn't seen that coming, and it bought me the split second I needed to hover-dash over to that bookshelf. I immediately began pulling out books to see if any were hiding crystal-adorned keys.

"So," I began as I worked, "you got a name, or should I just keep calling you snowhead?"

One by one, I tossed books to the ground. My foe made a frustrated grunt, dashing toward me. I prepared to block her next move.

But rather than come at me, she bent low to catch the book I'd just dropped.

Brows furrowed, she locked eyes with me. Then she pointedly shoved the book back into its place on the shelf before swinging her seaxe my way once more.

I blocked, cocking my head. "Passionate about books, are we, snowhead?"

She gritted her teeth. "My name's Meleya."

"Meleya," I repeated.

Meleya plowed on, "You can't just mess with someone's things like this." Pressing her blade into my spear, she reached down to clean up two of the other books I'd chucked.

I snorted. As if I was about to give the Black Valkyrie any courtesy. She was the person I'd spent the greater part of my teenage years so far hoping to kill.

To accentuate my point, I used my off-hand to deliberately grab another book. The snowhead—Meleya—gave me a warning look, and I raised one eyebrow in defiance as I dropped the book to the ground.

She cried out, something between a warrior's yell and that of a babysitter fed up with a disobedient child. One portal ripped to life to catch the falling book, and another tore open to replace it on the shelf.

One look at her told me it was on.

Our fight continued in full force, only now I found myself racing around the room, overturning boxes and throwing cloaks from their hooks on the wall. Naturally, I told myself it was all in search of the key.

Meanwhile, between strikes from her seaxe, Meleya was trailing right behind me, opening portal after portal to try to clean up the chaos I was wreaking on the room. Her mad, tidying escapades were working to my advantage, giving me more time to rummage through drawers and shelves, but there was still no sign of that key.

"I know you're a Knight of the Torch," Meleya said as she caught a framed painting before it crashed to the floor. She followed up with a swipe at me as I came racing by.

I hover-dashed out of reach on my way to a rack of black armor in the corner. "Oh! That explains why you keep trying to kill me. Us Knights don't exactly mix well with Mage Hunters."

For good measure, I bumped against a cabinet, causing a glass bottle to roll off the top of it. Meleya sent a portal racing across the floor to catch the bottle and return it to its place.

"Soot! You have problems," she cursed, training her seaxe on me once more. Her ability to multitask was objectively impressive.

"*I* have problems?" I said, batting away her seaxe while already looking for another place to search. "You're the one who can't help but compulsively clean up after me. It's like you're a forty-five-year-old trapped in a seventeen-something's body."

"Immature son of a dragonmutt." Meleya swung, and I blocked.

"Stuffy scale-in-the-mud." I swung, and she blocked.

"Scarfity scarf-wearer... person," she faltered.

"Wow," I feigned horror. "You always been this good at insults? You really got me there."

She roared and kicked me hard in the chest. I yelped as I stumbled backward directly through a me-sized portal.

Flailing, I reappeared across the room, where I fell over one of the few unopened trunks left in Swan Spire. Both me and the trunk's contents spilled all over the floor.

I gasped when I realized I was sitting in a huge pile of miscellaneous junk—including dozens of keys.

Large keys, rusty keys, shiny silvery keys… and several with crystals embedded in them.

Perfect.

I could hear Meleya rushing across the room toward me, and I knew I only had a few seconds. I rapidly sifted through random junk, pocketing each key that had any sort of crystal attached.

I was just reaching for one under a small stack of yellowed envelopes when my heart stopped. One of those letters was simply labeled, with smooth handwriting bearing a single name:

Zerana of Moss Falls.

I froze, my lips forming the word before I could stop them. "Mom."

I reached for the letter, but at the same moment, a certain infuriating, orange-cloaked, snowheaded Mage Hunter skidded to a stop in front of me, sending most of the junk—including the envelope bearing Mom's name—flying.

Meleya's long seaxe came slicing my way, and I burned ether to hover-launch myself straight upward. I floated there, expertly avoiding her swinging sword.

"Get down here and fight me like a normal person!" Meleya ordered.

"I don't think I'm capable of 'normal'," I chuckled, casually dodging her every attempt as I scanned the floor. I no longer gave a flying scale about any old key—I had to get that letter. Years ago, the Black Valkyrie had brought Mom to the Mage Hunter Academy… and her ultimate doom. What if that letter contained more information regarding Mom's death? I had to know.

Suddenly, I felt a sharp tug on my leg. I burned even more ether to keep aloft as I looked down to see that Meleya had dropped her sword and was now clinging to my leg, trying to pull me back to the ground.

"I said, *get down*," she ordered, dark eyebrows lowered over angry brown eyes.

"But it's so much more fun up here!" I replied. I gave her an unapologetically childish grin as I dropped my weapon as well, then shot toward the ceiling, hoping to both ditch Meleya and get a better view of where that letter had gone.

Unfortunately, Meleya's grip was tighter than I'd expected. Her legs flailed as we both hovered mid air.

"Anyone ever told you you're stubborn?" I grumbled.

"Anyone ever told *you* you're obnoxious?" she countered.

I made the mistake of trying to shake her off, which only made her start climbing up my leg like it was some kind of rope. Soot, she was stronger than she looked. I levitated back and forth to see if I could shake her off, but Meleya held fast.

Meleya gave another frustrated yelp as her hand flew through the air. Gold light trailed after her finger as a new golden Mystic rune shone over the center of her forehead.

Suddenly, a gold-rimmed Rifter's tear ripped open above me. Meleya made a yanking motion with her hand, and the portal dropped downward to encompass my head, shoulders, and torso.

Meleya had placed the exit portal flush with the ground below her feet. My upper half popped out of the floor like I was some kind of gopherdrake.

"Oh, so that's how you're playing it," I laughed. "Maybe you're not as stuffy and dull as I thought!"

"What do you mean stuffy and—hey!" Meleya protested as I reached up to grab hold of her boot as it hung in midair. She kicked to try and get me to let go, still somehow holding fast to my leg as my lower half hung suspended halfway through her portal.

The whole scene was absurd, but I didn't care. With a start, I realized I'd popped out right near that overturned trunk, where I spotted a certain yellowed envelope with Mom's name on it right there on the ground.

I strained, reaching for the letter. I could just feel the bottom corner with my fingertips...

That's when the door slamming open froze us both in place.

Meleya and I turned to see a group of stunned people standing in the doorway. Gleaming weapons hung from their belts, and I recognized at least a couple silver pauldrons with the Mage Hunters' symbol etched into them.

Oh stars.

The rest of the Black Valkyrie's entourage had arrived.

MELEYA

It was hard to tell if my face was so red out of intense frustration or pure embarrassment. Probably both.

"Meleya?" a few people asked when they saw me.

The rest of my team of Mage Hunters spilled into the Black Valkyrie's tower, their expressions ranging from shocked to befuddled to amused as they took in the sight of the trashed room. Despite my best efforts, my scuffle with Asher had left the tower in shambles.

Not only did the group seem astounded by the mess, but for whatever reason they were all staring at me. Yeah, I was still suspended in the air as I clung to Asher's leg, while his top half sprouted through the floor below me to grab *my* leg, so I guess that wasn't something they saw every day. Worst of all was my boyfriend, Jax, who looked almost angry to see Asher and me like this. Drak.

Our group leader cried out in anger as she pointed to Asher. "*You!*" Jaira's intense eyebrows hardened at the sight of him.

Asher gave an obnoxiously casual wave and spoke melodramatically. "This isn't what it looks like, Helga dearest! I swear."

Apparently, Jaira didn't find Asher's joke—whatever it was—funny.

"Get him!" she roared.

At her word, the others rushed toward us. Four of them surrounded Asher in a strategic quadrilateral formation, while Bjorn, my wild-eyed, mohawked ex-squadmate from the army, shot across the room like a bolt from a crossbow. He gave a horrible, maniacal yell that sent shivers up my arms and made Asher's eyes pop.

In an understandable act of self-preservation, Asher let go of my leg and scrambled out of the floor-portal at high speed.

I lost my grip on his leg as it vanished through the portal. I fell, dropping straight through that same floor-portal only to come out falling again through the one above. After looping through both portals twice more, I finally had the brilliant idea of turning off my rune. The portals dissolved into etherdust and I landed on the ground in a crouch.

I noticed Jax was still frozen in place by the doorway, unsure what to do. He stood out with his muscular build, his wild, steely gray hair sticking out from the maroon bandana he always wore wrapped across his forehead. Jax's midnight blue eyes were wide, staring at Asher like he was seeing a ghost. That made sense... I knew they'd worked together before, with a group of outlawed freedom fighters called the Knights of the Torch.

Not that I'd found Asher's behavior particularly knightly.

Meanwhile, the rest of the entourage was engaged in what appeared to be some kind of insane game of drake and drakalope. Excluding Jax and me, six Mage Hunters were all after one hyper-fast, swaggering, teenage Astromancer.

Asher's spear still sat abandoned on the ground, but he used his levitation powers to dart all around the room, gold light warping the air behind him like he was some kind of spastic shooting star. Even maniac Bjorn with his long legs couldn't hope to keep up.

I was puzzled. Asher was clearly outnumbered, so why wasn't he making a break for the window? What could possibly be worth sticking around for?

Asher strategically zipped past the four Hunters still trying to catch him and channeled more etherarchy to form rough starglass weights all along their boots. Lothar, Brigan, Solvai, and Shaya... they were all trapped, just like that.

Most of my fellow Hunters groaned, struggling against their new starglass bonds, but not my friend Brigan. Brigan squared his shoulders and extended his nobleman's jeweled seaxe toward Asher.

"Well played, stranger!" Brigan said, and Asher seemed surprised.

"I thought so," Asher shrugged, not missing a beat.

"Although," Brigan tapped his chin, "I can't help but notice an element of cowardice at play here. It'd be far more impressive if you were to release me and fight me man to man."

For a moment, I thought Brigan's bold argument was going to work. But after a split second of hesitation, Asher shook his head.

"Eight versus one? Nah, I'm good. But I'll take you up on a man-to-man fight with just you sometime!"

"I respect that," Brigan replied thoughtfully.

Asher saluted Brigan, but before he darted away, I couldn't help but notice Asher do a double take at the sight of Shaya—Clearly whatever memories the sight of her had stirred in Jax, Asher had been there as well.

Asher shook it off, then tried to snare Bjorn in starglass as well. But Bjorn didn't slow down at all as he chased his target.

"Fear not, my mohawked friend," Asher said, just barely levitating out of the way of Bjorn's pure silver dagger. "I have something special for you, too."

With that, Asher whipped two tiny crystal vials out of his pocket. Each was filled with a vaguely familiar greenish-gold liquid.

"Eat silverbane!" Asher cried as he chucked one vial at Bjorn's weapon. On contact, the vial shattered, and with a puff of orange smoke, the substance began eating away at his silver dagger.

"Scorch!" Bjorn cried out, frantically wiping the silverbane from the dagger with his pant leg. "Drak you, ethercursed!"

"Language!" Asher pretended to be shocked as he took advantage of the Hunters' distraction. He dove to the ground close to where I stood, and I automatically assumed a defensive position.

But Asher wasn't after me. Rather, he was reaching for something on the ground near my feet... That envelope that had fallen out of the Black Valkyrie's trunk during our earlier skirmish.

But Asher wasn't the only one taking advantage of his foe's distraction. Jaira's silver Mage Hunter's whip moved like lightning—In fact, it even *had* lightning crackling up and down its length. Jaira was a lightwielding magi, though unlike most, her powers didn't bow to silver, nor did they manifest in the usual gold.

Bright blue lightning ran down the length of her whip as she snapped at Asher's wrist to stop him. He recoiled, yelping in pain, both from the sparking lightning and the silver in her whip.

"There's more where that came from," Jaira warned, preparing for a second strike. As she did, her eyes narrowed. "What are you after, half-born?"

Her gaze traveled along the ground, searching. Just before it landed on that envelope, I stepped to the side to hide it beneath my boot so she wouldn't find it.

Asher cast me a grateful, somewhat-confused look. I was a little confused myself.

I wasn't entirely sure why I did it, but I was certain that if Jaira found that envelope, she'd do everything in her power to either destroy it or lock it up forever. Whatever was in that letter was valuable enough to Asher for him to risk his life, and I had a faint idea why. I'd heard what he'd involuntarily said when he'd first spotted the envelope.

Mom.

If there was one thing I understood, it was wanting to protect one's mother.

That's when Asher chucked his second crystal vial, this time at Jaira. With a puff of orange smoke, the odd substance began disintegrating the silvery armor of her Mage Hunter's uniform, from her oversized shoulder pauldron to the very buckles on her overtunic.

Jaira cried out. The substance didn't harm her skin, but she had to drop her whip to hold her shirt together. A few people snickered, and even I couldn't hold back a small snort.

With all of his active pursuers at least somewhat incapacitated, Asher scrambled to his feet. He leaped into the open window, turning around for one last look into the room.

First he locked eyes with Jax, who was still frozen near the tower's entrance. Next, Asher's bright, dragonfire green eyes settled on me, and he gave me an over-the-top salute.

Then, he jumped out the window.

For a ridiculous second, I wondered if he could survive a fall from this high. Then I realized he didn't have to.

Already racing westward into the Mirror Forest was Asher, sitting astride a large, black-and-copper wyvern. Within seconds, they'd disappeared into the thick foliage.

Inside Swan Spire, there was a moment of silence as we watched the thief get away. Then suddenly, Jaira screamed with rage.

"Chase him down!" she roared. "We can still nab him if we're fast. Riders, call your scorching dragons and let's—"

"No."

We all jumped at the sound of the smooth, even voice in the doorway. Standing proudly and wearing an all-black Mage Hunter's uniform, her cape adorned with inky swan feathers, was the Black Valkyrie herself.

She tossed her ash-colored hair over one shoulder as she calmly strode into the room. Aloofly, she observed the state of her sanctuary. Despite my efforts to keep it intact, Asher's mad search and the subsequent brawl with the other Mage Hunters had left Swan Spire in utter disarray.

The Black Valkyrie held our silent attention as she moved about the space. When she passed the Hunters still weighed down by Asher's star-glass, she casually used her silver-tipped spear to shatter it and free them.

I caught sight of Jax's expression as he stood across the room. His brow was knit, and I noted the tension in his sharp jawline as he watched the Black Valkyrie.

The Black Valkyrie had barely glanced his way upon entering the tower. She hadn't given him any more attention than the rest of us, but then again, how could she? Jax's relationship with the legendary leader of the Mage Hunters was a secret—Out of everyone here, only I knew that Jax was the Black Valkyrie's son.

"Did the thief take anything?" the Black Valkyrie finally asked.

I jumped when all eyes turned on me.

"Uh…" I began, "just a handful of keys from that chest over there." I pointed to the overturned junk trunk. "And… that's all."

A tiny bead of sweat formed on my temple as I kept my foot solidly rooted in place over that envelope. The Black Valkyrie's lower eyelids squinted slightly, but she didn't question me.

I breathed a sigh of relief as she turned away, continuing to observe the room. I felt an inexplicable obligation to keep that letter about Asher's mom safe.

Maybe it was because my own mother was the reason I was here at the Academy in the first place.

Mom's words from the note she'd left for me still rang in my ears:

Dear Meli… I spoke with the Black Valkyrie… Asked her if I could receive the magi cure. Once I'm free from this curse, I'll find you and Dad.

It was common knowledge throughout Evgard that the Academy was where they were working on perfecting the magi cure. The cure I'd once longed to receive myself. Now, the idea of someone stripping me of my etherarchy filled me with dread.

I had to find Mom. Even if I was too late to stop her from giving up her powers, I had to get her out of here and back to Dad.

"We have far more important things to worry about than a silly thief," the Black Valkyrie declared. She dramatically raised both hands into the air, using one to trace a rune. Like Jaira, her etherarchy appeared sapphire blue rather than the typical gold.

At once, dozens of scattered items began telekinetically rushing back to their places. Overturned trunks righted themselves as picture frames straightened. Within seconds, the room had returned to perfect order. I liked that rune.

Then I felt the envelope under my foot trying to zip back to its trunk as well. Rather than let it go, I ducked to grab it, crumpling it slightly when I stuffed it securely into my tunic pocket.

Only Jax seemed to notice anything out of the ordinary, and I winced when he gave me a suspicious look. Soot, we needed to talk.

"Now, on to business," the Black Valkyrie announced. "Welcome, new members, to my team of elites. Despite this most recent failure, you've proven your excellent potential as Hunters, and I'm glad to have you join me on our noble quest to protect the realm."

The Black Valkyrie made her way to the doorway once more as she went on. "I don't know what news you all have heard as of yet, so allow me to get you up to speed."

She turned to face us all, her posture impeccable and her expression proud. It made me want to stand up straighter myself.

"Evgard is on the brink of chaos," the Black Valkyrie went on grandly, as if she were performing for a large crowd "As you well know, the increase in skyfalls has not ceased. Wild dragonkind are a greater threat to the realm than ever before, and rather than pursue a common goal in unity as true Evgardians ought to, some have seen fit to form their own factions."

She nodded toward where Solvai, Brigan, Jax, and I stood. "I know those of you from Squad Reckless are all-too-familiar with the Coven of the Gray Ones." A shiver went down my spine as I thought of the gray-masked, hooded magi we'd battled multiple times in the past several months.

The Black Valkyrie looked down the bridge of her nose at each of us. "They have come to the conclusion that magi are superior to the regular citizens of Evgard."

Bjorn growled, narrowing his eyes at me and the other magi in the room. I tensed, ready to grab my weapon. I doubted he'd actually try anything right now, but Bjorn had long hated me for my etherarchy.

"In a way, they are right," the Black Valkyrie ignored Bjorn. "Magi have something that most do not. Etherarchy."

With that, the Black Valkyrie's irises flashed bright blue. As she accessed her archonic powers, black shadowfire ripped along the blade of her spear and she levitated just above the ground, her black cloak fluttering. The spectators, myself included, were fixated on her display of power.

"Etherarchy is a tool," she continued, "to be allowed only to the few strong and deserving enough to use it. We are among these few."

"And the rest?" Jax asked darkly.

The Black Valkyrie frowned, as if contemplating how she wanted to answer. In the end, she shook her head, then dismissed her shadowfire and landed back on the ground before us. Rather than reply to her secret son's question, she pushed right past it.

"But the Coven is not the only magi-related threat that Evgard faces in its hour of need," the Black Valkyrie went on. "The Knights of the Torch are equally dangerous." Jax was positively glowering at his mother.

"The Coven of the Gray Ones and the Knights of the Torch are two sides of the same coin." She traced a new rune, then flourished her hand to produce a shimmering, translucent illusion of a coin floating just in front of her. On one side of the coin, I saw a depiction of a blank mask with glowing blue eyes—the symbol of the Coven. The Black Valkyrie rotated her hand and the coin followed the motion to reveal another symbol on the back: A beacon of light.

The Black Valkyrie went on, "The Knights see the plight of the magi as an opportunity to usurp power, rather than follow their responsibility to aid their fellow Evgardians. In a flagrant act of war, they have attacked and pillaged three towns along the shores of the Capital Keepdom of Evgard itself just this past week."

"That's a sooty lie..." Jax mumbled under his breath, so quietly I doubted anyone but me heard him.

"It seems the Knights are finally bold enough to emerge from the shadows," the Black Valkyrie said, ignoring him. "For too long, they've hidden behind the smokescreen of myth, hiding out in Skygard, their beloved patron, the Farseer, only appearing every now and again to show off his power. But now... well, see for yourselves."

With that, she made another dramatic motion with her hand, and her coin illusion grew larger. Its surface changed to show a scene of a scowling woman with a Geomancer's silvermark on her left cheek. An army of men and women surrounded her, wearing red cloaks bearing that same beacon of light symbol I'd seen on the Black Valkyrie's illusory coin. The woman led her troops into battle, hurling shards of geomantic slate at the innocent people of the city as they tried to flee.

A fiery lump instantly formed in my throat as I watched the horror unfold. As a soldier, I'd been taught above all else that our job was to protect the citizens of Evgard. I hated what I was seeing, and tried to make eye contact with Jax. Could this be true? But even as an undercover Knight of the Torch himself, Jax seemed taken aback.

The Black Valkyrie's voice held the perfect amount of sorrow. "Even now, the Knights prepare to launch more brutal attacks such as this."

She let the illusion play out a little longer to drive home her point, then cut it off with a flourish of her hand.

"I hope you each can see the importance of our mission," the Black Valkyrie said, taking the time to make eye contact with each person in the room. When she got to me, she gave an understanding nod.

"Now, it's time we got you into your new uniforms. Jaira, it looks like you need one the most." The Black Valkyrie raised an eyebrow, and I realized poor Jaira was still holding the collar of her newly buttonless tunic together with her hands. Jaira shot the rest of us a glare, effectively getting everyone to look away.

"Come along," the Black Valkyrie beckoned for us to follow her out of Swan Spire. "It's time to turn you all into official Mage Hunters."

Like the rest of the grounds and the buildings, the Mage Hunter Academy's armory was imposing, grand, and positively jam-packed with silver.

Silver armor lined one wall, while silver weapons lay on racks set up throughout the vast space. And, of course, there was the ever-present silver in the mortar between the bricks of the walls.

I shuddered. As a magi, the presence of so much silver sent chills up my arms and made the whole place feel frigid and isolating.

The Black Valkyrie had told us to pick out our uniforms and new weapons, and I already saw Jaira, Bjorn, and the others eagerly selecting theirs. Jaira very much needed a new tunic after her brush with Asher's silverbane, and Bjorn had already selected a shiny silver pauldron from the racks, then moved onto the weapons section. Though Asher's vial of silver-eating substance had damaged Bjorn's dagger earlier, I saw him proudly clip the blade to his belt alongside his new silver long seaxe. The silver dagger looked even more terrifying now, with rugged, jagged points lining one side.

For a moment, I just stood there, looking over the wall of armor. According to the Black Valkyrie, there were a few shoulder pauldrons set aside for Hunters who were magi. Thankfully, they weren't forged from silver, but from shiny steel.

Unfortunately, it wasn't easy to tell the difference visually, and I didn't exactly feel like touching each painful piece of silver armor to find out.

Suddenly, a strong hand appeared on my back, and I turned to see Jax at my side. When he looked down at me, dragonflies hummed to life in my stomach.

"You okay, M?" he asked, his voice low.

"I could ask you the same thing," I replied.

"Wanna tell me what really happened in Swan Spire?"

"What do you mean?"

Jax grimaced. "I mean, uh, you know. With Asher. You remember who he is, right? That he and I are both..." He looked around to ensure nobody was close enough to hear us. "That Asher and I are both Knights of the Torch?"

I nodded.

Jax went on. "So, what was he up to? What mission was he on?"

I swallowed, sidestepping Jax and heading for the rack of tunics. He followed, and together we looked for uniforms in our sizes.

"Like I told the others, he was looking for a key," I said as I sifted through the rack to find the women's tunics. "And I don't know much more, since I was too busy fighting him."

"Fighting him?" Jax scoffed. "You knew I worked with him and you still fought him?"

"He was asking for it," I grumbled. "Just thoughtlessly messing up the tower like he *wanted* to be a jerk. And he was so... so annoyingly casual, I just panicked. I don't know." I pulled a tunic off the rack and held it against me to see if it fit.

"Drak," Jax cursed. He had a tunic in his hands too, and I watched as he whipped out one of the twin axes he always kept strapped to his back, then used the fanged point on the blade to cut at the seam where the sleeve connected to the shoulder. Once he'd torn through, he put away the axe and ripped the rest of the sleeve off with his hands.

The sound of tearing fabric drew some attention from the rest of the group. I particularly noted my two best friends from the army, and now fellow Hunters, watching us. Solvai chuckled and shook her head, brown waves falling around her freckled face. She'd been one of Jax's squadmates as well, and knew that his trademark look included going sleeveless to show off his incredibly toned, muscular shoulders and arms.

On the opposite scale, Brigan pressed his lips together with annoyance. As a proper nobleman, Brigan always wore his uniform exactly as intended, and even kept his dark hair perfectly smooth, other than the single corkscrew curl over one side of his forehead. Meanwhile, Jax's gray hair always stuck out of his maroon bandana at wild angles.

Brigan gave me a meaningful, almost longing look, and I found myself blushing and looking away. In more ways than one, Brigan and Jax were at odds.

Jax had slipped out of his guard's overtunic and was pulling on his new Mage Hunter's tunic. He was clearly flustered, and his large, rough fingers struggled with the smallish buckles.

Wordlessly, I put my hands on his. Then I began doing up the buckles for him. Luckily, they weren't silver the same way Jaira's had been.

"I'm sorry," Jax muttered. "I just hate feeling so disconnected from the other Knights. There's so much going on while I'm here undercover."

"You mean the Knights of the Torch's schism?" I whispered.

Jax nodded. "I don't know who's with Solrac and who isn't. I'd try asking Kai through the gecko mindlink, but..." Jax trailed off, squeezing his eyes shut. He seemed conflicted as he went on. "But I'm not entirely sure if Kai and Asher are on the right side, either. M, we have to get your mom and get the void out of here. Then we can find Solrac and join the rest of the Rebel Knights."

My fingers froze as I latched the last strap on Jax's tunic. I looked up at his earnest expression, guilt washing over me.

I knew that being at the Academy, so close to his estranged mother, was the last thing Jax wanted to be doing right now. But as far as his plans for *after* the Academy...

"Jax," I started, finishing with the buckle before gently laying my hands on his broad chest. "You know I'm not a Knight of the Torch."

"For now," Jax replied, looking deeply into my dark brown eyes. It might've been my imagination, but I could've sworn I felt his heartbeat pick up through his tunic. "But you will be soon," he continued.

"I'm not so sure," I said. "You heard what the Black Valkyrie said about those cities near the capital. You saw the Knights of the Torch slaughtering innocent people."

"Who gives a scorching scale about what that woman says?" Jax set his jaw.

"So you think she lied?" My dark brows knit. "Or you think it wasn't really the Knights of the Torch who killed all those people?"

"Solrac wouldn't allow that," Jax said, trying to convince both me and himself.

"Maybe not," I said. "But I'm not ready to choose a side right now. I've always thought the Mage Hunters were the enemy, but I saw what the Black Valkyrie did to help us stop the Coven in Rengard. And if she's right about what the Knights are doing... I just don't know what to believe. For now, all I want is to bring my family back together after years and years apart. I'm only here to find my mother."

Jax took a step backward, and my hands fell from his chest. There was a storm in his midnight blue eyes as he replied.

"And I'm only here for you."

I opened my mouth to respond, but before I got the chance, the Black Valkyrie's voice rolled throughout the armory.

"Finish up quickly, then gather around," she ordered.

Jax and I gave each other one last look, then hurried to gather the rest of our new uniforms. We found the steel pauldrons then chose our weapons. Every long seaxe was made from an alloy of silver, but most had a leather-wrapped handle so I could wield mine while still accessing my etherarchy.

Once the group had assembled, the Black Valkyrie ceremoniously gestured to a row of pegs along the wall. Hanging from each peg was a crisp, new Mage Hunter's cloak.

As I swapped out my orange guard's cloak for the dusky blue Hunter's cloak, I felt my chest constrict. I had to force myself to breathe evenly as I latched it on, and I couldn't help but feel as if I was trading one form of servitude for another.

First, I'd been forced to join the guard in order to keep my magi parents from execution. Then, the Black Valkyrie had given me little choice but to join the Mage Hunters. Meanwhile, Jax wanted me to join the Knights of the Torch, and I still didn't know which side was right. Would my choices ever be my own?

At the thought, a cold wave flowed through my veins like ice. Darkness filled my chest, and faint blue light played at the edges of my vision.

Oh no. Please, not now—

Meleya... a raspy voice whispered in my mind, and my breath caught. I hadn't told anyone about the wraith—At least, I hadn't told anyone that I'd been feeling a dark presence following me ever since that night on watch duty in Rengard Canyon's North Tower.

"Meleya?" Brigan's voice pierced my reverie, his warm, familiar brown eyes filled with worry. I realized my anxiety must've been showing through on my face.

"You okay?" Solvai appeared at my other side to put a hand on my shoulder. The shadows rapidly fled my mind, the coldness dissipating.

For now.

I turned to see Solvai giving me a meaningful look. She'd been my closest friend for so long, and I knew right away she could tell I was hiding something. Soot, Solvai had always been dangerously observant. It didn't help that I was the realm's most terrible liar.

Still, I gave it my best shot.

"I'm fine."

I bit my lip as I looked at my friend. I was hoping she'd move on without question, but I expected to see skepticism on her freckled face.

Instead, she looked up at me with so much hurt in her hazel eyes that I had to look away. She hadn't said a word, but I could tell that she felt betrayed.

I swallowed the lump in my throat. As much as I wanted to tell Solvai what I was going through, doing so felt impossible. I hated how powerless

I was against the mysterious spirit demon, and for whatever reason, that made me feel ashamed.

Besides, I cared too much about my friends to share this burden with them. Jax, Brigan, Solvai, not to mention Edrea and the other members of my squad… I had to protect them.

That was the other reason I wanted to stay at the Academy—The wraith wasn't the only dark weight I was carrying around. I had questions, and I got the feeling that the person who could best answer them was standing right in front of me.

"Very good," the Black Valkyrie said, looking over our new uniforms. "As members of my entourage, you'll spend each morning training with me or Jaira in Swan Spire. In the afternoons, you'll join the other new cadets in regular classes. For now, take your old things back to the dorm and get settled. It's been a long day, and you'll need your rest before training begins tomorrow at dawn."

She dismissed the group, and I was about to return to the dorm with the others when the Black Valkyrie called for me.

"Snowstorm," she said, using the title she'd given me after we'd fought alongside one another at Keep Rengard's Winter Solstice Ball. "If you'll stay behind, I'd like a word."

I immediately glanced at Jax, who had been about to leave the armory. He stopped in his tracks, then turned around with a look that made me think he'd rather don real, pure silver armor from head to toe than leave me with his mother for five minutes.

"Alone, please," the Black Valkyrie said, not looking at her son. I watched Jax's expression crumble at her words, and my heart ached for him as he hurried out the door.

As the Black Valkyrie telekinetically shut the door to the armory behind Jax, I sensed a hint of pain in her face as well. I got the feeling that it wasn't easy for her to pretend Jax meant nothing to her, but she felt she had no choice if she wanted to protect him.

As quickly as the crack in the Black Valkyrie's proud demeanor had appeared, it vanished as she turned to me. "I know it's only your first day here at the Academy," she said, "but I'd like to ask a favor, Snowstorm. You see, with your particular abilities, you're the only one suitable for the job."

A bundle of nerves jumped into my stomach. One look at the Black Valkyrie's proud, determined expression told me she wasn't likely to take no for an answer.

"What do you need?" I asked.

Her midnight blue eyes blazed with an inner fire. "I'd like you to join me on a highly classified mission. The Farseer has been spotted in the High Ridgebacks, and I need you to help me capture him once and for all."

I inhaled sharply, eyes growing wide as the Black Valkyrie continued. "We leave at first light."

The story continues in:
The Skystone Chronicles, Book 3:
Dragon Hunter

A Brief Guide to
EVGARD

By Blake & Raven Penn

the skystone chronicles

Mystic
Mind

Seer

Seers are Mystics that can access telepathic runes. Some of the more basic runes enable them, to read minds or see omens of the future, while more advanced runes can enable mind control, precognition, and memory wiping.

Method of Accessing Ether

- Mystic ether wells are located in their minds. They trace runes of golden etherlight in the air to achieve mythic effects. Mystics must know the correct runes and have the right intention behind them, and each rune requires a certain amount of ether. Once the rune is completed, it appears over the Mystic's forehead.
- Runes can also be carved onto objects to save time. This is most commonly seen with runemarked wands or staffs. We once met a certain Mystic who'd even carved psionic runes onto a whisk. The meringue was delicious.

Shared Power: Dreamweave

All Mystics can access the Dreamweave. In the most basic terms, the Dreamweave deals with illusions.

This can manifest through simple runes to trick the eyes, or more advanced runes to trick the other senses. Some runes enable the use of dreamblades—weapons made of focused, purple dream energy that passes through physical objects, but drains the soul's vitality and the victim's stamina. Quite inconvenient when someone blasts you midway through a meeting about the end of the world.

Additionally, the Dreamweave can be used to make illusory bodies for ethereal familiars, which, for lack of a better term, are almost like a solidified imaginary pet.

Psion

Psions are Mysitcs that can access telekinetic runes. More basic runes enable pushing, pulling, or holding objects in place. Psionics only work on non living things (like rocks or metal), and they require more ether to move things that were once living (like wood or leather.)

Rifter

Rifters are Mysitcs that can access teleportation runes. The most basic runes involve making portals through Etheria (the spirit plane), while more advanced runes allow them to make anchors, rift holds, and access the Sight to see into Etheria itself. Rifters can only open portals to places they can see or to an anchor.

The Skystone Chronicles

Sentinel
Body

Method of Accessing Ether

Sentinel ether wells are located in their core, near the belly button. Their mythic powers are more instinctually driven, and generally require a physical totem of some kind for use. A Geomancer's totem might be a volcanic stone or granite, while a Wildshaper's might be a wolf's fang or a dragonhawk's feather. A Woodweaver's totem could be a leaf or a piece of amber.

When Sentinels access their ether, golden patterns appear on their bodies around whatever area is being affected.

Wildshaper

Wildshapers are fauna-based Sentinels. They can take on aspects of and transform into animals for which they have a totem. This is commonly used to enhance senses or gain a creature's strength or agility. Full transformations are typically accompanied by a cloud of golden ethermist. Careful—that desert finch perched on your sill might not be what she seems.

Geomancer

Geomancers are earth-based Sentinels. Using a totem take from a certain environment can grant them aspects of power related to that environment. A totem of sandstone might be used to make sandstorms, while a stalactites totem could grow into a large club. A common use we've seen is to make one's skin hard as stone, so try not to make any Geomancer enemies. Trust us, they know how to take a hit.

Woodweaver

Woodweavers are flora-based Sentinels. They can use their ether to manipulate and even generate plants based on what totems they have. Some use this power to keep an endless supply of freshly-grown arrows in their quiver or grow diamondoak armor. Others maintain their crops even throughout the winter months. Some have even discovered the secret to making plant servants, called Folians.

Shared Power: Regeneration

All Sentinels share the power of regeneration. This enables them to use their ether to heal wounds. They can train to heal themselves more quickly or learn to heal others. Sentinel regeneration does not work on wounds caused by the anti-ether metal, silver.

The Skystone Chronicles

ARCHON
Spirit

Lightwielder

Lightwielders are Archons that manipulate light. Different forms of light carry different properties. Commonly, lightwielders use lightning for raw power or liquid light to heal. Lightwielding can reveal things hidden using etherarchy. Less commonly, these Archons can concentrate light into blades or barriers of a weightless, solid material called Luxite.

Method of Accessing Ether

- Archon ether wells are located in their hearts. They achieve mythic effects through the will of their spirits. When they command ether, their eyes glow gold. When an Archon learns a new way to use their ether, it is typically through a "breakthrough" during a moment of intense emotion.

Shadowbinder

Shadowbinders are Archons that manipulate darkness. Solid darkness forms shadowsilk, while darkness in its plasmic form makes shadowfire that slowly disintegrates anything it touches. It's actually quite useful in sewer systems. Shadowbinders can even use their affinity for darkness to turn invisible and pass through objects.

Shared Power: Levitation

All Archons share the power of levitation. This entails Archons using their ether to manipulate how they move. It's most commonly used to make themselves lighter and faster, through hover-jumps and hover-dashes. Levitation has its limits, and in the past thousand years, we've only met one who learned how to use this ability to fly. An Archon manipulating their movement in this way leaves a faint trail of warped golden light behind them as they go.

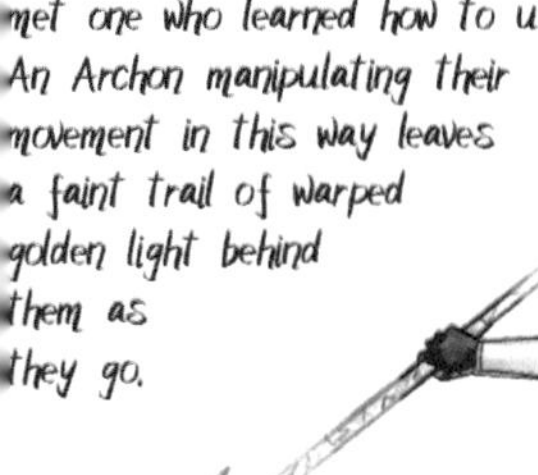

Astromancer

Astromancers use ether to manipulate ether itself. They can condense ether into starglass objects that will last a day, or blast ether directly. Ether leaves a white mark, and hurts both physical and ethereal creatures. It can stop dream energy as well. Some Astromancers can even sense where ether is, and what type is being used. Very few can give their ether away, and even fewer can take it from others. We think it's a latent astromantic sense in dragons that enables them to hunt magi by sensing their ether wells.

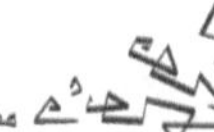

the skystone chronicles

True Dragons

True dragons are what your world generally thinks of as simply... dragons. They are great, intelligent, flying beasts with armored scales, four legs, two wings, and a tail. They vary in color, length, size, and style of horns. Every true dragons can command all nine types of etherarchy as well as breathe dragonfire, which produces an ultra-hot, emerald-green flame.

Since the Dragon Wars, true dragons are incredibly rare in Evgard.

Dragon Eyes

The eyes of dragons are a burning emerald green, just like their dragonfire. All dragons (as far as we know), even lesser dragons, share this trait.

A Note On True Dragon Eggs

Usually no larger than a fist, True Dragon eggs harbor immense power. Their shell tends to be scaly, with a color matching the scales that the hatchling will have. Hatchlings are always bigger than the space the egg could have contained, which implies they must have some form of rift hold within them. The shell ought to be saved for its mythic properties.

Dragon Blood

While true dragons have gold blood, the blood of drakes, wyverns, and evren is more bronze or copper in color. Some like a few drops in their draquila, but it was a little acrid for our taste.

DRAGONS

DRAKES

Drakes are dragons with four legs and no wings. They're commonly built like this worlds panthers or tigers, but more serpentine. They vary greatly in appearance, though most are large enough to carry two human riders on their first ascension.

Dragon Bonds

All dragons have a heartscale. It's found on their chest, near the heart. Dragons and humans can forge a bond if the dragon gives the human their heartscale. This grants the human power over the dragon, while enhancing the dragon's own cognitive abilities.

Evren

Evren are dragons with four wings and no legs. They have small claws on the joint of each wing which they can use to crawl, but evren are much more suited to the air. They tend to have more canine features, almost like this worlds flying foxes. Evren prefer to sleep hanging upside down from trees or cliffsides, and are usually only large enough to carry one human rider at a time until their second or even third ascension.

Wyverns

Wyverns are dragons with two wings and two legs. Their wings have well-developed claws at the wing joint, allowing them to navigate the ground far better than evren, though not as well as drakes. They are the most snakelike of the dragons, and tend to have longer necks and tails. When it comes to size, they're generally larger than evren, but smaller than drakes.

Ascension

Evgardian nobility jealously guard the secret to dragon ascension. Still, we suspect the trigger to a dragon's ascension has something to do with their hunger for ether. When a dragon ascends, their ability to communicate grows, and they advance in mythic power, if they have any. Third ascension is the highest level of dragon ascension that we currently know of.

Ether Hungry

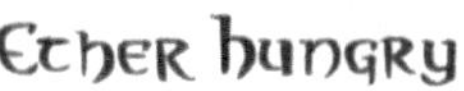

Dragons love ether. They will take it from any source they can find, even human magi. It is for this reason that magi are outlawed in Evgard—their ether is what draws wild dragons to the Keeps.

the skystone chronicles

Evgardian Creatures

Draconic Animals

There are countless draconic animals in Evgard. From draccoons to wyvernhogs to aldraka, the draconic lifeforms have supplanted most non-mythic animals. Some of our favorites are Kirin, which are draconic horses, and lutradons, which are large, scaly otters. There's nothing more fun than splashing around and riding a lutradon in the riverbank.

Ethereal Familiars

Ethereal familiars are not well understood. Born of etherarchy, these creatures act as an extension of the magi who created them. They develop their own distinct—and often strong—personalities as well (we once had rather an interesting encounter with a passive aggressive shrew). While all magi types technically have the capacity to create one, Mystics tend to do it most, using a complicated set of runes that manifest on the skin of their familiar.

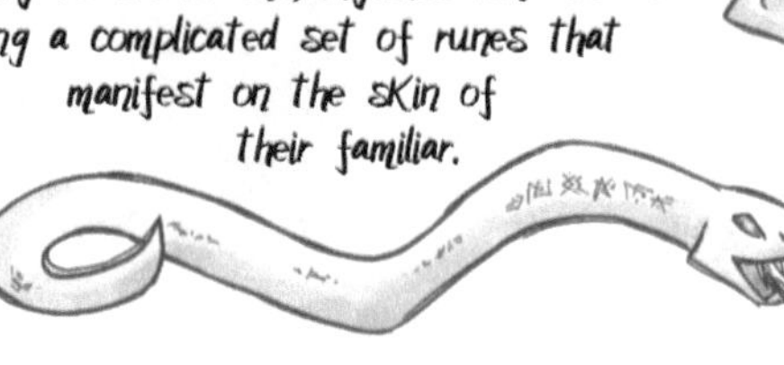

Umbrals

Umbrals are creatures corrupted by the shadow wasting. They fade until they become a smoky gray version of what they once were. They have lightning blue eyes. The bite of an umbral spreads the shadow wasting, though it will not turn humans or dragons fully umbral.

The Guard

The Canyonlands Guard, as well as the guards of the other Keepdoms of Evgard, fulfill one need above all others: Protect the realm from wild dragons. New recruits typically spend three years in basic training, followed by an initiation trial to weed out weak soldiers. After that, the captain and commanders divide the soldiers into squads of seven, each with a different, yet complementary skill set. A squad's performance during their first battle will (for better or worse) determine that squad's name. It's worked out well for soldiers on 'Squad Valient' and 'Squad Deathblade', while those from 'Squad Choke' would like a word with the creator of that tradition.

*note: Soldiers who ride flying dragons typically wear a lighter version of the guard uniform.

Soldiers train with each of the three common Evgardian weapons (long seaxe, dragonhook spear, and scaleslayer crossbow). Ultimately, soldiers will choose which to specialize in. Alternative weapons (such as fanged axes or warswords) are allowed.

the skystone chronicles

Outcast Outpost

Perhaps the most dangerous station in the entire realm, Outcast Outpost lies on the southern tip of Rengard Canyon, just north of the deadly Dragon Mists. The Dragon Mists are home to a constant stream of wild dragons and dragonKind. The border guard protects the canyon mouth from these monsters, but it's common Knowledge that only squads without a promising future are sent to the Outpost.

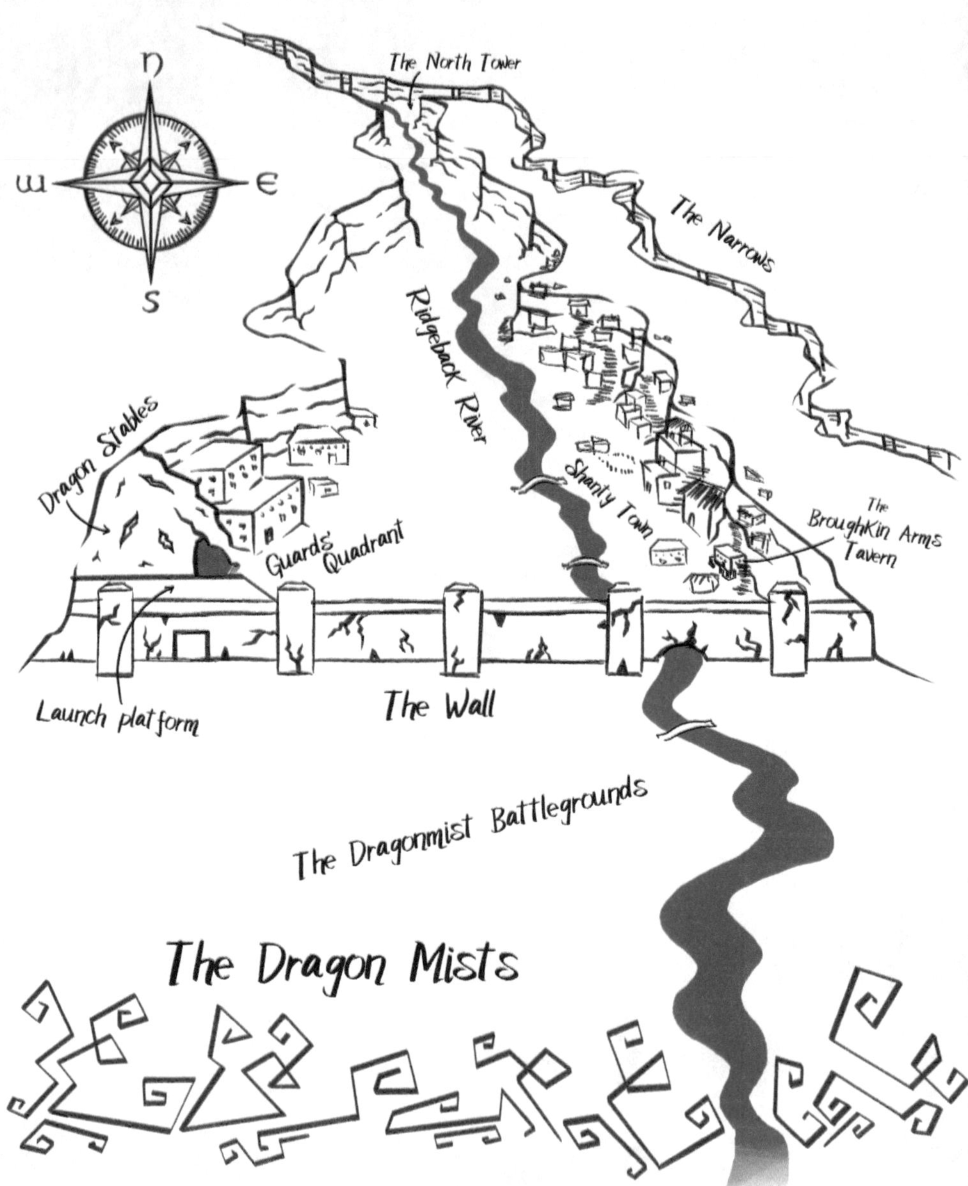

The Dragon Mists

the skystone chronicles

the COVEN of the GRAY ONES

The Coven of the Gray Ones is a shady cult based in southern Rengard. They're a dangerous group of magi supremacists who worship dark ethereal beings. They believe magi are the chosen vessels of the Gray Ones, and have discovered a way to use these mysterious creatures to increase their powers. Rather than the typical gold, the etherarchy they channel is a vivid sapphire blue. The cultists wear masks into battle, and commonly use mind control to force umbral animals or dreklings to fight on their behalf.

The coven members follow an extremely powerful magi known only as "the Liberator."

the skystone chronicles

The Evgardian Alphabet

The following depicts Evgard's alphabet, organized in a way those from your planet can easily understand.

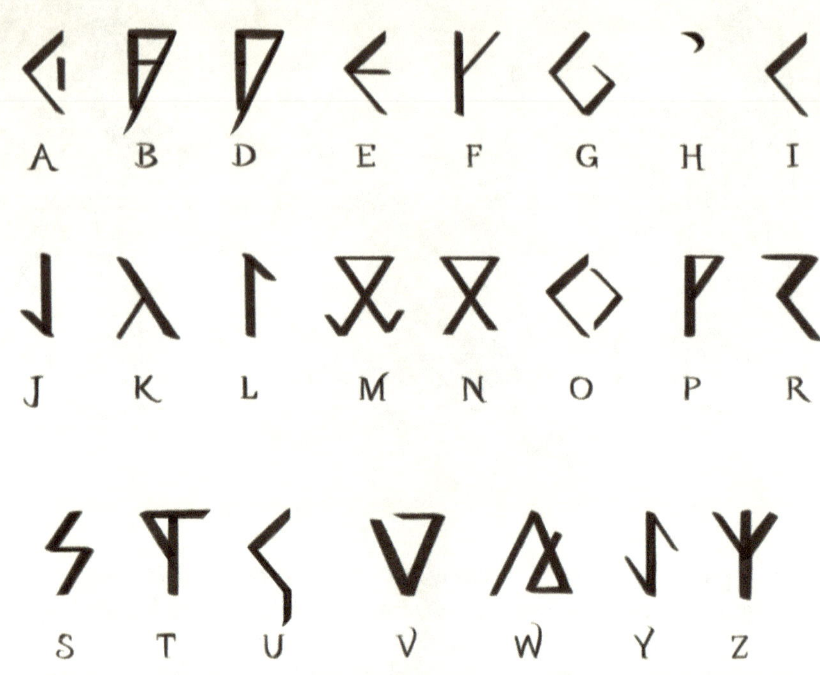

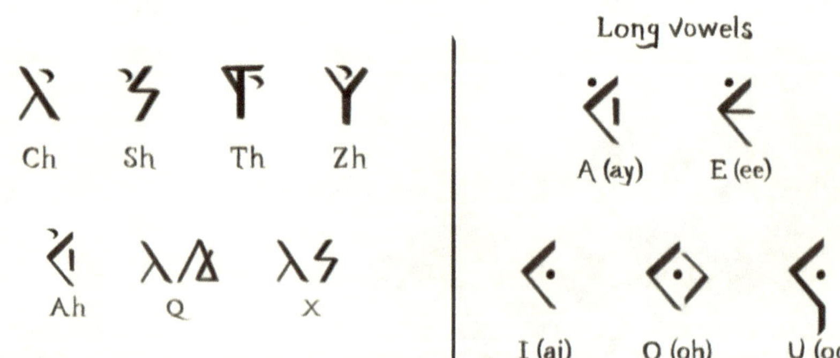

the skystone chronicles

Acknowledgements

Saddle up, dragon riders—It's time for some thanks.

First off, as always, a HUGE thanks to our parents for all their help and support.

Raven's mom, we love how invested you've become in this story, and how unapologetically 'Team Jax' you are.

Raven's dad, thanks for being our first fan, and for helping guide us through that first alpha draft that stunk worse than a drakalope with indigestion.

Blake's mom, thank you for all of your wisdom, prompt feedback, and more sage advice than even the Farseer could give.

Blake's dad, thank you for always letting us know how proud you are of us despite Blake not becoming a doctor.

Another big thanks is due to our beta readers: Kimball, Alex, Michael James, Michaela, Ella, Elissa, Ed, Amy, Brenden, Auriana, Bjorn, Sydney, and Cathy.

Without Alex as our 'character mood song consultant,' the scene where Meleya and Jax clean up the dragon corpses wouldn't have been anywhere near as intense—or fun. Oh, and thanks again to everyone who has let Blake continue refining the magic system on them—especially you, Tom, you've been pretending to care for the longest.

Another over-the top special thanks to our mad genius editor, Nadav Laemmle, for being a wonder to work with, and even dialing in some last minute changes for us. Nadav, you are the real MVP.

Once again, we want to thank J. Scott Savage and Brandon Sanderson for their courses on writing. J. Scott Savage, your formulas for book outlining have changed our lives immeasurably for the better. Brandon Sanderson, we have watched your scorching YouTube lectures so many times that your sped-up voice haunts our dreams... in the best possible way. And another continued thanks to Shad Brooks for helping us get the intricacies of our world building planned right.

And again thanks to George Nelson. We're still surprised all the time by how much your writing mentorship has impacted us on ensuring we make a story actually good. I still find myself singling out whole sections of sentences as "on the nose."

And finally, thank you to everyone who supported us by reading Dragon Thief. An even bigger thanks to those who liked and reviewed it! Hearing back from everyone has been so much fun, and we're so glad so many more people know the characters in our heads now.

But our most special thanks belongs to you—yes, you—for reading (or listening to) Dragon Guard. We hope you've enjoyed exploring Evgard as much as we have, and that you'll have even more fun with the Skystone Chronicles as they continue.

Now remember, if you liked Dragon Guard, please tell us by leaving a review. Reviews are to authors as skystone is to dragons—we're hungry for them, and the more we get, the more we'll ascend. Again, thank you so much for taking the time to read our book.

May you always choose light and burn bright.

Oh, and you can keep up with everything Evgard-related at <u>skystonec hronicles.com</u>.

(Direct Review Link)

Blake and Raven Penn fought through epic battles and twisted love triangles to finally find each other. They both studied script writing in college, and now deign to turn their film and comedy experience into novel writing. Through sunshine or the dreaded Utah Valley inversion, they spend their days tending their wild offspring and dreaming of dragons. Aiming to write fantasy adventures that would keep their former teenage selves up reading long past midnight, Blake and Raven hope to brighten a world in desperate need of light.

To contact them, you can reach out via skystonechronicles.com or follow them on social media @skystonechronicles. Also, be sure to join their mailing list and get a free short story set in the world of Evgard!